SHADOW CITY: SILVER WOLF COMPLETE SERIES

JEN L. GREY

SHADOW CITY: SILVER WOLF

Broken

MATE

BOOK ONE

USA TODAY BESTSELLING AUTHOR

JEN L. GREY

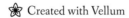

CHAPTER ONE

A SCREAM ECHOED in my ears, making my blood run cold. The noise originated from about two miles away, where my pack lived, deep within the mountainous woods outside of Chattanooga, Tennessee.

I stilled. *That was odd.* The trickling of the murky Tennessee River in front of me filtered back into my awareness.

Maybe some kids were playing or Dad was doing training rituals with the younger shifters. But that would surprise me because tonight was the new moon. Normally, we took it easy this day of the month when our kind was at our weakest—but maybe that was the point.

I hoped no one had gotten hurt.

Brushing the concern away, I leaned over the muddy edge of the riverbank and dipped my fingers into the cool water. The heavy storm from a few days ago had made the liquid more cloudy than normal, but I could still see my reflection. My long, silver hair, which signified my future as alpha, lifted in the breeze, and the olive tint to my skin contrasted with my light silver-purple eyes.

The noon sun warmed the back of my neck, and the tension melted from my body.

4 JEN L. GREY

"Attack!" The faint, desperate command resonated from the distance. "Kill as many as you can."

My body froze.

This was no exercise. We didn't shout frantically even when we wanted to during training. Revealing worry sounded weak. As silver wolves and protectors, we had to convey confidence at all times.

I spun on my heel and ran toward the neighborhood. Dammit, I shouldn't have snuck out and hiked the two miles away from home, but this was the one day of the month that I could be alone for a few hours.

The one day I had a reprieve from learning about my future responsibilities, which I'd inherit from my father.

What's going on? I linked with my pack, but there was radio silence. As though I'd been cut off from communicating with them.

That had never happened before. I probed my mind again for the link while panic clawed in my throat. The only solace I had was that my chest was still warm from my pack bonds.

Animals scurried in the opposite direction as me, and my already frantic heart pounded harder.

Something was wrong. The silver wolves acclimated into the world, but we kept our location and the type of wolf we were hidden from everyone, including other members of the wolf race. The only time we allowed someone from outside into our pack was when one of our own found their fated mate. To keep our pack secret, the fated mate always became one of us. It was our pack law and a way to ensure that the silver wolf race remained hidden. So, being attacked shouldn't have been possible.

Gunshots fired, and I drew magic from my wolf, increasing my speed with the animal inside. I needed to get back to my pack as fast as possible, but I couldn't risk shifting. In animal form, we revealed the kind of wolves we were to our attackers, our silver fur unmistakable. I couldn't take the risk of alerting them to our existence, in case they thought we were another regular wolf pack. The attackers could be from a pack led by an overzealous alpha who wanted to form a larger pack by strong-arming us into submitting to him. Dad had told me repeatedly that something like this could happen.

It was a possibility, but I couldn't be sure until I reached them.

Parts of my chest grew colder as members of the pack began to disappear, just like the time my grandfather passed.

No.

They couldn't be dying.

Any other day of the month, I could run twice as fast, but with the moon hidden tonight, my magic was weakened even more so than the other pack members' would be because alpha blood was more connected to the moon. Even in wolf form, I wouldn't have been able to run faster.

Not today.

Silver wolves were much stronger than standard wolves, especially at night and on a full moon. The fuller the moon, the stronger and larger we were. But this one day of the month, we were essentially like every other wolf in the world.

Nothing special.

More shots blasted, and I pushed myself harder, causing my side to cramp.

I had to breathe, or I'd be too winded to help my pack when I finally reached them.

The trees blurred as I rushed past, and my feet sank into the mulch-like ground, slowing me down. I wanted to scream in frustration.

Taking deep breaths of the spring air, I tried to use the floral scents of the woods to keep myself rational. Deep breathing was one of the calming rituals that had been instilled in me as a young girl. Learning airway control was one of the best weapons that anyone could have. It helped me think rationally and not make stupid decisions under pressure. Nothing was more powerful.

No matter how hard I pushed, it didn't seem to be enough. It felt like time stood still as I desperately tried to get to my friends and family.

With every step I took, the sounds of fighting became clearer. I had to believe that was a good sign. After all, we were born warriors.

I latched on to that hope and didn't let my fear take hold.

As the trees thinned, I almost shouted in victory. *I made it!* But the stench of copper hit my nose.

Blood.

The smell coated my throat, making it hard to swallow.

My feet stumbled, and I caught myself before I could fall to my knees. I didn't have time to come apart. I was an alpha, for God's sake, and my people needed me.

I opened my mouth and breathed without using my nose. The scent was still strong, but not nearly as bad. My wolf surged forward in my mind, helping me to remain emotionally strong.

As I got closer to home, modest brick houses peeked through the trees. I ran directly to the alpha house, its backyard connected to the woods. I had to find my parents and see what Dad needed me to do. He'd have a plan. He always did.

Needing to be as silent as possible, I slowed, not wanting to stumble upon an attacker. It wasn't as if they would be broadcasting their location to me.

The fighting sounded like a drum pounding.

Overwhelming.

Devastating.

Heartbreaking.

When I came close to breaking through the trees, an unfamiliar musky stench almost made me gag, stopping me in my tracks.

The attackers were definitely wolf shifters, but I didn't know their scents.

I squatted and removed the knife that I kept holstered around my ankle. Having it brought me comfort, and I never left the house without the weapon. Not even when Zoe, my best friend, gave me shit, asking what kind of critter would be brave enough to attack us.

I bet she'd changed her tune now.

"The girl has to be here somewhere," a male whispered. "I think I've found her scent heading into the woods."

"Maybe she ran," someone with a deeper voice responded. "The alpha, Arian, may have told her to leave."

I peeked from around a tree and saw two men dressed in all black and wearing ski masks, standing in my backyard. They were both over six feet tall, like Dad, and were muscled and stout, even more than most shifters. Whoever these assholes were, they worked out a lot, which alarmed me. That could mean they'd been training intensely for something.

A shiver ran down my spine as I realized they might know what we were.

But again, that shouldn't be possible. Everyone outside of our pack thought our kind had died off. Still... they knew my dad's name.

Breathe, Sterlyn. If I let my emotions get the best of me, they'd find me and do who knew what else. I clutched the hilt of the knife, holding it so I could use the blade easily if needed.

I couldn't see anyone else from this position, which aggravated me. I didn't want to shift—at least, not yet—in case they didn't know what we were. *Dad?* I tried to link to him again.

Instead of a response, more screams filled the air, sounding like they came from the front of my house. The breeze changed direction, blowing against me and toward the two pricks.

Dammit, I had to make my move fast.

"Her scent grows stronger this way." The speaker lifted his black mask, revealing an auburn goatee, and stopped it at his nose. He sniffed deeply. "She smells like freesia."

"Are you being serious?" The other guy reached over and yanked the first man's mask back down. "Freesia? What'd you do, go paint your nails with your mom before heading over here?"

My pack was being slaughtered by dumbasses who wore all black during the day and argued about scents.

The enemy didn't even feel bad about decimating my pack. What kind of heartless bastards were they? Rage coiled tightly around me, and I dug my fingernails into my free palm, making blood pool at my fingertips.

I took a few steps deeper into the woods and then moved toward them, hoping to catch them off guard.

"Don't be an asshole, Earl," Goatee scoffed. "I'm saying she smells pretty. Maybe I'll get a chance to breed with her."

Nausea rolled in my stomach. Why was he talking about breeding?

"Then say that. That's at least acceptable, and don't get your hopes up. They already have someone in mind for her." The other guy shook his head. "Stop being an idiot. I got you on this crew, and you better not make me look bad. One more stupid move, and I'll kill you myself." He headed toward me.

I crouched behind some brush. Once they got near, I'd strike at the smarter one—Earl—before going after Goatee.

Forcing myself to breathe slowly, I let calm float throughout my body.

Earl lifted his hand, signaling Goatee to stop. He stalked toward me, his yellow eyes searching the brush.

He was about ten feet away, but I needed him closer. With Goatee nearby, I needed to strike fast and hard. Taking him out on the first shot was crucial. Otherwise, it would be two on one, and I didn't like those odds.

Goatee moved gracefully beside Earl. Maybe he wasn't as stupid as I thought.

Earl glanced at his friend. "She's close—"

His distraction was all that I needed. I lunged forward and slammed the knife into Earl's chest, stabbing him in the heart.

"What—" His words garbled as he snapped his head back toward me. His eyes widened, and he looked at his chest, blood already soaking his shirt.

"Shit!" Goatee screeched.

I wrapped my hands around the hilt of the knife and pulled back hard. A sickening sucking followed by a crackle sounded before the knife slid from his chest.

Blood gushed as Earl pressed his hands to the wound, trying to stop the bleeding.

Walking past him, I readied the knife in my hand as Goatee charged.

"You bitch," he growled and reached for my throat.

I dodged him and straightened, slamming my elbow into the back of his head. He fell to his knees, and I grabbed the material and hair at the back of his head.

"You're going to pay," he growled.

Irrational anger. Perfect. That meant I had the upper hand.

He jumped to his feet and snatched my hair.

Dammit, I should've pulled it up. I jerked my head away, but he held tight and yanked me toward him.

Fighting dirty it would be.

I pretended to trip and fall toward him. He leaned forward, his chest helping to steady me, and spread his legs apart.

As my shoulders connected with him, I lifted my leg, kneeing the asshole right in the balls. I didn't feel much of anything, but he released his hold and grabbed his family jewels like he actually had some.

Interesting. Either way, my plan had worked.

I punched him, and he tipped over, landing face first. Unable to bring myself to kill the asswipe now that he was the only one left, I kicked him in the head, knocking him out.

I surveyed the area, anticipating another attack, but all I could see was the man I'd killed moments ago. Hysteria clawed inside me at what I'd done.

We trained to fight, but I'd never killed anyone. I'd prayed every night that I would never have to. Obviously, my prayers hadn't been answered.

"Sterlyn!" Dad called.

His comforting voice snapped me back to the present. I turned to face him...and almost wished I hadn't.

Blood stained his white shirt, and he clutched his side, grimacing with every move he made toward me. "You need to go *now*." His normally silver eyes looked more like steel, and his hair appeared a tarnished gray. The handsome man that I'd seen earlier today looked old.

"What?" I jogged toward him, not wanting him to hurt himself more. "No. I need to help protect our pack."

"Look." He reached out a hand slicked with blood. "They're here for you, and I can't let them take you."

"For me?" My brain fogged. "Why?"

"I think they want to force you into a mate bond." He glanced over his shoulder.

My gaze followed his...and my world crashed around me. I couldn't breathe as I tried to make sense of what I saw.

Bodies littered the ground. All from my pack.

Dad and I used the thick trees of the forest to hide us over a hundred yards away as my best friend Zoe army-crawled across the road onto the grass, trying to get out of the way of the attackers. Blood poured down her arms, and I could tell she was using all of her strength to survive.

A man dressed in black ran to her and placed a gun to her temple.

I have to stop him. I moved to intervene, but warm, strong hands wrapped around my waist and pulled me backward. Dad placed his hands on my shoulders and got in my face.

The loud blast of the gun made my stomach revolt.

The spicy scent of fear wafted from Dad as he jerked. "Sterlyn, focus on me."

"But—" I pushed against his arms. *I have to save them.*

He groaned in pain. "Those men have no intention of letting any of us live except you. There are too many for us to fight off. Most of the pack connections are now cold. Almost everyone is dead."

"What?" My body froze. "Mom?"

"Yes, and I'll be following soon." He nodded toward his side.

Now that he wasn't holding it, I could see his wound. The gash was so deep that the muscle was visible, and the way the blood was pouring from it, I knew they had to have hit a main artery. Even with shifter healing, no one could survive that. "No. I'll take you to the hospital."

"I'm barely hanging on as it is." A tear trailed down his cheek. "I had to keep it together long enough to find you. You have to run. Go to Shadow City. The alpha, Atticus Bodle, will protect you, but trust only him with what you really are."

"Dad, how do we know it's not him attacking us?" My voice cracked. Atticus was the only person outside of the pack who knew of our existence, so it would make sense if this assault had to be on his orders.

"Atticus is a good man. I have never sensed any negative intent in him. I'm certain he isn't behind this, but be careful, and don't trust anyone else. One of the attackers said they're here to find you. We can't let them catch you."

"I... I don't want to leave you." Not only did he expect me to leave him behind, but he wanted me to go to a city I knew very little about.

"Baby girl, I love you, but you have to." He kissed my cheek. "They're gathering a small group to search for you. Go. Before it's too late."

"The alpha is missing," someone shouted from not too far away. "He may be searching for the girl."

I looked at my father one last time, trying to remember his smell, his face, his touch. "Daddy."

"I'm sorry, but I have to protect you." His eyes glowed a brighter silver as he called his last bit of strength. Alpha will laced his words. "Leave. Now. And don't come back."

My wolf howled in protest as I turned and my feet moved on their own accord, following our alpha's command. I glanced over my shoulder to look at him once more. "I love you, Daddy." I placed the knife back in the holster on my ankle and took off as I heard him drop.

"He's here," another guy yelled.

My wolf surged forward, helping me run as sobs racked me. I didn't want to leave, but I could not disobey my alpha.

The voices grew louder as multiple footsteps rushed toward my dad.

"I smell her!" someone exclaimed. "She's in the woods!"

Breathing deep again to calm myself down, I focused on putting one foot in front of the other. I had to get out of here before they caught me. My pack's sacrifice couldn't be in vain.

CHAPTER TWO

"HER SCENT IS STRONG," one of the men yelled. "She can't be far."

Dammit, I didn't have even a quarter-mile lead on them. I had to get my head on straight or they'd capture me.

The urgency of my situation called for focus. At least, I had a reprieve from the overwhelming grief that wanted to suffocate me.

Wiping the moisture from my eyes and the snot from my nose, I increased my pace. They might have numbers on me, but I knew the land.

I veered left, staying deep enough in the woods that I couldn't be seen if they drove the roads. I ran a sporadic route, hoping they wouldn't guess that I was heading to the closest town, about four or five miles away. Luckily, the road led southwest toward Shadow City and allowed me to stay close to civilization. That would force the people chasing me to keep their animal sides at bay.

After all, humans weren't supposed to know about supernaturals. If someone let it slip, the punishment was death.

Footsteps pounded behind me, pushing me to move faster. I ran often for training, so I should be able to lose their asses. As long as I kept ahead, I should be okay.

I'd figure out what to do once I got closer to the city.

My legs grew heavy, and it took twice as much energy to keep going, but I pushed through the fatigue. From what I could guess, I'd run about fifteen miles, which meant Shadow City wasn't far ahead. If I maintained my current speed, I would reach the city in the next thirty minutes.

I was making decent time, but the assholes after me hadn't fallen behind as I'd hoped. I had to lose them.

Scanning the area, I searched for something that would slow them down. Staying close to the road wasn't a viable option any longer.

I cut to the right, farther away from the road, hoping the switch in direction would disorient them for a short while, and examined my surroundings. I wasn't familiar with this part of the woods. Even though our pack lived somewhat close to Shadow City, we'd always kept a wide berth from it, purposely avoiding anyone who lived near there.

I tried to remember everything I knew about Shadow City. It was a refuge that had been created over a thousand years ago. Anyone who needed help or asylum could go there. All shifter races lived there together, plus angels, vampires, witches... almost every supernatural race in existence.

When the city was founded, the silver wolves had been its protectors until corruption took hold. Unable to fight the corrupt leaders and unwilling to die for them, the silver wolves had chosen to leave.

At the time, Shadow City's alpha wolf had promised to clean the place up and had asked for us to not go too far away. Then, shortly after the silver wolves left, the city went into lockdown, not letting anyone in or out until the past few years.

Dad had gone there about two years ago, to meet with the current alpha wolf, Atticus, but he'd left me behind, telling me he needed to vet the situation and that I was to stay with the pack in case things went awry. I'd been sixteen then, old enough to step into the alpha role if necessary.

Despite the alpha's promise that things had gotten better, Dad had been wary of some of the other leaders in the city, specifically the angel, Azbogah, and some of the witches. Atticus had said to give him time, that we'd see more change. However, Dad never heard from him again.

For him to tell me to go there meant the Shadow City pack was my only hope for safety. That didn't sit well with me, but that was a problem for another day.

Right now, I had to get these assholes off my trail.

The rushing of the river helped me form an idea. I probably should've done it a while ago, but I'd foolishly thought I could outrun them.

Mistakes were forgivable as long as you could do something about them. And fortunately, I was alive and still moving, which meant everything in my current situation. No one else in my pack could say that.

"She's changing course," someone huffed. "She's heading for the river."

At least, they were showing signs of fatigue too. It would've sucked if they didn't sound as winded as I felt.

"Don't let her get there," another one yelled. "I'm calling for backup. We can't lose her."

The good thing about changing directions—it made their weight shift on their feet. I hadn't been able to get a good read on how many were chasing me, but with them pivoting, it sounded like about ten were riding my ass.

That was more than I'd expected. I'd hoped for a handful. With that many, my odds of getting away were a whole lot slimmer.

A problem for after I reached the water.

Watching the ground closely, I looked for patches of mud, roots, and tree branches that could make me stumble or fall. Unfortunately, this slowed me down, but that was marginally safer than taking a tumble. Another reason I'd stayed close to the road—more stable ground.

The downward slope helped me run faster. Tree branches cut my arms, causing some bleeding, but nothing that fazed me. I barely felt the burn and the sting, but what was all too easy to feel was that I was their fucking prey. Something that angered both my wolf and me.

Their footsteps grew louder, alerting me that they were catching up. They were larger than me, so gravity worked in their favor.

I hadn't thought the plan through, but the river grew closer.

As long as I reached it before they caught up, I should be good. My plan was to go underwater and swim for as long as possible so they'd lose sight of me and my scent.

"I see her!" one of them shouted, way too close for comfort.

Ignoring the overwhelming urge to look over my shoulder, I pressed forward.

Murky water appeared between some trees as the Tennessee River came into view. The water didn't appear to move fast, but that was misleading. In spring, there was so much rain that the current was strong. Luckily, the section down here didn't have heavy traffic. The boats stayed mostly north of us, so it wasn't risky to swim around here.

My attackers' breathing was so loud that I could tell they were almost on top of me. If things didn't change drastically, they'd catch me before I reached the river.

I hadn't run over fifteen miles to be captured now.

Concentrating on my goal, I threw caution to the wind and hauled ass, no longer caring about my footing. I pumped my arms at my sides, trying to make my feet move even faster.

As I reached the embankment, the mulch turned into muddy stone, and I leaped.

"No," a guy screamed as something snagged my right ankle.

Twisting my body to the right, I used my left foot to kick the punk in the face. His head snapped back, and his grip on me loosened.

I fell on my back, barely short of the water, my head dangling off the edge of the embankment. I raised my head to see nine men stalking up only a few yards away from me.

If I didn't do something, they'd catch me before I hit the water.

The guy I'd kicked was knocked out, so I climbed over and grabbed his gun. I hated using guns, but right now, it was a necessity. I stood and fired at the rest of the men, who were too close for comfort.

"Take cover," one yelled as all nine scattered. I waited a second before firing again, keeping a random pattern in hopes that they'd wait to ensure I was done firing before racing after me again.

Not far away, the river curved sharply. If I could hold my breath long enough, I could still lose them. After a few more random gunshots, I squatted so they couldn't get a good visual. I fired once again then let my natural instincts take over. I flipped backward and hit the water feet first, sinking under the surface, and swam as hard as I could, using the current to my advantage.

I swam deeper, hoping the extra cloudiness of the water left over from the storms would hide me. A few bubbles hit my leg, informing me that at least some of them had jumped in but that I'd gained some distance.

Swimming was one of my favorite pastimes, something I was grateful for now as I kicked as hard as I could with the current to get as far ahead as possible. My lungs began to burn, needing oxygen. I exhaled a little, trying to prolong the time before I would inevitably need to resurface.

After several more strokes, I had to emerge. Trying to be careful, I allowed only the top of my face to break through the water, hoping to stay hidden.

"Look, there she is," one of them yelled.

Dammit. I submerged once more and let panic push me harder than before. I couldn't let them catch me. If I did, then all the lives sacrificed for me would be in vain.

I couldn't live with that.

With each stroke, I expected to be grabbed, but it didn't happen... at least, not yet.

I swam diagonally, hoping to catch a stronger current. When my lungs began to scream again, the water pushed against my back, propelling me forward.

Good, but I needed to replenish my air supply.

I waited as long as I could before my instincts took over and my arms pushed me toward the surface. However, the current wouldn't release me, and I was too weak to break through.

Panic seized my body, and my brain grew lightheaded. If I didn't get a hold of myself, I'd drown. Quickly, I flipped onto my back and stretched out my body, feet first. All the articles I'd read about river safety said to float with my head upstream and my legs down. Being horizontal to the water should help, at least marginally.

Surprisingly, getting into that position was easy once I wasn't *trying* to break through.

Something brushed my hand, and I grasped it. For all I knew, I could be holding hands with a corpse, but I was desperate enough to use whatever was available for leverage. Hopefully, it was a log. I yanked it toward me with the little bit of energy I had left. The edges of my vision started to darken, and I pushed the maybe-log down toward the riverbed, trying to use it to propel myself upward.

The momentum shifted me from the current, and when I broke through the top of the water, I sucked in a breath. My head was still foggy, and I spun around, looking for the assholes who'd put me in this situation, to begin with. A large tree branch floated beside me, so I threw my arms over it, no longer strong enough to stay afloat on my own.

My eyes grew heavy with exhaustion. Fighting for awareness, I craned my neck around but didn't see the douchebags.

I was safe for now, so I propped my head and body on the branch as best I could and closed my eyes to rest for a moment.

———

AN ARM WRAPPED around my waist, causing my heart to race and my breathing to quicken. I opened my eyes and realized that my dumb ass had fallen asleep. I had no clue for how long, but it was obviously long enough for them to catch up to me.

I kept hold of the branch and slammed my elbow into the prick's stomach. "Let go of me!"

"Whoa," a deep voice exclaimed and then groaned. "You're going to drown. I'm trying to save you." His hold around my waist slackened.

Did he think I'd actually fall for that? He didn't smell of a lie, but that didn't mean he had good intentions.

Since he was distracted by his stomach ailment, I head-butted him with the back of my head. A sickening crack informed me that I broke something.

"Fuck!" he complained as he pushed the log toward the embankment.

My legs made contact with the riverbed, and I put weight on them before falling back into the water with a large splash.

"Hey, wait," the guy said as he swam over to me.

"Stay back." With trembling hands, I pulled my knife from the sheath and held it in front of me as I glared. "I will hurt you."

"Obviously." He gestured to the blood pouring from his nose. "You already have." Drops of water fell from his short, dark hair and dripped onto a once sky-blue shirt and jeans. The warmth of dark chocolate eyes caused me to lose focus, and my hand dropped a couple of inches. He had the musky scent of a shifter, but he was in human form.

He wasn't wearing black, but he could still be one of them,

messing with me. I had no clue how long I'd been out, and he could've changed into a different outfit and jumped in after me.

I lifted my chin and raised the knife. "Who are you?" I had no clue how I was going to get out of here. I didn't have the strength to stand, for God's sake.

"I'm Killian." He moved his hand slowly to his nose and pinched the bridge. "Killian Green. I saw you floating on a tree limb and thought you might be in trouble."

"Why would you think that?" I kept my body facing forward as I scanned for other possible attackers. They were probably hiding in the woods, waiting for the sign.

"Did you not hear what I said?" The corners of his mouth tipped upward. "You were passed out, floating on a tree limb in the middle of the river. It's dangerous to be swimming right now after the heavy storms that passed through."

"And you happened to be out here?" I had a hard time buying it.

He pointed toward a tree at the edge of the water. "Fishing."

Against my better judgment, my gaze followed where he motioned. And sure enough, a rod was propped against a tree with a worm dangling on the hook. The poor worm wiggled like it might have a chance to survive.

"So you aren't trying to capture me?" The words tumbled from my lips before I could stop them.

His brows furrowed, and he released his hold on his nose and wiped off the blood. "No, but now I understand why you beat the shit out of me." He chuckled.

"You find that humorous?" He had to be some sort of sick asshole to find the fact that I was almost kidnapped amusing.

He grimaced. "No, I'm sorry. It's just, there's only one girl who has ever kicked my ass like you did." He tilted his head as he examined me. "And funnily enough, you remind me of her." He frowned like he was remembering someone he didn't want to.

This was getting uncomfortable, and for me, staying close to the water wasn't smart. They'd be combing the area, looking for me.

"Look, I've got to go. It's not safe here for me." I placed both hands in front of me to bear some of my weight as I stood. Slowly, I climbed to my feet even though my legs wanted to buckle again. I took one step and dropped.

Before I could make impact, a strong arm caught me around the waist.

"Let me help you." He glanced around the area. "You're not going to make it far in this condition."

I hated that he was right. "Fine." I kept a strong hold on my knife, ready to use it at any given moment.

We slowly made it out of the water and to the tree line. But I wouldn't feel better until I was hidden. After a few steps on land, I stumbled into the woods.

"Hey, where do you think you're going?" Killian asked. "You can't leave like that."

And there it was. He hadn't been helping me after all.

CHAPTER THREE

I SPUN on my heel and tried not to fall over. Almost drowning had taken a hell of a lot out of me, but I had to push through and get to safety before I could fall apart.

My arm shook as I lifted the knife in his direction again. "So, you are working with them?"

"With who?" His forehead creased, and he lifted a hand. "You can barely walk."

"Don't worry." I took a slow step in his direction and almost pumped my fist in celebration when my knees didn't buckle. Who cared if it took every ounce of concentration to pull it off? Confidence spoke wonders. "I can still kick your ass."

"In fairness, I didn't fight against you," he said and rubbed his nose, emphasizing the crooked section that I'd broken. "You can barely stand, and even though you caught me off guard, I didn't hurt you."

"Stop rambling, and let's get this over with." I didn't want to hear about how pathetic I was. If he was going to force me to leave with him, we could bypass the chitchat.

"Look—" He walked slowly toward me like I was some sort of cornered animal.

Adrenaline coursed through me, making my body a little more sturdy. I swung my arm, trying to slice his chest.

He growled as he jumped back, the sharp edge narrowly missing him. "You need to calm down."

The momentum of missing him threw my body off balance, and I caught myself before I could fall. "Not happening." I stood back on my feet, ready to attack again.

"I'm trying to tell you—" he started, but I jumped toward him.

He spun away from my attack, and I landed hard on my feet, jarring my neck.

Before I could face him again, a hand gripped the wrist that held the knife, and an arm snaked around my neck. He pushed his weight on me so I had to kneel.

Here it was. What I'd been waiting for. My breathing grew rapid as I strained to hear some sign of the others.

"Calm down," Killian commanded. "I'm not going to hurt you."

"Really?" I spat. "Because this doesn't feel great." I'd never felt so weak before. I hated the feeling and never wanted to experience it again.

"You obviously have someone hunting you, and you almost drowned." He blew out a breath. "I was trying to be understanding, but you forced my hand."

"Where are the others?" I lifted my head, scanning the woods.

"There are no others," he said exasperatedly. "I keep trying to tell you this. You are safe. No one is here to get you."

I waited for the sulfuric scent of a lie to hit me, but nothing came. "So you came out here alone in human form to fish?"

"Yes." He sighed. "It was my sister's favorite spot."

Was.

She must be dead.

Dad's face flickered in my head. *Mom. Zoe.* Grief tried to wash over me, but I couldn't let it. At least, not yet. I wasn't safe. "I'm sorry about breaking your nose, but I need to leave."

"I gathered that," he said, but his hold didn't slacken.

"They'll be combing the river, and it won't take long before they get here." Actually, I had no clue where I was. "If you release me, I'll go without causing you any more issues."

His arm loosened slightly. "Are we good now?"

"Yeah." I dropped the knife, letting him know I had no intention of using it.

"Thank God." He let go of me and stood. "Who the hell is chasing you?"

That was a question I had myself. "No clue."

I picked up my knife, making him tense.

"I thought you said we were good." His eyes glowed faintly, his wolf peeking through.

I locked eyes with him as I bent down and placed the knife back in my sheath. "We are, but I'm not going to leave this behind." I placed a hand on a tree trunk, letting it brace my weight as I stood. When I felt steady enough on my feet, I strolled farther into the woods.

The sooner I moved out of the area, the faster my scent would dissipate, which would make finding me harder.

"Hey, wait up," Killian called as I heard him run back to the river.

There was no way I was waiting. Considering how slow I was moving, he'd be able to catch up to me in no time.

No matter how much I pushed myself, my speed never increased. I bet a freaking turtle could have beaten me.

"Of course she didn't wait for me," he grumbled. "She's too damn headstrong, like Olive." He trudged in my direction.

In a matter of seconds, he caught up to me, his fishing pole slung over his shoulder. He bit his bottom lip. "So, where are you heading?"

"I shouldn't tell you." If somehow they figured out he'd run into me, they'd torture him for information. "The less you know, the safer you'll be."

"Okay, so, if you don't know who, do you know *why* they're after you?" He slowed his pace to walk beside me.

"Once again, best if you don't know." What was with all the questions? "So, where exactly am I?"

"You don't know?" He pursed his lips. "How long were you out?"

I couldn't keep the venom out of my words. "If I knew that, I wouldn't be asking where I was now, would I?" I grimaced, immediately regretting biting his head off. I blew a raspberry. "Look, I'm sorry."

A smile flitted on his face. "For what exactly? Punching me in the gut, breaking my nose, trying to stab me, or being rude?"

Ouch. "In fairness, I thought you were an attacker. So, in this instance, I'm purely talking about biting your head off."

He chuckled. "Fair enough."

"Is withholding information my punishment?" I felt comfortable around him, which was odd. Normally, when I was around other wolf shifters, I got nervous and anxious, afraid I'd slip up and give them a hint of what I was.

"Maybe." He waggled his eyebrows. "But in all seriousness, you've landed in Shadow Ridge."

My shoulders sagged with relief. No way. Could I actually have gotten this lucky? Granted, after a day like today, I deserved some kind of break. "The bordering wolf shifter town to Shadow City?"

"The very one." He tilted his head. "You seem relieved."

"I am." I guessed there was no point in not telling him now. Maybe he could help me. "I was instructed to come to Shadow City, so all I need to do is get there."

"You do realize you can't go into the city without permission, right?" He wrung the hem of his shirt as if getting the excess water out would improve his situation.

"Atticus Bodle will see me." That had to be why Dad had mentioned the alpha's name. He'd be my ticket inside.

"Uh." He scratched the back of his neck. "Atticus won't be able to help you."

My stomach dropped. "Why?" Something bad must have happened. That must have been why Dad hadn't heard from him the past couple of years. "Is he in trouble?"

"That's one way of putting it." Killian cleared his throat. "He died almost two years ago.'"

This day kept getting worse and worse. "No." That was my entire plan. I'd banked everything on getting into the city and seeing Atticus. I hadn't even considered the possibility that Dad's instructions would have a flaw. He always knew what to do, but as of today, that officially had changed. The worst part was I didn't have him here to counsel me. "That's not possible."

"I assure you it is." He nibbled on his bottom lip. "Shadow City residents that attended his funeral saw his dead body. It was open casket.'"

"You didn't attend?" My stomach tightened even more.

"No." He shook his head. "I'm not allowed inside yet. They're slowly opening the city."

"How did he die?" I asked, even though the answer wouldn't help my situation.

He huffed. "Heart attack."

I must have misheard him. There was no way. "Wasn't he young?" Shifters lived to be well over a hundred, and Dad had made it sound like Atticus was only a couple of years his senior. A heart attack was very unusual.

"That's what made it so shocking." Killian took a few steps. "But being the alpha in Shadow City is a tough job. From what I've been told, navigating pack politics and trying to represent all the shifter races fairly while working with the council members is more stressful than anyone can imagine. The extreme stress made his heart give out."

I stopped in my tracks as my stomach dropped. I had nowhere to go. No plan to execute.

Nothing.

My heart pounded. My head spun, and my throat closed.

"Hey!" Killian said. "What's wrong?"

Not able to respond, I tried to focus on filling my lungs, but it was like my body had frozen.

"Girl." He grumbled to himself, "I don't even know her name."

I bent my knees, not able to stand upright any longer. I had to get control of this panic attack or I'd pass out again, but I didn't know how to. I'd never felt this pathetic before.

"This is going to hurt me more than it'll hurt you," he said.

A hard slap hit the side of my face. The sting broke through the suffocating haze. I sucked in a breath, filling my lungs.

"Are you okay?" He leaned over me as he examined my face.

"No, I'm not." The severity of the truth blasted like a bomb. I shouldn't have admitted it, but he would've known if I had lied. "Atticus was my only hope. I don't have any money or even clothing to my name. I don't know what to do." Here I was, pouring my heart out to a stranger, but it somehow felt right.

"Well, then I guess it's a damn good thing I found you." He brushed my cheek where he'd slapped me. His fingers were rough and warm.

I'd never been touched like that by anyone except my parents, but the different sensations I'd expected to feel didn't come. "What do you mean?"

"My best friend might be able to help you." He winked at me. "And I have a huge house all to myself."

"You own a house?" I asked with disbelief. He couldn't be that much older than me, but that didn't mean anything. Since I'd lived in such a small, close-knit community where generations of families lived together in the same house, anyone getting their own house was a big deal. Living situations were probably quite different outside of our hidden little world.

His face creased. "I inherited it when my family died three years ago."

Tears burned my eyes. "I'm so sorry. I lost my family too." And if I didn't start moving, I'd break down. The poor guy had already seen me ridden with anxiety and weak from almost drowning. I didn't need to add emotionally broken to that. Maybe I could push my breakdown out another hour.

He easily kept pace with me as the backside of a neighborhood came into sight through the trees. The houses appeared to be craftsman style, and one of them had a large pool in the backyard.

He frowned. "How long ago?"

"Earlier today." My voice ached with sadness. "The men chasing me—they killed everyone. My dad told me to run and find Atticus. That's why I came all the way here and why I thought you wanted to catch me."

"Well, that settles it." He smiled, but it didn't reach his eyes. "You'll be staying with me."

"I couldn't." I didn't want to be a burden. "That's asking way too much."

"First off, you didn't ask." He held up one finger then added a second. "And second, you have nowhere to go. You're not in the best of health since you almost drowned, and you have no money to your name. Not to mention, people are hunting you." He touched my arm. "And honestly, it gets lonely in the house, but I can't seem to get myself to move. You'd be keeping me company."

The word *yes* was on the tip of my tongue, but I didn't want to take advantage of him. "Are you sure?"

"Yeah." He waved a hand in front of me. "Besides, you're soaking wet. You won't be able to go anywhere without raising some eyebrows."

He was right. I wouldn't be able to go anywhere unnoticed, not that I had money anyway. "Okay, but I don't want anyone to know about me or what happened to my family." If word of that got out, it could help whoever was hunting me locate me.

"Got it. You can trust me." He led me to the yard that had the large in-ground pool with a diving board and water slide. "This is our stop."

"You live close." His fishing spot on the riverbank was only about a mile from his home.

He walked past the pool and up some brick stairs leading to a covered back porch. Thankfully, the porch's floor was cement, so I wouldn't ruin anything by dripping all over it.

"Let me grab you a towel, and I'm pretty sure my sister's clothes will fit you." He opened the door, which had been left unlocked.

"Your sister?" I cringed, thinking about wearing his dead sister's clothes. "Are you sure?"

"Yeah. I mean, they should do someone some good." His shoulders sagged, and he smiled sadly. "I'll be right back." He slipped inside, leaving me alone.

A chill ran down my spine, and I turned to face the woods. I rubbed my arms and assessed my surroundings. I needed to get a feel for the area and devise an escape plan in case they found me here. I couldn't stay and put innocent lives at risk.

The house next door appeared to have the same layout as this one, but instead of the hunter-green color of Killian's, it was pure white. A large fire pit had been dug out back with beer cans scattered around. Whoever lived there must be a drinker, or maybe they had people over routinely. That could be a good thing though—it would mix my smell with several others and help to obscure it.

Killian's footsteps grew closer to the door, and I turned as it opened.

He had changed into a white shirt and jeans. After handing me a large beach towel, he gestured through a pristine kitchen, past the wide-open living room with a picture of him and his family hanging above the couch, toward a hallway on the other end of the house. "If you go to the second room on the left, that's Olive's room. You can go through her closet and pick out something to change into. When you're done, come on out, and we'll get something to eat."

"Thank you." Even if I wanted to argue, I couldn't. He was being generous and helping me. I toweled off as best I could and hurried to the bedroom.

Inside, I shut the door and laid my head against it. I expected the grief to hit again, but numbness filled me instead.

Good. First step, get dry. I pulled off my clothes and walked toward the white queen-size canopy bed with a plum comforter, noting the matching white end tables and dresser. The walls were lavender, almost the shade of the purple of my eyes. The shaggy cream carpet felt amazing under my feet as I padded to the closet beside the bed.

As I surveyed the room, a picture on the end table caught my attention. It was of a younger Killian and a girl who must be his sister at the embankment, fishing together. They could almost pass for twins. Killian had his arm slung over her shoulders.

The fact that he'd lost his own family and now had found me had to be fate. We could both understand the pain of loss.

Choosing not to wear her underwear, I slipped on a thick black shirt and gray sweatpants. My stomach gurgled, and I grabbed my wet clothes and the towel then headed back to the kitchen.

Killian was nowhere to be seen, so I placed my clothes on the glass circular kitchen table and used the towel to dry the water I'd dripped on the hardwood floors. I'd squatted to finish wiping the floor when I heard him outside on the back porch.

"Hey, man," he whispered. "Yeah, I'm not going to make it tonight. Something came up."

Great, I was already interfering with his social life. I would have felt bad, but he had insisted on me staying.

After a moment, he spoke again. "Yeah, there's this girl I want to tell you about."

No. He'd promised he wouldn't tell a soul.

CHAPTER FOUR

IT WAS time to get the hell out of here. If he was already telling people about me, those men would find me easily. Leaving the towel on the floor, I gathered my wet clothes and moved toward the front door, my feet pounding on the hardwood. Then I came to an abrupt stop.

Dammit. I wasn't wearing shoes.

Should I leave without grabbing my soaked tennis shoes or take the extra time and grab them?

The longer I spent contemplating my options, the more likely he'd catch me before I escaped. A quick decision needed to be made.

Being barefoot would garner more attention, so taking the time to get them was the best option.

Making a mad dash back to Killian's sister's room, I tried to focus on one task at a time. Dad always said, *If you get too many steps ahead, you make mistakes on the most pressing ones.* I could almost hear his voice.

Almost.

And my heart somehow fractured a little more.

Focus, Sterlyn, I chastised myself as I slipped the shoes on. Water gushed around my toes, making me pause.

The back door opened, and Killian stepped inside.

There went my plan of sneaking out. Nonetheless, that didn't change my need to leave. I'd already been leery of staying here, and knowing I couldn't trust him made the decision to go so much easier. I hated that my instincts had been wrong, but I'd deal with that later.

Evolve and learn from your mistakes.

His footsteps echoed toward the room. "You're not changed yet?" Killian chuckled. "I figured you'd be out here, pacing the floor."

Dread pooled in my stomach. I'd had way too many confrontations today, but I might as well add another one. Putting it off would only make things worse.

I held the clothes harder against me, and more liquid absorbed into the dark shirt I'd put on. Apparently, there hadn't been a point in me changing after all.

"Uh..." He paused. "Dove?"

Dove? Maybe he hadn't been talking to me all along. Was someone else here? I sniffed, but all I smelled was him.

He knocked. "Are Olive's clothes not working?"

"Yeah, they're fine." I pushed my cowardice away and opened the door.

His eyebrows shot upward, and he smirked. "The point of changing was to get dry." He gestured to the wet clothes against my chest.

"And the point of asking you to not tell someone about me was for you *not* to call someone at the first opportunity and spill my secrets." My voice rose as my anger bled through. I shoved past him, marching toward the front door.

"Hey, wait," he said as he followed me and gently grabbed my arm. "It's not what you think."

"Oh, so the whole 'there's a girl I want to tell you about' wasn't actually about me?" I lifted my chin, daring him to deny it.

"Give me a chance to explain." He raised a hand and gave me puppy dog eyes.

And the more insane part was that it worked. My resolve crumbled. "You've got one minute."

"You know how you were talking about how you didn't feel right staying here?" He jumped right to the point.

"Yes." This had to be some sort of trap, and I was walking right into it.

His dark eyes turned milk chocolate. "What if you staying here helps me too?"

"How so?" I hated to admit that I was intrigued.

He rubbed his hands together. "Date me."

I jerked back. "What?" I had to have heard him wrong.

"Date." He touched his chest. "Me."

"You seem great." He had lost his mind. Maybe when I'd punched him, I'd caused a brain injury. "But my family and entire pack were slaughtered this morning, and I'm kind of running for my life. Dating isn't high on the priority list." I edged toward the door. I didn't want to startle him. I'd heard fast movements could aggravate insanity.

"There won't be strings attached, only exclusivity." He motioned between us. "You need a place to live, and I need the pressure to date someone to go away. It's a win-win."

"You don't want to date someone, but you asked me to date you?" My head spun, and I was pretty sure it wasn't from almost drowning.

"I can understand why you'd be inching toward the door." He shook his head. "But it isn't as insane as it sounds. Like I said, we would date and be exclusive, but we'll be friends dating without the romantic pressure. There's this girl eyeing my best friend, and she's pushing her best friend at me. I'm not interested, but I can't get Luna to leave me alone."

Wow, so much information at one time, but I had nowhere else to go. "So, you want to date me for real, but we're just friends. Nothing would be actually expected from me... in any capacity—physically or otherwise."

"Exactly." He blew out a breath. "I mean, you're gorgeous, and you're strong and direct, which reminds me of Olive. My sister. It's kind of nice being around you. It doesn't seem quite like she's gone."

Some of the discomfort fell from my chest, and surprisingly, his words didn't hurt my feelings. He was handsome, but I wasn't into him *that* way either. "If I agree, what does that have to do with the conversation with whomever it was earlier?" If he thought his weird proposal would distract me from that... it wouldn't.

"Well, this is where it gets awkward." He tugged at an ear. "I did tell Griffin—that's my best friend—about you, in the sense that I said I couldn't go out with that girl tonight because I was with you."

"You assumed I'd say yes?" My emotions were bouncing all over the place; I couldn't settle on one. I was equally horrified, angered, and flattered. It was a trifecta of conflict.

"Actually, it kind of came out, and I'm hoping you'll say yes, or I'm kinda screwed." He gestured to the house. "But this place is big enough for both of us. You can stay in Olive's room. Make it your own, and I'll stay in mine."

"This is a little crazy." And the funny thing was that I was down-playing it by calling it crazy. "I have nothing to my name—"

"Which makes this even more of a good plan." He took my clothes out of my hand. "I'm the alpha of Shadow Ridge, and I've got connections. I can help you get a fake ID and get you a job at the Shadow Ridge University coffee shop. You would have a secret identity with money and a place to live."

He was so young to have such a leadership role, but sometimes fate forced our hand. His help sounded a little too good to be true. "If you're alpha, that means others will be around a lot. I'm trying to blend in." Unless...maybe his pack being around would help with that. "Besides, why don't you tell that girl that you aren't interested? It would be a hell of a lot easier than doing all this other stuff."

"Don't worry about the pack. Honestly, I kind of stay out of their way. Even though I'm technically the alpha, I'm taking a hiatus, and my dad's beta is filling in. They're giving me space to go to college and grieve for my family, so you'll be more off the radar here than anywhere else." Sadness crept into his voice. "In regards to the girl, I've tried." He blew out a breath. "The problem isn't even her—it's her best friend, who keeps pushing for us to go out. The best friend is close with Griffin because her dad works with him. Griffin doesn't see that she's trying to force his hand to settle down. So, me having a girlfriend will make things easier with a lot less drama than continually refusing them."

He had no clue how girls worked. This would cause even more drama. Girls like that didn't back down without a fight. But a fake ID would be an amazing thing to have, and maybe his messed-up life could distract me from mine. "And I'd get to keep the fake ID?" With that, I could get a plane ticket or whatever else I might need when verifying my identity would be involved.

"Yup," he said and beamed as if he knew he had me. "I know we're being secretive, so I haven't even bothered asking your name. But is there a name you want on the ID?"

"Uh..." I chewed on my lip. I had so much on my mind; I didn't have the capacity to add anything else to it. "Surprise me?" I squeaked.

"Can do." He scratched his neck. "Any other information I should know?"

"Nope." I got that he was curious, but I'd told him enough for one day. "I'm facted out for now."

"Then let me make it official." He got down on one knee and lifted a hand. "Will you please do the honor of being my girlfriend?"

Somehow, he didn't look completely ridiculous. "Yes, I will, but why me? You're attractive. I'm sure you could find someone to date without bribing me."

"I'll be real. Like I said, I lost my entire family too. I know what it feels like, and maybe by helping you, I'll find some peace. Because I still can't look in the mirror." His eyes glistened, and he turned toward the living room and sniffled.

Absolution was what he was after. If I hadn't been leaning toward saying yes by this point, that would've changed my mind.

He pretended to scratch his nose when he was wiping under his eye before facing me again. "Our group is pretty steady. Not a lot of new faces, so me having a girlfriend will be more believable with a newbie in town. Especially since I sort of slept with most everyone here already."

Of course he had. "Wow. It's a good thing that sex is off the table." I wanted to make him smile again. "No telling what kind of STDs I could've gotten otherwise."

"Ha. Ha." He glowered. "We can't catch STDs."

"So...you've tried?" I bantered back, feeling oddly at ease.

"I believe in trying anything fun." He winked as he headed back toward the kitchen. "Now, go change again. I need to take a picture of you to send to my buddy for your new ID, and then I'll start some hamburgers. We need to get you fed."

AN ALARM BLARED, startling me from sleep. My eyelids were so heavy I almost had to pry them open with my fingers. I'd slept hard, but not well, the entire night.

Dreams had haunted me.

I'd lost count of the number of times I'd killed the guy behind my house. Each time, the pain felt fresh. Being a protector, I'd grown up knowing that the chance of killing someone was always there. But doing it was different than what I'd expected.

When I wasn't dreaming of killing, the images of my slaughtered pack were there.

So much blood.

So much hate.

Everyone I loved was gone. Almost like they'd never existed.

And the scariest part was someone was hunting me, and the only clue I had as to why was when Goatee had mentioned breeding with me. The thought of being forced to birth more silver wolves petrified me.

The memory of my dad bleeding out while commanding me to leave ended each cycle. Every time, that was the final blow. The last straw that had me falling apart.

Without them, I didn't know who I was anymore.

A rogue wolf with no one to turn to. Where my pack links had been was now cold. Completely cold. No-survivors cold. If I didn't connect again soon, insanity would start creeping in, and from what I'd heard, it might be only weeks before the madness took over. I had to find a pack fast...but that would mean letting someone in on my secret.

That wasn't possible. At least, not now.

The realization was the final piercing of my already unstable heart.

I didn't have time for this. Life moved on. The world still turned. And my heart still beat even if it felt like it shouldn't.

Somehow finding the strength within, I reached over and turned off the alarm. Even though my eyes stayed heavy, I forced myself out of the comfortable bed. I wasn't ready to face those dreams again.

I made the bed, trying to keep the negative thoughts at bay. Doing a routine task was comforting. I smoothed the bedspread into place before turning to the closet, trying to determine what to wear for an interview at a coffee shop.

Surprisingly, last night wasn't horrible. Killian had known what to do to help me process things. He hadn't asked about my family or pack but instead told me stories about his own, including their tragic deaths.

With tear-filled eyes, he recapped the entire nightmare. He was supposed to go with his parents, sister, and a few other shifters to a nearby lake to look into some strange occurrences that had happened there, but it was the same timing as some sort of senior high school party. He'd bailed on them last minute to attend the party instead, and everyone who'd gone had been jumped and killed. As soon as their pack heard through their links that they were in danger, people had rushed to help them. But they'd been far away enough that no one reached them in time.

There had been no survivors.

Similar to my own story.

He blamed himself. If he'd gone with them, maybe things would've been different. Because of that failure, he wasn't mentally ready to lead the Shadow Ridge pack like his father, Orion. He only attended meetings and made decisions when absolutely necessary, and he trusted his beta, Billy, to take care of the day-to-day pack matters. He kept himself somewhat isolated from the pack because he felt like he'd failed them already.

Part of me wanted to comfort him, but how could I when I felt the same way? If anything, I understood exactly where he was coming from.

When I'd stayed quiet, he'd popped popcorn and turned on a comedy featuring pure relationship angst. No killing, no family triggers, nothing but a girl and a boy finding their way to each other.

Pursing my lips, I flipped through the closet. His sister had drastically different tastes than me. There were several dresses, skirts, and flowy tops instead of the jeans and shirts that I always wore. All the other items were old worn shirts that looked like she'd used them for bumming around the house.

A college coffee shop should be pretty casual, but I didn't want to wear baggy clothes. Ugh. I was going to have to suck it up and wear something that I didn't want to. The best option I could find was a ruffled apricot dress. The sleeves were three-quarter length, which fit the spring season, and the hem stopped several inches above my knees. I paired the dress with some black flats that were a smidge too big for my feet.

When I received my first paycheck, I'd go clothes shopping.

Trying not to dwell on my misfortune, I glanced in the mirror. The fact that it didn't shatter astounded me. My hair was one huge rat's nest. I had bloodshot eyes and dark circles underneath.

The hair was my own fault. I'd taken a shower and fallen into bed without drying it. Now I had to get to work on myself to come off somewhat presentable.

A FEW MINUTES LATER, Killian knocked on my door. "Dove?"

That was the second time he'd called me that. What the hell?

I took one last look in the mirror, relieved that I looked nearly normal after working the knots from my hair. Inhaling sharply, I opened the door and found Killian leaning against the wall in front of me.

"Why do you keep calling me Dove?"

"You never told me your name, so I improvised." He gestured to my hair. "And your hair is gray, reminding me of dove feathers. I bet it's hard to keep that color up."

My name was on the tip of my tongue, but I didn't let it fall. And the fact that he thought my hair was dyed made things easier on my end. I'd never had a nickname before, and it was safer for both of us if he didn't know my real one. "That works."

"You like it?" He smiled. "It's unique, like you. You've already become Dove in my head, so even if you told me your real name, you'd be stuck with it."

In my pack, everyone had treated me as their leader, even though I hadn't yet taken the position. The only one who'd treated me like a regular person had been Zoe, but she never went so far as to give me a pet name.

The image of my lifeless best friend filled my mind—her gorgeous espresso hair disheveled and blood pooling from her mouth. What I'd do to be able to save her. To hear her give me shit once again.

"Hey," Killian rasped. "Are you with me?"

"Uh... yeah." That was such a strange question. "I'm right in front of you."

"I meant mentally." He booped my nose. "You seemed far away."

That wasn't good. I needed to at least give the illusion I was present. By not being alert, I was already failing at being a good protector. "Yeah, ready to go."

"Then your chariot awaits." He flipped his hands in the direction of the kitchen. "The garage is through here."

In the garage, I found a black truck that looked brand new. Within seconds, we were in the truck, pulling out and heading toward Shadow Ridge University.

Killian glanced in my direction, and I realized my leg was bouncing fitfully against the black leather. I forced it to stop and examined the truck's interior. This was a newer model that had all the bells and whistles. On a cold day, the seat warmer would feel like heaven.

As we drove through the quaint downtown, I scanned the buildings. The road was two lanes lined with parking meters outside of brick shops that connected for a couple of miles. There were restaurants, banks, and a movie theater. Everything that you'd expect to find in a town.

As we stopped at a red light, the door to a breakfast restaurant opened, and a guy wearing all black with an auburn goatee stepped out.

My heart froze as he locked eyes with me.

CHAPTER FIVE

THE CAR CLOSED in around me, and my lungs stopped working. The morning took on a surreal quality. If the attackers had found my trail, I'd expect them to track me straight to Killian's home, not go eat breakfast at a diner in the middle of town.

What was their end game? Maybe they needed to refuel before coming after me again.

My strength was returning now that the new moon was over, but that wasn't comforting at all. They should have struck hard and fast while I remained weak.

Killian spoke, but I couldn't make sense of his words. My attention was focused entirely on the man I was sure was Goatee. Our gazes were still locked, and the hair on the back of my neck stood on end. Could we have it out in the middle of the town square?

My hands clenched as the door to the diner opened and three men joined Goatee on the curb.

"We need to go," I said through gritted teeth as Goatee looked away and focused on his friends.

This would be where he warned them, and they'd attack. I hadn't brought my knife because of this stupid-ass dress, and now I regretted it. I had no weapon against these assholes, which proved my training correct. We learned to always have something on hand.

"Go!" I shouted. We were still sitting at the red light like bumps on a log.

"I can't." Killian gestured to people walking through the crosswalk in front of us. "Or I'm going to hurt someone."

Of course we'd be stuck at a red light. It was like the universe was pushing me toward these assholes, and I didn't know why. I'd lost everything. Wasn't that enough?

All I could do was sit here and wait.

Wait for the gestures and shouts.

Wait for them to drag me from the car.

Wait for them to finish the job and hopefully kill me too.

I'd rather die than be forced into a relationship with the sole purpose of producing offspring. Could I even love children that came from a forced union? I was afraid the answer would be yes, which would mean that watching them grow up into horrible people would be the final torture my would-be kidnappers could bestow upon me.

"Dove?" Killian leaned over to look at the four guys, who turned and casually walked away.

My breathing hitched. They were walking away. I shook my head and sucked in the breath I so desperately needed.

The fog began to clear as I blinked. If they were my attackers, they wouldn't have walked away like that. The people chasing me had been bound and determined to get me. They would've struck immediately.

I was being paranoid. Surely there was more than one redhead in the world who wore a goatee.

As my body sagged, the truck pulled forward.

Killian touched my arm softly, but his voice contained an edge. "Did those guys do something to you?"

"No." If he hadn't thought I'd lost my marbles by now, he would after this. "But the one that walked out first reminded me of one of the attackers. I thought—" My voice failed me, and I sat there with my mouth hanging open.

"Hey, you're going to see their faces and probably your packs' faces sporadically." Pain laced his words. "Believe me. It's part of the denial process, or maybe the trauma of it all. And I wasn't the one who found my family dead. You're going to have it so much worse than me."

"So that was normal?" I grimaced. I didn't want that to be normal for me—a trauma survivor. But no one would ever choose this road.

Dad used to say our trials made us stronger. I always believed him... until now. How did my pack being decimated make any of us stronger?

They were dead.

There was no reason for what happened other than brutality. Something that made my blood boil more than the moonlight ever had.

"Yeah, it's normal." He placed both hands back on the steering wheel. "It fucking sucks. It's one reason that Griffin tries not to go back to Shadow City. There are so many memories of his dad there and all the plans they made together for the packs."

"Griffin?" Wait... That was who he was talking with last night. "Your best friend."

"The very one." Killian chuckled. "His dad died shortly after my parents, leaving him with a whole lot of responsibility, like me. Despite us meeting only a few years ago when Shadow City opened back up, our losses bonded us together quickly."

"Then why do you feel responsible for helping me?"

"I don't feel responsible." He tilted his head toward me. "I want to help you. There's a huge difference. Besides." He leaned back in his seat and placed a wrist over the steering wheel. "You're helping me in return, so it's mutually beneficial." He waggled his eyebrows.

And I laughed. So odd. Ten seconds ago, I was on the brink of a breakdown, and now he had me smiling. Maybe I was certifiable. "No waggling eyebrows at me. This is completely platonic dating that so happens to be exclusive."

He huffed and rolled his eyes. "You're no fun."

"No, I'm not." And just like that, the sadness took hold of my chest again. "I've lost too much to be fun." Add in the fact that Dad had been grooming me since birth to be the perfect alpha. He'd repeat that, if I was a boy, it would be so much easier. Times were changing, with more women leading packs, but, not fast enough. For me to not get challenged, I had to be even stronger and more poised.

Because of that, no one had ever approached me for a date. Everyone my age had thought I was too perfect, or they were intimidated. Zoe had been my one and only true friend, able to see past most of the act. Though not all.

"Hey, it'll be okay." His hand tightened on the steering wheel, making his knuckles turn white. "It has to be."

Silence descended between us, leaving both of us lost in our own thoughts. Ones that I didn't want to have but didn't have the strength to push away. Arian and Cassie Knight had been amazing parents, even when they were hard on me. Mom had a way of making things better whenever I grew too overwhelmed with expectations or training. And Dad made me feel stronger and taught me to believe in myself. Because of them, I hadn't been captured and had found the strength to get away even when the enemy got too close to catching me.

As we turned toward the woods and the flowing river, several large brick buildings about a mile away popped into view. They looked brand new.

"That's the university." Killian answered my unspoken question.

It was picturesque with enough acreage that my wolf could happily run for miles. The lawn in front almost looked artificial with healthy green grass. "This place is gorgeous."

He smiled. "It really is. All the buildings were constructed at one time so the campus has a cohesive feel and branding."

"Do humans go here too?" From the little bit I'd heard about it, I'd assumed Shadow City was populated only by supernaturals, but I wasn't sure about the surrounding towns.

"No." He shook his head. "It's all supernatural based, but to maintain appearances, we allow humans to apply. We have a thorough screening process to weed them out from actually being accepted. We want this to be a college where supernaturals get the kind of education they need for their future, whether that's leading, fighting, healing, and so forth."

"So there aren't any humans in Shadow Ridge either?" Being around only supernaturals unsettled me. All of my experiences visiting the small town near my pack's home had involved a human presence, and any other supernaturals who might live or visit the town always had to be careful to not ask certain questions. Here, it would be harder to keep my heritage hidden. I couldn't risk running in animal form because, if anyone had even a vague memory of silver wolves, they would peg me easily. Staying human was going to suck because I was used to shifting daily. It was part of our training regimen, to fight in both wolf and human form. But I'd manage.

I had to.

"No humans live here, but tourists come into town." He pursed his lips. "It's good for businesses since they spend a lot of money, and having them around helps us remember our human side."

His wording seemed odd, but I let it go. The buildings were growing closer, and I could see now that a wrought iron gate circled the campus.

As we approached the wrought iron fence that served as the main entrance, I could see the emblem of a city etched into it with the words Shadow Ridge University underneath.

"Is that a drawing of Shadow City?" The emblem had modern buildings with a paw print and a symbol attached to the top.

"Sure is."

"So you've been there?" If he had a way into the city, maybe I could figure out another person to contact. I could find out who'd replaced Atticus.

"Oh, no. There's a large wall and dome that keeps the city from view. In order to get in, you need permission from one of the council members. They're letting residents out freely now, but it's still hard to get inside if you don't already live there." He slowed the truck as we approached a guard shack sitting between the entrance and exit lanes. "But I've been told that's the skyline of the city."

The gates to the university were closed, and Killian rolled down his window as he stopped.

The guard took a step toward us even as Killian pulled out a card key and swiped it against the reader. The gate clicked and slowly opened.

"Doesn't traffic get backed up if everyone has to stop and scan in?" I glanced over my shoulder to find no one behind us.

What time did classes start? It was almost nine in the morning. I'd figured this place would be a lot busier.

"Half the students stay in the dorms here." He accelerated and rolled up his window. "The other two hundred or so, like yours truly, live off-campus either in Shadow Ridge, Shadow Terrace, or Shadow City itself."

"Shadow Terrace?" I'd never heard of that city.

"Yeah, that's the city on the other side of the river. We didn't have a large enough population at first to protect both sides, so the vampires took it over." He shrugged. "The wolves protect our side for Shadow City since all the shifter council members are wolves. The vampires need human blood, and protecting the other side helps them stay under the radar and funnel blood in for the residents."

"Wait..." The thought turned my stomach. "Are you saying you all allow the vampires to kill humans?"

"No." He shook his head. "Not at all. They compel visiting humans to donate blood under the ruse of a local blood bank. They aren't allowed to directly feed from humans since that eventually makes them lose their humanity and can bring the kind of attention we don't want to our area. The whole point is to blend in."

There was so much I didn't know. "So only wolves are on the council?" That seemed surprising with all the races that lived there.

"No, there are twelve representatives. Three of each race," Killian explained. "Three vampires, three angels, three witches, and three wolves who represent all the shifter races."

I mulled that over as we drove down the tree-lined road, straight toward a large brick building that had to be at least a hundred yards long and two stories high. In front was a grassy greenway where a few students were sitting with breakfast and books while others were walking into the building.

As we got closer, the road bore to the right toward a large parking lot that looked mostly full.

This was more along the lines of what I'd been expecting.

Killian pulled into the parking lot and parked underneath a tree. "I have a ten o'clock battle strategy class, so let's haul ass to the coffee shop."

"How far is it?" I didn't want to complain, but these shoes weren't the most comfortable.

"In that building." He nodded to the building beside us. "It's toward the back, so not far. I want to be there to introduce you to the coffee shop manager, Carter. He's one of my pack members, and he owes me for helping him out on his English paper." He got out of the truck.

At least it wasn't across campus.

I turned to open my door and found Killian already there. He opened it and held out a hand to me.

"What are you doing?" I was more than capable of getting out of the truck by myself.

His eyes flicked toward the building. "Remember, we're dating." He took my hand and helped me down. "So I'm treating you like I would a girlfriend."

"Oh, right." That made sense. My irritation eased. "So that begins now?"

"Yeah." He chuckled and interlaced our fingers. "That is the arrangement, right?"

"I know. I forgot." That wasn't smart to admit to him.

He shut the door and guided me in the direction of the building. "Well, let's try not to forget around people, okay?"

He was counting on me. I couldn't let him down. "You've got it." I stepped closer to him, our arms brushing. I hoped I was doing this right, because I'd never dated anyone in my entire life. Watch him go to hold my hand, and I wind up shaking his. There were so many ways I could mess up.

The fact that his presence was comforting but nothing more than that surprised me. He was very good-looking. Probably the most attractive guy I'd ever seen, plus he was kind. Why didn't I find him more desirable?

My skin started buzzing, and I wasn't sure why. Anticipation? Something seemed to tug me toward the building, but maybe it was nerves. Shit had been getting weird lately, so maybe this was my new norm.

The wind blew, lifting my skirt. I managed to use my free hand to catch it before my borrowed panties were revealed to the world. I hated to wear someone else's underwear, but with a dress, I hadn't wanted to chance showing off my kitty. "How many classes do you have today?" I grumbled as I glared at the air around me.

"First off, I'm thinking the wind isn't scared of you." He smiled so wide dimples appeared on both sides of his cheeks. "And I have two—Battle Strategy and Supernatural History. Classes that are expected of me since my pack is responsible for defending Shadow City."

Well aware of the irony, I stared at those dimples. No wonder so many girls fell into bed with him. "And what am I supposed to do while you're busy?" The thought of hanging around all of these supernaturals by myself alarmed me.

"Trust me." He winked.

We walked past a girl who took a quick breath. I turned my head toward her and regretted the decision immediately.

If looks could kill, I'd be dead.

My internal joke fell flat. Death wasn't funny.

"You okay?" he asked.

"That girl is giving me a hateful look." I nodded behind me. "I have no clue what I did to make her dislike me." I sniffed toward each shoulder, wondering if I smelled.

He laughed loudly. "You don't stink, and I hooked up with her last weekend, so that's probably why. I don't want to be tied down, you know?"

"Really?" No wonder she was pissed. If it'd been me, I would've beat the ever-loving shit out of him. "How the hell are we going to get everyone to believe you drastically changed your ways?"

"When you know, you know." He smiled tenderly at me and brushed his fingers against my cheek.

"Save it for everyone else." I wrinkled my nose, trying like hell to hide my laughter.

We got to the large double doors, and he pulled one open.

This time, I knew to wait. When he waved me in, I stepped inside and took in my surroundings. The walls were the standard beige with forest brown tile floor. The hallway that branched off to the left held offices that looked like they were for admissions, financial aid, and all of the various types of administrative departments needed for a college of this size.

In front of me was a back entrance that led to picnic tables and the river. To the right was a bookstore with an attached coffee shop, and to the immediate left was a cafeteria with indoor seating.

"This way." Killian took my hand again and led me into Shadow Ridge Coffee.

There was an obvious theme around here.

Inside it looked like a standard coffee shop. There were a few tables that students had already taken over, and in the center were two espresso machines and someone taking orders. The line stretched outside the entrance and into the cafeteria.

Dragging me behind him, Killian went to the front of the line where an attractive guy who had to be close to twenty stood taking orders. His shaggy brown hair hung in his eyes and sweat beaded his forehead. He chewed his bottom lip like it was a piece of gum. The nice fact that he had a deep musky scent that identified him as a wolf shifter made me feel better.

"Carter." Killian leaned his hip against the counter.

"Dude, I don't have time right now." He hit some buttons on the machine and frowned. "It's rush hour, and that bitch Deissy called in sick. Now I have to work the cash register, and a demon lives in it."

"A demon?" I leaned over the counter, but nothing out of the ordinary appeared to be happening. I didn't realize that demons lived on Earth.

"Yes, because it won't work for me." He smacked the buttons like that would make everything better and then paused. He glanced at my and Killian's connected hands. "Uh... this has to be some kind of whacked-out nightmare. You're holding hands with a girl?"

"Well, yeah, but I didn't come here to declare my relationship status. I need a favor." Killian placed an arm loosely around my shoulders. "Dove needs a job, and you owe me one."

"Her name is Dove?" His forehead furrowed.

The girl standing in front crossed her arms and tapped her foot. "Are you going to get my coffee or not?"

Carter's moss-green eyes focused on me. "Do you know how to work a cash register?"

"It shouldn't be hard to figure out." It had buttons with words.

"Then you're hired." He held his hand out. "It's not like I could say no anyway since Killian is my alpha. Give me your ID so I can enter your information and you can get to work."

Shit, I hadn't thought that through. I didn't have anything to give him, and if I left, people would get suspicious. Anyone looking for a job would know to bring their ID with them.

How the hell did I get out of this situation?

CHAPTER SIX

MY EYES FLICKED TOWARD KILLIAN. I was at a loss as to what to say. The fact that I was already relying on him so much was unnerving. I hadn't even known him for twenty-four hours. I hoped my trust wasn't misguided by a desperate attempt to find someone to have my back so I wasn't alone.

Killian sighed exasperatedly. "Man, can we get it to you tomorrow? It's my fault that she doesn't have it at the moment."

"Of course it is, but I don't want any details. There's no telling what you two did to cause that." Carter rolled his eyes. "I'm desperate, so I'm willing to make an exception. But I need it first thing in the morning or no deal."

Thank God. I hadn't expected him to roll over. "So I can start tomorrow?"

"Fuck no." Carter pointed to the wall behind the counter where several black aprons were hanging on a hook mounted in the center. "Get one of those on and get your ass over here. We'll work the line together."

I moved quickly and snatched an apron before he changed his mind.

"All right then." Killian saluted me. "I'll let you get to work. I'll come by after my classes to get you." He kissed my cheek. "See you soon."

My cheeks warmed. I'd never received that kind of attention before, and a few girls in line gawked at his display of affection, making the entire situation even more uncomfortable.

"I like it when you blush." He brushed his pointer finger against my cheek. "But I'll get out of your way."

"Please do." Carter scowled. "I'm pretty sure PDA goes against sanitation rules, not to mention the cat fight that could break out."

"See you." I glared sternly. I didn't want my boss to get pissed at me during my first minute on the clock. Well, I was pretty sure he was my boss since he hired me.

Killian walked out the entrance, and the girl who'd been demanding her latte tilted her head. Her straight, long, mahogany hair fell over her shoulder, contrasting with her fair, unblemished skin. "Did you actually snag Killian?" She leaned over the cash register, and her rose scent hit my nose as her gorgeous dark purple stardust-colored irises focused on me.

She somehow smelled even more pleasant than the flower. She was breathtaking, but I had no clue what kind of supernatural she was. "Snag?"

She flipped her hair over her shoulder and tugged at the edges of her coral sweater, pulling it over her dressy white shirt. "Wow. You're a mindless bimbo like the other girls he's messed around with. And here I was intrigued by you. Obviously, you're not any different and aren't worth talking to." She wrinkled her nose.

What a jerk. I couldn't stand being talked down to. "Wow, that hurt," I said, emphasizing my sarcasm. "I mean a girl yelling at a poor guy who's trying to wait on her is always *super* classy. I really give a flying fuck what she thinks of me."

"Dove!" Carter gasped and his shoulders sagged. "I'm so sorry, Rosemary. She's new—"

"Yeah, I was standing here when that whole exchange went down. I know she's new." She licked her bottom lip and placed a hand on her hip. "But I'm glad you finally hired someone who has the balls to not take any crap." She grinned at me as approval radiated from her. "Do you think you can ring me up better than he can?"

"Of course." Girls like her respected others only when they demanded it. Granted, I wasn't sure how she'd take it here in front of everyone, but I went with my gut. Maybe I wasn't so out of sorts after all.

I sucked in a breath and stared the cash register down. I'd figure out how to work it. Another thing kicking my ass wasn't an option.

THE NEXT TWO hours passed in a blur. After initially struggling with the cash register, I finally conquered the beast, and Carter stopped grumbling about my bad attitude. He was happily helping make the drinks, leaving me alone in front.

We'd been nonstop, but the line was finally dwindling. Every kind of supernatural went to school here; it was a little unnerving. I'd seen almost every kind of shifter, plus vampires and witches. Even several I couldn't identify, which meant that I had never been around that race before. My guess was that most of the unknown races had been living in Shadow City and were only now integrating back into the world.

I needed to learn more about this city if I was going to survive and stay off the grid.

Something inside me *tugged*, and I looked away from the cash register toward the entrance. The most gorgeous guy I'd ever seen stepped into my view.

His honey-brown hair was slightly longer on top and gelled to sweep to one side. The fluorescent lights of the shop reflected off blond highlights. His golden scruff made his sculpted face perfect.

He towered over everyone, standing probably more than half a foot taller than me, and his hunter green polo shirt hugged his body, revealing chiseled abs.

And my heart fell when I noted his arm was wrapped around a girl.

Why in the world was I upset over someone I'd just seen for the first time in my life?

I must have been gawking because his light hazel gaze landed on me. His shirt brought out flecks of green in his irises. He dropped his hand to his side, and the girl pouted her overly done red lips.

Her long, golden blonde hair waved over her tight russet brown crop top. She slid one finger underneath her gold mini skirt, pulling it down a little to reveal more of her stomach. She pretended to stumble in her silver stilettos. "Oh, Griffin." She placed her hands on his chest, using him to steady herself.

They both smelled of musk, alerting me that they were wolf shifters, which further proved that her accident was forced.

He gently pushed her off him and marched past the line directly to me. A lopsided grin spread across his face. "Hey, you."

"Uh. Hi?" What was he doing up here?

Rubbing his thumb against his bottom lip, he nodded. "I'll take a coffee."

Was this a joke? It had to be. I kept waiting for the punchline, but he looked expectantly at me.

That wasn't how this worked. "The line starts back there." I pointed to where his girlfriend stood, her mouth hanging open.

"It's fine." He glanced at the guy in front of the line next to him, who happened to be another wolf. "Tell her."

"Uh... yeah." The guy averted his eyes, submitting to the asshole.

"The line is back there," I said sternly.

"Dove." Carter rushed over and scowled. "Please forgive her. She's new on the job *and* in town. I'll grab your coffee. Do you want cream?"

The alpha douche leaned toward me and winked. "I only like my cream in one place."

"Ew." Did that actually work for him? "Please stop. God."

"Some confuse me with him, but I assure you, I'm not." He took a step closer to me. "Granted, you'll be calling me that name again before the night—"

I turned away from him and focused on the guy in the front of the line. "What were you saying you wanted again?"

"Hey, I'm talking to you," the gorgeous asshole said as he reached for my arm.

My heart sputtered at the thought of him touching me. I had to rein this in. This guy was clearly a player, and his girlfriend was *not* happy about the scene going down. But I couldn't stop anticipating his touch.

"Dove!" Killian's comforting voice called from the entrance.

My tormentor stilled as Killian walked toward me.

Killian's eyes widened when he looked at the guy. "Hey, you two have already met?"

Wait. This had to be his best friend, Griffin. I almost threw up in my mouth. But Killian had said he slept around, and clearly this guy did too, so maybe it did make sense.

"Us two?" Griffin pointed at me and then back at him. "I was ordering a cup of coffee."

"So you cut the line again?" Killian smirked and nudged over to me, kissing me on my cheek. "This makes the whole first meeting thing easier. This is the girl I was telling you about yesterday."

Griffin frowned as his hands clenched. "Of course, it is." He took a step in my direction, and my traitorous heart picked up its pace.

Did he feel the *tug* too? The thought both thrilled and petrified me.

"You mean the one that you stood Jessica up for?" Griffin's girlfriend said as she sashayed over to us and looped her arm through Griffin's, stopping him from getting closer to me.

"Here's your coffee." Carter hurried back and handed Griffin a cup. "And Dove, maybe you should head out. The line is shorter, and you're making a scene."

"When should I have her here again?" Killian took my hand and pulled me toward him.

A low growl emanated from Griffin as his nostrils flared, but no one but me seemed to notice.

"Tomorrow. She got off to a rough start with Rosemary, of all people, but redeemed herself and did great until Griffin showed up." Carter held his hand out. "Give me the apron, and be here by nine. That's when things get crazy."

I looked at Killian. I couldn't commit to the time because I'd be relying on him to bring me here.

"She'll be here." Killian unlaced my apron and pulled it over my head. "Thanks, man."

"Please—" Carter placed his palms together, fingertips pointed upward like in prayer "—behave a little better tomorrow."

"Hey, I behaved today." I refused to be pushed around by some pompous student who thought his farts didn't stink, no matter how much I was drawn to him physically.

"That's what I was afraid of." He sighed. "I'll see you tomorrow."

Killian chuckled as he beamed at me. "That's my girl."

The blonde girl arched a perfectly styled eyebrow and held out her hand to me. "I'm Luna. Griffin's girlfriend."

"Friend." Griffin jerked his head in her direction and huffed. "Just friend. How many times do I have to tell you that?"

"Yeah, you made that clear when you hit on Killian's girl, didn't you?" Luna shifted her weight to one leg.

"You hit on her?" Killian grinned and interlaced our fingers.

"God, I hope not." I couldn't tear my gaze away from the sexy douchebag, so I bit out the next words for added measure. "Because if that's his game, it's subpar."

"I wasn't putting forth my best effort." His eyes glowed faintly, making the hazel stand out more as his wolf surged forward. "If I wanted you, you wouldn't be able to deny me."

The problem was I already didn't want to deny him, which meant I had to set clear boundaries more for me than him. "No means no." I placed an arm in front of my body. "Even if you try to force your alpha will on someone."

"I never have or would force anyone." Griffin lifted his chin. "They all come willingly, and some even beg."

Luna cleared her throat and frowned.

"Wow, okay." Killian rolled his shoulders. "We got it. Griffin wasn't hitting on you, and you didn't like the way he came across. I say we start over."

If I didn't feel so indebted to him, I wouldn't have been willing to drop it. But, for him, I would behave. At least for now. "Of course. Anything for you." I managed to pry my attention away from Griffin and turn my focus to him.

"Do you all want to go grab a bite to eat?" Killian gestured to the cafeteria. "I'm starving, and we can beat the lunch crowd."

"Really?" Luna sighed. "Here?"

"Why don't we go off campus to Dick's bar?" Griffin asked as he continued to stare at me. "I could use a beer."

"That sounds a lot better." Luna ran one hand along the top of her breasts. "Daddy has some wolfsbane we can use to lace the drinks too. I'm down for getting tipsy if everyone else is."

"I'm good with that." Killian faced me. "Are you?"

No, but I couldn't be an ass. "Why don't you go? I don't want to interfere with your friends' time."

"I insist," Griffin interjected. "After all, you're my best friend's girl. Clearly, we should get to know each other." He smirked, but there was something sparking dangerously behind his eyes.

He knew he was making me feel uncomfortable.

The asshole.

But the wolf inside me refused to cower. Alpha will and all. That had to be it. It couldn't be that I just wanted to be around him more. "I think I got to know you plenty well the first minute you spoke to me."

"Hey, I thought we were starting fresh." Killian glanced from me to Griffin with his brows furrowed. "That lasted all of ten seconds."

"I have to agree." Luna took my arm and pulled me toward the front of the coffee shop. "We're making a scene here, and it'll be *so* much more *fun* with you there."

The way she said those words made me cringe. Her tone was almost malicious, like she'd enjoyed watching Griffin and me fight. But why would she? I needed to understand what she gained by that.

She led us to the front door, keeping a firm grip on me.

"Dude, what's your problem?" Killian said quietly.

If I didn't have better hearing than most wolves, his voice would have been too low to hear, but with the moon waxing, I could make it out... barely. In a few days, I could've heard them with no problem.

"She was rude to me," Griffin grumbled. "She refused to serve me."

Killian snorted. "That's what all this animosity between you two is about?"

"Don't worry." Griffin sighed. "She's your girl. I'll make nice. After all, it's part of the politician degree that's being forced on me."

"Thank you," Killian said, sounding sincere. "It means a lot. She's important to me. And it's a political science degree."

"They're the same thing." Griffin sighed. "All I'm learning is to be fake and kiss ass."

I could agree with that. I hated politics. Be direct with a caring heart, and the world would be a much better place.

"Is she your fated mate?" Griffin asked with an edge. "You didn't say a word about her 'til last night, and all of a sudden, you seem kinda shoved up her ass."

"Because I bailed on you last night and then picked her up from the coffee shop?" Killian sounded amused. "That's a bit of a stretch, don't you think? And no, she's not my fated mate. But hey, I may never find mine, and she's gorgeous."

Fated mates were what every supernatural coveted. It was the purest kind of bond, and in my pack, the fated pairs who'd found each other clearly loved their mates unconditionally. That kind of love was breathtaking, and once upon a time, I had wanted that. But now, the pain I felt at losing my pack made me hesitant. If it hurt this much to lose my pack, I couldn't fathom what it'd feel like to lose my fated mate.

"So, where are you from?" Luna gestured to the door, indicating for me to open it for her.

Wow. Entitled much?

But I'd already rocked the boat with Griffin. I should probably shove the pride down and do it. Hating myself, I opened the door for her and gritted my teeth. "North of here."

She smiled brightly as she marched past me, knocking her shoulder into me.

She was declaring war between the two of us. She linked her arm through mine again and yanked me forward, putting more distance between us and the guys.

"I want to be clear with you." She cut her eyes at me. "Griffin is mine. Him hitting on you earlier doesn't make you special. He hits on all the girls who are relatively good-looking."

That was a backhanded compliment. Not only that, but she was also trying to mess with me because it was clear that Griffin wasn't that into her, and she was trying to force it. "I didn't think much of it, but since you brought it up again, maybe I should give him a chance."

She laughed without humor. "Look, you're dating Killian, which is tragic, but whatever. Don't get any funny ideas."

"If he hits on every girl that walks, why do you want him?" One thing silver wolves were good at was reading intent, and hers was all negative. The inkiness of her soul floated off her in waves. She wasn't a good person, and she enjoyed power.

"That's none of your business." She looked forward, her ass swinging with each step, no doubt in case Griffin was watching.

Fair enough. "Look, he's an egotistical asshole. Have at him." Whatever the *tug* was between us, I'd learn to ignore it.

"Oh, you think I was asking for your permission?" She giggled. "I wasn't. I was trying to help you out since Killian seems smitten with you. If we're going to be civil to one another, it's always nice to know the ground rules. I'd hate for you to make a mistake and something tragic to happen."

The air sawed into my lungs at the veiled threat. Maybe this place wasn't safer after all.

CHAPTER SEVEN

KILLIAN CLIMBED into the truck and shut the door. He turned and watched me buckle my seatbelt.

I could feel his scrutiny, and I didn't like it. Dad always did this when he was about to ask a question and wanted to read my body language before, during, and after.

"So..." He tapped his fingers on the center console. "You and Griffin don't seem to like each other. What happened?"

At least, he didn't sugarcoat it. "He told me he likes his cream in only one place. Be glad I had self-control, or his ass would've been on the floor."

"He *did* hit on you." Killian laughed so loud it hurt my ears, his dimples on full display. "That's his favorite coffee shop pickup line, by the way."

Ew. "You'd think after it didn't work the first time, he would've stopped and not continued to embarrass himself."

"You're the first girl it hasn't worked on." Killian turned the ignition and shook his head. "For the first time ever, not only did Griffin get shot down, but I got a girl that he didn't pass over."

"Pass over?" I'd regret asking.

"Everyone wants him over me. Partly due to his role in Shadow City." Killian shrugged like it was no big deal, but his shoulders sagged a little. "So, I usually wind up with the girls he doesn't look at."

"Why in God's name would someone pass you over for him?" Killian was loyal and kind. So much better than the sexy asshole that I refused to think about.

He laughed. "You don't have to sweet-talk me when it's the two of us."

"That's not it at all." He obviously didn't see himself in the right light. "He's arrogant and annoying." I managed to leave *dead sexy* out of the description, but unfortunately, he was that. And I hated that I found him that way.

"You do realize that's how people view me too?" He glanced over his shoulder and reversed out of the parking spot.

The way that girl had stared at me earlier kind of confirmed his point. I'd half expected her to come up and grab my hair for a cat fight. "Maybe, but you haven't acted that way toward me." And I couldn't judge him on anything other than that.

He put the car in drive and headed toward the campus exit. "Don't be too hard on him. Griffin is a good guy. He was there for me and got me through that first year after losing my family. He forced my ass to get out of bed and go for runs. Not only that, but he takes care of his mother, Ulva—she lives alone in this huge condominium since his dad passed—despite him hating being there. He doesn't show that side to anyone, especially not Luna. Thank God."

My feet were killing me, so I slipped off the shoes and rubbed my heels where blisters had formed. They'd heal within a few hours, especially since we'd be sitting down at the restaurant.

"What's wrong?" He glanced at where I was rubbing. "Her shoes don't fit you. Why didn't you tell me?"

"I can make do until I get my first check." I smoothed out the skirt of the dress. "Your sister and I have extremely different tastes." I cringed.

Killian's jaw clenched, but his expression smoothed a moment later. "Let me guess, you're a 'jeans and T-shirt' type of girl."

"Yes." I nodded. "Dresses and skirts are so restricting. What happens when you need to fight? Trying to make sure I didn't flash my panties at my opponent would hinder my abilities."

"First off, do you get into fights often?" He leaned against his door. "And second, even if you did, would you be focused on flashing as opposed to kicking ass?"

"Part of our training regimen was fighting every day, usually several times. And, yes, I would care if anyone saw my panties." Dad had taught me to be conservative and dress appropriately for battle. It could happen at any time.

He'd been right about that.

"Are you a—" He paused and faced me. He scanned my face and his mouth gaped. "You're a virgin, aren't you?"

Most supernaturals were pretty open about enjoying sex as much as they pleased, so the fact that I hadn't slept with someone probably was shocking. It was that, with my position intimidating everyone, I'd never found someone I clicked with, and I didn't want to have sex for the sake of having sex. "You make it sound like a bad thing."

"Hell, no." He perused my body. "It makes you hotter. How is that possible?"

"Well, you see, I keep my legs closed nice and tight." What kind of question was that? Plus, his attention was making me uncomfortable.

"You are a breath of fresh air." He focused back on the road. "Within the first few seconds of me meeting you, you elbowed my stomach and broke my nose. And you say whatever you think with no hidden agenda. It's nice."

I'd forgotten about his nose. He hadn't said much of anything about it when we'd gotten back to his place, but now that he'd pointed it out, I could see that it was a little crooked. His bones had healed that way. "I'm so sorry. We should've tried to straighten it."

"Are you kidding me?" He flexed the arm nearest me, making his bicep muscle bulge. "You've officially made me sexier. No girl will be able to let me walk by."

"Remember, we're exclusive." I teased him. "I will cut your pecker off if you cheat and make me look like a fool."

"I don't think I'm scared." He chuckled. "You probably wouldn't know what to do with it once it was unleashed."

"Oh, ha. Ha." He was right, but I'd never admit that to him.

We drove into the bustling downtown again, and he pulled into a small parking lot next to a brick building that stood separate from the others. A huge sign on the front read Dick's Bar.

"Really?" I gestured to the name. "That's the name of the bar? Let me guess. Griffin named it."

"Believe it or not, that's Luna's dad's name, and he owns the bar." He pulled into a spot next to a black Navigator on my side. "And want to hear their last name? It makes it even more epic."

I was officially afraid. Not of my life being in danger but that I would regret playing into Killian's hand. "What?"

"Harding." He cracked up. "His name is Dick Harding."

I snorted. "No. Tell me he goes by Richard."

"He does not." He opened the door and winked. "That's what makes it even more epic. Just a heads up, he's Griffin's Beta."

That was good to know.

I watched Killian move toward me, but my door opened, startling me. I'd been so caught up in Killian's and my conversation that I hadn't noticed Griffin come up to my car door and open it. I inhaled as that weird *tug* clenched inside my chest.

Griffin leaned over me and unbuckled my seatbelt. "Are you two having a good time?"

His fingers brushed my arm, and my skin buzzed. I inhaled deeply, smelling his musky myrrh and leather scent. My body warmed. What in the hell was going on between us? Maybe it was lust. That was all it could be.

Nope. Not happening. Shutting that down.

I grabbed his arm and pulled it away from me as the seat belt slid off. "Thanks, but I've got it."

His hazel eyes appeared to glow, making my palms sweaty. "Hey, you're my best friend's girl. I gotta make sure you're taken care of."

"Dude, back off," Killian said as he pushed Griffin away. "She's mine. Go find yourself another one-night stand."

Griffin leaned against the Navigator as I slipped from the car and took Killian's hand. I not only was emphasizing to him that I was with Killian but begrudgingly doing it to remind myself.

A frown formed on Griffin's face, and his shoulders drooped, making me feel guilty for holding Killian's hand. I hadn't done anything wrong, but I couldn't shake the feeling.

High heels clacked on the cement as Luna's overly ripe scent announced her arrival. She stuck out her bottom lip and glared at Griffin. "What the hell, Griff? You left me. I thought we were riding together."

"Sorry." His attention stayed on me. "I've got some things to do after this, so you needed to drive separately."

"You could've told me that, and besides, I'm not busy." She brushed a hand on his shoulder. "I can go with you."

My body tensed at her proximity to him, but I pushed the sensation away. He could let whoever he wanted to touch him.

Griffin removed her hand. "Nope, you can't."

The way he dismissed her made me way too happy.

"So, while you two figure out your plans, Dove and I are heading inside." Killian wrapped an arm around my waist and nudged me toward the entrance.

A low growl emanated from behind me, and I forced myself to keep my eyes forward and not look back to see what Griffin was upset about. If I confirmed he felt whatever this *tug* was between us, it would only make it harder for me to keep my distance.

"Don't you dare walk away from me," Luna yelled as her heels click-clacked after him. "You're going to talk to me. What the hell is your problem?"

"Hurry, let's get out of here," Killian whispered close to my ear.

Griffin sighed. "Can you stop being a drama queen?"

Oh, that wasn't smart. Calling a woman a drama queen was equivalent to calling a crazy person... well... crazy.

"I'll show you drama queen," Luna whispered threateningly.

Killian and I entered the building. The bar was one large open square with a cherry wood bar in the middle of the wall to the right. Three people were working behind the counter, and it looked like they had several beers on tap along with a cabinet full of wines and liquors. Cups of varying sizes were shelved below the cabinets. Stools lined the bar, and about twenty round tables were scattered around the main floor. The walls were made of varying neutral colors of brick with booths set against them. Televisions hung in every corner of the room, but they weren't blaring.

"I can actually hear myself think." This wasn't as bad as I'd expected. Between the tolerable noise level and lack of smoke, eating here wouldn't be that bad. Well, if Griffin and Luna weren't going to be joining us.

"This is a bar owned by wolf shifters in a mostly supernatural town." Killian bumped his shoulder into mine. "None of us like loud noises."

Fair point.

A beautiful sandy-blonde-haired girl headed in our direction. She wore a white button-down shirt and gray slacks that matched her eyes. She was a few inches shorter than me, but she walked with such poise that she appeared taller. Her hair was pulled back into a low ponytail with tendrils framing her face. "Hey, Killian." She smirked when her attention landed on me. "Who's this?"

"Sierra, this is Dove." He kissed my cheek and pulled back, gesturing to the girl. "Dove, this is Sierra. One of the few girls in town who knows how to handle both Griffin's and my asses."

"Handle?" She laughed. "I don't know if I would go that far, but I gotta say, you've never been one to take a girl out the day after a night of passion."

"She's different." He wrapped an arm around my waist. "She's tamed my wild ways."

"A girl after my own heart." Sierra leaned toward me. "You'll have to tell me your secret skills later, but for now, is it just the two of you?"

"No, unfortunately, Griffin and the devil incarnate will be joining us momentarily." Killian shivered. "Did you bring the holy water?"

"Between her and her dad, I always have extra on hand."

"Is her dad as bad as she is?" I couldn't imagine that.

Sierra grabbed four laminated menus and rolled her eyes. "He's worse in a different way. He wants everything to be perfect, but he's super nice. Luna demands all the attention. She's had her sights set on Griffin since she was a kid."

"That long?" I could kind of see it.

"Yes, that long." She waved for us to follow her. "Where are you from? I haven't seen you around."

"Oh, that's because I'm new." I had no clue what else to say. I didn't want to tell her how I got here, and I couldn't lie, mainly because she'd know. "Killian found me, and the rest is history."

"He tries to be a player like Griffin, but he could never quite pull it off." She stopped at a booth and turned to Killian, squishing his cheeks. "And now he has a girlfriend. My little buddy is growing up."

"You two act like brother and sister." I slid into the booth and scooted over to the wall.

Killian got in beside me and took my hand, placing it on the table. "We pretty much are. She was my sister's best friend. Sierra is my age, but she clicked with my younger sister because they had the same maturity level."

"Yup, Olive was way more mature than Killian." Sierra jutted her hip. "If she was here, she'd be kicking his ass into gear. Maybe you could do that job since he won't listen to anyone else."

"Olive had a way," Killian said with longing.

The *tug* pulled at me once again, and my attention went to the front door as it opened and Luna and Griffin marched inside. They radiated tension and avoided looking in each other's direction.

A man entered and walked around them, taking a seat at the end of the bar near a small hallway that had an exit sign.

Sierra frowned and blew out a breath. "I still miss her so much."

"Oh, God." Luna sighed as she slid into the booth on the opposite side. "Every time Sierra serves us, we have to talk about Olive. She's dead; it sucks. We've got to move on."

"So, when you die, you want your friends or family to never think of you?" I stared the entitled brat down. "We should roll our eyes and tell everyone to move on?"

One side of Griffin's lips tugged upward until Killian wrapped an arm around my shoulders. The smile slipped from Griffin's face, and he glared at us.

"I will take every opportunity to talk about my sister and celebrate her life and her friends." Killian wrinkled his nose. "If that bothers you, you can go sit at a different table."

"You are kind of being a bitch," Griffin said as he slid in next to her. "Don't take out your anger at me on them."

"Fine." Luna crossed her arms, her body language making it clear she wouldn't be apologizing. The tension grew thick between us.

The image of my pack members, bloody and dying, popped into my mind. My eyes burned with unshed tears, and I choked back a sob. I cleared my throat, desperate for my words to sound normal. "I need to run to the bathroom." I nudged Killian's arm, making sure he heard me.

"Oh, yeah." Killian stood.

I slid out and glanced around the room, looking for a restroom sign.

"It's over there before the back exit." Sierra pointed toward the small hallway I'd noticed earlier. "There's a men's and women's bathroom on either side of the hall."

"Thanks." I hurried in that direction, desperate for some time alone to compose myself. I didn't want to break down in front of Griffin and definitely not Luna. I didn't want either one of them to think I was weak.

"Is she okay?" Sierra asked the table.

Killian cleared his throat. "I'm sure she's fine."

The hallway was dark, not that it mattered with my wolf eyes, and longer than it looked. The women's bathroom was the door on the right. A few tears spilled over and trailed down my cheeks.

Dammit. My numbness was wearing off fast. Focused on getting into the bathroom to hide my imminent breakdown, I pushed the door open.

A calloused hand grabbed my arm and yanked. Another arm snaked around my neck and placed a knife against my throat.

"One sound, and I'll slit your throat," a deep voice hissed.

CHAPTER EIGHT

HE NUDGED the knife deeper into my skin. Warm liquid trickled down my neck as the copper scent of blood hit my nose. This prick was enjoying himself.

"What do you want?" I asked, trying to keep my fear at bay, hoping to learn something—anything—about why I was such a target.

"Absolutely nothing." He chuckled darkly, "Other than you need to move to the exit now." He pushed me forward, and I stumbled, causing the knife to dig a little deeper.

Asshole.

I'd rather die right there than leave. With a knife to my neck, there was only one way this could go.

Keeping my arms close to my body, I raised my hands toward his knife arm and relaxed my body into his chest. He loosened his hold, and I grabbed his wrist with both of my hands and pulled down and away from my neck.

"What—" He hissed.

His hold slackened and I slipped under his arm, keeping my grip firm on his wrist. When I broke free, I shoved the hand holding the knife back at him so the blade cut into his side.

"You stupid bitch," he yelled as he tried to recapture me with his free arm. Using his slumped angle to my advantage, I kicked his face and twisted his wrist, manipulating a pressure point by his thumb to make him release the hold on the knife. He stumbled back, and I kicked the knife away.

"Dove!" Killian yelled, but I didn't have time to answer him.

This guy wouldn't go down without a fight.

As he stood and faced me, I could see the spot where my foot had connected with his jaw. For the first time, I got a good view of him.

It was the guy who'd entered the bar behind Griffin and Luna.

His hair was dyed an awful ash blond, except for the dark brown sides. His long beard hit the top of the collar of his black shirt, connecting with the chest hair that spilled there. His hairy arms were almost as thick as his beard. I already suspected he was a bear shifter, and his grassy scent confirmed it.

"You're going to pay for that." He snatched my arm again and dragged me toward the exit.

Bear shifters were strong, but their arrogance worked against them.

"Let her go," Griffin commanded, alpha will lacing his words.

He was a fucking moron if he thought that would work on a bear, and massively egotistical if he thought that the bear would listen to him in the first place. He had no authority over them.

Confirming my suspicions, the bear shifter didn't loosen his grip on me. Instead, he tightened it and dragged me harder.

I might not have had a knife to my neck anymore, but that didn't mean I wasn't at risk of being taken. Doing the first thing that came to mind, I stuck my fingers into one of his knife wounds and made my hands like claws, breaking through fat and muscle. The wound needed to get worse, so I dug my fingers in hard, trying to get his brain to register the pain. With all the adrenaline pumping through his body, he probably hadn't even noticed he'd been stabbed.

He swung his free hand, aiming for my face, but I easily blocked it.

Dad had been right all along. If we didn't know how to protect ourselves, we were screwed. I wished I could take back all of those times I talked smack about him or complained.

Because of him, I still stood here, surviving.

As I straightened, I pulled my hands out of his side and round-kicked the asshole in the stomach. He fell against the brick wall.

"We can take it from here," Killian said as he got closer.

Oh, hell no. This was all me.

I scooped the knife from the floor as Killian and Griffin reached me. They grabbed the guy by the arms as I ran behind the bear shifter and placed the knife against his throat. I leaned in and saw blood well from beneath the blade. "Who are you, and what do you want from me?"

"Go to hell." He spat in my face.

Nope, that wasn't acceptable. I elbowed him hard in the temple, knocking him unconscious, and let him crumble to the floor. "Stupid prick."

"Uh. Wow." Killian snorted as he and Griffin released the guy, letting him drop to the floor.

I used the sleeve of my dress to wipe away the spittle. I wanted a shower *now*.

Sierra gasped, "She's freaking badass."

"Badass?" Luna scoffed. "Men are supposed to be the protectors, not us. That was extremely unladylike."

Oh, wow. Her beliefs were archaic. Good thing I wasn't raised that way, or I'd be captured or dead by now.

"Hey, are you hurt?" Killian rushed over to examine me.

"Look at her neck," Griffin said through clenched teeth. "The bastard cut her. I'm going to make him pay."

"I'm fine." Both of them were being a little too much. "Besides, I knocked him out cold. Everything will be okay, but I want answers."

I glanced down at my dress and cringed. Not only was I wearing this godforsaken thing, but I didn't have my knife on me because of the outfit. I needed better clothes and pronto.

Footsteps pounded in our direction. "What's going on here?" a deep, raspy voice asked.

"Daddy!" Luna sounded relieved. "A man attacked Dove."

So good ol' Dick Harding was here.

"Dove?" A tall man stepped into the hallway, and his ebony eyes landed on me. He ran a hand through his shortish salt and pepper hair. A frown marred his chiseled face, which was covered by dark brown scruff. "You're new in town."

"Yup." He was more focused on me being new here than the guy lying on the floor? That was a bit strange. "I am."

"I swear, Griffin." Dick looked past me to the bear shifter and shook his head. "We've got to do something about this. Obviously, people are growing more wary of letting residents out of Shadow City, and now you're trying to get me to promote letting people in. That's such a horrible idea for this reason here. Yet another attack targeting wolves."

"There's nothing we can do about it even if I wanted to undo Dad's decision." Griffin kept his attention on me. "The entire council voted, and there was a majority."

My brain struggled to catch up. Nothing they were saying made sense. "You're part of a council?"

"Yes, he is," Luna said and stepped over, placing a hand on Griffin's shoulder. "He's the alpha of Shadow City."

Laughter almost bubbled out of me. This had to be some sort of sick joke. From what I'd seen, he was more interested in getting into various women's pants than being a leader. Maybe his goal was to be a lead douchebag?

Griffin stepped away from Luna, making her hand fall. He cleared his throat. "My dad was the alpha, and he passed away right before the college was built. The alpha power and title fell to me, but Dick has gracefully stepped forward to help lead the city while I attend college and get my priorities in order."

Things clicked into place, and I groaned. I hadn't realized that I'd been holding out hope that Shadow City's new alpha would be my ally. Griffin wouldn't help me. At least, I understood why Luna wanted him and was willing to do whatever it took to lock him down. Hell, almost no one would turn him down. From what Dad said, the city had become the home of some of the strongest supernaturals he'd ever seen, and Atticus had been a beacon of power. If that was the case, that meant that Griffin was one of the most powerful wolves in the world, and snagging him would set his mate up for life.

Killian squatted next to the bear shifter and dug through his pockets. "He has no ID on him or anything."

"That's consistent. It has to be so no one can identify the attackers if something goes wrong." Dick sighed, but it seemed...off.

What he said had merit, but for some reason, I didn't buy it. This bear was cocky. He'd honestly thought he had me. He wouldn't think to leave his stuff in his car or wherever, so there had to be another reason he carried no ID. I kept my mouth shut, though, since I wasn't alone with Killian.

"Harold." Dick faced the front of the restaurant and clapped. "Take this jackass who attacked this poor girl to Shadow City jail. He's been roughed up enough, so try not to injure him much more. We need him to be able to talk."

A dark olive wolf shifter about Killian's height appeared and walked past us but avoided eye contact. He bent down, picked up the injured bear, and headed straight out the exit door.

He was gone within seconds like he couldn't stand to be near us or was scared. So strange.

"I'm impressed that you handled him without getting injured." Dick tightened his black tie as he addressed Killian and Griffin, ignoring my presence. "And thank God there are no other customers. That could've been a publicity nightmare."

"Actually, Dove took the guy out on her own." Sierra smirked and gestured to me. "Griffin and Killian didn't make it in time."

"Are you serious?" Dick's gaze landed on me, making my skin crawl. "That's *interesting*."

His negative energy nearly stole my breath. But I couldn't afford to alert him to that little fact. Dad had told me that at some point in my life, I'd meet someone truly evil. And that I couldn't let on that I could sense their darkness because it was a trait only silver wolves had. If I gave away my reaction, I could put not only myself in danger but the people I cared about. Granted, at this time, the total of people I cared about had dwindled to one—Killian. But I had to continue to play the game until I had a royal flush. Only then could I reveal my hand. "What can I say?" I forced my words to sound light, and I smiled. If my gut hadn't warned me, I would've thought he was concerned. "I believe that everyone should know how to protect themselves. Had I not been trained, this situation could've gone an extremely different way."

"So true." He smiled. "Even though men are normally the guards, not the women."

My skin crawled from his creepy-ass smile. Not only that, but he'd chastised me yet somehow managed to make it not sound too judgy. So he was the worst kind of villain—a manipulator—which meant Killian and Griffin were clueless. "In this particular instance, it's a good thing I didn't need a man, or he would've had me out the door." I refused to cower like Dick wanted.

Something unreadable crossed Dick's face before his features smoothed back into place. "Well, I should probably get back to Shadow City. I'd planned on working the books here for a little while today, but that obviously won't be happening."

"I'll go with you," Griffin said as his forehead lined. He scanned me before looking at Killian. "And why don't you take her somewhere safe?" His voice held concern, which shocked me.

"That's a good idea." Killian wrapped an arm around my shoulders and gestured to the exit. "Do you mind if we leave this way?"

"Sure." Dick waved him off, but his shoulders tensed. He turned to Griffin. "Stay here with Luna and have lunch. I can handle the attacker."

"No, I'll go with you." Griffin narrowed his eyes. "Technically, it's my place, not yours. And he attacked my best friend's g—" He cut off like he couldn't say the word and inhaled sharply. "Dove. He attacked Dove right in front of us. That's equivalent to him giving me the middle finger. I want to hear what he has to say."

"But—" Dick started.

Luna touched her dad's arm. "It's a good thing he wants—"

He cut her off with a glare. "Obviously, I can't tell you no, but I think it would be more prudent for you to stay here and enjoy a meal."

Griffin pursed his lips as he considered Dick's words.

"Yes." Dick blatantly didn't want Griffin to go with him, to the point where he was openly discouraging it. "Having lunch is *so* much more important than attending to alpha duties," I said sweetly as I smiled and batted my eyelashes.

"Don't worry, I'm not ready to step in permanently." Griffin straightened. "But like I said, he attacked her right in front of me, almost like a dare. One day, I will take back the role full time, and I need to show everyone I won't take any bullshit."

"Come on." Killian took my hand and opened the back door. "We'll see you guys later."

I let him pull me out the door, but I didn't want to leave. Dick was attempting to make Griffin stand down, and for whatever reason, Griffin had almost allowed it. If I hadn't butted in, I had a feeling he would have lost his nerve. But if Griffin was the true alpha and he wanted to be part of the interrogation, it wasn't Dick's place to tell him no or discourage him.

"You okay?" Killian asked, leading me to his truck.

"Yeah, why?" I focused on Killian. Everything inside me was telling me to go back to Griffin, which I didn't understand. The sensation *tugged* and itched inside me almost to the point of being overwhelming. He had some sort of hold on me, and I didn't like it one bit.

"Let's see, you went up against Dick." He chuckled. "And you were attacked."

"What is Dick's problem?" I tried to sound casual, but I desperately wanted to know.

"Well, he hates a woman talking back to him, but he's a good guy other than that." Killian opened the passenger door. "When Atticus died, the entire wolf pack in Shadow City landed on Griffin's shoulders. He was seventeen. My pack is large, around eight hundred wolves, but he's alpha, not only over the six hundred who live in Shadow City—but he also represents the over fifteen hundred various shifters who live outside. Not only did all the responsibility land on him, but he was grieving for his father while still learning to be a man, just like me. Dick offered to be his proxy. He's taken on a lot of the alpha responsibilities to let Griffin have a semi-normal college experience before Dick hands the reins back to him. That's why Griffin is majoring in political science, preparing for his inevitable role."

So that was the angle the older man was working. I had a gut feeling he had no intention of handing the power back to Griffin. "Is Griffin not your alpha too?" If Killian's pack were the ones protecting the city, it'd make sense that they were connected.

He chuckled. "No. With us living outside, we have our own pack. It works better that way. Besides, if we didn't, then we'd have to get approval from the council for any decisions we—or rather, I—make. It's easiest to stay separate."

"I see. And why didn't you tell me who Griffin was?" That kind of burned, but I didn't have a right to be upset. We'd known each other for only a day, and I had a ton of secrets that I hadn't shared with him. I slid into my seat.

"Because Griffin would rather pretend no one knows, though that's truly impossible." He pulled at his ear. I realized it was a sign that he was uncomfortable. "That kind of role isn't one you can hide from."

"What's going on with the attacks? It sounded like there was more to the bear shifter attacking me today." Maybe today's attack on me was coincidental, but that seemed convenient. Something about the whole thing bothered me.

Killian tapped his fingers on the steering wheel. "Ever since Shadow City began to open back up and the college was built, there's been at least one attack a month on wolves. We think it's because Atticus was the one who headed the charge." He shrugged. "Either way, your best bet is to stick with me, especially since you've been attacked twice in two days."

"I thought Shadow City was a place of refuge. How did it become so volatile?" That was the missing piece that I couldn't get a handle on.

"From what Griffin had told me one drunken night, that had been the intent, but they started recruiting powerful beings and approving only the strongest to move there before the border shut down." He shrugged. "I didn't push for more information, but essentially, only the strongest of the races were allowed into the city."

So much hidden history. But it wasn't my problem. I had something more pressing on my mind. "I need clothes." I lifted the skirt material. "This isn't cutting it. I need jeans so I can carry my knife around. I hate to ask, but can you cover me until I get my first paycheck?"

"Normally, I would argue with you, but after today, I won't." He pouted. "So I guess that means I'm taking you shopping."

THE REST of the day flew by, despite me looking over my shoulder at all times, expecting to be jumped again. I'd gotten two pairs of jeans, a few shirts, a pair of tennis shoes, and boots at a local thrift store, so tomorrow I'd feel more like myself.

Once my new-to-me stuff was washed, I put it away and then paced around the small bedroom. It was almost eleven at night, and I was restless. My wolf was edgy, not having a pack, and that damn *tug* was working at me again. I'd been waiting for Killian to settle in for the night so I could head out to the backyard and stand in the moonlight for a few minutes. The moon always seemed to soothe my soul and spoke to my wolf in a way that was almost inexplicable. It wasn't nearly as effective as running in animal form, but it would help ease the turmoil brimming within.

As quietly as possible, I opened my door and creeped out to the back porch. Low mumblings from the television from Killian's room informed me he was already in bed. My heart slowed as a sense of calm settled over me. I needed to be alone. He and I had been together all day, and even though I enjoyed his company, I needed space to function properly.

I slipped down the brick steps and around the concrete pool area until my feet touched the grass on the side of the yard. I lifted my face to the moon, feeling a little bit of its power wash over me. Even though it was a trickle compared to a full moon, it was enough to make my blood buzz.

That was when I heard the snap of a branch. I tensed.

I wasn't alone.

CHAPTER NINE

I SPUN on my heels and faced the direction of the white house next door. The scent of leather and myrrh filled my nose, and the *tug* from earlier reappeared.

Griffin was near.

Dammit. I came out here for peace, and the douchebag showed up here. Maybe he came for a swim. Either way, I had to stay away from him. For some reason, he grated on my nerves by being in close proximity. The fact that I was drawn to his playboy ways pissed me off even more.

No self-respecting girl would want someone like him. And I refused to become another notch in his belt, even if I would love to know how his lips tasted.

That was another reason I didn't need to be around him. I would never taste his lips. Ever.

Hoping he hadn't seen me, I turned to go back inside.

"What are you doing out here alone?" he asked as he stepped from the tree line.

I scowled at him. "Minding my own business, unlike you." I wished there was a privacy fence around the pool so I could've hidden, but shifters instinctively knew how to swim, so drowning wasn't a hazard.

"Noted." He shoved his hands into his pockets and stopped about five feet away from me. He still had on the same clothes from this afternoon, but he looked a little worse for wear. "You kicked that bear shifter's ass. But I wouldn't get too cocky. You probably couldn't do it again."

"Why, because I'm a girl?" Malice dripped from each word.

Griffin chuckled. "The guy wasn't expecting you to fight back, so you had the element of surprise."

What an arrogant bastard. Granted, I already knew that about him from earlier, but his smugness seemed to get worse each time I saw him, and that had been only twice so far. What would happen next time? Maybe he'd try to prove his point by tossing me in front of a car.

"We could fight now." I'd kick his ass, and that would be the end of it.

Hopefully.

"You think you could take me?" He touched his chest with a huge-ass smirk. His eyes flicked to my mouth, and I licked my lips in response.

Agh, I had to stop. I squared my shoulders and lifted my chin. "I know I can." Especially with the moon shining on me, I could kick his ass with my eyes closed.

"You want to shift into our wolves?" He grabbed the hem of his shirt, ready to remove it.

That was a big fat no. If I shifted, he'd probably know what I was. "Nope, I don't need my animal to make you scream like a girl."

"Well, all right then." He charged at me without warning, fighting dirty.

I wasn't surprised. He moved to wrap his arm around my waist, and I spun to the right out of his reach. He ran past me and almost fell since he had planned on my body to stop his momentum.

He huffed and faced me as his hazel eyes glowed. "You were lucky."

"You keep saying that." I couldn't help but antagonize him. His first move told me everything I needed to know about him as a fighter. He was strong, but he relied on his strength to win. Besides that, he had no form, no fighting technique, and bad general awareness of how to move. Maybe Shadow City had gotten spoiled since they had guards. This alpha was focused more on political studies and alliances than maneuvers, though I imagined with the proper training, he could be a force on the battlefield.

Rolling his shoulders, he stretched his neck side to side like that would make a difference.

I leaned back on my feet like I didn't have a care in the world. I enjoyed goading him. My body warmed, but I pretended it was from the brawl and not due to the handsome man standing in front of me.

"For what it's worth, I was trying to go easy on you, but not anymore." He shook his hands out at his sides and wiggled. "It's on." He lunged at me, dropping as he kicked out one of his feet with the intent to make me fall.

Wanting to end this, I let the moon charge through my blood and jumped over his leg. I landed behind him and dropped my elbow so that it touched the back of his neck and shoulder but didn't press down hard. "If I wanted to, I could knock you out. You still think I was only lucky earlier?"

He turned, and his chest brushed my side.

Goosebumps spread all over me as my body sizzled. *It has to be the moon,* I lied to myself. But the lie was pointless. This strange feeling had to do with the sexy guy right in front of me. If I didn't know any better, I'd think he was my fated mate. But a jerk like him *couldn't* be that.

His head lowered to mine, and I didn't want to move. Something coursed between us and made my head fuzzy.

That was what I needed to snap out of whatever spell was captivating us. I took three large steps away from him. The warmth vanished. "What are you doing here?"

"I went for a slow run and was heading back home." He nodded to the white house next door.

His words didn't make sense for a moment. "Wait, you're Killian's neighbor?"

"Right next door." He gestured to the house with all the beer cans littering the yard. "Did your *boyfriend* fail to mention that? I've lived next door to him for two years now."

"Why would he?" Normally men who had overinflated egos were short by shifter standards, so with Griffin's height, I wasn't sure what his excuse might be. Maybe small-dick syndrome. My gaze dropped to his crotch, and I could see the outline in his blue jeans.

No small dick. Maybe insecurity then.

"Because I'm his best friend." He scoffed like that should be obvious. "And we've been inseparable since I left Shadow City."

"Are you sure?" I tilted my head and shrugged. "Because it seems like you're busier hanging out with Luna and her daddy than trying to be a friend to Killian."

"Aw." He chuckled. "It's cute that you're so concerned."

He was enjoying getting under my skin. I wanted to snap back at him, but I'd already said and done too much. I'd come out here to be alone and calm myself. Fighting with him had resulted in the complete opposite.

The time had come for me to take control. I took a few steps toward Killian's house, determined to leave his ass behind.

"Dove." He sighed and caught up then stepped in front of me. "Give me a moment, please."

Wow, he was being nice...except for blocking me. "You have one minute."

A growl emanated from his chest at my demand, but his eyes softened. "I want to know how you really are."

The concern in his voice caught me off guard. I didn't like him sounding like a nice guy, especially when I got confused vibes from him. There was no evil inside him, which proved that he was a good person, unlike Luna and Dick. Once again, I was thankful for that perk of being a silver wolf—being able to sense someone's true intent. Hating him wasn't possible, despite him getting under my skin. That was why I needed him to be the douchebag from a few minutes ago. "I'm fine." The awful odor of a lie wafted off me.

"You're trying to lie to me?" He coughed and waved a hand in front of his nose. "Do you think I can't smell it or something?"

Man, I hated that he had me there. "The words came out."

And now I didn't have any of them. The hole in my heart ripped open even more. So far, my lone wolf status hadn't fractured me mentally, but the restlessness was a sign of that beginning. I needed to figure out my next steps, which should involve finding another pack, but I couldn't take the risk. At least, not right then. As soon as I joined one, the link would alert them all that I was different than a normal wolf.

Griffin's fingers brushed my arm. "Hey, are you okay? It's like you're somewhere else."

"Yeah, sorry." I would work harder to hold myself together. I couldn't break down, especially in front of him. "And I'll be fine." I internally cringed, waiting for the smell of a lie to reek again, but reassuringly, the air stayed fresh. I did believe that.

Strange.

I hadn't expected to.

"What can I do to make it better?" He inched closer to me. "I want to make things easier for you."

My body betrayed me, and I leaned toward him. I had to forget about his touch, smell, and proximity. "Tell me what you learned from the bear shifter." There. Even if he did affect me, I'd managed to keep our conversation strictly business.

"Well, that was a clusterfuck." His jaw clenched, and his hand dropped as he looked up at the night sky.

Wow, helpful. "Care to expand on that?"

Griffin met my stare. "I came over to tell Killian what happened, and I heard you two eating dinner together."

I studied him, at a loss. "Why didn't you knock?" He didn't seem like the type who would care if we were eating dinner. He'd barge on in.

"I expected him to be alone," he said tightly. "So I was waiting for you to leave, but here you are in the backyard in your pajamas. Are you staying with him?"

"A reminder, I was the one who was attacked, not him." I gestured to the house. "And how is my staying here any of your damn business?"

"It's not." He lifted his hands. "I was curious. And I wanted to talk only to him because I was trying not to see you."

His words stung, which made me even angrier. He shouldn't have this much of an effect on me. In fact, I should have been ecstatic that he didn't want to see me, but the fact that the air didn't smell told me all I needed to know. "Then why did you start talking to me?" If he didn't want to be around me, then he shouldn't have said anything in the first place. "I was about to go inside, and you wouldn't have been forced to have this conversation."

"Because I thought about it, and I figured you should know too." He blew out a breath and narrowed his eyes.

Wanting to get back to the actual point, I crossed my arms. "Then tell me—what happened with the bear shifter?"

"There isn't much to tell." Griffin ran a hand through his gelled hair, messing it up.

I grimaced. He was somehow even more breathtaking.

But I refused to be distracted. No good would come from it. "Well then, this should be a very short conversation," I snapped. One minute, I was trying to be nice to him, and the next, I was angry. My emotions had become a yo-yo, and I didn't know why.

"Remember how that guy who works for Dick—Harold—was taking the bear shifter to the Shadow City jail?" he asked.

"Yup." Maybe if I was brief, he would get to the point faster.

"The bear shifter somehow knocked him unconscious and got away." He clenched his hands into fists. "Which means we have no leads to whether he was the only person in on the attack or if it was a calculated move organized by others. Either way, the asshole is somewhere out here again."

"Wasn't he cuffed?" Surely the guy wouldn't have put the bear in the back of a car unrestrained.

Griffin laughed without humor. "Actually, he wasn't. Harold tied him up with a rope, but the bear shifter pretended to be unconscious and bit through it. He attacked Harold, making him drive off the bridge that leads to Shadow City."

"A bridge?" I hadn't seen more than downtown Shadow Ridge and the university, so I had no clue how many ways there were to enter Shadow City.

He waved his hand in a circular motion. "The river surrounds a large island that Shadow City is built on. The bridge leads to the gate to enter. Witches have spelled the city so that the Tennessee River around it appears narrower than it really is, which is why there isn't a lot of river traffic through here." He rolled his eyes. "Luckily, Harold came to before the car filled with water, but the bear shifter was already gone. His scent was untraceable. I'm sorry you got thrown into this mess. He attacked you because you were with me. They're trying to scare me so I'll try to shut the borders again."

"Then why were you out here alone?" If the bear could be anywhere, it made sense that he might try to attack me again, but we didn't know if I was the target or the most convenient wolf body at the time.

"You were too." Griffin pointed at me. "So, I think that's a little hypocritical."

"I thought he was in jail." In all fairness, if I'd known he'd escaped, my first instinct would have been to track his ass down. But I needed to stay put for a little while longer. I didn't need my hunters finding me, much as I didn't want anyone else suffering an attack. "What's your excuse?"

"My excuse isn't a good one." He closed the distance between us again, and he was so close his minty breath hit my face.

My breathing quickened, almost matching the racing beat of my heart. "I didn't ask if it was a good one. I asked what it was."

"I wanted to make sure that the bear didn't come looking for you. I was going to ask Killian where you lived. When I realized you were here, I was planning to follow you home." He sighed as if what he said next pained him to admit. "Seeing you hurt like that earlier almost made me go insane."

His words threatened to tear down my walls, but this couldn't happen. Whatever *this* was. "I'm with Killian." It helped that we'd agreed to be exclusive, so this wasn't a lie. Besides, Killian had helped me, and I couldn't let my inconvenient reaction to some hot guy screw up my relationship with the only friend I had.

"Yeah, I'm well aware." A vein between his brows bulged. "Thanks for the reminder."

"What the hell is your problem?" I didn't know what was happening between us. Lust? Would having sex with him get rid of this energy? *Absolutely not.* No way would my first time be with some playboy who got his rocks off by talking about his cream and where he liked it placed.

"Nothing," he said a little too loudly. "Nothing at all. I mean, I'm ready for him to get over his feelings for you and kick your ass to the curb."

"Says the douchebag who hit on me in front of the girl who's trying to manipulate him into settling down." If he wanted to hurt me, I could return the favor.

"She is not." He scoffed. "Don't be crazy."

Oh, *hell* no. He had a death wish. I stomped my foot, channeling Luna. "Griffin," I whined and pouted, sticking my bottom lip out as far as it would go. "You left me." I straightened, not able to keep up the charade, and patted my chest and rolled my eyes. "You're right. My bad. She totally isn't trying to manipulate you."

"Jealousy is a good look on you." He wrapped an arm around my waist and pulled me hard against his chest. "In fact, it's sexy. Maybe I should rile you up more often."

The *tug* strengthened to where it felt like two magnets were pulling toward each other.

My body warmed in ways it never had before, and I didn't even try to move away.

"You *are* attracted to me too." He dipped his head, and the world around us disappeared, the connection between us too strong to be ignored. His lips aimed for mine as my rationale left me. I couldn't remember why this was a bad idea.

The back door jingled and opened. "Dove?" Killian called.

CHAPTER TEN

I SHOVED Griffin away and jerked back as Killian stepped onto the back porch. He paused and rubbed his chin as he took us in.

"Are you two trying to wake up the neighborhood?" he asked.

"No." I'd been aware we were getting loud, but I hadn't realized the extent.

Griffin yanked at his shirt and glared at me. "Why the hell did you shove me?"

"Because you were all up in my face." And I'd loved every second of it. I didn't even want to consider what would've happened if Killian hadn't come outside. Griffin's lips had been only a breath away from mine, and I hadn't had the fight in me to pull away.

I couldn't be alone with him. Hell, I shouldn't be around him at all, but definitely not alone.

"You weren't complaining a few seconds ago." Griffin smirked.

"What the hell does that mean?" Killian tensed and ran down the stairs, joining us in the backyard.

My body felt like it was on fire, and not the kind I'd felt moments ago. This was the kind that made me want to cover my face in shame.

I'd almost broken a promise to the one person I could rely on. I had to figure out a way to salvage this. "He and I scuffled." That wasn't a lie.

"Scuffled?" Killian parroted, and his forehead etched with confusion.

"He didn't think I could kick his ass." I avoided Griffin's gaze, not wanting to see his expression. "So, I had to prove to him that I can handle myself."

"Dude, I could've told you that." Killian pointed at his face. "She broke my nose yesterday."

"Whatever," Griffin grumbled. "But it's her fault we're fighting. I was out here making sure the bear shifter wasn't around, and she came out all by herself. You'd think you wouldn't let your girlfriend come out at night alone."

"He's not my father, so I don't need his permission." God, I wanted to smack Griffin. I glared at him. "So why don't you go to Hell?"

Well, I escalated that quickly, but I couldn't control my emotions around him. This was going to be a problem.

"Oh, it's clear that he's not your father." Griffin laughed crazily. "You don't have to tell me that, but if he cares so damn much about you, then he needs to not let you go outside in the middle of the night by yourself. You could get captured or worse."

"Do we need to go over this again?" My body shook with so much anger. "I can take care of myself."

Killian touched my shoulder, and Griffin growled.

"Dude." Killian lifted his hand off me. "Are you okay?"

"I'm fine." Griffin straightened his shoulders and puffed out his chest. "More than fine. Great." The awful smell of a lie hit our noses.

"Yeah, right. If that's the case, then why are the two of you out here, yelling at each other?" Killian glanced at me before fixating on his friend again. "I mean, you say she shouldn't be outside, but if anyone was in the vicinity, they'd come check out the noise, and both of you could be in trouble."

Dammit, he was right. "Part of his concern is that the bear shifter escaped before they could get him to the jail."

"What?" Killian's mouth dropped. "How is that possible?"

Griffin's shoulders deflated, and he looked like the confused person I'd felt like earlier. He rubbed a hand down his face. "Apparently, Harold didn't follow standard police protocol, and the guy attacked him and got away." Griffin started the story from scratch, filling Killian in on everything he'd already told me.

"Why didn't you tell us this earlier?" Killian frowned. "He could try again."

"That's why I'm out here." Griffin glanced over his shoulder at the woods. "I wanted to make sure that no one was lurking around."

"We don't even know if he was targeting me." If the bear was one of the men who'd killed my pack, he would've known I was skilled and strong. He would've had backup, especially since it wasn't a new moon. I figured this had to be someone different, which made things even more complicated. "I could've been the closest wolf."

"She's right." Killian wrapped an arm around my waist as he watched Griffin. "The group that's unhappy are attacking wolves in general. Any of us could be next."

"I don't understand what's going on." I'd gleaned a lot earlier, but there were still crucial pieces of the puzzle missing. "I get that wolves are being attacked because you all opened the city back up, but I still don't understand—why only wolves?"

"Right before Dad died, he headed the initiative to open the borders, much to the chagrin of one of the angel council members and all three witch representatives. The vote was cast, and Dad got the majority by only one vote. Even though he died, there was no stopping the decision." Griffin winced with pain. "The alpha power transferred to me upon his death. At times, feeling everyone gets to be too much. That's why things have fallen apart since then."

"Any transition has road bumps." Killian tried to reassure him. "We've talked about this."

"And I told you that I'm not ready to be alpha. I could never be the kind of leader Dad was." Griffin rubbed his hands together. "The only reason I haven't handed the reins over to Dick permanently is all the turmoil going on. Once things are settled, I'll figure out my next steps."

Everyone fell silent, and after a prolonged moment, I forced a yawn. I'd come out here to find comfort and refuge, but all I'd gotten was drama and angst. "I'm exhausted. I'm going to bed."

"Shouldn't you go home?" Griffin rasped.

"Dude," Killian said, "she's staying with me for a while."

He raised both hands. "I was thinking if the bear attacked her because she was with us, staying away would be the best idea."

"I'm done having the same conversation with you over and over." I glared at him. "I've already kicked your ass, so drop it." I marched up the steps to the back porch and entered the house, leaving the two idiots outside.

When the door closed, I leaned against the wall, trying to find some sort of calm.

"Why are you being such an asshole to her?" Killian growled, and I startled, realizing I was in the perfect place to eavesdrop. I held my breath, trying to make sure I heard everything. Killian continued, "Is it because I got her first?"

"What?" Griffin said, sounding surprised. "No."

"Then what the hell is it?" Killian pushed harder.

My breath caught as I eagerly awaited his answer. I didn't know why, but his answer was so damn important to me.

"Man, I don't know." Griffin sighed. "She gets under my skin, and I have no clue why."

"Could it be because she shut you down when you tried hitting on her?" Killian asked.

"Maybe. I don't know, man." Griffin sounded conflicted. "I mean, don't get me wrong. I'm thrilled she shut me down since she has you, and I would've never hit on her if I'd known she was the girl you told me about last night. I think it's partly because she appeared out of nowhere, and now she's sleeping at your house. How much do you even know about her?"

I turned toward the door, ready to go back outside to interrupt their conversation. I didn't need Griffin learning about everything. He'd use it to his advantage. My hand reached the doorknob when Killian said, "Look, I appreciate you looking out for me. And there is a reason it happened so quickly. But it's not my place to tell you. Cut her some slack."

My hand fell to my side as my heart broke all over again. Killian had kept his word, but my gut said Griffin would start digging harder. I had to make sure I didn't let anything slip.

After all, my life depended on it.

A KNOCK on the door slammed me back to the present. I sat upright in the bed and glanced around, expecting someone to pop out from under the bed or out of the closet.

"Dove?" Killian said and knocked again.

"Come in." I pulled the covers over me for some dumb-ass reason. I had on a pair of pajama bottoms and a shirt. In fact, they were the same ones I'd worn outside during the whole weird conversation with Griffin. If I could even call it a conversation. It was more like rage, sexual tension, and me fighting off the urge to lick his entire body.

What the hell? Why was I thinking about licking him? That was wrong on all kinds of levels.

The door opened, and Killian sauntered in. He paused and glanced around the room, and I wondered if he was thinking about me living among his sister's things.

"Do you want me to come out instead?" I hadn't even thought about him not wanting to walk in here. He usually did stay in the hallway or in the living room.

"No, it's fine." He smiled sadly. "It's kind of nice to have you in her room. It brings a little bit of happiness to the space, the same way it felt when she was alive. Although she'd cry knowing that you didn't approve of her wardrobe. She and Mom loved going shopping together." He chuckled.

"Her clothes are great, just not my style. Did I oversleep?" If he was anything like me, he didn't want to continue that line of conversation. I glanced at the clock on the side table and read that it was seven in the morning.

"Nope, but we need to run and get your fake ID." He chuckled. "Carter will lose his shit if you show up without it again, so let's not stir the beast within."

I'd forgotten all about that. "Yeah, sounds great." Having an ID would mean I could open a checking account and other things. "I'll get dressed now."

Within thirty minutes, we were pulling into the breakfast diner where I'd seen the auburn-bearded man yesterday. I tried to calm my racing heart, but there wasn't much I could do about it. In the past, when I got nervous, I'd used my pack link to help calm me down, but I didn't have that now. Of course, that only made me panic even more.

"What's wrong?" Killian asked as he pulled into a metered spot alongside the road. "Your heart is pounding so hard I can hear it over the music. I don't think it could race any faster without you having a heart attack."

Yeah, tell me about it. "It's nothing," I said with a cracked voice as the smell of rotting eggs filled the car.

"No, seriously." He gagged at the smell. "What's wrong, and please don't lie. I haven't eaten, so it won't take much to make my stomach queasy."

"Remember when I freaked out yesterday?" I gestured to the red light we'd been stopped at.

He nodded.

"Well, that's the diner those guys came out of." I was being ridiculous, but I couldn't hold it in. Flashes of only two days ago replayed in my head, and the attack in the bar hadn't helped. I didn't want to go in there. I almost felt frozen in place.

"I'll be right there with you." Killian took my hand and gently pulled me so I faced him. "I won't leave your side."

He meant for that to be comforting, but he couldn't make that kind of promise. I hated feeling so weak and pathetic, but my wolf pawed against my head.

"Hey." He cupped my cheek. "Breathe."

But I couldn't even when I tried. I had to get away and connect with my wolf. It was the only way to become calm. "I've gotta go. I'm sorry." I pulled away from Killian and threw open the door. "I have to get away. Please don't follow me. I need a moment by myself. Just... get my ID please. I'll meet you back here in twenty."

"Dammit, Dove." Killian hissed as I slammed the door.

I'd apologize later, but the edges of my vision were starting to darken. I ran as fast as I could in the direction we'd come from toward the nearest woods. Maybe I'd regret it if I got caught, but I was about to lose myself.

My head swam as I pushed my legs to keep moving across the last road before the tree line. My eyes locked on my end destination.

A loud honk hit my ears, followed by squealing tires and the stench of burning rubber. I froze and faced the car as an older man stuck his head out and asked, "Are you okay, miss?"

I didn't have the luxury of responding, or I'd pass out before I could shift. Instead, I burst back into a run and continued on, thanking the gods that I hadn't gotten hit.

"Miss!" the guy yelled after me.

As soon as I'd run far enough into the woods to be out of sight from the road, I yanked my shirt from my body while kicking off my shoes and then pulled off the rest. I threw the clothes in one heaping pile so I could find them again easily. Then I called for my wolf.

She sprang forward with no hesitation, and I shifted faster than I ever had before. When I hit the ground on all fours, I ran deeper into the woods, needing to keep my wolf form hidden. I sniffed the air, making sure no one was close by.

Nothing smelled of other shifters or supernaturals.

Animals rustled around the woods, making my restlessness ease some. In this form, I could breathe, but the paranoia was still too damn close for comfort. I'd been packless for only a little over two days, and it was already beginning to take its toll.

I'd heard stories about how some wolves could go months before getting to this point, so why was I so different? The answer rang in my head—because I was an alpha with no pack to lead. It probably would have helped if I'd stayed under the moon longer last night, but with Griffin there, it hadn't been possible.

A rabbit jumped out from behind a tree, landing in my path, and my wolf grew excited. She wanted to be the predator and let our natural instincts take over. To lose our mind in the moment.

I chased the rabbit, the animal hopping off, running for its life. I didn't plan on eating it, just enjoyed the chase as nature intended.

The little sucker hopped faster than I expected, and my legs burned from the exercise. The paranoia receded as I lost myself in the task.

Minutes later, wings flapped, breaking my concentration. I skidded to a stop as I tried to figure out where the noise was coming from. I was used to worrying about creatures on the ground, not in the sky.

The thunder of large wings grew louder, and a familiar rose scent hit my nose. I looked up in time to see Rosemary descend between two trees, beautiful dark-feathered wings stretched out behind her back.

I wasn't used to looking out for angels, seeing as I'd never met one before her. I had to get out of here. I spun and took off in the direction of my clothes. I should've paid more attention to staying hidden, but I'd been trying to get myself under control before being stuck in the coffee shop for hours.

Hoping to lose her, I ran back toward the road. But suddenly, something was standing right in my path. I skidded to a halt, weighing my options.

"Well, isn't this quite interesting," Rosemary said as she crossed her arms. "I thought I smelled a strange wolf below."

No.

No one could know who I was.

CHAPTER ELEVEN

IF I COULD HAVE BEATEN myself up for my carelessness, I would have. I *knew* not to shift, but I'd been losing my damn mind and had needed an outlet. By letting my wolf take control, I hadn't stayed focused on my surroundings as I should have. I was having fun chasing down a flipping rabbit.

Rosemary's charcoal wings spread out, causing her hair to blow around her face. She was somehow even more breathtaking in this form, and I was almost thankful I was in animal form, or I'd have been gawking.

This was the first time I'd seen an angel with wings, and now her rose scent made sense. But I had no clue how her gray sweater wasn't torn to threads.

Thankfully, I couldn't speak to her in wolf form, so it wasn't like I'd be able to answer any of the questions that had to be churning in her mind. I could only hope that she didn't know who I was. Granted, whether Rosemary knew it was me or not, the news of a silver wolf being seen running around near town would cause a lot of excitement and would inevitably get back to the people hunting me.

"What is a silver wolf doing here? I thought they were extinct."

She arched an eyebrow as she examined my body. "You need to shift back into human form before someone else sees you.'"

Out of every possible scenario, I did not see that one coming. I figured she'd be eager to expose my existence.

"That means you better move your ass now." She waved a hand for added emphasis. "More people run in this section of the woods, so the longer you stay like this, the more likely others will see you."

She was right. These woods were near downtown and close to campus. My dad had been lecturing me about not thinking like a leader, and this proved he was right. Making dumb mistakes like this solidified that I needed him here with me. Not dead. I wasn't anywhere near ready to lead or even survive on my own without a pack.

Hysteria inched closer to the surface, and I took a deep breath, attempting to keep the negative emotions at bay. I couldn't afford to do another stupid thing.

Not wanting to get close to Rosemary, I nodded and took off, giving her a wide berth. I'd never been around angels before, but I had a feeling they would have an excellent sense of smell like most supernaturals, so the farther I stayed away, the less likely she'd figure out who I was.

Not altering my plan, I rushed back in the direction of my clothes. However, this time, I kept my eyes and ears peeled for sounds coming from any angle. Luckily, all I heard were the animals that naturally lived in the woods.

As I got closer to the edge of the woods near downtown, I slowed to a trot. When I reached my clothes, I scanned the area one more time before shifting back to my human form and getting dressed. I ran a hand through my hair, making sure there weren't any branches or grass stuck in it. I yanked my black top down over my jeans and forced my legs to propel me forward.

I needed to get out of here before Rosemary found me again. I didn't need to help her connect the dots.

This time, instead of almost getting hit, I checked both ways before crossing the street. If that car hadn't been able to stop earlier, I could've died.

What scared me was that dying didn't sound horrible.

If Zoe could hear what I was thinking now, she'd smack the hell out of me. But depression was a bitch, and I was at her mercy.

I got back to the diner as Killian exited. His eyes immediately found mine, and he hurried to me.

"I've been worried sick," he said when he caught up to me. "You freaked out on me."

That pretty much nailed my actions dead on. "Yeah, I'm sorry. The past few days kind of caught up to me, including not being part of a pack any longer. Being a rogue is beginning to take its toll."

"Shit." He ran a hand through his hair and shook his head. "I hadn't even thought about you being rogue. Maybe you can join my pack. Not that I want to be your alpha, but it's a good pack, and you have fighting skills."

"My problems aren't your responsibility." He'd already done so much by giving me a place to stay, finding me a job, getting me a fake ID, and being a friend when I didn't have anyone. He was taking all of this on like my problems were his too. "And, thank you. Let me think on that." The answer was no, but I didn't want to hurt his feelings.

"No, they aren't," he agreed and shrugged. "But I'm invested, and there's no getting rid of me. After all, you're my old hag."

A laugh slipped out, surprising me. I glanced around and lowered my voice so no one but Killian could hear me. "Old hag? Wow. No wonder you had to con me into playing this role."

"Con." He gasped and placed a hand on his chest. "That's hurtful."

"But calling me an old hag isn't?" I pushed his arm while smiling. "You turd."

"You keep calling me names, but look what I got for you." He pulled an ID out of his pocket and held it out of my reach. "Now tell me how much you love me, or you won't be getting this."

Enjoying the lighthearted moment, I sprang into action and elbowed him in the stomach, causing him to lean forward while trying to block me. I spun out, grabbing the ID as I moved. I looked at the picture, which was the one Killian had taken that first night on his phone, and read the name.

Dove Davis.

I tapped my finger on the ID and grimaced. "Dove *Davis?*"

"Yup." Killian nodded and waggled his brows. "Double Ds, right there."

The sexual innuendo rang clear. "That's why you picked Davis?"

"Think of it as an inside joke." His smile was full of pride. "I mean, it's not like you have to pull that out whenever you meet someone."

"Even if I did, I'm pretty sure most wouldn't think about boobs." At least, I hoped not.

"Come on, let's go." He took my hand and led me to the truck. "Before you're late and Carter shits a brick."

"Wow, your eloquence is on point today." I stuck out my tongue, trying to keep the conversation lighthearted.

When we got settled in the car, Killian pulled out of the parking spot and glanced at me. "You do realize that the longer you stay rogue, the more your mind will slip."

"I know, but what am I supposed to do?" I stared at my hands. "It's not like finding a pack that works for me is a simple thing to do. I'm an alpha." I wouldn't be able to submit to another alpha. Dad was the alpha when I was born, and he was also my parent, so accepting his authority over me hadn't been an issue. But I was born to lead, which made this whole situation complicated. I wouldn't be able to join a pack unless I could be the alpha. My wolf wouldn't let me, and there wasn't going to be a current alpha who would stand down... especially for a girl. Male alphas tended to frown upon women in leadership roles, although that made me even more determined to prove myself.

I got that Killian didn't want to be an alpha—at least, not yet—but

I didn't want to take over his pack. That wouldn't feel right. I could tell he was meant to lead.

"Why am I not surprised by that? That does make things way more complicated. Maybe we should try running together," he suggested.

"No!" I said quickly.

His face fell, and his hands fidgeted on the steering wheel.

Great, I'd hurt his feelings. I hadn't meant to. Rosemary already knew the truth; maybe I should let him in too. "There's another reason I can't run with you or join your pack."

"And what's that?" His forehead lined with confusion. He was making it abundantly clear that he wouldn't be dropping it, and in fairness, with the way he was helping me, he had a right to know. "Can you not shift or something?"

"You have to swear that if I tell you this, it stays between us. *No one* else can know. Not Griffin. Nobody." The last thing I needed was Griffin or Luna finding out unless they *had* to be let in on my secret later. Or if Rosemary figured out who I was and told people.

"If I haven't proven my trustworthiness by now, I'm not sure what else I can do." Killian scowled.

Fair enough, but I'd known him for only two days. It was kind of insane to think about revealing what I was to anyone after living my entire life in secret, but all I got was good vibes from him. I'd have to go with my gut.

"Have you heard of silver wolves?" Maybe he could figure it out on his own instead of me having to say the actual words.

"The race of wolves that once served as the protectors of Shadow City and were connected to the moon?" He nodded. "Atticus raised Griffin on stories about them. They sounded badass. It's too bad that they died off. I heard that they were powerful."

"Well, they all did die off—two days ago. Except for one, who managed to escape." I said the words quietly, bracing for his reaction.

He blinked a few times, staring straight ahead as the words settled over him. He inhaled. "You're a *silver wolf?*" He turned to face me. "How the hell is that possible? Your race left the city over one thousand years ago and vanished."

There had to be a piece of the story missing. "Atticus knew my dad, who was the alpha of our pack. My dad even visited the city at least once because Atticus wanted us to come back."

"Why did your ancestors leave?" He rolled his shoulders. "Did whoever attacked you know what your pack was?"

"All I know is that we left because things were taking a turn, and our race was being used for corrupt things." Dad never got into specifics. He'd said he'd tell me more when the time came for me to lead the pack. But that wasn't relevant now. "And the people who killed my pack knew. They attacked on the new moon when we're at our weakest and more in line with the strength of a normal wolf shifter. What I can figure is that they wanted to capture me alive so they could take me to someone to make babies with him."

"Why would anyone want to be forced into a mate bond?" He lifted a hand. "Not that you aren't gorgeous. I'd be all up on you if you didn't remind me of my sister."

For once, I was speechless. A car blew a horn, startling me. Both Killian and I looked out the windshield and found ourselves barreling down the wrong lane right toward a huge SUV.

"Fuck!" Killian yelled as he jerked the steering wheel hard to the right.

My breath caught as my head snapped sideways. I closed my eyes, bracing for impact, and forced my body to relax, remembering one of the training exercises Dad made us do regularly. When your body was relaxed, you didn't get as injured as if you tensed up. That was one reason that drunk drivers so often walked away from an accident without injury.

After a few seconds, nothing happened, and I opened my eyes to find Killian wiping his forehead then clenching the wheel extra hard.

He glanced at me. "Are you hurt?"

"Eyes on the road." I snapped, not wanting to experience that again. "If you can't stay focused, we can chat later."

"I'm fine now." He patted his chest. "I knew you had secrets, but I would've never guessed that."

No one would. "To answer your question, any child I bear will be a full-blooded silver wolf."

"How is that possible?" He grimaced. "I mean, wouldn't that be only if you mated with another silver wolf?"

"Let me repeat." I chuckled. "Any child I bear will be one hundred percent silver wolf. It has to do with our connection to the moon."

"How could you know that unless..." He trailed off. "Did your pack mate with normal wolves? Have you *not* been hidden all this time? Why haven't any of us heard you exist?"

He was asking a lot of good questions that I'd never thought about before. "Yes, sometimes, although we did stay hidden as much as possible. We integrated into society to find our fated mates—no one outside our pack was allowed to be brought home unless they were a pack member's fated mate. Because of that connection and the need to keep growing our pack, those were the exceptions. However, we'd go to the grocery store and school like any other wolf would. We just didn't shift with outside wolves or invite them to our homes. We kept a safe distance from them."

"That's insane." Killian turned the truck toward the entrance of Shadow Ridge University. "So whoever this person is wants you so he can father silver wolves. This is so much worse than I expected."

And that was when it hit me. Now that he knew my entire story, he might not want me around. I couldn't blame him, with the danger hanging over me. "I get it if you want me to leave."

"Of course I don't." He reached over and patted my arm. "You're only the second person I've truly connected with since my own family died. And honestly, the reason I live in the Ridge is because my pack became the protectors once the silver wolves left. Maybe with you by my side, I could become the type of alpha my pack needs and the two of us can work together."

"Really?" I'd never thought Shadow City would replace us. "And you do miss being close with your pack."

"Yeah, so I think it's cool that history has kind of come full circle." He rolled down his window and scanned his card. "And I do, but it's so hard to look at my pack members, knowing I failed not only them but my family. In a way, this has to be destiny."

My heart fractured. "My parents and pack being slaughtered was *destiny?*"

"Dammit. I didn't mean it like that." He cleared his throat as he rolled his window back up. "Let's talk about this more later."

"Okay, but there's something else you need to know." I stared at the building in front of us. "When I kind of lost it earlier, I ran into the nearest woods and shifted."

"While I was getting your ID?" he asked, his words careful, not conveying any sort of emotion.

"Yes, and someone saw me." If he got upset with me, he'd have the right. Since he was providing shelter for me, when I did anything stupid, it could fall back on him.

His jaw clenched. "Griffin?"

"*What?*" Out of all of the people he might guess, I hadn't expected that one. "No, not him."

"Thank God." His shoulders relaxed. "Then who?"

"Rosemary." The next words left my mouth faster than ever before. "But she didn't see me in human form, so maybe she won't know it was me."

"I take it back." He tensed. "I would rather it have been Griffin after all. If Rosemary figures it out, that's going to be an even bigger problem."

"Why?" If she was a bigger threat, then there was no telling what we could be walking into on campus.

CHAPTER TWELVE

THE CAR CLOCK showed two minutes 'til nine. I hated to cut this conversation short, however, I needed the job. I hoped that Rosemary wouldn't ruin it for me, but I couldn't hide like a coward. She seemed like she might not want others to know about me, so I'd hold on to that until she proved otherwise. "We've got to hurry or I'm going to be late."

"Are you sure it's smart going in there?" Killian cracked his knuckles. "Rosemary isn't known for being patient. And if she figures it out, she'll alert her mom, Yelahiah, who happens to be a council member of Shadow City."

Which meant every leader in the city would find out about me. Dammit. "If I don't show up, then it might confirm what she suspects. And if you're right and she doesn't keep her mouth shut, then I'm going to look guilty for not coming to work." If she did start talking, I needed to know as fast as possible. The longer she ran her mouth and I didn't know, the more at risk I'd be from whomever was hunting me.

My stomach churned.

Being a rogue wolf was already taking its toll, even with Killian by my side. I couldn't imagine what it'd be like all on my own with not even a friend. Relationships were so damn important to wolves.

"Fine, but one funny look, and we're out of there." He looked at me sternly. "You have to at least promise me that."

I was damn lucky to have found him. "Got it."

"Promise?" he pushed.

He already knew my stubborn ass too well. "Yes, promise."

He must have seen what he was looking for because he opened his door and climbed out. Normally he'd run over and open mine, but I had one minute to get inside. I got out and joined him behind the truck. Not missing a beat, the two of us rushed into the building and made our way to the coffee shop.

When we approached the shop, the line was already out the door and into the hallway. I shouldn't have been surprised—most of the people in line looked like they could fall asleep standing right there.

I sprinted to the counter where Carter stood grumpily in front of the cash register as one lanky crow shifter made drinks.

Carter sniffed as I got closer, and he let out a huge sigh, "It's about time you got here."

"Oh, come on." Killian chuckled as he caught up to me. "She's one minute late. I'm pretty sure that line didn't miraculously appear during the last minute."

"No, but Deissy called out sick again." Carter frowned. "I told her don't bother coming in ever again."

"You pulled the plug on her?" Killian sounded mildly impressed. "What made you finally do it?"

"Because you found someone to replace her." Carter held up a finger to the customer standing in front. "Please hold on one second." He turned to me. "But I need that ID now. I got screamed at by HR for letting you work yesterday."

The fact that he planned to keep me on helped with some of my turmoil. At least, I had something I could kind of call my own.

"Oh, here." Thank God Killian had come through for me. I handed Carter my ID and slipped on an apron. "Anything else?" At least, he was acting normal, not that he would've heard the latest gossip with the shop insanely busy.

"Yes." Carter hissed at the cash register like it was the demon he'd said lived in it. "Work that damn thing."

I grinned as I reached the register. Carter already seemed to rely on me, which thrilled me.

"When does she get off?" Killian asked.

"Come get her after the noon rush, but I'll want her here earlier tomorrow morning," Carter answered.

Killian blew me a kiss as he walked out the door, and then I focused on my task at hand.

FOR THE FIRST HOUR, my heart picked up its pace every time someone entered the shop. Each time, I expected to see the gorgeous dark angel who'd found me in the woods this morning. But she never came. Maybe she had no clue who I was after all. Or maybe she didn't care.

Angels were supernatural and could fly, and they had super strength and other magical abilities, but their nose wasn't as sensitive as a wolf's or a bear's.

Maybe I was safe after all. Maybe I hadn't needed to reveal my secret to Killian. In fear, I'd rushed to tell him, not wanting him to hear it from anyone else. Knowing what I was put him in so much danger, but I couldn't rewind and change the past.

But boy, I sure wished I could. That ability would have been so nice to have. My pack would still be alive, and I'd be with Dad, training for the day I took over the pack.

Someone cleared his throat, and I looked up to see a man who looked a few years older than me. "Are you okay, miss?" His sharp angular face brought out soft blue eyes that were full of concern. He pulled his wallet from his khaki pants and scratched his golden-brown hair. He had a regal presence to him, and he smelled like maple syrup, which screamed vampire.

"Yes, sorry." I forced a small laugh that sounded like a cough. "I spaced for a minute."

"Spaced?" His face lined with confusion.

"I was daydreaming." God, that sounded horrible. "But don't worry, it wasn't about you." *Come on, Sterlyn. Get your shit together.*

The vampire laughed and handed me his credit card. "I asked for a black coffee."

"Of course." I inhaled deeply, forcing my body to relax. I took his card and swiped it and then hurried off to fill a cup.

I didn't even know vampires drank coffee. Obviously, they did, or he wouldn't be here, asking for it. Generally, the vampires we had encountered were focused on one thing—blood. We had to protect the nearby town several times because of vampire outbreaks. When a vampire lost their humanity, they turned deadly, draining humans to death, and the sun began to harm them. Each kill weakened their soul to the point where even the moonlight could hurt them.

As the cup filled, a rose scent hit my nose, and the sense of peace I'd found evaporated like the feeling had been a figment of my imagination.

My hands shook as I put the lid on the coffee. Freaking out would only make the situation worse. I turned, plastering a fake smile securely on my face, and handed the attractive man his drink. "Do you need anything else?"

"No, thank you." He winked and headed out the door, walking up to what had to be shifter. I kept my gaze on him, not wanting to meet her gaze.

Rosemary *tsked* as she propped her hip against the counter. "I'm thinking Killian wouldn't approve of you checking out Alex like that."

"Alex?" What was she talking about? I'd expected her to throw her accusations at me. Not talk to me like nothing had happened.

"The vampire prince who got coffee and left. The one you watched walk out the door like he was the only thing you could focus on?" She tapped a finger against her lip and then wagged it at me. "That's right. You aren't from Shadow City or Shadow Ridge. Where exactly did you come from again?"

"A place not too far from here." The emotion wafting off her was confusion. Like she was trying to figure out something. I had to be very careful how I played this.

"How far?" She leaned closer to me. "Like an hour or several?"

Unfortunately, there was no lying now, so I was stuck in this conversation. "About twenty miles. Do you want something to drink?" Giving her an approximate mileage wasn't the best idea, but it would be hard for her to pinpoint. And if she was sniffing out silver wolves, no one would say anything. The only ones who knew, outside of me, Killian, and a bunch of murderers, were dead.

"Yeah." She looked around the register at Carter. "How about a mocha with four extra shots of espresso?"

"On it." He nodded like that request wasn't odd.

I almost wanted to say something about her heart not liking it, but I figured the joke would fall flat, and with her being one of the strongest supernaturals around, there wasn't much that would hurt her heart, to begin with. I rang up her order and prayed she wouldn't continue her investigation.

"Funny thing happened this morning," she whispered. "I flew over the woods and caught some shifter chasing a rabbit."

Yup, she thought it was me, but the confusion rolling off her calmed me. She was watching my reaction, trying to glean something from me.

"Depending on the shifter, that would make sense." I looked at her and smiled. She wanted me to slip up and say wolf to confirm it was me.

The edges of her mouth tipped downward for a second before she schooled her expression into a mask of indifference.

"That'll be $6.73," I said, forcing my voice to sound even. I needed her to drop this entire conversation, but I couldn't let her realize that she was affecting me.

She rocked on her heels as she pulled some cash from her back pocket. "You know, I love your hair. Do you dye it?" Her gaze remained on me.

Luckily, I had dyed my hair once. I was so tired of having the silver hair that continually reminded kids my age I was their future leader. I had wanted to blend in, but much to my horror, the color didn't stick. My hair stayed the exact same shade it was now. "Yeah, I've dyed it."

"Interesting." She handed the money to me.

I made sure to keep my hands steady as I made change. "Is your hair natural?" Everything inside me wanted me to change the subject, which meant I couldn't.

Her eyes widened marginally. "Yes, this is my natural hair color. Angels don't normally alter their appearance. We don't even wear makeup." The superiority of her tone grated on my nerves.

"I figured fallen might think differently." I was pushing her buttons on purpose. If I made her mad, maybe she'd drop the third degree. In reality, I wasn't sure if she had fallen or been born to fallen parents.

"Well, you obviously don't know much about angels, do you?" She lifted her chin in defiance before something settled over her.

She seemed more confused now than when she came in.

"Here you go, Rosemary," Carter said as he handed her the mocha while giving me the side-eye.

I'd get a lecture about being more professional when she was gone, my second one, and I'd been on the job only two days. This Deissy girl must be horrid if he was thrilled to hire me in her stead.

"Thanks." Rosemary took the drink but didn't leave. "There's something about you, *Dove*. Maybe it's not what I thought, but that doesn't mean I won't figure it out."

A small amount of respect filled me for this beautiful girl. She was direct almost to a fault, but I appreciated knowing exactly where I stood with her. One of the unique powers silver wolves got from the moon was the ability for us to read someone's intention. Rosemary wanted to be honorable, but she hadn't quite figured that out yet.

She turned to leave, and my gaze landed where her wings had been earlier. I noticed two slits in the back of her sweater, wide enough for the wings to spring from. The material almost hid them.

Another interesting fact that I learned today—angels had special clothing.

"How many times are we going to have this conversation?" Carter groaned. "You can't antagonize the customers, especially ones tied to the council."

He continued to ramble, but my focus remained on Rosemary as she left the shop. For now, she hadn't put it together that I was the silver wolf. She suspected it, but I'd managed not to confirm it. I had to keep it that way, or Killian and I could be in a world of hurt.

THE NEXT WEEK and a half passed in a blur. Each day, I grew jumpier, between my missing pack and, disturbingly, not seeing Griffin. What bothered me most was that missing the sexy douchebag kept him constantly on my mind and on alert for him.

I hadn't seen him since the night of our almost kiss. I tried not to look for him, but I couldn't help myself. His face, his smell, his presence...being without him had left a hole inside me, making me desperate to see him again.

He didn't appear to be staying at his house, and Killian had muttered that he hadn't heard from his best friend either. The last he'd heard, Griffin was going to Shadow City to spend time with his mom and try to determine who was behind the attacks on wolves, but every time Killian called, Griffin didn't answer.

The most concerning part was that Luna had been missing in action too. I didn't want to consider what those two were up to. It made me want to puke.

"Dove?" Carter called.

I was getting used to the name. I never would've expected that, but it had become mildly comforting. Probably because Killian had given it to me.

The coffee shop was dead. I'd been working longer days, and it was now nearly two in the afternoon, and we were closing up.

"Do you mind taking the trash out?" He pointed at the garbage can.

Carter acted like I wouldn't do it without him reminding me. "I've taken it out for the past five days." I finished counting out the cash drawer, headed over to the trash, and tied up the bag. "I'll be right back."

He nodded and continued wiping down the counters. "Holler if you need anything."

I walked through the kitchen, where the two kitchen girls were cleaning up the food mess from the day, and straight out the back to the garbage bin. The rancid smell of decaying food slammed into me. Since I was new, I got to be the one to deal with this. Something about seniority, and after the first time, I understood why. No one, not even a human, would want to come out here and smell this.

Holding my breath, I hurried to the large, blue dumpster outside the back door and threw the bag inside. I spun around...and silver paint on the brick caught my eye.

No.

This couldn't be.

Why would Rosemary do this to me? My breathing quickened. I was so upset that the awful garbage smell didn't even register any longer.

I rushed over and traced the drawing on the wall. It was of a wolf in silver paint, the combination telling. It couldn't be a coincidence. That would be too convenient at this point.

My vision grew hazy. I had to get something to clean this off or paint to spray over it. No one could see this.

CHAPTER THIRTEEN

TIME WAS TICKING, and I needed to get back inside. But I couldn't risk leaving this drawing out here where someone else might see it. This was a hidden message for me; it had to be. Most people probably wouldn't think much about it, but I didn't want to chance any sort of talk starting about a silver wolf painted on this building. The people hunting me could hear about it and come by to check it out.

I shuddered, remembering that whomever they worked for wanted me to have his babies.

A *breeder*.

The thought of what that would entail made a shiver run down my spine.

Every night, I dreamed that they found me, and I'd wake up in a cold sweat and not be able to go back to sleep. A run would make things better, but I couldn't risk it after last week in the woods.

To make matters worse, Rosemary had been feeling me out each day when she grabbed her morning coffee. Maybe this painting was how she was forcing my hand. She'd been growing frustrated with my evasiveness, so she wanted me to react and confirm it was me. She must be dedicated to getting to me to paint the wolf out here while enduring the smell, even if her nose wasn't as sensitive.

I hated to admit that her plan was effective. But I'd deal with that bitch later. I had to focus on the most immediate problem so I didn't get overwhelmed.

The trouble was I had no clue how to remove or cover up the wolf. I searched the area, trying to find something—anything—to help me fix this situation. I relaxed my arms and shoulders, trying to remove the panic from my mind. If I let the fear take hold, I wouldn't be able to figure out a solution... if there even was one.

Ignoring the putrid smell, I walked around the edge of the cement, staring into the distance, but there wasn't a damn thing that could help. All that was back here was the large blue dumpster, trash, and cement. There were a few trees not far away, but that wouldn't help me any.

Dammit.

Maybe the person had tossed the spray paint in the dumpster.

Holding my breath, I lifted the lid and stuck my head into the opening, but nothing but plastic bags of spoiled food and coffee grounds could be seen. I dropped back down to my feet and squatted, looking under the small crack of space between the bottom of the dumpster and the ground.

Small wheels on both ends of the dumpster caught my eye. I could roll it closer to the door, at least temporarily. Few people came back here, so there wasn't a *huge* risk of anyone else seeing it, but I didn't need to take the chance. The dumpster was large enough to block the painting from view.

The idea of touching that disgusting dumpster made me gag, but my life was way more important. Besides, the painting's existence put Killian at risk too. This wasn't about keeping me safe.

With renewed determination, I walked behind the dumpster and pushed it toward the wall, tapping into my wolf. At the first push, something brown drizzled from one of the crevasses and almost spilled on my shoe. I jerked my foot out of the way in the nick of time.

A glutton for punishment, I leaned over to examine the liquid more. It reminded me of the murky brown Tennessee River, which was disgusting in its own right. I pretended the liquid was coffee even though my nose screamed how wrong I was.

Footsteps sounded from inside the building toward the exterior door. I pushed harder, needing to get the dumpster over to block the painting and fast. However, even with my strength, it was slow going.

I hadn't gotten it over the wolf yet when the door opened. Thankfully, Killian's musky sandalwood scent covered up a portion of the stench.

He stepped outside and grabbed his nose. "Oh, God. Carter wasn't kidding when he told me to hold my breath."

He had a flair for the dramatic. "You can smell it in the hallway, so you should've known."

"It wasn't nearly as bad there. It's like someone magic-spelled the hallway to take down their enemies by luring them through it and then shoving them out the door." Killian shivered. "Carter said you've been out here for a while and that I should check on you. I thought he was overreacting until now."

I understood he was trying to be cute and funny, but now wasn't the time. "I've got a problem."

"This smell—"

"No, I'm being serious." I wasn't trying to be a bitch, but I needed him to focus. "Look." I gestured to the brick.

He pinched his nose, keeping up his antics, until his gaze fell on the silver wolf on the wall. "Holy shit." He glanced around and then sighed. "That could be awful luck."

"Let's see." The more I thought about the situation, the more I realized that this was done on purpose. "I've been the only person taking the trash out the past five days I've worked. Someone painted this back here where it smells like ass. And Rosemary has been sniffing around me since she found me in the woods last week."

"You had me at them coming back here and smelling this shit on their own terms." Killian sucked in a breath and pretended to dry heave. "I have got to stop doing that."

"Will you help me?" I nodded toward the other end of the dumpster. "The only solution is to use this to cover it until I can get back and spray paint over it."

"Of course. Let's do it." He clutched the other end of the dumpster and helped me guide it to the wall. Once it was positioned over the drawing, he frowned. "Go in before Carter comes back out here. I'll run to one of the hardware stores and get some spray paint. There's one not too far from here. I'll paint over the wolf and meet you out front."

He was already doing too much. "If Rosemary finds out that you know my secret, then she could lump you in with me too. I don't want the council to be out for you."

"If she knows, then she'll assume that I know too." He placed a hand on my arm. "Especially with how a girlfriend suddenly popped up."

Ugh, I hadn't thought of that. But he was right. "Fine, I'll go in before someone else comes out here and snoops around."

"I'll be back and meet you out front." Killian removed the keys from his pocket. "Finish closing up the shop."

"Are you sure?" Leaving him to clean up my mess didn't settle well with me, but at the same time, having someone come back here and see the painting sounded worse. "Thank you."

"Of course." He kissed my cheek. "You're one of my best friends now. I'd do anything for you." He walked around the building, heading to his truck.

How I wished we felt a romantic connection to each other. He was the type of guy my dad would've been so proud that I found. He was kind, considerate, and loyal. Although, if my dad was still alive, Killian and I probably wouldn't have become friends even if the silver wolves had returned to Shadow City. We'd bonded over the loss of our families and created a connection through that.

Forcing myself to go back into the building, I rushed to the bathroom to wash my hands. As I looked in the mirror, I almost didn't recognize the girl staring back at me. My silver hair was pulled back into a bun, and my silver-purple eyes had darkened to almost steel gray. Hell, with the paleness of my skin, I could almost pass for a vampire.

My clothes were a little baggy on me, due to all the stress. Every time I tried to eat, I'd lose my appetite after a few bites. Lately, I'd been living on coffee, which amped me up even more on top of everything else. At some point, I would have to risk shifting and taking a run.

Turning away from the mirror, I cranked the paper towel dispenser and wiped down my hands and face. I tossed the paper towel into the garbage and pinched my cheeks, trying to add a little color to my skin, then left the bathroom.

The two girls in the kitchen were gone, and when I walked out front, only Carter remained.

He leaned over, trying to see behind me, and sniffed. "How'd you lose Killian? I need you to teach me that little trick."

Carter and Killian loved giving each other hell, but I could tell there was mutual respect on both sides.

"He was whining about the smell and said he needed to run to the store, so he took off." I placed a hand on my hip and forced a smile, trying to act somewhat normal. However, my mind kept seeing the artwork I'd left behind. "I'm assuming the smell is why you sent him out there in the first place."

"Maybe." He shrugged. "He did leave me drunk off my ass at a party a couple of weeks ago with this girl I can't stand wrapped all around me." He shuddered at the memory. "All the things she did to me that night I can't take back. But I was hoping he'd puke."

"You do realize he's a shifter." Granted, that smell was awful out there, but our stomachs were sturdy.

"But the pain is real." He nodded toward the door. "Let's get out of here."

As we left the building, a certain dark angel caught my eye. Rosemary was outside all alone, lying on top of a picnic table like she was sunbathing. She had a bag propped under her neck and shoulders as she read some sort of textbook.

Anger spread through me like wildfire. "I'll see you tomorrow," I said to Carter as I headed toward her.

"Uh, yeah. See ya." He sounded confused, but I didn't have time to focus on that.

Of course, she would be perched outside the coffee shop to watch my reaction. I shouldn't confront her—that was what she wanted after all—but I was done playing this cat and mouse game with her.

It ended now.

I marched directly toward her, welcoming the righteous anger. The emotion was a soothing relief to the stress, anxiety, and pain that I felt most of the time.

When I reached her, I stood so that my shadow blocked her sun.

She dropped her book and sighed. "Can I help you?" Even though she sounded put out, interest seemed to spark in her eyes.

"You had to do it, didn't you?" My wolf brushed against my mind. She'd been struggling and cooped up, which was a dangerous combination to my already fracturing self.

"Do what?" She placed her book down beside her and sat fully upright. She examined my face and tilted her head.

"Don't play innocent." I lifted my hands. "You're getting what you wanted. A reaction."

"Dove, what happened?" she asked, sounding perplexed.

"You want me to spell it out for you, don't you?" My emotions swirled inside me so much that I couldn't get a read on her. I was losing control, and I wasn't sure how to rein it in.

She chewed on her bottom lip. "Are you okay?"

"You drew a silver wolf by the dumpster, knowing I'd take out the garbage and see it," I hissed as my hands shook. "And you're asking me if I'm okay?"

"What?" She jumped to her feet and looked all around us. "I did no such thing."

"Oh?" I wasn't buying it. "You expect me to believe that after you've interrogated me at every opportunity the past week?"

"You're a wolf." She tapped my shoulder. "You'd know if I was lying."

Dammit. She was right. "But if it wasn't you—" My mind circled and landed me right back on the last new moon in my pack.

They'd found me. But how...? I'd been so careful. Hell, Killian didn't even know my real name because I was afraid he might slip.

I had to get out of here, and now. This would've been an excellent time to have a car... or wings. "Do you have any idea who could have done it, have you noticed anyone lurking around? You've been here every day."

"Not at all." Her wings sprang from her back, spreading out. "I'll go see if I can find anything out. In the meantime, lie low."

"Wait!" The last thing I needed was for even more people to know about me. "How many people are you going to tell?"

"Zero." Her forehead creased.

Clearly, I'd misunderstood her. "Zero? Is that the number of people you *won't* tell?" I couldn't hide the sarcasm that laced each word.

"Believe it or not, I don't want anyone else finding out about you either." Rosemary tapped her fingers on her leg. "There's enough going on with the wolf attacks and another civil war brewing. The last thing we need is the story of an extinct silver wolf coming back from the dead. So many will consider you a traitor; it would cause tension to escalate."

"A *traitor?*" What kind of story was she trying to spin? "We left because people were using us to commit crimes!"

"We?" Her face fell. "How many of you are there?"

"None of your business." If I gave her a number, she would be able to tell I was lying. But I didn't want her to think she could kill me now and eliminate the problem.

She rolled her eyes. "Look, I'll come find you when I figure out all there is to know."

Yeah, I bet she would. "Why don't you try to kill me now?" Dad had told me stories about angels not being huge fans of silver wolves.

"I don't want you dead." She laughed. "You may be a pain in the ass, but I don't need Griffin and Killian as the angels' enemies. If anything, the races need to begin working together. Don't do anything stupid until we speak again."

She took off into the sky, leaving me with my thoughts, which wasn't a good thing at this point.

A howl sounded from the woods only a few yards away, making my heart stop. I spun around and found eyes glowing at me through the tree branches.

Good. Let's get this over with. I clenched my fists, ready to fight.

CHAPTER FOURTEEN

MY WOLF SURGED FORWARD, restless and ready to fight. Between the imminent threat and not training every day, my human and animal sides were easily excitable, and not in a good way.

I stepped toward the woods, but the wolf disappeared from sight. The padding of paws grew faint as it slipped away.

Dammit. That wolf could've overheard my entire conversation with Rosemary. And I'd been none the wiser to his presence because I was too overcome by my emotions. Dad had warned me that was what happened when you didn't think with a level head. Being rogue was clearly affecting my ability to be rational.

The urge to shift almost overwhelmed me, but I pushed my wolf back and took a moment to think. I couldn't allow my animal to take control away from my human side. If I let it happen, the rogue part I was already struggling with would get even worse.

For all I knew, the wolf shifter could've been the one who drew the painting and had been watching my next moves to confirm it was me.

Well, if that was his end goal, I sure made it easy for him.

I should've ignored Rosemary and waited for Killian in front of the building, but something inside me had snapped. Now I wished I could take it back. If that wolf was someone scouting me out for the men who'd attacked my pack, I'd placed a flashing neon light above my head that basically said, "I'm here."

Dad had to be shaking his head at me in heaven. I kept messing up. Everything he'd taught me I'd wildly abandoned.

Maybe me not being alpha of my pack was a good thing. I wasn't wise enough to lead.

Refusing to make another damn mistake, I inhaled, filling my lungs, and cautiously approached the woods. I wouldn't go far, just try to catch the wolf's scent better. At least, that way, I would recognize him when I ran into him again.

As I approached the tree line, I stopped and listened for anything that would indicate there were more shifters close by or anyone who could possibly jump me. My too-stupid-to-live moments were done from this point forward.

Nothing sounded or smelled out of the ordinary, so I pushed forward in the direction where the eyes had been. The closer I got, the stronger his scent became, but the smell was strange. The musk that confirmed it was a wolf shifter was there, but that was about it. There wasn't anything unique about it, which meant he'd used something to mask part of his scent.

Which told me everything I needed to know.

He could be part of the pack that slaughtered my family and friends.

I had to get out of here before he circled back and brought reinforcements.

Pivoting on my heel, I made my way back toward the main building, passing four vampire girls who were hanging out in the sun. The fact that they were sitting in direct sunlight meant they still had their humanity. That reassured me that they didn't kill for pleasure and were able to control their instincts. That was a requirement in order to attend school here, most likely due to the human visitors who came to hike the amazing woods.

One of them wrinkled her nose when she saw me, proving that, like angels, vampires didn't like intermingling outside their species.

Or it could be me. I did try to give off a fuck-you vibe. The more that people talked to me, the more likely I could slip up and say something that could hint at any one of my secrets.

Pretending that I didn't notice her sour expression, I pushed through the double doors and headed straight toward the hallway.

Luna's all-too-familiar voice rang in my ear from the tables in front of the cafeteria. "Aw, did Killian leave you?"

I'd gone a little over a week without seeing her, and still enough time hadn't passed. I stopped short, making my point clear that I wouldn't try to run from her. "Nope, he needed to run an errand, and then he'll be right back." I forced a sweet smile that felt foreign. The only reaction I wanted to give her was the middle finger.

"And he didn't take you with him?" Luna sashayed over, her dark sage maxi skirt flowing out around her. She tilted her head, causing her hair to fall in front of her shoulders, brushing against her cream top. "Sounds like trouble in paradise." She turned to face a girl a couple of inches shorter than me who was following right behind her. "Jessica, you may get Killian sooner rather than later after all."

The girl's forest-green eyes focused on me, and she gave me an uncomfortable smile as she twisted chestnut hair with natural light caramel tips around one finger. Her modest pale pink wrap top complemented her medium olive complexion. "I'm sure he needed something, and things are okay between them."

Wow. I hadn't expected that.

I'd expected this girl to be as hateful or even more so than Luna, but positive energy emanated from her.

"Oh, you don't need to be nice to her." Luna waved me off. "She doesn't live in the city and never will if I have anything to say about it."

I'd never disliked someone as much as Luna before in my life. Well, correction. I outright hated the people hunting me, but she was a very close second. "Killian doesn't live in the city either."

"His best friend—my future mate—" Luna said as she patted herself on the chest "—will get him into the city where he belongs. It's only a matter of time."

That was an odd thing to say, but whatever. I didn't have time to deal with her mind games. "Great, good luck with that."

"I didn't dismiss you." She walked over to me and lifted her chin. "I'm not done talking to you."

She was grating on my nerves. I'd come inside so the wolf couldn't spy on me, but I'd rather be captured than have to deal with her. However, I had to be careful, I didn't want her to follow me outside. "What?" I couldn't hide my annoyance.

"Look, I'm trying to be nice." She scoffed and crossed her arms. "I wanted to say thank you."

She was determined to tell me whatever was on her mind. However, I wouldn't give her the satisfaction of asking. "You're welcome."

"Don't you want to know why I'm thanking you?" She pouted.

Like that was going to work. "No, but I don't think that matters. Clearly, you want to tell me."

"Griffin's been spending a lot more time in Shadow City, which has been amazing for me. I was so upset when he bought that house by Killian, but now that he's avoiding staying there, I'm wrangling him faster than I'd originally planned." She ran her hands through her hair. "I'm thinking you had something to do with that."

My wolf howled in my head so damn loud that I almost whimpered. My heart felt like it was fracturing, but that made no sense. I'd seen the guy only a couple of times, and he'd been an asshole for most of it.

They were a match made in heaven. I should have been thrilled that he had a reason to stay away...but I wasn't. I'd have liked to pretend it was because Killian missed his best friend, but that wasn't the truth. I wanted Griffin around too.

A portion of my heart grew colder at the thought of him with Luna. Not wanting to risk sounding broken, I nodded and glanced at

Jessica. I forced my words to be smooth. "It was nice to meet you." And I turned and headed back out the front doors.

"What a bitch," Luna huffed. "I was thanking her."

"Well, you did tell her she'd never move into Shadow City and then in the next breath said her boyfriend would," Jessica said, "I'm thinking that hit her hard."

Not wanting to hear anymore, I stepped outside and walked onto the lawn in front of the building. The vampire girls were now watching a group of bear shifters playing football with no helmets. They had their shirts off, which almost made me laugh because their chest hair was so thick you couldn't even see their nipples.

Needing to be around noise so I couldn't hear Jessica's and Luna's conversation, I sat against a tree trunk close by and watched the idiots tackle each other over and over again.

FAMILIAR FOOTSTEPS MADE their way to me, and Killian's scent tickled my nose. I glanced toward the building and found his gaze on me.

"Are you ready to go?" he asked as his eyes flicked toward the bear shifters, who were putting on a show for the girls sitting around them.

The longer I'd sat out there, the more girls had congregated. I had to admit the bear shifters were sexy in their own right, and they were eating up the attention. Even a few angels, their floral scents giving them away, were standing around near the vampires, pretending to want to watch the game.

"Yeah." I knew I sounded terse, but, I hated being around people right now. My skin was crawling. Any time one of them made eye contact with me, I felt like they knew my secrets.

I needed to get control of my emotions because being rogue was beginning to cause even more problems. My hands kept growing sweaty, and my mind became hazy more frequently. At times, I felt a phantom pack connection that made my wolf restless. But it would vanish almost as quickly as it appeared. My wolf and I both needed to feel a connection to something, and the cold void seemed to be expanding and putting a wall up between my animal and human sides. If I didn't find a pack soon, I might go insane. Even Killian's comforting presence was having less of an effect on me. But if I became part of his pack, I'd connect with all the other hundreds, which wasn't an option. And the fact that he tried to maintain distance from his pack spoke volumes. I doubted they'd accept me—an outsider—so easily.

I had no clue what the answer was, but I needed to figure out something soon.

"Well, come on," he said and reached out a hand.

The stench of spray paint attacked my nose. I almost coughed but managed to hold it together. If the wolf was watching me, I didn't want to tip him off to what Killian had done. He could figure that out on his own. Granted, he probably wouldn't care that the image was covered. He'd painted it to get a reaction from me, and I'd already fallen into the trap.

Placing my hand in Killian's, I let him pull me to my feet, and the two of us headed toward the truck. We held an amicable silence until we were pulling out of the university.

"Were you able to cover it?" I tried not to let him know how nervous I was, but he knew me too well.

He nodded. "Yeah, I was. Sorry it took so long, but I had to make sure I didn't get caught."

"No, it's fine." His words weighed on me. "You shouldn't have done it. You're putting so much at risk by housing me and being my friend."

"Stop it." He pointed at me in warning. "That's what friends do for one another, and come on, you know I think of you as a sister."

"Because I remind you of her." Maybe he was investing too much in me because of that. "Even though we have different tastes in clothes."

"Olive wanted to fit in with Luna and Jessica." He sighed. "She dressed more like you until the last year or so before her death, but to be clear, I'm not helping you just because you remind me of her. Maybe at first, that was why, but not anymore. You've become a true friend."

I loved that he could be honest with me. I owed him the same. "I don't want anything to happen to you. There was a wolf watching me when I went off on Rosemary."

"What are you talking about?" His brows furrowed.

I filled him in on my embarrassing display.

"That doesn't change anything, other than that we need to figure out who the wolf is." He patted my arm as he said firmly, "And we're going to get through this together. We're each other's family now. That's final."

But the problem was I couldn't agree with that. If I were in his shoes, I'd have been saying that same thing. But he'd lost his family too. And because of me, his best friend hadn't been around.

Thinking back to the night before Griffin disappeared felt like a punch to the gut. One second, we were at each other's throats, and the next second, I wanted to rip his clothes off and do things I'd never done with anyone else. I still had whiplash from my emotions that night.

The worst part was that not seeing him was driving me crazy. And to know he'd been spending time with Luna was like mixing Pop Rocks candy and Coke. I was about to explode, or implode, and I had no fucking clue why.

I decided to change the subject from something I didn't want to talk about to something he didn't want to. It would make him shut down, at least for a little while, and I could use the reprieve. "Jessica doesn't seem all that bad." I lifted a brow at him. "In fact, she's quite breathtaking."

"How'd you meet her?" Killian pursed his lips as he glanced at me.

"Well, it involved Luna, which was very unpleasant." On so many levels. "Jessica was with her. She seems sweet."

"Jessica isn't the problem." He tapped his fingers on the steering wheel. "It's more of who her best friend is. Although honestly, what does it say about her that she chooses to be close friends with Luna?" He shuddered.

He did have a point. "They're from Griffin's pack, right?"

"Yes, and their fathers are close. They grew up together, but still. Also, my parents were fated mates, and I want to find my own. I don't want to settle for something other than that. A chosen mate is out of the cards for me. Why try to build a relationship with someone fate knows isn't for you? Why waste time in a relationship with someone when I know how it'll end?"

And he had a good point there too. If he knew what he wanted, then pushing him to do otherwise would only result in heartache.

Either way, with my secret coming out and the wolf now watching me, I knew exactly what I had to do to protect Killian and myself.

THE MOON SHONE through the window, alerting me that it was around midnight. I'd been lying in bed for hours, needing rest, but sleep wouldn't come. Each time I closed my eyes, images of my dead pack jumped vividly through my mind, but surprisingly, that wasn't the worst part. The worst part was Killian lying lifeless with them as well.

I got up and paced back and forth at the edge of the bed, trying to find some sense of calm, but it was futile.

My wolf howled in my mind, wanting to seize control, desperate to get out, and Killian's lifeless face was in every shadow of the room. Something *tugged* inside me, making my wits scatter, the sensation adding to my sense of losing control.

Terror took hold of me, and I couldn't regain my calm. My wolf surged forward, bucking against my hold.

Staying here wasn't an option any longer, but leaving would break my heart. I'd promised Killian we were in this together.

However, if I didn't do something, I wasn't sure how much longer I could hold my wolf at bay.

On the nightstand sat some plain white stationary and a pen. I grabbed it quickly and wrote a note.

Killian,

Earlier when you said I was your family, I know I didn't say anything in response. But I want you to know I feel the same way about you. You've been the one bright spot since that horrible day you found me in the river.

I planned on staying like I promised, but I realized tonight that I can't put you at risk. It would be selfish of me to stay and to risk the amazing future you deserve.

I'm sorry this is how I'm saying goodbye, but I'm not strong enough to say it to your face. You've become my home, and I love you.

Your sister always,

Dove

I placed the note on my pillow, and a sob formed at the back of my throat. I swallowed it down as I opened the window, making sure not to make any noise. The bag I'd packed earlier lay on the floor with a few changes of clothes, ID, and some cash. Of course, my trusty knife was strapped to my ankle.

After grabbing the bag and tossing it through, I slipped out the window and landed on both feet. Forcing myself to stay calm, I scanned the area.

Everything looked clear.

Sighing, I picked up the bag and slung it over one shoulder. My plan was simple. Get to the river and use it to find another city or town. I'd rent a car and get as far away from here as possible. Staying near my old neighborhood must have made it easier for them to find me.

As I jogged toward the back of the house, the back porch light at Griffin's house turned on, and the back door opened.

The *tug* was so hard I nearly fell to my knees. I stopped in my tracks as emotions I didn't understand surged through me—a mixture of desire, need, and desperation.

"Dove, what the hell are you doing?" Griffin growled. "That bear shifter could be out here. Get your ass back inside."

CHAPTER FIFTEEN

MY TRAITOROUS LEGS moved in his direction. Out of all the scenarios I'd imagined, Griffin being home wasn't one of them. He'd been gone for weeks, and all of a sudden, he reappeared tonight? *Figures. That's my luck lately.*

At least, he couldn't fight worth a damn, and the moon was already charging me. I'd kick his ass to get away if it came to that.

Not bothering to acknowledge his existence, I pressed forward, despite everything inside of me screaming to run to him and kiss his sexy mouth and touch his hard, muscular chest.

My weird attraction to him took my breath away. The time we'd spent apart from each other had only made this irrational desire even stronger. And those emotions I felt for him on top of the chaos already swirling inside made my throat dry as tears burned my eyes.

I didn't want to leave him either.

Stupid douchebag, always showing up at the worst times. Fate had a way of torturing me.

"Dove," he said, and it sounded like a warning. His feet hit the ground, coming after me. "Do not ignore me."

He moved faster than I expected him to, as if he was equally eager to get to me. But that had to be because he wanted to torment me or insult me further. My stupid legs didn't move any faster, almost as if they wanted him to catch up to me. Soon he grabbed my arm, forcing me to turn toward him.

I went to punch him but stopped short as his hazel eyes distracted me. They glowed, his wolf bleeding through and making him look even sexier. It took every ounce of my strength to keep myself from jumping into his arms.

"Does Killian know you're out here by yourself in the middle of the night?" His words held such concern. "I have a feeling he doesn't." He pushed the bag off my shoulder.

"He's not my dad—" That one word combined with Griffin's touch released the sob I'd held back, and the tears fell freely down my cheeks.

The sorrow of the past two weeks settled hard inside my chest. I hadn't truly broken down; I'd tried to focus on staying alive. But as of tonight, I'd genuinely lost everyone I cared about, one way or another. I couldn't even say *dad* without breaking down.

"Hey," Griffin said softly as he brushed tears from my face. "What's wrong?"

My skin warmed and buzzed wherever he touched me, and somehow, the bastard calmed me enough to get a handle on my emotions and stop crying.

His tenderness caught me off guard, and the urge to flee, to escape whatever influence he held over me, returned. I liked it better when we were fighting. I could channel the hate to ward off the *tug* toward him.

"I need to go." The longer I stayed, the harder it would be to leave.

"Tell me what's wrong." His words held a plea. "Or do I have to call Killian?" His nose wrinkled.

Dammit, if he called Killian, he would figure out I was leaving and ruin my escape. "Please don't. I'm doing this to protect him." I didn't want to give too much away, but I needed Griffin to let me go.

"How is running out late at night protecting him?" His brows furrowed, and he looked back at Killian's house.

"I thought you couldn't wait until my ass left him." I bit out the words, trying not to let him see how much it had cut me.

"You know I was being a jerk." His phone rang, and he pulled it from his pocket and rejected the call. "Regardless, you can't do that to him. You have to at least say goodbye. Do you know what you disappearing would do to him? He's already lost too many people in his life."

I didn't need this ass clown trying to make me feel bad. He treated people like shit, and he had the audacity to lecture me? I'd already struggled with this decision, so I didn't need him laying it on me too. "People are hunting me. I care about Killian too much to let him get caught in the crossfire."

"The bear shifter would've attacked anyone close to us that day," he growled. "You don't need to feel bad about that."

"I wish it was just him." If I had only one person to worry about, I wouldn't be so nervous or scared. I'd kicked that bear's ass that day all on my own, and I'd been holding back.

"What are you trying to say?" Griffin leaned toward me.

If I wanted to get out of this gracefully, I'd have to bare my soul to him. "I met Killian only a couple weeks ago." I stopped, needing to prepare myself for the inevitable questions that would come.

Much to my surprise, Griffin didn't rush me. Instead, he patiently waited for me to continue.

"In reality, he probably saved my life." And I'd never even thanked him for that. Another thing I didn't handle correctly. "I almost drowned when I tried to escape a group of men that had chased me from my pack home."

"Drowned?" His body tensed as a low snarl rumbled. "Why were they chasing you?"

"I jumped into the river, trying to hide my scent so they couldn't keep following me. They jumped in after me, and I found an undercurrent that helped me get away, but I almost didn't break free."

"But your pack. Why didn't they help?" he asked. "Is that why you're leaving? To go back to people who abandoned you?"

I laughed without humor. The bleak part of my soul flared. "No, I'll never go back home, but my pack didn't abandon me." I looked skyward at the moon, needing to find comfort in the one thing that I'd never have to give up. "Those men who chased me, they slaughtered my pack before running after me."

His eyes softened as he took a step toward me. "How did you escape?"

I told him the story of how I wasn't there at first and heard the screams. "You see—" I stopped short, bracing myself to spit out the truth. "My pack kept to themselves. We stayed at arm's length from all other supernaturals to keep our identity hidden. But, somehow, some wolves got wind of what we were and that a woman had been born to be the next alpha."

"So they didn't want a woman to lead?" He shook his head. "That doesn't make any sense as to why they'd kill the entire pack then."

"No, they wanted the woman for someone." I averted my gaze toward the ground. "I'm not sure who, but it doesn't matter. They want her to have babies with this man so he can lead her race."

"Why not lead the current pack?" Griffin tilted his head. "You're holding back key pieces of information. I need to understand how you leaving right now, in the middle of the night, protects my best friend."

He was right. I was dancing around the truth when I needed to get straight to the point. "The reason he killed the pack is because none of them—including me—would ever support someone corrupt. I mean, that was the whole reason my people left Shadow City centuries ago."

"There's never been a race that left Shadow City." He glared at me.

Interesting. But then how did Rosemary know about silver wolves? "There was. Your father knew about us. He invited my father to visit around two years ago."

"Your dad..." He *hmm*ed. "Silver hair, like yours?"

"Yes." He must have seen Dad during his visit, but why hadn't his father told him of our existence? Had he, like my father, thought he'd have more time? Atticus's death was starting to seem rather conveniently timed. "Your dad wanted our pack to come back and live in the city." My mind went back in time to the last time I saw my father, and I wrapped my arms around myself. "In fact, with his last breath, my dad told me to go to Shadow City and find Atticus. That he would protect me." I took a deep breath. "That he was an ally of the silver wolves."

Griffin held himself completely still. "Are you saying silver wolves are real?" He glanced at the moon and then back to me. "And you're the only one still alive—which means you're the alpha they want." He ran his hands through his hair, making it disheveled, which added to his allure. "But your children would only be half silver."

Our legacy was such a well-kept secret that even Rosemary hadn't known this. "No. Any child I have will be a full silver wolf. It's due to the power of the moon."

"And you're running away...because you love Killian."

"Yes. He's already done so much for me. I can't let him wind up dead like the rest of my pack." And here was the grand finale. The last bit of logic that would feed his self-serving side. "And I'll be out of your hair. You won't have to see me again, and you and Killian can go back to the way things were before my messy ass interfered. It'll be like I never existed." Damn, saying that hurt, but I had to seal the deal with him.

"Like you never existed," he said. He scanned my face as if looking for something.

I held my head high, trying to portray confidence. "All you have to do is let me go."

"No." He shook his head. "Absolutely not."

Relief filled me. "Thank—" Wait... he'd said no. "What? Why not?" He hated me.

"Call me selfish, but I don't want you to go." He sighed as his eyes faintly glowed and he took a step closer to me. "I can't."

My body warmed with anticipation as I got closer to him too. My hand itched to touch him, but I held it close to my side.

"Why not?" None of this made any sense. "You've been gone for weeks."

"With the wolf attacks and some council decisions being made, I had to stay in Shadow City for a little while. Also, Mom needed my help cleaning out Dad's old things. And, if I'm being completely honest, I was trying to stay away from you." He blew out a breath. "I feel something for you, and it's wrong on all types of levels."

My heart pounded. "What do you mean?" I shouldn't ask or encourage him to tell me how he felt, but a part of me had to know if what he felt was similar to what I was feeling.

"I can't get you out of my head, and seeing you try to run away—" He clenched his hands. "And the thought of never seeing you again —" He paused. "That would kill Killian."

We both knew he didn't mean Killian, but our hands were tied. He was with Luna, and Killian and I were supposed to be exclusive. "But I don't want anything to happen... to him."

"I'm the alpha of Shadow City, and if my dad would've protected you, then that's what I'm going to do." He cupped my cheek, and my skin felt like it was on fire. His touch warmed the coldest parts of me inside, and I never wanted him to pull away. "I've been putting off acting like the alpha for too long, and with you here, it's time for me to make some changes."

"I don't want you to change for me." I would never ask that of anyone. "If you aren't ready for that responsibility, then me staying here is a lot to ask."

"You didn't ask." His gaze landed on my lips. "I want to do it. Besides, I'm going to make sure that being with me is the safest place for you."

The air between us charged, and my mind yelled at me to step away. To run as I'd planned. But I was at his mercy. "How so? Someone already threatened me at the university."

"What do you mean?" His hand dropped.

I filled him in on the painting, Rosemary, and the wolf in the woods. "That's what I'm trying to tell you. I'm not paranoid. They've found me here, and that's why I need to run."

He unlocked his phone, and I saw he had over twenty-five missed calls. I hated that I looked, but I couldn't help myself. He cleared the log, pulled up a contact, and began texting. "I'm getting some Shadow City guards over here to protect you with more of Killian's coming. We'll make sure there are four positioned around the house at all times."

My heart quickened. He was taking care of me...and that thrilled me more than it should.

From our spot in the backyard, I watched a taxi pull into Griffin's driveway.

"Oh, hell." He grumbled and lowered his head. "She's fucking insane."

"Who are you talking about?" For him to have that kind of reaction worried me, but surely the group looking for me wouldn't take a taxi and pull into the Shadow City's alpha's driveway.

A car door opened and shut.

"Griffy!" Luna's fingernails-on-a-chalkboard voice called out. She sniffed loudly.

"Ugh, I guesss Griffy and Dove made up." The "p" popped on the last word, emphasizing her inebriated state.

"I'm so sorry about this." He met my eyes. "But you need to go back inside, and I have to deal with my drunken mess."

I'd *bet* he was going to deal with her. I bet he'd deal with her many times. Anger ignited inside of me at the thought. But I had no right. They were together, and sex was part of the equation.

I bet he was damn good at it too. "Yeah, okay. Have fun."

"*Fun* isn't the word I'd use." He winced. "She's a train wreck."

And yet, he was dating her. Some guys were attracted to people like that.

Luna stumbled in between the houses and stopped when her glazed eyes focused on me.

She was toasted, which meant she'd drunk a ton and had added wolfsbane to the mix. I had no clue why she'd let herself get this sloshed.

"You," she slurred and took a wobbly step in my direction. "Of course, he'd be out here with you." She leaned forward, one of her sharp-nailed fingers pointing at me.

Griffin stepped in front of me, blocking me from her view. "What are you doing here, Luna?"

"You din't answer my calls." She shook the finger in his face. "Whut would my daaaddy say?"

Was she threatening him?

"I don't give a flying fuck what he'd say." Griffin crossed his arms, looking unamused. "I'm the alpha, not him."

She laughed. "For suuumone so hawt," she continued, poking him in the chest, "yurrr stupid."

How dare she talk to him like that? I couldn't hold my tongue any longer. "Did you come all this way to insult him?"

Griffin tensed as Luna bared her teeth at me.

"Bish, doan *talk* to me." She waved her hand dismissively at me. "Not *worth* my *time*."

"Don't talk to her like that." Griffin growled. "You're the one who showed up here wasted. You called me over twenty times, and I didn't answer. Maybe you should've taken the hint."

"*You* din't git this way 'til *herrr*." Her bones began to break, and fur sprouted all over her body.

I gasped at the nerve. Was she crazy enough to attack me in this drunken state? I didn't like her, but that didn't mean I wanted to fight her. I wanted her to leave me the hell alone.

Within seconds, she'd shifted into her wolf form, leaving her clothes lying shredded around her paws.

"Luna, what are you doing?" Griffin said sternly. "You need to stand down."

She shook her large wolf head defiantly and ran toward us. Her eyes were locked on my neck.

She intended to kill me.

CHAPTER SIXTEEN

MY WOLF SURGED FORWARD, but this time, for protection instead of trying to take control. I allowed the shift to happen as Luna charged at me. My skin tingled as my fur sprouted, and I quickly removed the sheath seconds before my clothes ripped apart and fell from my body.

I hated shifting and ruining my clothes, but she would have an easier time hurting me if I didn't shift too.

"Luna, *stop*," Griffin growled as he stood protectively in front of me. He spread his legs in a fighter pose and tensed his shoulders. "Don't make me force you with my alpha will."

Her wolf made a choking noise that must have been a laugh. She obviously didn't think he had the balls to force her to stop. Given the way Griffin allowed Dick to treat him, it was no wonder she didn't think she had to listen to him. She continued to advance, clearly not concerned about his unveiled threat.

"Fine," he growled as he crouched.

The dumbass was going to get hurt, which infuriated me. If that bitch injured him in any way, I'd kill her. My wolf howled in agreement.

Luna ran around him and lunged, but in her drunken haze, she miscalculated, and her teeth snapped at Griffin's shoulder instead of me. He held his arms out as if that would prevent injury, but all he did was give her a better target for her teeth.

If my father was here now, he'd have been horrified at how clueless these two shifters were in the art of battle. At least, this time, my head was in the game.

In a bid to keep from adding another kill to my list and end up on the bad side of one of Shadow City's council members, I head-butted Griffin's ass, causing him to stumble out of the way.

"No!" he yelled. "I was handling it!"

If he'd let me focus, I would take down the drunken psycho in seconds.

A snarl ripped from her as she opened her mouth wider, going for my neck. I stood on my hind legs and let her fall, missing her mark completely. She managed to catch herself with her front paws, but they gave out, and she tumbled to the ground.

In order to prevent the fight from continuing, I jumped on her back and placed my teeth at the back of her neck, pressing them into her fur, though not enough to draw blood. If she moved, she'd cause herself injury.

Apparently, that wasn't a deterrent because she thrashed against me, determined to get up. The metallic taste of her blood hit my tongue.

She wasn't thinking clearly and probably didn't even feel the pain. I'd hoped this would be easy, but clearly, I'd been mistaken.

"Luna," Griffin yelled. "Stop it!"

She didn't even pause because she was too desperate to hurt me.

I was going to have to knock her ass *out*. There was no reasoning with her in this state. I jumped off her back, and she got to her feet immediately.

The pool gave me an idea, and I ran toward it. I heard Luna follow, stumbling the entire way. I forced myself to slow down so she wouldn't catch on to my plan. Granted, in her state, that was unlikely, but I knew not to underestimate my opponent.

For the first time in weeks, my mind cleared, and I was able to focus. That would've been nice earlier today with Rosemary and the drawing—and knowing what had caused the change would also be nice.

I'd focus on that later.

When I reached the deep end of the pool, I pivoted and spun out of the way.

Luna tried to stop, scrabbling and teetering on the edge for a second before her body fell over. Her eyes grew huge as she smacked the water, causing a huge splash to hit me and soak my fur.

She came up for air, doggy paddling in the center of the pool. But she treaded water and then sank instead of swimming to the side.

The back door to Killian's house opened, and he ran outside. "What the hell is going on out here?" He first looked at Griffin then me in my wolf form. "Uh..." Concern flicked into his eyes. "Dove, what's going on?"

Like I could answer him in animal form, but his message was clear. Why was I in wolf form in front of Griffin and Luna, of all people?

Luna whimpered, taking his focus off me. I glanced into the pool to find her struggling to stay afloat. I hadn't expected that. I'd figured she could get out—she'd been aware enough to attack me. Her head went under the water again, and it was clear that she wouldn't be able to tread enough water to get to the top.

That wasn't supposed to happen.

"I've got her," Killian yelled as he ran to the pool and jumped in.

As he swam to her, she didn't rise above the surface. I ran to the edge of the pool, whining. The whole point was for me not to kill anyone else, and yet, here she was, almost drowning.

"Hey, he has her." Griffin kneeled beside me. The myrrh scent that was all him filled my nose. Between that and his touch, my wolf and I calmed down. I leaned into him, needing to feel him closer.

Killian wrapped his arms around Luna, keeping her head above water.

My body sagged, and my lungs filled with air once more.

I didn't like her, but that didn't mean I wanted her dead.

The sound of an engine grew louder, and Griffin released me. "We need to get you shifted back to your human form before anyone else sees you."

That was easier said than done, seeing as my clothes were in tatters.

"Come on." Griffin rose, grabbed my sheath and bag and waved me to follow him.

He opened Killian's back door for me. Rushing inside, I ran to Olive's bedroom door, but reality hit me. I'd locked it earlier so that Killian wouldn't barge in and find me gone. At the time, it had seemed like the smart thing to do, but not so much now.

"What's wrong?" Griffin winced as he gestured to Killian's room. "Go change. Hurry before they come looking for us."

Ugh, this would cause so many questions, but my hands were tied. I trotted to the bedroom I was staying in and whimpered, looking at the top of the door frame where I knew the little metal emergency key was located.

"Whoa! Wait." Griffin's forehead lined with confusion. He followed my gaze to the top of the doorframe then snagged the key and unlocked the door. As he entered the room, he glanced at the skewed sheets on the bed. "You're staying in Olive's room?"

And the questions had already started. I should've put a spare set of clothes in Killian's bedroom in case something like this happened. But I'd never dreamed of *this* happening. At least, I didn't have to attempt to explain it right then since I was in animal form.

Pushing past him, I dug in the closet, not finding a damn thing to wear.

His chuckle forced me to turn around to find my bag on the floor and unzipped. Not looking at him, I rummaged through the bag carefully grabbing with my mouth jeans, bra, and white shirt.

Once I gathered my things, I turned to find Griffin sitting on the bed, watching me. One corner of his mouth tipped upward, and he looked almost pleased.

In other words, he looked drop-dead sexy, and the *tug* inside me seemed to coil and tighten.

Car doors slammed shut, alerting me that the guards had arrived. Welcoming the reprieve, I rushed out the door, not wanting to attempt to try to get him to leave my room. The way he was acting, he wouldn't budge, waiting instead for a show. So, I slipped into the bathroom to get some privacy.

My body tingled as I pushed my wolf away, and soon, I was standing back on two legs. I glanced in the mirror and, for a second, felt almost like myself, which was a welcome change. My emotions were more centered, and likewise, the dark circles under my eyes that had been there not even an hour ago had vanished. The shift and the moon must have done wonders for my mental stability. In fact, the overwhelming feelings of being alone that I'd previously entertained weren't suffocating at the moment.

I sagged against the dark granite sink and looked around the large bathroom. Beige tile complemented the light yellow walls. The tub and toilet sat against one wall, and across from the sink was a large linen closet that Killian kept stocked with towels. I grabbed a fresh hand towel, splashed my face with water, and patted it dry.

I could faintly hear the guards talking with Killian. They'd be coming in soon, so I quickly dressed.

Griffin knocked on the bathroom door. "Are you okay in there?"

His voice made goosebumps break out across my arms. Lord, I had it bad, but I had to keep my head on straight. "Yeah, I'm almost done." I put my bra on and pulled the white shirt down over my jeans. I took a moment and closed my eyes. There was no telling what kind of state Luna would be in, and I hoped that she didn't try to kick my ass again. I felt bad for dumping her in the pool since she'd obviously been even more drunk than I realized.

I heard Griffin walk down the hallway. The farther he moved

away from me, the more desperate I felt to get close to him again. This couldn't continue to happen. I didn't need to get to the point where I relied on him.

The back door opened. "What the hell happened out there?" I heard Killian rasp as four sets of footsteps entered behind him. "And why are there Shadow City guards here?"

I grabbed some bath towels from the linen closet and then ran into the living room. As I expected, wolf Luna was soaking wet. Killian was carrying her in his arms past the guards as water dripped all over the wood floor.

"Here," I said and held my hands out to take her from Killian so he could dry off.

"Uh, hell no," Griffin growled and took the towels away from me, the warmth of his body making the hairs rise on my arms as I swayed toward him. *Dammit.* "You're wearing a white shirt, and I'll be damned if you're giving them a show."

My cheeks burned, and I almost wanted to take her anyway to prove a point.

Almost.

But I didn't want to entertain the new men, so I let it go.

However, when Griffin took Luna from Killian, intense jealousy slammed into me. The irrational anger that surged through me when he touched her scared the shit out of me and luckily woke me up enough to keep my head in check. The girl almost died. I had to remember that.

Killian took a towel from me and dried off as I threw the two other towels onto the floor, trying to wipe up the water mess before his floors were ruined.

"What should I do with her?" Griffin wrinkled his nose.

There was only one option. "Put her in the bathtub, and I'll get her some clothes in case she shifts back."

He followed my instructions, which surprised me. Normally, he was more combative.

"Once again, why the hell were you outside when you were

supposed to be safely sleeping in bed, and why are there four guards here?" Killian's dark eyes locked on me and then glanced at the four guards standing at the back door.

I sucked in a breath, remembering the scents of the guards, and was about to tell Killian what I could when Griffin joined us back in the kitchen area. He filled in Killian and the guards on my wolf stalker and everything that had been happening.

Well... almost everything. Not the silver wolf part.

"We'll secure the perimeter," a bald-headed guard said. "No one will get by."

"Good, I'll stay here with them." Griffin motioned to Killian and me. "Let me know if you need anything, and I want you reporting in every hour."

"Yes, alpha." The oldest guard nodded and headed out the door.

When the four of them left, Killian rubbed his arms. "You were running away?" He sounded hurt as he touched my shoulder, making me meet his gaze.

"I don't want anything to happen to you." He had to understand that. "Think about it—if someone was hunting you, and they were willing to kill me in order to succeed, what would *you* do? And I couldn't tell you goodbye. If I tried, I knew I wouldn't leave." I felt like a huge asshole. If he was this upset from me contemplating it, what would've happened if I'd managed to go through with it?

"It doesn't matter." Killian stepped toward me, his face set with determination. "You are one of the most important people in my life now, and I refuse to let some assholes take that from me. Do you understand?"

"Yes. I'm sorry. But I wasn't trying to hurt you." I wanted him to know that. "It was just...every time I closed my eyes, I saw you dead, along with everyone else I love."

Killian pulled me into his arms and kissed the top of my head. "I know that feeling too, but you can't get rid of me. Okay?"

A deep growl emanated from Griffin as he stepped closer, pulling Killian's attention away from me.

"Dude, what the hell?" Killian frowned.

Griffin must have been feeling the same thing that came over me when I watched him carry Luna away. I pulled out of Killian's arms, trying to calm the situation.

"It's been a long night." Griffin rasped, as if trying to smooth out his reaction.

"Let me go get Luna to drink water and eat something, or she's going to feel like hell in the morning."

"And I'm going to dry off." Killian picked at the shirt that was plastered to his chest. "I'll change and come back out here to make her something to eat."

He had the better end of the deal. I watched him walk off, feeling even worse that I'd almost left without saying goodbye.

I'd taken one step toward Olive's bedroom to get Luna some clothes when Griffin cut me off.

His hazel eyes glowed, emphasizing the flecks of green as he came close enough that his minty breath hit my face. "If you leave, I will find you. I will use every resource I have until you're back here where you belong." He tucked a piece of hair behind my ear, which made a shiver run through me. "If you so much as *breathe* the wrong way, one of the guards will alert me. There's no escaping me now, Dove."

My breath hitched, and my body grew warm all over. I never dreamed possessive words would turn me on, but here I stood, wrong.

CHAPTER SEVENTEEN

THE SWEET SCENT of arousal wafted from my betraying body. I had to shut down whatever was brewing between us before he thought I was down for a one-night stand. I still hadn't changed my mind about that, and to be honest, if I let myself go there with him, I wasn't sure I'd be able to pick up the pieces afterward.

He had a hold on my mind, body, and soul.

I despised him for it.

A cocky smile appeared on his sculpted face. He knew *exactly* what he was doing to me.

Humiliated, I pivoted to walk around him, but he countered, staying in front of me. He placed a hand on my waist, and the *tug* grew even stronger.

"What are you trying to prove?" I asked quietly. "My boyfriend is in the other room."

"Boyfriend?" He stepped closer.

His scent overloaded my mind, turning me into a bundle of nerves. His own sweet scent slammed into me, making it clear I had an effect on him too.

"Hmmm..." he whispered as he placed a finger under my chin, tilting my head upward.

I licked my lips as my brain stopped working. "What?" I couldn't remember what he'd asked.

"Killian is your *boyfriend*?" His nose wrinkled as his hands wrapped around my waist.

"We're exclusive." I nodded my head. He already knew this. Why was he asking the question again?

His face fell, but he was close enough now that his chest brushed against me. "Are you attracted to him like you are to me?"

There was absolutely no way to get out of this gracefully, and he knew that. The asshole was setting me up to admit it either with my words or the stench of a lie. "It doesn't matter." I somehow found the strength to step back, putting distance between us, despite my body and my wolf warring inside me.

"Really?" He chuckled. "Because it kind of does to me." He moved right back into my space and kissed me, catching me by surprise. His lips were soft and warm, so damn inviting. My body hummed, wanting more of him.

When he slipped his tongue into my mouth, his delicious taste overwhelmed my senses, and a moan escaped from my throat. Thankfully, the noise startled me enough to snap me out of the moment.

I pushed him in the chest, hard. "Stop," I said as instinct and emotion warred inside me. A large part of me wanted to kiss him again and let him do things to me that had never been done before, but another part of me felt so much guilt. Even though Killian and I were only friends, we had promised to be exclusive. I'd broken his trust with my momentary weakness.

"Why?" he asked, licking my taste from his lips.

"I'm with your *best friend*." He knew why. We had this conversation not even five minutes ago. "You can't kiss me when I'm with him."

Griffin shrugged. "Break up with him."

"And have a fling with you?" Oh, look. His douchebag side was coming out again. This I could handle. I circled him slowly, preparing to get away to help Luna. "You're saying you would do that to your best friend and to Luna?"

I had never despised someone as much as I wanted him before. I wanted to slap him and kiss him at the same time.

"I wouldn't be doing anything to them." He countered my movements, remaining close. "So, I'm going to ask—"

A whimper escaped from the bathroom, alerting us that Luna was stirring.

For the first time ever, I was ecstatic to hear her. I pushed past him and rushed into the bathroom. Anything that would give me distance from Griffin so my mind could focus once more.

She hacked as she lay, head raised, on the plastic floor of the tub. Her brown fur was drenched, and her head bobbed like she was dizzy.

I'd never been in that condition before, but Zoe had, one night when her parents had gone out of town. She'd invited me and a few more people to hang out, and they'd all gotten so drunk they were puking all over the floor. I refused to join them because Dad would've lost his shit—alphas didn't behave stupidly.

Wow, if only he could see me now. Behaving stupidly was all that I'd done, despite not meaning to.

Rubbing a paw over her face, Luna groaned.

"Let me grab you some clothes, and I'll be right back." I said the words, though I doubted she'd care. I remembered what it felt like to almost drown. Maybe being intoxicated on top of it was a blessing in disguise for her.

I hurried into Olive's room and grabbed a pair of black sweatpants that had Juicy written on the ass and a matching top. It looked like an outfit Luna would wear herself, so at least there was that. If I'd had clothes to spare, I would've made her wear mine out of spite, so it was probably a good thing that I had only a couple of pairs of boring pants to my name.

When I turned back toward the door, I found Griffin standing against the wall, watching me. His eyes were so dark I couldn't see any of the green. His smoldering expression sent chills up and down my body.

Focus, Sterlyn. He could break you, and you're already struggling to keep your shit together.

I tried to ignore him as I marched past, heading back to Luna, but it was so damn *hard*. The *tug* was now almost a *yank*, and every one of my cells seemed to be on fire. The need that surged through me nearly overwhelmed me.

Killian's door opened, and he stepped into the hallway. He frowned but didn't say a thing, which made me feel even more guilty for the stolen kiss.

"You need any help?" he asked.

"Wow," Griffin said sarcastically. "Is that your way of telling Dove that you want to see other people naked?"

"Dude," Killian said as he faced his best friend. "What the hell? I didn't mean that at all!"

"Are you sure?" Griffin lifted both hands. "Because you know she's trying to get Luna to shift and get dressed, so I'm not sure how that could be taken any other way."

Oh, great. They were going to have a pissing match. I didn't want any part of that. "I'm good. Thanks." I was a little shocked that Griffin didn't volunteer to help get Luna changed, but I didn't overthink it. I despised the idea of him being near her anyway.

I left them scowling at one another and entered the bathroom, shutting the door behind myself. I laid the clothes on the bathroom sink and walked over to her.

This time, she was sitting with her wolfish head lying against the side of the cool plastic. When she sensed me, she turned toward me and let out a low growl.

Great. For all I knew, she was going to try to attack me again. "Come on, you need to get some food and water into you. Otherwise, you'll get sick again." I tried using a nice but not over-the-top tone with her.

She huffed and tossed her head.

I had no clue what she was trying to tell me to do, but if I was a betting woman, I'd say she was telling me to go to Hell. "I'm trying to help you."

She growled again in response and stood on shaky legs. Her eyes flicked from the door to me and back to the door.

Of course, she didn't want my help. "Okay, I'll go outside. I put the clothes on the sink in case you want to shift." I pointed to them. "Let me know if you need anything." When I opened the door, she huffed, making it clear that she wouldn't ask for my help even if she needed it.

Fine, let her struggle. I refused to kiss her ass.

When I stepped back into the hallway, Killian and Griffin stood in the living room, still glaring at one another. The drama was getting overwhelming. At this point, all I wanted to do was get Luna out of here and go to bed.

"You can't stand it that I got her first." Killian sneered. "Well, too bad. You need to stop sniffing around her."

Great, they were fighting over me. The last thing I wanted to do was come between the two of them. No girl should ever do that.

"If I hadn't been sniffing, she would've slipped away tonight since you obviously weren't paying attention to her." Griffin lifted his chin, daring his friend to disagree. "So maybe a 'thank you' is in order."

Oh, dear God. Did Griffin think that logic would work? If anything, he'd made the entire situation worse. I decided to intervene before things got even more upside down. "Hey, you two, cut it out." I stepped over to them, avoiding Killian's gaze. Each passing second caused more guilt to settle over me. "We have too much going on to be at each other's throats."

"Now that I can agree with." Killian grabbed my hand and pulled me beside him.

Griffin bared his teeth, making it clear that he didn't like Killian touching me.

Dammit. Luna was his girlfriend, and he'd kissed me. Not only had I betrayed Killian, but what did that say about Griffin? He had way too much influence over me. Hell, he got me to agree to stay.

We couldn't let our emotions get the best of us. "The entire day has been a shit show." That was the only way I knew to explain it. "All of our emotions are everywhere, and between me almost leaving and Luna almost drowning, we all need a time out." I dropped Killian's hand, not wanting to antagonize Griffin more than he already was, which was way too telling. I should be more worried about Killian than him, but I'd analyze that later. Right then, I needed space. "I'm going to my room for a second." I grimaced, realizing that this would lead to more questions.

"Speaking of which." Griffin pointed a finger at the two of us. "If you two are together, why is she sleeping in your sister's room?"

The bathroom door opened, and Luna stomped down the hallway. When she saw the three of us, she sighed with what looked like relief. She weaved over to Griffin and threw her arms around him. "Thank you fur shaving my liiife."

I clenched my hands into fists as I worked to keep myself from grabbing her by the hair. I wanted to yank her the fuck away from Griffin, and I hated that she got to smell his delicious scent.

"That wasn't me." He removed her arms from him and took a step back. He wiped the spot on his shirt that she'd gotten soaking wet from her hair. "You can thank Killian for that."

"What?" she asked and blinked, turning to face Killian and me. When her gaze landed on me, rage filled her eyes. "Thissiz all yur fault." She shook her head hard from side to side. "You *attacked* me, and yur fur was siiilver."

Great. Even drunk, she remembered that I had silver fur, but not that it wasn't Griffin who saved her. She had it out for me, and I had no clue why. "You think I had silver fur?" I forced laughter, trying to make it sound like that was the funniest thing I'd ever heard.

Her face turned sour, and she ran her fingers through her hair. They got caught halfway through where there was a large knot. "I doan feel so good."

Yeah, I bet she didn't.

"Come on." Griffin walked to the back door. "Let's get you taken care of."

Her eyes lit up at his words while pure rage coursed through me. My breathing quickened, drawing Killian's eyes to me.

Way to go, Sterlyn

"'Kay," she said eagerly and looped her arm through Griffin's.

His face twisted, but he didn't remove himself from her clutches.

I wasn't sure if that was better or worse. At least, he didn't seem to be enjoying the contact, but he was letting her touch him. What if he continued to let her touch him when they got back to his house?

My wolf surged forward, howling with hurt and anger, and I clenched my fists so hard that my nails dug into my palm. However, it was enough to cause some rationale to flit back into my mind. What the hell was going on with me?

"I'll come back in the morning," Griffin said as he opened the door. "And I'll let you know the guards' schedule." He winked at me before leading Luna out the door and shutting it behind them.

The asshole *winked* at me as he was taking another girl to his house. What the *hell*? And why did it enrage me so much? He'd kissed me, and I told him no. If anything, that kind of made this partially my fault, but I'd made a promise to Killian.

"Hey, what's wrong?" Killian asked, and he touched my arm.

Like I would be answering that question. I couldn't admit to him how I felt about his best friend for so many reasons, although, granted, he probably had an inkling based on the scents of our attraction earlier. But Griffin was a player, and I had to remember that.

"Dove?" He squeezed my arm comfortingly. "Are you okay?"

"No." I wasn't okay for so many reasons. "My whole life keeps falling apart. Right when I felt some semblance of normal, I find a painting of me near a dumpster. Then I confirm Rosemary's suspicions while letting some random wolf overhear me admit to everything!" He already knew all this, but I couldn't stop. "*Then* I try to leave and get caught by that ass-clown—" I pointed toward Griffin's house "—and then his drunken girlfriend attacks me. There is no part of this that's okay." Not to mention the kiss, which I would have to tell Killian about.

"Look, I get that we're more friends than lovers." Killian placed his hands on my shoulders, making me look at him. "But Griffin isn't good for you. This isn't me being jealous—I'm telling you as a friend. He doesn't want to settle down, and he makes a point to prove it at every opportunity. I don't want to see you get hurt. He has a way of making a girl feel special, and he seems to be focusing that on you, which pisses me off because we're best friends, and you're supposed to be my girl."

His words were like a slap in the face, even though I already knew that they were all true. And here it was. I had to tell Killian the truth. I'd made a promise to him, and I broke it. I had to take the blame and deal with the consequences. I didn't want to ruin their friendship. "Killian, I need to tell you something."

He tilted his head and inhaled sharply. "What?"

"Griffin and I kissed."

CHAPTER EIGHTEEN

A TENSE SILENCE swallowed us whole.

His jaw twitched as he processed my words, and I braced myself for the inevitable blow.

"Who initiated it?" Killian huffed. "Was it him?" He started pacing.

That was the exact question I'd hoped he wouldn't ask. There was already a ton of tension between them, and I didn't want to cause more, but I'd broken my promise to Killian and had to tell him. "What matters is that it ended almost as soon as it began, and I'm so sorry that I betrayed your trust." In reality, the kiss had lasted seconds, but I could still feel his lips on mine.

"So...he kissed you." Killian stopped and stared at me. "Dove, he's bad news."

Something snapped inside me. "He brought four guards here to protect us. How is that bad news?"

His brows furrowed as he sighed. "No, I mean he's bad news to girls. Look, apart from his dating habits, Griffin is a great guy and a good friend. Well, at least he was before he kissed you." He laughed without humor. "Either way, he has made it abundantly clear that he doesn't want to settle down, and I don't want you to get hurt."

He was right. Somehow, I *had* opened myself up to getting hurt by Griffin, but I couldn't help it. No matter how loud my head screamed, my heart and wolf wanted to be next to him. I was at war inside, and my brain was losing. "No, I get it. He did hit on me horribly my first day in the coffee shop."

"I'm not trying to be ugly or mean." Killian touched my arm. "But I'm afraid he did that because I claimed you first. And don't forget that he left with Luna."

That was like a punch to my gut, but sometimes the truth was hard to hear. Everything he said made sense, but it didn't erase the crazy connection I had with Griffin. "I know."

"Look, I know you're helping me out with the pretend relationship thing, and if your fated mate or some other great guy came along, we'd end the ruse immediately. But Griffin is not the one." He kissed my forehead. "And I don't want to see you get hurt more than you already have, losing your family and pack."

"Not to mention that I have some wacko threatening me." I had to stop thinking about Griffin and what he and Luna were probably doing right at this moment.

The thought of them having sex, or God knew what else, kept trying to creep into my mind, making me want to march over there and kick Griffin in the nads. At least then, he'd be hurting and thinking of me.

Whoa. That was a violent thought. And why did I care if he wanted to be with Luna? I needed to keep my head level.

And that right there spoke volumes.

My reaction to Griffin wasn't rational, which confirmed my nagging fear. "Look, I want to be honest with you. Griffin and I... we have a strange connection, and even though it's probably a *very* bad idea, seeing as he left with Luna... I need to explore it."

"Dove—" His face pinched.

"I get it." Boy did I ever, but after going two weeks without seeing

Griffin, my heart hurt from wanting to be close to him. "But I'd rather have your blessing than do something behind your back."

"All I'm saying is, you deserve someone who's going to treat you with respect, loyalty, and kindness." Killian hugged me. "And if this is something you need to explore..." He sighed and ran a hand down his face. "Then you have my blessing. But if he hurts you, I will kick his ass and not have anything to do with him anymore."

I chuckled, but it sounded a little watery. "I'm so glad that I met you. You're like a piece of my family I didn't realize was missing."

"And I kinda love you too." He pulled back and arched an eyebrow. "But no more running away, or you *will* be sleeping with me in my bed. Got it?"

"Maybe I'll misbehave then." I winked, totally messing with him.

"Yeah, yeah." He rolled his eyes. "But seriously. The fact that you were planning to run away hurts. We're family. If you go, then you better take me."

"But you have your life here, and your pack." Although...he didn't talk about his pack much, now that I thought about it.

"It's my dad's pack. All I've done is let them down and allow them to lose their alpha before his time." He frowned.

I hated that he felt responsible, but that was something he'd have to work out himself. "You know that you're the alpha, and you haven't stepped down for a reason. I see how Sierra and Carter look at you, and it isn't with hate or disgust. They love and respect you, which shows you're doing something right."

"Maybe, but I'm not ready." He yawned. "Look, I'm exhausted. I'm going to bed. We've got to get to the university early tomorrow."

Shit, I'd forgotten all about work. I was going to be dead on my feet. "You're right. I'm sorry about all this." If I hadn't tried to sneak out, then none of tonight would've happened, including the kiss.

"No, it's actually a good thing." Killian nodded toward the back door. "We now have four guards protecting us, so we'll know if anyone tries anything."

That was true. "Yeah, Griffin said that I'd be safer here than on the run by myself."

"I hate to admit it, but he's right." Killian yawned again, and I heard his jaw crack. "Now let's go get some rest."

We walked to the bedrooms, and he opened his door all the way. "I'm leaving this open to make sure I catch you next time you try to do something—"

"Smart? Selfless?" I interjected. "Loving?"

"Foolish." He squeezed my arm tenderly. "Good night."

"Night." I left my door cracked open too and crawled into bed. Surprisingly, I fell right to sleep.

MURMURS from the kitchen woke me.

"Sir, she needs to stay here and not go to the university." A voice I didn't recognize spoke. "It'll be too hard to try to keep her safe with all those people around her."

Sir? Was Griffin here already? I glanced at the clock. It was almost seven.

"You're right," Killian's voice replied. "That coffee shop is always busy. I'll link with Carter and let him know and then run by and make sure everything is okay with the painting."

Yeah, I had to be part of the conversation about what I'd be doing all day. I got up and made my way toward the voices.

A tall man who had to be in his mid-thirties stood in front of Killian. He had his arms crossed, emphasizing his muscular biceps through his black shirt. He had two guns strapped around his waist, and his amber eyes homed in on me. A blackish eyebrow arched high enough that his matching longish hair hid it. "I take it this is Dove?" His attention went back to Killian.

Yeah, that wasn't going to happen. I could answer questions about myself just fine. "Yes, I am. And you are?"

"Lucas," he said curtly. "I'm part of Killian's pack. We were discussing your safety."

"Were you?" I tried to keep the sarcasm out of my voice but failed miserably. "I didn't realize that either of you could make decisions on my behalf." I probably would've been willing if the asshole hadn't laid out what I was going to do without discussing it with me.

"It wasn't quite like that." Killian glowered at the man. "Lucas made some very good points about you staying home. The coffee shop will be so packed with people that anyone could slip in and get to you. It'll be hard to keep an eye on everyone without making it obvious that you're under guard."

Establishing security measures would be hard; I couldn't argue with them there. "Carter will be pissed." But honestly, I didn't want to go back there yet. Call me a coward, but taking a day to recover might be a good thing. A day to work through my issues, instead of continually making poor decisions. I hadn't sat back and reflected on anything.

"I'll handle him." Killian winked. "Don't worry about that. And I better get moving because I wanted to check on the paint job I did and make sure nothing bled through."

"Is there anything else we need to discuss, sir?" Lucas asked.

"Nope, make sure no one gets inside to hurt her." Killian patted my arm as he walked by, leaving me alone with the guard.

I didn't like being around people I didn't know, but I couldn't be rude when this guy was protecting me.

"Well, I better get back outside." Lucas opened the door to the porch. "Let us know if you need anything."

"Will do." I strolled over to the couch and picked up the remote then turned on the television.

I'D BEEN THERE by myself for all of thirty minutes, and I was already restless. I flopped around on the couch, trying to get comfortable, but nothing helped.

Footsteps pounded on the back porch and the door opened once more. Between the rhythm of the feet and the *tug* that took hold, I already knew who it was...and I hated it.

Despite him not being the massive creep he'd appeared to be the other day, I still wasn't thrilled that fate had chosen *him* of all people. He'd left with Luna last night, so what did that say about our connection? Something had to be wrong, and I had to be misreading the situation.

The problem was after tossing and turning all night, I was pretty damn sure I knew what this overwhelming, horrifying connection was.

Griffin had to be my fated mate.

Which didn't make any sense and shouldn't be possible. In fact, I hated that the thought had even crossed my mind, and yet...it resonated with my soul.

Of course, he'd show up now, after Luna must have left. The anger inside me at what they might have done put me in a combative mood.

When he stepped into the living room, I somehow prevented myself from getting up and running toward him. He looked fresh with his hair gelled to the side and his maroon shirt fitting him like a second skin. He placed his hands in his jeans pockets as he scanned me from head to toe.

My body warmed.

"Hey, you," he drawled as he sauntered over to me. "A little birdie told me that you were staying home today."

"I know that little birdie wouldn't be Killian." It had to be one of the guards. "He's pissed at you."

"Oh?" He looked amused. "How come?"

I sat up, surprised at his cavalier attitude. "Because I told him that we kissed."

He shrugged and sat next to me, throwing his arm over my shoulders. "I'm thinking there is more to the story between you and Killian."

"Are you trying to be funny?" I scooted away from him, needing him not to touch me. I lost my mind that way. "As far as you know, he and I are dating." I wanted to see how he reacted to my words.

He smirked. "I don't think that you really are. I would even go as far as to say you two view each other more like siblings than anything."

"What?" I said in a way too high-pitched voice. "I don't have to explain anything to you." Shit, why would he say that? Were we not convincing? "Besides, it's not just Killian that's part of this equation. Speaking of which, how is *Luna?*"

"Probably hungover as hell." He laughed. "Her dad was not pleased. He called me, apologizing profusely when she got home."

"Well, I'm sure she made up for the inconvenience she caused you many times over." I crossed my arms and turned my head, cheeks burning, refusing to meet his eyes. I didn't want to see what was reflecting back at me.

"What are you talking about?" He sounded bewildered. "When I left here, I dropped her off at her house and immediately left."

My heart leaped with joy, and I told it to sit the hell down. I wasn't going to fall for the innocent-playboy act. I stood, needing to get away from him, but he grabbed my waist and brought me down beside him, the *tug* pulling us together.

"I asked you a question," he rasped.

"She's your girlfriend." I inhaled sharply, trying to keep my act together. I wanted to explore things with him—I couldn't help but want to be with my fated mate—but not while he was with someone else. "It's fine. But you shouldn't be here with me alone."

"Why the hell would you think she's my girlfriend?" he asked as he cupped my face and turned me to look at him.

I expected to see malice, contempt, or something, but instead, I found concern. His eyes were tender, and the cocky man I'd met that day in the coffee shop appeared to be gone.

"Because she told me that, during those weeks when you were gone, you'd been spending them with her." That conversation had devastated me, even though I didn't like to admit it. "That she'd been able to get you to settle down sooner than she expected."

"Are you fucking serious?" he snarled. "She's such a bitch. Killian had her pegged all along."

"So you aren't together?" I wanted to take that back because the answer was way too important to me. But there it was, hanging out there for him to answer and potentially to break me.

He smiled. "No, but she did have part of that right." He leaned so his lips hovered over mine. "For the first time ever, I do want to settle down."

My heart raced, and butterflies took flight in my stomach. "That's funny, after all I've heard about you."

"Oh, everything you heard is true, but this silver-haired girl walked into my life, turning everything upside down." He brushed his lips against mine. "The first time I met her, she challenged me, infuriated me, and was so damn alluring. The first moment I laid eyes on her and she cut through all my bullshit, I was a goner."

"You expect me to believe that?" My head didn't believe him, but my heart and wolf did. The awful stench of a lie was missing. My wolf whimpered, wanting to get closer. "You fought with me constantly and disappeared until last night. You didn't even come into the shop."

"When I lost my dad, it was the worst day of my entire life," he said as he took my hand. "And I swore I would never grow close to anyone else again. But then you came here, and not only did I care for you, but I fell for you so damn hard that the thought of losing you makes me insane."

Happiness surged through me stealing my breath. I never thought I'd even feel a fraction of this ever again, but that was the kind of effect this man had on me.

"So you ran?" He and I were more alike than I'd thought.

"Yeah, but every day, the urge to see you again got stronger and stronger. Watching you with Killian would have killed me." He turned his body fully toward me. "But yesterday, I couldn't stay away any longer. It was like something pulled me back here in the nick of time. I'd only been home a few minutes before something told me you were outside. And there you were, running away."

"Griffin—" I started, but he placed a finger over my lips.

"Please let me get this out." His irises darkened to a brown.

I nodded, wanting to hear what he had to say.

"Between you confiding your secret to me and Luna trying to hurt you, I knew my heart was done for. That I would have to watch you with Killian, from the sidelines." He rubbed his thumb against my wrist. "But then I came into the house to help you get shifted back and realized that, not only are you sleeping in Olive's room alone, but you don't love Killian in the way I feared you did, and I didn't need to worry about betraying my best friend any longer. You are fair game."

"What are you talking about?" There was no way he could've known that Killian and my relationship was based on pure friendship.

"Because I found this." He pulled a piece of paper from his pocket and unfolded it.

My breath caught as he showed me the letter I'd written to Killian. Griffin did know everything. "That's why you kissed me."

"Yup." He waggled his brows. "The only thing standing between you and me wasn't a problem after all. I wouldn't be betraying my best friend, and I had to see if you felt the same way about me."

"And what did you determine?" My breath caught as I looked at his lips.

"That you do." He kissed me, not holding back any longer. My stomach fluttered, and my head grew dizzy as his tongue slipped inside my mouth. His hands went to my waist, dragging me onto his lap. He began to whisper against my lips.

"At first, I thought it couldn't be possible, that this feeling was lust. Each time I see you... touch you... kiss you, I can't focus on anything else." He pulled back, and his eyes stared into my soul as he whispered, "We're fated mates. Tell me that you feel it?" He peppered kisses down my face.

His words crumbled every wall I'd built up around my heart. Maybe he'd been a player before, but everything inside told me that we'd changed each other. The *tug* between our souls was painfully blissful, as if we needed to connect to make us whole. "I feel the same way."

I straddled him, needing to be closer, but I still couldn't get close enough. My body caught fire as I slipped my tongue into his mouth, and he matched me stroke for stroke. The sweet scent of arousal coursed between us.

Between his minty taste and his smell, my head swam in a way I never wanted to end. I moaned when his fingertips brushed the bare skin of my stomach, and my need for him slammed through me.

His hand slipped under my shirt, cupping my breast as I rocked against him. I had no clue what I was doing, but he bucked against me, making me feel as if I was doing something right.

As I kissed down his neck, he sighed. "Wait. We can't do this."

The rejection stung as I pulled back. "What? But I thought—"

"I *want* to." He removed his hands from under my shirt and growled. "But you deserve better than this. I don't want to take you in Killian's house while he's out. You deserve to be courted and pampered. I want to give you all of my attention and go back to an empty house so we can take our time in my bed." He kissed me and ran his fingers through my hair. "I want our first time together to be the best memory possible because it'll be the start of our whole life together."

"You do want this?" The tug had become an overwhelming leaping sensation that made me yearn for every inch of him. For him to want to wait made me fall even more.

"There's no doubt in my mind." He gently pressed his lips to mine. "So, Dove, what are you doing tonight?"

"Sterlyn," my name fell from my lips.

"What?" His brows furrowed. "Sterlyn?"

"It's my real name." No one had called me that in so long. "I didn't tell Killian my name, so he started calling me Dove."

"It's beautiful." He brushed his lips against mine. "So, what are you doing tonight, Sterlyn?"

"Pretty sure some desperate alpha is going to wind up showing up at my door, begging me to be his for the night," I teased him, unable to stop myself. In this moment, I was so damn happy.

"You better make him grovel." He sighed and leaned his forehead against mine.

The garage door rumbled open, indicating that Killian had arrived home.

"Well, it's a good thing we didn't take things further now," Griffin said as he pecked my lips. "I guess there's no time like the present to inform my protective best friend I'll be taking his sister out tonight."

I tensed. Griffin acted confident that this was all going to work out, but I wasn't so sure.

CHAPTER NINETEEN

I JUMPED TO MY FEET, not wanting Killian to walk in on me straddling his best friend.

Oh, dear God. That sounded horrible, and what Killian had said to me last night about Griffin not being the right guy for me made this entire situation surreal. But I'd been honest with him, and he knew that I wanted to explore things with Griffin. Granted, I was pretty sure completing the mate bond with him tonight wasn't *exploring* so much as committing to each other.

My gut screamed that something uncomfortable was imminent, but this was something Griffin and I should do together. Either way, Griffin had become determined that I was going to be his.

The thought both thrilled and terrified me.

Griffin chuckled as he stood next to me, taking my hand.

A pause in Killian's footsteps told me he'd figured out that Griffin was here. A low growl emanated from him as he hurried into the room and stopped short.

"What's going on?" Killian straightened his shoulders as he stared at his best friend.

"I came over to ask Ster—*Dove* out tonight." Griffin leaned closer to me.

"Griffin, she's important to me," Killian said. "I don't want to see her get hurt."

I hated that these two were arguing over me again.

"That's fair. And I know I've been behaving like an asshole, but that's changing from now on." Griffin lifted our joined hands. "She's my fated mate."

Killian closed his eyes and exhaled. He looked up and met first my eyes, then Griffin's. "I can't stand between something special like this, but no more fucking games." Killian's shoulders sagged. "She's lost so much already."

"There won't be." I straightened my shoulders, standing tall beside Griffin. I couldn't let him be the only one fighting for us. "I told you last night that I felt the connection. It's real."

Killian's jaw tightened as he glared at his friend. "Remember when you told me you're not the 'settling down' type of guy?"

Wow, I figured this was going to be tense, but I hadn't expected Killian to call out his friend directly. Though I guessed I shouldn't be surprised that he was protective of me after all we'd gone through.

"Yeah, I remember, but ever since she walked into our lives, I've been pulled in her direction." Griffin faced me. "That damn *tug* had me going into that coffee shop the first day without Luna having to nag me. Then I saw the most beautiful girl standing behind the counter, and I froze—then acted like a dirtbag."

"I can't argue with you there." If he wanted me to comfort him, he'd come to the wrong person. He had been an asshole that day.

"He hits on every woman that way." Killian dropped his backpack on the floor and locked eyes with me. "He tries humping anything with two legs when the mood strikes."

"This is *different*," Griffin rasped. "When I realized what she was to you, it drove me insane. Every time you touched her, I wanted to punch the shit out of you. That's one of the reasons I left for so long. I had a ton of stuff that I needed to do with Mom and the council, but also, I couldn't stand to see her with you, and I didn't want to be tempted to interfere. You're my best friend. If she made you happy, I had to leave in order to respect that."

Killian rolled his eyes and crossed his arms. "Dude."

But I wasn't sure if that was the only thing. Maybe his reasoning was a tad bit selfish. "Griffin and I decided to pursue this, but know you will never lose either of us."

"If you break up, I will." Killian hung his head, but then he stalked over and hugged me. "You're my family now, and I don't want to risk that."

Griffin growled but didn't do more than that. "Man, I would *never* hurt her. I know I have a bad track record, but I'm serious about Dove. She's it for me."

"If you were being all noble and left out of respect for the relationship that you thought she and I had, then why did you come back last night?" Killian released me and faced his friend.

"I couldn't stay away any longer. Hell, Mom told me if I didn't stop frowning and snapping, she would personally put me in Shadow City's jail. I could barely pay attention to the council meetings because all I wanted to do was come back here to her." Griffin sighed. "I wasn't going to act on it. I wanted to see her for a few minutes to subdue whatever this urge was inside me. But then the whole Luna thing happened, and I found this note that our little runaway left you." He pulled the piece of paper back out of his pocket.

I inhaled and held my breath, guessing how Killian would react.

"Note?" Killian asked and took it from him. His eyes scanned it, and I saw when realization sank in. "*This* was how you were telling me goodbye?"

"We've gone through this." I didn't want to talk about it again. "I couldn't say it to your face because I wouldn't have been able to leave. But I had to make sure you knew I left of my own free will—and how much your friendship means to me."

"Don't make her feel bad," Griffin said as he touched my arm. "She thought she was doing the right thing."

Killian's jaw tightened, and he folded my letter up and put it into his back pocket. "Can I talk to you alone for a minute?" He pointed at Griffin.

"Whatever you have to say, you can say it in front of Dove." Griffin tightened his hold on me. "She and I are a package deal."

"No, it's fine." Griffin was already acting like we were together, and though I loved the sound of it, I had to make sure Killian was okay with it. After all, he'd been there for me first. "I'll go outside and get some fresh air."

"Stay close, please, and make sure the guards are in sight," Griffin said. He kissed my cheek and released my hand. "There've been enough attempts on your life to last a lifetime."

That was a very true statement. "I don't plan on venturing far." Not wanting to affect their conversation, I slipped out the back door and made my way around to the side of the house near the living room. They still had no idea how strong my hearing was, and I couldn't help but want to listen to what they had to say.

"Do you realize how important she is to me?" Killian asked. "If you ever hurt her—"

"I couldn't. It's not possible." Griffin sounded so sincere. "The connection is real. I swear it is."

Hope blossomed in my stomach. The scary truth was that I was at the mercy of our connection. I had no clue how powerfully the bond would impact us, but the more time I spent with him, the harder it was to leave his side. Each kiss and touch made the *tug* so much stronger.

"Oh, I believe that you think that." Killian sighed. "That's the only reason why your ass hasn't been beaten to a bloody pulp."

A smile slipped into place, and I made my way toward the wood's edge, not wanting to hear any more. They were coming to an agreement, and Killian hadn't wanted me to listen.

I focused on the sounds of the animals in the forest and glanced at the sun. It was midday when the sun was at its highest point in the sky and the moon farthest away, which meant I was at my weakest for the next few hours. At some point, I wanted to be able to shift and run free.

A *crack* sounded about a mile away and I jerked to a halt. Was that a gunshot? I scanned the area, realizing that the guards weren't in position. I'd been so caught up with Killian and Griffin that I hadn't been paying attention.

The noise took me back to the day when my pack had been murdered. I scanned the area, looking for one of the guards to alert, but I couldn't find one.

That was odd. They were supposed to be surrounding the house.

Another shot echoed, this one closer, followed by a low grunt.

Somebody was in trouble. I started to run in the direction of the shot, but I stopped. I couldn't leave Killian and Griffin and run off on my own. They'd be pissed, and rightfully so.

I rushed to the back door and threw it open. "Someone is in trouble, and the guards have disappeared." I stuck my head in to find them running toward the kitchen. Good, they were moving. "Call for backup. I'm going to go see what I can do."

"No," Griffin said absolutely. "You're staying here. It could be a trap."

Oh, hell no. "I may be attracted to you, but that doesn't mean I'll hand over my decision-making to you. I *am* going out there. It's up to you whether you come along for the ride."

A scream pierced the air, urging me back outside.

"Dove!" Griffin yelled as his footsteps pounded behind me. "Stop. We need to wait for backup."

"They can find us by following the noise." I spun around to face him. "We'll do recon first. We need to see what we're up against."

Killian stepped out of the house. "More of my guards are on their way."

"So are Shadow City guards," Griffin said.

"Great, let's go." I took off again and heard Griffin grumble something, though I couldn't make out the words.

Dad had taught me never to go on a mission without at least one other person knowing where I was headed.

I pulled magic from my wolf and picked up my pace with the guys on my heels as the trees flew by. We were headed in the direction of Killian's fishing spot from that day not too long ago.

When I crossed a path that appeared to have been made recently, the scent of the guards hit my nose, along with at least six others. Judging by how the branches were broken and scattered, someone had been dragged to wherever they went. Had someone gotten the jump on the guards?

It had to be the same assholes who'd attacked my pack.

The surrounding area was creepily quiet now that we'd stumbled across the trail. I slowed and lifted my hand, pivoting toward the two men. I placed a finger to my lips and gestured at the worn path.

Killian nodded as he walked over and touched the grass where it'd been flattened. I squatted next to him and held up four fingers, one for each guard. How the hell did they take the four guys?

"What—" Griffin started to ask quietly, but I covered his mouth with my hand. There was no telling how close anyone was.

This would have been when a pack bond would have come in handy.

"Come on out, Sterlyn," the voice of the auburn-bearded man called to me. He must have been at least a half-mile away, but I could hear him clear as day. "Or should I say Dove? We know you and those two guys that are always sniffing around you aren't far away."

Great, these assholes knew my names.

For them to know we were here meant someone was either listening for our progress or watching us. I tapped into my wolf more and scanned the area with precision. That was when I noticed a crow sitting on a tree branch not too far away. I sniffed the air, looking for a human smell mixed in with the vanilla of the animal.

When the bird flapped its wings and cawed, that confirmed all I needed to know. He was gloating, knowing we'd overlooked him.

Dammit. Crow shifters normally flocked in small groups and stayed out of matters unless it benefited them. What in the world were my hunters offering all of these different kinds of shifters to get them to work for them? They must have some incredibly enticing plan to get others to follow across races.

Another piece to the ever-growing puzzle.

There was no point in pretending that we weren't there. "How do you know my name?"

"What are you doing?" Killian whispered. "And when did you plan on telling me your name?"

"That crow—" I pointed to it "—already spotted us and reported back to Auburn Goatee." There was no point in pretending that we could do recon now. We were all-in, and I hoped the new guards would follow us soon. "And I was going to but got a little distracted."

Paws padded in our direction, and I assumed wolves were circling to trap us. The best thing we could do was try to get them talking. We needed to buy time for backup to find us. If we ran, they might take us down before the others could reach us.

"Please, come and join us." Goatee chuckled, no doubt loving that he had the upper hand.

"I'll come if you let the other two go." If I could protect Griffin and Killian, I would.

"Like hell." Griffin took my hand and shook his head. "There's no way I'll leave you."

Killian arched an eyebrow, and his mouth dropped slightly before he schooled his expression into one of indifference. "I'm with him. We aren't leaving."

"You need to go. They want me—you can't help me if they capture all of us." If I lost them, I wasn't sure I could stay in my right mind. "You two are alphas, for God's sake. You have to stay safe for your packs."

"Stop bickering," Goatee commanded. "They aren't going anywhere, and they aren't shifting. "

Four wolves stepped through two trees and circled us. The one right behind us growled and nodded his head forward, his milky brown fur blowing in the slight breeze.

Great, they were herding us to Goatee.

We started walking, slowly, Killian and Griffin flanking me as if they could protect me better than I could protect myself. They should be linking with their packs, pulling more guards toward us. But it could take time before they got here. I didn't know what skills either had, but I'd guess Killian might have been trained to fight similarly to me, given he was the alpha's son of the protecting pack. Griffin hadn't seemed to have formal training, but he was strong.

The river grew louder, and after a few more minutes, the trees grew thinner as we neared the embankment, close to the spot where Killian liked to fish. The four guards and Lucas lay dead on the mulchy ground, bullet holes between their eyes.

The present-day picture merged with the memory of my pack, and my legs grew shaky.

CHAPTER TWENTY

"WHAT'S WRONG?" Goatee chuckled darkly. "Does this remind you of something?"

The asshole was gloating. He knew exactly what this was doing to me. That was probably why he'd had these five guards slaughtered this way. He wanted to break me and flaunt what they'd done to my pack. He had no remorse. "You had twenty guards on these five guards. From my standpoint, it was a small-dick move like the guns you used on my pack."

"Instead of insulting me, you should be thanking me. After all, we didn't kill you or your two boyfriends." Goatee *tsk*ed. "And these five deaths, well, they're on you."

"How so?" I wanted to understand his delusional justification. The next thing he would tell me was that I was to blame for my pack's death too, but I wasn't some weak-minded wolf. None of this was my fault, and I wouldn't let some self-absorbed asshole tell me otherwise.

"Because you ran away." The guy sneered and took a few steps in my direction. "Do you know how damn hard it was to find you?"

Killian and Griffin moved in front of me as if they could actually protect me. A laugh almost bubbled out of me, mainly due to what I'd seen of Griffin's fighting skills. I would need to train him if we did make it out of here alive.

Here I was, doubting myself. I had to believe that we would come out of this breathing, all three of us, or I might as well lie down and give up. But we needed backup, so I had to stall.

"I'm pretty sure you found me that second day." That had to have been him exiting the diner that morning when I had my meltdown. "Granted, you made me doubt it when you walked off without a second glance."

"We had been at a loss until that moment." Goatee scowled. "We actually were passing through the city and didn't think you'd run here of all places with the number of people here that could identify a silver wolf. It was a good strategy, but this was obviously fate. By the way, what did you think of the little calling-card we left for you?"

Of course. That explains seeing the wolf right after I found the painting on the wall. "Fuck you," I spat.

"Gladly," Auburn Goatee chuckled. "But we can get to that part as soon as we get you settled in your new home."

My skin crawled at the insinuation.

"She is *not* yours," Griffin said with menace. "She's mine, and you won't be taking her anywhere."

"You have no influence over me, alpha boy." Goatee rubbed his hands together and gestured to the five dead guards.

"If you hurt Sterlyn or injure another one of my people, you will have made an enemy out of Shadow City." Griffin straightened his shoulders, standing tall. "If you stand down now, we can come to an agreement. I have the power to protect you from the punishment you deserve and *will* receive if you try to take Sterlyn or harm any of us. Tell us what you're looking for. Entry to Shadow City? A place in a new pack?"

"Oh, no." Goatee placed a hand over his mouth and forced his body to shake. "What ever shall I do?" He glanced over his shoulder as ten more men slipped through the trees behind him and joined us.

"We have no other choice than to leave right now. After all, the big powerful Shadow City alpha might not like us. Oh, wait. He already doesn't, and Shadow City only lets in wolves that can benefit them. So I guess that means I don't give two fucks about negotiating with you."

A few of his men chuckled, clearly enjoying watching the alpha wolf of the elusive city being made fun of.

Griffin had to see that this group of idiots wasn't afraid of consequences. Either their own alpha had commanded them to retrieve me, or they were getting paid big bucks. There was no negotiating with them because they didn't work in diplomatic ways, so I'd cut straight to the chase. "I'm not going with you. I refuse to be some dickwad's personal breeder."

A low growl escaped Griffin. "You'll have to kill me to take her."

The fact that they hadn't killed Griffin both worried and relieved me. They obviously didn't want him dead, but why? There had to be more going on than we even guessed originally.

"We can arrange that," Goatee cooed. "Or we can walk away here as friends, and you get over your little-boy crush. Either way, she'll be coming with us."

"My sister isn't going to be some guy's sex slave," Killian said. "Griffin is right; you'll have to kill both of us."

I couldn't let them sacrifice themselves for me. That would be something I couldn't live with. "If you don't hurt them, I'll willingly go with you." The fact that they hadn't yet hurt or killed either guy made me think there was a reason, that maybe they had orders not to. If I went willingly and played the part for a while, they'd possibly let Killian and Griffin go, and I could determine a way to escape. It would no doubt be hard, but under the moon, I might be able to swing it.

"No." Griffin shook his head. "You aren't going with them. Absolutely not." He clenched his hands into fists, and some honey brown fur sprouted across his arms. He was dangerously close to shifting.

The time still wasn't right to start the fight. I couldn't hear any additional guards running in our direction. And that stupid crow would probably know they were coming long before we did, what with being perched on that damn tall tree not ten yards away.

"See, this is why I tried to leave last night." If I got Griffin to focus on me, that should hold him back. "I didn't want you and Killian to get hurt foolishly for me."

"Well, then, a thank you is in order." Goatee rubbed his hands together. "She would've gotten the slip on us since I was gathering the troops after confirming it was her at the university yesterday."

Of course, he'd done the drawing and watched me make an ass of myself with Rosemary. The memory of the wolf in the woods triggered—he'd been in the shadows, and I hadn't noticed that his fur had a red hue to it, but thinking back, it was pretty damn clear.

The crow flew off the branch, crying, "Caw! Caw! Caw!"

That was when the noise of multiple feet pounded on the ground, heading in our direction.

"They have backup." One of the lanky guys in the back called as he stood, pulling out a machine gun.

Dear, sweet Jesus. This wasn't going to end well, and not enough guards were heading this way. Maybe more were coming, but Goatee's men would try to pick them off one at a time, which meant a fight was inevitable. We'd have to distract as many as possible so the guards wouldn't end up like these other five.

Doing the only thing I could think of in this moment, I called my wolf forward. I had no weapon because I foolishly hadn't planned to come outside, so my animal was the only option I had.

I was born for battle. I had to trust my instincts.

My skin tingled as my silver fur sprouted all over my body, and my bones cracked, contorting me to my animal form. My clothes ripped away as my four paws hit the ground.

"Dammit, she shifted." The scrawny shifter swung the gun in my direction. "What do we do?" His voice held a slight tremor.

Good, at least, they weren't comfortable with me.

Goatee spun around and knocked the gun away from my direction. "You do not shoot her unless there is absolutely no other choice. Got it? If we don't get her there alive, you'll be taking the blame."

That little bit of information was music to my ears. They didn't want to kill me, which meant I had a little leeway before they'd be willing to do it.

Deciding to use their distraction to my advantage, I ran through Killian and Griffin and locked on the scrawny guy who'd been foolish enough to show weakness. That would make the others pause around me.

What I wanted was to attack Goatee, but he was in control of this little pack, which meant I had to be smart.

A few of the men froze as I ran past them. It was clear that they'd never been around a silver wolf in wolf form before. Since we were close to a full moon, I was larger than all of them. My pack called a full moon a silver moon, in celebration of the strength of our connection.

Killian and Griffin followed my lead and shifted behind me while the others stayed focused on me. I hated that they were here with me, but I knew they wouldn't leave.

Even though time seemed to move slowly, only a few seconds had passed. I lunged at the lanky guy and sank my teeth into his neck, jerked my head to the side, and killed him on the spot. Blood dripped down my mouth, covering my fur as the taste of copper stuck to my tongue and the metallic scent hit my nose.

My stomach churned. I hated death and being the one to cause it, but I had to hold it together. It was us or them, and there were twenty-three enemies in human form, four wolves, and a crow to go. I'd seen what they were capable of and refused to let anyone else I loved die because of a moment's hesitation.

Dad had told me that we should never celebrate killing others and do it only when absolutely necessary.

I'd challenged him, asking how you would know whether it was necessary or not. And he'd patted my arm and replied that I would know. That our wolves would guide us because they were good and thus made of pure light as well. That we were a reflection of the power inside us.

I never believed him until now, but there was no question in my mind that these assholes had to die. They got off on hurting others and asserting their dominance, and I refused to let the cycle continue. The cost of their sins was their lives.

"What are you standing around for?" Goatee yelled. "Attack to incapacitate. Don't kill the girl."

Dark fur rushed past me as Killian went into battle mode. He jumped on one of the closer men, sinking his teeth into the arm that had been going for his gun.

Killian made decisions like a fighter, so that was one less person to worry about.

An arm wrapped around my neck, cutting off some of my oxygen. The man who had me jerked me upright, pulling me up to my hind legs. I turned my head, trying to bite some part of his arm, but the enemy had me in an iron-clad hold. I dug my front claws into his arm, which made him groan. But no matter how deep I dug into his skin, his hold didn't slacken.

"You're not getting out that easily," the guy cackled. "You aren't the only one who knows how to fight."

I loved having an arrogant opponent. There was nothing quite as motivating as proving their asses wrong and watching them squirm when they realized they were outmatched.

The enemy chuckled as if he'd gotten the upper hand. That was my cue to push backward and let my entire weight fall on his chest. He wasn't prepared for it, so he fell on his back with me right on top. I rolled off him quickly and stood on him.

His soulless eyes widened as he realized I'd outsmarted him. Not giving him a chance to react, I clawed his neck deep, letting the blood pour to the ground. At least, I didn't have to taste it this time.

I glanced in Griffin's direction and almost cried in relief when I realized he was holding his own against three guards. His wolf was very strong and knew what to do. So fighting was a weakness only in his human form. I could work with that.

A guard squatting between two trees five feet away lifted his gun in Griffin's direction. My wolf howled, and we ran with blinding speed toward the guy as his finger tightened on the trigger. I lowered my head and rammed it between his legs, lifting him up like he was riding a bull.

He fell forward as the gun fired, and the bullet missed its mark—short by three feet, and the guy landed on his face.

A rustling forced my attention back to Goatee. He loaded some kind of tranquilizer dart into a gun and pointed it at me. "This has gone on far to long."

Shit. I had to time my movement, or my fight would be over. I inched toward a tree, as he aimed right at me.

Taking a deep breathe, I tried to remain calm and act scared, like I'd given up. I lowered my head, but not enough that I couldn't see what he was doing. His finger pulled the trigger, and I channeled every ounce of speed into racing behind the tree.

The breeze of the dart hit my tail as I narrowly escaped impact.

"Fuck!" Goatee screamed as his face turned red. "The tranq missed the mark, so all of you need to get your asses in gear."

Goatee charged Killian, who was fighting off a man with a knife.

It was clear these were all shifters who were more comfortable using their weapons than their animals, which boded well for us in a way. No matter how bad things got, they would shift only if that was their last option.

My animal knew that Goatee was trying to trick me. She took note that he wasn't moving as fast as he could, and he had his head turned slightly in my direction as if waiting for me to charge. All of that told me he had no intention of attacking Killian.

I couldn't let him know that I was on to his plan. I rushed toward him like he was expecting, but as I reached him, I spun out of the way.

He turned on his heel and swung a knife where my shoulder

would've been. However, all he did was hit air as he turned in a complete circle, expecting an impact. He sneered at me as his breathing increased.

"You stupid bitch," he growled. "You won't get away this time, no matter what kind of game you try to play."

Game? That was what he called this? This *game* was not only about the fact that my life was at risk, but it involved the lives of the two people left that I cared dearly for. I risked losing everything. *This* was about survival.

I hunkered down and bared my teeth at him. Our guards were getting closer, at least, giving us some more backup. I glanced around and noted that all four wolves and eight enemy shifters were now missing, probably gone to stop our guards. I hated that the guards were being ambushed, but for the moment, that helped Killian, Griffin, and me. With Killian and Griffin pack linking with the guards, they should be somewhat prepared for what they were walking into.

Gunshots fired, and a sharp pain pierced my hind leg. I staggered back a few steps, trying to keep my balance, but placing weight on the injured leg caused me to collapse. The sharp pain morphed into fire as if my leg were being burned. I turned to find blood trickling down my silver fur.

I'd been shot.

"We tried to do it the nice way." Goatee squatted beside me and held his knife in front of my face. "But you wouldn't have that. So you're forcing our hand... again."

My heart hammered. Maybe they didn't have to bring me in alive after all.

CHAPTER TWENTY-ONE

MY FOCUS LOCKED on the knife Goatee wielded in my face as my training kicked in. This guy was insane, and there was a glint in his eyes, informing me he loved the hold he had on me. He placed the knife against my throat, letting it cut through my fur and slice my skin.

My skin burned, but that was the wake-up call I needed. He would hurt me little by little, which would lead to me losing my mind.

Fear could paralyze and make someone irrational, which meant if I didn't get a hold of myself, I would be playing right into his hands.

I refused to do that.

To make it easier for him.

I had to make them pay for what they'd done. Being smarter than them shouldn't have been hard. They relied on terror, weapons, and surprise attacks.

In my peripheral vision, I could see both Killian and Griffin holding their own, but we were each fighting multiple enemies. Goatee's men outnumbered us by eleven, and the enemies were attacking Griffin and Killian in groups of five while four were locked on me. But that was both good and bad. Good because they thought we'd have backup imminently, so they wanted to end the fight quickly, and bad because they'd do whatever it took to end it as quickly as possible.

Goatee had to be my first priority. I needed to get out of his clutches to help my guys and the other guards who were on their way.

The other three men on me circled, watching their leader subdue me. Or so they thought.

"Don't worry." Goatee leaned forward like he was telling me a secret. "They won't see us take you. We'll knock them out before we drag you away. And we *will* kill them if we have to—if you don't cooperate."

Like hell that would ever happen. I refused to be a puppet in this sick game. But that was the problem. I had no damn clue what game they were playing, which put us at a disadvantage. Who was the man behind all of this who desperately wanted me as his own?

The knife slackened against my neck as Goatee turned his head to watch what was going on with Griffin and Killian.

This was the distraction I needed. Going with pure instinct, I clamped down on the wrist of Goatee's hand that was holding the knife until my teeth hit the bone. This was my opportunity to even out the fight.

He hissed as his blood dripped down my chin, mixing with that of the lanky guy I'd killed only minutes earlier and my own blood where Goatee had cut me. My mouth tensed as I waited for him to yank in desperation to free his hand, but his face only contorted into rage.

Shit. I'd miscalculated. Maybe he had some brains after all.

His free arm moved toward my body as he aimed for my bullet wound, but since I was in wolf form, I was a little faster.

I released my hold on him and rolled out of the way as his hand only skimmed my fur. I stood on all fours, placing most of my weight on the three uninjured legs.

The three other men began to move toward me, but Goatee yelled, "Stop! This bitch is mine."

He wanted to make a statement, not only with me but with his men too. He could take down a silver wolf all by himself.

"You got lucky." Goatee clutched his injured hand close to his body as he bent down and grabbed the knife. "But don't worry. I can use my left hand just as well."

I had a feeling he wasn't bluffing, which meant I had to injure that hand too.

Game on.

I snarled, wanting him to know that he didn't scare me. We were on even ground, even though I didn't like to admit that my hind leg was as much of a strategic liability as his injured hand.

He swung his knife at me, making it clear that he wasn't scared. This wasn't only a battle of skill but of proving something to each other.

Breaking me was his end goal, whereas mine was proving that he couldn't.

I stumbled back, avoiding the blow, but that had been his real intent. I placed more weight than I could handle on my back leg and almost fell.

Goatee scowled when I managed to stay on all four legs.

My silver wolf healing abilities worked faster than other wolves, which worked in my favor. My leg still hurt like a son of a bitch, but I could already feel it knitting together and was able to put more weight on it. Unfortunately, the bullet was still lodged inside, which meant that I'd have to reopen the wound to get it out, but that was yet another problem for later.

Needing to strike first, I charged his right side. He would be weakest there and not able to counter as well. Before I connected with him, I noticed a tree with a low-hanging branch a few feet away and changed my plan mid-stride. At this point, I didn't care about making him suffer, I only wanted this entire thing over so I could help the others.

I lowered my head and bulldozed him into the branch. The sound of ripping skin and a groan of pain told me that I'd hit the mark. I took a few steps back and saw the end of the branch sticking through his shoulder. My intent had been to skewer his heart, but at least, he was worse off than me now. Even though the wound seemed to have missed the main artery, there was so much blood his subclavian may have been nicked.

"Attack her!" Goatee demanded. "She can't get away. As long as she can survive, do whatever is necessary to make her leave with us. Take them down and kill them if she doesn't yield."

The three enemy guards sprang into action like they'd been waiting for this moment. Additionally, one guard from both Killian and Griffin spun in my direction with hunger in their own eyes. Each one wanted to have a claim on taking down the almost extinct silver wolf line. At least, that helped both Griffin and Killian with their own battles.

One pointed his gun at the side of my body that wasn't injured. They were going to try to weaken both sides.

Shit, I didn't know how to get out of this. I scanned the woods desperately for an idea, but there wasn't a damn thing I could think of. My best bet was to run and make them chase me. It might hurt like hell, but as long as I survived, that was okay.

I took off running toward the water as more gunfire echoed farther away from where Griffin's and Killian's additional guards were coming in.

Someone fired at me, missing by mere inches. The bullet lodged in the dirt, making it splatter.

I had to run faster.

Trees blurred by as I pushed harder. With each step, my leg grew a little stronger, which was a blessing in this hellish situation.

When an opening between two trees came into view, I made a sharp left, planning to double back to where Killian and Griffin were. The five men chasing me were falling behind.

As I rushed toward Griffin and Killian, one of the enemies yelled, "I'm going to shift. Otherwise, she'll outrun us."

Even though that sucked, at least, it would be one less person with a gun or knife.

When I broke through the clearing, an enemy had a gun to Killian's head while two others were laughing despite one of their own being dead at their feet. It was as if their friend's life had meant nothing.

My world wanted to stop, but I pushed through the mental block, racing toward the enemy. I growled low and threatening, making him pause and glance in my direction. His mouth dropped in shock like he hadn't expected to see me, and the other two stumbled back a few feet.

They weren't so cocky when they were the ones being surprised.

That was the distraction Killian needed in order to spin around and pounce on his attacker. The man screamed in agony as Killian ripped him apart while his two friends stood there and watched the gruesome attack with open mouths.

My heart hurt to see so much death and destruction, but this was the cruel necessity of war. I blew past Killian, heading toward Griffin and the others. We had to level the odds as fast as possible. The longer they outnumbered us, the more deaths there would be on our end.

Three feet away, Griffin was fighting two men who had knives instead of guns. He'd managed to take down two during my run, which meant our numbers were getting more favorable by the minute.

Gunshots were still firing not too far away. The fact that the enemy fighters hadn't returned meant that Killian's and Griffin's guards weren't being decimated as I feared.

My eyes flicked to where Goatee had been to find him gone. The branch remained covered in his blood and pieces of muscle and skin. The bastard had been determined to get free, I had to give him that.

But right then, I needed to help Griffin. I struck at the enemy nearest me, biting into his leg. The guy screamed as he turned his attention to me. He swung his knife toward my side, but Griffin attacked, sinking his teeth into the guy's jugular. The man's eyes widened as he dropped the knife and grasped his throat as if that was going to prevent the fatality of his injury.

The other man used our distraction to pick up his friend's discarded knife. I released my hold, allowing Griffin to finish the job, and turned my attention to the uninjured guy, taking advantage of the angle and biting deep into his side. The wound reminded me of the one they'd given my father.

Poetic justice.

Griffin sniffed me over, focusing on my wound. His hazel eyes filled with concern as he nuzzled his head against me. His closeness centered me, bringing me back from the horrible memory. The comforting *tug* of our connection made me feel whole.

"Aw, how cute. You think you might actually win, but my men and I have been holding back." Goatee croaked and waved to his men to come toward him as he stepped into view along with the remaining four men in human form and the lone wolf. "But this is over." Blood trickled down his shirt, soaking it.

Killian growled and stepped in front of me, sides heaving. Griffin flanked my injured side, baring his teeth through the blood coating his muzzle. Those two were showing that they would protect me no matter the cost.

The two men that had been fighting Killian joined Goatee as they regrouped and stared us down. Each one tensed and poised, waiting for their instructions.

"Fuck the orders. Kill them." Goatee glanced down at his fatal wound, and his nostrils flared. Pure hatred reflected as he locked eyes with me. "I want her to watch them die."

At this moment, there were seven of them and only one wolf against our three. At the rate we were going, we could have kept chipping away at their numbers as long as we continued to hold on. But we'd foolishly given them time to regroup, and they circled us with weapons.

I shook my head no. I would do anything to be sure Griffin and Killian lived. At least, they would have a chance at happiness, and I'd figure out a way to escape. It might take days or months, but eventually, these people would let down their guard.

"No?" Goatee walked to me and grabbed my snout. "You going to behave then?"

Griffin growled as he inched toward the prick.

"Don't come another step closer or you'll regret it," Goatee threatened.

Griffin ignored him, but I bumped him away.

"I tried to warn you." Goatee sighed as he wrapped his uninjured hand around my leg, jabbing a finger into the healing bullet hole.

Intense pain coursed through my body, and even in animal form, my stomach revolted from the intensity. A whimper wanted to escape, but I clamped it down, refusing to show weakness.

"I gotta say, I do enjoy that you force me to do these things." Goatee smirked as the engine of a boat purred toward us. "You gave me a plausible excuse for my alpha when he demands to know why I had to do this to you."

Dammit, the getaway vehicle was on its way. If we didn't figure out something fast, then I'd be going with them.

Goatee dug his finger deeper into my wound, determined to make me cry out. He wanted these two guys to hear my pain. He was messing with me, trying to make me believe that they might get out alive if I cooperated.

Gathering all of my strength, I pushed back the pain and focused. That was when I realized that he'd actually opened himself up to an attack. He'd been banking on me being too overcome with pain to try to attack him.

Arrogance was a blessing.

I bit into the shoulder of the arm he had wrapped around me and shredded his skin, biting as deep as possible. This time, he couldn't ignore it, and his hand slipped out of my wound as he yelled and jerked forward, trying to stick the bloody finger into my eye.

"Jimmy," one of his men called out. "What do we do?"

Their uncertainty fueled my adrenaline, and I bulldozed him over onto his back, knocking the breath out of him.

A loud howl hurt my ears as I watched Griffin attack one of the enemies who was holding a gun. The weapon fell, and when the guy reached down to get it, Griffin lunged, slashing his teeth through the back of the guy's neck with a sickening cracking noise. The guy crumbled.

Goatee used my distraction against me as his finger connected with my eye. As the pressure increased, my heart sank, and I realized that I could lose my eye.

Killian attacked another man with a gun while Griffin ran toward me.

I hated that he was running to me instead of attacking the other guard, but right now, I was at a huge disadvantage, and the guard seemed confused as to whether he should help Goatee or fight Griffin.

The boat motor grew louder, and the pungent smell of gas wafted around us. It was that damn close.

"Shoot her other leg before she kills me." Goatee cried as his voice began to slur from blood loss. His finger's pressure reduced on my eye as his strength finally began to fade. "Now!"

The gun clicked as it was cocked, and I braced for the pain. I only hoped that the guy missed his mark and killed me.

Death would be more welcome than living through whatever they planned to do to me.

A loud, heartbreaking howl pummeled my ears as Griffin jumped in front of me.

No, what was he doing? The guy was going to shoot!

As the gun fired, I jerked away from Goatee, desperate to get Griffin out of the way. Considering the angle at which the enemy guard was trying to shoot me and the way Griffin landed in front of me, it would be a kill shot for him.

But my legs fell out from under me, and Griffin's wolfish body took the bullet in his chest. The momentum knocked him backward, and he fell hard next to my legs.

CHAPTER TWENTY-TWO

THIS HAD to be some crazy dream. A horrible nightmare that I could wake from. I couldn't have lost Griffin before we even had a chance to embrace our relationship.

Watching him bleed out forced me to realize my biggest regret.

Being too scared to bond with him.

A loud howl vibrated all around us, and it took a moment to realize that the cry was coming from me. My heartbreak shattered my soul, and hatred flowed through my body.

I'd be damned if I left with these assholes. After everything they'd taken away from me, I'd rather die than give them what they wanted.

The thrumming of the boat engine indicated it was almost upon us. We were running out of time, no one more than Griffin.

"Ssseee," Goatee slurred, barely able to keep his eyes open. "We will always wiiinnnn."

Not if I have anything to do with it.

Anger fueled my body, and I gathered enough resolve to put weight on my front paws and reach his neck to rip out his throat. For the first time ever, I didn't feel remorse. Numbness took over.

Large black wings rushed past me, helping rage ward off the strange haze I was locked in.

That damn bird topped my shit list, seeing as he'd probably been watching me for longer than I'd ever realized. I'd pluck him feather by feather until he couldn't handle it and turned back to his human form.

I turned to attack before the crow could hurt Griffin more but stopped short when my gaze landed on Rosemary instead. All of the enemy guards lay dead on the ground except two. One was engaged in battle with Killian while the other swung his gun in the dark wolf's direction, ready to shoot.

No. I can't lose him too.

I tried to stand on both legs but fell hard on my stomach. Whether I wanted to admit it or not, Goatee had done a number on me. All I could do was lie there in agony as the last man got ready to shoot Killian.

As the gun fired, Rosemary circled her wings, making her feathers blend together and surround her. She stepped between the bullet and Killian.

Did she have a death wish? I watched in horror as the bullet hit her...and bounced off her wings.

"What the—" the guy stuttered as he dropped his gun.

She unfolded her wings, a smirk on her face. "Angels are hard to kill." She jumped, flying directly at him, and the guy had enough sense to turn and run.

The idiot ran in the direction of the boat, like that would protect him.

Before he could escape from view, Rosemary caught up and grabbed him around the neck. A loud *crack* followed, and his body smacked to the ground, clearly dead on impact.

Thank God she was here because Killian would have been dead if she hadn't arrived.

Killian.

I turned to find his dark fur soaked with blood, but the last enemy lay dead at his feet. For the moment, we were safe, so I crawled toward Griffin and laid my head next to his. I whimpered as both my wolf and I mourned the man beside me.

He brushed his head against mine and nuzzled my face.

This was wrong. We couldn't even communicate in this form. I couldn't tell him my regrets or how I wished things had gone differently. All I could do was lie beside him as he died.

"I need you to move," Rosemary said as she squatted on Griffin's other side. She reached her hands toward him, and I growled.

No one but me could touch him right now. I needed to be the one he was with when he transitioned out.

Rosemary arched a brow and tilted her head. "Did you growl at me?"

I bared my teeth, emphasizing my point. My wolf surged forward. I wasn't sure how much clearer I could get.

"Do you want me to save him or not?" She bobbed her head as she tapped her fingers on her jeans. "Once he's dead, I can't bring him back."

I lifted my head and stared at her. She could save him? Was this some sort of joke? I looked at Killian, wanting him to give me a sign.

He nodded, alleviating some of my concern.

Griffin's breathing began to slow, and his eyelids fluttered close. He was fading, and I had to put his life before my own possessive tendencies.

Everything inside me screamed for me to not allow her to touch him, but I reined in my animal. Of course, being injured made it more difficult for me. If she did do something to him, I wouldn't be able to protect him, and that made me more volatile.

"I'm going to try again." Rosemary narrowed her eyes at me. "And if you bite me, this will be the last time I help you."

She might not be the nicest person in the world, but she was blunt, and I knew where she stood. I did respect her for that. Not many people were that forthcoming. I scooted away, letting her know that I wouldn't be a problem.

"Good girl," she chuckled.

Great, she'd already gotten cocky enough for dog jokes, but if that was what it took to save Griffin, I'd gladly take them.

She placed one hand on Griffin's wound and the other on my hip. Her skin began to glow.

White light poured from her fingers, and a warm buzzing sensation smacked me straight in the chest—a fluttering feeling of safety and security like everything would be okay. It reminded me of when I was a little girl and my mom would hold me in her arms.

Rosemary's stardust irises glowed a brilliant white as her power charged all around us. If I'd thought she was breathtaking before, I was wrong. Now she was transcendent.

I watched in awe as Griffin's chest rose once again. After a long moment, Rosemary's skin began to fade into her normal pale complexion. She dropped her hands and faced me. "Your leg should be better also."

That was why I'd felt so safe. She'd healed both Griffin and me at the same time. I'd heard that angels were powerful beings, but that was downplaying their abilities.

Griffin slowly sat up on his hind legs, and the relief that burst through my heart was jarring. I jumped on him, forcing him to his back. I was so damn happy that he was okay. He licked my face as he rolled over on top of me, his tongue hanging out of his mouth.

"As much as I hate to interrupt your play, your guards are still under attack, and a boat pulled up to wait for these idiots to get away." Rosemary stood and brushed the dirt off her jeans.

She was right. We needed to help the others. There wasn't as much gunfire, but no one had made it to us. Our new priority was protecting Killian's and Griffin's packs.

I jerked my head in the direction where the others should be and took off running. There was absolutely no pain in my leg, which surprised me. Rosemary had been able to heal my leg completely, even removing the bullet.

The only question was: Why had she helped us? In general, people didn't go into battle willingly for anyone who wasn't a friend or an ally. Even though we weren't enemies, our interactions hadn't been the best. She must have a reason for helping. Yet another issue to deal with later.

Rosemary flapped her wings, ascending into the sky. "I'll meet you there." She flew in the opposite direction faster than my four legs could take me.

As we followed our trail back toward the guards, the sound of fighting grew louder. I wasn't sure if I should be relieved or not, but at least, some of their guards had to still be standing.

The crow fluttered into the sky again, cawing over and over, letting the enemy guards know that we were approaching.

Forcing myself not to waste any more negative energy on that stupid thing, I scanned the area, taking in the damage. There were bodies littered everywhere.

This whole attack was eerily similar to the one back home. Maybe I should've gone with Goatee and kept all these people safe.

Killian took the lead, racing toward a wolf who was surrounded by three others. He growled loudly, drawing the attention of the enemies from their target.

I followed Killian's lead with Griffin running beside me. The attackers didn't outnumber the lone surviving guard any longer. In fact, they were now the ones who were outmatched.

Running to the side, I targeted the large milky brown wolf who'd been with Goatee earlier. The cruel glint in his eye matched the abyss deep inside him, revealing a sickness even worse than Goatee's. Maybe Goatee wasn't the one I should've been most focused on. Discovering two souls so full of hatred made me even more worried about whomever they were working under.

At least, I could get rid of one more jerkwad.

He faced me in a clear challenge. He knew who I was and

sneered at me with determination, examining me, waiting to predict my next move. He was probably the most skilled fighter of his group.

Not wanting to give away my plan, I slowed as if I had nothing to prove. Technically, I didn't, but I did want to survive.

Killian and Griffin attacked two of the wolves as I sat in front of the larger one, pretending I wasn't fazed in the least. We were in a standoff. He wanted to see what he was up against while I wanted to see what strategy he'd use.

The best way to piss off a man who was trying to prove himself was to belittle him. I forced my shoulders to shake and made the choking bark sound of a wolf laughing.

He snorted and shook his head, giving me a sign that I was getting under his skin. His quickened panting let me know that his anger was beginning to get the best of him.

I glanced at Griffin and Killian, making sure they were doing okay but also to indicate that I wasn't fazed by the increasingly angry wolf watching me. Even though I could see him in my peripheral vision, not paying attention to him was the final straw.

Inching toward me, he kept his eyes locked on my face. I pretended to not notice his approach, despite my entire focus now being on him since Griffin and Killian were holding their own.

With each stride toward me, he grew bolder and angrier when I didn't bat an eyelash. His body grew rigid, and I knew he would attack at any moment. How he charged me would tell me the most about him.

Now only ten feet away, he growled, wanting me to acknowledge he was there. When I turned my head his way, he lunged.

Brute force. That was his plan, which was what I'd suspected.

I rolled out of the way as he landed on all four legs where I'd been. He snarled and pivoted, teeth bared, drool dripping down his chin. He reminded me of a rabid dog.

Hell, he might have been truly rabid.

Not bothering to change strategy, he lunged at me once more, aiming for my shoulder. Like Goatee, he didn't want to kill me, just injure me severely. But he wasn't thinking it through because Killian and Griffin were here as well. Even if he took me down, how was he going to get himself and my injured body to the boat when they were both here?

The one surviving guard on our side barreled toward me. He was coming to help me fight this wolf.

Where I differed from this crazed wolf and Goatee was that I didn't have to prove myself. They enjoyed dominating others to get ahead, but real protectors fought to win, not to come out on top. Protecting was about doing what was best for everyone, pushing vanity and self-worth aside. There was no room for ego. I'd welcome the help as long as it stopped more innocents from dying.

The enemy wolf didn't even bother turning in the guard's direction. He was focused solely on me, which was both stupid and scary. How could someone have such a one-track mind when their death could be imminent?

But that was the thing; he didn't see anything outside of me.

The guard jumped on the milk chocolate wolf's back and stuck his claws into its side as his teeth sank into the spot between his neck and shoulder.

As if realizing the magnitude of his injuries, the enemy wolf stood on both hind legs, trying to fall back onto the guard so he would release his hold.

I refused to allow him the opportunity, I jumped forward and sank my teeth into the front of his neck, ready for this whole damn fight to be over. The guy's eyes widened, and I jerked my head hard, assuring he would die instantaneously.

At this point, I didn't care about them paying for their sins. I wanted the fight done.

With the weight of the guard on his back, the wolf landed on his face but was already dead before impact.

The world seemed to pause as I surveyed the area and realized that all of the enemy fighters were dead. But the heartbreaking fact was that Killian, Griffin, this one guard, and myself were the only survivors on our side. I had no clue how many of their pack had come to aid us and died.

A caw and the flutter of wings caught my attention as the crow flew high, away from the mess on the ground.

We had to catch him before he alerted whoever was behind this ambush.

CHAPTER TWENTY-THREE

OF COURSE, the damn bird was flying back toward the boat, probably to alert the people on board that everyone was dead. There was no way we could beat him to it.

But dammit, we had to try. I howled and took off in the direction of the river once more, Griffin, Killian, and the guard right behind me.

I kept my eyes forward, refusing to glance at the bodies as I passed. So much death and destruction, and it was all because of me. If I'd gone willingly, would this have turned out differently?

I had to push those thoughts aside. Focus on the here and now.

Within seconds, I passed through the trees, and the river came into view. I stepped into puddles of what could only be blood, the metallic scent confirming my suspicions.

But I powered through.

The three wolves behind me panted, trying to keep up, but I couldn't slow. If I wanted to have a chance at catching the people on the boat, we had to get there fast.

A loud caw sounded again, closer than I expected. It was a call of fear and desperation. I glanced skyward only to see the crow fly over our heads back in the direction we'd come from.

What the hell would have caused that?

Large wings whooshed behind me, answering my question. I glanced over my shoulder, surprised to find Rosemary landing a few feet away.

Blood covered her arms, and the shoulder of her shirt was ripped. "The shifters on the boat are dead." She nodded in the direction of the water. "I figured I could take them out while the rest of you focused on saving your men and yourselves."

I couldn't speak to her in this form to tell her I was grateful. All I could do was nod.

Even though I hated that the bird got away, at least the boat hadn't managed to leave.

"Why don't you four go back and shift to human so you can get more help to clean up the bodies?" Rosemary said with authority. "I'll meet you at the house in a few minutes."

Normally, being told what to do would irritate me, but after the way she'd helped us and all of the fighting, shifting back and regrouping sounded nice. We needed to take care of our dead and figure out our next moves, but for the moment, we didn't have to worry about another attack.

I turned around and found Griffin waiting for me and Killian and the guard trotting off together, leaving the two of us to head back alone.

My heart warmed and welcomed the sensation of the *tug*. For a minute there, I thought I'd never have the chance to walk beside him again. I hurried to him, not wanting to stay out here another second.

STEPPING out of the shower was one of the hardest things I'd had to do. Between needing to wash the blood from my body, the deaths I had caused, and just being sore from not training as I should have, all I wanted to do was stay in the warm spray of water.

But that wasn't an option because of a certain dark angel pacing the living room.

"What the hell is taking her so long?" Rosemary complained. "When she said she was taking a shower, I didn't think I'd be stuck out here with you two idiots for this long."

"First off, this is my house," Killian growled. "And second, she's been in there five minutes. Give her a break."

Ugh, maybe I should turn the water back on. She seemed to be in a mood.

Granted, she was always kind of like this, so I shouldn't have been surprised. I quickly dried and got dressed.

"Do you know what I risked by helping you fight those wolves?" Rosemary's tone grew angry. "If that jackass Azbogah learns what I did, he'll give my parents hell. I risked a lot—"

Griffin's anger was palpable as he said, "The water has turned off, so you can slow down. No one asked you to help, so don't come in here, demanding certain things. If my mate—"

"Your *mate*?" Rosemary snorted. "Are you kidding me? This gets better and better."

"What's so funny about that?" Griffin rasped.

"You don't even want to be alpha, and now you're mated to a wolf like *her*." She sighed. "Can you get any luckier?"

Inhaling sharply, I quickly dressed in the jeans and shirt I'd worn the day when Killian found me. I'd been avoiding wearing these clothes, but after destroying the new ones, I didn't have much choice. I opened the door and strolled into the living room.

I straightened my shoulders and stared the angel down. "Thank you for fighting alongside us and helping, but you don't get to come in here and treat us like we're worthless." She and I had a very odd relationship, to say the least. I didn't dislike her, but she was abrasive and rash.

"See, that's why I like you." Rosemary turned her back on Killian and Griffin. "You get straight to the point without trying to prove you have a dick."

A smile broke through my face. "It's kind of hard to prove I have one when the appendage is missing."

"It makes things easier that way." Rosemary laughed.

"Uh... what's happening?" Killian asked Griffin.

"No clue, man." Griffin shook his head as he walked over to me and took my hand. "But her being nice is kind of freaking me out."

"And they wonder why I don't want to bother talking to them." She shook her head. "But I'm assuming they're kind of a package deal?"

"Yeah, they are." I stepped closer to Griffin, needing to feel him. "So how did you know we were in trouble?"

"I didn't." Rosemary strolled to the windows overlooking the pool and backyard. "I was actually on my way to find you about our little talk the other day."

My eyes flicked toward the tree line where several shifters were heading out back to take care of the dead. After we'd gotten back to the houses and shifted, more Shadow Ridge and Shadow City shifters had arrived. Luckily, I'd already gone inside, so none of them saw me in my silver wolf form. However, I needed to hurry and get out there to help them. After all, this carnage was all my fault. "Well, you found more than you bargained for."

"You do realize you need to tell Zac that he can't tell anyone about what she is." Rosemary scowled at Griffin. "The more people who realize she's a silver wolf, the more at risk she'll be."

"We've already handled that." Griffin stood tall beside me. "I commanded him with the alpha will. He can't tell anyone, not even his family."

Killian leaned against the wall on the other side of the window. "Not that he would've anyway."

"Don't be so certain." Rosemary rolled her shoulders. She looked at me. "But that's not why I'm here. Fortunately, if you can keep these two and the guard quiet, it appears no one else knows that a silver wolf has rejoined our society. At least, not on the angel side of things."

"That's good news, right?" The fewer people who knew about me, the safer we all would be.

"For now." Rosemary gestured to Griffin as she continued, "But if you two are fated mates, how long do you think your little secret can last?"

My heart sank. I hadn't even thought about that.

"I'll leave with her." Griffin made it sound so simple.

I jerked my head toward him. "You can't do that." Especially if what Rosemary had said about a civil war brewing was true. "You are their leader. Fate has determined that. You can't leave when there's so much at stake and wolves are being attacked."

"You're more important." He brushed his fingers along my cheek. "I'd rather do that than lose you."

"Dove is right," Rosemary said, making me cringe.

I was so damn tired of that name. "It's Sterlyn." She at least deserved to know that after everything that went down.

"Thank God. Because Dove is a horrendous name." Rosemary groaned.

"It is not." Killian frowned. "I thought it was fitting because of her hair."

"Of *course* he gave you that name." Rosemary took her phone out of her pocket and then glared at Griffin. "With the wolf attacks, if you were to step down, it would cause anarchy, and you know it. The best thing we can do is figure out who's after Sterlyn and go from there."

"That crow is heading back to whoever wants her." Killian's hands clenched into fists. "And we're at a disadvantage, but I'm hoping we'll find something on the boat that can point us in the right direction."

"I've got to go, but are you working tomorrow?" Rosemary faced me.

There was no reason not to right now. If I didn't go in, things would look even more suspicious. "Yes, I am. We need to pretend everything is as normal as possible after the shit show today."

"I agree." She nodded. "I'll run by and talk to you then. I've got to get back to Shadow City—Mom is looking for me." She hurried out the door and took to the sky.

Griffin pursed his lips. "Was it me, or was it like we weren't even in the room?"

"Get used to it." Killian pointed at me. "Ever since she came into my life, I'm the chauffeur."

That was kind of true. "As fun as this is, I'm going to head outside and help the others."

"Nope, you're not." Griffin pulled me into his arms. "They have enough people, and they know what they're doing. After almost dying, I'd like to take you on that date."

"I don't feel like going out." I'd been so excited earlier about spending time with him, but between what we'd gone through and my subpar outfit, all I wanted to do was crawl into bed.

"Then you two go over to Griffin's and chill while I go help the others." Killian gestured to the door. "Between you getting injured and Griffin almost dying, I say you've done enough today. Besides, I'm thinking it's time that both Griffin and I start stepping up to our responsibilities."

In other words, it was time to be the alphas they were destined to be.

"He's right." Griffin started to pull me toward the back door.

Unable to say no, I nodded but stopped in front of the man I viewed as my brother now. "Are you sure you don't need me there? I don't mind helping."

"I know." He booped my nose. "But I want you to get to know him —the side of him that I know. I'm giving you my seal of approval."

"With the womanizer?" I asked and pointed at Griffin.

"Hey," Griffin growled.

"He took a bullet for you," Killian said as he opened the back door, waving us out. "I figure if that doesn't prove he meant what he said, nothing will."

The truth of his words made my heart pound, and I turned to

face the sexy man who now held my heart. My wolf howled, and my body warmed, leading to the scent of arousal wafting off me. I locked eyes with my mate. "No more waiting." I'd had enough. I got that he wanted to do things right, but I needed him. And now.

"Oh, dear God." Killian shut the door and headed to the trees. "That's my cue to go."

A smirk fixed on Griffin's face as he led me toward his home. Within seconds, we were entering his kitchen. I had no idea what the room looked like, and I didn't care. He slammed the door shut, and I slammed my lips on his.

He growled as he grabbed my ass and I wrapped my legs around his waist. The feel of his hands and mouth on me made both my body and wolf go wild.

I wrapped my arms around his neck, fisting his hair. He stumbled down the hall. In my half-lucid state, I realized his house was exactly the same floor plan as Killian's.

We entered the master bedroom, and he kicked the door shut behind us then tossed me on the bed. The cool blue of the walls was the shade of the ocean. I ran my hands over light muted gray sheets that reminded me of the sky on an overcast day.

But when Griffin stood over me, my eyes saw only him. He stared back at me, his hazel eyes glowing, and removed his shirt. His abs looked even more muscular than I'd imagined as they bunched and coiled. He leaned over me, trapping me between his arms.

"You're so beautiful," he said, sounding raw.

My breath caught as he kissed me, and his fingers pressed into my sides, turning me on even more. "You're not too bad yourself."

"Not too bad, huh?" He chuckled as his lips pressed against my throat and his hand lifted my shirt. "You've seen more handsome?"

"Define handsome," I teased as he unfastened my bra and removed both it and my shirt from my body.

Then I tensed, realizing we had one more thing to discuss.

"Stop." He froze, and I smiled to reassure him. I hated to interrupt our moment, but before we did this, we had to make sure we were on the same page. Normally, when fated mates completed their connection, they linked to the strongest wolf's pack. If the pair were two alphas, the packs remained separate unless the two alphas agreed to merge with only the fated mate bond linking the mates. But since I didn't have a pack, that meant I'd be linked with his...unless I purposely put up a barrier. "I want to complete our bond, but I can't submit to you and become one of your pack." I hoped that didn't anger him, but it was better to have this conversation beforehand. My wolf wouldn't submit to him, and even if she could, the rest of his pack would realize that I was different. My secret wasn't ready to be revealed.

At least, not yet.

"I want you any way I can have you. My goal isn't to be your alpha." He kissed my lips sweetly. "I'm all-in. Nothing will change that."

My stomach fluttered at his words, and somehow, my desire for him grew even stronger.

When his mouth captured my nipple, pleasure like I'd never experienced before waved through my body. I gasped as my fingers dug into his strong, muscular back.

My head swam from his unique scent and the hand he trailed slowly down my body. I'd never been touched this way, and I never wanted him to stop.

Slipping my hand between our bodies, I unbuttoned his jeans, needing to feel all of him.

"I'm trying to take care of you." He sighed, his breath hot against my skin.

But the problem was I *needed* him. "Slow can come later." The *tug* inside me was desperate—he had to make me whole and now. "Please."

"Fine." He stood up and removed my yoga pants and panties. "But we *are* going slow next time." He groaned as he scanned my body and removed the rest of his clothes.

He was even more delectable than I'd ever imagined. His body was hard in all the right places, and I did mean all.

He slipped his hands between my legs and rubbed.

My breathing caught as waves of pleasure gripped me. My body convulsed as he slipped his fingers inside.

With each movement, he had flames licking my body. "Oh, God," I cried out, about to lose my mind.

His tongue circled one breast and flicked over my nipple, causing sensations to shoot through me and bring me dangerously to the edge. I pushed him back and flipped us around, needing to take control. He was dominating me, and I loved it, but it was my turn. I straddled him and started to slip him slowly inside me.

"Whoa... wait." His irises glowed even more as he stilled. "You're —are you...?"

I writhed and started to press down, but his hands on my waist stopped me. "Am I *what*?" But then I realized what he meant, and my cheeks flushed hot.

"You're a virgin. We need—"

"No, I need *you*." My wolf howled. We'd waited long enough. I slipped him inside, filling me, causing the connection between us to grow.

"Wait," he rasped as he scooted us both to the headboard and propped himself up. His hands caressed my breasts as I began to ride him. Each time, he filled me more, going deeper and deeper.

Moving faster, he soon bucked underneath me, and my wolf surged forward, needing to cement the bond between us. My mouth went to his neck, and my teeth raked his skin, but I didn't want to completely break it until he gave me permission to claim him.

"Do it," he groaned. "Please."

That was all I needed to hear. My teeth broke his skin, and his blood seeped onto my tongue while a part of my soul reached out and slammed into him.

"My turn," he growled, and I tilted my head willingly, offering my neck.

"Yes," I sighed, giving him my consent.

When his teeth entered me, his feelings and emotions collided with mine.

If I'd had any doubts about how he felt about me before, they were gone. All he saw was me, and he'd lay down his life to protect me again without a moment's hesitation.

My heart grew warm once more now that I wasn't alone, and my wolf put up a barrier to prevent the further pack connection.

Pleasure built within our bodies, and soon, orgasms ripped through both of us, our pleasure molding us into one.

Something snapped inside our chests, and our connection strengthened as our emotions poured into one another. Love merged us into one being, warming my chest and filling the space that had been cold for all too long.

I don't deserve you, Griffin linked.

His voice in my head caused happiness to surge through me. *No, you don't,* I teased. *And yet, you still have me.* I kissed his lips, so happy to be in his arms.

Completely exhausted and satiated, I rolled onto my side, and he pulled me into his strong, comforting arms. His fingers brushed my arm, up and down, and soon, I was out cold.

IF I'D THOUGHT WALKING into Shadow Ridge University with Killian had been strange, this was a whole different matter.

Everyone we passed turned and stared as Griffin, the alpha of Shadow City, held my hand and walked me into the coffee shop.

Of course, it didn't help that as of yesterday, I'd been *dating* his best friend.

As we walked past the long coffee line, Carter's mouth dropped open, and he pointed from Griffin to me. "What the hell, Dove? I can't figure out if I'm impressed or disgusted. Weren't you with Killian yesterday?"

A growl emanated from Griffin's chest.

Behave. I understood comments like these weren't fun for Griffin, but we'd both known this would happen. "Killian and I were more friends than anything."

"With friends like that--"

Griffin snarled. *I never have liked him anyway. I may kill him.*

I laughed, not able to conceal my happiness.

"Stop," I warned Carter. "He's my fated mate. He's not enjoying your commentary."

"*What?*" he said loudly, causing the entire coffee shop to go silent. "Griffin completed the mate bond with you?"

"Yes." Griffin stepped in front of me and glanced at each person in line. "She is my mate, officially, in all ways. No hitting on her, and no hitting on me."

Well, that was pretty much equivalent to him peeing on me, but at least he'd included himself in that equation.

A few girls pouted, riling my wolf, but I pushed her down. There was no reason to let her get too worked up. If anyone tried something stupid, we'd kill them. Easy-peasy.

I hate to do this, but I've got to go to Political History and then International Relations. He kissed me a little longer than necessary. *I'll be back when classes are over.*

I'll be counting the seconds. I pulled away and gave him a smile.

He licked his lips and winked before walking out of the cafe while I enjoyed the view.

"Uh... Earth to Dove." Carter pulled me back into the present. "That cash register won't work itself."

I turned around and got to work.

A COUPLE of hours later when the line finally calmed down, Carter tapped my shoulder. "Hey, do you mind going into the back and getting more Italian roast beans? We're running low."

"Oh, yeah, sure." Usually, another co-worker got the beans because I was always so busy at the register, but Susan was on break. I remembered seeing the Italian roast when Carter showed me around the first day I started working here.

I walked past the kitchen to the small hallway closet next to the exterior door that led to the alley where they kept that smelly dumpster. I opened the storage door and started glancing through the inventory.

"That's weird," I whispered to myself. "It was on this shelf the last time I saw it." The third shelf held some of the dark roasts but not the Italian.

I had just squatted to check the bottom shelf when I heard footsteps coming my way. Carter must have needed something else or wondered what was taking me so long.

"Hey, Carter. Did you move the Italian roast? It's not on the top shelf," I asked, searching the labels near the floor.

I felt the hairs raise on the back of my neck as he stepped behind me, and then something sharp stuck into my neck, right above my collarbone. A familiar voice I couldn't quite place whispered, "I'm so sorry."

I tried to turn around, but the world began to spin.

My vision turned hazy, and all I managed to do was link to Griffin. *Help.*

SHADOW CITY: SILVER WOLF

Rising
DARKNESS

BOOK TWO

USA TODAY BESTSELLING AUTHOR

JEN L. GREY

CHAPTER ONE

MY BODY BOUNCED, causing my restrained wrists to move and burn.

What the...

I attempted to open my eyes, but my head lolled to the side as my body jarred again. Heat surrounded me with the faint stench of exhaust, making my head swim even more. If I didn't know any better, I would think I was drunk or had lost a lot of blood, but that couldn't have happened. I'd been in the coffee shop just a few minutes ago...

Griffin, my fated mate, linked, *Sterlyn. Please tell me you're awake.*

Wow, he'd called me by my real name. *I like you saying my name.* He'd always called me Dove before we'd become mates.

Oh, thank God. Griffin sounded relieved. *Where are you?*

The question nudged me to focus a little more. I pried my eyes open and took in the dimness around me. At first, I saw double, but slowly, my brain filtered the picture into one. Gray upholstery was smashed against my face and silver metal outlined the ceiling, which was about a foot above me.

Holy shit. This was the kind of nightmare I'd had as a child. *I'm in the trunk of a car.*

What? he growled. *I'm going to kill whoever did this to you.*

Not if I got to them first. I took a deep breath, trying to get my head on straight. The first task I needed to address was getting my wrists unbound. Luckily, Griffin had gotten some guards to run to the store and purchase me some shirts and a few pairs of jeans, so I had my security measure strapped to my ankle.

I turned on my side, bending my legs as far back as they could go. While I was growing up, part of my alpha training regimen had included daily stretching, so I was more flexible than most wolves. Something my father had drilled into me from birth.

In the eyes of male alphas, I already had one disadvantage just by being a woman, so I had to be stronger, better, and faster than all of them.

Sexism was real—especially in the supernatural world. Unfortunately, I had no pack to lead because they'd all been slaughtered, not even a month ago.

But that didn't mean I'd give up. My mother had taught me better than that.

My fingers fumbled on the handle of my knife, and at this odd angle, the rope dug into my wrists even more.

At least, the pain helped clear my head. I inhaled, enduring the sting of the rope, and managed to pull the knife from the sheath. My best friend growing up, Zoe, had always teased me about carrying the knife everywhere—but the habit had served me well, especially during the past few weeks.

Are you hurt? Griffin asked, as misery laced his words.

Getting the knife's sharp edge onto the rope proved difficult, between the jarring from the road and the awkward placement of my hands. *No, not really. They drugged me with something that's still affecting me. How long have I been gone?*

About an hour. You linked me with "Help," and when I got to the coffee shop, Carter was frantic and told me that someone took you.

Whoever it was drug you out the back door, and then your scent disappeared.

At his words, something tickled the back of my mind, but I was at a loss as to what. Either way, the car had to have been waiting for me. After we'd been attacked yesterday by the men who'd murdered my pack, and we'd killed everyone, I hadn't expected them to strike again so soon. But someone had come back to capture me.

My skin rubbed against the rope, and blood dripped down my hands, making it difficult to keep a good grip on the knife. If I didn't get out of here, I'd be rolling up to God knew where, and my chance of escaping would be greatly reduced. *Carter asked me to grab some coffee beans, and that's the last thing I remember.* I felt like there was more to recall...but I couldn't access the memory.

Someone had gotten the drop on me—which shouldn't have been possible—and the encounter was a blur. That had to be due to whatever had knocked my ass out.

Gritting my teeth, I continued to saw at the rope and, after what felt like an eternity, it began to loosen. *My hands are almost free.*

Do you have any clue where you're going? Griffin sighed. *Rosemary is looking for you, but we don't know where to search. Killian went north, and I'm heading south.*

I'll get you some sort of location in a second. I was getting my ass out of here. I wasn't going to wait for one of them to find me—they might not be able to. From the rhythm of the car, whoever was driving was going the speed limit and not driving wildly, which meant there probably weren't any visible signs that he'd kidnapped someone.

When I cut through the last bit of rope, I came damn near close to crying. I placed the knife beside me and flexed my wrists, trying to get some circulation back. They were raw but would heal quickly on their own.

After wiping the blood onto my pants, I searched for the emergency release. My gaze landed on a white handle that had arrows pointing to pull right to open.

Griffin linked, *What do you mean, you're going to get a location?*

I'm jumping out. The closer I got to wherever they were taking me, the less chance I'd have to get free.

Are you insane? Griffin growled. *You're going to get hurt.*

If I don't, I'll wind up wherever they want me, which could be worse. He wasn't trying to be an asshole; we were newly mated. On top of that, he wasn't trained in battle strategy. But dammit, that was something he'd need to rectify, and soon, now that he was with me. Unfortunately, people had found out my kind—the silver wolves— still existed, and they had come after me. We had to find out who "they" were and neutralize them, because the thought of living my entire life on the run didn't sit well with me.

Not wasting another second, I placed my knife back in its sheath and grabbed the release. I gathered my wits because, as soon as this trunk opened, the driver and whoever else might be in the car would know. At least the driver would be in human form and not animal; I only prayed they didn't have any guns.

The only way to know what I was up against was to go through with the plan, so I yanked the release, and the trunk cracked open. Wind blew inside, whipping my long silver hair into my face. I pulled it to one side and looked out of the trunk.

There wasn't a car right behind me, so at least there was that. If I had to jump out, I wouldn't be playing Frogger, trying not to get hurt. The area was thick with trees, and we were driving on a two-lane road. My captors were either avoiding the interstate or taking me to some backwoods area. Or both. *There's a county road sign.* I read off the numbers to him.

You're going south, but more important—how the hell do you know that? Griffin growled. *Please, don't do anything stupid.*

I decided to stop overthinking and go for it. I pushed the trunk all the way open, and the car swerved. *I'm jumping out now.*

No—don't, he said, sounding frantic. *Just wait for one of us to catch up with you.* A whirlwind of emotions slammed into me. He was scared and felt helpless.

It's too late. The tires squealed as the driver slowed down. *They already know I'm escaping.*

I wanted to shut down the bond between us, but I couldn't do that to him. If I'd been in his shoes, I wouldn't have been much better off, and it wouldn't be right to worry him more than he already was. But I had to ignore his emotions and focus on escape.

The car was almost at a complete stop, so I jumped out and rolled to prevent injury. I jumped up and ran to the tree line, hoping to hide and see what I was up against.

Pushing my legs as hard as they would go, I raced toward a tree with a large enough trunk and vibrant new spring leaves to keep me hidden for a moment. I welcomed the adrenaline pumping through me, partially clearing my head of whatever they'd injected me with. I flung myself behind the tree trunk then peeked my head around toward the road.

Lurching, the car came to a stop, leaving gray smoke rising from beneath the tires. The driver's side door opened, and a tall, muscular man jumped out. He was almost as large as my dad with dark, cinnamon-colored hair.

He had to be a bear shifter, which didn't sit well with me. All of the attackers in the group we'd recently faced down had been wolves, except for one crow, and now this guy. Unless the bear who'd attacked me in a bar in town not long ago was connected with them too.

So many races being involved in this scheme complicated matters. That meant that multiple races that usually were divided were working together, which happened only when the enemy of their enemy was their friend. Did that mean they were working together to eliminate or control the last remaining silver wolf? I didn't like the implications.

"You aren't going to get away," the guy bellowed, his bear growl bleeding through his words. "So why don't you come out now and make it easier on the both of us?"

I rolled my eyes. Did he think that would actually work?

He sniffed, catching my scent. His eyes focused right where I was hiding.

That hadn't taken long, but I hadn't expected it to. At least I knew that he was alone, which struck me as odd.

"How did you wake up so fast?" He sneered as he strolled toward me, placing his hands in his pockets as if he didn't have a care in the world.

But he wasn't fooling me. I could feel the tension rolling off his body. He wanted to appear confident to try to make me nervous. Maybe I should play the game right back at him. "Not sure." I stepped out from behind the tree and forced a smile. "Maybe you didn't use enough."

My casual demeanor must have hit the mark because he paused. Instead of him throwing me off guard, I'd managed to do it to him.

"Well, it doesn't matter now." He gestured to the car. "Let's get going, and you won't have to be hurt again."

"Can I sit in front?" I smiled, but my body was coiled, ready to fight.

We both knew how this would end. Right now, we were playing some stupid game of who was the most dominant.

"No, but I'll let you choose the music."

"Going to have to say no." I took a few steps toward him, wanting to get this done. I was so damn tired of fighting.

"Then I'm going to have to insist." He marched forward but stopped about ten feet from me. "Now."

"Good luck with that." I spread my legs and got into a fighter's stance.

"You think you can take me?" He chuckled, but there was an edge to it. "I'm not some weak wolf shifter like the ones you fought yesterday."

So, he knew what had happened, and he was nervous. The vileness of his soul rolled off him and into me. "Good. They were easy." Needing to intimidate him as much as possible, I charged first and punched his jaw.

His neck snapped back, and his eyes widened with rage. "Fine. Let's do this." He lunged toward me, using his weight as his weapon.

Good, that was what I wanted him to do. That was what all men did—tried to use their strength against me. But I was faster and more agile than they were.

I spun out of the way, and the bear ran into the tree I'd been standing in front of. I twisted around and kicked his back, making his head slam hard into the trunk.

A loud growl shook his body as he pushed off and pivoted toward me. A large cut had opened on his forehead, and the blood dripped down his face and into his eye.

Not bothering with threats, he leaped at me and wrapped his hands around my waist, tipping me over. I landed on my back with his full weight on top of me.

"You won't win against me," he spat as he grabbed my arms, pulling them up on both sides of my head.

Yes. Irrational rage. That was what I wanted.

I forced myself to ignore the pain in my shoulders and kneed him in the balls. His face blanched as agony radiated through his body, and his hold on my wrists slackened.

Tapping into my wolf strength, I rolled him off me and kicked him in the stomach. He groaned as he curled into the fetal position, one hand wrapping around his belly and the other going to his family jewels.

As if he wasn't sure which one needed protecting more.

My biggest problem was that I had a decision to make, and one that I couldn't take lightly. I pulled the knife from my ankle and lifted it as I approached him.

Should I kill him or let him live? He wasn't a great person, but could I kill someone in cold blood?

"Do it!" he yelled. "Kill me."

And that answered my question. He was desperate for death. "No, you're coming with me." But I had no clue how to take him. I didn't have handcuffs or rope. How the hell would I restrain him?

My mind ran over possible scenarios as the guy reached for his belt buckle. My body coiled, ready for another round of fighting. *I'm on the side of the road. I took down a bear shifter who's getting ready to attack again.*

I'll be there shortly, Griffin said. *Just stay alive.*

Easier said than done. I held my knife, ready for battle, but the guy didn't remove his belt—rather, he pulled something out. It looked like a pill.

No! Surely that couldn't be what I thought it was.

I rushed toward him as he put the pill in his mouth.

"What are you doing?" I screamed, as I reached him.

I squeezed his cheeks, trying to make him open his mouth, but he clamped it closed. His eyes widened as his body jerked.

"Spit it out." I smacked his face like that was going to make him listen to me. "*Now.*"

His mouth finally opened, but spit bubbled out as he choked. His eyes bulged, and his body convulsed.

Tears dripped down my face as I watched the life fade from his eyes. I didn't know the guy, and he obviously wasn't a nice person, but that didn't mean he had to die. Not like this.

Who the hell was after me? They had to be bad if this guy was willing to kill himself instead of facing their wrath.

CHAPTER TWO

WINGS FLAPPED OVERHEAD, and I tore my gaze from the dead man. I wiped away my tears and stood, knife in hand.

My mind still felt fuzzy from whatever drug remained in my system, so being able to fight as well as I had was a godsend. My breathing became labored as I scanned the area, waiting for whoever was coming to appear.

At least, the adrenaline was helping ward off the fogginess threatening to overtake me again.

With my luck, it'd be that damn crow that got away yesterday from the battle scene. He must have reported straight to their leader in order for them to have sent more people to capture me so quickly.

As the flapping grew louder, my body tensed. Whoever was coming wasn't trying to be quiet. Instead, they were announcing their arrival.

When a familiar rose scent wafted toward me, my heart started beating once more.

Rosemary.

As if she'd heard her name, the dark angel flew between the two large trees and landed several feet away. Her long, straight mahogany hair was pulled into a low ponytail, emphasizing her piercing purple stardust eyes. She wore a black shirt that matched the color of her feathers and contrasted with her fair skin.

Her forehead wrinkled as she took in the scene.

I blinked a few times, trying to wrap my head around the fact that she was here. "How did you find me so quickly?"

"I've been flying around ever since I was alerted that someone had kidnapped you." Rosemary pulled in her wings, which then disappeared into her back. "I was about to turn around to head north when I heard squealing tires. I thought I'd better check it out."

"Well, I'm glad you did." I ran my fingers through my tangled hair. "Luckily, he was alone, or I might not have gotten the upper hand."

She strolled to the bear and squatted next to him. "He killed himself?" she asked in surprise.

"Yeah, he did." I was still reeling over that fact, too. "I took him down, and he went for his belt. I thought he was getting ready to fight again, but he took a pill."

"I swear, things have gotten even more interesting since you showed up." Rosemary stood. "We need to get out of here before someone finds us."

"Yeah, but how?" If a human pulled up right now, we would have a huge problem—but it wasn't like I had a shovel handy. "There's no way we can hide the car and him." It was daylight, so anyone driving by would be able to see us from the road. "But we need to check the car out before we leave. He might have left something important in it."

"Fine. See if you can find anything incriminating. I'll deal with the bear." She bent down and picked up the huge man all by herself.

"What are you going to do with him?" I got that we needed to divide and conquer, but that bear was huge—and dead weight, now.

Her wings appeared behind her once again. "I'll figure something out." She took off, flying low and using the trees as cover.

I watched her disappear—gaping and shocked at her show of strength—before reality snapped back around me.

There was no time to stand here idly.

The driver's door remained open, and the engine was still running. The bear had been so focused on reaching me that I was almost surprised to find he'd put the car in park.

Rosemary found me. I linked with Griffin as I surveyed the tan interior of the sedan. The car looked to be several years old, but in good condition. I ripped off a piece of my shirt, using it to avoid leaving fingerprints, and leaned over to pop the glove box.

Where is she? Griffin asked. *Are you hurt?*

No, but the bear shifter who kidnapped me killed himself. I filled Griffin in on everything as I searched the car. There was no registration, which didn't surprise me. They could've stolen the car, for all I knew.

A shrill ringtone came from the backseat, and I glanced over my shoulder and saw a phone. I reached over the seat and grabbed it, but before I could answer, the ringing stopped.

This had to be a burner phone, which would come in handy. Maybe when things settled down, we could call the person who was trying to capture me. At least I hadn't come up empty-handed.

Rosemary stepped from the trees again. She hurried to me, alarm etched on her face. "A few cars will be passing by soon—we need to go. Otherwise, you'll have a ton of questions to answer." She stretched her arms over her head. "Unfortunately, I can't carry you after dealing with that bear. We're going to have to take it by foot."

"No worries." I appreciated that she'd handled him by herself. She'd managed to do it faster than if I'd tried to help. And she was right, we had to move. But unfortunately, I couldn't shift into my animal, which would make everything take longer. There were already enough people who knew that I was a silver wolf; I didn't need to add more to the equation. And I didn't want to take the possibly stolen car, so, walking it was.

"Well, come on." She grabbed my arm and pulled me toward the tree line.

We walked in silence until we were deep enough into the woods that no one could see us from the road. I kept an eye out anyway, thankful that the trees and bushes were in full bloom. I was moving slower than I liked, still impacted by the drug they'd given me. At some point, this stuff would have to wear off. It didn't help my paranoia that there was a tickle in the back of my mind, hinting that I was forgetting something important.

After a few minutes of silence, Rosemary said, "Tell Griffin that we'll be at Shadow Lake shortly. We're about five miles away. He can pick you up there."

Being told what to do rubbed me the wrong way, but I pushed my annoyance down; she'd come and helped me when no one else had been able to find me. I followed her instructions—alerting Griffin to the plan—then paused, trying to determine the best course of action.

"Why are you here?" I finally asked, rather bluntly. The few times I'd been direct with her, she seemed to appreciate the straightforwardness, so I'd go with that.

"Let's see." Rosemary pursed her lips. "A girl went missing on Shadow Ridge University's campus in broad daylight."

"A wolf." If she thought just telling me facts that I already knew would halt my line of questioning, she would soon learn otherwise. "Not an angel."

"What?" She gasped and placed a hand on her chest. "You've got to be kidding me."

"Seriously." I wasn't in the mood for witty banter. "This is the third time you've helped me, and I have no clue why." When someone had spray-painted a silver wolf on the brick wall outside my place of employment in an attempt—a successful one, I was still annoyed to admit—to draw me out, she'd gone back to Shadow City to figure out who knew about me. She'd helped us fight the attackers yesterday and had healed Griffin from a near-fatal gunshot wound, and today she'd helped me with the bear shifter and was now escorting me to my mate.

"Maybe I want to stay on your mate's good side." Rosemary kept her gaze forward, not meeting my eyes.

"Bullshit." I was done playing games. "You insult him at every opportunity, and you don't seem impressed with wolves, in general. What do you get out of helping me?"

She chuckled, her irises lightening in the sunlight. "You're right. I think Griffin is a tool. He's caused a lot of problems for Shadow City because of his reluctance to take his father's place."

"Among the wolves?" Apparently, there were random attacks on wolves pretty consistently. I had been the target of one such attack at Dick Harding's bar.

"No, not just the wolves." Rosemary inhaled sharply. "There's an order to the city. Each race has a handful of representatives, but the city itself has an overall leader. Griffin is supposed to be that leader but has refused to step up, and it's caused discord among all the supernaturals. It's just been messy."

"Which brings me back to my question." I arched an eyebrow.

"There are a few reasons." She wrinkled her nose. "And at this point, I don't want to explain them to you."

"Then why should I trust you?" That was the real question I needed answered. I didn't sense bad vibes from her, but I didn't necessarily get warm fuzzy ones, either. She was strong, which I respected, but I needed to understand where her loyalties lie.

"I know one of your secrets, so I guess it's fair that you know one of mine." She stopped and faced me. "But this stays between us, do you understand?"

"Of course."

"I grew up believing that the silver wolves were dead." She nibbled on her bottom lip. "But Mom would tell me stories of the past and about this special race of wolves."

"You grew up hearing stories about us?" That was a little surreal.

"Yes, and each story centered on the fact that silver wolves were special. And that if they were still alive, we would be doing anything we could to protect them like we should have done before." She shrugged. "So I figure, if Mom believes that angels should have helped the silver wolves, then there has to be something to it."

"So, you told her about me?"

"No, I did not." She shook her head and picked up the pace. "There's enough going on with the angel members of the council—I didn't want to add your secret to it. Mom already has her plate full. Right now, only the handful of us know, and it should stay that way."

I was okay with that. The fewer people who knew about me, the easier it would be to determine who might be working against me. "Well, thank you."

"You're welcome." She gestured to the right. "The lake is there."

Lapping water affirmed what she said, and I scanned the murky lake water, looking for any signs of people out here besides us.

The rest of the trek was made in silence, and soon, a familiar Navigator came into view.

My heart rate increased as my legs took on a life of their own. The connection between us *tugged*, and Griffin climbed out of the car, staring straight at me.

My breath caught as his hazel eyes met mine, glowing with his surging wolf. His sculpted face held a strained expression, and his honey-brown hair looked completely disheveled. He rushed toward me and caught me, lifting me up against his six-and-a-half-foot frame. He pulled me into his arms as his scent of myrrh and leather comforted me. His scruff brushed my face as he kissed me. *Thank God, you're okay. I was so damn worried.*

I eagerly responded to his kiss, trying to calm him down. *I'm fine. We're back together now.*

Rosemary cleared her throat. "You two aren't alone."

"Clearly," Griffin grumbled as he pulled away. He ran his fingers down my cheek and checked me over for injuries. "Thank you for finding her."

"No problem. Now, we need to figure out our next steps." Rosemary's jaw twitched.

"What do you mean?" Griffin wrapped an arm around my waist. "I'm taking her home where she belongs."

Rosemary huffed. "She was just attacked there yesterday. She's not safe there, or at work."

"I'll get more guards." Griffin puffed out his chest.

Rosemary lifted a hand. "Oh, because that went *so* well yesterday."

Great, they were already arguing, and it hadn't even been a minute. "She's right." I faced him and touched his shoulder. "Going back to your or Killian's house isn't the best idea. They know where I'm staying, and they have a lot of manpower."

"Then we'll go to the alpha house in Shadow City." Griffin intertwined our fingers. "That's the safest place you could be."

"Not while we don't know who's behind all the attempts to capture me. It could be someone inside the city." We had no clue who we were up against. "Before we alert anyone else that a silver wolf is alive, we need to figure out who's hunting me." A chill ran down my spine.

I truly was being hunted.

"She's right." Rosemary nodded. "I know for a fact that Azbogah and his angel backers wouldn't be thrilled about her existence. We need to focus on one problem at a time instead of having everything come to a head."

Her words resonated with me. "We need to go where this whole thing started." My heart sank, but there was no getting around the truth.

"What do you mean?" Rosemary arched an eyebrow.

"My pack was...*slaughtered*." My voice broke, but I managed to keep it at least somewhat together. "That's how I ended up in Shadow Ridge, to begin with. My pack home is where we need to start."

"Are you sure about that?" Griffin cupped my face, ignoring the dark angel beside us. "I'll station fifty guards in front of our door at all times if that's what it'll take to keep you safe."

"But that's the thing." His concern warmed my heart. So much had changed between us in a short amount of time. "I wouldn't be truly safe. I'd be more of a prisoner." I refused to live like that, which meant I had to face my biggest fear. "For our future, I need to go back to the pack neighborhood right outside of Chattanooga and see if anything was left behind. The answers may be in the past."

My stomach revolted the entire way to my family home. Rosemary was going to meet us there later after checking in with her family, and Killian would be there a few minutes after us.

The memories of that day were crisp and clear. The sound of the guns firing, all of the dead bleeding out on the ground, and my own father being attacked while I slipped away to safety; nightmares that still haunted me whether I was asleep or awake. For the past month, with all the death and heartache that had come my way, a reaper might have been following me around. I'd heard that there were a few that got involved when life became unbalanced, but there hadn't been any signs, so that wasn't plausible.

"Are you sure about this?" Griffin's hand tightened on mine. "We don't have to go back there, or I could at least have some people go first and check everything out."

"No. I bet they gave up on me coming back, but we'll be careful, just in case." Hell, I'd never expected to willingly go back. "And the more people we alert to the plan, the more likely the wrong person will find out. If we want to see if something was left behind, going now is our best bet."

Griffin took the all-too-familiar turn that bent around a section of woods leading into the pack neighborhood. The bright sun sparkled in a cloudless sky, almost as if the past few days had all been just a nightmare. But the pain that gripped me as I prepared to see the death and destruction I'd left behind reminded me that it was, in fact, reality.

When the neighborhood came into view, I sucked in a breath... and couldn't believe my eyes.

CHAPTER THREE

"I... I DON'T UNDERSTAND." My brain was still fuzzy, but that wasn't the problem. I scanned the road leading into the pack neighborhood—there wasn't a body in sight. From what I could see, each modest brick house looked untouched, as if the slaughter had been only a dream.

The image of that day blurred with today, and I shook my head, trying to keep a hold on reality.

Griffin clutched the steering wheel, his knuckles turning white as he slowed the car just outside the pack neighborhood. "What's wrong?"

I bit the inside of my cheek so I wouldn't laugh. The question wasn't funny, but I was teetering on the edge of insanity, which unsettled me. "That day...there were so many bodies." They'd littered the ground every ten feet, if that. "Where did they all go?"

"Do you think there could be survivors?" Griffin pulled over to the side of the road under the shade of several large oak trees grouped together at the edge of the woods and stopped the car. "Maybe they were able to fight back after you left."

His words gave me foolish hope that I had to squash down. "No. I don't feel any pack connections. If there were survivors, I would know." I got out of the vehicle, leaving the door open. A cool spring breeze stirred around me, carrying the familiar scents of magnolias and redbuds of my home.

"Should we head back?" Griffin asked.

"No, going back to Shadow Ridge won't be safe." We'd already had that conversation, but I understood his instinct to go somewhere he knew. "This is the safest place to be." At least, for the moment.

"Okay." He sighed. "Let's check things out while we wait on Killian."

"How long until he gets here?"

He pulled his phone from his pocket and glanced at the text. "Probably ten to fifteen minutes."

That would give us enough time to run around and make sure there weren't any surprises before pulling Griffin's Navigator into the neighborhood, alerting watchful eyes. "Sounds like a plan."

"I'll let him know what we're doing in case he gets here before we get back." He turned off the car and shot off a text before getting out.

As I waited on him, I inhaled and exhaled slowly, focusing on calming breaths to keep my racing heart from exploding. I didn't want to be here. In fact, this was the last place in the world I wanted to be. I'd figured seeing my pack's home would be hard, but it was so much more than that. Everywhere I looked, memories of my child-hood replayed in my mind.

We'd used the large circular grassy knoll for our training sessions that dad led, and the faint laughter of playing chase in the woods tickled my ears.

This safe haven had been turned into a place of anger, hatred, and so much remorse. What I wouldn't give to run in the woods with Zoe again, or for my dad to yell at me for flinching and giving away my next move. Or to experience, again, how Mom always listened when I felt like Dad—or anyone else—was being unfair, guiding me into considering the other person's viewpoint, which had molded me into the person I was today.

"Hey," Griffin rasped, as he pulled me into his arms. "We can find a hotel room or something. We don't have to stay here."

"That would put us around people and other shifters, which could make it easier for them to locate us." I appreciated what he was trying to do, but this was where we needed to be. I could feel it, even if I didn't like it.

I kissed him, using our bond for comfort. I needed him in order to get through the next little bit. "Let's scout around before Killian gets here." I faced the neighborhood. *Why don't you go right and I'll take the left?*

You want us to split up? Griffin sounded less than thrilled. *I figured we'd go together.*

If we find something—or someone—it'll be better if they think we're alone. I didn't want something to happen to both of us. *That way we'll have the element of surprise.*

Do you not realize what I went through when you disappeared? What we all went through? he linked as his fingers tangled in my hair, making my body warm. *I went insane looking for you. I don't think I can go through something like that again.*

My fingers trailed over his chin, his scruff biting the tips. I couldn't imagine how it had felt, and I hated that he'd gone through that. *I understand, but this is for the best. You won't be far, and we'll be linked the entire time.*

Fine, but if there is any sort of sign that we aren't alone, you let me know immediately. Griffin stared into my eyes. *I get that you're trained to fight and I'm not, but you're my mate. I need to know that you'll let me protect you, if it comes to that.*

We're a team. I stared into his eyes and pushed my emotions hard toward him so he could feel my sincerity. We'd had a rocky start with me pretending to be Killian's girlfriend and both of us trying to fight our connection. But we were finally here and on the same page, and we had to start trusting one another. *If even one thing seems out of sorts, I'll let you know. Also, we should stay in human form so we can talk with Killian when he gets here.*

He must have seen whatever he was looking for in my eyes because he nodded. *All right. Let's get this over with.*

I pecked him one last time and took off toward the tree line on the left.

His footsteps grew farther away as he followed my lead, heading in the opposite direction.

The neighborhood is one huge circle. I ran into the trees, trying to push away the memories that hung at the forefront of my mind. *We'll meet up on the other side.*

Got it, he responded.

Silence descended as I ran through trees that I knew like the back of my hand. Woodland animals fluttered and rustled around me like they hadn't a care in the world, which seemed unjustly cruel. Life had moved on. It shouldn't have been possible.

It wasn't fair.

The stain of my pack's murder should have had some sort of impact on the world.

Each silver wolf who'd died had vowed to protect the entire supernatural world—not just the wolves—so their loss should've been mourned by everyone. And yet, it was as if they had never existed.

It was as if the silver wolves had been erased from history. Atticus had known about us, but he hadn't shared the information with Griffin. So...who else knew?

Something wasn't adding up, and unfortunately, neither Griffin's dad nor my own were here to answer questions.

I tapped into my wolf, trying to keep my emotions in check. I ran a little faster than normal, afraid that if I slowed, the memories would catch up to me and crash all around.

However, when I turned toward the alpha's home—*my* home—there was no saving me.

Even though it wasn't possible, I was back in time, reliving that horrible day.

Dad stood in the center of the yard, grimacing as he clutched his side. Blood stained his white shirt, and his silver eyes—so similar to my own—stared at me. I could hear his voice clearly. "You need to go *now*." His irises had darkened to steel, and his silver hair had become a tarnished gray. The handsome alpha I grew up knowing had looked so damn old.

"Daddy?" I whispered, rushing toward the mirage. A part of me knew that he wasn't here—that it was a figment of my imagination—but I couldn't see past it. All I wanted to do was hug at least one of my parents, at least one person I missed more than life itself, and have him tell me everything would be okay.

But when I reached him and tried to hug him, all I touched was air.

His image vanished right before my eyes, and the overwhelming sense of loss coursed through me again.

I didn't know what to do or how to proceed. How I wished I could go back in time and cherish our moments together. I'd thought I still had so much time left with him—that he'd be here to teach me so much more—but I'd been so damn wrong. Instead of being annoyed with every new lesson for the day, I should've worked harder.

When he'd told me I needed to push through, I should've listened.

At the end of the day, he and Mom were the two people who always made me feel safe, and those gunmen had taken them away from not only me, but the entire world.

They couldn't get away with that. I refused to let the pack's sacrifice be in vain. If there was one thing I could do right by for all of my pack, it would be to become the very person Dad had hoped for, and the alpha Mom had known I could be.

A kickass alpha who every man would submit to.

Babe? Griffin linked. *Did you find something?*

The concern in his voice forced me to center. I sucked in a breath, trying to push back the raging emotions inside. I needed to calm down. *I'm fine. I'm sorry.*

Why are you sorry? he asked, almost frantically. *Did something happen?*

I could hear his footsteps now, rushing toward me. There was no telling how long I'd been standing here. *I... I just...* My inner voice cracked, and his concern wafted through our bond.

No matter how hard I tried to center myself, it was like I couldn't stay above water. My emotions flowed underneath, trying to drown me. *I'm home and...*

Griffin stepped into the yard and raced toward me. He pulled me into his arms, holding me tight as he pressed his face to the top of my head. *I'm here,* he whispered. *You're not alone.*

Tears fell like a waterfall as I mourned the deaths of my parents and pack. I'd thought I had grieved for them, but I'd been wrong. I'd been pushing it off to stay in survival mode. Focusing on the threat and surviving day to day. But being here and having to face what had happened... their deaths were catching up.

But Griffin's words stuck with me.

I wasn't alone.

Somehow, in this harsh new reality, I'd found not only my fated mate, but a brother, too. And even though neither one of them could replace my pack or parents, they were so damn important. With them by my side, I would be able to continue on and become the daughter my parents always wanted me to be.

Returning Griffin's embrace, I filled my nose with his comforting scent. There was no place I'd rather be than in his arms. *It just kind of snuck up on me.*

I know that feeling all too well. Griffin leaned back and smiled sadly. *So, this was your home?*

Yeah. I steadied myself, almost expecting to see the broken memory of Dad again—but this time, when I looked at the house, the backyard remained empty of ghosts.

But not the memories.

I turned to the red and yellow hibiscus and purple hydrangeas that lined the entrance to my house. "Mom and I planted those flowers last year, and we were so excited to see them bloom." Yet another thing she and I wouldn't ever do together.

Tears threatened my eyes, so I turned toward the woods. The healthy green leaves of ash, oak, and maple trees contrasted with the death I now associated with this place.

The sound of Killian's truck alerted me to his presence.

"We better go meet him before he gets concerned." I scanned the area, looking for any sort of sign that we might not be alone. Nothing stirred.

The two of us took off back toward the Navigator, quickly running the two miles to the vehicle. When we reached the Navigator, we found Killian leaning against his black truck, which he'd parked behind Griffin's SUV.

His warm, dark-chocolate eyes lit up when he saw me, and he pushed off his truck and hurried in my direction. His cappuccino-brown hair hung in his face, and with each step he took, it flopped to the side. He hugged me tight against his athletic body, and his musky sandalwood scent helped calm a part of my soul.

"Don't ever scare us like that again," Killian growled.

"Hey, it wasn't her fault," a familiar female said as she climbed down from the truck.

My body tensed as I stared at Sierra. Her sandy-blonde hair was pulled into a ponytail, and her gray eyes scanned me. She was a few inches shorter than me, but her big personality compensated for it.

"Wait...I thought you were alone." I didn't like the fact that Killian had brought someone with him. I got that Sierra had been his late sister's best friend, but the fewer people who knew about me and my pack, the safer we all would be. I scowled at Griffin, wondering why he hadn't told me this little fact.

"Hey, I didn't know." He lifted both hands. "When I tore out of the coffee shop, Killian was alone."

"I'm sorry. I didn't mean to intrude, but when I heard about you being taken, I told Killian I wanted to help." Sierra put her hands in her pockets. "There have been so many attacks. The other day, my sister got injured in one of the outbreaks, and Killian told me about your pack being killed." She paused as her jaw clenched. "It's got to stop. The unrest is spreading farther and farther."

"I promise she's trustworthy—and worst case, I can command her not to share." Killian placed a hand on his heart. "I wouldn't have brought her here if I doubted she was trustworthy."

"Okay." It wasn't like I'd planned on shifting to my animal form anyway. I needed to stay human as much as possible so there weren't any other accidental sightings.

"Besides, I thought you might need a friend who doesn't have a penis." She pointed at Griffin and Killian. "Because even though they try to be good guys, they're kinda assholes."

I laughed, surprising myself. "We all have our moments." Maybe it wasn't a bad thing for her to be here. If she could make me laugh like that, she could be a godsend.

"True that." She lifted a hand, but there was sadness in her eyes. "So what's the plan?"

That was the real question. "We need to find clues. Anything that might lead us to whoever killed my pack and attacked me in Shadow Ridge. The problem is someone came here and cleaned up the bodies."

"Which means they were making sure they didn't leave anything behind." Killian pursed his lips. "That means it's someone organized."

"Yes, but we already knew that," Griffin sighed, "between the attack outside our houses and them taking her from the coffee shop."

We could stand out here and speculate all day. "Our best bet is to look for answers. They have to be here somewhere." I hated to suggest it, but the first place to look would be the last place I wanted to go. "Let's start at my house. After all, my father was the alpha, and he had a study. A few days before we were attacked, he was going in there and locking the door a lot." I couldn't believe that it had taken me until now to remember that little fact.

"I agree." Sierra waved to the vehicles. "That's the place to start. Let's go."

We got into the vehicles and Killian followed Griffin to the house.

As we drove past the neighborhood houses, my pain somehow increased. And the closer we got to my house, the more hurt coursed through me. I didn't know what kind of state I'd be when we arrived back at home.

House after house looked untouched. The only sign that no one was around was the overgrown grass that now covered the yards. Soon, the turn to the back of the neighborhood and my house appeared. I felt as if I couldn't breathe again when we pulled into my driveway and got out.

I made my way to the side of the house where the air conditioner unit sat. I bent and picked up the key that was hidden under the rocks surrounding the unit. As I straightened, a branch snapped not ten feet away.

CHAPTER FOUR

I SPUN AROUND, searching for the source of the noise. My heart pounded so hard my ears rang, and I sniffed, searching for any scents outside the norm.

Nothing.

Needing to make sure, I slowly walked to the tree line...and a faint scent of musk tickled my nose. However, it wasn't strong enough for someone to have been there moments ago. This scent was a few days old, probably from whoever had cleaned up the pack neighborhood. A squirrel or something must have run by and caused the disturbance.

Is something wrong? Griffin asked as he made his way toward me, following my gaze into the woods.

That was a tricky question, even though he hadn't meant for it to be. *I heard a branch snap, but it must have been an animal.* I forced myself to turn back to the house that I dreaded entering. I was tempted to say we needed to scout out the area more, but that would only prolong the inevitable. Searching the house was the best bet for finding clues or, at least, something that could point us in the right direction.

Putting one foot in front of the other, I made it to the sturdy, red chestnut door of my childhood home, but the door was already slightly ajar. I pushed the door open the rest of the way, trying not to freeze. If I paused, there was no telling when I'd finally get going again.

The living room looked the same as it had that morning when I'd left to walk to the river. The beige, cloth couch sat against the tan wall with Dad's brown, leather recliner in the corner. The news flickered on the television with the sound muted, and the remote control sat on the arm of the recliner. That was where Dad always sat.

Sadness tugged on my heart, but I pushed it away. If I started crying now, I wasn't sure if I'd ever stop.

I entered the house, stepping onto the dark walnut floor. The scent of lavender—Mom's favorite fragrance—overwhelmed me.

My throat went dry as I held back the tears burning my eyes. I didn't want to break down in front of everyone.

I had to be strong.

Sierra stepped beside me. "This is kind of creepy."

That was one way of putting it. "It feels like they should be somewhere in the house." I tried to keep the emotion from my voice, but it leaked through, so I pushed forward through the room and toward the hallway.

The three of them followed me, and I paused at the large eat-in kitchen on the right. All of the maple cabinets were closed—which was the norm—but the large empty pot on the black stove and a sink full of washed-off dishes made it clear that something was wrong. Mom hated a cluttered kitchen and always told me that the trick was cleaning as you cooked.

Just another reminder that they were truly gone.

"What time of day did they attack?" Griffin asked as he took my hand.

"Midday on the new moon." I noted that two of the chairs at the round table were pulled out; probably due to Mom and Dad sitting down with their coffee. *When we are at our weakest,* I linked with

Griffin. I got that Killian trusted Sierra, but I didn't yet. Trust had to be earned at this point.

"New moon?" Sierra parroted. "I guess that's one way of remembering the date."

I wasn't going to touch that comment. Anything I could've added would have exposed me further.

Killian cleared his throat. "So, where should we begin looking?"

"Why don't you and Sierra search the woods and see if they left something behind or, at least, find what they did with the de—" I couldn't finish the sentence. I wanted to know where the pack was buried...or if they even were.

Sierra grimaced. "Yes, we can do that."

She understood my meaning, which relieved me. I didn't have to say it after all.

Needing to change the direction of the conversation, I said, "Griffin and I can search here." I wanted to be the one who went through Dad's stuff—there was no telling what I might find.

"Are you sure?" Killian asked. "We can help—"

"No, I need to do this." I had to. Depending on what I found, I might need to process it a little while on my own.

"You heard her." Griffin stood behind me, placing his hands on my shoulders. "If you guys need anything, we're only a phone call away."

"That sounds like a plan." Sierra saluted. "We can circle deeper in the woods and see what we find. They had to leave something behind."

"Let's hope so." I needed answers.

The two of them headed to the door as Killian called out, "We'll be back soon."

When the front door closed again, I spun around, placing my head on Griffin's shoulder. I needed a moment to brace myself for what came next. It was hard enough being in the house, but going into Dad's study and my parents' room would make things even worse.

I'll be right here with you the entire way. Griffin pressed a kiss to my forehead. *We can take as long as you need.*

But the longer I put it off, the harder this would be. *No, let's get moving before Sierra gets back.* I headed back down the hallway, straight to my room on the left. I wanted to look in there and make sure nothing had been left behind by the hunters.

Going through my own room shouldn't be as hard as the others, so it made sense to start there.

I stepped inside, and the scent of unfamiliar shifters hit my nose. I hadn't smelled anyone until this room, which meant they'd spent a lot of time in it. The silver walls of my room felt as though they were mocking me—like I'd tempted fate by matching them to my hair.

The collage of me and the pack was missing, and the teal sheets of my bed were crumpled. Mom had been a drill sergeant when it came to cleanliness, so it was another sign that people had gone through the house.

"This is your room?" Griffin asked, as he stepped in behind me.

"Yeah. It was." It didn't feel like home anymore. There were too many horrible memories for that...at least, for now. "Our pack has lived in this town ever since we left Shadow City."

"Why did the silver wolves leave Shadow City?" Griffin asked as he walked to my small bookshelf, scanning the titles of the classics that I loved to read.

"Honestly, I'm not sure." Dad and I had assumed we had so much more time for him to teach me things. "I know we were in danger there, but I have no clue why, or from who."

"It's strange that my dad knew that you existed." Griffin slowly turned, taking in the room. "He never told me about you all, either, but your dad did come and visit. I vaguely remember him."

I walked to my closet and looked through my clothes. Nothing seemed to be missing, except for my pictures, which made sense. They'd probably taken them back to wherever they were based to get additional resources looking for me. "I think we're good here. Let's go look at Dad's study. I'm assuming that's where they did most of their searching."

He followed me into the study, and I took in the scattered papers on Dad's huge mahogany desk. "This was the third bedroom. He converted it into his office." I flipped through the papers, finding bills and other records, but nothing substantial. Yet, I knew he hid stuff somewhere.

Griffin walked to the filing cabinets that lined the wall. "I guess I'll start here, and you search his desk?"

I didn't have a better suggestion. "Sure." I opened the top drawer of the desk, expecting to find the cabinet keys, but instead, I found it bare. Yet another sign that someone had searched the house.

However, Griffin was able to open the cabinet drawers without any problems. Whoever searched it hadn't taken the time to lock it and put the keys back. Either they didn't care if someone figured out that they'd been here, or they thought no one would show up and realize what had happened—beyond someone from the electric or water company looking to get paid or turn off the water.

Either way, we had a lot to dig through. I sat in my dad's chair as a heaviness seemed to press on my shoulders.

My entire life, I'd known that I would be sitting at my father's desk one day, but I could never have imagined it like this. He'd been taken from me far too soon, and I didn't know how to recover. A piece of me had died that day—along with him and the others—but I refused to cower. Whoever was after me wanted to break me and have me as his own, personal breeder. But what he didn't know was that silver wolves reproduced slower than normal wolves. Dad had explained that our slowness to reproduce was due to our stronger powers—that nature had a way of balancing power so that it didn't swing in favor of one race alone.

That didn't matter. The man hunting me didn't give a damn about the logistics. He wanted control, or at least the illusion of it.

So, I did the only thing I knew to do.

I rolled up my sleeves and began digging.

––––––––––––

THE ENTIRE DAY had been one emotional ride.

The four of us sat around my kitchen table in silence. Killian had run out to get some all-meat pizzas, so I choked down a slice—only because both Griffin and Killian kept watching me. But the food sat uncomfortably in my stomach.

"Are you sure you're good staying here tonight?" Griffin asked, for the fifth time.

"It's the safest place for us." And it would keep us close to Dad's study so we could continue our search in the morning. "I have everything I need here." Except for my pack.

Killian and Sierra hadn't found much in the woods. They'd searched about half the neighborhood's perimeter before calling it a day and going to grab the food for dinner.

If I hadn't known better, I would've thought I got run over by a train. I felt incredibly hungover—probably from the drugs—plus, my emotional well-being was subpar. Every so often, I thought I heard Dad's footsteps coming down the hall, and the realization that I would never hear that again slammed into me.

"Since that's settled, let's get you to bed." Griffin's face creased with concern. "You've had one hell of a day."

Bed did sound nice. I stood and glanced at Sierra and Killian. "Let me get you two some sheets for the couch and recliner."

"Nope, we're good. I saw some blankets in the hall closet." Sierra waved me off. "You go get some rest. I'll take care of it."

I sort of wanted to argue but just didn't have it in me. "If you do need something, just let me know."

"Will do," Sierra said as she pointed at Griffin. "Now go get your mate in bed."

"Yes, ma'am." He chuckled and took my hand.

When the two of us entered my room, I climbed into bed, not even worrying about changing clothes. My body seemed to weigh a ton, and the thought of standing any longer didn't hold any appeal.

Griffin lay down next to me and pulled me into his arms. His fingertips brushed my arm, making me sigh. I rolled toward him and stared into his eyes.

I'd never get tired of looking at him, and I wasn't sure what would've happened if he wasn't here with me. A part of me knew that I wouldn't have been nearly as strong.

He kissed me gently, parting my lips with his tongue.

I responded to his kiss in earnest, needing to feel him.

Hey, you need your rest. He pulled back a little. *You almost passed out while eating.*

I did need my rest, but I also needed him to help me feel alive. *I want you to make me forget this shitty day.* I kissed him eagerly, making my intentions clear. *I need you.*

Why don't you take a nap first? he growled, trying to remain strong.

My hand unbuttoned his jeans as I deepened our kiss. *No.* I slipped my hand inside his boxers, stroking him.

Dammit. He groaned as his hands gripped my waist and pulled me on top of him.

I rocked against him, needing to feel the friction. I grabbed the hem of his shirt and yanked it over his head; then, clawed down his chest, enjoying the feel of his skin.

His hands slipped under my shirt and removed it from my body. He reached around me and unfastened my bra, and my breasts fell right into his face. He captured a nipple between his teeth, flicking it with his tongue.

The ache grew deeper inside me as my body warmed. He rolled me off him and stood at the side of the bed. Then he grabbed my jeans and panties and dragged them off my body.

"You're so damn beautiful," he rasped as he kicked off his jeans and boxers. He leaned over me and kissed me to the point that my head grew dizzy.

The scents of our arousal mixed, making the room smell intoxicating. I tried getting up, wanting to take control, but he grabbed my arms and held them at the sides of my head.

We're supposed to be going slow, he chastised me, as his fingers pinched my nipples.

A low moan escaped as my body caught on fire. *This is slow.*

He chuckled, sounding so damn sexy. *No, it's not.*

I wrapped my legs around his waist, enjoying the feel of him rubbing against me.

He groaned huskily, nearly making me come unglued.

Please. I begged, not even embarrassed.

Fine. He placed his hand between us, positioning himself, and thrust into me hard.

Pleasure rocketed through me as he lifted my hips, hitting deeper inside. With his free hand, he rubbed circular motions between my legs, making every cell in my body ignite.

He surrounded my senses; every smell, touch, and taste belonged to him. I opened myself up, wanting him to know everything I felt—between everything that had happened that day, and this moment. The words *I love you* passed through my mind.

His emotions poured into me like a dam breaking. *I love you too,* he linked as orgasms surged through both of us.

We breathed out together and stilled. My body was completely satiated, and finally, a sense of peace settled over me.

Eventually, I stood and put on my pajamas. Griffin followed my lead, and soon, we both crawled back into bed. He cuddled me in his arms, and my eyes closed of their own accord. Within seconds, I began dozing off. My body relaxed, but before sleep completely overtook me, a memory popped into my brain.

I sat straight up in bed and clenched my teeth. "I remember who drugged me."

CHAPTER FIVE

GRIFFIN'S EYES glowed brightly in the dark room as his wolf surged forward. "What do you mean? I thought the guy who kidnapped you killed himself."

"Well, yes, but he wasn't the one who knocked me out at the coffee shop." The memory of the familiar footsteps replayed in my mind, followed by the prick and the apology. "Carter injected me with something."

"What?" Griffin growled. "When I reached the coffee shop, trying to find you after you asked for help, he told me someone took you."

"Because the bear shifter did take me. He was the one driving the car." The betrayal sat hard on my chest as the reality of the situation landed on me. I got that Carter and I only worked together, but I'd thought we were at least somewhat friends—and I hadn't sensed any bad vibes from him. The next words hurt to say. "He knocked me out for him."

"I'm going to inform Killian, since Carter's part of his pack, and then kill him." Griffin stood, and a vein popped between his eyebrows as his body tensed with anger. "I'll rip him limb from limb, starting with his dick."

Okay, he actually went to the male appendage first, but I had to admit the thought had merit. Even though Killian was Carter's alpha, technically, Griffin ruled over the pack because he was the Shadow City alpha. So, Griffin could yank Carter's dick off without penalty.

I rubbed my arms, trying to fight off the cold sinking into my bones. I was even more exhausted; I'd almost been asleep when the memory woke me. The day had been long and hard—both physically and mentally—but this was something that couldn't be ignored.

"Killian should know." Griffin opened the bedroom door and marched down the hallway toward the living room. Each step rattled the pictures that hung on the walls.

"Dude, what the hell?" Killian asked, alarmed. "Are you trying to wake up the dead?"

"The only thing louder than your walking would be someone playing the drums," Sierra complained. "I was almost asleep."

I realized I better get in there before Griffin did something stupid. I forced myself to get up and hurried into the living room, despite my legs feeling like they weighed a hundred pounds each.

"Sterlyn remembered something about her attackers in the coffee shop," Griffin rasped. "And we've got a huge problem."

I joined them in the living room as Sierra sat up on the couch and blinked, asking, "Sterlyn?"

Yeah...we had to be more careful, or we'd wind up having to tell her everything. "That's my real name."

"Thank God. Dove is atrocious. Sterlyn fits you so much better with your hair and silver-purple eyes." She grinned. "Your parents nailed naming you."

She had no clue how true that statement was.

"'Attackers?'" Killian's brows furrowed. "As in plural?"

"Yeah, I thought there was only one, but when I was dozing off, a memory came back to me." I dreaded telling Killian who it was. He and Carter had some kind of bromance I didn't want to interfere with, but we were working as a team, so they all needed to know.

He scowled at me. "Well, then who attacked you?"

I opened my mouth to respond, but Griffin cut me off, "Carter. Your bestie."

"What?" Killian scoffed and shook his head. "No way. He linked with me and told me that someone took her."

God, how many times was I going to have to hear the same thing? "Because the bear shifter took me. That was the only thing he could say without his lie coming to light. But he injected me with God knows what while I was in the pantry, getting the coffee beans that *he* asked me to get. He even apologized before I completely passed out."

"That doesn't make any sense." Killian pulled his phone from his jeans pocket like he was going to make a call. He set it on the edge of the recliner and grimaced. "Look, I'm not trying to be a dick here—"

"Normally, when someone starts off with a comment like that, they're going to be a dick." Sierra placed her feet on the ground and got upright. "So don't even try to qualify it. Just own your damn statement."

Killian glowered at her. "You aren't helping."

"I didn't know I was supposed to." Sierra crossed her arms as she leaned back on the couch.

"Just say what you want to say." I wanted this conversation over with so I could go back to bed. I was struggling to stand on both feet at this point.

Killian scratched the back of his neck. "Are you sure it was Carter? If you were drugged—"

The question stung. "Do you honestly think I would accuse someone if I wasn't one hundred percent sure?" My feelings were hurt that he was second-guessing me. I got that he'd known Carter longer than me, but I thought we'd developed a bond. Maybe I'd misread the situation.

"Dammit, I didn't mean it like that." Killian ran a hand down his face. "You were drugged, and maybe your memory got distorted. That's all I'm trying to say."

"Dude, if Sterlyn says that he did it, then why are you trying to brush it under the rug?" Griffin wrapped an arm around my waist, glaring at his best friend. "Are you really willing to ignore what she remembers because you don't want to consider the possibility that your pack member hurt her?"

"I don't mean it like that." Killian groaned with frustration. "It's just...Carter and I have been friends since childhood. We grew up in Shadow Ridge together. I know his entire family, and that just doesn't sound like him."

"Maybe he didn't have a choice." Sierra lifted a hand, trying to be the voice of reason. "There's no telling what happened, and I agree with Griffin. Sterlyn is no fool, and if she remembers something, we need to check it out."

My heart warmed from both Griffin and Sierra having my back. Usually, I could count on Killian—but not now. My emotions were raw from the entire day, so I couldn't help but feel vulnerable. Being objective wasn't possible for me right now.

"You're right." Killian's shoulders sagged. "I'm being a dick and not thinking objectively. So, there's only one way to find out, and I want you all to hear what he says to me." Killian swiped his phone.

"No, don't call him." I understood that Killian wanted to confront him, but that wasn't the smart way to handle it. "If you call him and ask, he could disappear. We need to see him in person so we can get a good read and he can't hide, lie, or warn whomever he might be working with. If he is involved, he won't hang around just because you two are friends."

"Then how the hell do we get him here?" Killian threw his hands up. "I can't wiggle my nose and make him appear."

"You do seem kind of witchy." Sierra stuck out her tongue at him. "Especially tonight, so maybe it could work."

Those two really did act like siblings. It was clear that they had grown up together.

"I have Rosemary's number." Griffin paced in the center of the room. "I'll call her and see if she's willing to bring him here."

"Why would she help us?" Sierra arched an eyebrow. "You know she's one of the more difficult angels, seeing as who her parents are."

"Who are her parents?" That could mean so many things.

Griffin exhaled. "They're council members who oppose me. They think I'm not strong enough to be the overall leader of the Shadow City and Shadow Ridge wolves."

"I'm not sure what that even means." They tended to forget that I wasn't raised in Shadow Ridge or Shadow City and didn't know the hierarchy.

"From what I've gathered from my history classes, it's similar to the humans' political structure that you've grown up with." He rubbed his hands together. "Like the House and the Senate. Technically, I'm the Senate, while the other two wolf representatives are in the House. So I can veto anything they bring to the table."

"So, what is Rosemary's family?"

"Her mom and dad are the House of Representatives, with Azbogah being the Senate. So, he can't get anything passed without at least one of them agreeing, and vice versa. They're kind of at odds and at a standstill. Nothing is getting passed on the angel side of things because they're fighting one another."

"Which means I doubt Rosemary will want to get involved with wolf stuff." Sierra waved a hand. "All it would do is cause more of a divide between the angels if they found out."

Interesting. No wonder she was trying to be discreet about helping us. "She and I have an understanding." I wasn't willing to go into more detail than that. "Besides, she'll be willing to help out because of all the attacks going on. The more wolves who are attacked, the more likely a civil war will start."

"True, and if the council members find out that some of our own people who are supposed to be loyal to the city are working against it, things will escalate across the board." Griffin sighed. "Ever since Dad died, things keep going from bad to worse."

I understood that sentiment all too well. "Look, if Rosemary grabs Carter now, his entire family will know something is up. Why don't you call her and see if she can run by the coffee shop in the morning and pick him up? He won't be able to get out of it that way, especially with everyone around as witnesses if he makes a scene."

Griffin's face fell. "I want to question him tonight."

"I know." I did too, but sometimes you couldn't let your desperate need for answers ruin a sound strategy. "But I'm exhausted, and I could really use some sleep. If we aren't well-rested, then we could miss things when talking to him."

"She's right." Killian yawned, though his irises darkened with concern. He was still struggling with the thought of Carter hurting me. "Just call the angel and see what she says."

"Fine." Griffin pushed some buttons, and soon, a phone was ringing on the other end.

Rosemary answered on the second ring. "Is everything okay?"

"Of course not," Griffin said, annoyingly. "Why else would I be calling?"

This conversation was already starting off great. *Be nice.*

"You call me and then get rude within seconds." Rosemary scoffed. "Give the phone to Sterlyn. I'm done talking to you."

"Gladly." Griffin held the phone toward me.

Well, all right then. I took it and cleared my throat. "Hey, sorry we're calling so late."

"What's wrong?" Rosemary asked, as a door shut on her end.

"I remembered something about the attack earlier." I wasn't sure why, but I didn't dislike her as the others did. She was blunt and said exactly what was on her mind. Maybe the protector side of me appreciated that, because what she said and how she acted mirrored what I felt from inside her; she tried to do the right thing, even when it was difficult. In a way, she was a warrior like the silver wolves.

She remained silent, waiting for me to continue.

"Carter's the one who drugged me."

"That's why the idiot was freaking out." Rosemary sounded disgusted. "He tried to pretend it was because you'd vanished, but I wasn't buying it. I thought it might've been because Griffin was panicking about you being missing, but this makes more sense."

Just like that, she believed me. "Do you think you could run by the coffee shop in the morning and...grab him?"

"You don't want me to get him now?" Rosemary asked, with surprise.

"They could be watching him." The last thing we needed was for her to alert whoever was hunting me to our location. "So it'll be safer if we wait until morning."

"It'll be easier for me too," Rosemary huffed.

"We have to be careful." Bringing him here was risky. "He can't know where we are. We either need him brought here in a way that he can't figure out our location, or we need to meet you somewhere else. But if we do the latter, he could have backup following him."

"Don't worry. I'll take care of it. He won't have a clue where you are," Rosemary reassured me. "Text me your address, and I'll be there early."

We hung up the phone, and I sent her the address.

Then Griffin and I went back to bed...and I fell fast asleep.

A LOUD BANGING WOKE ME. My eyes popped open, and I sat upright, trying to remember where the hell I was. It took a second for me to realize that I was actually in my room back home.

"What the hell?" Griffin grumbled as he stood, and almost tripped over his feet.

"I don't know." I glanced at the clock. It was barely after eight in the morning.

Carter's voice sounded high-pitched. "Where are we? Why did you kidnap me? I need to get back to work."

"Shut up," Rosemary grumbled. "Before I make you."

"You can't just take someone without their permission," he said wildly. "Wait until your parents find out what you did!"

That was wild, coming from him. Granted, he had no clue what he was walking into.

"They aren't going to know," Rosemary bit back, as she pounded on the door again. "Because you aren't going to tell them."

We needed to get out there before Rosemary killed him; I needed answers before she slit his throat.

Rosemary opened the front door as Griffin and I joined Sierra and Killian in the living room. Carter's shaggy brown hair was a knotted mess, and his moss-green eyes almost bulged from his face when he saw the four of us standing there. He spun around, rushing past Rosemary to try to get away.

Rosemary grabbed the back of his shirt and yanked him into the house. He stumbled backward, tripping and falling on his ass in front of everyone. As he stared up at us from the ground, he looked more like a child than a twenty-year-old man.

"Uh... Why did you bring me here?" he asked Rosemary, as she shut the door and twisted the lock.

"You know why," she said as she rolled her shoulders and looked at me. "And you owe me. I had to fly his ass here to make sure we weren't followed, and he screamed the whole way."

"Wolves aren't meant to fly," Carter yelled. "They are meant to have their feet on the ground. It's unnatural, what you did to me."

"I'll show you unnatural if you don't shut the fuck up," she sneered.

"Come on, man." Killian held his hand out. "Calm down. There's no reason to freak out."

"Yeah, okay." Carter's arm shook as he took Killian's outstretched hand to stand up.

But his initial reaction proved that my memory was sound. Which meant I had to get a confession from him before he somehow manipulated Killian into believing whatever his story was. That was one thing that I loved about Killian—he was as loyal as they came... but that was also his weakness.

"Yeah, there is." I shifted my weight and placed a hand on my hip. "Because I want to know why you drugged me and handed me off to a bear shifter."

Carter's mouth dropped open, and he took in a shaky breath. "What? No, I didn't."

The sulfuric scent of a lie wafted in the room, confirming what everyone except Killian had already known.

Killian's face twisted into an expression of disappointment, and he closed his eyes.

"You son of a bitch," Griffin yelled, as he punched Carter in the jaw.

CHAPTER SIX

THE IMPACT of Griffin's knuckles on Carter's jaw was practically ear-splitting.

Carter's head snapped back and he stumbled, trying to get out of reach. He grabbed his jaw and winced with pain. "What the hell?"

"That's what you have to say for yourself?" Killian's jaw twitched as his nostrils flared. "'What the hell' is all you have to say?" He rushed over to Carter and punched his friend in the gut.

"Ugh." Carter leaned forward, wrapping one arm around his waist as his other hand continued to rub his chin. "Just stop," he groaned.

"Oh, well... Since you asked." Rosemary rolled her eyes. "You're more moronic than I thought."

To prevent them from continuing the beating, I stepped between the two guys and Carter. I scowled at the person who I'd thought was at least sort of my friend. "You've got one second to spill or I'll let Griffin and Killian continue."

Carter tried to straighten up, but he winced, stopping before he reached his full height. "Look, it was nothing personal," he rasped.

"Dear God." Sierra barked out a laugh and sat on the couch like she was ready to watch a show. "I never thought I'd see the day where I agreed with Rosemary, but hell has officially frozen over. He really is an idiot."

Carter frowned. "Hey! My family is at risk."

"We're well aware," Rosemary said with disdain.

I pushed aside my natural inclination to beat him to a bloody pulp. Acting on emotion would work to our disadvantage, and we already didn't know who we were up against. We didn't need to stack the odds even more in their favor. "Nothing personal is getting the wrong type of cake, or taking a longer lunch break than you were supposed to. Drugging me and passing me off to someone who put me in the trunk of a car is the *definition* of personal."

"I didn't know he was putting you in the trunk!" He at least had the sense to cringe and avert his gaze to the floor.

For him to act so flippant irritated me even more. Who the hell did he think he was? Maybe he was clueless, and we could learn nothing from him.

"Obviously, that makes the entire situation better." Rosemary took a menacing step in his direction. "Because the drugging part wasn't bad enough."

"You know what?" I stepped out of the way and waved both Griffin and Killian on. "Beat the living shit out of him. If he isn't going to talk or doesn't know anything useful, we might as well at least get even." I prayed that he didn't call my bluff.

"What? No!" Carter lifted a hand in front of his body—like that would save him. "There's no need to beat me up. I didn't mean for any of this to happen."

"How so?" I lifted my chin and stared down my nose at him. "You stuck me in the neck with a needle and injected something into my bloodstream. That seems pretty purposeful to me."

He took a step toward me. "Dove—"

"Shut up," Griffin bellowed and shoved him in the chest. "Don't even say her name."

"I didn't have a choice." Carter's bottom lip quivered.

Killian shook his head. "You always have a choice. You happened to make the wrong one."

"They have Randall," Carter said. "And they threatened to hurt him if I didn't help them get Dove."

"Randall?" I hadn't heard of anyone by that name.

"His younger brother." Killian sighed, but the tension didn't leave his body. "What do you mean they have him? As in they still do? Why the hell wouldn't you tell me or Billy?"

It took me a second to remember Billy was the pack beta who was stepping into the alpha role while Killian figured things out.

"I was told not to alert anyone—I couldn't risk it. They said that he'd be released once Dove got to wherever the hell they wanted her to go." Carter waved a hand toward me as he continued, "And I'm pretty sure this isn't where they wanted her."

"She got away." Griffin gritted his teeth. "No thanks to you."

"What was I supposed to do?" Carter asked, as his shoulders sagged. "They were going to hurt my brother. Correction... They *are* going to hurt him."

"Why didn't you come to me?" Killian clenched his hands into fists.

"I didn't want to get you tangled up in this." Carter blew out a breath. "I mean, you already lost your entire family. I didn't want to make you choose between Randall and Dove."

"She's my fucking *mate*." Griffin stepped in front of me. "Did you think that we would just be like, 'oh well, it sucks that we lost her?'"

"In my defense, I thought she was still with Killian when I agreed the day before," Carter said, wringing his hands.

"That's a very weak defense." Sierra wrinkled her nose, looking disgusted. "It shouldn't matter whether she's Killian's girlfriend or Griffin's mate."

"It kind of does." Carter ran his fingers through his hair and yanked on the ends. "I knew she wasn't Killian's mate, so he would get over her. When she walked in with Griffin yesterday, it completely threw me, but I was already in too deep. Randall is a good kid. He doesn't deserve to be hurt."

"And she does?" Griffin asked, shoving Carter.

"No, that's not what I meant." Carter plastered himself against the wall. "But he's my *family*."

I understood that all too well. If there had been a way I could've saved my parents or pack, I'd have been tempted to play along, too. Granted, I would've tried to find a way so no one else would've gotten hurt, but Carter clearly didn't have leadership potential. He wasn't an omega, but he definitely wasn't dominant; he did well managing the coffee shop, but his wolf was submissive. "Let's give him the benefit of the doubt." It was hard saying those words, but if I didn't, Griffin wouldn't calm down. "He made the best choice he thought he could under bad circumstances. Whoever we're up against is smart; think about how they managed to take out those four guards that disappeared at the start of the fight two days ago with us none the wiser."

"That doesn't make it okay." Griffin sneered. "He deserves to have his ass beat."

"Maybe, but this gives us a strategic advantage." I had to put on my fighter hat. Making smart choices was the only way we could get a step ahead of the enemy; we were in the dark right now. I faced Killian and Griffin. "Were we able to glean anything from the boat that was left behind?"

"No." Killian sat on the other end of the couch. "There was no registration or anything personal on it."

"That's how the car they used to kidnap me was, too." We'd left the car on the side of the road for someone to find. Hiding it would have raised more questions. "So I'm betting the boat and car were stolen, which strengthens my case for recruiting Carter to help us."

"How can that ding-a-ling help us?" Sierra leaned forward.

"Because they have leverage over him, and he's already proven that he's willing to do whatever it takes to save his brother." I gestured to Killian. "Even going against his alpha and the Shadow City alpha as well."

"In fairness, he doesn't think of me as his alpha." Killian pursed his lips. "I mean, I haven't really been alpha material."

"Well, it's time for that to officially change." If we were going to figure this out, we were all going to have to do things we didn't want to—like me being here, facing the death of my pack—Griffin and Killian were going to have to step up and be the leaders they'd been afraid of being. "We need to pool our resources to have a fighting chance...unless you two want to walk away?" I had to give them an out. This wasn't something they'd ever wanted, and I was asking a lot.

"That question has to be a joke." Griffin's irises darkened. "You're my fated mate. I'm not going anywhere."

"And you're my family now." Killian nodded. "We're all in, and we're going to figure this out together."

"It's about damn time that you two finally step up." Rosemary placed a hand on her hip. "There's been so much turmoil, between your families dying and you two messing around instead of taking charge. You committing to your alpha roles should, at least, cause tensions to die down among the Shadow City representatives."

"You know, sometimes it'd be nice if I could at least wonder what you might be thinking." Griffin scowled at the angel. "But you've never given me the opportunity."

"Sorry if I've ruined your fragile ego several times now." She flipped her hair over her shoulder. "But no one dares to give it to you straight, so I figured I would."

Dear God, I didn't want to listen to their bickering right now. "The point I was trying to get at is they'll wind up calling Carter again to help them out."

"You think so?" Carter cleared his throat and pulled at his collar. "I mean, you're okay with being captured again?"

"No, idiot." Rosemary huffed. "You're not actually going to go through with it."

"But my brother—"

"You're going to tell Killian—using the pack link or whatever—and we'll set it up so we catch whoever is there to collect me, instead of them actually taking me." I had to be careful or he might not be willing to help us. Instead, he could tell whomever it was that we were on to him. "How did they get a hold of you the first time?"

"Some robotic voice called my cell phone." Carter tapped his foot. "Randall must have given them the number. It told me that since you worked at the coffee shop, I got to be the lucky person to help them."

That was what I'd figured. They'd been watching me and knew that Killian and Griffin wouldn't turn me in; the only other person who had influence over me was my manager. "So, you'll be that lucky person again—which means Carter needs to get back to the coffee shop before they suspect anything." I looked at Rosemary.

"I... I can't risk Randall." Carter slumped over. "If something happens to him—"

I was trying to be nice, but it was time to lay it out for him. "They aren't going to give up your brother willingly. In fact, once you deliver on your end of the bargain, he's as good as dead."

"But they said—"

"They lied," Rosemary interjected. "They've gone out of their way to make sure no one can identify them and that they can't be located. Do you really think they're going to just hand him over if he has any sort of clue who they are? They definitely won't if he's seen some of their faces. The only reason he's still alive is to manipulate you into compliance."

I appreciated that Rosemary had said it instead of me. She had an excellent bad-cop approach, which helped me appeal to Carter's softer side. She and I made a good team. "So, if you help us, we can capture whoever shows up to get me, and we can locate your brother before it's too late."

"Do you believe this?" Carter asked, looking at Killian. "Do you think my brother is at risk?"

"Yes, I do," Killian said curtly. "That's why you should've come to me from the very beginning. Not only would St—Dove be okay, but we could have already gotten Randall back."

I felt bad for Carter. He hadn't known what to do, and he had put so many people at risk. We were all being hard on him, but he needed to learn the lesson.

"Let me be very clear," Griffin said, as he grabbed Carter by the neck. "If you make *any* sort of decision that puts my mate in harm's way again, you will suffer immensely. I don't care what it takes; I'll make sure you go through hell. Do you understand?"

Carter's face turned red, and he nodded his head, as if unable to speak.

"I want to hear you say it." Griffin rasped.

"I..." Carter coughed a few times. "I understand."

Griffin released his hold, and Carter fell back, inhaling sharply.

"Do you mind taking him back?" I asked Rosemary. I didn't want to tell her to do it because that would just irritate her. I needed to be diplomatic in order to keep the angel on our side.

"Yeah, but if he screams the whole way back like he did here, I can't promise I won't drop him." She rubbed her temples. "He gave me a headache."

"Huh." Sierra blew a raspberry. "Can supernaturals get headaches? I never heard someone complain about one."

"This was a first for me." Rosemary reached the door and paused. "So, I'm guessing if we're around someone super annoying, it is possible. Something I wished I hadn't learned firsthand. I might need ear plugs."

Her dramatics were exactly what I needed at the moment. The corner of my mouth tipped upward. "Sorry, I'm fresh out."

"Damn tragedy." She snorted and shook her head.

"Uh...maybe you guys can blindfold me and take me by car." Carter put his hands together like he was in prayer. "Then Rosemary won't have to go through the torture of carrying me."

"You've already been gone too long." They did need to leave, and now. "She'll get you there faster."

"Just come on." Rosemary marched over to him and grabbed him by the ear. "I'll take him back. Call me if you need anything else."

"Ow," Carter whined, as he followed behind Rosemary and out the front door. When it closed, the four of us looked at each other.

"Do you think he'll be able to pull it off?" Sierra tapped a finger against her bottom lip. "I mean, he seems nervous."

"He'll have to if he wants his brother to survive." That was a cold, hard fact—whether we liked it or not.

Killian puffed his cheeks. "He'll be able to pull it off. He loves his family and will do whatever he can to protect his brother. He'd told the pack that Randall had gone on a camping trip, so now it adds up. Randall must be far enough away that we can't use our pack link to connect with him—or he's being drugged. Between that and Carter being willing to face Griffin's and my wrath to do what he thought would save Randall, he'll make it work."

I sure hoped so. "Well, we need to keep digging because, once they call him, we'll have to head back to Shadow Ridge." Luckily, we weren't that far away, but I was afraid to leave before we had searched through everything. There was no telling what we might come back to.

A phone rang from my bedroom. I faced Griffin and said, "You better go answer it."

"It's not mine." He pulled his phone from his pocket.

My stomach dropped. "It's the bear shifter's burner phone." I rushed down the hallway and ran into my room. The phone buzzed on the nightstand and rang for the third time. I snatched it up and pressed the green button.

CHAPTER SEVEN

THE LINE CONNECTED, and my stomach dropped. I didn't want to say hello, or they'd know right away something was wrong. They had to already suspect it, or they wouldn't be calling.

Silence filled the line at first, until a deep, menacing voice said, "Samuel, where the fuck are you?"

I'd been afraid the voice would sound familiar, but it didn't. Relief coursed through me that another person I trusted hadn't been working against me. Granted, the two people I trusted most were here with me.

"Samuel?" the man said in a lower tone.

Griffin, Killian, and Sierra entered the room, and we all looked at each other, at a loss as to how to proceed.

What's the plan? Griffin asked as he glared at the phone.

"Who's there?" the man demanded. "I take it the silver wolf is listening."

Sierra's head snapped in my direction, and her mouth dropped open.

Well, there went keeping Sierra in the dark. I only hoped Killian's judgment was sound with this one...because it hadn't been with Carter.

"For some supposed 'fierce warrior,' you're sure scared to talk to me." The guy chuckled, clearly trying to get a rise out of me.

He already assumes I'm here, so I might as well speak. Maybe I could wrangle some sort of information from him. "I'm not scared, just trying to decide if you're actually worth the effort."

"Ah, I heard that you had a smart mouth." He *tsked.* "Very unbecoming of a lady."

I let disdain drip from each word. "I'm sure I'll lose sleep tonight over disappointing you."

"See, that's what's wrong with having a female who thinks she's destined to be alpha. You don't respect the natural balance of the hierarchy."

No. He *didn't* just go there. "You mean I should be willing to submit to any male wolf?"

"Exactly." He scoffed. "This whole women's rights movement doesn't work, especially in the supernatural world."

This guy was a dick and the exact reason Dad had been so hard on me growing up. Assholes like him had to be put in their place, and I couldn't wait to be the one to teach him that lesson. "Yet, you're the one hiring people to come after me while you stay behind, all safe and snug in your secret hideout."

"There are reasons for that," he growled. "And none of them have to do with me actually being worried that you could best me. There's a lot at stake here, more than you even know."

"All I'm hearing is that you all are too scared to let your identities be known." This situation had been one hot mess after another— along with many different races getting involved—which made it even more complicated.

Maybe you shouldn't goad him? Griffin frowned, as concern flowed from him through our mate bond.

He wanted to protect me, but this person wasn't going to stop. Whether I spoke to him or not, whoever was behind this would continue to come for me. They had this grand plan that centered around me; they wanted to control the silver wolf population. We had to figure out the end game—if we could do that, it should help us determine who might be pulling the strings. *If I anger him enough, he might reveal something, or react without thinking. It's the best strategy we have right now.*

"We aren't scared, and our identities will come out sooner rather than later." The guy sounded amused, not angry. "I applaud your efforts to rile me up. However, you have no clue what you're up against. If you're free, that means Samuel failed, which is unacceptable. Death is a blessing compared to the punishment he would have received for coming back empty-handed."

The reference to Samuel killing himself was clear. This guy was feeling me out—trying to determine if the bear shifter had given up anything. I wouldn't let him know that the bear shifter wasn't alive any longer.

"Noted." I inhaled sharply. "I'll relay the message to Samuel for you."

"Oh, is he near?" His tone took on an edge. "I'd love to hear his voice to confirm he's still alive."

"Why would I do you any favors?" He was calling my bluff. We were in a game of chess where we were trying to outsmart one another.

"Because I don't believe you have him." The guy chuckled. "He's too smart to do something that would negatively impact his family. Well, this conversation has been fun, but I've got other pressing things to attend to. I'll talk to you soon."

Now the bear being desperate enough to kill himself made sense. He'd been protecting his family, just as Carter was trying to protect his brother. Whoever we were up against was heartless and cruel. They didn't mind taking whoever they needed to in order to get their pawns to comply. Though, I imagined the bear shifter's family *wasn't* safe. We needed to locate these assholes so we could free everyone they'd taken prisoner.

Before my finger hit the red hang-up button, the guy spoke again, "Oh, and Sterlyn."

The fact that he dropped my name made me uneasy. He was about to say something that would trip me up. My gut screamed a warning, but there wasn't a damn thing I could do. "Yeah?"

"Tell the Shadow City alpha and the Shadow Ridge alpha that I said hi." He ended the call; the silence was harsh—a screaming in my ear.

He wanted the shock value, and he'd gotten it.

"There were so many things wrong with that conversation." Sierra walked past me and paced in front of my bed. "No one thought it might be a good idea to tell me that Sterlyn is a fucking silver wolf?"

"No one was supposed to find out. Only Atticus was supposed to know we still existed." I had no idea how this group had found out about us, but being slaughtered and attacked reaffirmed that our ancestors were right to have hidden us. We'd wanted no part of the corruption that had taken over the supernatural world. We'd kept to ourselves and stayed peaceful so that others wouldn't try to use us as pawns.

Guess that hadn't worked out so well.

"Everyone thought the silver wolf was a myth." Sierra shook her head. "You're one of the strongest supernatural beings there are, which is why these people want to capture you. But why did they kill off the entire pack? You'd think they would want to control all the silver wolves."

There was no use keeping things hidden from her at this point. She knew my secret, so I might as well fill in the gaps—especially since she was in harm's way now. "Because we could kill them if we decided to fight, and my father would refuse to work with them."

"Then why not kill you, too?" She waved her hands like she had a sword. "It doesn't make sense."

"They plan to use me as a breeder." A shiver ran down my spine as Sierra gasped. "And break me so I'll submit to whoever is in charge."

"Which is never going to happen." Griffin pulled me against his chest and wrapped his arms around me.

"He purposely dropped that he knew Griffin and I were with you." Killian cracked his knuckles as he nibbled on his bottom lip. "Which means someone must have realized we found you."

I hadn't considered that. The thought sat like a hard lump in my stomach. "You're right. We probably need to get back to Shadow Ridge soon since they could see if we were hiding here." But there were still some spots unturned in my dad's office. "Let's finish searching the house. Maybe Killian and Sierra could keep an eye out to make sure no one comes through before we're ready to go."

"Yeah, we should probably get out there now, after that call." Killian stepped into the hallway and looked at Sierra. "Let's warm up the leftover pizza and load Sterlyn's things into the vehicles. That way, if someone comes, we can leave."

"Let me pack some stuff." There was no reason to leave here without my clothes and personal items. It would save me a ton of money.

"Sounds like a plan," Sierra said, as she followed Killian down the hallway.

Sighing, I grabbed two duffel bags from under my bed and began filling them with all of the essential things I needed.

"DID YOU FIND ANYTHING?" Griffin asked, as he slammed the drawer to the last cabinet he'd searched through in my dad's office.

"No." I'd dug through the entire desk multiple times, hoping to find *something* that could hint to who could be behind the attacks, but nothing looked even a little bit promising. Most of it was bills and a few piddly things that had to do with the land surrounding us. As I'd guessed, the town's land had been passed down over generations, and he had several offers from people wanting to purchase it from us.

"That's so strange." Griffin glanced around the walls. "Dad's office was like this too. He handled a lot of political stuff, but when Mom and I looked through his files, it was like he hadn't kept any paperwork on the packs and Shadow City."

"Well, he knew where we were located. The knowledge had to pass down somehow." My gut said there had to be something that had gone unfound or was missing. Dad was paranoid—always thinking about ways to hide things in case something happened—and we were found; that told me that he had information secretly hidden somewhere. We had lived here for centuries—something of importance *had* to have been kept here, somewhere.

"At the time I didn't know that...but yeah, exactly." Griffin stood behind me and rubbed my shoulders. "You're tense."

"Being drugged and kidnapped after losing your entire pack will do that to you," I bit out, and immediately regretted being a bitch to him. None of this was his fault, but my nerves were frayed. "I'm sorry. I have no right to talk to you that way." I was also on edge from expecting Killian to call at any moment telling us to move, but luckily, he hadn't. We had at least a little more time to look—I just didn't know where else to search.

"Hey, it's okay." He kissed my forehead as his fingers dug deeper, working out the knots.

The pressure both hurt and felt amazing, relaxing me enough to clear my mind. "Maybe we're thinking about this all wrong." If I knew Dad like I thought I did, he wouldn't leave information where someone could easily find it. He'd leave enough—like the land offers —to make people think that was all there was.

Like I almost had.

Griffin's hands stilled. "He'd have a hidden compartment or location."

"Exactly." But where the hell would that be? I looked around the room for something that seemed a little out of place.

Nothing stood out.

"Maybe it's not in this room." Griffin dropped his hands. "This would be kind of a dead giveaway location-wise, right?"

"I bet it'd be in their bedroom." I had avoided going into their room so far, but fate kept nudging me that way. She must have a sick sense of humor.

"Do you want me to look?" Griffin squeezed my arm. "You don't have to go in there if you don't want to."

The fact that I would love to take him up on the offer proved that this was something I had to do. "Yeah, but I'm going with you." I wouldn't have been strong enough to do it on my own.

"Are you sure?" Griffin tucked a stray piece of my hair behind my ear. "I don't mind looking alone if you aren't ready."

"I can't keep letting their deaths impact me this much." I would never get over losing them, but I had to face reality. "Otherwise, these guys will continue to have leverage over me, and that's not acceptable."

"You're stronger than anyone I've ever known," he whispered, placing a hand on my cheek. "You make me want to be a better man."

I couldn't keep the giggle from bubbling out. "Really? You're going that cheesy?"

"Any other girl would've loved to hear words like that from me." He lifted his chin, pretending to be upset. "But not you. You always make me work for it, even when I mean what I say."

"No, that's sweet." Even though he was trying to keep our conversation lighthearted, I could feel a little bit of hurt wafting through our bond. "I'm sorry. I just never thought I'd hear you say something like that, especially since the first time you spoke to me, you informed me you only liked your cream in one place."

He grimaced and closed his eyes. "Please don't remind me of that. That was definitely not my finest moment."

"No, it definitely was not." I pecked him on the lips and smiled. "And yet, here we are."

"I wouldn't trade it for anything," he said, as he winked and took my hand. "Come on, let's go see if we can find anything."

The moment of lightheartedness vanished, and I followed his lead. We did need to finish our search.

I headed to the very last doorway in the hall. My hands grew sweaty as I reached for the doorknob. I wasn't ready for this—I never would be. I was going to have to push through.

Trying not to overthink it, I opened the door. My parents' bed was made, the navy-blue comforter, wrinkle-free, contrasted with the white bed frame. The sky-blue walls made the room feel too bright for the staggering hole they'd left behind. My heart fractured further, feeling the pain of their loss even more in the moment.

"Any idea where they would hide something?" Griffin entered the room, running his hand along the wall.

"No." But at least there weren't any cabinets or desks to go through.

I scanned the room, trying to think like my dad. He was always so straightforward and said what he meant.

Griffin walked around the room, stepping purposefully on various parts of the floor. He listened to the noises the floorboards made, trying to find a spot that sounded more hollow. He bent over and knocked on a low portion of the wall. His gray boxers peeked out from his jeans.

Some of Dad's words of wisdom played inside my brain. He'd always told me that people's underwear drawers held the best secrets; that they could tell you more about a person than anything else. I'd always thought the comment was odd and would roll my eyes, exclaiming he was weird.

Wait.

What if that had been a clue? I might be losing my mind, but...at this point, what did we have to lose?

I rushed to his chest of drawers. The underwear drawer was at the very bottom. I pulled it open, then moved his boxers out of the way.

Gross. I tried not to think about touching my father's underwear as the bottom of the drawer came into view. I inhaled sharply as the outline of a hidden compartment became visible. Had I not been looking for it, I would've missed it. With a shaky hand, I dug my fingernails into one side and lifted.

I couldn't believe my eyes. Documents and a photo album sat inside.

Griffin's phone rang, startling me back to the present.

"It's Killian," he rasped as he answered the phone. "Hello?"

"There are cars heading this way," Killian yelled.

CHAPTER EIGHT

DAMMIT. They'd figured out that we were here—but how? My first thought was Carter, but it didn't feel right. He'd seemed genuinely sorry for betraying me, but maybe that was remorse for being caught instead of for helping me get kidnapped.

I could stew on the how later. The looming threat was all that mattered right now. We had to get out of here without any more deaths, and before the enemy trapped us.

"How many vehicles are there?" Griffin asked as he stepped over next to me.

"Four huge SUVs. You two need to get out and into your car, now —they'll be here in minutes. We're heading your way."

Of course, they were. At least I'd found Dad's stash, even though it would've been nice to figure out the riddle earlier; we could've bypassed this encounter. Thankfully, we weren't leaving empty-handed. "I think I've found what we were looking for." It'd be nice to confirm it by looking through the stuff, but we didn't have time. I had to trust my instinct. Dad wouldn't have hidden something if he didn't think it was valuable.

"Why am I not surprised?" Griffin kissed my cheek, as he glanced around the room. "You're kind of amazing. Let's find something to put it in."

"Let's not go overboard with the compliments." I was definitely not amazing—if I were, we wouldn't be in our current situation. I stood and picked up the drawer. "And we don't have time to pack it. We're taking it as is." I rushed out the door and headed down the hall-way. Thankfully, the vehicles were already loaded, so we just needed to get in and go.

Griffin followed me, and I heard the jangle of the keys as he pulled them from his pocket.

As I entered the living room, the front door opened, and Killian's strained face appeared. He glanced at the drawer and then at Griffin and me. "Come on. They're pulling into the neighborhood now."

"Do we know how many there are?" I jogged past him and stepped outside.

I glanced at his truck, finding Sierra in the driver's seat. Her hands clutched the wheel, and her chest heaved with each breath. She looked petrified, and I kind of hated that Killian had included her in our mess.

They'd lump her in with me now, which meant there was no telling what the enemy would do to her family. It was clear that they weren't above hurting or abusing innocent people to get what they wanted.

Enough people had been hurt or threatened because of me, and I hated to add another person to the ever-growing list.

"I have no clue," Killian answered as Griffin ran outside.

Griffin pressed the unlock button on his key fob and the car doors clicked. I rushed to open the passenger door and set the drawer on the floorboard. Fortunately, the vehicles hadn't turned down the dead-end road yet and hadn't seen that we'd carried something out, and they probably wouldn't be looking for anything in the car.

"Let's go," Griffin commanded as he hurried to the driver's side door and opened it. He leaned over the seat like he was searching for something.

The sounds of engines rumbled, and the vehicles took the turn and rushed toward us. One of the windows rolled down, and the barrel of a gun poked out, aiming in our direction.

Shit. We would be huge targets in the vehicles.

"We need to go into the woods." Everything inside me screamed to get into the car and go, but the protector side knew it was a horrible idea. If we tried, they would blow out our tires, and then we'd be even more at their mercy. I couldn't let panic take over. "Otherwise, we're sitting ducks. The trees will offer some protection."

As if reinforcing my words, the gun fired, and a bullet hit the back tire of Killian's truck. Air poured out as the vehicle drooped.

"Dammit." Killian opened the passenger door and yelled, "Sierra, crawl over here and get out *now*."

Don't press the lock button on the fob, or they'll wonder why we cared enough to lock the vehicle. I pressed the lock button on the inside of the door panel so the horn wouldn't beep, and then slammed it shut.

Griffin shut the driver's door and ran toward me. He took my hand and tugged me toward the trees. "We've got to move."

The tires squealed as the vehicles came to a harsh stop.

We were about to run out of time. Killian and Sierra ran past the Navigator, and Griffin and I ran hard behind them.

A few shots were fired and hit the ground beside us, breaking up dirt.

We ran at an angle, using our cars for coverage. Car doors opened as the enemies climbed out in hot pursuit.

At least I was on land that I knew all too well. Worst case—if we had to—we could run all the way back to Shadow Ridge, but that would be hard with the four of us. When I had been alone, they'd almost caught me. With four of us, it would be a miracle if we all got away.

A loud *caw* sounded overhead, and I looked into the sky to find a black crow hovering there. It paused directly over me, flapping like it was taunting me. It held a branch in its talons and dropped it, making a faint *crack*. The crow cawed again, mocking me.

Dammit, we hadn't been alone when we'd arrived here, after all. That branch I'd heard must have been the crow. I'd been so focused on a threat at ground level that I hadn't thought about looking in the damn trees. I should've known better, but the emotional strain of being here had gotten the better of me—that was why I hadn't sensed anything out of the ordinary. The bird had been God knew how high in the sky, so I couldn't smell it.

At least that told me that whoever it was didn't live close by. Granted, they'd have to take time to group and get here, but if they lived in a city close by, they would've gotten here during the night.

Killing that dumbass bird jumped even higher on my priority list. He had flown under the radar way too many times, but I wouldn't make that mistake again. At least, Carter hadn't betrayed us again. That was the silver lining, if there was one.

"We all need to split up," one of the enemies commanded. "Remember, do not kill the girl, but stop her by any means necessary."

So in other words, shoot, but not to kill.

"What about the other three?" another man asked, bullets jangling as he loaded his gun.

"They don't matter," the first man responded. "Our mission is to get the girl."

Follow me. At some point, we would need to split up—but right now, I needed to get us far enough away that we all could talk. The first priority was getting past the crow.

I took off running deeper into the woods. A small cave sat about four hundred yards away that we should be able to use for shelter for at least a little while.

The three of them ran after me. I zigzagged, hoping to confuse the crow. Its wings flapped overhead, confirming what I already knew...it was tracking us to alert the idiots.

We were going to have to split up. We couldn't shake the crow.

Coming to a stop, I faced the other three and spoke quietly. We'd gained enough distance from our pursuers that if we talked softly enough, they wouldn't be able to hear. "We need to split up. That damn crow is following us. I'd hoped to hide out in a nearby cave for a little while until their group split up to look for us, but that won't work."

"So, what do we do?" Sierra asked with trepidation.

I took a deep breath so I wouldn't snap at her. It was clear that the only one besides myself with any sort of training was Killian. But Sierra was here, trying to help, and I had to remember that. She was definitely proving her loyalty. "First off, what weapons do we have?" I bent and pulled my knife from my ankle sheath.

"Even though I didn't want to, I did bring something when you went missing." Killian lifted his shirt, revealing a gun.

If I wasn't mated to Griffin and didn't consider Killian a brother, I would've kissed him right then. I'd expected to be the only one with a weapon. "Anyone else?"

"Believe it or not, me too." Griffin pulled out a gun from his waistband. "I'm learning that, when it comes to you, we all need to be prepared."

"What?" I couldn't believe my eyes. "How the hell did I not know you had that on you?" We'd had sex the night before, and he hadn't had it then. It was like it appeared out of thin air.

"It was in the Navigator," he said with pride. "That's why I opened the door in the first place."

We actually had a better chance with two guns. The men tracking us wouldn't expect that, based on the last several fights they'd had with us. We'd never had guns in the pack before; only the handful of our guards that they'd taken out had carried them.

"Do you know how to shoot?" I didn't mean to come off condescending. Griffin was a strong wolf and a good fighter in animal form...the problem was when he was in human form. He didn't have strong skills then—although, that one punch he'd given Carter had shown good form.

"Yes...believe it or not, I do." Griffin sighed. "I didn't grow up training for battle, only politics, but the Shadow City leaders are all about target practice for leisure."

I'd take any wins we could get. "Okay, then let's split into two groups." I'd initially thought we'd all four separate, but that would be too risky—especially with Sierra weaponless. Killian was a trained fighter, so it made sense for her to go with him. "Griffin and I will stay together. You two head off that way." I pointed in the direction we'd been heading. "If you stay straight, it'll take you to a cave that you can use for cover. If you go to the side where the opening backs up to a wall, there's a section that's covered all around except for in front of you. You can use it to keep these guys at bay."

"What about you two?" Killian frowned. "We could all go there together."

"The cave isn't large enough for all four of us." We didn't have time to debate everything. "And if they stay grouped together, they can strategize more. If they split up, they can't make as much of a coordinated effort. You've gotta assume they have tranquilizer guns and can mind link. We can't."

"She knows the area and is a fucking silver wolf. She was born for this kind of thing." Sierra took a step in the direction I'd indicated. "And the longer we stay here, the faster they'll find us."

"Fine, but text us if you get in trouble." Killian hugged me tightly. "And please don't get captured." His body was rigid with tension and concern.

"Same to you two." I returned the embrace.

The sound of footsteps broke the moment. The enemy was coming, and faster than I'd given them credit for. Not willing to speak again, I gestured toward the cave.

Killian nodded and patted Griffin on the back before taking off. He and Sierra kept in step with each other as they ran in the direction I'd told them to.

Any ideas for us? Griffin held the gun at his side with his finger on the trigger.

I moved southward, away from Killian and Sierra, making sure our enemies would hear us and split. Even though I was their end goal, they'd have to keep an eye on the other two. No fighter would ignore two people who could be threats. *Unfortunately, there isn't a spot like that for us. We're going to have to run so they'll at least split up, and then fight.*

As if they'd figured out our plan, their footsteps paused, and the leader spoke quietly, "They split up. It's clear the silver wolf went that way, so let's separate. This half goes with me, and the rest of you follow Bo's lead."

They were speaking out loud, which made me think that maybe they weren't pack, either. At least this put us on more equal grounds.

"Got it," a guy responded, and half the group moved in the opposite direction from us.

"From here on out, we don't talk," the leader commanded. "We need to be as quiet as possible to try to surprise them." The group took off again, but they were noisier, probably because they didn't know the terrain. Luckily, they wouldn't get the drop on us.

Is there a way we can round them up or lock them in somewhere? Griffin kept pace with me.

I wished there was somewhere like that, but it was going to be hand-to-hand combat. *We can get to the river so no one can sneak up behind us. I could maybe shift and have them focus on me so you can pick them off one at a time.*

In other words, use you as bait? Griffin's anger was palpable through the bond. *Hell, no. Unacceptable. Absolutely not.*

The problem was this wasn't up for debate. *They're gunning for me...the rest of you are collateral damage. We have to think strategically. If we dangle me in front of them, they'll be more focused on capturing me than hurting you. It's our best chance of making it out with minimal injuries.*

Griffin growled. *It sounds like you've already made up your mind.*

Having him upset with me didn't sit well. This was our first disagreement, but I knew using me as bait was our best and safest strategy. I owed it to all of us to take the least risky approach. *If things get too dicey, I promise to shift back to human and fight alongside you.*

The suggestion seemed to appease the beast, and his anger receded. *Okay. I'm not thrilled with this suggestion, but I trust you. If you think this is best, I'll go along with it. Just...please don't make me regret it.*

My heart warmed. *Thank you. I'm going to shift now, but take my knife so I don't lose it.*

I handed him the knife and sheath, and he put it in his pocket.

The sound of our pursuers' feet hadn't gotten any closer—probably because they were moving slower, making sure they kept on our trail. They hadn't caught wind of us yet, which was miraculous.

Not bothering to strip, I called my wolf forward. She obliged willingly, sensing the trouble we were in.

My bones cracked as I shifted from human to wolf, and my skin tingled as fur sprouted all over my body. My clothes ripped away, and soon I stood on four legs.

A loud *caw* grated on my nerves, followed by the flapping of wings.

I lifted my head to see the crow flying over us, making enough racket that the enemy wolves would be able to find us. He hadn't made that move until I shifted, which meant he knew I was up to something.

I'd hoped to be closer to the water before they picked up our trail. *I can't wait to kill that bird. Maybe you can shoot it.*

It would be my pleasure. Griffin kept pace beside me.

If we ever got some downtime and I could work with Griffin, he would be an excellent fighter in both wolf and human form. Maybe when we got out of this horrible situation, I'd demand we take time for him to train. It'd be good for both of us—it would help me maintain my skills, and he would learn some important moves that would help in situations like this one.

The enemy heard us and moved faster, as if not worried about sneaking up on us anymore.

We weren't going to make it to the water, but we at least knew no one was circling around us. I stopped running and turned in the direction they would appear.

It was time to fight, and I prayed that Griffin was a good shot.

CHAPTER NINE

THE ENEMY WAS close enough that I could hear each intake of breath. Being in wolf form amplified my senses, and I could make out ten distinct gaits that raced toward us.

Killian was right about the numbers. I was mildly impressed that he'd read the situation so accurately—I wouldn't have been correct if someone had asked me to predict how many people would come after us. *Ten are approaching us. With the way they're shuffling, there are two in front, so we'll need to take them out fast. If we do, it should make the others hesitate.*

Okay. Griffin aimed his gun in the direction they would appear. *I've got this,* he reassured me...and himself.

My confidence in his ability faltered, but I held my doubt close, not wanting him to feel it through our bond. If he had to talk himself up, that meant either he wasn't sure he could pull the trigger, or he was that inexperienced. Either way, doubt was dangerous in war, and whether we liked it or not, these battles were leading up to just that.

I threw my head back and howled. The enemy felt invigorated and in control; they knew their numbers and weapons exceeded ours. We had to hit fast and hard to show them that we weren't afraid at all.

As expected, their pace slowed. They hadn't expected me to alert them to where we were, and I'd thrown them off.

Good, my plan was already working.

"At least one of them has shifted," one of the men whispered, but he might as well have spoken in his normal voice. "Do you think it's her?" His voice raised in trepidation.

"Shhh," the leader hissed and slowed down.

One of the enemies was scared enough to speak out loud, confirming they weren't part of the same pack, which would make the situation even more problematic long-term—but in our current circumstances, it would help.

If multiple packs were working together, they'd have more resources at their disposal. That thought made my stomach sour. At some point, we had to get on even ground with them. They knew a whole hell of a lot about me, but I knew very little about them. If we wanted a chance at succeeding, we needed to figure all this out...and fast.

The crow flew several feet above my head, making a ton of noise. He was giving away my exact location. That bird was the gift that kept on giving. I couldn't wait to return the favor. I still relished the idea of plucking out each feather, one by one. After all of the pain and suffering he'd put us through, that kind of torture seemed fitting.

The footsteps sped up now that they had a little bit going in their favor again.

That damn bird has got to go, Griffin rasped.

A loud gunshot rang out, and the crow screeched before dropping. His dead body fell right in front of my face, landing mere inches from my body.

Holy shit. Griffin had shot the bastard...and he'd hit him on the first try. He was a good shot, after all.

Comforted that we might have a chance, I focused on the trees the enemies would soon be crashing through. I was a little disappointed that I hadn't been the one to kill the crow, but at least he was dead. That definitely leveled the playing field.

The enemy was upon us, and the first one stepped through the trees. I growled, bringing his attention to me and not Griffin. The fur at my ruff stood up as I let every bit of my anger shine through.

He swung the gun at me, aiming for my shoulder, but Griffin shot immediately—the bullet hitting between the man's eyes. He fell hard with a resounding thud.

"What the—" someone gasped from behind the tree.

"Don't just stand there," another one said, "*move.*"

Chaos descended among them, and two men charged into the area.

Knowing they would be looking for the gun, I lunged toward them, forcing them to pay attention to me. One guy tripped over the man who was already dead, as the second guy swung his gun toward me and pulled the trigger.

Move right! Griffin yelled, and I listened, jumping to the side.

The bullet missed me by inches, and Griffin fired two shots, one after another, each hitting its mark. Both were kill-shots in the same place as the first. Griffin had taken out three men.

"What do we do?" one guy blubbered.

"Attack, dumbass," the leader barked. "Now!"

Get behind a tree and use it as coverage, because they're going to try to take you out now. I needed to know he was protected. I pivoted in his direction as Griffin raced behind the largest nearby tree. Most of his body was covered—the only part visible, his hand holding the gun.

Three more enemies stumbled toward us, and, as I'd suspected, neither glanced my way. That worked, too, because I could get closer and take a few out. If we injured them to the point of not fighting, we could get the hell out of here.

I wished there was a way to handle this without killing, but if Griffin didn't shoot to kill, we'd be overrun in seconds. My dad always told me that the fact that we didn't relish killing made the silver wolves different...and after going through all I had, I agreed. I couldn't kill that bear shifter when he was lying on the ground all vulnerable; I couldn't kill maliciously like that. Granted, he still wound up dead, but that was a whole different scenario.

The taller of the three had his gun aimed at Griffin the quickest, which meant he was the one I needed to take out. He fired a shot at my mate before Griffin could respond.

Are you okay? I asked, as I lunged at the guy's gun hand. The other four men were already moving in this direction, probably realizing that coming one by one was allowing us to pick them off more easily.

Griffin fired as he responded. *Yes, thank God you told me to get behind the tree.*

The taller guy looked at me right as my teeth sank into his wrist. His eyes widened as he yanked his arm back, but it was too late; he released his hold on the gun, and it fell. His other hand came around and punched my face, causing my jaw to slacken enough for him to pull his wrist out.

I snarled as his blood dripped down my chin. My jaw throbbed, but with my shifter healing, I'd be better within minutes. All I needed to do was weaken as many of them as I could so Griffin could take them out.

Arms wrapped my neck with the butt of a gun digging into my throat as another enemy attacked me. He tightened his arms, trying to cut off my oxygen. I grew dizzy, and if I didn't get out of his hold soon, I'd faint.

Extending the claws on my hind legs, I kicked the asshole in the stomach, digging the nails in as deep as I could get them to go.

He grunted in pain and released his hold. I slashed his skin as I stood back on four legs, and the guy tripped over a tree root and fell. With shaky arms, he raised his gun, and my instincts took over. I bit into his neck, ripping it out.

His body convulsed before going limp.

My heart hurt, but I didn't allow myself to whimper or show any regret. The others would attempt to use my sympathetic side to their advantage, and they didn't need more leverage.

Gunshots fired as our last four enemies joined the fight. I scanned the area to find one left from the last batch locked on Griffin. There was a total of five who were still standing, and they were coordinating their attack.

Instead of attacking just one, I needed to cause pandemonium and swipe at everyone. That way, all of them would have to keep an eye on me.

Unsure what I was going to do, I tried not to overthink it. I charged at each man, running into them before moving on to the next. I kicked my legs and bucked my body, imitating a bull.

All of my years of training had officially been flushed down the toilet.

Griffin continued to fire as I distracted as many of them as I could.

"What the hell is she doing?" the leader grumbled as I kicked a leg higher and hit his face. My claws slashed his cheek, and blood welled up.

"You stupid bitch," he spat and swung the butt of his gun toward my head.

Nope...I already got nailed there once, and it still hurt. I wouldn't allow myself to be injured a second time. I threw my body into his, which made the gun miss my head—barely—but his forearm hit me instead. It hurt, but not nearly as bad as if it had been metal.

Lowering my head even more, I bulldozed the leader into one of the tree trunks.

Duck, Griffin commanded.

Obeying, I dropped and looked upward as his gun fired. A bullet buzzed over my head and into the leader's heart. He jerked as his eyes widened. He glanced at his chest and then focused on me. He lifted his gun, ready to shoot me—but then his head bobbled to the side, and he slumped against the tree.

I spun around to find my next target and realized that there was only one remaining. The guy must have noticed the same thing because he turned and ran back in the direction they'd come from.

No, we couldn't let him get away—we might get some answers out of him. I chased after him, and he glanced over his shoulder at me. Seeing that I was catching up, his face hardened in determination. He reached for his belt buckle, and I knew exactly what he was going to do.

The same thing that damn bear shifter did. He even kept it in the same place.

I pushed my legs harder, urging myself to get to him before he took the damn pill. Once he got it in his mouth, there was no taking it back.

He spun around and fired. The bullet lodged in my shoulder. My leg crumpled underneath me, and I skidded into the ground.

I howled and linked with Griffin, *He's about to kill himself.*

What? Griffin sounded surprised. *I'm hurrying.*

But he wouldn't get there in time.

I forced myself to stand, my leg throbbing with sharp, excruciating pain. But I somehow managed to hobble toward him.

"I'm so sorry, but I had no choice." The enemy put the pill in his mouth and a tear dripped down his face. "You have no clue who you're up against."

Ugh. I wanted to ask questions, but I was in animal form and couldn't communicate with him. He seemed like a decent guy who'd been put in an impossible situation. I was beginning to see a common theme.

His body shook as the drug worked into his system. There was no saving him now.

My eyes burned, and my throat constricted with frustration and anger at whoever had created this mess. All of these people we'd killed might not have been here truly willingly, but at the end of the day, their goal was still the same.

Capture me.

Kill the others.

They'd forced us to do whatever was necessary to survive. Letting these men capture me would only make whoever the enemy was stronger and would cause even more unrest and hate to spread throughout our world.

Griffin raced toward me and stopped short when he saw the blood dripping from my shoulder. *I felt you were in pain. What happened?* He dropped to his knees and examined my wound. *Did you get shot?*

Yes, but I'll be fine. It was superficial, but I needed the bullet removed. *Do you have a way to get the bullet out? It's not deep.*

No. His jaw twitched. *I've got nothing but keys and a gun.*

You have my knife. I nodded to his pocket. *Use it and get it out before I heal. It'll hurt worse if we do it later, and if I shift to human with the bullet still inside, it could make my injury worse. I need to shift back to human form now that we have their guns so we can help Killian and Sierra.*

Fine. He placed his gun beside him and pulled out my knife. He inhaled sharply and cracked his neck.

If I wasn't in so much pain, I'd have laughed. He looked as if he was preparing for battle.

He held the knife right at the edge of the entry wound, and I forced myself to look at the fallen man, who had died while we were preoccupied. Bubbles poured out of his mouth and down his face.

On the count of—

Just do it. I didn't want to know when. Anticipation was not my friend right now.

Griffin stuck the knife in, and pain coursed throughout my shoulder. I'd thought getting shot wouldn't hurt much, but I'd been so damn wrong. A whimper escaped me, and I was at the pain's mercy.

The edges of my vision grew dark as Griffin dug around for the bullet.

Maybe I should pull out, he said as he paused.

We've already gotten this far. I took deep breaths, trying to prevent myself from passing out, and attempting to keep nausea at bay. If I got sick, I wouldn't be able to help Killian and Sierra.

Griffin continued his efforts, and his guilt and concern flowed into me, making my already raw emotions even more frayed.

I feel it, he said excitedly. *I've got it.*

Then get it out. I groaned.

He angled the blade—cutting the wound larger—but within seconds, the bullet fell out, and the knife finally exited my body.

I sagged with relief. Even though the pain was still excruciating, it didn't come close to how it'd felt with the knife inside me. *Thank you.*

Let's make a pact that this is the last time you get shot. Griffin rolled the bloody bullet between his fingers while his other hand ran through my fur, making my skin buzz from our connection.

It'd be nice to sit here and enjoy the peace and quiet, but we needed to find Killian and Sierra. We hadn't heard anything from them.

Can you take the guy's shirt off him? I asked. I had ripped my clothes, not considering that we'd have access to extra guns, and I'd need to be able to use one. *I want to shift back so we can grab some of their guns to go help Killian and Sierra...and I'd rather not be completely naked.*

Griffin growled, *Hell no. You're wearing mine.* He pulled his hunter-green shirt from his body as I shifted back into my human form. His abs contracted, making my body warm at a very inappropriate time. I looked away, needing to keep my head on straight and not drool.

When I was on two legs, he helped me put on the shirt without using my injured arm too much. The garment was huge on me, and the hem hit around my knees, much like a dress.

Being shorter came in handy, at least for the moment.

When I felt comfortable, I bent down to pick up the dead man's gun. "Now let's go help our friends."

CHAPTER TEN

I HATED the way the gun fit into my hand. Weapons like these went against my animal instincts because they were the opposite of natural. They tore down communities and more, but they were highly effective in battle.

That reason alone was why Dad had trained us with firearms. He had emphasized that learning to fight with them was just as essential as learning to fight without them. He was right...but I hated the fact that we might have to use them again if we were all going to come out of this alive.

I preferred a bow and arrow, but there weren't any on hand, and they were bulkier to carry.

We needed to get to Killian and Sierra, but grabbing a few more guns might be worth taking a few extra minutes. Even though my shoulder throbbed, I pushed through the pain. *Let's go grab another gun each.*

Not waiting for him to respond, I turned and ran back toward the others we'd killed. Griffin ran close behind me, his anxiety flowing through our bond. He probably never expected to go through something like this, and here I'd waltzed into his world, turning his entire life upside down. I couldn't help but think that maybe he would've been better off if we hadn't met. He'd almost died once and was already in another battle—not even three days later. If we hadn't stumbled upon each other, he would probably be sitting at Dick's bar with Killian and Luna, drinking a beer.

Despite the thought being hypothetical, flames of jealousy flickered through me. I hated that Luna had gotten her claws into Griffin for so long. We hadn't seen her since the night she'd shown up drunk at his house, but she had clearly intended to hurt, if not kill me. Had I not caused her to fall into Killian's pool, there was no telling how that confrontation would've ended. Granted, she'd almost drowned because I hadn't realized she was that far gone until it was too late. Killian had jumped in and saved her.

I ran through the last section of trees. Looking at the bodies littered across the ground made my heart hurt, and somehow looked even more gruesome than I remembered. So many of these deaths could've been prevented.

Squatting next to the closest two bodies, I pried the guns from their cool hands—I could already detect the faint smell of decay. Holding my breath, I turned and handed another gun to Griffin while keeping two for myself.

Griffin's fingers brushed my bullet wound.

Blood had soaked through the green shirt in that spot, and there was still an ache, but it was dulling. Silver wolves healed faster than any other shifter, and even faster than vampires when they drank blood. With a wound this deep and irritated, it'd probably take a day or two for it to be completely healed, but I should be able to move without wincing by tonight.

Maybe you should rest. Griffin's eyes deepened to a brown. *You can head back to the Navigator while I get them out.*

No way in hell would I let that happen. They were still grossly outnumbered, and even though Griffin was an amazing shot, I couldn't, in good conscience, run to safety while the three of them were in danger. *I'm fine. I promise.* I kissed him, taking an extra moment to reassure him. He had been almost panicked with worry ever since I got shot. *It's already not hurting as bad.* I slowly peeled the shirt away from the wound. *See, the bleeding has already slowed.*

In other words, you're refusing to stay behind. Griffin huffed as he caressed my face. *Fine, but if it starts hurting worse or bleeding again, promise me you'll let me take the lead.*

Promise. I couldn't deny him that, as long as I was there with him.

The air remained sulfur-free, which caused him to relax marginally.

Now, let's go. I was chomping to get away from all the dead people, as well as check on Killian and Sierra. If I wasn't worried about their cell phone distracting them or giving away their location, I'd have been texting them now. But we had to go in blind.

We sprinted through the woods in the direction of the cave.

The sound of shots firing echoed all around. I hadn't even noticed that it had been quiet until then. Maybe they weren't in over their heads yet.

I held my arm close to my side, attempting to ease the jarring of my steps. I gritted my teeth, trying to make sure that Griffin couldn't feel my discomfort. I planned on keeping my promise, but the pain wasn't unbearable...

At least, not yet.

Ten distinct scents hit me when we intersected the route the enemy had taken to reach our friends. I sniffed and tapped into my wolf so I could maintain a decent speed. Soon, Killian's and Sierra's scents mixed with theirs, which wasn't surprising. The enemy had been tracking them after all.

Unlike what I'd told them to do, Killian and Sierra seemed to have run in some sort of random pattern. There were sections where their smells veered off in two different directions. Killian must have been trying to confuse the enemy on where their end goal was by having them run in circles.

The tactic was smart but risky. They were lucky that the others hadn't figured it out and caught them before they got to the cave. But it must have bought them some time, and was probably the reason the fight had just started.

We need to move quietly. The men stalking them would be more focused on what was in front of them instead of behind. They'd expect their friends to have taken us down. *Where's my knife?* I stopped and faced Griffin.

Here, he linked and handed it to me, along with the sheath.

I squatted and fastened the sheath around my ankle, already feeling more like myself. For some reason, this knife always made me feel safer. More grounded. Maybe because it had been my grandfather's. *Okay, we should take out as many as we can without shooting.*

Your shoulder, he growled.

I'll use my left hand. We'd been trained to use weapons with both hands, just in case our dominant side was injured. There'd been so many times I'd thought Dad was being dramatic, but all of those lessons were coming in handy now. *It won't be a problem.*

I wished I could tell my dad I was sorry and that he was right. I'd been so disrespectful at times—rolling my eyes and complaining to Zoe about how stupid it all was. Had I known what our future held, I would've taken it all more seriously.

Pivoting in the direction of the cave, I took off slowly. The sheath rubbed my skin a little more than normal because I was barefoot. Not only had my clothes ripped off my body, but so had my shoes. I was able to move more silently than I would have with the rubber soles of my tennis shoes, but I had to take Griffin's footwear into account as well.

Gunshots kept firing, which brought me peace of mind. If the enemy continued to fire, that meant Killian and Sierra were alive. They hadn't been taken out or hurt yet.

"What's the plan?" a guy asked, from not even a quarter-mile ahead. "They've got coverage, and every time we try to move so they're in view, they shoot. I don't know how the hell we're going to get to them."

Thank God my plan was working. Sometimes, even the most well-thought-out plans went awry.

A row of thick bushes appeared a few feet away, and I got down on my hands and knees and crawled toward them. Griffin moved beside me, following my lead, and soon, we were peeking through the branches.

Two enemies were standing about fifty feet away near a large redwood.

"We have to figure it out," the shorter one said hatefully. "We all have too much on the line if we fail. Besides, we don't need some woman alpha thinking she can rule over us. She needs to be put in her place like any bitch with visions of grandeur should be."

He sealed the deal.

Shorty would be my first target. Maybe I should stand over him all alpha-like as he choked on his own blood.

Okay, I didn't mean that. Even the idea of killing that dickhead turned my stomach, but I would kick his ass.

What's the plan? Griffin lifted his gun, aiming for the one on the right.

The problem was I had a hard time with the concept of killing people who weren't even aware that they were in danger. Call me a glutton for punishment, but it just never felt right. *We'll charge them and try to incapacitate them by hand. If they raise their weapons at us, then we shoot in order to survive.*

I love that you don't want to just kill them, but wouldn't that be the safer solution? Griffin asked as he touched my arm, bringing my attention to him.

Then we'd be the same as them. We couldn't throw our humanity aside and kill because they might attack. What if they didn't? Some of these guys didn't have horrible intentions radiating off them. They might be at the mercy of whoever had leverage over them.

Okay. Griffin sighed. *Let's do it your way.*

Our relationship had changed so much in such a short amount of time. He used to argue and fight with me, and now he was giving in because he could sense my inner turmoil. *Let's go. I'll take Shorty and you take the other guy.*

Rising to my feet, I adjusted my grip on the guns in case we had to fire. I couldn't foolishly pretend these men weren't going to attack. In fact, I knew they would, but I had to see it with my own eyes.

The two of them were so focused in front of them that they didn't see us move until the breeze shifted and blew our scents toward them.

Shorty stiffened and turned, his cold, dark eyes focusing on me. He hissed, "Stupid bitch. But this makes the job easier for us." He raised his gun, but before he extended his arm completely, a gun fired, and a bullet hit him between the eyes.

"Bo," the other guy hollered, and he charged at me. "You're going to pay for that."

However, he focused his attention on the wrong person. I wasn't the threat.

The next shot fired, and the guy's eyes widened as he realized his mistake. Griffin fired off two shots, each hitting the center of the enemy's torso. He clutched his chest—as if that would stop the blood—then dropped his gun. Tears streaked his cheeks, and he dropped to his knees as the life began to leave his body.

But I couldn't feel bad. They'd forced our hands. We'd tried not to come at them with weapons first thing.

Forcing myself to turn away now that neither of the men was a threat, I raced with Griffin toward the cave. The gunfire had stopped, and fear dug inside me.

Please let them be alive, I chanted internally, over and over again.

The cave came into view, and I scanned the area for threats. All I found was body after body of the enemy, dead on the forest floor. However, I couldn't see Killian and Sierra from my position. All I saw was the dark opening.

"Who's there?" Killian called out. "Don't take another step toward us or you'll force us to shoot." He could hear us but wasn't able to tell who we were.

I counted bodies and realized that, between the two groups we'd killed, all twenty of our enemies were dead. "It's us. They're all gone."

"Sweet Jesus," Sierra gasped. "I didn't think we were going to make it out alive."

That made two of us. "We need to get out of here in case they have backup coming." If their leader didn't hear back from the crow or someone soon, there was no telling how many people they would send next time.

The two of them stepped from the corner of the outside wall of the cave and into view. Neither appeared injured, so that was another miracle that we all had to be thankful for.

"Why didn't you guys go inside?" I asked.

Killian shook his head. "They were firing right at us, and if we ran in, it would've been directly in the line of fire...so, we found a divot in the side where we could shoot from our angle, and they had to come into our line of fire to see us." Killian frowned when his eyes landed on the spot of blood on my shirt. "What happened?"

"I got hit, but it's already healing." I took Griffin's hand and squeezed lovingly. "Griffin removed the bullet—that's why it took us longer to get back to help you."

"You shouldn't have gotten hit in the first place," Griffin grumbled, as his guilt slammed into me.

"It wasn't your fault." There was no way my injury could've been prevented. He and I had done the best we could under the circumstances.

"Come on." Griffin tugged me back toward the house. "You're right. We need to get moving."

If he thought I'd be dropping this conversation, he'd soon learn differently. But getting the hell out of here had to be our number one priority.

"Grab more of their guns." The more we had, the fewer they had. "At least the ones nearby."

"Good idea." Killian bent down and picked up several guns.

Sierra grabbed one and held it awkwardly away from her body.

"Here, give me that." I took it from her. "You're going to get shot like that, which means you need to learn how to shoot when we get back."

"Uh, I'd rather not." She lifted a hand and blew out a breath like she was relieved that I'd taken it from her.

"Unfortunately, you're lumped in with us now, which means you must learn how to protect yourself." There was no room for negotiation. "Now let's go before we have to fight again."

The four of us trekked through the woods, running as fast as we could with our hands full of weapons. When my house came back into view, I had honestly expected to see more vehicles there, but no one new had shown up. Hope ballooned in my heart that we might get out of here without another battle.

"You two need to ride with us," Griffin commanded as he pulled the keys from his pocket and unlocked the car.

"No, I have fix-a-flat. We can be ready to roll in a few minutes." Killian sped up, running faster than I could with my injury. He reached his truck and got out what looked like a metal canister.

Griffin opened the Navigator's passenger door and helped me get settled. My shoulder screamed at the movement of climbing into the tall car. By the time Griffin jumped into the driver's seat, Killian was done with the tire and getting into the truck, Sierra already buckled in on the passenger side.

We peeled out of the driveway, heading to the neighborhood exit, with Killian squealing right behind us. My breathing grew rapid as we sped around the final turn.

When both vehicles turned onto the main road, racing away from my old home, my heart began to settle. That was until my gaze landed on the drawer that sat between my legs. There was no telling what I might find in there, but there was no time like the present. Who knew if we would make it back to Griffin's home?

I inhaled sharply and bent down, resolved to figure out everything I could from the hidden compartment below.

CHAPTER ELEVEN

GRIFFIN PLACED his hand on my leg, making the buzz of our connection spring to life. "You don't have to look at that now. We just went through hell back there—you can lie back and close your eyes. We'll be home in about fifteen minutes."

Home.

The place we'd left behind had been that to me for eighteen years —but last night, it had felt almost foreign. Maybe because Mom and Dad were missing, and they were what made it home. Or maybe I'd changed so much that I didn't recognize my prior life any longer.

Who knew?

At the end of the day, home was now wherever Griffin and Killian were. The fact that I was so emotionally invested in two people scared me, but what was done couldn't be undone. I loved each man deeply, but for very different reasons. Killian was like a family member I hadn't even known I was missing until I found him. Well, correction... He'd found me floating in the river and on the run for my life.

Griffin... How did I even explain what he was to me? He was the oxygen I craved—needed—and couldn't live without.

"No, I need to." My gut told me that when we got to the house, I'd crash—my eyes were already beginning to droop. And the longer we kept this drawer of secrets, the more likely something could happen to it. These assholes kept coming at us hard, which meant they'd be striking again.

I placed the drawer in my lap and removed the hidden-door compartment. I reached for the small journal and two loose pieces of paper, leaving the photo album for last.

Selecting the brown and yellow stained sheet of paper, I slowly opened the frayed edges. It appeared to be the oldest document of the bunch, so starting there made the most sense.

The letter was handwritten, and I read each word slowly.

ARIAN,

Things are improving slowly in Shadow City. There is still corruption, but the angels are settling into the new normal. It only took them close to eight hundred years. The loss of our silver wolf protectors is still felt by everyone.

Orion does a fine job guarding us, and no one has gotten in illegally to our city, but Orion's pack doesn't have the extra skills and blessed magic that your pack does. He is raising his son, Killian, to be the next Shadow Ridge alpha, but I hope it doesn't come to that anytime soon.

Just as my father wished, my goal is to reacclimate your pack into our society—but don't worry, your existence will remain a secret until we're in agreement. Even though we are both new alphas, I believe we're destined to meet and make a difference—for the sake of our children. Shadow City was meant to be a safe haven but, instead, has become a place of entrapment.

Together we will right the wrongs of the past.

Sincerely,

Atticus

. . .

Holy shit. "I found a letter between our dads."

"Really?" Griffin looked at the paper in my hands. "What does it say?"

I read it to him, and somehow kept a level voice. "That's insane. Your dad even referenced their children." Little did he know that their children were fated mates. I wished we could've seen both of their reactions when that little fact was brought to their attention.

"What else is there?" he asked.

I pulled out the next piece of paper, and as expected, it was another letter from Atticus. This one looked more recent, and the handwriting, more rushed. I read the words out loud.

Arian,

The votes have been cast and counted. The gates of Shadow City will open in a week's time. The hope of reuniting with the supernatural races outside of this city has finally come to fruition. Even though people won't be able to move into the city for a while—and even when they do, they'll have to be approved by the council before admittance—we are allowed to have visitors.

I'd love for you to be my first. Your pack identity will be kept secret, but I would love for you to see how much our city has changed and that this place can be a safe haven for the silver wolves once again.

Please come in two weeks and inform the gatekeeper that Atticus has invited you. I will ensure you are ushered straight to me. Let us make this the kind of world our children can be proud of.

Sincerely,

Atticus

"Dad tried to keep a level head, but he really dreamed of our pack making a big impact on the wolf community." Griffin smiled sadly, but there was so much pride reflected in his eyes. "He wanted to help the struggling wolf packs and bring harmony to our world. He'd show me maps of the packs that we knew about prior to the border closing and share his plans with me about how he and I, together, were going to visit and help make things right since we'd been closed off for so long."

"I still don't understand why the gates were closed."

Griffin sighed. "There was some sort of political unrest that made the city go into lockdown, but I don't know the details. I hope Mom knows. Dad hadn't gotten around to telling me since it seemed certain we had so much more time."

"Your father sounds like a kind and amazing person." Griffin had never talked to me about his father, and hearing him open up to me warmed my heart.

"Yeah, that was one reason his death shook me so hard." He frowned and inhaled. "We had all these plans, and the thought of doing them alone hurts a lot. Everyone thinks I'm not interested in leading, but it's not that. I want to carry out his plans, but the thought of doing it alone... It was easier to let Dick Harding handle things while I ran off to school and fucked around."

"I know I'm not your dad, and I would never want to replace him...for many reasons." I tried teasing him because I missed seeing his handsome smile. "But I would love to carry out those plans beside you."

"Since the moment we stopped fighting our bond, I've felt like I'm finally ready to be the kind of leader my dad saw in me." He took my hand and squeezed lovingly. "With you by my side, I want to not only follow my dad's plan, but make our own, too."

"That sounds amazing." And it made our current situation piss me off even more. "We have to find whoever is attacking us and kick their ass so we can actually focus on those goals." Although that certainly sounded a whole lot simpler than it would be.

Irritated, I pulled out the journal and flipped to the first page. Dad's familiar squiggly handwriting hurt my heart. For some reason,

I'd expected this to be Mom's. But the journal was in his hidden compartment, so, it only made sense that it was his.

I scanned the first few pages, finding nothing earth-shattering. He mentioned that the new alpha of Shadow City had begun sending letters and how he was concerned that, because of his eagerness to connect, others would learn about us.

But the next entry made my breath stop. Dad described the day his brother left the pack.

He'd never mentioned a brother to me. I had an uncle somewhere in this world and had never known about him. The date of the entry was a year before my birth.

Somehow, I'd thought if I learned that I wasn't the last silver wolf, a part of me would be relieved... I wouldn't be alone. But this news made me feel even more hollow.

A shell of myself.

Not only was I not the last of my kind, but potentially, I had family who were still alive. Family I'd never met and had no way of finding or contacting. The thought made me feel more isolated than ever before.

The onslaught of emotions hovered over me, and I wasn't ready to deal with them, so I flipped several more pages and paused when I saw the date of my birth.

At least, this should be a happy entry, but the very first sentence didn't make sense to me.

The witch who attended my birth to help heal my mother is the same attending my wife to help birth my son and daughter. I'm so thankful for this because birthing an alpha from our pack is hard enough, let alone another child right after. Never has the same witch assisted with two generations of alphas, but because of this unique circumstance, stronger magic is warranted. I only hope that everyone comes out of this healthy and unscathed.

I stopped reading, completely baffled. Was this even my dad's journal or was it someone else's? But the handwriting was unmistakable. Needing for things to make sense, I continued.

Surprising us all, my daughter, Sterlyn, was born first. For the first time in our history, the alpha heir will be a female. If that isn't a sign that change is coming, my son, Cyrus, dying shortly after birth was. The witch tried to revive him with her magic, but she wasn't successful. If it wasn't for our precious little girl, we'd be falling apart right now. Even though the death of our son will always linger, our little girl will pull us through. She's special. We can already feel it.

I had a brother, and my parents never told me. The realization settled over me, making my stomach turn. The feelings I'd been holding off swept over me like a tsunami. Nothing made sense, and I couldn't help but question if I even knew my parents at all.

"What's wrong?" Griffin asked with alarm.

I'd been trying to keep my emotions in check—not wanting to distress him—but I couldn't any longer. Even if I tried pushing them back, it wouldn't work. The force of my reality crashed over me.

My body grew numb, and I felt like I was suffocating from the turmoil coursing through me. The two odd feelings warred with each other as I seemed to drift out of my own body. I dropped the journal and rocked in my seat, wishing the pain of my injury would take over. That pain I could understand—but not whatever was rooting inside me, taking control.

Sterlyn. Griffin almost screamed. *Come back to me.*

His words might've been in another language because I couldn't process them. All I could focus on was this deep, dark void.

My body jarred and a breeze hit my skin, but I still couldn't shake the feelings inside. I was trapped in my own body, and I didn't know how to break free...or if I even wanted to. If I did, I'd have to filter through these raging emotions that were colliding inside me.

COLD WATER PUMMELED MY BODY, forcing me back to the present. I groaned and tried to jerk away, but strong arms had me locked in place. My head rested against a muscular chest, and the scent of myrrh and leather comforted me. I blinked, finding myself in Griffin's arms under the showerhead in his bathroom instead of in the Navigator.

How did I get here? He must have carried me.

The familiar light-gray tile almost seemed too bright in the room.

"That's cold." My teeth chattered. "What the hell are you doing?"

"You went into shock," he rasped, and kissed my forehead. "You scared the shit out of us. I didn't know what else to do."

"Us?" My mind tried to catch up. It had been only the two of us in the vehicle.

"Yeah, Killian and Sierra are here. We were at a loss about how to snap you out of it, so I told them I would try this. Killian wasn't thrilled about not helping, but no one but me gets to see you in the shower," Griffin growled. "I told them we'd be right out. They're getting cleaned up too."

The reminder that I had a member of my family out there that I didn't know hit me hard, making the emotions that had been held at bay by the shock of the water stream back inside. My eyes burned with tears, and my throat had dried, but I wasn't able to hold them back any longer.

I almost wished I could recede again as I had in the car, but the protective barrier wouldn't lock back in place. Instead, the feelings coursed through me, and a large sob broke free.

"Baby, what's wrong?" Griffin asked, as he gently put my feet on the cold tile floor. "I don't understand...what happened?"

Not able to verbally speak, I used our mate link to fill him in on the information I'd learned. When I was all done, my soul felt fractured. *All this time, Dad didn't tell me anything. It had to be because he didn't think I was strong enough to handle it, and he obviously was right. I feel broken.*

I may not have known him, but I know that's not true. Griffin leaned back and cupped my face in his hands. *You're the strongest person I've ever met. He may have been waiting to tell you everything, thinking you all had more time. No one would expect your pack to be decimated.*

The cold water turned warmer as it ran down my body. His touch comforted me, and I remembered that Dad had told me there were things he needed to share with me in due time. *Maybe, but that doesn't mean that I'm not at the end of my rope.*

Then lean on me. He stepped closer to me. *I'm here to be your rock and your strength. Let me take care of you in a way that you've been able to do for both Killian and me.*

I nearly laughed. *All I've done is put you two in danger. In fact, it would probably be better if you'd never met me.*

That is not true. His words held such conviction and his eyes locked with mine. *Killian and I were going through the motions. We've both been floundering since the loss of our families, then you came along and gave us purpose. He views you as a sister, and you're the love of my life...my soulmate. You've made him happier than he's been in years, and I'm the happiest I've ever been. Without you, I'd never become the man my father envisioned. And now, not only do I want to become that, but I want to be even more for you.*

But... I still couldn't get past everything they'd gone through.

No buts. He kissed me firmly. *You are stuck with us—especially me—and we have your back. The same way you have ours.*

His warm lips ignited something inside of me—a deep, aching need. He was the light in the dark. My life vest in the raging sea. He was my happiness when I almost lost hope.

My sweet scent of arousal floated around us, and a deep growl emanated from his chest.

"You're injured and upset," he said, but his fingers dug into my arm. "Now isn't the time."

"But I need you." I wrapped my arms around his neck, ignoring the pain in my shoulder. This moment was so much more important. "I love you and want to show you how much," I breathed, pushing every ounce of my affection toward him. I didn't want him to doubt my words.

He responded to my kiss, slipping his tongue into my mouth. *I love you too.*

In this moment, there was no doubt about how we felt for each other. He slowly set me on my feet and turned his head, kissing me deeper. His scruff brushed my face, making my body warm even more.

Grabbing the hem of his shirt, which I was still wearing, he stepped back and slowly removed it from my body, paying close attention to my injury. I stood before him, naked now, and my hands rubbed over his bare chest, down toward his jeans. With shaky hands, I unbuttoned them and pushed down his pants and underwear.

Hold on. He released me and yanked his jeans down his legs. The wet material clung to him, and he leaned against the wall, prying them from his body.

For the first time, he didn't look like the confident alpha I'd always known...but all that did was turn me on more. Finally, he pulled free of his pants and threw them outside the glass shower door. *Okay, maybe that was worth it to see that smile.*

One hand caressed my breast as he backed me into the now warm spray. With his other hand, he grabbed a bar of soap and twisted it into a lather. He placed the bar down and gently cleaned my injured arm. The white froth turned pink, and I washed the soap off.

Him caring for me made my heart beat funny, and not able to wait any longer, I jumped up and wrapped my legs around his waist, primed and ready.

"Let me take care of you," he rasped, as he pressed my back to the tile wall. "You need to make sure not to reinjure your arm."

He entered me slowly, making my mind grow fuzzy. I leaned my head against the wall, closing my eyes, enjoying how he overwhelmed my senses.

As he slipped into me, his teeth nicked the sensitive area of my throat where my mate bond mark was located, driving my wolf to howl in pleasure. He nipped and sucked all the way down to my breast.

I bucked against him, making him groan in pleasure.

The two of us moved as one, completely in sync. He sped up his pace as the friction increased between the two of us. I threw my head back, panting as his teeth nipped my breast.

Our feelings intermingled, and I wasn't sure where he began and I ended, but I wouldn't change it for the world. We climaxed together, our pleasure merging and exploding between us.

We stayed still for a moment, lost in each other, when we heard a pounding on the door. Killian's grave voice said, "Get your asses out here *right now*."

My heart dropped. There was no telling what we had to face once we left this room.

CHAPTER TWELVE

OUR MOMENT of peace was over, and anxiety wove through me again. The temporary reprieve that only Griffin could provide was gone.

Griffin's arms tensed around me. "What's wrong?" he called.

"We have a visitor." Killian rapped his knuckles on the door. "I put Sterlyn's clothes in your room so she'll have something clean to change into." His footsteps receded, leaving Griffin and me alone again.

"Of course, he couldn't wait until we got out of the shower," Griffin grumbled.

"Well, someone is here." That thought scared me. Who could be here that he didn't want to name drop? "We better get out there."

"Whoever it is can wait a second." He squirted some shampoo into his hands and rubbed his fingers into my hair, working up the bubbles. "You were shot and need a second to get clean. We don't need an infection setting in."

I bit my tongue, not bothering to mention that my wound was already scabbing over. The point was, it didn't matter—he wanted to

322   JEN L. GREY

take care of me, and I did want to get clean. I had dirt in places it shouldn't be, which was fine in wolf form, but not human.

He quickly washed me, and soon we stepped out of the shower. It hadn't taken more than a few minutes for both of us to rinse off since we'd been under the water for a while. After drying off, I stepped onto the cold, gray tile floor and hurried to the bedroom.

Griffin's bedroom was one of my favorite places on earth for two reasons. The first was that his scent was everywhere; that alone calmed me and made me never want to leave. And second, the room felt like him, but also me. It wasn't a standard bachelor room, but wasn't girly, either. It was as if he'd decorated it with me in mind. The walls were a warm blue that reminded me of the ocean, and the furniture was a dark walnut...even the comforter and sheets were a light muted gray, similar to an overcast sky.

The duffel bags holding my clothes were on my side of the bed, which didn't surprise me. Killian would have been able to smell which side held most of my scent. I dug through one bag and pulled out a pair of dark jeans and a maroon shirt, which I purposely chose in case my wound began bleeding again. Even though the spot would be wet, at least it wouldn't visibly stick out like it would on white or a light color.

I put my underwear on first, knowing that—considering where my injury was located—dressing my bottom half would hurt less than my top. Even though I wanted to rush, I forced myself to not go too fast in case I wound up hurting myself worse.

Griffin walked out of the closet and toward me. "Here, let me help you."

He snatched my bra and helped me put it on, followed by the shirt. His help made the process so much easier.

"After our guest leaves," he said with frustration, "we're going to get you situated in here. There's plenty of room in the closet and drawers, and if you need more space, I'll move my stuff around."

"No, I wouldn't want to put you out." This was his room, after all. I didn't want to cause any problems, and him wanting me to stay here was enough for me. "I can make do with whatever you aren't using."

"Put me out?" He grimaced as his nose wrinkled. "This is your bedroom, too. You have as much right to have whatever you want in here as I do."

A huge smile spread across my face, so wide that my cheeks hurt. Hearing him consider this to be our room made my heart happy.

"Wait..." He ran his fingers through my wet hair as he frowned. "You don't think of this place as your home?" Hurt wafted through our bond.

"I just never wanted to force myself on you like that." I hadn't meant to upset him. "Of course, I do, but I didn't want to push things between us too fast."

"You're my fated mate, whom I've claimed and confessed my love to," he growled and kissed me. *I'm yours, which means everything I have is now yours, too. Get it through your head.*

Feet pounded on the floors, and Sierra said, "You better get your butts out here before Rosemary and Killian go at it. They've been staring at each other, lobbing insults back and forth, and I'm not sure I can hold off the impending argument much longer. Unlike him, I'm not afraid of coming in there—Sterlyn doesn't have any parts I myself don't have."

"Uh...but I do." Griffin released me and winked.

"I'm not so sure," she said. "You've always been kind of wussy."

His mouth dropped open, and he marched to the door and yanked it open. "You don't think I have a penis?"

"No, I do, but it got you to open the door." Sierra gloated as she sashayed into the room and looped her arm through mine on my uninjured side. "Which was the whole point. I figured you two were dressed by now." She tugged me toward the door. "Please get out here because Killian is irritable and worried about you. You scared us all."

"What?" I hadn't done anything. "How?"

"The little freak-out state you were in." Sierra sighed as she leaned toward me. "Killian didn't think Griffin's shower plan would work, but obviously it did. I told him no one would know better than the person's mate."

"For a second, I thought he was going to try to join us," Griffin said protectively. "And that would've caused some problems. But he was wise enough to not follow me into the bathroom with you."

"Oh, he thought about it." Sierra laughed as we entered the den. "But he knew you'd kick his ass out of the house."

Killian was pacing in between the two couches in the center of the living room but stopped when we entered. His dark eyes focused on me and his shoulders relaxed. "Thank God you're back to normal."

I wasn't sure if *normal* was the right word, but I was in a better state of mind than I had been twenty minutes ago. "Let's not push it."

"What the hell happened? They refused to tell me anything," Rosemary bristled, crossing her legs as she angled her knees toward me on the large pearl-gray couch. "Griffin texted me, asking me to come, and then I got the silent treatment when I got here."

"Wait." I turned toward Griffin. "You asked her to come? *Again?*" That surprised me. The two of them didn't like each other very much.

"She can heal people, and you weren't yourself." He shrugged as he sat on a matching loveseat perpendicular to Rosemary. "I asked her to come in case the shower didn't work. Besides, we need an update on Carter, and I don't trust hearing it from him."

"He's a good guy." Killian crossed his arms as his jaw ticked. He looked an inch from having a meltdown of his own.

"Well, thank you for coming so quickly." She'd already helped us more than I'd ever expected anyone to. "And I'm sorry that they didn't fill you in. They should've." I scowled at Killian.

"I was a little preoccupied with worry over you," Killian said as he tugged me away from Sierra and hugged me. "What happened? I haven't been scared like that in such a long time. You took at least ten years off my lifespan."

"Oh, stop." I wrapped my good arm around him while keeping my injured one close. When he squeezed me, I hurt a little, but I wasn't going to complain. "You're healthy as a horse. Nothing could shave off those years."

"This is sweet and all, but why don't you fill me in on what's going on?" Rosemary motioned for me to come to her. "And if you want me to heal your injury, I can."

Under normal circumstances, I'd have said no; I didn't like taking shortcuts. But we could be facing some sort of fight again by tonight, so getting back to full strength would be smart. I pulled away from Killian and faced her. "Are you sure you don't mind?"

"I wouldn't have offered if I did." She arched a brow and leaned against the back of the couch. "I took you as someone who would know that."

And there was the directness that I admired so much about her. "You're right." I sat next to her, turning my body in her direction.

She waved her hand at my shoulder. "Where exactly is it?"

I moved the collar of my shirt until it showed the dark scabs that covered the wound. They were dark red because of how deep the wound had been.

"You two get shot more than anyone I know." She placed her hand on it, and her hand began to glow.

A warmth soaked into the injury, easing the pain. The healing was coming from the inside out, and within seconds, my shoulder felt normal again. "Thank you." I rotated the joint, enjoying the movement without pain. "That feels so much better."

"No problem." She dropped her hand and pointed at me. "So, obviously there was a fight. Spill."

I sat back and told her everything, wrapping up with the little bit I'd learned in the car. At this point, she deserved to know just as much as Killian and Sierra. Everyone here had sacrificed in more ways than one for me.

"Wow, you had a twin brother and an uncle you knew nothing about." Sierra shook her head and plopped into the seat next to me. She laid her head on my shoulder. "That sucks. I'm so sorry."

"I don't get why you mortals apologize for things that aren't your fault." Rosemary pursed her lips. "Like your insincere apology would make a difference in how a person feels. You didn't do anything wrong, so why would you even fathom saying it? That would be like me apologizing for your darker-blonde hair."

"Wait." Sierra tilted her head and glared at the angel. "What's wrong with my hair?"

Oh, wow. That had regressed quickly. "There's nothing wrong with it."

"They call it dirty blonde for a reason." Rosemary threw both hands up. "That should tell you something, but it's not my fault. It just sucks for you."

"It's *sandy* blonde." Sierra huffed and crossed her arms. "Not dirty blonde."

"That's what all dirty blondes say." Rosemary shook her head. "Call it whatever you want, but it doesn't change facts."

"Dude, I think they might have a catfight over this," Killian whispered, as if no one but Griffin could hear him. "This could get kind of hot."

"Maybe I would've thought that at one time." Griffin's gaze landed on me. "But there's only one girl here who makes me feel that way, and it's neither one of them."

If I hadn't had an out-of-body experience earlier when I was overwhelmed with grief, I'd think I was having one now. The craziness going on around me didn't make any sense, but at the same time, it was comforting. Things almost felt normal.

Girls argued over stupid stuff, and guys wanted to fantasize about a catfight.

"Where is this mysterious uncle of yours?" Rosemary asked, coming back to business.

That was a good question. "I have no clue. He left, and there was no hint about where he might've gone. Maybe when things settle down, I can try to find him." It'd be nice to have him now, but I could focus on only one major thing at a time. "So what happened with Carter? You haven't filled us in yet."

"I swear I don't know how that guy isn't an omega." Rosemary groaned dramatically. "He screamed the entire way back, begging me not to drop him, saying that he was sorry. He clutched on to me so hard he ripped my shirt."

"There're a couple of wolves weaker than him." Killian winced and leaned against the wall. "But not by much."

"That's one reason they targeted him." Rosemary rubbed her temples. "They target people who are easily intimidated or have a lot to lose. There's no telling who might be next."

"But they will contact Carter again." They already had leverage over him. They didn't have to risk being exposed by kidnapping someone else. "I'll need to go back to work and pretend I don't suspect a thing."

"Which means people will know we're back." Griffin sighed. "Not to mention you being bait."

"We've already gone over that." There was no getting around it. This was our best plan.

"Everyone already knows you're back." Rosemary twirled a finger. "The guards positioned outside the house were talking about you pulling in like a bat out of hell. If you wanted to stay under the radar, you should've taken that into consideration."

"Sterlyn was unresponsive." Griffin crossed his arms defensively. "I didn't know what was wrong. I panicked, but once we got settled, I did inform them that everything was okay."

"Tomorrow they'd know, anyway." So what if they'd learned a day early? "It'll be fine."

"Well, it's best if we all stay here," Rosemary said. "That way, if there are any attacks, the five of us are already together."

"You're going to stay with us?" She had her own family and life. "I mean, I'm not complaining, I'm just surprised."

"I told you why." Rosemary's eyes tightened in warning. "And you can't seem to stay out of trouble, so it only makes sense to be close by."

"What are you going to tell your parents?" Griffin blinked in surprise.

"That I'm staying with a friend." She shrugged. "I mean, I consider Sterlyn that anyway, so it wouldn't be a lie. The city is a little tense right now anyway, so it'd probably be a blessing that I was out of their hair regardless."

Wow. She thought we were friends. I liked her, so I'd roll with it. "And we have three extra bedrooms."

Griffin beamed at my words. *That's right. We do.*

"You said five." Killian pushed off the wall. "Sierra doesn't need to be wrangled into this. She already survived an attack."

"They might not realize who she is yet." Rosemary glanced at the blonde shifter. "If she goes back home though, they might locate her family, and she could put them at risk."

I hadn't even considered that. Killian should've thought about that before bringing her with him.

"It's fine," Sierra reassured everyone. "It makes sense for me to stay. I want to help you all. It's just a benefit that I could be protecting my family by doing it."

Griffin's phone dinged. He looked at it and groaned. "It's Dick. He's pulling into the neighborhood."

"Then that's my cue to run home and grab some clothes." Rosemary stood and headed toward the back door. "I don't want him to see me here—it'll raise too many questions. Text me when he's gone." She exited the house, and I watched as she took flight.

The fact that an angel was hanging out with us shouldn't raise questions. We were all supernaturals and should be friendly. Maybe that could be part of the plan Griffin and I worked on together.

"What does he want?" Killian asked.

"He said we need to talk. That it's important and involves Luna." Griffin complained.

My heart dropped. What had the bitch done now?

CHAPTER THIRTEEN

"WHAT DO WE DO?" Sierra stood and rubbed her arms. "I'd rather not run into Dick if I can help it. He hollers at me enough at the bar, and I called out sick because of the whole Sterlyn thing."

"Go into one of the guest bedrooms." Griffin pointed at one of the doors back down the hallway. "I'll meet him outside and try to keep him from coming in."

"I don't care if he knows I'm here," Killian scoffed, and took Rosemary's spot on the couch. "*Dove* can stay in here with me while you take care of business."

"No, she's going outside with me." Griffin shook his head and took my hand. "She's my mate, and we've claimed each other. We need to be seen as a united front."

"Are you sure?" Sierra furrowed her brows. "From what I'd heard, your mom didn't rule by your dad's side, or at least, that's the perception we had on the ridge."

"That's true...but unlike my dad, I have the strongest wolf by my side, and one who can lead in her own right." Griffin kissed my cheek. "And we will not be seen as alpha and alpha mate, but as their leaders together." He stilled. *If you're okay with that.*

The fact that he wanted me beside him in all ways somehow deepened my affection for him. This was more than a mate-ship—it was a true recognition of the alpha wolf in both of us. A weak man couldn't handle a strong woman beside him, but Griffin was anything but that. *More than okay.* I kissed his lips, letting him feel how much that meant to me.

"Yeah. On that note..." Sierra walked out of the room, pretending to dry heave.

"Thanks." Killian groaned. "You're leaving me alone in here and making me watch those two like a creeper."

"If the shoe fits," I teased and gave Griffin a huge kiss, making loud noises.

Griffin's shoulders shook as he wrapped his arms around my waist.

"My eyes!" Killian cried and grabbed a couch pillow, putting it over his head.

A knock at the door turned our moment of fun into thick tension.

Dick was here—and I didn't mean the one that had given me a good time in the shower.

Come on. Griffin intertwined our fingers. *Let's get out there before he gets pissy. He hates waiting.*

A little bit of anxiety flowed into me, alerting me that he was trying to hold the emotion back. That didn't make sense. Why would he feel that way, talking to this man? Griffin was the alpha, not the other way around.

Another round of knocking happened even though we were almost at the door. The asshole could smell us through the door at this point, but he was still being impatient.

What the hell was wrong with this guy? I'd met him for only a few minutes at the bar right after I'd been attacked on my first day here, and something had felt off about him—but it had to be more than just *off* given the way he was acting, and the emotions churning inside Griffin.

Unable to stop myself, I yanked open the door and stepped outside right into Dick's space, forcing him to take a step back.

His strong, musky sandalwood scent overwhelmed my nose. His short salt and pepper hair was gelled to the point of looking greasy, and he was rubbing his fingers along his dark beard. The suit he wore was the same color as his ebony eyes, and matched the vileness that radiated from inside him.

The bear shifter's attack had thrown me off-kilter. This man had something worse than Luna did stirring inside him. No wonder Luna struggled. She must have inherited it from him.

"What are you doing here?" Dick bit out, before smoothing his face into a charming smile. "Shouldn't you be with Killian?"

"Why would you ask such a thing?" I batted my eyelashes and asked lightly. If he wanted to play games, I could keep up.

"Aren't you dating him?" He chuckled, but annoyance flashed in his eyes. "I wouldn't want you to cause problems between him and Griffin. Killian will take over as alpha of Shadow Ridge's guards one day...surely...so it wouldn't be in Shadow City's best interest for him and Griffin to be at odds—especially over a girl." He reached through the door and patted Griffin's arm.

Wow, I had to admit he was good. He came off like the concerned father type.

"I'm sure you can smell that she's not his any longer," Griffin said stiffly at the suggestion of me being with Killian. "So you have nothing to worry about."

"That's what I was afraid you were going to say," Dick replied as he glanced at me, before focusing back on Griffin. "Can we talk?"

Griffin lifted his chin. "Anything you have to say can be said in front of my mate."

"Look, I understand what you think you feel, but I think it's best if we speak alone." Dick cleared his throat, pulling at his tie. "Maybe she can go back in the house or something. Or, better yet—go to Killian's."

The asshole was dismissing me. Yeah, that wasn't going to

happen. "No, I think I'm good here...and don't worry." I couldn't help but try to fracture his façade. "Killian is in the house, watching a movie, so he's close by."

"Oh, so he knows about this." Dick's shoulders tensed, but he sighed like he was relieved. "Well, at least that's something."

"Yeah, it is." Griffin wrapped an arm around me and led me to a round, black-wire table and chairs stationed on one side of his concrete front porch. We sat down, facing the front yard, the white siding behind us. Some sycamores were positioned in front for privacy and to provide shade.

"Okay, if this is how this conversation will go." A vein twitched between Dick's eyebrows as he strolled over to us. Other than that slight sign of annoyance, he appeared calm—but there was a storm brewing inside him.

"What's so important that you felt the need to leave Shadow City and drop in on *our* home?" Griffin asked, as he took my hand and laid it on the table in view of Dick.

Dick sat at the edge of his chair with his back completely straight. "Maybe you two are moving a little too fast...and she hasn't been officially introduced to the council yet to solidify things, so I thought I should tell you that I'm worried about you, Griffin."

"Why are you worried about me?" Griffin asked as he looked at me with adoration. "This is the happiest I've been in a long time—maybe ever."

"How much do you actually know about this girl?" Dick leaned forward, waving a hand at me, but still somehow pretending I wasn't even there. His eyes stayed locked with Griffin's as if they were the only two people at the table. "Don't you find it funny that she appears from nowhere, starts dating Killian, and then somehow puts the alpha of Shadow City under her spell? She's climbing the ladder."

Yeah...no. Him not acknowledging me ended now. I refused to be dismissed and treated like I wasn't an equal. "*She* is right here and finds your accusations offensive and boundless."

I'm sorry about this. Griffin linked, stroking my hand with his thumb. *I'm not sure what's gotten into him. He's not normally like this.*

In other words, Dick was normally better at keeping his charade in place. *You have nothing to apologize for.* Now I sounded like Rosemary...but it was true.

"I'm sure you do." He rolled his eyes and rubbed his hands together. "Griffin, I think of you as a son, and I'm concerned. This is a conversation that Atticus would have had with you right now. You and Luna have been friends since childhood, and she loves you—"

"There was never a me and Luna," Griffin interrupted, speaking slowly. "I know that you and Saga—" *That's his mate,* Griffin linked to me, "—hoped that she and I would wind up together, and I stupidly didn't discourage either of you. That's my fault, but it ends now. Dove is my fated mate, and we've claimed each other. Everything is final, and you need to let this go."

"Sometimes lust can be confused for a fated mate connection." Dick lifted a hand as he shook his head, playing the concerned father role perfectly. "You wouldn't be the first who was confused, and Luna is willing to forgive—"

"Are you saying that Griffin doesn't know the difference between lust and a fated mate bond?" I growled as my wolf howled inside; Dick even insinuating that Griffin should be with someone else enraged me.

He must be acting like this because Luna is upset, Griffin justified.

Whether Griffin realized it or not, this prick was insulting his intelligence. I might not have worldly knowledge, but that didn't give Dick the right to disrespect or disregard me. There was no doubt that Griffin and I were fated mates. The feelings were similar—attraction-wise—but lust didn't explain the immediate connection and love that you felt for the person; the acknowledgment of both halves of the same soul seeing each other for the first time.

Dick glared, and the vein somehow appeared larger. "I'm saying that attraction can be a confusing thing and that he wouldn't be the first that thought with his—"

"Dick?" I couldn't stop my mouth from running. "It's funny and fitting that it so happens to be your name."

Babe. Griffin sounded both horrified and amused, which was an odd combination. *I love your sense of humor, but he has been good to me. He's helped me so much since Dad died, so let's at least give him a break and not poke fun at his name, please.*

Oh, shit. Griffin had no clue what this man was really like. He was completely buying Dick's act. I had to tread carefully because this could become a problem between us. It wouldn't break us, but I didn't want to force my opinions on him and make him bitter or resentful. I had to get him to see the truth gradually because Griffin trusted Dick.

Of course, he did.

He was letting this man make decisions on his behalf. He wouldn't do that if he didn't trust him. I needed to warn him about his intent, but honestly, this gift was newer to me, so I wanted to make sure I was reading people correctly before throwing around accusations. Prior to coming here, I was almost always around the same people—none of whom had read negatively to me.

Thankfully, he was talking about taking back control.

"Do you think that's the first time I've ever heard that joke?" Dick lost his calm, and his body turned rigid. "It's very unoriginal, which already confirms my suspicions about you." He held out a hand toward Griffin. "Someone like that wouldn't be the fated mate of the strongest alpha of our species."

Wow, he'd laid it on thick. I had to give him props, he wasn't half-assing. "Look, you're right. That was uncalled for...but you came here, insulting not only me as a person, but my bond with Griffin."

"The fact that you're calling it an insult should prove that you don't have his best interests at heart like I do." He placed a hand on his chest and closed his eyes. "If you were his mate, you would appreciate that I'm worried about him."

Okay, that's too far. Griffin's annoyance flared. *I've given him enough leeway.*

Griffin opened his mouth, but I cut him off; I had to call the guy out on his crap if I wanted Griffin to see things for what they really were. "If you didn't come here and essentially call my mate stupid and insult my intentions, maybe I'd feel differently. To add insult to injury, you tried to pimp your daughter out to him—despite him telling you that he was never interested—and that our bond is final since we claimed one another. To me, that comes across as pushy and manipulative." I smiled sweetly at him, trying to play one of his own hands against him. "I'm sure you appreciate what I'm saying since it's out of concern, much like your words are."

"Now listen here." He locked gazes with me, challenging my wolf. He planned on forcing me to submit to him. "You don't get to come here and talk to me that way."

"Actually, you came here." I held his stare, effortlessly. This guy might be strong, but he was nothing like a silver wolf, or even Griffin. He had an inflated sense of self-worth, which made him more danger-ous. But I refused to look away. Griffin said he wanted us to lead together, so that was exactly what I would do. "You're more than welcome to leave." *I hope I'm not making you angry.* I did care about upsetting Griffin.

No, he's being an ass to you, even if it is out of concern for me. Griffin squeezed my hand lovingly. *You need to stand your ground. It's not okay, what he's trying to do. He has to respect not only me and you but our relationship. So do whatever you feel needs to be done.*

That was exactly what I'd hoped he'd say, but I was relieved that we were on the same page. *I love you.*

I love you too.

Sweat sprouted along the top of Dick's lip as his wolf began to struggle against mine.

My wolf growled inside—but not because she was feeling the strain. She was angry. She could feel the darkness in him too and was both annoyed that he'd questioned my and Griffin's bond, but further irritated that he expected us to submit to him. "Are you feeling okay?" I tilted my head while maintaining eye contact. "You seem to be getting overheated."

"I'm fine," he rasped, his words shaking. He had to be on the brink of submitting to me. The fear reflected deep inside.

In my peripheral vision, I saw him reach a hand into his pocket. A few seconds later, his phone made a noise. He pulled it out and glanced at the screen. "Oh, my phone rang." The smell of a lie was nonexistent because he had, in fact, made his phone ring.

He was a clever asshole.

I wanted to call him on it, but I'd pissed him off enough for one day. "Is everything okay?"

Dick ignored me once again and focused on Griffin. He said, "Consider what I said, and maybe call Luna tonight? She's been worried."

"Look, I've let you have your say." Griffin stood and stepped behind my chair, placing his hands on my shoulders. "I've even watched you be disrespectful to my mate, but that ends now. You are like family to me, but Dove is my claimed fated mate. There is no confusion on either of our ends, and Killian is very happy for us. If you insinuate one more time that Dove is not, in fact, my mate, it will cause problems between you and me, which I would hate."

"You're letting a girl..." Dick sputtered, seeming at a loss for words, "come between us? Luna *loves* you—"

A deep, threatening growl emanated from my chest. If he said that bitch's name one more time, I would attack his ass.

"No, you're going to let my mate come between us." Griffin emphasized each word. "Dove is my mate. She will be moving in with me here, and in Shadow City."

Dick took several deep breaths and then nodded slowly. "Fine, I understand." He pulled on his suit jacket. "Do you by chance have that paperwork signed?"

"Oh, yeah." Griffin relaxed. "Let me go grab it. I'll be right back." *You okay staying out here?*

Not really. The guy made me very uncomfortable—but if I ran in after Griffin, I'd look weak. *Yup. I'm good.*

When Griffin entered the house, Dick smirked, "It would be in your best interest to not get involved with certain decisions. Griffin and I have a system that works. I wouldn't want you trying to interfere more than you already have."

The unveiled threat hung between us. "Or what?" My wolf surged forward, ready to fight.

CHAPTER FOURTEEN

I INHALED DEEPLY as I stood, trying to keep my heart from beating too quickly. I didn't want Dick to think he had some sort of power or influence over me—even if he did. Granted, the emotion he inspired was anger, not fear—but egocentric males like him always tried to make themselves feel more powerful.

Even though it wasn't fear, he would pretend that it was.

"Look, I don't know what you're up to, but Griffin will come around." Dick's nostrils flared as he marched over, crowding into me.

He wanted to make me feel threatened and to step back, but I refused to budge. Instead, I lifted my chin and looked down my nose. "Yeah, he will. I agree. He's smarter and stronger than you give him credit for."

A frown peeked from the corners of his mouth, and he inhaled sharply, making his chest touch mine.

Even though he had multiple layers on, and I was wearing a thick shirt, I still felt dirty. An ickiness coated my skin, and my natural inclination to jerk away almost took over.

Almost.

But I used every ounce of self-control I had to prevent that. He was doing anything possible to force me to be the one to cower first, and I couldn't let the asshole win—even though my desire to jerk away had nothing to do with me actually wanting to submit to him, but rather to get away from the maliciousness that wafted from him and coated me.

Griffin's footsteps grew louder as he approached the front door once again.

Unfortunately, Dick was smart enough to take a step back, an amicable smile replacing the scowl from moments before. He was going back to his little persona that worked on my mate. But it wouldn't last for long.

I'd make sure of it.

The front door opened, and there was Griffin with a stack of papers in his hands.

I wanted to ask what they were, but it didn't matter—I could see his signature on the back few pages, so I could only hope that he'd read the documents thoroughly before signing.

"Thank you," Dick said as he swiped them from Griffin's hand. "I should be getting back to Shadow City now so we can file these with the council."

"Very well," Griffin said as he nodded, and placed an arm around my waist. "And I understand that Luna may be upset, but she'll be okay. Don't worry. With time—and when she finds her fated mate—things will get better."

"Not everyone finds their fated mate." Dick cut his eyes over at me. "You know that."

He must have thought that if he kept insinuating we weren't fated mates, Griffin would believe him. The arrogance behind the strategy was insane. Even if we weren't fated mates, we'd claimed each other. Our bond was complete, and the only thing that could break it was...

Death.

My heart sank.

Could that be his plan?

"But that was before we began leaving the city and integrating back into the world." Griffin kissed my cheek and continued, "If we hadn't done that, then I would've never found St—Dove." *Shit, I'm sorry. It's just...Sterlyn fits you so much better.*

Dick's eyebrows rose, but what made me most nervous was that he didn't comment. That meant he'd noticed Griffin's near slip and stored the information.

I cringed. The less Dick learned about me, the safer we all were. At least Griffin had caught his slip before my whole name came out. *It's okay. Just got to be more careful.*

"Well, then. I guess I better go." Even though Dick's face was smooth, there was a slight edge to his voice. "I'll see you soon." He turned around and strolled toward the black Mercedes.

That was when I noticed there was someone in the driver's seat—like a chauffeur.

Who the hell did this guy think he was? The president or something? *Why does he have a driver?*

No clue. Griffin chuckled. *He's had one for as long as I can remember.*

But you don't? You'd think out of the two of them, Griffin would be the one with that kind of luxury. I understood that the guy was on the council, but Griffin was the alpha heir.

God, no, he replied as we watched Dick's car pull out and drive away. *I like being behind the wheel. Dad was the same way, but from what I understood from Dad, Dick's whole family is like that.*

Dick had to be who my dad had sensed was still corrupt. The amount of negativity coming off him was enough to upset my stomach. There was a little badass in everyone, but I'd never encountered something that awful before. Even the people attacking us weren't that negative—though, granted, we'd learned that some of them weren't doing it willingly.

Griffin opened the door, and I entered, brushing past him.

Killian remained on the couch, watching television. He paused the show. "So, what'd he want?"

Oh, this would be all me. "To inform Griffin that he thinks our fated mate bond is only lust and that Griffin belongs with Luna."

"Wow." Killian pursed his lips. "Took a long time for him to say those two things."

"He was long-winded." Griffin plopped onto the loveseat and patted the space beside him. "But don't worry, Sterlyn put him in his place and had a semi-standoff with him."

"That he ended." At least the dumbass was smart enough to know when he couldn't win. "Sierra, it's safe to come out now."

The bedroom door opened, and she padded down the hallway toward us. "That didn't take as long as I was afraid it would. Did he catch my scent?"

"He didn't say anything." That was the one good thing about the entire situation. "He was too preoccupied trying to get Griffin to leave me for *Luna*." It angered me that I even had to say her name in the same sentence as my mate's.

"And I always thought he was smart." Sierra shook her head. "But everyone can smell your scent on each other. He knows that you're both claimed."

"Oh, he knew." I tried to pretend like I wasn't watching Griffin's reaction. "And he mentioned how I'd better not get involved with any council or city decisions."

"What?" Griffin's face tensed as his jaw twitched. "Where was I?"

"Where do you think, dumbass?" Killian deadpanned and crossed his arms. "In here getting whatever paperwork he had drawn up for you to sign."

"Speaking of that." I had to ask. There was no way I couldn't, especially now that Killian had brought it up. "Please tell me you read over the documents before signing."

"Of course, I did. It's authorization for some of the Shadow City guards to get more training." Griffin waved off the concern as he turned his body toward me. "But he threatened you, and you didn't use our link to tell me?"

"It wasn't a big deal." Right now, Dick was the least of my

concerns. Well, that was an exaggeration, but considering how few people could actually leave the city, I doubted that my attackers were Shadow City residents. "I can handle him. Dad prepared me to handle sexist wolves my entire life."

"Really?" Sierra sat on the other end of the couch from Killian, closest to me. "He's kind of over the top. At work, he pretends that I don't exist unless he has to talk to me. Of course, it's usually to tell me to go clean the bathrooms or some other sort of 'woman's work.'"

Griffin's brows furrowed. "That's surprising. He never treats the women on the council that way."

"That's because they aren't wolves, and he needs something from them, man." Killian leaned back and placed his hands behind his head. His arms flexed, revealing how muscular he was. "Have you not noticed this before now?"

"No." Griffin ran a hand through his hair. "But it kind of makes sense. We were locked away, and our culture is archaic because of that."

"Shadow City isn't the only place like that." I'd been prepped and warned. "Dad told me I'd experience that kind of sexism in the world, and honestly, there was some even in my own pack. But it doesn't matter because, at the end of the day, I'm stronger than Dick, and there is absolutely nothing he can do about that."

"Girl, I knew I liked you from the get-go." Sierra leaned over the end of the couch and patted my arm. "Change is coming, and poor ol' Dick will wind up a limp noodle before it's all done."

"What?" Killian's face smooshed in disgust. "Really? You two are like sisters to me, and you're making sexual innuendos in front of me?"

"Would you rather we act them out?" Sierra gave me a huge smile, revealing both rows of her teeth.

"Maybe bringing you here was a bad idea." Killian pouted and bounced a leg. "Between your comments and Griffin pawing at Sterlyn, I'm going to have nightmares." He pointed at me. "What happened to keeping your legs closed nice and tight?"

344   JEN L. GREY

Laughter spilled out of me, and I hadn't realized how much I needed the release. During the first week I'd stayed with Killian under the ruse of dating him, he'd found out I was a virgin and been shocked. I'd made that comment to explain things to him.

"Oh, don't worry." Griffin wrapped an arm around my shoulders, pulling me into his side. "She still does for everyone else but me."

Killian huffed and stared at the television like he was too disgusted to look at any of us.

"Well played," Sierra said, as she saluted Griffin. "He's speechless for once."

Comforting warmth expanded in my chest. In this moment, things felt normal; four friends hanging out, trying to get a reaction from one another. In fact, I'd never gotten to experience things like this until I found Killian and Griffin. They'd given me a piece of normalcy that I hadn't been able to find with my birth pack—a sense of belonging that let me know that life might be shitty, but there were bright spots.

Spots that I cherished more because of the bad.

Not that I wouldn't love to have my parents here with me, along with the brother I'd never gotten to meet. I would—so damn much—but that wasn't possible, no matter how much I wished it.

There's a sense of happiness ebbing from you. Griffin intertwined our fingers. *I've never felt this from you before.*

Is that a problem? I teased, able to feel how pleased he was. *Should I be broodier?*

God, no. He tucked a piece of my hair behind my ear. *I hope you feel like this more often. You look even more breathtaking right now.*

"Ew," Sierra groaned. "Maybe I was wrong to give you hell. It is kind of sickening to watch them be all lovey-dovey."

"Nope, you sided with them." Killian crossed his arms and bared his teeth. "You don't get to complain. That right is solely reserved for me."

The flapping of wings notified us that Rosemary had returned. The back door swung open, and her rose scent swirled into the room as she stepped inside with a black duffel bag slung over her shoulder.

"Well, come on in." Sierra snorted. "Make yourself at home."

"I believe I just did." Rosemary strolled to us. "Which bedroom am I staying in?"

As usual, we could count on her to get straight to the point.

"The bedroom down that hallway on the right." Griffin gestured in the same direction that Sierra had come from. "You'll be on the other side of the hall from Sierra's and Killian's rooms. Sterlyn and my room is at the very end of the hallway."

"Good, I'll be close to Sterlyn." Rosemary frowned and gestured to me. "If someone attacks, I'll be her best ally."

"Uh...I'm the alpha of the protectors of Shadow City." Killian pounded on his chest. "If anyone—"

"You and your pack are the protectors by default." Rosemary flipped her hair over her shoulder. "And only because angels have more important jobs than watching for potential threats. We come to your aid in wars, but Sterlyn's pack was always meant to be the true protectors."

Killian growled.

She'd kind of insulted me and praised me in the same breath, and made Killian feel inferior. "We need to work on your manners."

Are you sure that's wise? Griffin asked.

I trusted my gut. *We'll find out.*

"Excuse me?" She frowned, her twilight eyes blazing. "I'm only speaking the truth."

"Being rude and speaking the truth are two different things." That was part of the problem—no one ever tried to explain to her why what she said was uncalled for. If no one was going to correct her, I would. "Killian and his pack have sacrificed a lot to protect Shadow City and their own. To the point of losing his entire family. Do you think calling him weak and telling him he does something you find worthless is the way to make him want to help protect you?"

"It's not worthless." Her face fell. "I just meant that angels—"

"Stop." I stood and placed a hand on her shoulder. "Angels have other things they are responsible for, but they don't mind coming to help fight when an adversary rises."

"That's what I said." She blinked and looked at the others.

"No, it was most definitely not." Sierra pinched the bridge of her nose. "You said that angels have more important jobs."

"Which is—" Rosemary started, but I raised a hand.

"Not true." I leveled my gaze at her. "You don't think protecting Shadow City is an important job even though Killian's pack aren't silver wolves?"

"Oh." She bit her bottom lip as realization dawned on her. "Yeah, okay. I see what you're saying." She pivoted toward Killian and frowned. "I'm sorry. I didn't mean it like that. Sterlyn is right—the way I worded things was inconsiderate. It's just—"

"That's good." I had a feeling if she kept going, it would negate everything she'd just said; I was surprised that she'd apologized on her own. "That was very nice of you. Wasn't it, Killian?" I glared at him, daring him to not cooperate.

"To say I was shocked would be an understatement," Killian offered.

"All you all have to do is point things out like Sterlyn does." Rosemary blew out a breath. "If something bothers you, just say it. That's what's wrong—"

"Let's get you situated." I grabbed her hand and pulled her toward the bedroom Griffin had pointed to. "And then we all need time to relax before tomorrow." And I meant that, even if we relaxed separately.

I YAWNED as Griffin and I walked into the coffee shop on the Shadow Ridge University campus extra early the next morning. The night before hadn't been as relaxing as I'd hoped because Rosemary had watched a movie with us. I'd been on edge, waiting for her to make

Killian or Sierra angry again. She hadn't, and the night had been pleasant, but the anticipation had kept me a little tense.

The inside of Shadow Ridge Coffee looked like a standard coffee shop. A few tables were scattered around the room, and two espresso machines were positioned in the center of the counter, with the cash register on the right.

Carter walked out from the back, and his face fell when he found the two of us there. I snatched an apron from the hook on the wall behind the counter, refusing to let his reaction bother me. Of course, my return made him tense because whoever had ordered him to drug me was probably watching.

"It's so good to have you back." Carter tried to sound sincere, but the sulfuric stench of a lie wafted around us.

"Just act normal," Griffin growled, lowly. "Or you're going to get us all killed." *Maybe this wasn't a smart idea after all.*

We got here early so you could hang out and get comfortable before your classes. I kissed him and then went to the cash register. *We have to act normal if we want this to work.*

"God, remember no PDA here." Carter stomped a little and grabbed some of the items needed for the espresso machine. "And I thought you and Killian were bad."

A loud rumble bellowed from Griffin.

Great, this day was starting out wonderfully.

"Right, Killian did kiss her often." Luna's voice rang in my ears. "I wonder what else they might have done in here when no one was looking."

And there she was. I'd figured she and I would have it out soon. No better time than the present.

CHAPTER FIFTEEN

THE INSINUATION that Killian and I might have had sex had Griffin visibly shaking beside me. I touched his arm, trying to calm him. *You know that's not even remotely true.*

Luna sashayed to the cash register and flipped her golden bronze hair over her shoulder. Her Caribbean blue eyes landed on my hand, and she straightened her back, probably trying to appear as tall as possible despite being two inches shorter than me. She smirked and said, "I wonder where you've touched Killian prior to you and Griffin getting together."

That bitch wanted to cause problems, but little did she know that my relationship with Killian hadn't been like that. We'd been exclusive, but only to prevent her from trying to hook Killian up with her best friend. Griffin was fully aware, so the only person he was getting angry with was her. "For someone who has so much interest in Griffin, you're very focused on Killian's and my *former* relationship."

"Well, I just want to make sure that Griffin has fully thought through the implications of being with you." She lowered her head and pushed out her breasts so the cleavage framed by her skimpy, thin, royal-blue sweater's low neckline was available for view. It was a miracle her nipples didn't pop out.

I swear, if she doesn't shut up— Griffin was so enraged that he couldn't finish the sentence.

"He has, just like he thought out *not* wanting to be with you." My skin tingled as my wolf got riled too. If I wasn't careful, I'd shift, and we didn't need Luna knowing more about me than she already did.

"It's funny." She crossed her arms, lifting her boobs even more. "You're doing a whole lot of talking, and he's remaining quiet."

"Luna, we're not open yet." Carter hurried over and wiped sweat from his brow. "Why don't you come back in ten minutes when everything is open and ready?"

She didn't even acknowledge the poor guy and took a few steps closer to Griffin. She pouted and lowered her voice as she reached for him. "It's not too late—"

Griffin stepped back out of reach and glared. "Do *not* touch me. In fact, don't come near me or Dove ever again."

"Are you fucking serious?" She dropped her hand and sneered. Unlike her dad, she didn't have a good poker face—but maybe that would improve the longer she practiced. "She's an outsider who screwed your best friend, and you want her instead of me?"

"He not only wants me...he *chose* me." I was going to make this crystal clear. If I had to pee on Griffin's leg, so be it. I pointed at the faint teeth-mark scar on my neck. "The decision has been made, and Killian has given his blessing, so why don't you leave like Carter asked, and maybe don't bother coming back."

Her mouth dropped open, and her breathing increased. "Tell me this is some kind of joke." She looked at Griffin. "This can't be real."

"It is real, and you need to get it through your head that you and I will never be together." Griffin walked behind the counter and wrapped an arm around my waist. "I never wanted you, and you knew it. The only reason I became your friend in the first place and tolerated your grand delusions was because of your father; I didn't want tension between him and me. But I was being a coward."

"That's not true." She huffed, not noticing the trickle of people entering the coffee shop now that we were open.

Carter groaned as if realizing that, once again, I was causing a scene. In a way, he should have been thankful. I'd bet that my employment here was helping business because people wanted to come by in case something else happened. I probably should get a raise.

"We kissed that one—" she started, and a low threatening growl escaped me.

The fact that his lips had been on hers rattled not only me, but my wolf as well. *You kissed her?* I didn't have a right to be angry. The instance obviously occurred before we committed to each other—but the thought of his lips on anyone else's made me see red.

She smirked, thrilled with my reaction.

"Don't change the story," he snarled. *It wasn't like that, at all.* His fingers dug into my waist a little as his anger increased. "You got me drunk and kissed me, trying to do more. Even in my drunken state, I pushed you off me."

"That's not true." But the sulfuric smell of a lie wafted around us.

A few of the shifters who had walked in coughed at the rancid smell.

Her body stiffened, and she glanced over her shoulder, seeming to realize that we had an audience. She must have been so caught up in her anger that she hadn't noticed when they'd entered.

"Look, it's obvious that he's never been into you." I was so tired of people not telling the truth; people needed to be direct. Like Rosemary. The angels had that right. It was something we shifters should embrace too. "Ever. It's not my fault, even if you can't see it that way."

"He's confused." Luna spread her arms out. "That's all. It makes better sense for him to be with me. I'm going to be part of the council in the future—taking over my father's spot. I know how things work in the city. I decided to come to college to get the best education so I can be valuable in the future."

I'm going to follow your lead. Griffin waved his hand in front of his chest. "Maybe that's all true. But you didn't make those plans until I decided to come here."

Okay, he had laid it out there for her. Sugarcoating only got you so far.

"Griffin..." She stomped a foot, reminding me of a child. "Don't do this. We're good for each other."

"Listen, I'm not sure how much clearer I can make this for you." Surely if I ticked off everything on the list, the truth would finally click. Something had to work or Griffin and I might hurt her. And even though I didn't like Dick, we had to be strategic—hurting his daughter was not part of a good strategy.

I lifted one finger. "He's claimed me." With each point, I lifted another one. "I've moved in with him. He's never been interested in you, and you're coming off pretty pathetic right now."

"You're such a bitch." She leaned across the counter, getting into my face. The corruption emanating from inside her seemed to darken to nearly the same shade as her father's. "You will learn your place sooner or later."

"Or maybe you'll be the one who actually figures it out." One of the first alpha lessons Dad had taught me was when I started elementary school. Another shifter there didn't like me immediately; some boy who was the alpha heir of his father's pack. He could sense my strong wolf, and because of our animal nature, he tried to assert his dominance. Dad told me that standing down from a bully, especially a supernatural one, only encouraged future mistreatment. I hadn't believed Dad at first, but each day, the bullying grew worse until I finally made the boy submit to me. He didn't return to school the next day.

This was the same situation—but instead of a boy, it was a girl vying for her sexist father's approval. There was no telling how she'd grown up, and judging by the way Dick had acted at the house yesterday, he was probably the reason that Luna was so desperate to be with Griffin.

But Dick was never going to change, and she probably didn't

want to see that. Maybe at one time, I could have felt bad for her, but not now. Not anymore. She was old enough to make her own decisions, and her soul was darkening on her own accord.

"You don't want to mess with me," she threatened, her face turning slightly red from her anger. "You have no clue what I'm capable of."

But that wasn't true. I did. It wafted from her and slammed into me, making me feel gross. "And you don't know anything about me. You may not like me—hell, the feeling is mutual—but I'm Griffin's mate, and I'm not going anywhere." I leaned over, getting even more in her face; she had to realize that I would not be intimidated by her or anyone else.

"I want to add," Griffin rasped, "this is the last time you get a reprieve from talking to my mate like that. If you so much as look at her in a hateful manner, we'll become enemies. I don't give a flying fuck if Dick is your dad. Do I make myself clear?"

Her bottom lip quivered, and she stood up straight. "This isn't over."

"Oh, but it is." I lifted my chin and laid my head on Griffin's shoulder. We had presented a united front, and there wasn't a damn thing she could do about it.

Her irises turned navy before she spun on her heel and marched past the growing line of people and out the door.

"Dove, I swear." Carter sighed and waved to the next person in line. "There is never a dull moment with you around."

"Yeah, I have to agree." I wished that wasn't the case. At some point, things had to calm down...surely.

THE NEXT FEW days flew by. Luckily, Luna didn't come back. She'd left with her tail between her legs—but if she was anything like her father, that wouldn't last long. She'd come back at me, but when Griffin wasn't around.

I counted out the drawer as Griffin entered the shop. He scanned the area like he expected to find Dick or Luna inside.

Stand down, Cujo, I teased. *Only Carter and I are here.*

That does not make me feel any better. He strolled over to me with a frown on his face. *He's the one who injected you with a drug and handed you over to that bear shifter.*

He did have a point. *True, but he's on our side now.*

Supposedly, Griffin growled as Carter walked out of the kitchen and behind the counter.

"Oh, yay." Carter sighed. "Your boyfriend is here while we're clos-ing...like he has been the entire week."

"Mate," Griffin corrected, and kissed me. "And sorry if I don't like her being alone with you."

"I made a mistake." Carter's shoulders sagged.

"Let's not talk about this now." We were supposed to be acting normal, and if anyone was watching closely, our cover was blown. "Carter has been a good friend." Hopefully, that last sentence would throw anyone off if they were somehow listening or keeping an eye out. No one would expect me to call him that if we knew what he'd done.

I closed the till and smiled sweetly at Griffin. "Are you ready to go?" We needed to act upbeat and not worried.

"Yeah, we'll see you later, man." Griffin stood and waved at Carter. He took my hand, and we walked out the door together.

If you keep acting angry with him, he'll be hesitant to help us if they call. Carter might feel like it would anger Griffin more, and we really needed him to be comfortable informing us.

I usually agree with you, but not on this one. Because he knows I'm pissed, he'll call first thing. He kissed my cheek as we entered the hallway between the campus bookstore and cafeteria.

The seating inside, and the picnic tables just outside the glass back doors, were full. The view out back was beautiful with the scenery of the river and woods. The scents of maple and redwood swirled in the air. Most of the shifters were outside while the vampires were mostly inside.

Maybe he had a point. Carter did seem upset that Killian and Griffin were mad at him. In a way, those two had been angrier than I had been...and I was the one who'd been kidnapped. Granted, if something happened to either one of them, I wouldn't be quick to forgive either.

We turned down the hallway to the front doors. The walls were the standard institutional beige, and the floor a warm, gray tile. A few students passed by us, heading in the opposite direction as we passed by the second hallway, which housed various administrative departments.

Griffin opened the wooden front double doors and waved me through. Of course, the scent of honey vanilla musk overpowered my nose.

The bitch was here...again.

My gaze found Luna sitting on one of the benches in front of the school. Her focus had already been set on us, like she was waiting for us to come outside.

Ignore her, Griffin said, as he angled us so that he walked in front of her like a barrier.

My natural instinct was to move so I was on that side, but he wanted to make a point to her that he would protect me. I couldn't dissuade him even if I wanted to. He wasn't trying to make me look weak—he was showing that he had my back.

She growled faintly as we walked by but didn't say anything, which unnerved me. She liked to run her mouth, and her not doing so made me think she had ulterior motives.

We continued past her and soon climbed into Griffin's Navigator and headed home.

"Should we be nervous that she didn't say anything to us?" I already knew the answer but wanted to hear his take.

"No. She gives me the cold shoulder whenever she's mad at me."

He shrugged. "She'll be trying to talk to me again soon enough. Just enjoy the quiet."

He sounded so sure, but the quiet was what scared me. I reached over and took his hand, enjoying the feel of his skin.

A FEW DAYS LATER, I found Rosemary in the living room. "How did everything go at the coffee shop?" Rosemary asked, pacing the room like she'd been on edge.

"Luna hasn't come in since the incident," I said as I walked to the loveseat and dropped onto it. "So other than her staying away, nothing out of the ordinary." The girl did like being the center of attention.

Killian walked out of the kitchen and joined us. "Well, Rosemary here has been pacing the room since she got back. Each day, she gets more amped up. She's been a whole lot more nervous about Sterlyn going to the coffee shop than she let on." He took his usual spot on the couch and smiled at the angel.

Wait...he was smiling at Rosemary. What dimension had I entered? They had seemed to be getting along more amicably the past few days, but I hadn't expected them to be friendly.

"If you've been that worried, why didn't you go keep an eye on her?" Griffin asked, angrily.

"Because Carter and I flew off together the morning I brought him to talk to you." Rosemary scowled back at him. "So if I looked protective and whoever is behind all this was watching, they might become alarmed. We have to be smart."

Killian tensed, somehow adding more tension to the air. He glanced at us and cleared his throat. "Carter just linked with me. He said Rosemary needs to meet him. They finally made the call."

CHAPTER SIXTEEN

THE RIDE to Shadow Lake passed in a tense silence. One of Griffin's hands was on the Navigator's steering wheel while the other one gripped my leg like I might disappear. As if his grasp was the only reason I was still sitting beside him.

Killian sat behind my seat, breathing heavily with his own anxiety. "I can't believe I'm coming back here."

"Wait... What do you mean?" Something must have been bothering him more than I realized.

He didn't respond, and Griffin linked with me, *His family died where we're heading.*

Oh, my God. "Killian, you don't have to come—"

"Hell, yes I do," Killian growled. "I'm not having the two people I consider family go here without me. Never again."

I already felt like I was suffocating, and their stress-filled demeanors only increased mine—but there wasn't anything I could do about it. If I reacted, it would cause them to become even more stressed. Besides, to be fair, if one of them were in the same situation, I'd feel the same way. "Okay, but if it gets to be too much—"

They were upset because they cared, and even though I was

miserable because of it, I wouldn't change them feeling this way for the world.

Both of them were my family.

"Please stop." Killian exhaled. "I'm going. It'll be fine. We aren't going to hang out—we'll be dealing with shit so I won't have time to think about it."

Griffin glanced in the rearview mirror. "Are you sure he won't fuck this up?"

"Dude, how many times do we have to go through this?" Killian grumbled. "He's meeting Rosemary in the woods behind the pack neighborhood, and he's willingly letting her fly him to Shadow Lake to meet us to ensure he isn't followed. You need to keep your attention on the road and make sure no one is following us."

"Including any damn crows." I still hated that one. I'd been staring out the windshield, paying more attention to the sky than the road behind us. My stalker's first crow was dead, but there was no telling whether he had another that had stepped in.

Wow—he... I might be as sexist as Dick. Why couldn't the bad guy be a girl?

Great, I was losing it. Scolding myself and having internal debates revealed that little nugget.

Griffin smirked. "I'm so glad I shot that bastard."

"That was too kind after everything he'd done." I had wanted to be the one to end him. "I planned to pluck out each feather one by one before providing a slow and painful death."

"Damn, Sterlyn," Killian chuckled. "And here I've been thinking that you were kind and empathetic—only killing when required—but then you spout off something like that."

"I'd planned on killing the bear shifter who attacked me." I'd been ready to get my revenge. "But when he was lying helpless, crumpled on the ground...I just couldn't do it." To actively kill someone like that in cold blood... I didn't have it in me.

"Hey, I was teasing." Killian placed a hand on my shoulder and rubbed. "I know—when it came down to it—you wouldn't have been able to kill the crow, even though he deserved it."

Maybe not, but...the crow was a little different. He'd put not only me but the people I loved in danger.

"I won't be nearly as kind as her if Carter tries to put one over on us again." Griffin's hand tightened even more.

Hey, everything is going to be okay. If he didn't breathe, he could have a heart attack like his father. "He told us they called; I think we're good."

"Yeah, man." Killian's hand disappeared, and I heard him sit back in the seat. "When he does come through for us, you're going to have to let that go."

"Nope." Griffin shook his head as his left leg bounced. "I won't. I get that he grew up with you and Sierra and is part of your pack, but I've known him for a couple of years—ever since I started at Shadow University—and I've never been impressed."

"Because he was petrified of you." Killian sighed. "But I know he'll come through. That's all that matters."

"I think he will, too." I pried my fingers under Griffin's, trying to get him to release his death grip on my leg. If he didn't let go, my leg was going to fall asleep. "At least we'll know what we're working with this time."

"I'd feel better if Sierra was here too." Griffin frowned. "If we're walking into a trap, the more people we have, the less risky it will be."

"If she called out or left work early again, that could make whoever is behind this more suspicious." We couldn't be reactive. We had to keep level heads or the plan wouldn't work.

Killian said, "Don't forget that Dick is already pissed about her missing work the other day. He's been riding her ass ever since."

"Dick riding ass, eh?" I tried lightening the mood in the vehicle. "Why am I not surprised?"

"Dear God," Killian groaned. "Between you and Sierra... Hell, Rosemary even made a similar joke the other day, which freaked me out."

Not even the corner of Griffin's mouth tipped upward, revealing how stressed he really was.

I feel like, ever since you met me, you've been a bottle of nerves. Sometimes I worried that my presence in his life was more problematic than good.

Griffin looked at me for a moment before looking back at the road. *First off, it's only because I care about you so much, but second, I've always been kind of uptight.* He kissed my cheek. *I promise I have never felt happier and more content in my entire life.*

You sure? The scent of a lie was missing, but that couldn't stop me from asking. Each day felt like we were waking up to some sort of hidden threat. *I just don't see how.*

I'm positive, he reassured me as he turned onto the road to the lake. The trees were thick on both sides, taking us to a spot in the lot that the shade from the trees covered. Rosemary and Carter were meeting us in a part of the woods a few miles in the direction that the bear had taken me.

A few visitors would, no doubt, be at the lake, so we were going to meet off the path where no one would see us together.

Griffin pulled into a parking space, and I gazed around. Several people were swimming in the lake. When I opened the door, the grassy and maple scents informed me that the two who seemed to be a couple were bears, and the other four were vampires.

My body tensed. I'd been attacked by two bear shifters already and was feeling particularly wary of them.

The three of us got out of the car, and I grabbed a bag I'd packed for keeping up our charade. Shifters loved to run, so us heading into the woods with extra clothing would help create the façade that we were just there to shift and enjoy the outdoors. This place was only about thirty or so minutes away from Shadow Ridge, so we had to pretend to be there for a day of fun.

Scanning the surroundings, I looked for any crows or falcons; those were the only two birds that could shift into both human and animal forms.

The only thing that stood out was the group of vampires distorting their beautiful faces to scowl in our direction.

I spoke softly, even though we were at least a half-mile away and they wouldn't be able to hear. "Uh...what the hell is their problem?"

"They have to be from Shadow Terrace," Killian spat.

"The town on the other side of the river?" Someone had mentioned it in passing, but not much more. All I knew was that the town was protected by a vampire clan that provided humans to the vampires in Shadow City when needed.

"Yeah. Between us throwing a fit about them funneling humans into Shadow Terrace, and the university being built on our side of the river, things are a little tense between the races." Griffin lifted his chin and ignored the vampires. "Things between us and the vampires are tense inside the city, too. We have conflicting agendas—except for everyone being on board to build the college. However, with so many humans applying and wanting to visit the campus, we didn't want the school located on the vampire side—we knew it would increase the number of human visitors by a lot, and that would be very tempting for them. So, between the wolves and vampires vying for the spot as best protector, and since they both guard a side of the city, the university being located on the wolf side added even more animosity between us."

We stepped into the woods, leaving the scorned vampires behind us. A memory from my first week at the coffee shop passed through my mind. "Doesn't the vampire prince, Alex, attend the university? If there is so much animosity, why is he there?"

"He does, and it's partly to keep an eye on things," Killian said, catching up and walking on my other side. The trees were still spread out enough for us to walk next to one another. "Which was a whole thing within itself. During the first few months the university opened, he fed off one of the humans who was touring the school. Ever since then, a shifter has been assigned to escort every vampire around campus so that doesn't happen again."

"What? Really?" The day I'd met him, he'd seemed nice...but that was part of a vampire's allure. They were manipulative and practiced at hiding their true intentions because darkness was already a part of them. A bloodthirsty monster that tried to make each of them lose their humanity. "He can still walk in the sunlight, or at least tolerate it."

"He's only drunk from the tap a few times." Griffin laughed harshly. "And has never killed anyone. So he's actually pretty clean. Apparently, one of the students had cut the girl or something, trying to make him lose control."

"Wait, they *tried* to make him lose his humanity?" No wonder Dad said vampires were too corrupt to be around. Granted, I was learning that the shifters and vampires needed the silver wolves' help to suss the vilest people out. Just like how Griffin didn't sense Dick's true intent—if he had, he wouldn't be letting Dick make decisions on his behalf. Maybe the silver wolves leaving the city had been the wrong move after all.

I needed to talk to him about that, but there was always something more pressing going on.

"Yes, Shadow City has come far, but there are still some circles trying to get ahead." Griffin shook his head. "It's hard at times to figure out who is friend or foe."

"This could be a soap opera," I tried teasing, but the joke fell flat. Sometimes the truth wasn't all that funny.

Silence descended between us as the trees thickened. Griffin took the lead, heading to the spot Rosemary had directed us. He reached back and held my hand like he needed to make sure I remained there.

Killian walked behind me, and when I looked back, I saw him glancing around—no doubt looking for any signs that we were being followed or at risk of imminent attack.

I kept my eyes skyward. No way was another damn bird going to spy on us.

Luckily, I didn't see or hear anything suspicious. My heart couldn't help but balloon with hope. Could we actually get ahead of whoever was hunting me after all?

We're almost there, Griffin linked, his pace increasing.

He was as eager to arrive as I was. In fact, I was beyond ready for it all to be over. I'd love to see what a relationship with Griffin would be like without this constant threat hovering over us. I understood his position within the council would always make things tense, and he'd always have enemies, but hopefully not people who'd put our lives at risk every single day.

"Are they there yet?" Griffin asked.

"Yeah," Killian responded. "Carter linked me when we pulled into the lot. They're waiting on us." He chuckled. "He's scared that Rosemary will kill him."

Almost as if on cue, I heard Rosemary's voice. "I swear to God, if you scream like that on the way back, I won't drop you gently."

"You need me," Carter said, cockily. "At least until this is over. I ain't scared."

"You can still do what needs to be done with a broken leg." Rosemary's voice grew deep and threatening. "So don't get cocky."

"You wouldn't." He squeaked. "Dove wouldn't like that."

"Dove isn't my boss." Rosemary retorted. "I don't need her blessing or permission."

Oh, dear God. She was going to make the poor guy piss his pants before we even had a conversation.

The three of us hurried toward them, and I purposely stepped on a branch, hoping that would prevent them from going at it.

"Well, they're on their way," Carter gloated. "So—"

A loud *smack* echoed through the trees.

"Ow!" Carter whined. "You slapped me!"

"Why do you always feel the need to state the obvious?" Rosemary grumbled.

Okay, there went that strategy. Obviously, Rosemary didn't care if we were close. Which wasn't surprising.

The two of them came into view, and Carter was holding a hand over his left cheek.

"I swear the two of you bring out the worst in each other." I shook my head. "And to think you took Rosemary's shit at the coffee shop when I started working there."

"Because I'm a professional." Carter placed his free hand on his chest. "And all bets were off the first time she flew my ass up in the sky. All I could see were clouds, not even the earth below."

"Let's focus," Griffin barked. He stood in front of Carter and crossed his arms, glaring at the guy. "Now spill."

"Fine." Carter lowered his hand. A bright red handprint marked his face.

She'd slapped the shit out of him. I kind of felt bad. Kind of.

"They want it to go down tomorrow." Carter inhaled and winced. "Dude, this still hurts."

Killian rubbed his forehead. "Carter, man, if you know what's best for you, focus."

"They want me to send her out back to take out the garbage around seven in the morning so they can kidnap her before the campus gets busy." Carter took a deep breath. "If they don't get her, my brother loses a hand."

"Well, at least he has another one," Griffin rasped.

"Stop it." I smacked his arm. "He will not, because they're going to capture me."

Griffin's nostrils flared. "Like hell they are."

"If they don't, we won't find out who they are." I wasn't sure what else to do so he would get on board with this. "And they're going to keep attacking. This is the one time we have a heads up on their plan. They take me, and you all will be prepared to follow."

"I can be nearby in a tree." Rosemary nodded and rubbed her fingers together. "I can stay high enough that they won't see me, and I won't lose her." She looked at Griffin. "There will be absolutely no risk of me losing her."

"And you two can be in the parking lot in the car. Hell, we can even rent a car so they won't know it's yours." We had a whole day to plan. We could get a rental car tonight and already have it parked on campus. "You follow us, and worse case, if you can't keep up, Rosemary can text you the location when they stop."

"You expect me to be okay with you being used as bait?" Griffin asked as his forehead wrinkled and his mouth dropped open. He looked completely flabbergasted. "There's no *way* this is going to happen. Tell her, Killian."

Killian lifted a hand. "I'm not thrilled about it, but Dove has a point. This may be the only chance we have the upper hand. We're clueless, and this could lead us straight to the organizer."

I placed a hand on Griffin's chest and turned toward him. "I'm not asking for permission. I *will* be doing this because it's the best plan we have and may be the only time we'll have this kind of advantage. They've been one step ahead of us the whole way. They'll be arrogant and not expect it."

"So, that's the plan." Rosemary nodded. "I promise, Griffin, I won't lose her—and I'll be watching over her so nothing bad happens."

A *kak* sounded, still far away, but my blood ran cold. That was the sound of a falcon.

CHAPTER SEVENTEEN

THE SCENT HADN'T HIT, and the noise was at least several miles away. Luckily, the falcon couldn't hear us—as birds didn't have exceptional hearing like wolves and angels—but their vision was better.

"We need to get out of here before that falcon finds us." Granted, the bird might not be working for our enemy—but we couldn't risk it. "Rosemary, when you get back to Griffin's, we can make more concrete plans. It's probably better if Carter doesn't know the details in case anyone comes poking around ahead of time."

"True," Rosemary agreed and picked up Carter, throwing him over her shoulder as her black wings sprouted from her back.

"What the—" he gasped, and she placed a hand over his mouth as his eyes grew wide. She took flight, using the trees as cover, flying in the opposite direction from the bird. She flapped her wings hard and disappeared from our sights within seconds.

Killian chuckled. "That was one way of handling it."

"At least she knew to stay hidden, but we better change the subject." I walked back toward the Navigator.

"Shouldn't we stay out here for a little while?" Killian asked as he glanced at the sky. "Not that I want to."

Ideally, we would go deeper into the woods for a hike to keep up our pretenses. "The bird could be leading others over to attack us. Maybe they caught on that Carter was alerting us to their plans and this was the true strategy." Too much was at risk to stay, including the memories that haunted Killian.

"You're right." Killian nodded.

Let me take the lead. You're the one they're after, so please let me lead with Killian following you. Griffin moved in front, not bothering to wait for my answer.

I wanted to argue, because he'd only pretended to run that by me, but we didn't have time to spare. All it would potentially do was put us in more danger, and I cared too much about these two to let pride get in my way. I swallowed the hurt feelings, even though the lump in my throat refused to go down. Being an alpha wolf myself, I didn't like people taking decisions away from me.

I stayed between the two men, focusing on getting back to the car. We moved at a much quicker pace than we had when entering the woods, so if the bird caught up to us, we'd be safely around others.

The next *kak* sounded much closer because he did have the advantage of traveling through the sky, but he wasn't gaining as much on us as he might expect. The three of us were comfortable in nature, and even in unfamiliar territory, we could cover a lot of ground quickly.

Water splashing could be heard, which meant that we were nearing the lake with the bears and the vampires. Right now, they'd be a welcome sight...even with the vampires' hateful expressions.

When the trees began to thin, my heart returned to a normal rhythm. We would definitely make it back before anyone could attack.

Sprinting even faster, we reached the tree line in minutes. Griffin slowed down before the other supernaturals could see us. They'd probably heard our approach, but that shouldn't seem odd due to the kind of supernaturals we were. The only thing that might seem strange was the short amount of time we'd been gone; wolves tended to enjoy running for a while, not minutes.

As expected, the vampires looked at us with varying puzzled expressions. One was visibly upset, stroking his short beard while watching us the entire way to the vehicle.

The three of us pretended to not notice their stares, our focus on getting to the Navigator. When my hand clutched the door handle, the falcon flew overhead.

Unable to stop myself, I looked up and saw a mostly white-feathered falcon. He didn't seem to be paying any attention to us as he swooped down toward the bear shifter couple, who were locked in a lingering kiss.

He landed right in the girl's thick black hair, causing her to jerk back and swat at him. She yelled, "Ollie! What the hell?"

As I climbed into the vehicle, my body sagged in the seat. I was so paranoid, every bird shifter was potentially evil. That was how prejudice started—but right now we had to be careful. When this was all over, I would befriend some bird shifters and prove to myself that most of them were good.

Dad had told me over and over that the main problem with our supernatural world was that we were still segregated; we lived independently from one another and came together only when necessary. When I first got to Shadow Ridge, I'd found his words hard to believe, especially that first day at the university. The place was full of all kinds of supernaturals, and I knew the council was a mixed bag as well. But the longer I stayed, the more his words began to make sense. Each race was fighting for their best interests and not for the greater good of the community. Shadow City had started as a refuge, but when the angels took over, they'd recruited and let in only the strongest supernaturals in the world. The original intent of a safe haven had been thrown out the door.

"All that, and he came to hang out with bear shifters." Killian shut his door. "I'm not complaining, though. I'd rather we be severely risk-averse and alive instead of the alternative."

"Now that's something we agree on." Griffin put the car in drive. "I feel like we haven't been on the same page lately."

"Why? Because of Carter?" Killian huffed.

I did *not* want to hear this argument again. "That's the only thing you two disagree on. So please, stop. I don't have the energy to listen to you bicker like an old married couple again."

No one responded, and Griffin placed his hand back on my thigh.

You better be glad I love you, Griffin teased, and pretended to glare at me. *Because if I didn't, I might accuse you of taking his side.*

I've made it clear that I agree with him on this one. I kissed his cheek, not wanting to truly upset him. *So, there.*

Yeah, I know. He watched the road once again, and the rest of the ride was silent.

"Where the hell is she?" Griffin paced in front of the couch and loveseat. "You'd think she'd be back by now."

"Chill." Sierra snorted as she plopped next to me on the loveseat, taking Griffin's usual spot. She smelled of grease from her shift at the bar. "I've only been here for ten minutes, and you've already got me so tense that I might snap at any second."

"That's my spot," he growled and pointed at her.

"You weren't sitting here." She stuck out her tongue. "That means it's fair game."

Moments like these were my favorite. These were the small pockets of time where things felt almost normal. They were the ones that gave me enough hope and strength to waddle through the shit. A little bit of clarity among the chaos.

Killian entered the room with the burger Sierra had brought for him. "Did you roll around in the fryer before coming here? We could smell the grease on you before you even walked in."

"Don't hate." She lifted her head high. "Unlike you two, some of us have to serve bar food in order to make ends meet."

"Hey, we work hard, too." Killian gestured his burger in my direction. "It's a full-time job keeping this one alive. I swear I've never worked this hard, even when Dad was alive."

"Does that mean when things calm down, you're officially going to take over?" Sierra tugged at her bottom lip. "The both of you?"

I already knew Griffin's answer, but I'd never directly asked Killian. We didn't get alone time as we had before, with Griffin, Rosemary, and Sierra always around.

"Sterlyn and I have already discussed this." Griffin winked at me. "When we've taken down the enemy, we're going to continue Dad's original plans and make some of our own."

"Really?" She faced me. "I love this. You two will make a fierce team." She leaned closer to me and whispered, despite her voice still being loud enough for Griffin and Killian to hear, "Honestly, you're the one I'm excited to see lead. You keep his head on straight...and girl power."

"I'm standing right here," Griffin deadpanned.

"Oh, she knows." I bumped my shoulder into hers. "She's trying to get a rise out of you."

"True, but I did mean it." Sierra blew her bangs out of her face and focused on Killian. "Now, what about you?"

"Yeah, I think it's time I stop being afraid." Killian inhaled. "It's important that we protect this part of Shadow City, and with Griffin and Sterlyn in charge, I feel like it's time for me to step up and take my rightful place. How do you think Billy is going to take it?"

Sierra snorted loudly. "He'll be dancing the macarena."

Killian pursed his lips. "You think so?"

"Don't get me wrong, he's been a great leader in your absence, but he doesn't have that alpha edge." Sierra shrugged. "You'll be fine. He is an amazing second-hand. Your dad always said so."

Feet landed outside the back door, and Rosemary entered the house.

"What the hell took you so long?" Griffin bellowed as he pivoted toward her.

He should have known better than to talk to her that way. The angel wouldn't put up with that kind of attitude.

"Excuse me?" Rosemary turned her head in his direction and pointed at her ear. "I did hear 'thank you,' and 'how did everything go', right?"

"No." Sierra leaned forward, shaking her head wildly. "You did not. In fact, you heard—"

"He might not have said it, but I will." We didn't need to alienate the one person who gave us an edge—especially when the other side had crows, bear shifters, and wolves. And those were the ones we knew about. "Thank you. I hope Carter didn't drive you too insane on the flight back to wherever you dropped him off." He lived somewhere in this neighborhood, but I didn't know where.

"Oh, it went fine." A rare smile flitted across her face, making her even more breathtaking. "Covering his mouth was something I should've done from the get-go, and I may have given him a little hint of what could happen if I have to take him somewhere again and he screams."

Killian frowned, but that didn't stop him from taking another huge bite of his burger. With a full mouth, he asked, "Wha dijoo do?"

"I may have dropped him from ten feet up when he whimpered loudly." Rosemary rubbed her ears. "I can't handle him being a freaking lunatic anymore. I think he learned his lesson."

"Did he get hurt?" He shouldn't have, but with Carter, anything was possible.

"No. It may have stung a little when his feet hit the ground." She shrugged. "No biggie."

"Can we focus here?" Griffin massaged his temples. "We need to make sure we have a solid plan for tomorrow. I am personally against this plan, but obviously, I'm outvoted."

"Outvoted doesn't matter." This was my decision. No one else's. "I'm the one putting my life at risk."

"Exactly," Griffin growled.

"What about that bird?" Rosemary asked, and then snatched

Killian's burger from his hands. She took a large bite out of it before handing it back to him and sitting on the other side of the couch.

He blinked several times, looking from his burger to the angel. "What the hell just happened?"

"What?" Rosemary asked and lifted both hands. "I'm hungry."

Sierra laughed. "I brought you a burger too. It's in the kitchen."

"Thank God." Rosemary sighed. "Because that's really good."

"It's from Dick's." Sierra wrinkled her nose. "Which I hate to say, but see—if you angels tried some of the shifter restaurants, you might find that you like them."

Even though shifters would eat at each other's restaurants, we still kept to our own races. No other supernaturals frequented shifter establishments.

A pink hue tinted Griffin's face.

He might spontaneously combust if we didn't keep on track. This was hard enough on him even without their squirrel moments. "We're pretty sure the falcon wasn't spying or scouting us out. He playfully attacked a bear shifter couple who were making out."

"Okay, good. But I'll be careful and go to campus early to scan for any suspicious birds or anything else before I hide in a tree." Rosemary licked her lips. "We all need to take precautions."

"We rented a car on the way home." Griffin's jaw twitched. "And parked it in the lot. Killian and Sierra will get there early, as well, and I'll sneak over after walking Sterlyn in like normal."

Rosemary nodded. "Good—that's key. We have to make everything appear completely normal."

Easier said than done. Tomorrow morning, I'd be riddled with anxiety...but I'd have to hide it. "So, I play the part of the unsuspecting target." I only hoped that I didn't wind up in a trunk again. That had been horrible and hot.

"How the hell is Carter going to pull off you taking out the garbage?" Sierra sat back and crossed her legs. "I mean, every business that serves food takes the garbage out each night. How is he going to justify a morning trash run?"

"That isn't my problem." I shrugged, at a loss.

"It's Carter." A vein in Griffin's neck stuck out. "You can't count on him to figure out something like that. He's an idiot."

"In all fairness, he did get me into the supply closet and drug me." I hated to admit it, but the truth was just that.

The truth.

"I'm sure we can find something to throw out." One more thing to determine in the morning.

Can I talk to you? Griffin asked, his mesmerizing eyes locking with mine as his feelings of anxiety and worry slammed into me. *Alone?*

Crap. *Of course.* I stood, wishing I could tell him no. But I couldn't. I knew how concerned he was about this plan, and I needed to hear him out. I just hoped the rest of our night wouldn't be ruined.

CHAPTER EIGHTEEN

I FOLLOWED Griffin into our bedroom while the other two stayed with Rosemary as she ate her dinner. Luckily, we'd eaten our food prior to Rosemary getting here.

Well, correction... Killian and I ate while Griffin glared at him. I could feel how much this all bothered him, but there wasn't a damn thing I could do about it. When I looked at it from every angle, this strategy was what I kept coming back to.

When I entered the room, Griffin shut the door behind me a little too hard. The doorframe shuddered at the force.

I'd been expecting his outburst, having felt it brewing inside him ever since Carter made the call informing us that the enemy had contacted him. For a second, I'd falsely hoped that we wouldn't argue. Hell, we hadn't officially had our first fight.

I guessed that changed now.

I want you to call this off. Griffin jumped right to the point. *This is a bad decision. You being captured isn't the right answer.* His hazel eyes darkened to all brown, as if the warm green flecks had simply disappeared.

I kept a clear head and didn't react as I wanted to because I had to put myself in his shoes. If he'd suggested using himself as bait, I wouldn't be thrilled, either. In fact, I would be doing everything possible to find a different course of action. But, unlike him, I would see the plan for what it was—our best chance.

This, again, went back to him not having the same battle strategy training I'd had my entire life. Without that training on his side, I would have to help him see things in a different light. *Okay, then what do you suggest?*

His head tipped backward as the tension around his eyes slackened. He nibbled on his bottom lip as his brows furrowed in confusion.

He hadn't expected me to respond like that. He'd been prepared to argue.

Uh... Well, I can get Dick involved and see if he can help us find the culprit. Griffin nodded like he was convincing himself that what he said was the best course of action.

Dammit, I understood his gut reaction, but I needed to figure out a way to help him decide that it wasn't a good idea to include that bastard. *So, you want to put the person who is currently running Shadow City at risk and potentially lose not one council member, but two?* The words tasted sour in my mind, but talking down to him wouldn't work. Dad had used this strategy with me while I was growing up, and I believed it had helped me learn to think things through more objectively. *I'm not sure he has our best interests at heart. I have a feeling about him.*

Fine. Okay. I trust you. He blew out a breath as he ran his fingers into his now disheveled honey-brown hair. *Then we wait until they contact Carter again when he doesn't deliver you. Maybe you can say that was an odd morning request and you have other things to do.*

They won't give Carter a second chance, and he would be more likely to inform them that we knew the plans and that he was compromised in order to save his brother. Not to mention his brother probably will lose a hand or worse. I sat on the bed and placed my hands in my lap, staring straight ahead. *Then they could attack us again, knowing that we lost our temporary advantage over them.*

Then we fight. Griffin nodded as he sat next to me. *And you can stay somewhere safe like Shadow City in the meantime.*

And leave others here to fight when these people are coming for me? That was the one option that I would never accept, even if Griffin tried to demand it. *What kind of leader would that make me? If we want to lead Shadow City, side by side, that strategy is the worst option. No one would respect me or be able to view me as their alpha or, hell, even the alpha's mate.*

His hands clutched mine to the point of near pain. He practically yelled through our bond, *Who fucking cares? At least you'd be alive and safe!*

My wolf growled, infuriated that he'd spoken to us that way. We weren't his pack member, but his equal. If I wanted to, I could force him to submit to me. But the silver wolves weren't meant to lead regular wolves. They were meant to lead the other protectors and make the calls that were the most difficult to make.

War strategies.

Like these. But I would never talk down to him and insult him that way. Even if he had just done that to me. His reaction stemmed from emotions and caring; a good place, even if it was uncalled for.

Look. I tried to stay level-headed, but my irritation bled through. *I can only imagine what you're feeling.* I turned my body and fully faced him, cupping his cheek with one hand. Our eyes caught and held. *But your people not respecting me isn't an option. My dad raised me to be the kind of warrior that people would respect, and what you're asking me to do is something that would make him turn over in his grave.* If he had one. That was yet another thing I had to figure out—what those assholes had done to my pack's bodies. If I could find them, I wanted to give each and every one of them a proper burial, as any shifter and fighter deserved.

The anger faded from his eyes, and his whole body sagged in defeat. *I'm sorry. I didn't mean to do that, but the thought of you walking into something and getting hurt when I could've done something to prevent it...it almost paralyzes me.*

His honesty was what I needed to get to the root of the problem. *But you have to know this is the strategy that makes the most sense—and asking me not to do it isn't right. I get that we're mates, but I'm still an individual who believes this is the best decision. I'm not trying to be a martyr. I don't have a death wish. In fact, because of you, I'm determined to make it out of this alive. But I need you to trust me and my instincts.*

You weren't supposed to argue with me. He leaned his forehead against mine and continued, *Or use logic.*

I'll always listen to your concerns. He was my mate, and even if I didn't agree with him, he deserved the respect of being heard. *I love you.*

He ran his fingers through my hair and kissed me. The feelings of love between the two of us intermingled as we opened to each other to show how much we cared.

You are something I never prepared for. He pulled back, locking on to my gaze. *Had I known what was tugging at me that morning in the coffee shop, I would've tried not to be such an ass to you. You didn't deserve to be talked to that way.*

I smiled, remembering his cringe-worthy pickup lines. *Our first conversation was not a good way to introduce yourself, but I wouldn't have it any other way. After all, I got to tell you right away that I wouldn't take that shit from you.*

He chuckled. *I didn't know how to react. I never had a girl shoot me down like that before, and then Killian walked in, marking his territory.* He shuddered. *I almost tore him a new asshole right then and there.*

At least, you didn't pee on me, I teased. To think about how our relationship had changed since then was crazy. He was now my other half in all of the ways that mattered. The thought of being without him terrified me.

He kissed me again. *Oh, believe me, I thought about it. In fact...*

He grabbed my waist and hoisted me onto my back on the bed before crawling on top of me. He took both of my wrists, and placed them beside my head, holding me in place. *Maybe I should do it now.*

No, he wouldn't. *You've bitten me. I think we're good.*

Better safe than sorry, he said as he raked his teeth against my neck.

My body heated between being restrained and the slight pain. *I'm okay with how you're making sure.*

This time we get to go slow. He sucked hard, making his intentions of leaving a hickey obvious.

For some reason, the fact that he wanted to mark me thrilled me. The bruise would be gone by morning, but the effort he put forth for even a temporary branding excited me in ways I'd never imagined.

His hand slipped under my shirt, then my bra, and pinched my nipple. I inhaled sharply as the two sensations overwhelmed my senses.

Is this okay? he asked, caressing my breast more firmly.

I nodded, not able to speak even in my mind.

He kissed his way down my neck slowly and lifted my shirt. His mouth replaced his fingers as his teeth scraped against me.

A low moan escaped, but I wasn't embarrassed. I tried pushing against him, but his hand kept me secured in place.

Instead of loosening his grip, he bit down, which had me bucking beneath him.

Take me, I growled, primed and ready for him.

No, he said sternly. *Not yet. I'll be in agony tomorrow, so it's your turn tonight.*

What the hell? I couldn't believe that he'd say something like that —but then his tongue began to work, making my mind foggy. Need flowed through me, short-circuiting my brain.

He released the hold on one of my wrists and rolled to the side as his hand slid down to my jeans and unbuttoned them. Within seconds, his fingers were between my legs, rubbing and setting my body on fire.

The glorious torture of his mouth and hand was unlike anything I'd ever experienced. My body quivered with powerful desire. *Griffin,* I whispered, not above begging. *Please.*

He removed his hand and stood, dragging my pants and panties away from my body as he moved. After they lay crumpled on the floor, he discarded his own.

He pulled his shirt from his body, and I enjoyed watching his six-pack contract. My mate was the sexiest man I'd ever seen, and the fact that he was all mine added to the lust coursing through me.

I lifted high enough so I could yank my shirt off. I wanted to feel his skin on mine; it was the best sensation in the world. He snaked a hand around me, unfastening my bra and tossing it aside.

Ready for him, I moved to spin around, but he caught my waist, holding me in place.

I get to be in control this time. He slid between my legs and thrust deep inside me.

Throwing my head back, I wrapped my legs around his waist, and he moved in and out slowly—over and over again. He captured my breast in his mouth as he continued in a slow but strong pace, making tension build steadily inside me. I'd thought the emotions coming fast and furious couldn't be matched, but this was intense in a different kind of way. No matter how I tried to quicken the pace, he held firm.

The sensation strengthened inside me, overwhelming me. The intensity of the friction both hurt and felt amazing. I dug my fingers into his back, and a sharp metallic smell hit me as warm drops of blood puddled under my nails.

"Oh, God," I groaned, as he finally began to increase the rhythm. His body shook as an orgasm rocked through both of us. His thrusting became quicker, pounding even deeper inside me. My body contracted as the strongest release shook me. My head went light, and my vision blurred.

He slowed as we both came down from our shared high. His lips devoured me as he chuckled in my mind, *I told you you'd call me that.*

It took a second for his meaning to sink in. That first time he saw me, he'd told me I'd be calling him God later that night. I giggled and smacked his arm, rolling him off me. I arched an eyebrow as I growled, "You better be glad I love you."

"Oh, I am," he said seriously, as he pulled me into his arms. "I'm happier about that than you'll ever know."

THE NEXT MORNING, Griffin walked me into the coffee shop. His grip on my hand was extra tight, mirroring the fear and anxiety that riddled him.

We'd enjoyed our night together, but his chaotic emotions had woken me up this morning. If I were a betting person, I'd put money on him not having slept at all.

Hey, Rosemary called and told us she doesn't see or sense anything out of the ordinary, and she's in the tree. I tried reassuring him because I hated that my decision was causing him to feel this way. *Killian and Sierra are in the rental car, and you'll be with them soon.*

Just promise me that if anything we haven't prepared for happens, you'll let me know. He rolled his shoulders, at least trying to act normal. *And that you'll be okay with me stepping in if there's any indication that we won't be able to follow you, or if the danger escalates.*

As long as you make sure it's not you being overly paranoid. If he could promise me that, I'd be okay.

Some of the tension did leave his body, and he faced me. *Really?*

I trust you. I kissed him and forced myself to walk behind the counter and put on an apron. *So, if you truly believe something isn't going as expected, then do what you feel like you need to.*

"Oh, look." Carter's voice cracked, and there was sweat on his upper lip. "Your boyfriend is here...again."

His attempt to sound normal was coming across more as scared. Someone was probably watching us, given the kidnapping was

382 JEN L. GREY

supposed to take place in the next little bit. I hoped they'd expected Carter to be nervous.

"Mate." Griffin tried to sound annoyed, but his delivery fell a little flatter than normal.

Hopefully, if anyone was close enough to hear, they wouldn't notice.

"You two be nice." I tied the apron and shook my head, trying to act better than them. "One day, you're going to wind up friends."

"Fat chance." Griffin wrinkled his nose and scowled at Carter.

You need to leave. For the plan to work, he had to go get breakfast like he normally did. *I know it's hard, but after today, this should all be over.* At least, that was the goal.

I love you. He kissed me again, lingering a few seconds too long. *This is the hardest thing I have ever had to do in my entire life, and it proves I'm willing to do anything for you.*

Brushing my fingertips across his cheek, I smiled. *You proved it the time you jumped in front of that gun to protect me.* I was talking about the ambush we'd survived together in the woods outside his and Killian's houses just one day before I was abducted.

And that wasn't a hard decision at all. He kissed my fingertips and looked at me a second longer. *You better come home to me.* He pivoted and walked out the door.

I'd prepared to get hurt and be put in threatening situations, but I hadn't been prepared for how damn hard it would be to watch Griffin walk away. Even though I knew this was the best strategy, there was a chance that I might not see him again.

"Hey, Dove." Carter cleared his throat. "I forgot to take out one of the trash bags yesterday afternoon. Would you run it out back before the others get here? I'd hate for them to think it's okay to slack off."

My heart sank. His request had come sooner than we'd planned. *I'm heading out to the dumpster now.*

What? Griffin sounded tense. *I'm not in the car yet. Take as long as you can so I can get there. I need five minutes.*

Carter mouthed 'I'm sorry. They texted me a few minutes ago.'

Dammit. He was being an idiot. *They changed the time on him.*

We need to abort. Griffin sounded tense. *They could be suspicious.*

No, they're just being careful. It was something I would do if I were them. *It's smart.* I took the bag from Carter. "Okay, but I won't cover for your ass again."

I walked through the kitchen, taking my time. *Are you there yet?*

Yes, I just got into the car. I wasn't followed—I went out a side door I never use, he rasped. *Killian started the car. We're ready.*

All right. It was time.

I pushed open the back door and stepped out...and someone grabbed me from behind, spinning me in the direction of the garbage can so I couldn't see them. Before I could even scream, a cloth bag went over my head, obstructing my vision.

There was no going back now.

CHAPTER NINETEEN

MY WOLF TOOK OVER, and I yanked against the man holding my arms. It would be suspicious if I didn't try to fight him off...but that wasn't why I was doing it. I didn't like being confined with my vision taken away.

The full moon was approaching, which meant I was growing stronger each day. I almost broke free, but managed to rein myself in.

Barely.

Griffin's face popped into my head, which made me remember what was at stake. If I ruined this abduction attempt, there was no telling what other attacks would happen—and who might die as a result. So many of Killian's and Griffin's men had already died because of me.

Fingers dug into my arm as the man held me tight. The smell of grass hit my nose, telling me that this was a bear shifter.

"Open the car door before she breaks free," the guy growled.

The voice was all too familiar to me, although I'd heard it only once before.

From the horrible frosted-tips bear who'd attacked me at Dick's bar.

I knew now that the attack hadn't been some sort of attempt to instigate a civil war as Dick and Griffin had assumed about Shadow City and its affiliated civilians. According to them, people were rioting due to the opening of the gates, and shifters were attacking their own kind.

The faint musky smell of a wolf shifter coated the air, and a few seconds later, a door opened.

"Let me go," I growled. Playing the part of an angry wolf shifter wasn't hard; rage coursed through me in sync with my heartbeat. I tamped down my extreme desire to escape, trying to keep a level head. I took a deep breath like I'd been taught, but it didn't help. It was humid and dark, and I was breathing more carbon monoxide than oxygen, adding to my panic rather than relieving it.

Frosted Tips chuckled darkly. "Not going to happen."

The enjoyment in his tone rattled me to the core as the cold realization that he was as twisted as Dick filled me.

When someone shoved me toward the car, I almost stumbled, but somehow managed to stay upright. I had no clue what kind of vehicle we were getting into or who was in it. Even though I hadn't wanted to get in the trunk, I wasn't quite sure getting in the car with God knew who would be better. At least in the trunk, I'd be alone.

The musky smell tickled my nose again as the wolf shifter gasped, "Wait. Her hands. We need to bind them unless you plan on her sitting in your lap the entire way there."

God, please, no. I yanked against his hold again as my skin crawled. I didn't want to sit in anyone's lap.

"Calm down," Frosted Tips growled. "You're hot, but I know you pack a mean punch." His weight shifted, and he addressed the wolf again, "There are some handcuffs in the front—grab them, and let's restrain her."

"On it." His footsteps rushed only a couple of feet before another door opened.

This had to be a smaller car, which kind of surprised me. I'd figured they'd have several men with them, but maybe, like the other bear shifter, they expected this to be an easy job and didn't have more backup. That was a good thing. Maybe their numbers would be small—wherever they were taking me—since they thought I was subdued.

The quick shuffling of feet headed back toward us, and within seconds, my hands were yanked behind my back, and cool metal was fastened around my wrists. When Frosted Tips released my arm, a little bit of sanity came back to me. Some of the desperate need to escape was gone.

A large hand shoved me, making me fall forward in shock. Luckily, I hit the seat of the car instead of landing on the ground. With my hands behind my back, I could've been severely injured.

"Get all the way in, now," Frosted Tips demanded. "We've got to go. We've been here too long. That pathetic alpha wolf is probably already almost here. She must have linked him right away."

I stayed put, pretending to try to drag the whole situation out like he was right.

Large hands grabbed my waist and placed me on my ass. He grabbed my legs and tossed them inside. I tried to stick them back out, but he slammed the door, causing it to hit my ankle. Pain radiated for a second, but it'd only clipped the side. It should be healed in minutes.

"I know what you're trying to do," he said disgustedly from outside my window, knowing I could hear him. "And it's not happening."

When the front door opened, I startled. I'd expected the bear to be driving, but instead, I heard him climb into the passenger seat.

Tires squealed as the car jolted forward.

"Dammit, you're going to alert everyone around to us," Frosted Tips snapped, clearly not impressed. "Maybe you should pull over and let me drive."

"And waste more time?" Clearly, the wolf had had enough of being talked down to. "We're good. Besides, the campus is pretty much dead. Most students opt for later classes these days."

"Yeah, but her mate is around." Frosted Tips snorted. "So trying to stay below the radar is our best damn strategy."

"We're pulling out of the university now. Slow your damn roll," the wolf bit back.

Please tell me you're okay. Griffin's comforting voice filled my head.

That was subjective, but I was in the back seat alone. I didn't sense anyone else around me...and at the moment, I'd call that a win. *I'm fine. Please tell me that you guys are in place.*

Yeah, we're hanging back, but you're in our vision. The tension was so thick from him that he could've been sitting right beside me. *Do you know who they are?*

Well, they were waiting for me as soon as the door opened, and they put a bag over my head. At least, when I'd been thrown in the trunk, my head hadn't been covered. *But I recognized one of the voices. It's the bear shifter who attacked me in the bar.*

So he's working with the ones hunting you. That's how the bastard got away. Griffin spoke so low through our link that it was hard to hear. *I'll kill him...slowly.*

Now wasn't the time to focus on torture. No matter how appealing it sounded. *Just make sure you don't ride too close. They mentioned you, saying they needed to get me out of there before you caught on to me being gone. So they're paranoid.*

They should be. When we get there, I'll put a bullet in their heads first thing.

Wait, when did you pack guns?

Killian brought them this morning. Griffin sounded offended. *Do you think you're the only one who can make smart decisions? We were surprised when you didn't bring it up.*

Because I didn't want to risk it if we were being watched. It didn't matter now. They'd done it, and these two idiots appeared none the wiser. *But I'm glad you did. We have no clue what we're walking into.*

Remember, I wasn't thrilled with this plan, to begin with. But I got outvoted, and you had your mind made up.

He was right. I did. And I didn't regret it.

Let me see if I can weasel out any information that might help us. Any sort of heads-up we could get as to what we were walking into would be helpful.

Just be careful. Griffin pleaded.

Always. I love you.

He sighed. *I love you too—that's why I'm struggling so damn hard.*

I know. That wasn't new information. *And I'm sorry. I'm going to work these two and hope they aren't smart.* I turned my attention away from Griffin and closed my eyes. There was no reason to keep them open, it didn't make a bit of difference. "So...where are we headed?"

"That's none of your concern," Frosted Tips snapped. "Do you really think we'd tell you something like that? I bet you're already linked to your mate, begging him to come find you and save your life."

"I don't know what you're talking about?" The sulfuric stench of my lie filled the car.

"Oh, God." The wolf coughed and rolled down the window. "You'd think she'd know there was no point in doing that."

"She's a woman." Frosted Tips chuckled. "She doesn't know any better. They're born stupid."

He was trying to rile me up, but I refused to play along. Instead, I focused on the breeze whipping around me. I pretended that I could actually breathe the fresh air through the bag on my head, trying to use my deep breathing technique to help calm my racing heart.

My wolf was angry and scared, not liking that we were acting weak. She was used to dominating, and being complaisant went against everything ingrained in us. Dad had wanted us to prove these sexist assholes wrong, not bend to their will. I tried to reassure her that it was just another strategy of war, but she wasn't appeased.

Honestly, neither was I.

"So... how did you escape from that car?" I forced my voice to shake a little like I was petrified and trying to be strong. I needed them to underestimate me. That would make things easier when the time came to act.

"Once again, not answering," Frosted Tips said with annoyance. "Why are you asking questions?"

He was smarter than I hoped. That was unfortunate.

"I can't wait to see her reaction," the wolf babbled. "It's going to be epic."

"Why?" That didn't sound good. My breathing quickened, and I hoped they'd think it was due to the bag and not fear.

A loud *smack* sounded, shocking me. The car swerved like the driver had lost control for a second.

"Why the hell did you hit me?" the wolf growled. "You touch me again, and I'll kick your ass. I don't care if you're twice my size."

"Don't be a dumbass, then." Frosted Tips didn't sound scared or threatened. "You're running your mouth, which is dangerous. All it takes is one little slip, and her mate could figure it out. We have to get her far enough away that he can't use the mate bond to find her."

Whoever was making the calls had thought it through. They knew Griffin and I were mated and that they'd need to put enough distance between us to slow him down. If Carter hadn't alerted us, I would have been screwed. I also had a feeling they had backup in case I did break free again.

There was no point in continuing the conversation. I'd have to let events take their course if I wanted to learn anything.

TIME MUST HAVE STOPPED. There was no other explanation. My numb ass and sweaty face were almost too much to bear. Sweat puddled between my breasts as the heat took me to the point of almost suffocating.

I was sure there was plenty of oxygen, but I'd been under the bag for so long I was dizzy. I laid my head on the back of the seat, trying to let a breeze in from the bottom. No such luck.

All I got for the effort was a crick in my neck.

The car slowed and turned onto another road. The sounds of gravel crunching under the wheels told me we were likely close to our destination. *Hey, I think we're getting close to wherever we're heading.*

Yeah, we see that. Griffin sounded nearly unhinged. *I swear, if anything happens to you before we can get there—*

His concern warmed my heart, and I wished I could take his discomfort away. Unfortunately, I was hanging on by a thread too. The entire ride had been torture, and neither one of them had spoken again, so I'd had absolutely nothing to distract me. I hadn't wanted to talk to Griffin because all it would do would be to rile him up more, which would result in bad decisions.

We couldn't risk that, so I cut him off. *Rosemary will be there if I need help before you arrive.* He tended to forget we had more people helping us and it wasn't all up to him to save me.

You're right, but, please, keep me informed on what's going on. His thoughts broke. *We've pulled over, and we're getting out now. We'll be there soon.*

The ride became bumpier, causing my neck to jar. I sat up straight, bending my head side to side while wiggling my fingers. I needed to get my body ready to fight. I was pretty sure if I channeled my wolf hard enough, I could break through the handcuffs.

As the car slowed, my heart picked up its pace.

"We're here," the wolf shifter said as he shifted the car into park. "You're going to take her, right?"

"Yeah," Frosted Tips growled as he opened his door.

Mine soon opened as well, and he curled his fingers around my arm and yanked me out of the car. I fell on the gravel, but luckily, my jeans protected my legs.

"Oh, sorry about that," he deadpanned, the insincerity of his words clear.

"It's about damn time that the two of you got here," a deep voice rasped as feet pounded into the gravel. "I thought you fucked up retrieving her again."

The bear's hold tightened, yet again. "I don't underestimate my enemy more than once."

"You shouldn't do it the very first time, either." The new guy sounded disgusted, and his musky pine smell tickled a memory in the back of my head. Did I know him?

"Are you planning on standing here and insulting me, or are you going to tell me where to put her?" Frosted Tips snarled.

I needed the damn bag off my head. I tried climbing to my feet and pushed my pride aside as I fell.

"Wow." The deeper voice sounded unimpressed. "She outsmarted you once? Why aren't there holes in the bag for her to breathe? And how long have you left the bag over her head?"

"He left it on her the entire way," the wolf gloated. "And he said she didn't need air."

Footsteps moved closer, and I could hear the new guy squat in front of me. His hand grabbed the bottom of the bag, and he removed the material from my face.

I sucked in a breath, trying to clear my head, but when I looked into this new person's face, my heart and lungs stopped working.

Squatting before me was a younger version of Dad. His silver hair was a little darker than mine, and his silver eyes were the exact shade of my father's. That was why he smelled so familiar—his scent was a combination of Mom's and Dad's. Just like mine.

There was only one explanation as to who he was...but it was impossible. "I thought you were dead."

CHAPTER TWENTY

"OH, DID YOU NOW?" The man chuckled. "You expect me to believe that?" His eyes hardened, turning a granite color.

He had to be kidding, but my mind sputtered, not quite able to catch up with this development. *I think I'm looking at my dead brother. Cyrus.* I had to say the words, and my gut told me that saying them out loud was the wrong move. "You'd know if I were lying."

When she'd gone to clean us both up, the witch who'd attended our birth had told my father that my brother had died...and yet, this man was standing here in front of me, and the resemblance couldn't be denied. Something tingled inside my chest, and I had no clue what the hell it could be.

Your brother? Griffin sounded as bewildered as I felt. *The one who died at birth?*

The very one. I mean, I'm not absolutely sure, but he looks like Dad and smells like him and Mom. Like me.

Frosted Tips scratched his head and glanced back and forth between the man and me. "You two know each other?"

"No, we don't," Maybe-Cyrus spat.

"I can't keep up." The wolf kicked at the ground, making a dust cloud. His cornflower-blue eyes filled with confusion as a slight breeze ruffled his pecan-colored hair. He wasn't nearly as large as my brother or Griffin but more slender and athletic, reminding me of Carter. "She said you were dead, so how do you two not know each other, Julius?" Scrawny looked small compared to the other two guys.

Frosted Tips crossed his thick, hairy arms over his massive chest, straining the top two buttons of his shirt where even more chest hair spilled out. Just like I remembered, his hair was an awful vanilla color on the tips, with dark-brown everywhere else. His long, dark-brown beard reached the top of his chest hair, and he puffed out his chest—which made him look nearly the size of a truck. He wasn't much larger than Cyrus, though.

"It's none of your damn business," Cyrus retorted, and turned his hate-filled gaze back on me. "I'm taking her inside. You two idiots keep an eye out for anything that seems abnormal. We can't be too careful since she went and got fucking mated. Like that was actually going to save her." He chuckled nastily.

He was definitely a silver wolf...but maybe he wasn't my brother. Scrawny had called him Julius—which wasn't my brother's name—and he wasn't old enough to be my uncle. Maybe he was a cousin? Various ideas ran through my head. Negativity rolled off him, but it wasn't as overwhelming as the bear's or Dick's, so maybe there was hope. "You think I was trying to save myself and that's why I got mated?" I focused on the safest topic.

"That's what I would've done." He shrugged his shoulders. "But the boss wants you whether you're tainted or not. I mean...he doesn't want you for love."

Frosted Tips growled. "Get one of your flunkies to stand guard. My ass—"

Julius almost blurred as he rushed the bear and punched the guy's jaw. The force of the impact caused the bear shifter to fall back on his ass and clutch his face.

Even though it was daylight, the silver moon would soon be upon us. The power of that moon was already sizzling through my blood, so it had to be doing the same thing inside Julius.

"One more word and I'll withhold your pay and get the joy of teaching you a lesson." Julius's nostrils flared as he stood over the bear. "Got it?"

"Yes." Frosted Tips nodded so fast I was surprised his neck didn't crack. "We'll stand guard." He averted his gaze to the ground.

"If he gives you any lip..." He turned to Scrawny. "You let me or one of the guards in the house know. I will not have any of my men challenge me."

My stomach dropped. I didn't know why I hadn't realized it immediately—probably because of his familiarity—but this silver wolf was in charge. Which shouldn't be possible. We were born inherently good and were protectors of good for all supernaturals. Of course, we felt most comfortable around wolves because we were part of them—but we still had the best interests of all in our hearts.

"I'm taking her downstairs before she gets even stronger." Julius clutched my arm and dragged me toward the door.

Something inside me popped as the tingling grew warm—it reminded me of when fur sprouted across my body, but inside me instead. I tried to move my hands to rub the spot, but the handcuffs restrained them.

He hissed but didn't release his hold. Instead, he yanked harder, causing my feet to drag. I had to get my shit together if I was going to make it out of this. Maybe the connection I felt was because he was a silver wolf like me, and not because he was actually part of my family? It felt similar to my pack bond, but more intense. Maybe because he was one of the last of our kind?

Pushing the horrible thoughts away, I managed to steady my feet underneath me. If I played off like I was pathetic, this guy would know; I had to come across as strong...but not too strong. Hopefully, he'd think I was weaker due to being female—his followers thought that way, so maybe that was a reflection of him.

A large, one-story brick house sat about a hundred yards ahead.

It was easily twice the size of Griffin's, which wasn't small to begin with. As we reached the front door, I could see around the edge of the house and saw that there were at least ten cars parked at the side.

This had to be their home base, which meant the rescue mission just got trickier. The sun was beginning its descent from the midday point, which told me it was shortly after noon.

"One wrong move and I'll make you regret it," Julius promised, as we reached the door. "You may be strong, but between me, the bear shifter, and all my men inside, you won't make it far. Silver wolf or not."

He was expecting me to fight but, right now, it was more important for me to focus on every single detail I could. I needed to absorb everything and relay good intel to Griffin...and form a plan of escape in case it came down to me having to get myself the hell out of here. "Noted," I snapped.

We reached the large wraparound porch, and he swung open the oak door and pushed me inside. We entered a gleaming, high-ceilinged foyer that led into a modern living room, confirming my suspicions. This house must have been built in the last ten years.

The walls were a light gray that seemed more commercial than homey. The natural wood floors made the room seem even brighter. There were two large, dark-gray couches in front of a flat-screen television centered on one wall. Other than that, the room was bare; I guessed that only men lived here.

No one else was in the room, and some of the tension in my body slackened. Maybe there were only three of them, after all.

"You're not getting the lay of the land," he said, as he jerked me across the living room to a door in the center of the wall, to the left of the television.

The door swung open, revealing narrow stairs that led down to a basement. Not bothering to turn on the lights, he pushed me forward, making me stumble a few steps down the stairs.

Somehow, I managed not to fall, even though I didn't have my hands at my disposal. I took the first few steps fast, trying to maintain my balance.

He followed closely behind. "You're more nimble than I expected."

That was why he was yanking and pushing me along—he was gauging my capabilities. I should've realized that, but I had been too shocked by his existence and had let him get the best of me.

Again.

How did this asshole keep getting the upper hand? My connection to him pulsed and nagged at me. I wasn't sure what was causing it, but it needed to stop. I didn't want any sort of bond with this monster who was shoving me into a basement so some douchebag could come and force me to be his breeder.

My stomach roiled.

Babe, what's wrong? Griffin linked, and his anxiety mixed with mine.

I would never shut down our bond, but I did try to even out my emotions so he wouldn't feel the turmoil that brewed inside me. That was an alpha tip Dad had given me growing up. Our mates could feel our emotions and could be overwhelmed by them when we lost control of our own minds.

That problem had been steadily increasing since I got here—and by losing focus, I'd given Julius more control. *Other than being led into a basement by a silver wolf who might be my not-so-dead twin brother, nothing,* I tried to joke...but it fell incredibly flat. I should've just given him an update.

What? His voice was girl-shriek level through our link. *We're getting you now.*

No, not yet. I wanted to get out of here and away from Julius, but we couldn't be rash.

Rash would get us killed.

He laughed hysterically. *Not yet? There's no way we aren't.*

Just give me five minutes. I took a deep breath as I approached the bottom of the stairs. I focused on calming myself so I wouldn't upset him more than he already was. *Let me see what we're up against. There are a ton of cars out front. If you come in here and we're outnumbered, then our worst fear will come true: I won't get out of here.*

This is what I was afraid of. His anger and concern grew thick between us. *That we won't be able to get you out. We just handed you over to them without a fucking fight.*

He had every right to be upset. We'd been put in an awful situation. When I thought about the fate of my pack, so much hate rumbled inside me. *I know, but we're going to get out of this.* I refused to accept any other option. *We're going to get through it and stay alive. Is Rosemary with you?*

Yes, and she said the same thing. He growled, not pleased. *That she saw a ton of vehicles when she did her fly-by, and that we needed to wait. There's a crow on the lookout, too. She was almost spotted.*

That confirmed what I'd already suspected. *We're going to have to do the escape at night; otherwise, if there is a bird watching, they'll be alerted since they can see excellently during the day. I'll also be at my strongest, since it's a full moon.* I hadn't wanted to remind him of that last night because he'd have wanted to know why I thought I had to be at my strongest. All it would've done was add more worry.

Yeah, she said the same thing.

When I took the next step, the entire basement came into view. My stomach swooped and churned with nausea. A group of five men were sitting around a table on the right, and straight ahead were two rows of what looked to be six open, barred jail cells with a walkway in the middle.

One of them had a person in it.

"So, this is the girl that you've been obsessing over?" One of the burly men's dark-chocolate eyes perused me as he leaned back in his chair and bounced his foot. His grassy bear scent was strong. "I mean...she's hot, so I get it, but you two look like you could be siblings."

"So, what I'm hearing you say is that you think Julius is attractive too." I ran my mouth, wanting to get under both of their skins. Just as Julius had tested me, I needed to see what I was working with.

"You stupid bitch," the bear sneered, his mouth gaping open with a crazed smile that reminded me of a hyena. "You got a mouth on you. Maybe I should teach you some manners." He stood and rolled his shoulders like he was preparing to hurt me.

"Don't touch her," Julius spoke low and menacing.

Wait. Was he actually protecting me?

I must not have been the only one surprised by his reaction.

A wolf shifter leaned forward across the table, placing his elbows down. He wasn't as large as Julius but was similar to Killian in size. His butterscotch hair hung in his eyes a little, resembling a llama. "Since when do you care if we bust up the prisoners?"

"I don't," Julius barked, as he shoved me again. "But I have someone picking her up tomorrow, and she can't be beat-up, or we won't get paid for the job."

Not bothering to pay attention to the others, I glanced at the prisoner we passed. He looked like a younger version of Carter with the same shaggy brown hair and moss eyes. It must be Randall. The only difference between them was that he seemed stronger than his brother. A bruise circled one of his eyes, making the iris seem brighter.

Great, this was going to be fun. *So, we need to plan on rescuing Carter's brother, too.*

I love that you want to save people. Griffin didn't sound like he loved it at all. *But we have no clue where he is, and we know where you are.*

We do know where he is. I'm looking right at him. He's in the basement with me—in a cage.

Of course, he is. Griffin sounded defeated. *And you won't leave without him.*

I hadn't even considered the possibility, but now that he said it, I realized he was right. *Yeah, pretty much.*

Choosing to divert the conversation, I pressed forward. *There are five large guards down here. One is a bear shifter, and the other four are wolves. That's in addition to the bear shifter and the other wolf who are stationed out front, keeping an eye out for you.*

Rosemary saw at least ten men in the woods before she noticed the bird. He paused. *I want to rush in and get you now, but Rosemary and Killian won't budge. They're threatening to tie me up.*

We're outnumbered. Once again. I was sick of getting into these situations—but at least, having fewer people allowed us to be more flexible. We could hide more. However, having a pack link between all of us would be even more helpful. Something we needed to figure out when this was over with. *We're going to need the darkness.*

Fine, I'll tell the others. Warmth spread through the bond as he said, *I love you.*

I love you too. I pushed back my feelings toward him.

Julius unlocked the cell across from Randall's and pointed inside. "Get in there now. And no funny business. I've got to patrol the area."

Once I was locked in the cell, he spun on his heel and walked back up the stairs, leaving us down here.

Once again, time moved at a snail's pace. There was no visual indication of it passing because we were underground—but the moon was close to rising.

My blood told me that.

Ignoring the pain in my wrists, I sat on the floor of the prison. I hung my head down, pretending to be defeated for the five guards who glanced my way and snickered, from time to time. I'd named the other three. The one with dark-auburn hair who kept reaching for a red solo cup, made the obvious choice, Solo. Then, the sandy blond guy who kept picking his nose with his left hand became Leftie. And the last guy, fidgeting in his seat the entire time, was dubbed Twitcher.

I ignored them and considered all I knew about Julius. I hated that he knew things about me that other wolves wouldn't. Of course, the best way to hunt a silver wolf was with another one, but who the hell was he? My pack had been the only one of our kind, so I could think of only two options; they'd been swirling inside my head, creating chaos, because one of them wasn't plausible.

The most logical one would be my uncle, who ran. He must have run for a reason—and maybe working with assholes was his motive. But Julius was too young to be my uncle, which left two options but, with the similar features to Mom, really only one viable one.

He was my brother.

The very one who supposedly died at birth—which meant the witch had lied to my parents and kidnapped a member of our family. But why?

However, the *why* didn't matter at the moment. I had to get out of here and take Randall with me, but I couldn't alert him to anything without tipping off the guards.

I had too much damn time to think, and it wasn't good. My wolf itched to take action, and I along with her.

Footsteps pounded down the stairs in Julius's leisurely rhythm. Others probably didn't notice that he purposely walked that way—pretending to be calm for the masses—as any leader would do when they were worried or scared.

"Something wrong, boss?" Hyena, the bear shifter, asked as Julius reached the bottom.

"No." His words were clipped. "But the cavalry is pulling in shortly. They're showing up early to take her." He nodded at me as he headed over. "It's time for you to learn your place in the world."

They're here. I linked with my mate, not able to keep my panic hidden. *Randall and I gotta get out now or never.*

CHAPTER TWENTY-ONE

ONCE JULIUS'S fingers bit into my arm, our connection strength-ened and snapped between us even more. I tried not to focus on that, which was easier than it might have been, because I was damn tired of being manhandled. The raw rage hit me so hard that my skin began to tingle, alerting me to how close I was to shifting. I had to force myself to stay passive so I could surprise them when I needed to. I might have been stronger than any one of them, but even with the full moon's charge, taking down six men would be a challenge.

"But I thought the moon—" Hyena's face scrunched in confusion, making him resemble a bulldog.

"Apparently, they don't care," Julius bit as he dragged me to the stairs. "They say they're prepared and can handle her. They want to bring her to some witch to cut the mate bond before that alpha dumbass gets a read on her." Something like hesitation wafted off him.

The bond between us grew stronger, almost in pace with the moon charging through our blood. A warm spot in my chest formed, but not completely—almost as if something hindered it. The silver moon amplified all our magic, including the link we now had with one another. Whether Julius and I wanted to face the truth about our connection or not, the choice was being taken from us.

Fate always forced her hand.

I used to think that it was poetic. That destiny was mapped out for us. That our lives served a specific purpose. Some wolves liked to complain about their decisions being predetermined by a manipulative bitch—their job, their ranking, their mate—but I refused to think of it that way.

In my mind, fate knew the decisions I would make...almost like foresight. They were my decisions—she just helped solidify the plan for me.

A helping hand.

But for the first time ever, I understood the manipulative bitch sentiment. Because I would've never chosen my pack being slaughtered, my potentially dead brother still being alive, and a constant threat that wanted to ruin my mate bond and use me for their own corrupt desires.

His hand gripped my arm harder, like he wanted to virtually cut the connection off at my skin. Under normal circumstances, I'd have been pissed, but right now, I welcomed the pain. It helped me focus on something other than our bond and my anger.

In other words, it kept my wolf in check.

"Follow me." Julius snapped his fingers with his free hand. "I want all of you up there in case something goes down. Those idiots who are picking her up aren't trained, and there's no telling if they were followed. Another reason they were supposed to wait until tomorrow."

Some of my anxiety ebbed. At least Carter might not be blamed for Killian and Griffin following me. After all, he was only trying to protect his family.

"Angus, take the lead." Julius gestured at Hyena. "Make sure nothing looks funny. The others are probably running their mouths instead of keeping an eye out."

"Yes, sir." He walked in front of me and took the stairs two at a time.

He was an eager one. He must be hoping for a fight. Men like that enjoyed the rush that only fists could achieve and looked forward to inflicting harm on others.

Silver wolves naturally sought out peaceful solutions to conflict. We chose war only when absolutely necessary.

Well, every silver wolf I knew besides Julius. But that glimmer of light inside of him had to be the ways of the silver wolf attempting to influence him.

"Get your ass up those stairs now," he said threateningly. "Or I'll push you up them."

"Shouldn't he come too?" I gestured to Randall.

He pushed me toward the stairs. "No. Now move."

Dammit. I had to think of a way to get Randall out of the basement, but nothing was coming to me.

At least, I could tell that my growing connection with Julius was getting to him. I could sense a portion of his feelings. Not like I could with Griffin, but stronger than a pack bond. Hell, I had no clue what was happening. But the more unsure Julius felt, the edgier he became, which meant he was unpredictable.

And dangerous.

Unpredictability was the thing Dad taught me to be wary of the most. Opponents like that were either unsure how they felt or were completely unhinged. Sometimes, they were one and the same.

I had a feeling Julius was the latter. He wanted to keep his emotions in check, and right now, they were riding a tidal wave, pulling him under.

A feeling I understood all too well—but I had my father's teachings whispering in my mind. He anchored me even in death. Who knew whose teachings were going through Julius's head.

Rosemary killed the crow, so we're making our way in right now. Griffin had a calmness to him that I hadn't felt since last night. *We're getting your ass in the car and taking you home.*

Ah... Taking action appeased him. I put a foot on the first step, moving slowly but steadily. I didn't want to stall so much that I made Julius suspicious, but I wanted to give Griffin and the others as much time as possible to reach me. If Julius got me into the next car, there'd be no going back.

I could feel it in my bones.

Deaths would be rampant, and the thought of who might be willing to die to save me didn't sit well in my stomach. If anything happened to Griffin, it would kill me. Even injury or death to Killian, Sierra, and Rosemary would hurt like losing a pack member.

All of those walls I'd been determined to keep intact had crumbled all around me. Not only had I let Griffin in, but the other three as well.

Julius huffed. "Get your ass moving, *now.*" He shoved between my shoulder blades, forcing me to fall forward. My hands were still cuffed behind me, so my chin hit the steps; the pain shot through my jaw and teeth. I had to get out of these handcuffs. I'd been moving my fingers constantly, trying to help keep my blood flowing. Being able to move my hands comfortably to fight as soon as I broke free would be necessary for our survival.

The copper taste of blood filled my mouth, making the smell twice as strong. My stomach roiled as I got on my knees and slowly stood again. "You push me like that one more time, and I'll kick your ass." Just because he couldn't handle our connection didn't mean he got to be a bigger bully and asshole than he already was. I could be complaisant, but I refused to be his punching bag.

"Oh, really?" He snorted. "What are you going to do about it?"

Yeah, okay. I was close to the top of the stairs, and he was being cocky as hell. *Please tell me you guys are ready. I'm about to kick someone's ass.*

What do you mean? Anger laced each one of Griffin's words.

Forcing myself not to turn, I took another step toward the main floor. There were only three steps left until I reached the top, and the front door was only about twenty-five feet from there. I could be outside in less than a minute. *How long until you get here?* I didn't have time to answer all his questions. It was time for action.

We're almost there. Killian and Rosemary are taking out two wolves who were running the perimeter. Sierra and I are coming through the woods in front of the house. A Suburban just arrived with at least four additional guards.

Okay, so they were pretty much in position. None of the wolves here were alarmed, which meant the two Rosemary and Killian were attacking either weren't part of the same pack or they'd taken them down before they could alert anyone. Either option was fine with me as long as no one was aware that an attack had already begun. *I'm kicking ass, starting now. I'll be running out the front door soon.*

I spun around and kicked Julius in the stomach, channeling my wolf and alpha power.

His eyes widened in shock as he fell backward. He reminded me of a bowling ball taking down pins as he tumbled against the guards behind him. All five of them slammed down the stairs, and I pivoted toward the door, taking the last three stairs in one leap.

As I landed on the main floor, I tugged power from the moon and jerked apart my wrists, shattering the handcuffs that had bound me.

"How the hell did you do that?" Hyena's mouth dropped as he stared at the shattered metal on the ground.

"A full moon is rising." I gestured out the window where the moon peeked between the trees. It was twilight, just when the sun and the moon swapped spotlights.

The dumbass turned to see if I spoke the truth, turning his back to me.

Maybe these guys weren't as well trained as I thought. That would be beneficial.

I charged at him before he could spin back around, elbowing him hard on the neck. He dropped and grasped his neck in pain.

However, he didn't go down as I'd hoped. Instead, he rolled his neck like he was working out a kink and lowered his body. Then he ran straight at me.

Hunkering down, I braced for impact. I forced myself to wait until he was about a foot away before moving into action; I didn't want to give away my plan. I pivoted, bringing up my leg and then snapping my foot out to kick him in the stomach. His weight almost knocked me over, but my wolf surged, harnessing my strong magic. His body flew into the wall behind him, and he dropped, groaning.

Footsteps raced up the stairs toward me. Now I had to get the hell out of here. I swung the front door open and paused.

Six men turned toward me. Frosted Tips, Scrawny, and four new enemies dressed like the men who'd attacked my pack that day. All in black and with ski masks.

Scrawny blinked and shook his head. "That shouldn't be possible."

"Well, it is, dickwad," Frosted Tips growled. He grabbed a pistol from his back pocket and pointed the barrel at me. "But it ends now. One wrong move, and I'll shoot your ass." He shook his head as he chuckled. "Dumb bitch."

Rosemary swooped silently into view and dove toward Frosted Tips.

She was going to be able to attack before they saw her.

A shriek filled the air as Rosemary caught Frosted Tips and lifted him into the sky.

"They've found her!" the shortest of the four new additions yelled, his voice sounding like a toddler's. "Everyone get your guns!"

Every single one of these idiots liked to state the obvious—like, if they didn't say it out loud, no one would know what to do. No wonder they'd had to surprise-attack my pack in the middle of the day of a new moon cycle with machine guns in order to win. We would have slaughtered them otherwise.

"Put me down!" Frosted Tips yelled. They were at least a hundred yards high at that point.

"Gladly." Rosemary retorted, and released him.

The phrase "he screamed like a girl" had never made much sense to me until this moment. The bear shifter sounded like a five-year-old throwing a tantrum over a Barbie doll.

A sickening *crack* sounded as Frosted Tip's body made impact. It bounced a little and a *thump* sounded as the body caved in on itself. Blood spilled from his mouth and eyes, but his death had been immediate. There was no sound of a heartbeat.

I'd never seen anything more disgusting in my life.

"Holy shit," a taller guy in black said, his voice so deep it sounded like a bass guitar.

A gunshot rang out, and Toddler Boy in black grunted as he dropped. Blood puddled under his head from where he'd been shot between the eyes.

The other three men in black pulled guns from their holsters. This was going to be another bloodbath—the very thing I'd hoped to prevent by coming here. Obviously, good intentions didn't matter. Death was inevitable whenever I was involved.

Julius and the four men from the basement barreled out the front door with their guns already in hand. Hyena gimped after them, rubbing his neck and the back of his head with his face fixed in a grimace. His pupils were dilated, meaning he had a concussion.

Once again, we were outnumbered, which seemed to be the norm lately.

Another shot made its mark as Bass Guitar moaned and clutched his shoulder. The bullet hadn't landed a kill shot, and I guessed it must have come from Killian or Sierra.

"Get her now," Julius screamed and pointed at me. "Make sure she stays alive, or all of our asses are toast."

If I could make it to the woods, I would be able to shift and be more helpful. But Julius's four men ran right at me as the three remaining black-clothed guards shot back at my friends.

Julius lifted his gun skyward, pointing at Rosemary.

Normally, I'd have been worried, but I remembered from that night in the woods that Rosemary was able to use her wings to shield us from bullets. She would be fine; it was the others I had to worry about. These men didn't care about killing them.

Griffin, Killian, and Sierra kept shooting, distracting all but Twitcher.

Twitcher made the first move, swinging a punch aimed for my face. I dropped and spun, kicking him in the stomach.

Stumbling back, he gripped his middle and his nostrils flared.

Solo moved to attack, but Twitcher rasped, "Stand down. She's mine." His breathing became labored as he straightened and took slow, deliberate strides toward me. "You're going to pay for that," he threatened.

"Come at me," I smirked, channeling my crazed side. "Back up those idle threats with some worthy action," I wanted to make him mad and embarrassed that a woman had mocked him. Taking him down would be so much sweeter.

"Keep it up," he spat. "I'm going to make you beg for forgiveness."

"Oh, wait." I'd always thought Dad had exaggerated the standard male alpha elitist, as if trying to purposely enrage me. The sad truth was he hadn't at all. We were stuck in an old hierarchy where women were expected to submit and obey. Boy, did I have a lesson to teach them all. "You kidnapped me and held me against my will, and I'm supposed to be the one who begs?" I lifted my hand and gestured for him to come on. "Bring it, prick, so I can put you in your place. But unlike me, you'll be crying for mercy. Don't waste your breath asking for forgiveness."

Gunshots fired, and the three guys in black ran toward the tree line, while Scrawny turned and ran down the driveway toward the main road.

Julius shot at Rosemary, and as expected, she blocked the bullets, but couldn't get any closer since she had to use her wings for protection and not flying.

Unfortunately, the angle of the house and our positions meant my allies didn't have a clear shot at Julius or the four assholes surrounding me.

I was on my own. At least, for now. I had to figure out a way to give us the advantage—but we were outgunned. I needed to take down these four clowns so I could help the others.

Leftie was at least three times my size. He hissed and ran toward me, no doubt planning to use the force of his weight against me. There was no room for error. One misstep, and he'd have me right where he wanted me.

CHAPTER TWENTY-TWO

"AUGH," Leftie grunted as he lunged, aiming for my body.

I dropped to the ground on my back. As he flew over me, I kicked him in the nuts and lifted him, causing him to flip over and land on *his* back.

A loud thud and groan confirmed that I'd hit my mark.

I climbed back up and into a fighter's stance with my feet shoulder-width apart, shuffling backward to keep an eye on everything going on around me while I moved into sight of Griffin and the others.

If I wanted their help, I had to position myself so they could see me *and* my attackers.

Leftie rolled over and vomited chunky bits of whatever he'd eaten; the stench stole my breath away. My own stomach rolled like it wanted to sympathy barf beside him.

Yeah, not happening. I breathed through my mouth and kept my eyes averted from him. He'd be down for a while.

The firing stopped, and the other three descended on me. They weren't underestimating me as the other two had.

"Watch her," Hyena warned, and rubbed his neck. "She's stronger than she looks."

"Yeah, dumbasses." Llama smirked. "She's a fucking silver wolf. What did you expect? You've fought Julius."

"But he's a man." Hyena waved a hand toward me. "She's less than half his size, but she delivers a stronger punch."

Dammit. I'd fooled them at first, but the ruse was over. They were aware of what I could do...granted, they didn't know to what extent. I smiled, hoping I looked crazed. If they were attacking me in groups now, then they were at least a little nervous, so I needed to play into it.

Act deranged.

I forced laughter from deep inside my belly while shaking my head. The sound chafed my throat due to the anxiety mixed within it. As much as they were scared, so was I. Not only for myself, but for my friends.

I was so tired of putting us all in danger.

My blood pumped with the moon's magic. I took a second to glance in its direction, noting that it was above the trees now. The light shone on me, giving me a silver moon high.

Raising my hands, I watched my skin glisten silver. On nights like these, I could take on the world.

"Dude, her skin and eyes..." Solo sounded awed. "I've never seen anything like that before."

Wait. If they'd been around Julius, then they should've seen this before now. I glanced at the other silver wolf and noticed a faint hint of silver around him, but nothing like my alpha shimmer, or even like my pack members had. Alpha blood contained the strongest magic, and thus, Dad and I always looked more silver than the others—but they'd still shone brightly in the moonlight.

Maybe he wasn't my brother, after all.

The thought both comforted and upset me. I didn't need a family member who was out for my blood, but at the same time, having any sort of family would be nice...even a cousin. I understood that Griffin was my family now, but he couldn't understand the struggles of being a silver wolf. No matter how hard he might try, he would never fully get there, just like Mom.

"What are you doing?" Julius yelled, turning to face us. "She's leading you right in front of her friends. Get her ass back over there." He glanced at Rosemary, who was swooping toward us again, and fired a few rounds, stalling her. He shoved me back toward the front door, where Griffin and the others didn't have a clear view of me anymore. However, when his hand touched me, the warm spot in my chest solidified as our bond snapped into place.

His conflicting feelings slammed into me almost as powerfully as Griffin's. He inhaled sharply, and his gunfire halted as he shifted his entire focus to severing the connection between us.

Solo, Llama, and Twitcher descended on me like I was the prey they desperately needed.

Llama moved behind me and clutched my arms like he could restrain them permanently behind me. I played along and leaned back against him as Solo pulled out another set of handcuffs—as if those could hold me.

They hadn't seen what I'd done to the other pair. They'd been downstairs.

As Solo got closer, I leaned back on Llama and kicked Solo in the jaw. He twisted through the air and landed several feet away, his head hitting the ground with a sickening crack.

"Don't waste your time with handcuffs," Hyena said as he bounded off the porch, already recovered enough to join the fight. "The bitch shattered the other ones."

I was tired of being bullied and called derogatory names just because I was female. I pulled more power from the moon, making myself even stronger. I leaned forward and threw Llama over my body. His hold released as he tried to catch his fall, but he landed hard on his back, hitting his head and passing out.

"Julius," Twitcher shouted. "She's kicking our asses."

Dammit, are you okay? Griffin linked.

Yeah. I glanced in his direction for a second and could just make out the three of them squatting in the tree line. *How about you guys?*

We're trying to get to you. He sounded frustrated. *We hit another one of them.*

I'll be there to help in a second. It was time to end this.

Not wanting to be on the defensive any longer, I decided to take control of the situation. I no longer had any reason to not go all out. I called to my wolf, asking for her to come forward. She gladly obliged, and within seconds, my bones began to crack and reform. Before long, I was on four legs, completely shifted into my animal form.

"Holy shit." Hyena stopped and stared.

On nights like these, my wolf was huge; on all four legs, I was the same height as I was in human form. I bared my teeth and stalked toward Hyena, letting him know that he was the prey, not me.

His bottom lip quivered as he seemed to realize he was on the wrong side...at least, at the moment.

That wasn't going to win him sympathy. He'd proven that he had no remorse about handing me off to a horrible fate. The only reason he had regret now was because of his fear.

As if realizing his best chance of survival was in his animal form, he began his own shift.

I'd never fought a bear before, so this would be interesting. More hair sprouted along his body even though I wasn't sure how. The asshole had been hairy as fuck, to begin with.

He roared at me in his beast form.

However, he didn't have the size advantage he would on standard wolves—because I was the same size. He barreled toward me, probably planning on using his brute strength against me. I easily dodged him, and he ran past me several feet before he could stop. He skidded in the gravel and spun back around.

Drool dripped from his teeth as his chest heaved. He lumbered back in my direction but, this time, didn't race like before. He antici- pated that I'd dodge him again. So, when he got close, he stood on his back two legs and wrapped his arms around my body, countering my move.

He'd surprised me...and it infuriated me. I'd been trained better than that.

As he tightened his hold, pain coursed through my body, alerting Griffin.

Sterlyn. Griffin cried through our bond.

I'm fine. If he did something stupid, then both of us would get hurt. There was no way in hell I'd let anything happen to him. *He doesn't have me.*

As Hyena wrapped his arms around me, I sank my teeth into his upper shoulder.

He grunted as he stumbled back and then attacked again, swiping a paw at me. I tried to get out of the way, but his claws slashed into my leg. Pain radiated, but luckily, I'd gotten out of the way enough that it wasn't detrimental—only a minor inconvenience, since I could heal quickly under the Silver Moon.

Not wanting him to gain the upper hand, I lunged at his neck. He swung an arm, swatting me like a fly. I flew back several feet and landed on my side. Fighting through the ache, I forced myself back onto all fours.

Hyena scuffed his paws in the gravel, throwing out small rocks and dirt that hit my face and legs. The rocks stung, but the dirt in my eyes was the bigger concern.

Dammit, he was fighting dirty. Of course, he was.

I closed my eyes and focused solely on hearing as heavy paws pounded my way. Hyena was running at me at an angle. At the very last second, I dropped and rolled in the opposite direction, forcing him to fall with a thud. I then jumped on his back and sank my teeth into his uninjured shoulder.

Growling, he bucked like a bull in a rodeo, trying to fling me from his back—but I dug my teeth in deeper, along with my claws. I shredded the skin all along his back, and he whimpered in pain. Eventually, he dropped and rolled, capturing me under his weight.

For a second, I couldn't breathe, but it was just my mind playing tricks on me. Getting my head on straight, I stretched, reaching the side of his neck. That was all I needed. I bit down right where the artery was. Even though I wasn't fully ripping out his throat, he'd bleed out too quickly to heal this way. It wasn't an instant death, but it wouldn't take long.

Blood poured from his wound, coating the fur around my neck and chest crimson. He lurched to his feet as if he thought that would reverse the fatality of the injury. Within a few steps, his legs gave out, and he succumbed to the inevitable.

Not worried about him anymore, I turned my attention to find Llama back on his feet. He'd been trying to sneak up on me while I'd been preoccupied with Hyena.

His eyes widened, and he shook his head and raised his hands. "Look, I don't mean to cause any trouble."

But that wasn't the truth, according to the horrible stench swirling around. Everyone here had a darkness within them that told me otherwise. And, unlike Julius, they didn't seem to have any redeeming sensibilities. They'd be after me again in a heartbeat. Hell, to be fair, Julius probably would be, too.

"Don't be a damn pussy." Leftie climbed to his feet, his face red with either pain or rage. Most likely a combination of the two.

My natural instinct was to focus on Leftie, but Llama had proven he had no problem trying to attack me while I was preoccupied. Since he was pretending to surrender, I couldn't force myself to kill him, but I could knock his ass out.

Using the element of surprise, I kicked at his head, forcing his body to spin hard to the ground.

Leftie said with disgust, "That asshole deserved it."

Not wanting to hear any more of his lip, I lowered my head and bulldozed him, past Julius—who was still shooting at Rosemary—and five feet away into the trees where Griffin and Killian were located.

Leftie tried to get a grip around my neck, but his hands slipped on the fresh blood. I picked up my pace and slammed his body into a tree trunk, and his arms jerked with an accompanying *crack*. When I stepped back, his body crumpled at my feet. I realized that I must have broken his neck, and his heart wasn't beating any longer.

I spun back around to locate Twitcher, only to see him racing down the gravel road. One of the men dressed in black growled and shot at him, and he cried out as he fell.

"You know there is no escape," Bass Guitar yelled at him. "Now you're going to wish you'd died."

I imagined they planned on beating the shit out of him, and God knew what else. No wonder the first bear shifter to kidnap me had killed himself that day.

Rosemary landed beside me, her twilight eyes filled with worry. She touched my fur, and her power entered me, but after a few seconds, she sighed with relief.

My heart raced with fear from her being here since she'd been fighting Julius. However, I could feel the connection still between me and Julius, and I turned to find him lying still on the ground. My body tensed, then sagged with relief when I realized he was breathing.

She must have understood because she wiped the blood from her hands onto her pants and sighed. "I was told to protect the silver wolves no matter what."

She'd told me that before—and I realized it applied to Julius, too. The weight that lifted from my shoulders once I understood that told me I already cared about this man more than I should. The connection between us *was* familial.

I nodded and focused on my next few targets. Once we eliminated them, we could get the hell out of here.

Rosemary ran next to me, pointing to the man on the far right, and gestured at herself. Then, she motioned at the one on the left and at me. The message was clear. We'd get the two on the outside, and Bass Guitar, who was in the center, was already hurt and not able to react quickly; because of his injured shoulder, he wouldn't be able to train his gun in opposite directions, so when he turned to shoot at

Rosemary, I could take his ass down. They wouldn't shoot at me first since they were supposed to keep me alive.

Moving as quietly as possible, I trotted toward the man on the left. Of course, that was the moment that the breeze changed directions and blew my scent his way. He tensed and pivoted toward me. His attention flicked to the bodies that lay scattered around, and then to the angel who was about to attack his cohort.

"How the hell do you all keep doing this?" he asked, his voice thick with anger. "We were told if we couldn't take you alive, we should kill you on the spot." He pulled out his gun and aimed it right at me. I pushed my legs, trying to reach him before he could fire.

The mixture of my parents' scents invaded my senses...almost as if I was trying to remember them one last time before I died. Panic sank deep inside me and seeped through the bond connecting me and Julius. But that didn't make sense. He was passed out behind me.

Griffin's cry filled my ears as gunfire went crazy, and I linked to him. *I love you.*

Rosemary flapped toward me, her hand reaching out for me.

The sound of a gunshot echoed loud, and a flash of silver slammed into me as Julius's voice popped into my head, *No! She can't die.*

I landed hard, my breath knocked out of me by either the force of the impact or the fact that we had some sort of bond that now allowed him to mind-link with me. Julius held me down, his face set with pure determination.

Gunshots rang from Bass Guitar and his two friends, back in the direction of Griffin and the others. So, when Griffin reached my side and shoved Julius off me, I couldn't believe my eyes. I had to be imagining him in my final moments alive—but I didn't care as the mirage pulled me into his arms, tears running down his face.

Grateful to be with my mate, I focused on what had just happened between Julius and me. *But how?* I linked to Julius, even though my mind was reeling from everything else. I wasn't sure what I was addressing—him saving me or talking in my mind. Our eyes locked as some sort of battle sprang up between us like our wolves were fighting to dominate one another.

Was it that important to him to get paid and hand me over to whoever had hired him?

It didn't matter.

He'd soon regret saving me from that bullet...because our fight had just begun.

THE SILVER WOLF TRILOGY

Silver

MOON

BOOK THREE

USA TODAY BESTSELLING AUTHOR

JEN L. GREY

CHAPTER ONE

THE MAN—WHO could pass as my brother—stood over Griffin and me as my mate held me in my wolf form. The joy of having Griffin beside me eased some of the aches that racked my body, despite his concern wafting through our bond.

I loved him so damn much.

The full moon was high in the sky, shining as if informing me we'd been in battle longer than I realized. It had to be just after midnight, and there was still a chill in the late spring air that felt good on my hot skin.

Because of the full moon, my wolf body was twice the size of a normal wolf, which made me a larger target; that was partially why I'd almost been shot in the first place. Julius had just pushed me out of the path of a bullet fired by one of my enemies, but the reason why was worse than death.

In fact, he was the worst enemy here. A man from my own race, working to hand me over to someone who wanted to use me as his personal breeder.

Someone who wanted to take me from my fated mate and hold me hostage for personal gain.

Who wanted to rule over my race—the rare silver wolf—because we had ties to the moon and were stronger than other wolf shifters.

Who wanted to breed his own personal army.

It was a future that I refused to accept. I'd rather die than submit to someone like that.

The only person whose children I'd ever bear was my mate, Griffin's.

You're hurting. Griffin's deep, sexy voice rang in my head. *We have to get Rosemary to heal you.*

I'm okay. The words were bitter despite them not being spoken aloud. *Julius...knocked me out of the way.* I'd almost said *saved me*, but that wasn't what he'd done at all. He wasn't saving me from evil— he was just making sure that I survived long enough to fulfill the evil plan that would benefit him.

I bared my teeth at Julius, allowing my wolf to surge even more. We were in some sort of stare-down, and this asshole wouldn't win. Whether he realized it or not, I was more dominant—my brighter silver hair told us everything.

He'd also mind-linked with me, which shouldn't have been possible.

I lay in the grass only a few yards away from three fighters dressed in all black. Two of them were still shooting at Killian and Sierra, while the third held a phone to his ear. I couldn't hear what he was saying, though, because I was in some sort of stunned state when I *should* have been ripping out Julius's throat. It would be so easy while he was in human form and I was still a wolf. It would eliminate yet another threat—but I couldn't get myself to do it. The bond that had formed between us was causing both of us issues.

His silver eyes had darkened to a gunmetal gray, and his smoke-colored hair was disheveled from all the fighting. Only alphas and their bloodlines had silver hair, with the true alphas having the lightest shade, like mine.

"I'd heard you caused problems, but I didn't believe it until now." Disgust wafted off him and into me through whatever demented bond we shared as he clenched his hands at his sides. His scent—a mix of Mom's and Dad's—made my eyes burn. "But the world revolves around you, so I shouldn't be surprised." *She must have done something to me.*

Griffin growled, "If you say one more word about her, I'll kill you even slower than I'd already planned."

Wait...

Julius thought *I'd* done something to *him.* The idea was laughable. I'd been minding my own business—trying to live my life and move on from the slaughter of my pack—and he'd kidnapped me. Now he blamed *me* for something happening to *him?* Annoyance flared through me, calming some of the inner turmoil. *I haven't done a damn thing to you.*

Eyes widening, Julius stepped back like I'd slapped him. "Stop doing that."

"Like hell I will." Griffin's hazel eyes glowed with his own alpha wolf.

My mate thought Julius was talking to him, but it was me.

Before I could intervene, black wings whooshed past me, and someone slammed into Julius, forcing him past me. Rosemary screamed with unbridled rage as she punched him in the jaw and kept swinging. "There's more where these came from if you don't get in line." Her long mahogany hair fell over her shoulders, and her large angel wings stretched behind her. She turned her head, and her purplish twilight eyes scanned me for signs of injury.

Watching her punch Julius bothered me way more than it should have. After all, she'd refused to kill him earlier because she'd been raised to protect silver wolves. However, she wasn't using fatal blows, so he wasn't at any risk of dying.

The ski-masked gunman dressed in all black, who had just fired at me, must have been in shock because he suddenly yelled, "What the hell, Julius? We were told to kill her if things got out of hand."

Of course they'd be more upset over Julius knocking me out of the way of the bullet than care that he was getting the shit beat out of him by the angel. And the idiot just stood there like he expected an answer.

Gunfire hadn't ceased, even if it felt like time had stopped for those few moments. Bass Guitar and the other gunmen continued to fire at Killian and Sierra, ensuring they couldn't advance here to help us, while the gunman Julius had thwarted continued to gape at him.

"Get her off me," Julius grunted at me as he grabbed Rosemary's wrists, restraining her for the moment. *She's going to stand there and do nothing.*

The angel used her wings as weapons, curling them around her body and stabbing him with the tips of her feathers. For feathers that looked so silky, they sure turned into armor or a weapon when she needed them to.

His pain radiated through me, and I hated that the silver moon had connected the two of us tonight. Our mind-link was going to cause problems.

But once again, how were we able to link? We weren't mates or pack. This shouldn't have been possible. *Maybe you shouldn't have tried to capture your own kind,* I retorted back to him.

He gasped and released his hold on Rosemary, his eyes searching for me. One eye was already swollen from her attack, and blood dripped down his arms. *This is so strange. Why do you keep talking to me like this?*

My heart broke with the realization that he must have been raised as a lone wolf for him not to understand how mind-linking worked—but at least that meant he couldn't link with anyone else to alert them to what was going on. Or he was playing some sort of demented game? I couldn't rule out the latter.

The guard who had just shot at me raised his gun, pointing it at Rosemary. *No!* I screamed in terror.

"Move, Fallen," Julius growled. "He's aiming at you."

Rosemary paused and snarled, "Don't call me that." She jerked her head toward the guard and wrapped her wings around herself as he fired at us once more. The bullet bounced off her, leaving her unharmed.

"What the hell?" The guard's eyes widened, and he glanced at the gun barrel.

How I wished the damn man would shoot himself in the eye. What an idiot. You never pointed a gun at your face—even if it was empty.

I got back to my feet and forced myself to step away from Griffin's warm embrace.

"Hey, easy," Griffin said softly.

Yeah, I was about to piss him off, but the battle wasn't over. Pushing away the pain, I raced toward the gunman who'd attempted to shoot me and then Rosemary. The other two guards were still focused on keeping our allies at bay, so this guy didn't have help.

He pointed the gun back at me, but it was too late. I lunged at him, and he fell back and shot skyward, completely missing his mark. I landed on top of him and ripped out his throat, and even more blood coated my silver fur, mixing with that of the bear shifter I'd killed just minutes ago.

For whatever reason, these men were trained to fight with guns and knives and not their animal sides. Using my wolf was always my first instinct, with my knife being second. I'd been trained with weapons because we couldn't ignore them...but these people used their animals only as a last resort. It was a weakness that we'd been able to exploit in our defense.

"If you want my help, you better stop beating the shit out of me," Julius rasped to Rosemary. "Their numbers may be dwindling, but they should've already called for backup. We've got to get out of here."

My stomach sank. Just when we had only two opponents left... the threat of more coming meant we'd be back to being outnumbered. He was right, we needed to leave. I wasn't sure we could last another round.

But did that mean he planned on coming with us? Surely not.

"And we should trust you *why?*" Rosemary asked. "You could be trying to trick us so you can attack when we're fighting."

We didn't have time for a strategy discussion. I turned my focus to Bass Guitar, who had just smelled his friend's blood. He jerked his head in my direction, then stiffened and winced a little, probably due to the pain of his shoulder injury from where he'd been shot. That little bit of a reaction was all the extra time I needed to get to him.

"Ernie, we're the last two left right now." Bass Guitar's voice didn't sound quite as deep with panic setting in.

Great, he was going to get his buddy to help take me down. Maybe I wouldn't make it out alive after all, but that would be a better alternative than some mystery asshole thinking he could use me to make a silver wolf army.

"They're going to kill her if we don't help." Concern laced Julius's words, and it must have been enough for Rosemary to somewhat trust him.

She stood and hissed, "One wrong move, and I'll punch *you* without a moment's hesitation."

The two guards stopped firing as they turned their focus on the most immediate threat. Bass Guitar's dark eyes flicked toward Julius. "Get her. Don't just stand there." He turned his focus back on me and put his finger on the trigger, but Griffin lunged straight toward him.

His sculpted face was tense with anxiety, and his normally perfectly styled honey-brown hair flopped with each step. His light, hazel eyes with flecks of green locked on Bass Guitar. My mate was twice as large as my attacker—his six-and-a-half-foot frame towered over the guy, despite him being about twenty feet away.

Griffin aimed his gun, ready to take on the enemy. Seeing him like this, with so much raw power, filled me with adoration. Despite us not having the same sort of training growing up, Griffin was formidable with a gun.

A millisecond before Bass Guitar pulled the trigger, Griffin shot the guy through the head. He crumpled dead on impact.

Another gunshot fired, and I turned to find Rosemary's wings wrapped around her once again. I was jealous of her ability—getting shot hurt like hell.

Griffin turned toward the man focused on the angel and shot him between the eyes. The last guard in black dropped.

Do you know how damn anxious I've been? Griffin ran back to me and pulled me into his arms. *That blood. Are you injured?*

His unique scent of leather and myrrh filled my nose, easing a part of me now that I was back in my mate's arms. Just minutes ago, I hadn't known if I'd see him again or feel his skin on mine once more. I rubbed my head against his chest, needing him close. The fight wasn't over—not yet—but I needed to take a moment for my own sanity. Being in human form would have been ideal right about now, but if I shifted back, I'd be completely naked, and I wasn't comfortable with that.

"We've gotta get out of here in case what he said is true," Rosemary said as she marched toward Julius again.

I begrudgingly pulled away from my mate, but I needed to shift back to human form. *I need my extra set of clothes.*

Griffin nodded. "I'll be right back." He jogged off in the direction of the car as Killian came into view.

Killian's warm, dark-chocolate eyes lasered in on me, and his jaw relaxed. He rushed over, his cappuccino hair flapping in the wind. He stopped when he reached me and looked me over. "Next time, I'm with Griffin. This was way too stressful. I can't do that again."

My head nearly came to his shoulder tonight as I nuzzled against him, letting him know that I was fine. Nothing bad had happened—well, except for everyone we'd had to kill.

Before Griffin reached the tree line, Sierra stepped from between the cedars and redwoods and passed him with a black duffel bag hanging from her shoulder. Her gray eyes sparkled as if all the stress had left her body. Her sandy-blonde ponytail bounced with each step she took as she raced toward me, with Griffin following close behind.

He reached for the bag, and she turned, leaving him to grab air.

She winked at me and threw the bag in front of me. "He's pouting," she said. "He wanted to bring you your clothes, but I was coming back with the bag already. I saw you shift and figured you might need this."

I nodded and took the bag in my mouth, then ran into the trees. I quickly shifted back to human form and dressed, listening to Griffin get louder while talking about Julius. "You expect me to just let this asshole walk away after he planned to kidnap my mate? She almost died—yet again—because of him!"

"We can't kill him," Rosemary said, upset. "I'm supposed to protect them."

"You just punched the shit out of him, girl." Sierra chuckled. "I'm thinking that doesn't count as protecting him."

"Well...I didn't kill him," Rosemary retorted. "I mean, I wanted to do much worse, and if he doesn't tell us all he knows, then I might make an exception."

"I can't stay here." Julius tensed. "I have to go with you."

"Nope," Killian growled, sounding almost as upset as Griffin. "He can't be trusted. We leave his ass here for someone to find him."

"No!" The word was out before I could take it back. But I couldn't let anything happen to Julius. The two of us were connected, and I wanted to understand why. What if he really was my brother and had been kidnapped at birth? It wouldn't be his fault that he'd wound up like this, if that was the case. I locked gazes with Griffin. *He saved me.*

So he could give you to the asshole who wants to control you, Griffin growled, and his jaw twitched with rage.

Maybe, but he and I can mind-link. He had to understand that this was important to me. That if Julius was hurt, I'd feel his pain, too. *My hands are tied.*

Griffin closed his eyes and rubbed a hand down his face. *This keeps getting better and better.*

"Look, if I don't go with you, I'm dead," Julius slurred from behind a fat lip. "One of them called their alpha and ratted my ass out while I was preoccupied with Sterlyn. Besides, I know how these guys work, so I can be an advantage to you." One of his eyes had swollen shut. "Backup will be here within thirty minutes. The farther away we get, the safer we all will be."

"We?" Killian laughed maniacally. "You think you're actually going with us?" He walked over to Julius and clenched his fist.

It was time for me to do something before things got out of hand.

CHAPTER TWO

I STEPPED in to stop Killian before he punched Julius and made things worse. Since my friends and I weren't all one pack with mind-links, no one but Griffin realized that Julius was the only reason I wasn't dead. "Stop, please." I winced, preparing for his inevitable reaction. "He saved me from being hit by a bullet."

"So he could hand you off to God knows who!" Killian didn't budge. "This asshole better be glad that you and Rosemary want him alive, or I'd rip out his throat right now." He turned to Julius. "Who is after Sterlyn?"

I understood why he was reacting this way. He was the first person I'd met in this group. He'd found me floating on a log in the flood-swollen Tennessee River, asleep after nearly drowning while running from the men who had decimated my pack. He'd pulled me out and taken me in. We'd become close in that short amount of time while we were pretending to be a couple; he felt like a missing part of my family I'd never known about until that fateful day. Because of him, I'd met Griffin, my fated mate and the love of my life. "Look, he's a silver wolf, which means I'm not alone." I didn't want to spill my guts in front of Julius, so I was choosing my words carefully. "But I agree." I spun around to Julius. "Who are you working for?"

Julius glanced at me, and something unreadable crossed his face. He knew we had a connection, but I didn't want him to know how much that affected me. He said, "If you take me with you, I'll consider telling you."

"Not good enough," Griffin rasped as he punched Julius in the eye and dropped him back to the ground. "We want to know everything you know. Now!"

"Girl, this asshole doesn't care that he's silver." Sierra shook her head, looking disappointed. "They're still coming after you, and he's helping them. Don't go making me think you're not as smart as I thought. I'm not sure my heart can take it."

"He's coming with us." Rosemary nodded, backing me up. "And I'll keep watch on him the entire time—but one way or another, this asshole will tell us everything."

Killian growled, low and threatening. "He's coming over my dead body."

"Well, that can be arranged," she retorted. "I agree with Sterlyn. We can't kill him, and he admitted to knowing he'll be dead if we leave him behind. So, if he comes with us, he'll have to answer our questions, or I'll kill him myself once we get settled."

"Dude, why am I the only one getting all up in arms?" Killian asked as he turned to face Griffin, looking for an ally. "She's your mate. Don't let me be the bad guy."

"I'm not thrilled about any of this." Griffin rubbed his temples and closed his eyes. "But Sterlyn wants him to come with us, and if that's what she wants, then so be it. The closer we keep him, the more easily we can keep an eye on him."

"Are you fucking serious?" Killian's mouth almost hit the ground. "What, is she your alpha now?"

I'd never seen Killian act this way, and his words cut deep. I tried to hold in my hurt, but it flowed into my bonds with Griffin and

Julius, which pissed me off even more. I marched over to Killian and slapped him, stealing some power from the moon to make a point.

His head snapped back, while Sierra gasped.

Emotions were becoming charged, and horrible things were going to be said if I didn't keep a level head. "You're being an asshole. How dare you speak like that to your best friend, who would do anything for you *and* me?" I glanced at my mate, who gave me a tiny nod. "But it doesn't matter. You're outvoted. And even if you don't like that answer, I don't care. He's coming with us. We'll keep him under watch the entire time if that's what it takes." I stared Killian straight in the eye, ready to make him submit if that was what it came down to. I never liked playing the alpha card, but I'd do whatever was necessary to do what was right. And everything inside me told me Julius coming with us was just that.

Killian rubbed his cheek and grimaced.

"Sterlyn's right," Griffin said as he took my hand, scowling at his friend. "If she hadn't slapped you, you'd be dealing with me right now. You don't get to disrespect her that way, even if it's because you're afraid of losing her." *I'm actually kind of disappointed that you beat me to it. I've been wanting an excuse to punch him ever since I learned you two weren't romantically involved, but I've been trying to be the bigger person.*

My heart warmed, and some of my anger disappeared, nearly making me chuckle. I was afraid that we'd fight over Julius, but once again, Griffin proved that what I needed was the most important thing to him. *I love you.*

And I love you. He squeezed my hand affectionately. *If I hadn't proven it before, this should damn well show you how much.*

The man had taken a bullet for me. *You have nothing to prove.* I kissed his lips, pouring my love into him.

"Really?" Rosemary wrinkled her nose. "They're doing that even at a time like this?"

"Have you ever been in love?" Sierra countered. "You know

what? Never mind. It's obvious you haven't. There's always time for kissing."

Rosemary was right, though. We needed to get a move on. Despite me wanting Julius to come with us, I didn't trust him, so we needed to spend a few minutes making sure bringing him wasn't putting us even more at risk. "Are you part of anyone's pack?" He'd seemed surprised earlier that I could hear his thoughts, but I couldn't assume that meant he wasn't linked to anyone else.

"No, I'm not." Julius met my gaze as if he didn't have anything to hide. I watched for any signs of abnormalities beyond the horrible sulfuric smell of a lie, but nothing seemed out of sync with his natural inclinations.

Dad had taught me that over ninety-nine percent of society couldn't hide the obvious stench of a lie, but there was less than point one percent that somehow could manage to mask that standard tell. However, no lie was completely perfect, and the slightest change in heartbeat or breathing for a split second—or even an abnormal swallow—could give it away.

"Then how are you mentally stable?" Even during the short time I'd been rogue, I'd shown signs of going insane.

"Why wouldn't I be mentally stable?" He shrugged, his brows furrowing. "Is that some kind of wise crack?"

Sierra gestured at Julius. "He obviously isn't mentally stable since he's working with sick assholes."

His eyes darkened. "And you guys are so outstanding. I mean, you just killed a ton of men yourselves."

"To protect ourselves," I countered. This was once again turning into a highly volatile situation. "What I meant is, since you aren't part of a pack, how are you able to keep a sane mind?" I had to give Sierra some credit. He had obviously been manipulated, given how much hatred he held, but I didn't think it was his fault.

He chuckled darkly. "I've always been alone. I grew up that way. I haven't known any different."

Appeased, I turned my attention to my next task. This one would get the reaction from Griffin that Killian had given me. "Carter's brother is downstairs in the prison. We have to free him, too." The teen, Randall, had been taken hostage for leverage to force Carter to set me up to be kidnapped.

"Let's go." Griffin tugged me toward the car. "It's bad enough that we're taking dipshit over there, but now we're going to stay here even longer to rescue Randall and risk backup finding us?"

"That person is your responsibility because he's part of Killian's pack." Granted, Killian was Carter's direct alpha, but their pack protected one side of Shadow City. The very city that Griffin was supposed to be leading. "Killian's pack is our responsibility, and it's time we start acting like one pack and not two separate ones. Would you leave Killian behind?" A lot of the Shadow Ridge wolves felt slighted by the Shadow City packs...or that was the rumor I'd heard at the coffee shop. They were good enough to live outside the city and protect Shadow City supernaturals, but in return, the Shadow City wolves acted like they were above the Shadow Ridge pack. Now that Killian was taking over Shadow Ridge and Griffin was leading Shadow City, it was time to act like one pack again.

"You know I wouldn't," Griffin huffed, realizing that I'd already proven my point. "Fine, but dickhead here is going to go with Killian to get Randall instead of Killian having to stumble around, looking for the keys or a way to get him out."

"No, it's too risky." The best thing was to keep Julius right in front of us where he couldn't pull some sort of trick. "The keys to the jail cell are on the table. It shouldn't be hard to figure out."

"All right, I'll go. I'm linking with Randall so he doesn't get scared," Killian said as he ran off to the house.

I turned to Sierra and Griffin and said, "You two head back to the car."

"I'll keep an eye out for incoming vehicles. I'll be two miles southbound, so you shouldn't have any issues with hearing me if I see something." Rosemary took off into the sky, heading toward the road.

"They'll be here shortly," Julius growled, clearly annoyed. "We need to go or we're going to get caught. I offered to come with you all because I thought I'd get away from here faster, not be stuck waiting for my imminent death."

"With Rosemary gone, I'm staying here with you." Griffin crossed his arms, refusing to leave. "Sierra, hurry and go get the car." *After almost losing you, I can't leave you right now. And that way, two of us are watching Julius.*

His words softened me. He'd already agreed to so much, despite not being thrilled about it. *Okay.*

"Uh, why me?" Sierra asked and pointed at him. "You have two legs."

"You know Griffin would never leave here without me," I said. Sierra also wasn't the best fighter, so for her to not be in front of the house if their backup rolled up would be ideal, but I also didn't want to offend her. She'd been loyal and jumped into danger to help and be part of the team. Disregarding her would be a mistake. "We need you to get the car ready so we can get the hell out of here if things go south. Or worst case, you'll still be free and can get help if the rest of us are caught."

"Oh, okay." Sierra nodded, and her back straightened. A glint of determination darkened her irises to charcoal. "I can do that." She pulled the keys from her pocket and headed toward the car

I kept my gaze on Julius to avoid looking at the bodies that littered the ground. If I paid attention to them, I'd have flashbacks of my own slaughtered pack, and unlike these people, we hadn't done anything to warrant an attack.

When Sierra disappeared back into the tree line, I stepped toward him. "Now tell me who's after me. Who are you working for?"

"Why would I tell you now?" Julius sneered. "You could just leave my ass behind. I need to make sure you're invested in keeping me around."

Griffin clenched his fist. *That jackass.*

Yeah, I couldn't disagree with that sentiment. "We could still leave you here. Maybe you should give us something so we know your knowledge is worthwhile."

He smirked arrogantly. "Yeah, I'm not falling for that." There was so much animosity wafting off him, it was almost suffocating. I had no clue what I could've done to make him hate me so much.

The problem was that Julius knew he had us. We couldn't risk leaving him behind in case he actually did know something. And even if he didn't, I couldn't turn my back on one of my own. It would've been so much easier if I'd never found out he existed.

The front door swung open, and Randall and Killian ran outside.

Randall's shaggy brown hair clung to his face, sticky with greasy sweat, and when he saw us, his moss-colored eyes widened in horror, emphasizing the light purple bruise around his eye. "He's still here." The spicy smell of fear emanated from him.

Then Rosemary's scream filled the air. "Incoming!"

CHAPTER THREE

HER WORDS RATTLED me as we sprang into action.

We crossed the gravel driveway, and Randall was able to keep up, despite the younger wolf's injuries. If his face was bruised like that, I could only imagine what the rest of his body looked like. They hadn't given us any food or water since I'd been there, so there was no telling the last time he'd eaten, which would slow his healing. A weaker shifter might not have been able to push through.

More confident in Randall's stamina, I kept my eyes forward, trying to ignore the corpses lying all over the ground. Even though we'd killed in self-defense, death still haunted me; there had been too much of it, and I was raised to always mourn the dead, regardless of the situation. In our attackers' minds, they weren't the bad guys, and in fairness, we could be viewed as the bad guys through another lens. It was all about perception.

By the time we reached the tree line, the rumble of an engine was purring faintly in my ears. Shit, they were getting here faster than I'd anticipated. They couldn't be more than a couple of miles away now.

Wings flapped overhead, and I glanced up. Rosemary's dark feathers almost blended into the night sky, which was saying some-

444 JEN L. GREY

thing, given my better-than-normal vision. She grunted, "Hurry up. They'll be here in minutes if not sooner."

Even if the trees hid us, they'd pick up our scent easily. It was fresh and strong, and though Julius and I could easily outrun them on a night like this, we would be held back with Randall's injuries. He might be a trooper, but they would catch up to us, even with our head start.

Griffin ran faster as the crunching of gravel grew closer. The other two kept a steady pace behind us.

The only reason I wasn't panicking was because I could hear the engine of the car Griffin had rented to trail my kidnappers' car from the coffee shop where they'd grabbed me, which meant we were getting closer to Sierra. We'd known the kidnapping was going to happen because Carter—the shop's manager, and my boss—had informed us this time around. We couldn't risk our enemies identifying Griffin's or Killian's vehicles, so we'd rented one and left it in the school parking lot overnight. Griffin had driven me to work at the shop like usual in his car so that nothing would seem suspicious, and then he, Killian, and Sierra had been able to stay under the radar in the rented car. Rosemary had followed in the sky.

Fortunately, the plan had worked. They'd remained undetected until we had to act when four additional men came here a day earlier than expected to retrieve me from Julius.

The trees grew thicker, helping to cover us from the silver moon's bright light. That would buy us a few minutes before the new arrivals realized what had happened. Well, maybe not that long—the bodies were easy to see.

A small break in the trees came into view. That had to be where they'd hidden the vehicle. *How close to the road is it?* Maybe we'd have a chance to get out of here after all.

It's a cutout, so not even a quarter-mile, Griffin answered, not missing a beat. *I want you in the front seat with me, okay?*

Julius needed to be in the far back seat so he wouldn't be close to a door. *I wouldn't have it any other way.*

The enemy vehicle had arrived at the house, and the sound of doors opening and closing made my skin crawl.

"What the hell happened here?" one guy asked, clearly at a loss for words. His baritone voice sounded worried. "How the hell did this happen with Julius being a fucking silver wolf?"

"I don't know," another guy spoke as he sniffed. "But they aren't far away. He must be chasing them because his scent blends with theirs. Do you smell how fresh it is?"

They would be on us soon if we didn't move our asses. They wouldn't be able to catch us, but if they were anything like the others, they had guns and could blow out the car tires.

Black peeked through the thinning trees, revealing the rental car about fifty yards ahead. They'd rented a Chevrolet Traverse to go unnoticed. The car didn't stand out, and no one would expect these young alphas to drive something so standard; everyone was used to Killian's fancy truck and Griffin's Navigator.

Our group increased the pace, but one guy's raspy voice yelled, "She came this way."

"What do we do then?" the baritone asked.

"We were instructed to kill the Shadow City alpha, too, if he interferes," the raspy guy answered. "Don't chicken out now. We're in too deep."

Don't chicken out? And now Griffin was a target. My being his mate had put a target on his back. The realization sank in before I could do anything about it.

"I'll distract them," Rosemary huffed, and flew toward them, trying to buy us time.

I hated that she kept putting herself in danger for me, but I'd gladly take her help. I normally wouldn't be as accepting, but her wings protected her in ways that none of us could equal.

Our breathing grew ragged as we rushed ahead. I could now see Sierra jump out of the driver's seat and dive into the back. She was as ready to get the hell out of here as the rest of us.

"Angel!" the baritone screamed. Rosemary must have begun her attack. "I'll take her, the rest of you go after them!"

At least that would keep one of the guards busy. Gunfire started once again, which wasn't surprising. These guys had the one consistent way of fighting, which still seemed so strange to me: they fought like humans instead of animals. Yes, guns were deadly, but our animals empowered our magic and made shifters the most formidable enemy. I used my wolf as much as possible, which I believed was one reason we kept winning, despite being outnumbered.

We reached the car, and Griffin pointed at the front seat. "Sterlyn goes there. The rest of you get in the back." He ran straight to the driver's seat and got in. "Sierra, move so that Killian can sit in the far back with Julius."

Sierra nodded and climbed into the middle bench seat as I opened the back door, hoping to help speed up the process. Julius frowned, pausing.

Get your ass in there. He obviously didn't want to sit in the very back, but he was going to have to learn his place in our circle...sooner rather than later. *I might have pushed for you to come, but if you put my family at risk, I'll leave you here without a second thought.* I shoved forward those feelings, wanting him to know that I meant them. *If you don't believe me, then test it.*

He huffed and climbed over the middle seat into the back while his conflicted feelings of both respect and hatred hit me. I wasn't sure why he felt either, but I could analyze all that later.

Killian and Randall reached the car door, and the poor kid jumped in headfirst, no doubt desperate to get out of here. I couldn't blame him. My skin crawled after being in that basement half a day, and he'd been there for a week, if not longer.

Grunting, Killian climbed over Sierra and into the back with Julius. He growled, "No funny business, jackass. One strange look, and I'll kick your ass."

The three guards darted toward us and broke through the thinning trees. They raised their guns and fired at us as Sierra reached for the door.

Griffin gunned the engine, causing the SUV's wheels to spin and fling dirt before we lurched forward.

"Close the door," Julius yelled, as Sierra bent and grabbed the door handle.

"I'm doing it, dumbass," Sierra growled back as another shot fired and Killian yelped in pain. The door slammed shut, but the metallic scent of blood filled the SUV.

Our attackers continued to shoot as Griffin spun onto the road, taking off toward Shadow Ridge. The bullets hit the plastic of the SUV, but luckily didn't hit the tires or any spots that would make the vehicle stop. Though their shots continued, we were out of harm's way as Griffin pushed the car, making the engine redline.

Since we were out of immediate danger, I turned around and scanned Killian, looking for the injury, as Randall leaned over the back of the seat to help his alpha. Killian bent forward, helping Randall survey the injury.

Blood soaked Killian's shirt at the shoulder. "Did the bullet exit?" I asked. The memory of when I'd been shot flashed through my head, the sensation of the phantom bullet turning my stomach. Griffin had gotten it out, but the extraction had hurt like a bitch, worse than when I'd been shot in the first place. But it was better to get the bullet out before your shifter healing set in, instead of having to reopen the wound later.

"I have no clue," he whispered, in pain.

"Aw." Sierra glanced over her shoulder, her face slightly pale. However, she felt good enough to make a jab. "Do you need some tissue?"

Ignoring her, Julius rolled his eyes. "Of course he doesn't. Lucky for you, I had to learn how to tend to injuries," he grumbled as he leaned over and lifted the sleeve of Killian's shirt. The material was soaked and sticking to his skin, and I was surprised when Julius gently moved the fabric away, taking care not to hurt him even worse.

Killian hissed and grimaced.

"What are you doing?" Randall asked, and shoved Julius away.

The silver wolf's hand dropped, yanking the shirt with it.

"Damn it," Killian huffed as his face tensed. "That hurt."

"You asshole," Randall yelled as he punched Julius in the face. "I'm going to kill you." There was so much hatred in his voice, it unnerved me.

Get him off me, or I'll hurt him, Julius linked. *I swear to God, I'm about to lose it.*

"Randall!" I shouted, leaning over the center console and catching his arm. "Stop. He wasn't hurting Killian. He was checking out the bullet wound and needed to move his shirt. Of *course* it's not going to feel good." I barely knew Randall, and I hated talking to anyone like that, but he needed to get his shit together. There was no telling what he'd endured in that house—and Julius probably deserved his anger—but there was too much going on to be acting this way.

"She's right." Killian backed me up. "He wasn't doing anything on purpose to hurt me. At least, not this second." Mistrust dripped from each word.

"Can I proceed, or are you going to start hitting me again?" Julius's jaw twitched, and he sneered at the young man.

"Fine," Randall snapped as he jabbed his finger in Julius's face. "But one wrong move, and I'll punch you again."

"Do you think you could actually beat my ass? Don't you remember what happened back in that house?" Julius's expression filled with disgust. "I'm holding back because you all let me come with you, but that's it. Do one more thing out of line, and I'll hit back. And you know my punch is going to hurt you worse than yours did me."

"Boys!" Sierra snapped her fingers and gave each one a level look. "Behave, and concentrate on the man who's injured and not the pissing match you two have going on. There are more important things than revenge and personal agendas."

At that moment, I could tell that Sierra was an oldest child. She'd obviously helped look after her siblings, and thus, she knew how to put misbehaving idiots in their place.

Griffin glanced in the rearview mirror at Randall and said, "Julius is going to check Killian because he's the one with experience. If he pulls any funny shit, I'll handle it. Got it?"

"Yeah." Randall nodded and sat back in his seat, crossing his arms. His lips mashed together as he glanced out his window, staring into the darkness.

"Okay, let's try this again." Julius rolled his neck from side to side and reached across Killian's body. This time, he was able to move the shirt completely out of the way while Killian gritted his teeth.

"He'll be fine." Julius put his shirt back in place and sat back in his seat. "There's an exit hole, which you can see at the back of his shoulder. I wanted to make sure it was there. The wound is far enough from any main arteries, so it may hurt like a bitch for a while, but he'll be fine."

His heartbeat remained steady, nothing indicating a lie. "Thank God." I blew out a breath as I looked at the man who was my brother in every sense except biologically. "You scared the shit out of me."

"Welcome to our world," Killian said through clenched teeth. "Now you know how you make Griffin and me feel at all times."

I didn't want to keep the focus on his discomfort, so I smiled and turned back around in my seat.

"Dude, don't even try to compare yourself to me," Griffin teased, trying to ease the tension. "She's my fated mate; there's no competition. Think about how I've been suffering."

"Yeah, okay." Killian snorted. "She's my sister, so it's pretty much the same thing."

Julius huffed loudly in the back. *He's your brother?* He laughed bitterly in my head.

Not by blood. For him to act this way pretty much confirmed my suspicions. He didn't like Killian calling me sister, but there was no reason he should care...unless *he* was my brother. But how could he know about me and not try to find us? The questions were on the tip of my tongue, and my mind reeled. There were so many damn unknowns.

"No, it's not." Griffin wrinkled his nose. "When you meet your fated mate, you'll understand."

"Okay, boys." Sierra chuckled. "We got it. You both care about her. Can we just be quiet, for the love of God? After all that commotion, a little silence would be nice."

"I agree." I leaned my head back on my headrest and closed my eyes.

"Uh...what's going on?" Griffin's words startled me from my doze. "Killian, those are some of Shadow Ridge's police cars."

I blinked a few times before reality came crashing back in. We were passing by Shadow Ridge University, and there were indeed a few police cars parked in front of the school with flashing lights. My chest tightened.

What the hell had gone wrong while we were away?

CHAPTER FOUR

THE FLASHING blue and red lights reminded me of a scene from a movie or some horrible news clip on television. We were still far away, but the lights were almost blinding in the darkness.

Killian groaned, still in pain. "This night keeps getting better. I'm covered in blood and injured. Isn't that bad enough?"

"It's nice to see my alpha being so strong and brave." Sierra snorted.

"Well, we can't leave the Navigator there. It's already been over twelve hours at this point." Griffin's knuckles turned white as he clutched the steering wheel.

Ugh. Once again, it felt like we were in an impossible situation. My mind began to race, causing my sanity to crack. I was so damn tired of us being put in difficult positions.

No. I couldn't break down. Not now.

"Let's park somewhere downtown and take the woods into the school," I suggested. "We can climb over the fence relatively easily." The huge gate and fence were only for the front part of the campus, in order to appear secure for the humans coming to visit, despite them never being admitted. This was a supernaturals-only college, but I knew they had to keep up the charade that everyone had a chance of attending. In truth, because of Griffin's father leading the charge, supernaturals from all over the world could attend. The admissions staff just weeded out the human applicants. Living this close to a powerful, hidden supernatural city would raise human suspicions and threaten to expose our races' presence to the human world.

Though we were much stronger than humans, they outnumbered us by leaps and bounds. And the few humans who had learned about us had developed weapons that could take us out. We didn't remain hidden for noble reasons—it was a means of survival.

"I can't go in there," Julius insisted. "We need to go somewhere else and forget about your damn cars."

"Except that Killian and Griffin disappeared, leaving their cars behind. This could be all about finding them." I had been so arrogant. I'd suggested they get a rental car so they could follow me without easily showing up on the enemy's radar. I'd thought that we'd return before nightfall, but I'd underestimated my enemy and might have caused this new situation. "If that's the case and we don't get their cars now, it could escalate things. You two should check in with your packs."

"Then how are you going to explain me?" Julius's voice took on a wild edge. "The people who are hunting you—well, now us—have spies everywhere. I can't be spotted."

"Killian introduced me at the university, and it wasn't a huge deal." He was freaking out over being seen, which made me wonder who was involved. Maybe this was a bigger group than we realized... or there were more people we trusted who could be wrapped up in this. What had those people done to Julius? "It's not like they're going to be able to tell you're a silver wolf on sight. If that were the case, they would've known about me."

Julius snapped, "We need to keep a low profile, which is the opposite of strolling up to police officers with a new person in tow, another who's been missing for weeks, and a Shadow Ridge alpha who's been shot up."

My stomach dropped, and bile rose in the back of my throat.

"What are you trying to say?" Griffin stopped the car in the middle of the road and turned toward the back. "That we run and hide? You obviously don't know Carter well. If none of us show up with his brother, he'll start running his mouth to anyone who'll listen."

"Regardless, if they're looking for Killian and Griffin, the longer we wait to show up, the more cops they'll have searching everywhere, which means you could be discovered, anyway," I said.

"It's not like I can hide in the trunk. They'll smell my scent. I guess I need to make it on my own." Julius's nostrils flared.

"Not happening," Griffin growled, and his eyes darkened. "Do you think that after you tried kidnapping Sterlyn multiple times to hand her over to some self-absorbed prick, we're going to trust you and let you go? There's no way in hell. In fact, you're going to tell us who the prick is, or we'll beat it out of you when we finally get back to the house."

"He must think we're idiots." Killian's face tightened, and he glanced at Julius, giving a small flinch as the only sign that his shoulder pained him. "Maybe we should just kill him and lose the threat."

"That wouldn't be smart." My chest squeezed at the thought of something happening to Julius, but I couldn't let my emotions factor into this any longer. I needed to keep my head on straight but make sure I didn't lose my heart.

Dear God, if Dad knew how many times I'd repeated his little teaching moments that I used to roll my eyes at, he'd tease me and tell me he was smarter than I ever gave him credit for. But that was the problem with pure warriors who pushed their hearts aside. For whatever reason, they left their hearts outside the equation and made decisions based on logic, and that was when what was right became blurred concerning what they wanted done. Both parts were equally important—one shouldn't outweigh the other. "Right now, let's figure out our first problem, because he's afraid."

Julius's gaze met mine, and his pointer finger tapped on his leg.

He was uncomfortable that I'd called him out. Being afraid was hard for silver wolves to admit. Being confident and steadfast was ingrained in us.

"Okay, she has good points," Sierra jumped in, surprising me. She normally stayed out of strategy conversations. "So what do we do?"

"I still say kill the asshole," Killian grumbled and scowled. He looked a little green and sweaty, and I wondered if his wound was feeling worse.

Randall lifted a hand. "Hey, if that's what my alpha wants, who am I to disagree?"

Despite the horrible situation, his response made me smile. There was a little bit of Carter's smart mouth in him after all.

The sound of fluttering wings notified me that Rosemary was near. She tapped on my window, and I rolled it down.

She crossed her arms as she glared at me. "What the hell is going on? You're sitting in the middle of the road, stopped after midnight, not far away from a school crawling with Shadow City and Shadow Ridge guards."

"Shadow City?" Griffin leaned back against the headrest. "I figured it was only Shadow Ridge."

That could mean they were looking for Griffin. "What do we do? We can't show up with Julius as our prisoner and Killian injured."

"I'll take Julius with me to Griffin's." Rosemary rolled her shoulders as she prepared for his extra weight. "And I'll heal Killian. As long as you have an extra shirt, we should be good."

I kept forgetting she could heal. "Are you sure? You've been sticking your neck out for us a whole lot more than I could ever ask of you."

"That's one reason I don't mind doing it." Her gaze softened, and her beauty became even more breathtaking. She was so gorgeous that someone should have erected a statue of her. "You embody everything Mom told me about silver wolves, and thus, it's an honor to help you." She cleared her throat, seeming uncomfortable with her moment of vulnerability, and yanked open the back door on the passenger side. "Pull your shirt off," she ordered, and leaned over Randall toward Killian.

"Uh..." Killian seemed baffled for a second, and he swallowed nervously, still looking a bit green. He moved toward her, lowering his voice as if that would make any difference with all our supernatural ears. "I mean...I'm not saying no, but is now the time? Maybe a date first—"

Uh...does he have a thing for Rosemary? I snorted, somehow keeping the noise solely inside mine and Griffin's heads.

Griffin's shoulders shook, and his amusement flowed into me. *Not that I'm aware of, but who knows? I've never heard him say something with so much sincerity.*

I knew they'd gotten closer, but I hadn't realized it had come to this. Normally, races stuck to their own kind, but the thought of those two being together didn't bother me. They'd make a great team.

"Oh, dear God." Rosemary's eyes sparkled with humor before her perfectly veiled expression snapped back into place. "Didn't you just hear that I'm going to heal you? Your shirt is drenched with blood, and it works faster if I touch the actual wound."

Killian laughed loudly and winked, but I suspected he might be trying too hard to convince us. "Of course. I totally knew that."

He slowly removed his shirt, and Rosemary made a point of locking eyes with me as if she were making sure we knew that she wasn't watching him, which seemed odd. *Something has to be going on between those two.*

"Damn it." Killian groaned as he pulled the shirt over his head. "That still hurts a lot. Shouldn't I be healed more by now?"

"They laced their bullets with wolfsbane," Julius muttered. "To make you die more painfully."

Great, we had sick, *sadistic* assholes hunting us. No wonder Killian still looked shaky. I shouldn't have been surprised—they *did* want to capture me to either force me into birthing babies or kill me. Little did the general wolf population know that silver wolves reproduced at a slower rate. That was one reason why Dad and Mom had only me...and, well, Cyrus. Even the males were affected by a low reproductive rate. A regular wolf could birth a baby a year, but it took a silver wolf ten years, if not longer, to conceive once we began to try, and our window of fertility was drastically reduced, as well. Realistically, Griffin and I would most likely have only one child, two max. My pack had been the only one in existence, and we'd kept how little we could reproduce a secret. We were already living in hiding since we'd always feared people would hunt us for this exact reason—to manipulate us and use our strength and magic against everyone else to control all the races.

Dad had told me that we were gifted by the moon to not only be stronger but to also make us pure in intent. Great power comes with responsibility, and magic had a way of balancing itself. Silver wolves would never want to rule over the supernatural world because we wanted the best for everyone, not just ourselves or our race.

"Lovely," Rosemary retorted as she placed her hands on Killian's wound. Her hands glowed an iridescent white as she pushed her magic into his injury. "Thankfully, that won't impact my magic."

"Oh, thank God." Killian sighed as his body began to heal in earnest. "That was almost unbearable."

She kept her hands on him for a few more seconds, then dropped them and stared at Julius. She commanded, "Get out. You're coming with me." Glancing at Griffin, she added, "And get the hell out of the middle of the road. You're lucky no one else has come through here yet."

"It's the middle of the night." Griffin lifted both hands. "We should be good."

Julius blew out a breath and squeezed past Randall out of the car.

Rosemary still blocked most of the doorway, proving I was right to trust her to take the silver wolf. She knew that if she moved even a foot too far away, Julius could take off. Yes, she was fast, but on a full moon, he could outrun her. Thankfully, she could outfly him, but she needed to stay close and always on alert.

When he climbed from the SUV, she grabbed his arms and took off toward the sky. "I'll meet you at Griffin's!" she called, but they were out of sight before I could respond.

I watched as Sierra climbed into the far back seat by Killian then started digging through the trunk as Griffin followed Rosemary's instructions, pulling to the side of the road.

"Here. Please." Sierra tossed Killian a shirt and covered her eyes with her hands. "You're like a brother to me, and I prefer you clothed."

I cringed, trying to keep my eyes averted. Killian was an attractive man, but I viewed him as family now. And no one wanted to see their brother naked.

"Me too," Griffin deadpanned and winked at me, trying to help with the emotions he could feel brimming inside me.

I loved him so much for it, but I wouldn't feel at ease until we were back home safe in our bed. "It might be best if Sierra and Randall don't come to the university with us. Maybe they can hang out in the woods until we come back and pick them up. It would be safe for them here, especially in wolf form."

"We can shift and run back to the pack neighborhood. It's only about a twenty-minute run from here," Sierra said as she stretched and patted Randall's arm. "I can drop Randall at his house. And I bet I'll still beat you back to your place."

"Yeah, I linked to Carter now that we're close enough." Randall rolled his eyes. "He's a hot mess and needs to see me. I love him, but damn, he can be high maintenance."

"Thanks for that." Killian groaned. "He's been nagging nonstop."

"Wait...isn't it supposed to be the younger brother bugging the older one?" Sierra climbed back to the middle row and gestured for Randall to get out.

Randall laughed, but it held an edge. "Yeah, that's what I always thought, but that hasn't been the case."

458 JEN L. GREY

"I hate to ask, but before you go..." I turned my body, wanting Randall to feel my sincerity. "Do you know or remember anything that could help us?"

"I don't think so." Randall exhaled and grimaced. "I mean...it was those five guards most of the time. Julius only dropped by every now and then. They talked about some guy in charge that only showed his face to Julius, but they were all promised large sums of money and a nice place to live. Other than talking shit about each other, they were kind of tight-lipped."

That didn't surprise me. They wouldn't want to divulge too much in case Randall did get free. But I'd had to at least try. "Well, if you think of anything later, let us know."

He opened the door and got out, then paused. "Thank you all for saving me." His attention locked on me. "And I know it's because of you that I got out. If you hadn't seen me..." He trailed off, and his face filled with horror. "I...I don't know what would have happened." He moved out of the way, heading to the tree line.

"I'll see you at Griffin's." Sierra climbed out of the car, but before shutting the door, she stuck her head back in. "And be careful. The three of you attract crazy like I've never seen before." She slammed the door and hurried after Randall.

"You know, you could go with them." Griffin put the car in drive but didn't press the gas. "And keep an eye on them."

In other words, he wanted me to stay protected. But they were safe in the woods, and we both knew it. The enemy wouldn't have regrouped yet. They would attack again—and soon—but not tonight. "Did you mean it when you said you want us to lead your people together?"

His shoulders tensed, knowing his answer would only reinforce that I should go with him. Instead of answering, he blew out a breath and turned back toward the university.

"If you're going to be mad at anyone, it should be fate." Killian chuckled behind me, but it was devoid of humor. "She's the one who put you together with a headstrong, independent fighting machine." I heard shuffling as he moved from the far back onto the middle seat.

"Yeah, but I wouldn't have it any other way." Griffin rubbed his eyes and sighed. "The truth is, we protect each other. Not just her and me, but you, too. We're stronger together."

The truth of his words hung in the car the entire way to the university. We *were* stronger together. The three of us were not just friends, but family...a pack. It was about damn time we started seeing each other that way. The divide among shifters, particularly our kind, only weakened us. It was a self-inflicted injury.

The university came into view as we followed the black wrought-iron fence to the empty guard station. Griffin pulled the entry card from the rental's glove box and scanned it, opening the gates.

He slowly pulled to the front of the main office building. Guards shouted at our approach, not familiar with the SUV, and Dick Harding marched out in his black suit with a guard right behind him.

I sucked in a breath. Of course Dick would be here. He was a council member and vying for Griffin's top spot, even though my mate hadn't quite figured that out yet. But he was beginning to.

If that asshole was on campus, that meant he was using whatever situation we'd just driven into to gain more control. But I wouldn't let Griffin fall victim to some narcissistic, power-hungry douchebag. It was time to take a stand together in front of everyone. The moment to show that Griffin and I would lead together without outside influence was now.

In other words, it was time to take back what was rightfully Griffin's.

CHAPTER FIVE

DICK TUGGED at the lapels of his black suit as he marched toward the rental car. The windows were dark, so he couldn't see in. His salt and pepper hair was over-gelled to the point of looking greasy, and he ran his fingers through his dark scruff as his ebony eyes squinted, like that would help him see inside.

Dumbass. He didn't have X-ray vision, just wolf vision.

"Whoever the hell it is, get out of the car," Dick growled, his face squinched. "Now."

You better roll the window down before this gets out of hand. This entire situation was odd. Why were there so many cars out there? And the fact that Dick was here in the middle of the night didn't add up.

Griffin rolled the window down, and when his face came into view, Dick's eyes slightly widened as his musky sandalwood scent floated into the SUV.

"Griffin?" Dick asked, sounding truly shocked. "What are you doing here?"

"Uh...I go to school here and needed to get my car. I left it here today." He arched an eyebrow at his fatherlike figure, then looked at a guard who'd joined Dick. "Is there a problem?"

"Of course not, sir." The face of the guard stretched into a smile. He extended his hand to my mate. His black clothes were crisp with no signs of wrinkles, and his matching black hat sat on dark chestnut hair that spilled from the edges. The hat was marked with a crescent of two buildings and an upside-down paw print above it, the logo for Shadow City. "My name is Lars. We've been searching for you."

"For me?" Griffin tapped his chest. "Why?"

"Because Carter called, informing us that Dove disappeared," Dick said, as he gestured to me. "And then you couldn't be found."

"Did you expect him to just sit back and twiddle his thumbs when his fated mate had gone missing?" I asked. I bet he hadn't. In fact, I'd have wagered that he'd hoped that Griffin got hurt along with me. I mean, here he was, in the middle of the night, dressed to the nines. He'd put time and thought into what he wore on campus, which signaled some kind of power play. "Would you wait around if your mate went missing?"

"Probably," Killian chuckled, causing Dick to flick his gaze to the back seat. However, Killian didn't miss a beat as he continued, "They're chosen, anyway, so they don't have as strong of a connection."

I bit my cheek, desperate to find a way to keep my smirk from spreading. Killian had pretended to justify why Dick wouldn't feel as passionate about his wife by effectively reminding everyone that he had a chosen mate rather than a fated one. Every shifter knew that a fated mate made a person stronger in a way that a chosen mate never could. He'd weakened Dick's status compared to Griffin's with me by his side.

"That doesn't make a difference." Dick's nostrils flared as he glowered. "I'd..." He trailed off.

He and his mate barely get along. Griffin linked. *They're good at pretending, but behind closed doors, they're awful. They live next door to my family in Shadow City, and we can hear them yelling through the walls. But Dad and I never confronted Dick about it.*

That was information that I could hold close to use when it might be advantageous. Sometimes, keeping the tidbits quiet helped make a bigger impact later when you needed it. For now, Killian had sufficiently called Dick out, and I didn't want to anger the beast more than he already was. He might explode...

Hmm...that made it so much more tempting.

"Well, he's here," I said. If we kept pushing Dick, he could play the victim, claiming that he'd stormed the halls, looking for their alpha, and all we'd done was show up and insult him. He'd use whatever he could to cast Griffin in a bad light to prove that he wasn't fit to actually lead. "And thank you for your concern. It's nice to know that Griffin has people who have his back." I smiled sweetly because I knew Dick understood that I hadn't been referring to him, but rather to myself and Killian. He'd soon learn he wasn't the only one able to play the nice guy.

"Of course." He forced a smile, but all it accomplished was making him look constipated.

"So, what happened, sir?" Lars took a few steps closer.

If we wanted to sniff out who was behind all of this, we'd have to be vague and keep our ears alert. That way, if anyone knew more specific details, we could identify them. I needed to be careful and make sure I didn't say anything that could be a lie. "We're not sure, exactly," I said before Griffin could answer Lars. "Someone put a bag over my head, so I couldn't see much, but I know my kidnappers drove me about an hour east from here. Luckily, these two guys"—I beamed at Griffin and then Killian—"found me before anything truly horrible happened."

"Oh, man." Lars's sea-green eyes sparkled with admiration. "You're lucky that they found you in time. Do we need to go check out the area? And what's with the rental car?"

"We don't have jurisdiction over that area," Dick growled. "So unfortunately, we can't check it out. The last thing we need to do is get more involved and make our city a target."

Of course Dick didn't want us to check it out. Every meeting with him made him more suspicious than the last.

"Are you sure the city is a target? Or is it just my mate?" Griffin asked, his brows furrowed.

Don't push too hard. We didn't want to alert Dick that we were suspicious of him. *He needs to hang himself naturally.*

Dick laughed loudly.

Fine, I'll let him off the hook, Griffin replied. "As for the rental, we thought it'd be nice to have something different so people couldn't easily identify us." He shrugged and reached over the center console, taking my hand as he stared lovingly at me. "Good thing we had the crazy idea, or we might not have been able to track her, since they'd probably have recognized my car."

"You're going to have a hard time returning it." Lars gestured to the back of the SUV. "You have at least three bullet holes on this side."

An older man ran out the front door of the school, heading straight to the car, his bald head glistening in the moonlight. A brown shirt with the Shadow Ridge crest of a paw print on the front covered his large, muscular chest. He was only slightly smaller than Griffin, which meant he was huge by wolf standards. His face was lined with concern as he beelined to us. "Are they okay?"

"Yeah, Billy." Killian's voice softened to the tone he only used for me. "Sorry if we caused a problem."

"As long as you three are safe, that's all that matters," he replied. Goodness radiated off him, especially standing next to Dick. This must be the man who'd been holding things down on the Shadow Ridge side since Killian's parents passed.

"Well, as you can see, they are." Dick nodded curtly at us. "So you and the other guards are dismissed." He wrinkled his nose as if speaking to Billy was beneath him.

Billy lifted his chin, and his acorn eyes narrowed. "Shadow Ridge guards were here before Shadow City's personnel. If—"

"Now listen here." Dick pivoted toward the beta, looking ready to unleash the rage he was barely containing.

Do something, I encouraged Griffin. It was important for him to be the one to put Dick in his place, not me. The Shadow City guards needed to see their true leader take control. *We should be one pack, not divided.* I must have sounded like a broken record, but going against the established norm was hard. I finally understood how Dad had felt all those times our pack rolled their eyes at him being insistent the day would come when we'd need to fight and protect not only our own kind, but the entire supernatural world. None of us had believed it because nothing had happened for centuries. Now here I was, harping at the guys, trying to encourage them to embrace change.

Maybe nagging them was more accurate, but...harping sounded a *little* better.

"No, he's right," Griffin said. "If Shadow Ridge arrived here first, they deserve to be part of this conversation. After all, not only were Dove and I at risk, but their alpha, too." Griffin straightened his back, his trepidation wafting into me. *You're right, but damn, why is this so hard?*

Because it's easier not to upset anyone. And I had a feeling the more we rattled Dick, the quicker he'd show his true colors. But a confrontation had always been inevitable. That man was determined to take control. He'd been going slower and easier only while Griffin had been compliant. *Especially someone you grew up believing had your best interests at heart.*

Dick huffed, and his jaw twitched as his composure slipped. "Now, Griffin, you asked me to handle things while you finished school and goofed off. Why don't you stay out of this and let me take care of it like usual?"

God. He was such a prick. He'd purposely used that term to

undermine Griffin in front of everyone. I opened my mouth to defend my mate, but he surprised me.

"You're right. I did." Griffin's face was smooth as if he didn't have a single worry, but the vein in his neck bulged. "And effective as of this moment, Dove and I plan to become more involved."

You handled that perfectly. If he had told Dick we were ready to take back control, it would have pushed him over the edge, and we weren't ready for that. Not yet. We needed to move the needle slowly and gauge the fallout. Someone as vile as Dick could cause even more chaos for us, and the others needed to see Griffin begin to take the reins so they'd feel comfortable backing him when the time came.

Dick's mouth dropped before he closed it, and his beady eyes landed on me—Griffin had taken him by surprise. He swallowed hard and rolled his shoulders as if the suit was suddenly too much. "I think you have something to do with that decision."

I'd never had someone look at me with such disgust. It both unsettled and thrilled me. Dad always said that whenever someone met you, if they didn't either love or hate you, you'd done something wrong because you'd blended into the background—been unmemorable. Silver wolves were about taking a stance and doing the right thing, so we should never go under the radar unless we did so purposely. Between Dick and his daughter, Luna, I'd definitely followed Dad's advice. "Nope, this was all Griffin." And that was the truth. I'd only grounded him, which enabled him to see what the future should be.

"Whether she did or didn't is irrelevant," Griffin said with annoyance. "The fact remains that it's solely my decision to make. On that note, my mate has been rescued, and we almost didn't make it through, so I think it's best if we get our cars and head home. We'll take care of the rental tomorrow."

Dick's jaw twitched, but he nodded, unable to do much else.

"Billy..." Killian leaned forward and placed a hand on my shoulder, effectively showing I was under his protection too. "We need a handful of guards available at Griffin's in case something goes awry."

Unlike Dick, Billy flashed a proud smile. "I can send them there now."

My body tensed. Julius was there. If the guards saw him, there was no telling what kind of problems that could cause. I understood we needed protection, but if the enemy found out where Julius was staying, they could try to kill him. We had no clue yet who was working against us—we needed those answers from Julius. And the fact that there were at least two people who'd killed themselves rather than be caught spoke volumes about what his controllers would do if they got ahold of him.

The thought of Julius being injured upset me way more than it should.

It'll be fine. Griffin obviously understood what was roiling inside me. *Rosemary should already be there with Julius. I gave her a key this morning in case we had to split up, so no one will see him come in.*

I hadn't considered that. The enemy wouldn't expect an angel to be flying Julius around. Having the guards could work in our favor. I heaved a sigh. We should be okay.

"If you're okay with that plan, I'll link them myself." Killian rubbed my shoulder for a second before removing his hand.

"Kill, they're your pack." Billy patted the hood of the SUV. "You don't need my permission to act as the alpha."

And that was the largest difference between Dick and Billy. I already liked Billy and could easily view him as a friend or even a family member in the future.

"Lars, do you mind coordinating a few Shadow City guards, too?" Griffin didn't even bother looking at Dick and spoke directly to the guard. "It would be good for the two forces to work together."

"Of course, sir." Lars's face reminded me of a kid's on Christmas morning.

"Wait." Dick shook his head as his hands clenched. "Why do we need to involve our guards when Shadow Ridge's can do the job just fine?"

"Because pooling resources is always smart, and Shadow Ridge has already given lives to the cause," I said. I hated the man. "Why should Shadow Ridge always risk themselves and their pack for both cities? Don't you think there should be more of a partnership?"

"This is how things work," Dick spoke through gritted teeth. "I don't expect you to understand."

"Excuse me." Griffin's voice laced with alpha will as he stared the prick down. "You will not speak to her like that again. Do I make myself clear?"

Dick grimaced and growled. "Perfectly."

"As I was saying, please send at least two guards to help out the Shadow Ridge guards," Griffin said stiffly to Lars. "If you have any questions or problems, link me directly."

Lars's head bobbed like a doll's, and Griffin pulled forward, heading straight to the vehicles.

This whole day had been a shit show, and it still wasn't over.

GRIFFIN PULLED his vehicle into his garage, passing three pack members standing guard out front.

The guards had officially circled the house, which both stressed and comforted me. As long as Julius didn't do anything stupid, we should be safe. But he seemed to be a hothead, and the moon was still full, despite it descending in the night sky.

The two of us climbed out of our vehicle just as Killian entered the garage. As the door lowered, I exhaled and relaxed, feeling so damn glad Rosemary was near. We might not have made it out of that place if not for her. She was a powerful ally, and I wanted to know why she was helping us. Why would her mom be so insistent that they should help protect the silver wolves? We were missing a chunk of the story.

"I said get out of their room now!" Rosemary commanded so loudly we could hear her in the garage. "You might be a silver wolf, but I *will* kick your ass."

Just when I thought I might be able to crawl into bed, there was already another fight brewing. I ran toward the interior door, needing to know exactly what Julius was snooping for. Maybe he was one of the less than point one percent of our population that could lie, but I couldn't fathom it. My gut said differently.

There was only one way to find out, so I marched into the house.

CHAPTER SIX

THE COMMOTION WAS COMING from mine and Griffin's bedroom, so I stalked through the kitchen, down the hallway past Sierra, who was flipping the station on the TV, and into the room. Griffin and Killian were only a few steps behind me, ready to fight.

Usually, this room, with its warm blue walls that reminded me of the ocean and the dark walnut furniture that reminded me of the forest, was my sanctuary.

But not today.

Julius had dug through Griffin's room and found the family album, journal, and notes that I'd hidden under the bed. Angst, confusion, and hurt swirled inside him, spilling into me.

The album lay on the floor, open to the picture of Mom holding my brother and me on a bed. Blood spotted our bodies, proving that we'd just been born. Dad had his arms wrapped around Mom's shoulders, and they both looked so damn happy.

Each time I looked at this photo, it stole my breath.

My brother having been stripped from us was horrible, whether it was due to death or kidnapping. The man who sat on the floor was rocking himself as he read Dad's journal, his face crumpled in agony.

For him to be looking so desperately for answers, he had to be Cyrus.

Rosemary stood over him, her body coursing with anger. The angel wasn't the most empathetic person, and being ignored didn't sit well with her.

"You heard her," Griffin growled as he appeared to the right of me, with Killian flanking me on the left. "Get the hell out of here. What do you think you're doing?"

All they could see was a threat inside our house, but I saw a lost, broken man. "He's looking for answers." It was that simple.

He wanted to find himself.

"Well, this is the wrong fucking way to do it." Griffin waved his hands around the room. "He's in our bedroom and digging through my drawers."

Sierra entered the room with a smile—or grimace—I wasn't sure. She arched an eyebrow at me as she inhaled sharply.

"I'm so sorry," she said in her usual talking-shit voice. "But when you say drawers, do you mean the shelf or your actual under-wear?" She waved a hand to the still-open drawer with his boxers shoved to the side and spilling out. "You can see where I'd be confused."

Killian closed his eyes and shook his head. "Now isn't the time."

"Get out," Griffin rasped with rage, directing it toward her and away from Julius. "Now."

I couldn't help but grin, appreciating Sierra diverting some of his anger toward her. But Griffin would have to come to grips with Julius. He wouldn't be leaving anytime soon, and there was too much other shit to focus on for us to waste energy on something that wouldn't change. *Hey, give me a moment alone with Julius.* I already knew how he'd react to that comment, but I needed a chance to talk to Julius alone.

Hell, no. Griffin turned his icy glare on me. *Not happening.*

His outright refusal pissed me off. *That wasn't a request,* I snapped. *But if you'd rather I leave with him, that can be arranged. I* wasn't some meek mate who would bend to his will—I was my own person. Whether he liked it or not, I made my own decisions.

He organized a kidnapping to hand you off to some limp-dick prick who hoped he could get a hard-on long enough to impregnate you. Griffin's body was so tense, he could pass as a statue. *So excuse me if I'm not thrilled to leave you alone with him.*

Forcing myself to take a deep breath, I thought through my next words. He was my mate and deserved some sort of consideration for how he was feeling. I had forced him to watch me walk into a dangerous situation earlier today, and he saw Julius as a continuation of that threat. *I understand, but I can feel him spiraling out of control. Stay right next to the door, and if anything feels wrong, you can barge right in. Just give us the illusion of privacy.* I knew in my heart that he loved me and that he was reacting from fear.

"Why aren't you listening to me? I told you to get the hell out of here." Rosemary faced us with her brows furrowed. She pursed her lips as she tilted her head. "Do you think he's deaf? Can wolves suddenly go deaf?"

"It's called selective hearing," Sierra hollered from down the hall. "All men suffer from it. I'm surprised it took you so long to learn this."

"She can't keep her mouth shut," Killian grumbled, and ran a hand down his face. "It's like she gets worse instead of better. She used to only be this bad with Olive."

Olive—his late sister. She'd died a couple of years ago, along with the rest of Killian's family. He rarely spoke of them, so for him to say her name startled me.

Griffin sighed, making it clear that he wasn't happy. "Let's give Sterlyn a few minutes alone with *him*."

"You wolves have such a weird sense of humor," Rosemary said as she crossed her arms and stared at Griffin. His somber expression didn't change. "Wait...you aren't joking?"

"No, unfortunately, I'm not." Griffin's voice was strained, and he stomped over to Julius, sneering, "But one wrong move, and we'll be back in here in a flash. Don't get any stupid ideas."

Julius's irises darkened to gunmetal as a stormy expression crossed his face. "I'm here with a stronger silver wolf and an angel. That alone would give anyone pause." He made it clear that he wasn't scared of Griffin and Killian.

Great, these guys were going to have a power struggle, which wouldn't result in anything good. Just more anger and tension. "Okay, we got it. You're both strong alphas. Noted," I said. "Now I'd like to have a few minutes with him."

Rosemary strolled over to me and spoke into my ear. "Do you think that's wise?"

"Yes, I think it might help," I replied, and placed a hand on her shoulder. "But thank you for your concern."

Her face tightened, and she picked at her nails like she was suddenly uncomfortable. "I just...like you better than most. Even those of my own race."

My heart seemed to keep growing, making room for more people. Whether the angel admitted it, she cared for me and probably every other person in this group. She and Killian didn't argue nearly as much as they had when I'd first met her, and she'd even smiled at some of Sierra's absurd comments. This was one reason the great divide among the races had to come down. Inherently, we'd always remain more separate, but we didn't have to work against each other. "I feel the same way about you, but I need you to trust me."

"Fine. Shout if you need me." She nodded and marched out the door, not even giving a backward glance.

Why couldn't Killian and Griffin be that conciliatory?

"If you so much as fart weird, Griffin and I are in here," Killian warned Julius as he pulled me into a huge hug, wrapping his arms securely around me. "And I swear, you're trying to see how far you can push us."

I returned the embrace, knowing that this whole situation had been hard on him, too. "Not on purpose. I promise."

"All right, let my mate go," Griffin grumbled, and he kissed my cheek. "You don't have long. That's even pushing it, considering the way I'm feeling."

That was something to start with. Julius and I wouldn't be able to discuss everything in one conversation, anyway, and I was exhausted. Now that the bed was only a few feet away, all I wanted to do was climb into it with Griffin. "Okay."

One thing out of line, if he's even breathing funny, you let me know. Griffin linked, staring deep into my eyes, looking like he could see into my soul. *I can't chance losing you again.*

I'm not going anywhere. I kissed him gently. *He has to be my brother. I need to talk to him and connect with him. Otherwise, he's not going to help us. He's vulnerable right now, and he needs me.*

Griffin nibbled on his bottom lip and looked away. "Come on, man," he said to Killian.

The two of them exited, and Griffin glanced at me one last time before shutting the door.

The room somehow seemed overwhelming with just Julius and me inside, despite there being fewer people.

He didn't acknowledge me, but instead kept flipping the pages of the photo album. I casually walked over to him, trying not to seem threatening. This was something I couldn't alpha out of him. He needed to come to grips with it on his own terms, but that didn't mean that nudging him in the right direction was out of the question.

Pictures of me at my first birthday party was where he'd gotten to in the book. A birthday he should've been a part of.

"I didn't know you existed until I found the album and journal barely a week ago." I sat next to him and pointed at a picture of me with pink icing and chocolate cake all over my face. Mom and Dad stood on either side of me. My eyes had been more purple then, before the silver set in, and my silver hair was pulled into short pigtails. I had a large smile on my face, proving that I was happy and loved. However, now that I knew about my brother, I noted a sadness in my parents' eyes. That must have been both a horrible and joyful day for them, remembering the death of one child while celebrating the life of another.

His jaw flexed, and he flipped the page to the next set of pictures. "Do you think that makes me feel better? It makes it worse."

"Did you know that you're my brother?" And yet, he'd still tried to hand me over to God knew who.

"My parents gave me up because they only wanted you. The girl alpha." Disgust and hatred rang clear in his words. "I was reminded daily by the person who took care of me that I should be grateful that I had them, since my parents didn't want me. That despite my uselessness, they still took me in."

My heart hurt for him, but he couldn't be angry with me over that. "Did you not hear the part about me not knowing you existed until a few days ago?" Maybe Rosemary was right. Could he be hard of hearing?

"And what's *their* excuse?" He pushed the picture album away. "They didn't even tell you about me."

"They thought you were *dead*." His accusation stunned me. "The witch assigned to heal Mom told them that you died while she was cleaning us up. The witch *had* to be in on it. She brought you back out with me, and you didn't have a heartbeat. She must have spelled you or something."

"I want to hear this from them." He climbed to his feet and waved his arms around. "I'm assuming they'll be here at some point. They wouldn't want to leave their precious *daughter* unattended for long."

Wait. He thought our parents were still alive? He had no clue that they were dead. But then who else was in play? I wanted to break the news to him gently, but I wasn't sure how that was even possible. In some ways, their death would be worse for him because he'd never have the opportunity to know them. At least I'd had that, and selfishly, I wouldn't change it for the world. "They're no longer living."

"What?" He sagged against the wall. "They're *dead*?"

"Yeah." I couldn't hide the pain in my voice. I missed them so damn much.

"But...when?" The strong young man I'd met today now looked broken. Like every bit of hope he'd clutched had been destroyed.

"A few weeks ago." I should tell him more, but I wasn't emotionally ready for it. If I tried, I'd fall apart. And that was something I couldn't do. Not in front of him. Not yet. I didn't trust him, and the only people you should ever show weakness to were the ones who had your back even in the worst of times. Killian, Griffin, Rosemary, and Sierra had proven that. I deflected the situation. "I'm curious about who raised you in their absence, though."

"Just some person who was paid and forced to do it. Don't worry, she wasn't the one who wanted you. When I got old enough to take care of myself, she disappeared just like everyone does with me." He frowned and glanced around the room like the answer would magically appear. "How did you find out about me?"

I wanted to push the conversation more, but there was so much pain in his words. Besides, this was where I'd hoped we'd land from the very beginning. He could read the stories in Dad's own words. That would mean so much more than coming from me. He'd be able to read the heartbreak in them and maybe find a sense of peace over time.

I gestured to the journal that lay closed on the shaggy carpet. "In there. I found the journal and album back at my pack house." I grabbed it and opened it to February fourth of the year we were born, then handed it to him. "Here, read it."

Julius took the worn leather book in his hands and turned it around. As his eyes scanned the pages, my heart broke in two, watching and feeling his pain.

His hands tightened on the book, and I forced myself to remain quiet. I didn't want him to hurt the pages, but he had to go through his process, and I didn't want to interfere.

His jaw clenched, and he began to swallow like his throat was dry. When his eyes watered, I wasn't surprised; everything he'd ever wanted to know was right in his grasp. But sometimes, no matter how badly we wanted the truth, we weren't nearly as prepared for it as we thought.

"This has to be some sick joke." Julius slammed the book closed but didn't put it down. "There's no way that happened. You're manipulating me, trying to turn me into one of your brainless followers like those idiots out there. I won't fall for this act."

I could only imagine what he was going through. I took a deep breath and sighed. "Cyrus—" I hated calling him by his fake name.

"No!" he yelled, and his face turned red. "Do *not* call me that! That's not my name. And even if it was, your lying ass better not call me that. All those years, my caregiver told me the truth about you. You're just a piece of shit who'll do everything possible to be on top. You're only good for breeding an army." He shook his head and marched to the door. "I can't do this."

He yanked open the door, revealing Griffin. My mate snarled, "What the fuck is your problem? You can't yell at her like that."

And he was right—Cyrus couldn't, but only I would be able to demand his respect. Griffin couldn't command it for me, so I knew exactly what I had to do.

CHAPTER SEVEN

I GRABBED Julius's shoulders and slammed him into the wall, causing the door to rattle. I allowed my wolf to surge and felt alpha will begin to bubble within me, but I pushed the urge down, needing to make him respect me without that influence.

Alpha will should be used only as a last resort, when nothing else would work, or if there was a deadly risk if someone did not obey. Respect should be earned, not forced, whenever possible.

"I get that you're upset." I did. Hell, I was upset, too. My life hadn't been bad, and though he'd had it a lot worse than I had, my past hadn't been a walk in the park, either. "But you can't act out like that. I didn't cause this. Why would you think I was involved? I would've loved having a sibling growing up."

He held his chin high in defiance as his lips flattened. Despite the rage pouring from him into me, he held the picture album and journal tight against his chest and snapped, "Are you going to let me go now?"

Keeping my gaze locked on his, I shook my head. "Not until you tell me that you understand."

Griffin stepped beside me and cracked his neck from side to side. "And apologize before I have to make you."

Oh, dear God. *Please stop. You're going to make this worse.* I loved that Griffin wanted to have my back and support me, but all he was doing was antagonizing Julius—and all I wanted *him* to do was calm down. He needed time to process his emotions, but not in an explosive, disrespectful way. All we'd done was help him.

"You and what army?" Julius sneered at Griffin, while a faint glow lightened his silver irises.

They were having yet another pissing match. "Yeah, we get it. You're a big, mean, silver wolf." I let the sarcasm drip from each word. "But I'm one, too, and stronger than both of you." I glared at Griffin as well. There, I'd insulted both of their manhoods. Maybe that would wrap things up more quickly.

If I didn't love you, that would infuriate me, Griffin linked.

All strong wolves desired to be the strongest alpha. That was how most supernaturals were wired and one reason why there was so much corruption in our world. In wolves, alphas not only wanted to be the strongest, but also to protect their pack. It was an internal struggle that was always at the core of our wolf.

Dad had taught me that each supernatural race had some sort of inherent conflict it struggled with. Angels had their lack of emotional range—they were built to be warriors and tended to be colder and more closed off, making them seem heartless at times. Vampires were born or turned with humanity, but they had a thirst for blood and power that was always at war with their empathetic side. The list went on and on.

For silver wolves, strength and weakness were tied to the same thing: the moon.

The larger the moon, the more powerful we were, but the less the moon glowed until it waned to a new moon, the weaker we were. Our power grew and lessened. Naturally, our kind had dubbed the full moon "the silver moon."

"You don't think I know that?" Julius growled as his nose wrinkled in disgust. "Your power is the only reason you kept escaping."

"That's not true." Strength was great, but that wasn't how I'd survived. Maybe it had been at first, but not now. "I have a mate and friends who love me and would sacrifice anything to keep me safe. Because of that, we brought you with us. You should remember that, since you were afraid of being killed." He needed to come to grips with the fact that we'd saved him.

He thrust out his chest and remained silent.

Yeah, this was pointless. Me holding him here would only make things worse with us relationship-wise. "I'm going to let you go, but if you treat anyone in this house, including me, horribly again, then I'll kick your ass. You can be angry, stomp, cry, or scream at the moon, but not at any of us. Got it?"

Just when I thought he wasn't going to acknowledge me, he negligibly nodded his head. *Got it,* he linked with me, probably not wanting Griffin to hear.

I wanted to roll my eyes at his childish antics, but I'd scolded him enough for one night. I wasn't his parent, after all, and he was an adult. I couldn't help but wonder who'd raised him. Someone had put a roof over his head, but he was packless and had abandonment issues, so they'd messed with him. That was the one thing I knew for sure.

Not wanting Griffin to chime in, I linked with my mate as I released my hold on Julius. *He said he got it, using our strange bond.*

Of course he did. Griffin wasn't pleased.

None of us were happy at the moment. Too much shit was going on, and even though we'd gotten closer to the bad guy, we still had no clue who we were up against. Time to try to gain some knowledge. "So...we're here, and you're safe," I said to Julius. "Who's trying to kidnap me?"

"That information is the only reason for all of you to keep me around." Julius sneered. "I'm not telling you a damn thing until I learn more about who created me. If you want information, then I need mine first."

Dear God, this was going to be never-ending. But I wanted to try to cooperate with him—after all, he was my brother.

Rosemary stepped into the room. Her face was set into her customary mask of indifference.

"Is everything okay?" Griffin asked as his shoulders sagged. Lately, it seemed like we couldn't catch a break.

"Yeah." Rosemary arched an eyebrow. "I wouldn't walk in like this if there was something we had to address."

And there was my blunt angel friend. She could come off as aggressive, but I found her refreshing. She didn't shy away from the truth or confrontation. "I think what he meant to ask was is there something you need?"

"No." She pointed at Julius. "I figured I could take him to sleep in my room. I can keep an eye on him."

That, actually, was the best plan. We couldn't trust Julius, so we needed someone to watch him. Since she was the strongest of us, it made sense. I was just glad she'd offered instead of one of us having to make the request. "Okay, you know where the extra covers and pillows are if you need them." Under normal circumstances, I'd have offered to get the blankets and help out, but I was exhausted; I wasn't sure how I was still standing. Before I could crawl into bed, though, I needed a shower. Being locked in that cell for half a day hadn't been pleasant—the entire basement had smelled like piss and body odor.

"Or he could just sleep on the floor without any luxuries." Rosemary shifted her weight to one leg as she looked at Julius with cold disregard. "I mean, after all he's done, that's better than he deserves."

I didn't have the energy to argue with her, nor was she wrong. I turned and headed toward the bathroom and waved a hand. "Do what you have to do." At the end of the day, as long as he was safe, that was all that mattered. Maybe being a little harder on him would make things more bearable for him. He seemed to struggle with us being nice, like he was afraid that we'd take it back.

"Come on, Beta," she teased. "Let's get you settled."

Julius *harrumphed* but followed the angel out of the room.

I'm going to make sure he doesn't cause any problems. I'll be back in a minute, Griffin linked as I made my way into the bathroom.

Don't be long. I needed him after the day we'd had. For a second, I'd thought that I wouldn't be able to make my way back to him.

I removed my pale pink tennis shoes and socks and relished the cool gray tile that my feet now touched. Walking past the dark granite bathroom sink, I turned on the shower and pulled off my clothing.

Steam billowed from the top of the glass door of the shower, and I climbed into it and let the warm water hit my tight, sore muscles for a moment before quickly washing myself. Even though I wanted to stand in there forever, my body required sleep.

After getting clean, I wrapped a fluffy white towel around myself and strolled back into the bedroom. Clean clothes in hand, I dropped the towel right as Griffin came into the room.

He shut the door quickly and took a rapid intake of breath before the spicy scent of arousal hit my nose. *I'm so damn lucky,* he rasped.

My body responded to his smell and sexy voice, and I turned to face him.

His lips parted as he erased the distance between us. He kissed me with so much passion, my mind grew hazy.

I can't risk losing you again. His arms wrapped around my body, and his fingers dug into my ass. *I almost went insane. It gets worse each time.*

Our bond strengthened every time we had sex or spent time together. I'd heard that mates fell in love more each day, and now I knew it to be true. At first, it was lust, with love taking root within our hearts, but the lust never went away. Fated mate bonds ever deepened within each other.

You know I wish things weren't like this. In a perfect world, we'd have only regular pack issues to take care of, not someone breathing down our necks, wishing captivity or death on me. *Maybe fate messed up, putting the two of us together.* Griffin deserved to not live under constant threat. He should've been given a mate who could not only make him happy but didn't put him at constant risk.

He growled and lifted me, his body pressing my back against the wall. One hand snagged my wrists and held them over my head. *Don't ever talk like that again.* He pulled his mouth away from mine and kissed down my neck, all the way to my breasts.

Last time we'd almost lost each other, he'd demanded slow and tender lovemaking, so when he bit my nipple, I gasped in both surprise and delight. His tongue flicked out, giving me the sensation of both pleasure and pain, and my fatigue left me.

All I wanted and needed was him.

My wet hair clung to my shoulders as I leaned my head against the wall. He nipped and teased me as one of his hands slipped between my legs.

Now that one hand was free, I took a fistful of his hair, pulling his head toward me. I wanted to taste him.

No, he chastised me as his fingers increased both the pressure and pace, rubbing the place that built the friction inside me faster.

My breathing grew ragged as his mouth devoured me and his hands pushed me toward the peak. Every time I tried getting closer to him, he pulled away and bit and touched harder. My body was teetering so damn close to the edge. *Fuck me now.* I growled.

I was done playing nice. There was only one way that I'd get fully sated.

Take it back, then. His teeth grazed against my skin, making my body somehow warmer. *Tell me you're glad that you're mine.*

Of course I am. I had trouble even forming the words in my mind —my body had never been through so much torture and excruciating pleasure before.

Say fate had it right, he linked as he slipped a finger inside.

Right as my body almost contracted, he removed his hand, causing the building sensation to stall.

I bucked under his hand, wanting that release so damn badly.

Say it, he growled, commanding me.

I'd never been so turned on in my life. As an alpha, I thought I wouldn't like being dominated, but Griffin was the exception to the rule. *Fate had it right, okay?*

Good. He stumbled back and yanked off his clothing. His scent of arousal was as strong as mine, though I hadn't even touched him. He grasped my waist and tried to turn me around so I wasn't facing him, but it was my turn to dominate him.

My wolf surged, and I pivoted so that we switched sides with him against the wall. His eyes widened, which meant my plan had worked. He thought he'd be in control the entire time.

I climbed him, and he bent his knees enough that my legs could touch the floor on either side of him. When he slipped inside of me, I rode him fast and hard. After the torture he'd just put me through, I wouldn't take it easy on him.

He thrust into me, slamming deeper, and soon, I was close to falling over the edge again. My fingers fisted his hair, and I pulled, wanting to give him a taste of the pain he'd given me as I sucked on his neck. He shuddered against me, making me feel even more powerful and sexy.

One of his hands slipped between us, pinching my nipples as I pierced his skin with my teeth. Our bond filled with raw attraction and need, and I could feel him as he orgasmed with me. Our bodies rocked in sync as he filled me, and we stilled as we floated back to reality.

Damn, that was amazing, he said huskily, as he started to pull back. He scanned my breasts. *I didn't hurt you, did I?*

Just the perfect amount. We'd done "fast and hard" before, but *that* was something a little different, raw and carnal. *And that was amazing.*

He chuckled and kissed my lips sweetly. *Yeah, you can say that again.* He scooped me up in his arms and carried me to the bed. He laid me down and pulled the covers over me. *Get some rest. I'm going to jump in the shower and then join you.*

My eyes grew heavy, and before he even made it into the bathroom, I'd fallen asleep.

I woke cuddled in Griffin's arms. On mornings like these, life felt normal. The exact way things should be.

His chest rose and lowered steadily, indicating he was still asleep, but he pulled me closer in his arms. I took a moment to breathe in myrrh and leather, his unique scent, which had quickly become my favorite smell in the world.

The essence of home.

But footsteps stomped down the hallway, and soon, we heard a loud knock at the door. Julius's urgent voice called out, "Sterlyn, we need to talk. *Now.*"

CHAPTER EIGHT

GRIFFIN GRUMBLED, and his arms didn't slacken. *Couldn't he wait a little longer before waking you up? You went through hell yesterday and need your rest.*

I glanced at the clock and saw that it was after ten in the morning. *In fairness, he kind of did, too. Besides, we need to get moving and get Julius to talk before something else happens.* One thing was certain: whoever it was who'd come after me would attack again. I couldn't help but suspect Dick, but I couldn't prove it yet, so I'd keep those thoughts close until there was more to go on. Griffin was already struggling with coming to grips that Dick wasn't as helpful to him as the man pretended to be.

"Sure, give me a minute," I called to Julius, and kissed Griffin. However, when I tried to pull away, he tightened his arms around me even more.

Just a few more minutes, he whined and buried his face in my hair. *I don't think we've ever been able to lay leisurely in bed together in the morning.*

We hadn't. With work, his class schedule, and everything in between, we were constantly on the go. *I know, but the sooner we can take down whoever keeps hunting us, the quicker we can live out that fantasy.*

Using logic on me shouldn't be allowed before noon. He groaned and released his hold on my waist. *I hate it. But the only reason I'm appeasing you is that I want to figure out who it is before they strike again. Allowing you to put yourself at risk is not an option.*

Annoyance surged through me, but I squashed the sensation down. He wasn't trying to be bossy but rather hated thinking we'd all have to go through this mess once more. However, I couldn't let the comment go by completely without addressing it. I didn't want him to think my silence was agreement. *I get it, but we all have to do whatever is necessary for the greater good of the people.*

His jaw twitched. Clearly, he wasn't thrilled with my response, either.

This was one of those situations where the two of us were going to have to agree to disagree and hope the situation didn't present itself. "I love you." I kissed his cheek, hating that he was already tensing up and we hadn't gotten out of bed. Hopefully, that wasn't a sign for how the rest of the day would go.

I love you, too. His face softened as his fingers ran through my hair.

My body protested as I pushed back the covers, but I persevered and quickly grabbed the pajamas that I never got to put on the night before. After Julius said whatever was on his mind, I'd get dressed for the day. I didn't want to chance taking too long and Julius doing something stupid.

I shut the door behind me and found the rest of the crew in the living room. The television wasn't on, and Killian stood in the corner of the room, leaning against one of the blue-gray walls. His white shirt and blue jeans contrasted starkly, making him appear even more on edge. He didn't even acknowledge me when I entered, as his gaze was focused on Julius.

The blinds were drawn against the wall of windows so no one could see in, but the tension in the room was nearly suffocating. If I didn't know any better, I'd think we had an enemy lurking in our midst.

In fairness, we could, but I meant a much bigger threat than just my brother.

Wow. That was still strange to say.

Rosemary perched on the large pearl-gray couch that sat across from the flat-screen television mounted on the wall. Her long hair was pulled into a braid, and her face was set in a scowl that she directed at Julius.

The only person who seemed like her normal self was Sierra. She sat on the matching loveseat perpendicular to the couch, dressed in her purple Dick's Bar shirt and jeans. She'd be leaving for work soon, and in a way, I was kind of jealous. Despite her getting involved in the craziness with us, she still had a somewhat normal life. The only thing that made me uncomfortable was that if Dick was, in fact, the person behind everything, he'd have a better opportunity to harass her.

"What's going on?" Maybe Griffin and I should've gotten up earlier.

"Well, Julius here is determined to go to your pack neighborhood." Killian frowned and cut his gaze to me. "And I told him there's no way in hell. That the last time we went, we almost didn't make it out alive."

My stomach filled with dread. I hadn't told them yet that Julius was my brother. After last night, he'd confirmed it, so there was no reason to withhold the information. "Well, he was taken as a newborn, and he wants to see our family house."

"Family house?" Sierra parroted. "Are you saying you're *related* to him?"

"Yeah...he's my twin brother." The words felt weird passing my lips for the first time out loud.

A strange combination of hope and warmth exploded in my chest through the connection I shared with Julius. But after just a second, the sensations were replaced with skepticism, as if he were afraid to hope.

He cleared his throat. "I didn't realize we were going to let everyone in on that little fact." Discomfort wafted through him as if he didn't like them knowing. "But, yeah. Exactly, and I want to see the house I would've grown up in." Julius tensed next to the back door. "I at least deserve that."

"You don't deserve shit." Rosemary leaned over and gestured at him. "All that went out the window when you hurt your own kind."

"I never hurt her." He waved a hand toward me. "In fact, I tried to protect her as much as I could, despite knowing better. I don't know why, but it was like something inside me couldn't bear the thought of something bad happening to her. Hell, I saved her from being shot."

"True, but you were going to hand me over to some sort of sick, demented asshole." No matter how he tried to make it sound, he still wasn't truly protecting me. He just didn't want me to die, and honestly, that could've been because he didn't want the wrath of the big boss. There was a truthfulness to his words, but I had to be careful. I was desperate to connect with him—after all, he was the only blood family I had left. But I was still wary. I would keep that in mind moving forward.

"Wow. Now that you mention it, you two look similar, but, damn, your personalities are completely opposite. Ugh. I want to ask so many more questions, but I have to get to work," Sierra said as she leaned over, tying her tennis shoes. "This conversation is not over."

"Be careful." I was pretty sure she hadn't officially been lumped in with us by my enemy, but there had been times when we'd been watched and hadn't been aware. If she didn't show up to work, that would raise questions, so we were in one of those impossible situations where there wasn't necessarily a good choice. "If anything seems suspect, link with Killian and let him know." The fact that we all weren't linked was getting very inconvenient. There had to be a way to at least have our group interconnected.

Luckily, we didn't have to keep Sierra and Rosemary hidden like Julius. The guards wouldn't find it strange to see them coming in and out, as they'd been staying with us for a while.

"Of course." Sierra stood and hugged me, then went to the front door. "I'm heading over to my house to grab my car, and if you guys need me, don't hesitate to contact me."

The four of us watched her walk out. I welcomed the silence, trying to gauge how I felt. I understood both sides of this argument.

Our bedroom door shut, and Griffin strolled into the living room a few seconds later. He scanned the room, taking in the varying stances and body language. "What's he done now?" Griffin sighed as he turned toward Julius.

To prevent either side from starting, I jumped in. "Julius wants to go back to my pack neighborhood and get a feel for what the place was like before everyone died."

"What?" Julius gasped as his face went pale. "The entire *pack* is dead?"

"Like you didn't know." Rosemary snapped. "Don't even try to come off innocent."

Being a silver wolf was his only saving grace with Rosemary. She clearly didn't like him, never mind her mother's strong words about protecting our kind.

"But you said it was only our parents!" He blinked and swallowed, and I saw a suspicious glimmer in his eyes. "I had no idea that the pack was annihilated. They promised—" He cut himself off, as if realizing he'd already said too much.

"*Who* promised?" Griffin pushed up the sleeves of his mustard-colored shirt like he was preparing to fight.

"No, you have to be lying." Julius raised both a palm and his voice. "This has to be a sick game you're playing."

Each side accusing the other was unproductive; we could go back and forth like this all day. "No one is lying," I said. "We'd all know if we were. We're supernaturals, for God's sake." And if we wanted him to trust us, we had to give him a reason. One that wasn't convenient for us. Besides, I felt a tug to go home, too, now that the topic had been brought up. "I think we should take Julius back to the neighborhood. Besides, I'd like to find where they buried the dead." I glared at Julius. "But you have to give us something after this. Do you understand?"

My words hung in the air.

"If what you say is true, then I might be more inclined." Julius nodded, though he still wasn't committing.

Killian's shoulders slumped, and Rosemary placed a hand over her stomach as she sat upright.

God, I'm such an asshole. Griffin wrapped an arm around my waist, and regret wafted from him. *I hadn't even thought about that. You haven't gotten any closure or a chance to say goodbye.*

His simple statement was obvious, but I hadn't been able to nail down the negative emotions coursing through me.

Until him.

"Well, I guess that means we're heading to your pack house." Killian pinched the bridge of his nose. "But we need to be careful this time."

"I'll fly ahead." Rosemary stood and headed toward the back door. "Wait to hear from me before you drive into the neighborhood. I'll meet you at the entrance."

"Thank you." I hoped she could feel my sincerity. One day, I'd have to do something to pay her back for all she'd risked and done for us. "We'll be there shortly."

"See you soon." Rosemary exited the house.

"Okay, if we're going to do this, we have to be smart." We needed to get out of here with Julius staying hidden. "Griffin's Navigator is our safest bet. Julius can lie down in the back so none of the guards see him."

"You do realize some of the guards are going to want to come with us." Griffin pushed his shoulders back as he rubbed his fingers together. "What do we tell them?"

"That we have something that we need to do alone." Killian and

Griffin were their alphas. It was as simple as that. "As long as you don't come off unsure, they won't challenge you."

"And we can reassure them that we'll link them if anything goes wrong." Killian shrugged.

"Fine. Let's just get this over with." Griffin bared his teeth at Julius. "One wrong move, and I'm bringing our asses back here."

"I figured that was coming." Julius rolled his eyes. "But I want to go too badly to argue with you."

They'd go back and forth all day if I let them. "Let's get going. We'll be safer in the daylight, and we all know Rosemary isn't famous for her patience."

"You got that right." Killian clasped his hands together. "We'll never hear the end of it if she has to wait long."

I quickly dressed, and then the four of us made it to the car. Julius followed my directions without any prompting, lying down in the back with a blanket over his body so that he'd barely be seen if Griffin had to roll down his window. Killian took his normal spot in the middle row behind me as Griffin got into the driver's seat.

Once we were all settled, he opened the garage and backed out. Griffin rested his hand on the gear shift when he paused. After a second, he linked with me. *They're asking questions. Are we sure that it's smart to go there? The last time, we were attacked.*

I can't promise it will all be okay. For some reason, I wasn't too concerned about what we might face. *And this time, we have Rosemary standing guard. Killian wasn't able to alert us until it was too late. With Rosemary, we should be able to get in the car and out of the subdivision before they get close.*

"My pack wants to know where we're going, like we expected they would." Killian sighed. "At least they're asking through the pack bond and not in person."

Even though Julius should be out of sight, stopping would be risky. "Well, we'll get there and back quickly. We don't need to spend all day there." The longer we stayed, the greater our chances of someone ambushing us, but this was something Julius needed.

Between the way he reacted to the entire pack being killed and learning that he'd been stolen, maybe this would be the final turn to get him to warm up to us.

Can I get up yet? Julius linked as discomfort slammed into me.

He always got more edgy when he connected with me telepathically. I guessed if I'd been a rogue my entire life, I wouldn't be enthused with someone having a link inside my head, either. Back in the day, I'd hated that the pack could have access if I wasn't careful when I got upset, and this had to feel completely foreign to him. *Give us another few minutes to get out of our neighborhood.*

As Griffin put the car in drive, six guards stood in his front yard with huge frowns on their faces, watching us pull away. I didn't need a pack link with them to know they weren't thrilled.

When we pulled onto the main road that would take us to my former neighborhood, I turned toward the back. "You can get up now. We're clear."

Julius's head popped up, reminding me of the whack-a-mole game Mom and I played together when I was little and she'd take me to the arcades. I turned forward before the smile broke across my face. Maybe things would be all right after all.

THE RIDE to my pack neighborhood took less than twenty minutes. As soon as Griffin neared the entrance, he stopped and waited for Rosemary to give us some sort of sign.

"Where is she?" Julius complained.

And here I'd thought Rosemary was the most impatient person I'd ever met. I'd been proven wrong. "We just got here. Give her a few minutes."

He groaned as he sat back in the seat.

"And I thought women were dramatic," Killian deadpanned, and leaned between the seats and over the center console with his fist pointed toward Griffin like he expected a bump.

I arched an eyebrow and glared at my mate as he raised his hand. I warned, "You touch his hand, and you'll see something dramatic." I was teasing, but at the same time, I was tired of the sexist comments that somehow got thrown my way.

Rosemary landed by my car door and scanned the area like she was expecting some sort of threat to jump out at her. When she chewed on her fingernail, it put me on edge. She was uncertain and nervous about something.

I rolled down the window and asked urgently, "What's wrong?"

The area around her eyes tightened as she looked at me straight on. "We have a problem."

CHAPTER NINE

IF I NEVER HEARD THOSE four words again, it would still be too soon. There were so many damn problems—we didn't need to add more to the mix. "Are there enemy shifters here?" If there were, I was surprised that Rosemary hadn't started kicking their asses. Maybe she wanted backup; that would make sense.

"I'm not sure if *enemy* is the right word." She gritted her teeth, which wasn't like her. She normally ran her mouth without regard for what came out.

This change made my skin crawl. Something was horribly wrong. "Just tell us," I commanded.

She squinted at me, clearly not appreciating how I'd spoken to her, but she pushed it aside. "There are about fifteen shifters walking around your neighborhood."

"Of course there are," Griffin groaned. "And let me guess, they have guns."

"No, they don't." She pursed her lips. "One of them has darker silver hair, like Julius back there."

"Wait..." My mind raced to catch up. "Are you saying one might be a *silver wolf*? But how? All the links are cold." Unless...could it be my uncle?

"Based on finding both you and Julius, finding more wouldn't be that farfetched at this point." Rosemary shrugged. "If it was one of Julius's buddies, they'd be loaded up."

"Maybe we should turn around," Killian said uneasily. "Maybe having them pop up is fate's way of telling us to stay away. We could stand to catch a break."

"No. I need to see them." Julius climbed into the center aisle and out the driver's-side back door. "There might not be another chance."

Everyone grew uneasy, which was affecting our logic. We couldn't let emotions rule our decisions. That was how mistakes were made. "If there are more silver wolves, they could be allies," I said.

"But they might not be," Griffin countered, and pointed at Julius, who surprisingly hadn't marched toward the neighborhood.

A little bit of self-preservation was bleeding through his eagerness. Good, I didn't need him running headfirst into a bad situation.

"He has a point." Killian fidgeted in the back seat. "Julius is a silver wolf, and he was definitely working against us."

"I get your concern," I told him. Everything we'd experienced had taught us to be cautious, especially around new people. Every time we turned around, somebody else was trying to kill us. "But I think we have to check it out. If there are more of us, we could have a hell of a lot better chance of surviving and overcoming my would-be kidnapper."

"You can't guarantee they'll work with you," Rosemary said, and nibbled her bottom lip. "I didn't take you as overconfident."

Her words stung. Dick and Luna were overconfident; I'd never want to be lumped in with them. "I'm now the silver wolf alpha. My dad was the ultimate alpha, and his abilities transferred to me. My light silver hair signifies that. Worst case, I make them submit to me."

"And if they attack all at once?" Rosemary's forehead lined with worry. "I don't think we can hold off fifteen of them."

"If I challenge their alpha directly, it's against wolf nature to organize an attack." Only a coward would refuse or organize a group attack when faced with the alpha challenge.

Griffin swallowed and scowled. "If they're silver wolves, that doesn't mean they'll be ethical."

But it kind of did. I could feel the turmoil in Julius when he was solidly working with the other side. He was in constant conflict, and our bond only added to the chaos. It didn't create it. Like Dad had explained, our race was inherently good. I had to believe that. And if that was my uncle, maybe he'd have some answers. "Let's drive through the neighborhood. If we spot them, I can roll down the window and feel them out. If they charge or act shady, I'll tell you, 'Let's roll.' They might be fast, but they can't outrun a vehicle, especially for a long amount of time."

"Don't even bother trying to argue." Killian sighed and leaned between the center console yet again. "You know you're going to cave, and she does have a point. If there's a slight chance they're good —that they're on Sterlyn's side—we'd be stupid not to try."

"I know that." Griffin tapped his finger on the steering wheel. "But that doesn't mean I'm happy about the situation." He jabbed the button that rolled the window down and barked, "Are you getting back in the car or not?"

"Are you going down there?" Julius asked warily, but he opened the car door as he waited for a response.

Griffin groaned. "Yeah, she'd kick my ass if I didn't."

"I'll take to the sky and make sure nothing strange happens." Rosemary stepped back as her wings spread behind her. "If I see anything, I'll holler and let you know."

"Thanks." Every conversation I had with her always seemed to end the same way.

She took flight as Julius got back into the car. As soon as the door shut, Griffin rolled into the neighborhood.

He gripped the steering wheel so hard his knuckles turned white. "The first sign they might attack, I'm getting our asses out of here."

"Okay." If I fought him, he'd be even more hesitant to go. And honestly, he had a right to be wary. "But let's at least give them a chance."

"All you have to do is tell me," Killian grunted. "I'll roll the damn window up for her."

Those two were insanely protective of me. If I didn't love them as much as I did, I wouldn't be able to tolerate being around them.

"You do realize she can take care of herself, right?" Julius didn't sound amused. "If it weren't for her and the angel, you two would've been killed by now."

Not helping matters, I linked to Julius. *Let's not threaten their manhood when they're already going into a situation they aren't thrilled about.*

Agitation rolled off Julius. *If they can't handle the truth, they need to learn how to. Sometimes, the truth hurts.*

Says the guy who exploded on everyone last night when you learned about your past. You *didn't know how to handle it.* He had no right to get all high and mighty. Every single one of us had flaws, and in this instance, Griffin's and Killian's was that they cared so much about me. *Maybe some self-reflection would go a long way.*

He remained silent. In fairness, he couldn't have a good retort.

The modest brick houses came into view, and my heart twinged. With each house I looked at, the image of the family who had lived there popped into my mind. Every person meant so much to me. We'd been one large family, the way every smaller pack should be.

These houses were all one-story structures, similar to those in Killian's pack neighborhood, but missing the Craftsman feel. These were simple and built to be low maintenance. The only sign that the town had been abandoned was the tall grass and weeds in everyone's yards, now that the weather was warming with spring.

Griffin drove slowly, but soon, we took the curve leading to the back of the neighborhood and my family home.

In front of my parents' house stood fifteen wolves. They didn't hide but rather stood side by side, staring us down.

The tallest man stood in the center of the group with seven

flanking each side. His hair was a shade darker than Julius's but silver nonetheless. He appeared to be a few years younger than Dad and held himself in a similar way. And his golden flecked silver eyes zeroed in on me.

Could he be my uncle?

Griffin huffed as he turned the Navigator so that I faced the group head-on only a few feet away. When I rolled down my window, the faint floral, musky scent of the silver wolf filled the car.

I lifted my head high, making sure my posture exuded confidence. "Who are you, and what are you doing here?"

"Maybe we should ask you the same questions," the man who obviously was the pack alpha retorted. He lifted his head high, mimicking me. "You don't look as if you belong here."

A loud laugh escaped me. This had to be some sort of joke. "I grew up here."

"Really?" The alpha placed his hands inside his jean pockets and tilted his head. "You've let the place go to shit, then."

The insult burned. He was right. I should've done more. I shouldn't allow my childhood neighborhood to deteriorate like this. "I've been kind of preoccupied. Once again, who are you, and why are you here?"

"We thought we should check out the area." The alpha shrugged, but there was something strange wafting off him. His intent was good, but he was trying to hide some sort of pain. "See if we could find a place to land."

I wasn't in the mood to play games. Dad had told me that political maneuvers were an important piece of leading, but all they did was convolute things. I hated it. I got that there was a time and place, but now didn't feel like the time. "I'm Sterlyn Knight. Are you my uncle?"

Babe, I know you want him to be part of your family, but maybe you were a little too forthcoming. Worry pulsed from Griffin. *Now he could pretend to be your family.*

If he lies, we'll know. There were some things you couldn't hide. *He looks like my dad, and he's the right age.*

And he left for a reason. Griffin placed his hand on the gear shift, ready to pull away. *We don't know what it was.*

The alpha's mouth dropped open, and he quickly scratched his nose as if trying to cover up his reaction. "You cut straight to the point, huh?"

"I figure there's no reason to beat around the bush." I scanned the entire group. The other men were around the same age as the alpha, so they weren't his children. There was no way a silver wolf could reproduce like that, and their mates couldn't be silver. "So my question is, what was my father's favorite dessert?" Dad's favorite was odd. Mom and I gave him hell, but he said his grandmother introduced him to it at a young age.

The alpha remained quiet for a moment, as if he were considering my words. "Jalapeno orange marmalade cupcakes. Grandma's specialty."

Even though I'd suspected this was my uncle, having him confirm it was surreal. "You're really him."

"And you're really her. I thought you died..." The emotion grew thick in his voice, and he trailed off, unable to finish the sentence.

"I escaped." I sounded like such a coward. "I was out in the woods when the attack happened. When I finally reached home to help, the slaughter was over. Dad was mortally wounded when he found me, and he told me to run. He had a huge gash—" I choked off.

"Look, I'm not trying to be an asshole," Griffin said, and glared at my uncle. "But why the hell are you here now?"

"That's a long story." He ran a hand through his hair, making it stand on end. His focus landed on Griffin and the other two men in the back seat. "And one that Sterlyn deserves an answer to. I was hoping to check out the house. Would that be all right?"

"How do we know we can trust you?" Killian asked. "If we walk in there, we could be walking to our deaths."

My uncle nodded his head in approval and looked at me. "Who are these two?" He gestured from Killian to Griffin. "They aren't silver wolves."

"No. I met them after I escaped." Even though we might be family, I wasn't going to tell him my entire story. At least, not yet. Complete trust had to be earned, and I had learned that being family didn't always mean someone had your best interests at heart.

"And who's the other guy in the back?" my uncle asked.

"My brother." If he knew my name, then his reaction to this little tidbit would tell everything.

"Impossible." My uncle marched over to the car and scowled. "That's not funny."

His disbelief settled me. "Apparently, the witch who attended our birth spelled him to appear dead." I could throw Julius under the bus and tell our uncle that he'd been trying to kidnap me for the bad guys, but I wouldn't...for now. "We just found each other, but that's a long story. I'm more interested in why you're here now."

"Decades ago, murmurings arose about reopening Shadow City to the world, and the city's alpha began writing letters to your dad to see if he was interested in returning. We knew there was a chance that someone would try to control us, so since I was the pack beta, we decided that it would be best if I split off with a small number of wolves to form my own pack. This was a few years before you were born." He motioned to the fourteen men behind him. "About two years ago, your dad contacted me to tell me that he was heading to the city to meet with the alpha. We've checked in once a month since then as the murmurs got louder."

"That's why you're here." It'd been almost a month since I ran that day. "You reached out, and he didn't respond."

"Yeah." He clasped his hands loosely behind his back and stared at the ground. "When we got here, we searched the area and found several men dead in the woods. I'm assuming they were part of those who attacked the pack since they appeared to be military and had weapons on them, and they weren't silver wolves. And then we found—"

My breathing quickened. For him to not finish the sentence told me everything. "Did you find the bodies of my pack?" Last time I'd been here, with Griffin, Killian, and Sierra, I hadn't had a chance to find my dead because we'd been attacked again.

"We did." He closed his eyes and rubbed his forehead. "And it was awful. The way those assholes tossed them..." He blew out a breath and looked back at me. "Let's just say they're buried now in the cemetery."

"Are there markers so I can find them?" I opened the car door, wanting to see where they'd been laid to rest.

The shortest man behind my uncle took a step forward. His midnight-brown hair fell to the side like long bangs, and his blood-orange eyes glazed over with sadness. Dirt coated his arms and smudged one cheek. He was close to my height but thicker. "We put a cross in front of each and did our best to bury family members together."

"We were wondering where your body was." My uncle touched my arm. "I didn't let myself hope that you were still alive. I'm just so damn glad that you're here."

"Me, too." Having more silver wolves and finding my uncle was a very good thing, especially since my attackers shouldn't know about them. Not only that, but maybe he could help me get through to Julius so we could get some answers. We'd finally have something up our own sleeves. "But the question is, do you plan on staying?"

"We don't have a choice." My uncle lifted his arms and gestured around the town. "They tried to exterminate us. We won't take it lying down."

Good. I'd been worried they wouldn't feel that way, but they were here for a reason.

"Do you mind going inside the house with me?" My uncle glanced at the front door and then back at me. "There's something I need to show you."

Whatever he wanted to show me must be important, which made me wonder what we'd missed the other day when we'd had to rush away so quickly. Were there more secrets hidden inside?

CHAPTER TEN

DO you think it's wise? Griffin asked, feeling my determination through our bond.

I was glad he was challenging me. Sometimes, people needed to be questioned to ensure they were thinking things through. *I think if we don't go, and there's something in there that's valuable, we'll risk more by not finding out. Besides, I don't feel anything menacing coming off him like I do Luna, Dick, and even Julius.* I hated that my brother had such a darkness shrouding him, but it had to be a product of the environment he was raised in.

I met my uncle's gaze. "Are you sure no one's watching us?" I didn't want to get into the same situation as last time when we'd stayed in the house and couldn't get to the cars before we were attacked. "Our enemies have bird shifters on their team, and I overlooked them before."

"We checked for everything once we found all the bodies." My uncle shivered. "We're safe, and there are no recent scents."

"No odd noises that can't be explained?" Killian asked.

The last time, we hadn't smelled the bird because it had stayed high in the trees, but it had knocked a branch onto the ground. I'd overlooked the odd noise then, and I wouldn't make the same mistake twice.

The man who'd spoken earlier raised his head. "We're good."

This time, we have Rosemary, I linked to Griffin.

"All right, let me park." Griffin put the car in reverse and backed up.

We pulled into the driveway, and the four of us were out of the car within seconds.

After shutting the door, I turned to find my uncle staring at Julius and me like he'd seen a ghost.

He shook his head as the corners of his mouth tipped downward. "You two look like the spitting images of your mom and dad. It's uncanny."

I'd been told that a lot. My pack always teased my parents, saying there was no mistaking that I was their child. Those comments used to irritate me, but not anymore. I cherished them. "Thank you."

A few of the silver wolves looked at me a little longer than felt appropriate, and Griffin placed an arm around my waist. "I'm Griffin Bodle, Sterlyn's fated mate."

My uncle's eyes twinkled. "A good mate always stakes his claim when it comes to other men." He laughed good-naturedly and took Griffin's hand. "My name is Bart Knight. It's nice to meet you."

That was when it hit me. I'd had no clue what my uncle's name was. At least Griffin got it out of him before I had to ask.

"And I'm Killian Green." Killian didn't budge, just stared each of the wolves down like he expected them to attack at any minute. "The alpha of Shadow Ridge, so if anything strange goes down, my pack will be here in minutes."

"Noted," Bart replied as he shook Killian's hand. "Which means you are Cyrus." Bart turned his attention to my brother, using his birth name. "I don't know how you two found each other, but thank God you made it out alive."

I cringed, waiting for the explosion, but nothing happened other than Julius stiffening before nodding his head.

"Yeah, that's me." Julius tilted his head and sighed. His demeanor reminded me of Dad so much that it hurt.

"Well, these are my men." Bart waved his hand at the fourteen people standing behind him. They were all over six feet tall and about as burly as Griffin and Killian, except for the one other guy who'd spoken earlier. My uncle gestured to him. "This is my beta, Darrell Hart." He did seem to have more confidence than the other thirteen.

"It's nice to meet you all, and I'm sorry to say that we don't have a ton of time to stay here," I replied. "We have to get back to Shadow Ridge before people get worried."

Even though we weren't trying to hide that Griffin was the Shadow City alpha, I wasn't going to offer that piece of information unless we had to. If Bart had split from our pack because of rumblings of Shadow City opening its doors, that could mean that he wouldn't be as forthcoming with Griffin in our presence—or potentially, even me—since we were mates. I wanted to see what information they had before risking them not sharing it with me.

Surprisingly, Julius hadn't ratted us out. My guess was that he was afraid we'd force him to leave before he got to see everything and that I would inform Bart and the others of exactly what his dear, sweet nephew had done. We both had leverage over each other, which worked for the time being. I hoped that one day, we could move past all that.

"All right, let's get moving." Griffin took my hand and led me to the door. "We do need to hurry." His expression remained indifferent, keeping his unease hidden from everyone but me, but it flowed through our bond.

I swung the sturdy red chestnut door open, trying to push away the suffocating sense of nostalgia.

The living room remained untouched from the last time we were here. The beige cloth couch still sat centered against the tan wall, with Dad's brown leather recliner in the corner. Mom's favorite orange-red throw was folded on the couch from when Sierra had slept there.

Sadness tried pushing through once again, but I couldn't appear weak, especially in front of these other silver wolfmen. I needed to be a confident alpha so they wouldn't second-guess my abilities more than they already did because I was female.

Dread filled me as I stepped on the dark walnut floor, and Mom's lavender scent caused my eyes to burn. God, how I missed her.

When I reached the center of the room, I blinked a few times to hold back tears before spinning toward the men marching in behind me. "So, here we are." Luckily, my voice sounded strong and didn't break.

Griffin winced as he sensed all the emotions raging inside me. He moved to stand next to me and reached for my hand, but I stepped back, which made him miss. Hurt etched on his face at my rejection.

I'm sorry. I hated that I'd made him feel that way and embarrassed him in front of the others, but I didn't have a choice. *If you comfort me, I won't be able to hold back my sadness. I feel safe with you, but I can't let my guard down in front of these strangers. Silver wolves or not.*

As long as that's the reason. He rubbed his hand on his pants leg.

As arrogant and vulgar as he'd acted the first day I'd met him in the coffee shop, I'd never have expected him to be insecure, ever. But there were hints like these that proved he still needed to realize the strength he had inside him. I was determined to get him to see the man he was. *I promise. Don't make me punish you for doubting me,* I teased, trying to make him smile.

As Bart's fourteen men began to enter the house, Bart commanded, "Stop. Spread out around the house and keep watch. Alert us of anything out of the ordinary."

Darrell's forehead pinched, showing he clearly didn't like being sent outside. Those two must have shared almost everything together, so not being privy to whatever Bart wanted to show me must not have sat well with him.

"Now." Bart's voice was laced with alpha will.

"Yes, Alpha." Darrell grimaced and turned, the last one to leave.

The door shut loudly behind them, and Bart nodded toward it. "Why don't you three go out there and help keep watch while Sterlyn and I have a few minutes to talk."

"Not happening," Griffin growled, shaking his head. "I'm her mate. I'm not leaving her side."

"And same." Killian marched over, flanking my other side. "Where they go, I go."

"Interesting." Bart tapped a finger against his lip as he faced Julius. "Why is Killian protecting her and not you?"

Silver wolves were intuitive, so the fact that Bart already caught on to my strained relationship with my brother didn't surprise me. I'd have been more worried if he hadn't.

"*He's* her brother," Julius spat and scowled. "Not me."

Great. We were going to let our family drama hang out with a man we hadn't even known for ten minutes. Things were already going so smoothly. "They can stay." I wanted to add *but not him* about Julius, but that would only make him feel more alienated. Whatever there was to find, Julius should theoretically have the same right to know as Bart and I.

"Okay, then." Bart shrugged. "You're the top alpha," he said without bitterness, catching me off guard.

I'd almost been afraid that he might challenge me for that title, but maybe there wouldn't be a problem after all.

Bart gestured to the hallway. "Let's visit the basement room."

"The basement room?" I had no clue what he was talking about. Maybe he wasn't who I thought he was.

He stepped back, looking startled. "Your father never showed you?"

I took a deep breath. I didn't like being left in the dark, especially since it sounded like I should know about it. "There's no basement room. This is a one-story house with a crawlspace." Either I was stupid, or he was. I had a feeling it was me, and that didn't sit well.

He lifted a hand for a moment and tilted it side to side as if he was trying to figure out what to say. "There's a secret room where our ancestry is hidden. Only the alpha heirs know about it. No one beyond them."

"If that's the case, then how do you know about it?" Maybe he would challenge me after all.

"Until you were born, I was the second in line to lead." He licked his lips and gazed at the wall above my head as if he was lost in memories. "I needed to learn everything about being alpha in case your father died. When you were born, you took my place. Now you're the true alpha with Cyrus as the spare. You two need to learn about our history. It's how things have always been done so no one is left without the knowledge."

Whether I liked the situation or not, Bart knowing about the secret room was a very good thing. That information could've been lost forever if both he and Dad hadn't been told. "Then why didn't he tell me?" Hurt laced my words. Dad had left me without all the facts.

"The transition should've happened by now, but knowing my brother, he wanted to protect you as long as possible." Bart rolled his shoulders, displaying his discomfort. "The more someone knows, the more at risk they are from people who are desperate to know all about us."

I laughed humorlessly. "At one point, I might have agreed with you, but not now. I was spared only because someone wants to use me as a breeder, so my limited knowledge hasn't saved me."

Bart's jaw twitched. "Some things never change. There's always someone out there trying to corrupt the world. It makes me sick."

"Maybe the silver wolves going into hiding wasn't the right call." I'd been thinking that for a while. We were meant to be just and fair. By running off to hide, had we allowed the supernatural world to become more corrupt? "We should've stayed and helped to fix the problems."

"You say that now, but you don't understand the whole story." Bart rubbed his hands together. "You're about to learn everything."

That was something I could get behind. "So where is this hidden room?" I'd grown up in this house and knew every nook and cranny. There was no way I'd missed it.

"Let me show you." Bart gestured to the hallway. "Do you mind if I lead?"

I waved him forward. "Go for it."

"But no funny business." Griffin straightened his shoulders. "There are four of us against you."

"Math is one of my strong suits." Bart chuckled and stalked down the hallway. "But thanks for clarifying."

"You stay here with us." Killian sneered at Julius.

Between Griffin and Killian, my brother sure couldn't feel the love. However, my uncle calling him by his birth name didn't seem to bother him. He was dying to fit in but wasn't sure how to go about it. Maybe if we let him come along, he wouldn't feel so alone. I couldn't fathom growing up without a pack; he'd had a rougher childhood than any of us could relate to. "No, let him come," I said.

"What?" Julius's lips parted as his breath hitched. "Is this some kind of cruel joke to get back at me?"

"You can't be serious." Killian ran his fingers through his hair. "He hasn't done anything to prove himself."

"Because we haven't given him the chance to. And Bart's right—he should know this, too." In order to prevent Julius from feeling any more uncomfortable than he already was, I took off after Bart.

There's no way in hell I'm letting you go down those stairs with your resurrected brother who's tried to kidnap you multiple times and an uncle who just recently appeared. Griffin sounded broken as he ran after me and took my hand. *Please don't ask that of me.*

Even though I hated considering breaking tradition, how could I tell my mate no after that? If anything, he and I were stronger together. *Fine, but just you.*

And Killian. Regret wafted from my mate toward me. *Because you can't take on two silver wolves on your own, and let's be real, I'm not even a match for just one. It'll be best if we don't split up.*

He was right. I had to think with logic, and beyond that, I trusted Killian and Griffin more than the two men in front of me. They'd proven they had my best interests at heart, and after all that we'd gone through, that had to mean something. I paused and waited for Bart to look back at me. "I respect that under normal circumstances, only Cyrus and I would go with you. But not many silver wolves are left, and Killian and Griffin are my family, too. I want them to be part of this as well."

Bart frowned but nodded his head before he took off again.

Griffin and Killian followed me, with Julius's hesitant footsteps several feet behind.

I glanced over my shoulder and watched my brother pause and look at every picture that he passed. Most of them were photos of me through varying stages of childhood, but then he spotted two family pictures of Mom, Dad, and me. I sensed his pain through our bond as he saw everything that he'd missed out on. And for some reason, that was what it took for me to understand even a fragment of his pain. How would it feel to look at pictures you should've been a part of but weren't? To see the life you could've had but that someone had stolen from you? If this didn't get him on our side, I wasn't sure what would.

I didn't want Bart to be alone for too long, so I quickened my pace and entered the very last doorway in the hall.

Bart had left the door open, and my parents' made bed immediately came into view. The navy-blue comforter was wrinkle-free, contrasting with the white bed frame and the sky-blue walls.

Bart stood in front of the white chest of drawers where I'd found the hidden false bottom in dad's underwear drawer, which had contained the picture album, journal, and letters from Griffin's dad to mine.

The other three men entered behind me as Bart smiled and said, "This is when your entire life changes." He reached down to where the drawer had been and slipped his hand inside at the top. A loud *click* sounded, and the chest of drawers jerked.

Bart grabbed the right side of the heavy furniture piece and pulled it toward us. A large, gaping hole appeared with steps leading down to what must be the hidden room.

What was it with Dad and his fucking underwear?

CHAPTER ELEVEN

"YOUR DAD'S underwear has its own story." Griffin shook his head. "At least his hint was a good one."

Dad's words about a person's underwear speaking volumes about them made sense, especially now. Between the false bottom of the drawer and the button that unlocked the hidden door, his saying was obviously meant to stick with me to help me find everything. The only flaw in his plan was that I was pretty sure I wouldn't have found the hidden door if not for Bart. "You're telling me."

"Um..." Bart's brows furrowed. "I have a feeling that I don't want to know."

"Are we sure it's safe down there?" Killian walked to the door frame. He peeked his head through the hole, looking down the stairs.

Bart took the first step and looked over his shoulder. "Yes, the room is safe. Most likely a little dusty and small, but safe nonetheless. There's even a light switch, so we won't be in the dark."

I paused, taking a moment to collect myself. I had a feeling that whatever we'd find would alter my reality.

We don't have to go down there. Griffin comforted me. *We can head back home and come back later, or not at all.*

The idea was appealing, but leaving would be the coward's way. Whatever was down there was important, and it might answer some questions that had taken root in my mind. *That's not an option.* Even if I wanted it to be.

I'll be right here beside you, he linked as he placed a hand on the small of my back. *If it gets to be too much, we can head back up.*

Even if it became difficult, I'd push through. Not knowing things had been a problem this entire time. Everyone else was several steps ahead of us, and even though we were slowly leveling the playing field, time was running out. We needed something to use to our advantage instead of playing defense all the time. *And I love you for being right here with me.*

Bart continued the trek down the stairs with Killian right behind.

I rushed forward, following Killian before I lost my nerve. Griffin stayed close behind me with Julius taking up the rear.

The stairwell was small, even for me, and I was the smallest of the five of us. I folded my shoulders as I took each step slowly. The wood creaked underneath us but remained secure.

Dust floated around us. *Dad must not have come down here for a while.*

Well, if he wanted to keep it hidden, he might not have had many opportunities.

Griffin stayed so close that I could feel his body heat on my back. I had a feeling that if he weren't with me, I wouldn't have found the strength to come down here. *Yeah, I wonder if Mom knew about it.* My gut said no. She would've insisted that Dad tell me or would've shared it with me herself. The day I turned eighteen, only a couple of months ago, she'd told me that I was now a woman and that I needed to take my training with Dad more seriously. My excuses wouldn't work any longer.

Unfortunately, you'll probably never know. Remorse poured off him. *But maybe whatever is down here will shed light on everything.*

That was the entire reason I was making myself go through with this.

"Watch your head," Bart said as he turned to the right, ducking.

Killian reached the bottom and laughed dryly. "You weren't kidding about a small room." He glanced at me and winked, but the tension in his shoulders spoke volumes. He was on edge just like Griffin and I were, but he wanted to relax me. He lowered his head and entered the room.

Light flooded the opening as I touched the cement ground and turned toward the room. The rectangular space was around three hundred square feet, which wasn't large, but not as small as Bart had made it sound. The walls were all beige stone, and there was an air vent in the ceiling, so the area was cooled. In the middle sat a large white marble statue of an angel—a man with strong, chiseled features who stood as tall as Bart. His wings fanned behind him, but that wasn't what caught my eye. It was the moon sitting in the palm of his hand.

Griffin and Julius brushed past me, and I tried to move, but my legs were frozen. I stared blankly at the statue. "Why is there an angel in my basement?"

The absurdity of the statement would've made me laugh under normal circumstances...or at least, I thought so. Hell, I wasn't sure I knew what constituted normal anymore.

"That's one reason you're here." Bart strolled to a desk in the corner of the room where a journal sat with a note on top.

Another damn journal.

Hadn't the last one done enough damage?

Anger fueled me, and my strength returned. I marched to the desk and found my father's neat handwriting once again.

Sterlyn,

If you're finding this, that means that my worst fears have come true. Shadow City has opened the gates once more, and something bad has happened.

Our location has been revealed. I'm working on negotiations for another property, but they aren't final-ized. I hope that I'm being paranoid, but if one group

found us, that means others could follow. I'm writing this letter in case something happens before I can get us relocated.

I know you must have so many questions, and I hope you never find this. I plan on telling you everything on the new moon. I've been putting it off because when I learned everything, I learned it with my brother. How I wish you had someone to rely on like Bart and I had each other, but fate didn't have that in your cards.

None of this matters, but if I don't tell you this, I know you'll always be curious. Kevin's new mate came from Shadow Ridge, and she told her former alpha about our location, not realizing the severity of our situation. You'll soon read the journal I left behind that will detail what I'm referencing, but just know her mistake wasn't intentional.

So read the journal, and at the very back, I have details on how to contact your uncle for help. Unfortunately, if you're reading this, that means I am dead. Just know that you are a true alpha, and never let any man or woman doubt your capabilities. There is something special in you. Both your mother and I see it. You have a just heart, even more so than most others, and you will be a leader who understands what's best for the entire supernatural race, not just the silver wolves. You are the true embodiment of what a silver wolf is meant to be.

I love you, baby girl. And I will always be watching over you. You deserve to be happy and find a fated mate who will make you even stronger. Please don't be angry with me because everything I've ever done has been out of love.

With all the love of the moon,

Dad

My throat dried as I blinked back tears. I'd read the letter with his deep, vibrating voice in my mind. I *was* angry with him, but he had planned on showing me this room and whatever it contained. He'd died the day he was going to bring me down here.

"Babe?" Griffin asked with concern.

"He was going to tell me." Bart had been shocked that he hadn't, but the explanation was right there in the letter. "The night of the new moon. He died that day."

"Well, at least you got a letter," Julius snapped. His nostrils flared as his nose wrinkled with disgust. "Why are you upset?"

That was the final straw—I couldn't handle his nastiness anymore. "You aren't the only one who gets to hurt." My hands shook as I sneered at the selfish prick. "Just because a witch spelled you and said you were dead doesn't mean that I can't hurt, too. I lost my parents, and you never knew them to feel this kind of sting. And as much as it hurts that you never knew them, I hurt because I *did*. I'm tired of being patient with you. If you can't be civil to me, then you can go run back to whoever the hell took you and left you as a fucking rogue wolf your entire life."

Julius inhaled sharply, but his demeanor didn't change.

"I have a lot to get caught up on, it seems." Bart rubbed the back of his neck. "And if they have a witch working for them, that means other races know about us as well. But if Cyrus didn't connect with another pack, I don't understand how you didn't know he was alive, especially with your twin connection."

"Well, I wasn't alpha, and Dad probably thought he was imagining things." If I were him, that was what I'd think. "He probably didn't want to get Mom's hopes up. When Dad died, I felt, at times, a pack connection, but I thought it was a phantom echo because I'd just lost my pack and I wanted to feel them again." I paused and thought through what he'd said. "What is a twin connection?"

"It's a special bond twins have. You two are only the second ones in the silver wolf line and the first twin alpha heirs. You sense each other more than regular linked pack members do, though it's not as strong as a fated mate bond." Bart paced in front of the angel statue. "How close by was he?"

Julius cleared his throat, obviously done remaining silent. "I was about fifty miles away, holed up by myself."

"Far enough that neither link would be strong." Griffin's head lowered, and he sighed. Then he lifted his head and glared. "But close enough that you could coordinate attacks on Sterlyn."

Bart stilled. "You attacked your sister?"

Though Julius answered Bart's question, he addressed me. "I was told my parents didn't want me and cast me aside. They said that my parents favored you because you were the rightful alpha heir—that they didn't want to keep me around in case I tried to challenge you. That my parents were more concerned about your well-being than anything else. That you were their moon," he said agitatedly. "A woman was hired to take care of me, and some arrogant man said they wanted to help make things right and that they wouldn't harm any of the silver wolves."

"A woman and a man?" That piqued my interest. That was the most I'd gotten from him so far. "Who are they?"

"I...I don't know their names." Julius frowned and tugged at his ear. "I called them Grace and Topper, but I've only seen him a handful of times, and I haven't seen either of them in years. I only get calls now, but Topper promised that we were righting the wrongs done to me."

"Well, clearly they were *so* trustworthy," Killian deadpanned, his irises turning dark chocolate. "Didn't them not accepting you as part of their pack tell you something?"

His words made the question pop into my brain. "Why *didn't* they make you pack?" I asked Julius.

He chewed on his cheek and averted his gaze. "They were going to after my first shift, but..." He trailed off.

"But what?" Griffin growled with impatience.

"He never shifted." Bart chewed on his finger, then dropped his hand.

Griffin blew out his cheeks and released his breath. "How is that possible? His wolf would eventually take over."

I hadn't even considered that. No wonder Julius was so angry—he wasn't in sync with his wolf. He had to be at internal war most of the time. "Because the alpha blesses each wolf cub, and they shift with the pack."

"When they realized I couldn't shift, that's when Topper stopped visiting and resorted to phone calls." Julius's mouth pinched. "And then, a few years ago, they realized that I wasn't the true alpha. That *you* were." He nodded toward me. "So to pay for my keep, he put me in charge of training their guards, since he used so many resources on having me trained from the time I was small."

"That's why all the men hunting us have been fighting with guns more than their animals." Killian spoke slowly. "You couldn't train their animals."

"Yeah. Over the years, I've tried to prove my worth and specialized in weapons. I learned quickly and easily."

Silver wolves were like angels in easily learning the craft of battle. My blood ran cold.

The angel statue in the room had to explain part of that, and I wasn't quite sure I wanted to know what it was. Or who.

"Well, as soon as we get out of here, we'll get you to shift before we go home," I said. That would most likely be why he was so volatile. His wolf must feel confused, and to make matters worse, trapped. Wolves weren't meant to be contained inside the human form.

"You'd do that for me?" His lips parted as he flinched. "After everything?"

The answer was simple. "Of course. You're family."

Something unreadable crossed his features, but I didn't want to stare at him and make him feel even more uncomfortable.

As much as I hate to ruin this touching moment, we do need to get back soon. Griffin nodded at the leather-bound journal. *Do you want to grab that and head home?*

No. I had a feeling that I'd need Bart to answer questions. *I need to read it here.* But Griffin was right. I needed to stop wasting time.

I sucked in a hasty breath and placed the letter back on the table. I picked up the journal and rubbed my hand over the front. The leather was soft and worn. Gathering my courage, I opened the book, which revealed yellowed pages. I'd expected another of my father's journals, but this wasn't his handwriting. In fact, the first entry was dated 1125.

My eyes scanned the page...and the world seemed to shift. I read the first paragraph over and over again. There was no way I understood the words correctly.

Griffin's anxiety oozed from every pore. *What's wrong?*

The question was simple, but the answer was anything but. The first paragraph had changed everything I'd ever known, and that alone made me afraid to continue. What other truths would be revealed that I'd rather remain oblivious to? By the end of the book, I might not ever understand who we truly were.

You're scaring me. Griffin's body coiled like he was about to fight whatever was bothering me.

But the truth was just that. Truth. Nothing could change it. I'd read it, and I could never undo it. When Bart had said that the life that I knew would change, he hadn't been kidding.

This changed *everything.*

I cleared my throat. I didn't want to have to repeat the information multiple times, so I might as well get the words out so everyone could hear.

My uncle gave me a sad smile, nodding his head in encouragement.

Now I understood what Dad had wanted, and I was so damn glad Griffin and Killian were here with me. In reality, I was glad Julius was here, too, both of us about to process this new information together. "There is a reason the silver wolves are tied to the moon and stronger than other wolves."

"Okay," Killian said carefully. He tried to sound patient, but I could hear his frustration. "Which is?"

"That guardian angel, Ophaniel, impregnated a wolf who lived in Shadow City." The words sounded foreign to my ears. I'd grown up just accepting we were stronger without questioning why. "She got pregnant, even though it was supposedly impossible. Their offspring was the first silver wolf."

Griffin gasped. "But that actually makes a whole lot of sense. That's why you're tied to the moon and so strong."

"Not to mention warriors." Killian moved closer.

"But that's not all." The next part was the real kicker.

CHAPTER TWELVE

"WHAT IS IT?" Julius asked, clasping his hands together as if he was trying to prevent himself from yanking the journal from my grasp.

I read the last sentence again, ensuring that nothing had changed. But no, the words glared back at me, mocking me. "This can't be right." My attention flicked to Bart.

I wanted him to tell me this was some sort of elaborate scam or that I'd wake up from this crazy dream. But he gave me a slight nod, confirming something that should've been unfathomable.

"What is Rosemary's mother's name, again?" I was pretty sure she'd mentioned it in passing one day, or maybe I'd seen the name flash on her cell phone.

"Yelahiah," Griffin answered, and he tipped his head back. "Wait...if Ophaniel was the angel that fathered the silver wolves, that means you're related to Rosemary. Yelahiah is Ophaniel's sister. She's refused to talk about her brother ever since his death."

I focused on the most important part of the sentence. "He's dead?" Of course he was.

"Yeah, he died centuries ago." Griffin's forehead wrinkled, and his foot bounced. "I can't remember how."

"It's all in there." Bart pointed at the book. "Keep reading."

I inhaled sharply, steadying myself. I read a few more paragraphs, and something hard landed in my stomach. "Apparently, the angels were angry that he had a child with the wolf. Angels can only reproduce every couple of decades, and Ophaniel had a child born only a decade before the silver wolf was born, so the timing was an anomaly, making it appear as if the silver wolves were destined to be created."

"Things don't happen at random." Bart faced the statue and reached out, touching the moon that the angel held in his palm. "There's a reason for everything, even if it's not apparent at first."

Maybe. I used to believe the exact same thing—that we all had free choice, though fate already knew what our choices would be. Would fate be that cruel?

Surely not.

A slaughtered pack, a kidnapped brother, attacks that rocked my entire world—these should never have been set in stone. Only those who had grown up privileged and never faced the cruelness of the world could think that such horrors were meant to be. When all you'd been given were minor trials and tribulations, it was easy to think something good was in charge. But bad things happened to good people, and communities unraveled or were besieged by terrible events.

The world *had* to be a crapshoot. Just a random series of events that happened, and you either got lucky or not. Your fate could change in an instant, but in my darkness, I'd found light. I'd found a part of me that I didn't know existed.

I'd found my strength, my perseverance, and a new family.

I'd found something I'd never been sure I had inside me, despite Dad's insistence it was there. I finally believed I was meant to be an alpha—the silver wolf alpha—and I'd take down whoever threatened our world.

"Whether silver wolves were destined to be created or not, we're here." Resolve coursed through me. "And they won't kill any more of us. Not if I'm breathing."

"Well, it's not like we have huge numbers anymore." Bart grunted. "There are only eighteen silver wolves left, outside of you and Cyrus, and our pack totals twenty-five."

"Twenty-five?" There were seventeen here now, including Julius and me. "Where are the other eight?"

"Five of us found our mates, and Darrell and I each have one child." He licked his lips. "We left them behind with one of the men as guard."

Of course the children and the mates that weren't silver needed protecting. They were mated to silver wolves, which meant they were regular wolves and not as strong as our kind. The children were full silver wolves—the magic of the moon was dominant and passed to them fully—but they were still young and vulnerable.

"What happens if they're attacked?" We'd thought we were safely hidden here, and we weren't. I'd hate for the others to be ambushed and butchered.

Bart's body became more rigid. "The guard will alert us, and we'll head back as fast as possible. We wanted to check this area out and bring them to meet the pack here if it was all clear. They're all packed and waiting for the nod."

"I wouldn't bring them here—this town is compromised. But Dad was planning to move us to a new location not too far away that should be safe."

"He told me." Bart rubbed his temples. "That's where I planned on us heading next."

The book grew heavy in my hands, reminding me that I wasn't anywhere near finished. "Good." I flipped to the next page.

The once neat scribbling was now a jumbled mess, the chaotic swirls making my heart pound from whatever secrets they held. "Apparently, the angels weren't thrilled that the male hybrid was able to reproduce and that his child was as powerful as him. But Ophaniel protected his son, his grandchildren, and his great-grandchildren. The wolves were able to reproduce every five to ten years, which angered the angels even more. Apparently, the wolf side of them made it easier to reproduce, and once again, their powers weren't diluted. Each generation angered the angels even more."

"Well, they are kind of elitist." Killian chuckled. "They think highly of themselves, similar to the fae."

I'd never met a fae, though I knew they existed. Most of them stayed in their own realm and rarely crossed over to Earth. If you weren't of fae blood, you couldn't travel to their land.

"What else does it say?" Julius asked as he shuffled to my other side and glanced over my shoulder. He stiffened and blew out a breath. "What the hell?"

"Uh..." I had no clue how to answer him. "No?" That certainly wasn't what the book said. I looked around, trying to figure out what had set him off.

"There are no words on the page." He swiped the book and turned it upside down, making a few pages fall and land on the cement.

"Are you insane?" He had to be. I grabbed the book from him and clutched it to my chest. "You're going to mess it up!"

Griffin squatted and picked up the papers. "Babe. He's right." He stood and held the papers toward me. "There's nothing there."

"This isn't funny." Now wasn't the time for games. The letters seemed even more frantic, but they were legible. It took just a little bit of focus to make out the words. I took the pages from him and placed them back inside the book. I'd figure out where they went later.

"They can't see the writing." Bart smiled sadly as he pivoted toward me. "And this confirms what your father knew all along. Only angels and the true alpha of the silver wolves can read those words."

"Is that why you didn't tell me?" Another stupid-ass test that he needed to perform because he didn't believe a woman could be alpha. "How do you know I'm not pretending?"

"Our father read the entries that day because neither your dad nor I were alphas yet." He kicked at the cement as if he were ashamed. "We had him read the journal to us so many times that I have most of it memorized. You didn't know anything about this room, and your dad's letter confirms that he never told you about it."

"Is it because I'm a woman?" I was going to make him admit it. Dad told me to never back down. Maybe he was preparing me for the first time I met Bart.

"No." He grimaced and lifted a hand. "But I thought maybe the witch lied to your dad when she planned on stealing Cyrus. I just had to make sure."

I guessed that made sense, but it didn't completely settle me. However, the stench of a lie was missing.

"Another thing she gets that I don't," Julius grumbled, sounding jealous.

Maybe I wasn't as safe with him as I'd hoped. He might have alpha aspirations of his own, which meant he could stab me in the back. He'd already done it twice. "Considering how much you whine, you could never handle being in charge." I was done being nice.

Killian snorted while Griffin chuckled.

I waited for a smart-ass retort, but Julius's face only turned red.

Not wanting to keep going down this horrible road, I read some more. "The angels grew disgruntled and tried to overtake the city. The silver wolves realized that the angels had to be stopped, and for more than just their own protection. The angels were trying to control everyone and using the city that had been built for refuge as a place to dominate and control. The silver wolves strategized and got the other supernatural races to work together and overthrow the angels."

A smile spread across my face. "Ophaniel writes that it was the most amazing process to watch. The silver wolves had an even more cunning strategy than the angels because they were able to feel and relate to the pain of the races all around them. They energized an army that stormed the city and demanded justice for all."

Julius bounced on his heels. "What happened next?" He sounded like a kid listening to his favorite bedtime story.

He must have had so many questions growing up as a silver wolf that he was thrilled to get answers. Questions I should've had but didn't because I'd taken things for granted.

"Yelahiah intervened and called a truce, with the majority of the angels backing her, but at a cost." I forced the next words. "Azbogah claimed the silver wolves were an abomination, stating that his judgment was final and that they all needed to die. Ophaniel tried to protect the silver wolves from the angel attack, but all the other angels were afraid to stand up to Azbogah. After all, the angels were forced to stand down to the other races because of Ophaniel's offspring. The angels rallied and attacked, killing five silver wolves. Ophaniel helped the remaining ones flee in the middle of the night." I paused, needing to collect myself. The past seemed like a deadly soap opera. "Who is Azbogah?"

"He's part of the angel council." Griffin frowned. "He's the one who makes decisions for the whole angel community, overriding Yelahiah and her husband. He calls himself the judge and executioner."

"Sounds like a stand-up guy." Pricks like that had huge egos. "I bet he and Dick get along great."

"You know what?" Griffin tilted his head as if something clicked. "They actually do."

"Of course." Killian rolled his eyes. "I've been telling you forever that Dick's an asshole. Assholes stick together."

Hoping to keep the insults from starting, I turned the page to find different handwriting looped across it with a date a few days later. Red-hot anger filled me. "Apparently, after the silver wolves escaped, Azbogah called a meeting of the angels and declared Ophaniel a traitor. He proclaimed the only acceptable penance was death."

"For protecting his family?" Killian sounded shocked.

I nodded, needing a moment before I could continue.

Griffin interlocked his fingers behind his head. "Did someone stand up for him?"

"No. The silver wolves weren't there to help them regain control, so they let the angels proceed." Cowards. That was what they all were. "Yelahiah says she tried to stop the execution, but it was too late. Azbogah chopped off Ophaniel's head, and Ophaniel didn't even try to fight back, wanting them to take their wrath out on him instead of his family."

"No wonder Azbogah and Yelahiah are at odds." Griffin sounded disgusted.

And I couldn't blame him. For Yelahiah to watch her brother die, knowing she'd done nothing to stop it...I imagined that would make her hate not only Azbogah, but herself, too.

A low growl emanated from Griffin's chest, and he cleared his throat. "I hate to interrupt, but we have a situation."

That was just a variation of us having a problem, and I'd lost count of how many times I'd heard it today. "What's wrong?"

"There's trouble within Shadow City's gates." Griffin pinched the skin at his throat. "We're needed there immediately, along with Killian."

I shut the book. "Then I guess we need to go." I turned to Bart. "How do we contact you?"

"Easily." Bart walked to me and lowered his head, submitting to me. "I am now part of your pack, and you are my alpha, as it should be."

A warm spot popped into my chest, followed by twenty-four more. My heart swelled until I thought it might burst. I could feel not only a connection to them but also their well-being. I hadn't expected him to do that. This must be how my dad had felt every day. I sensed anxiety, worry, and love wafting through each connection, identifying each person's mental state. I couldn't hear their thoughts, but the general gist of their mental states flowed into me. And my uncle pulsed with pride. "You didn't have to do that."

"I know, but I wanted to," he said and closed the distance between us to hug me. "You're even stronger than your dad realized, and I'm so lucky I finally got to meet you and Cyrus." He released me and hugged my brother.

Julius stiffened and patted Bart's back awkwardly, but then he stilled and looked at me. "I can't come with you to Shadow City, or people will see me." He gestured at Bart. "Why don't I stay with him?"

Ugh, he was right, but I didn't want to put that burden on Bart. "We can drop—"

"No, it's fine." Bart tapped his head. "I'll link you and tell you where we land. He can stay with us. In fact, if you bless me, I should be able to help him shift and run for the first time."

"Bless you?" I had no idea what that even meant. "Like sneezing?"

Killian burst out laughing. "I've never heard you sound anything less than smart until this moment."

Nope, I was *not* taking any shade from him. "Then what does it mean, asshole?"

His laughter cut off as his face smoothed. "Um...I'm not sure."

"So I'm not the only idiot." I stuck my tongue out at him. It'd been a while since he and I ragged one another. It felt nice, even though this wasn't the best time.

"But I didn't—"

Bart pinched his lips together like he was trying not to smile and cut off Killian. "Just push some of your alpha will toward me, allowing me to borrow a little bit of your power until the shift is over."

That sounded so simple, but I was clueless about how to do it.

"Let your wolf guide you." Bart encouraged. "She's mixed with your angel side and knows exactly what to do."

"Like an angelic wolf?" Killian asked, wide-eyed. "With wings and all?"

Now I couldn't not give him shit. "And *I* sound like an idiot?"

"Hey." Killian frowned, but there was warmth in his eyes.

Griffin took my hand and chuckled. "She's got you there, man."

I closed my eyes to focus, tuning everyone out. I needed to get this done. I tugged on my connection with Bart...and my wolf pushed a little bit of our magic toward him. *Use this to help Cyrus shift and send it back to me.* Alpha will laced the words, and a small part of me passed to Bart.

"Perfect." Bart squeezed my arm. "Take the book and go. I'll handle everything here."

His sincerity flowed into me, and I turned without hesitation. We had another crisis to face, and the longer we took to get there, the more Dick would take control, which was unacceptable.

CHAPTER THIRTEEN

THE FIVE OF us ran up the stairs and into my parents' room. As soon as Bart slipped past the door, I pushed the chest of drawers back into place and heard a faint *click*.

I still couldn't believe I'd lived in this house my entire life and had no clue about the secret compartment. Whoever'd thought to build the entrance into furniture was brilliant, and Dad must have taken extra precautions to ensure Mom and I didn't walk in on him whenever he visited downstairs. In fairness, he could've kept the journal in the hidden underwear compartment and rarely ventured down until he feared the rumblings.

"We tell no one about this door," Bart said quietly. "This is meant only for the alpha bloodline to know, so by letting those two down there as well"—he gestured to Killian and Griffin—"I've already broken protocol."

"Because your alpha asked you to." Now that he'd come clean with us and was part of my pack, we owed him the truth. "And I'm sorry, but we're in a rush. Griffin is the alpha of Shadow City. His father was Atticus Bodle, the alpha who contacted my dad about opening the city. And Killian is the alpha of Shadow Ridge. There's a crisis and we're needed. We can meet up soon, but at least now we can communicate, as long as you all don't venture too far from Shadow Ridge."

"Your mate is the alpha of Shadow City?" he asked, slowly turning toward Griffin. "Are you sure magic wasn't involved in that union? It seems awfully convenient that the Shadow City alpha is mated to you."

"Oh, trust me." Killian snorted. "We know. They hated each other at first, and both he and I had no clue what she was."

Griffin growled as unhappiness pulsed off him. He didn't like the accusation.

Now wasn't storytime, and we didn't have time to waste for them to brawl it out. "I'm positive, and you need to get that thought out of your head." I stared Bart down and continued, "He's my mate, and we've completed our bond. The decision has already been made and is final. That's your one pass. Make sure it doesn't happen again." I touched Griffin's arm, hoping to calm him.

Be glad he's your uncle, or I'd kick his ass. Some of the tension left his body, but a scowl remained. "Since you're worried about her best interests, I'll let it go," he told Bart, then interlaced our fingers, tugging me toward the hallway. "And she's right. We have to get moving. Dick is asking where I am. The guards told him that we left the house."

Of course they did. Granted, we hadn't asked them not to say anything to Dick—that would've raised a lot more flags. We rushed down the hallway with Julius taking up the rear. Once he stepped out the front door, I paused long enough to lock it.

"I'll link you the address to where we're heading. We're still staying close by," Bart said, and pulled me into a small hug. "If you need us, let us know. We won't hesitate to come."

"We need to keep you hidden. For once, we have an ace up our sleeve." My attention landed on my brother, and I allowed my wolf to rise, lacing my next words with alpha will. I wasn't going to chance him ratting us out. Whether he liked it or not, he was both my twin and part of my pack, which was probably why he hadn't gone insane. "You will not communicate in any form with anyone outside our pack with the exception of Griffin, Killian, Rosemary, and Sierra until I state otherwise." I wasn't going to allow him to backstab us. There was way too much at risk. And if he didn't tell Bart anything that would help us, I would use my alpha will to make him talk. But I wanted him to come clean on his own. I was going to give my uncle a day or two because otherwise, it'd fracture my already broken relationship with Julius.

Julius sneered but kept his witty banter to himself.

Good. He needed to earn his place in my warm regard.

I'll keep an eye on him, Bart assured me. His inside light comforted me. *And I'll try to reach him. Even though I wasn't abandoned like he was, I had to leave my family behind. I can at least relate to his situation. My own father died while I was gone, and I couldn't risk coming back here for the funeral. So I understand what it's like to not get the chance to tell someone goodbye.*

I hadn't even considered the implications of what him leaving the pack had meant. I remember Dad saying something odd the day of Pawpaw's funeral. Something about how he wished that the entire family could be there. It hadn't made sense then, and I thought he'd been feeling regret and turmoil over the death of his father. Now, I understood clearly—he'd meant Bart. *I'm sorry and appreciate your sacrifice. If you hadn't done it, I might be the only silver wolf standing.* Well, me and Julius, but I didn't officially consider him a silver wolf yet. He still had negativity roiling inside him, which didn't fit our kind.

"Let us know if you need anything, too," I said out loud, not wanting to make Julius feel even more alienated. "It goes both ways."

Darrell stalked out of the woods, heading in our direction. His eyes turned to slits when they locked on me.

He must have felt our new connection.

Even though I hadn't replaced Bart as their direct alpha, there was a hierarchy to things, and I would never override Bart's leader-

540   JEN L. GREY

ship unless I felt it necessary. Maybe Darrell thought I had forced Bart to submit, but I'd let Bart handle this one. The more I got involved, the more he'd believe that had been the case.

I turned, forcing my legs to move to the Navigator. As I opened the passenger door, I called out loudly enough so Rosemary could hear. She was still in the air, keeping a lookout. "Meet us in Shadow City—there's an issue." I climbed into the vehicle and slammed the door. Now we had to focus on getting there.

As we pulled into downtown Shadow Ridge, my gaze landed on the enormous bridge over the Tennessee River that connected this bank to Shadow City. Its immense towers jetted toward the sky, looking graceful and reminding me of the pictures I'd seen of the Golden Gate Bridge, especially with the afternoon sun shining down on it. About a hundred yards from the city's main entrance was the section that could be raised in order to prevent anyone from getting inside.

I'd never been inside the city, nor even on the bridge, so I hadn't thought much about the security and the surrounding protective walls of the city. Probably because what I expected to lie within were corruption and deceit. I wanted to stay far away from it all.

"I've never asked, but there are always humans visiting Shadow Ridge." I glanced at the small two-way road that ran through the heart of downtown, where humans and supernaturals alike loitered along the sidewalks and passed by the picturesque brick buildings that made you feel as if you'd gone back in time. "Why do they not ask about Shadow City?"

"It's spelled from within by the witches." Griffin's finger tapped the steering wheel. He was on edge, and he'd driven faster than he should've to get here. "Only supernaturals can see it. Humans see the Tennessee River flowing through, and the place where the city sits just looks like water to them."

Interesting. I figured it had to be something like that.

He drove to the section of land where the bridge connected and turned onto it. The bridge obviously had been built with care without even a bump, but I shouldn't have been surprised.

Only the best for Shadow City.

The closer we got, the clearer everything came into view. The massive walls stood over one hundred stories high, with the city's emblem carved on them over and over again. The emblem was simple but breathtaking in its own right. The picture must be a skyline view of the city, and hovering over the tallest two skyscrapers was a huge paw print. "Why is there a wolf print on top?" I asked. This was a supernatural city, so it seemed strange that only one race would be represented in its emblem.

"Because of the silver wolves." Griffin's lips smashed together. "That was what Yelahiah demanded when the council was formed in memory of her brother."

No wonder Rosemary had turned out to be such a good ally. I couldn't help but wonder if she knew the story. For some reason, I didn't think she did. But finally, the kinship we felt for each other—which neither of us had understood—made sense.

I glanced at the top of the city, which was covered by a large glass dome so that not even supernaturals who could fly would be able to enter unless the city authorities wanted them to. "I'm assuming the glass is spelled?" Dad had taught me that witches were damn powerful when they worked together. It was both their strength and weakness, as all it took was one turning against the coven to fracture them.

"Yes, they reinforce it with their magic. From what Dad told me, there's been only one occurrence of someone trying to break in, a century or two ago." Griffin nodded toward the top. "Some power-hungry fae dragon king wanted to take over the city. All I remember is that even against fae magic, the dome held tight."

"So only one attack here?" I'd expected several. There was always at least one crazed, power-hungry supernatural alive at any time. Probably more than one, but I chose to think optimistically. Dad always said to prepare for the worst-case scenario, but think positively. Positivity was stronger than anyone realized.

"No, there have been several," Killian said, and he leaned forward, staring out the windshield in awe. "But the last one was during the time when my grandfather had been alpha for only a few years. It was a coordinated shifter attack of a few races that lived in a bordering town. Our pack was able to hold them off, though we lost a lot of lives. Shadow City raised the bridge, and the witches spelled the water to kill the few who got past us when they reached it."

"How many did you lose?" Griffin asked stiffly.

"About half our numbers." Killian sighed. "That's one reason that half our neighborhood is vacant and why you were able to buy the house next to mine. We're still trying to get back to those numbers."

"Dad told me about an attack, but he said the loss was minimal," Griffin said with disgust. "That doesn't sound minimal to me."

"I think there might have been one Shadow City death—one of the city guards in charge of the drawbridge." Killian scratched the back of his neck and smoothed his features, becoming unreadable. "The bridge got stuck, so he had to hang over it to get the rope unhung. The enemy took him out then, and Shadow City gave up on raising it higher. It was up high enough that the shifters couldn't jump to it."

In other words, the Shadow City deaths were minimal. That perspective was yet another example of why we shouldn't be separate packs. "You all have done so much to keep that city safe," I said to Killian. Every time there was an incident, Killian's pack reacted without hesitation. And still, they weren't worthy of being officially invited into the city, only to protect the exterior. To Griffin, I asked, *They came from Shadow City—why are they viewed as outsiders?*

I...I don't know. Griffin squirmed, and regret wafted from him into me. *I never questioned any of this before you arrived. Things had always been that way.*

Now *that* was a sentiment we both shared. We believed in our fathers and hadn't thought to question how and why things were done, or how we were raised.

As children, we'd thought of our parents as heroes. We'd put them on pedestals, but the more we grew and learned, the clearer it became that they were just people. They had strengths and weaknesses and didn't always make the best decisions.

They were flawed.

They were real.

They were the type of people who should lead because a perfect person wouldn't have the empathy to relate to others or the convictions of what was right and wrong. Their imperfections made them better leaders, and I was beginning to understand that. Besides, as I did so, I also realized everything that I'd done wrong along the way.

Questions were meant to be asked. A situation should be looked at from every angle. Supernatural races should work together because we all saw things differently, which could show us that sometimes the way things have always been wasn't the way they should be now.

Things had to change. Each bit of information I learned strengthened my resolve, because Rosemary, Griffin, Killian, and I were going to make it happen. We'd find other allies along the way, but for now, we had a diverse group formed: an angel, the alpha from Shadow Ridge, the alpha from Shadow City, and the alpha silver wolf. Even if I didn't plan to recruit more races for the cause, no one would be able to argue that we didn't have the strength to usher in change.

As we approached a large wooden door that would allow us entry into the city, Griffin slowed. When the car came to a complete stop, he waited, his eyes glowing faintly.

He must be linking with people inside.

Confirming my suspicions, gears ground, and soon, the door began to lift. The process was slow and loud, as if the weight of the door were too much for its cables.

The city came into view inch by inch...and it was gorgeous. The buildings seemed modern, despite the city being closed off for almost one thousand years, and they filled the skyline. A stucco-like building with a huge, round, purple stained-glass roof stood directly in front. The light shining from the top of the city's dome made a beautiful color streak inside, and it seemed like we had entered a different realm.

"Holy shit," Killian gasped. "It looks unreal. Almost like a drawing from an artist."

That wasn't enough to describe the beauty.

"It has to be beautiful to hide all the snakes inside," Griffin murmured as he drove forward.

When we pulled into the city, the place somehow became even more beautiful. Supernaturals milled through a town square, seeming to have not a care in the world.

Instead of heading toward them, Griffin took a hard right, keeping to the outskirts near the walls where buildings were only on our left side.

"Where are we heading?" I hadn't asked him many questions before now—he'd felt determined but on edge, communicating internally with his pack, and I hadn't wanted to pester him. But now that we were here, I needed a little bit of background.

"To the barrier protection building." Griffin's jaw twitched. "Something bad happened, and they need our assistance."

"Are you going to expand on that, man?" Killian asked, clearly annoyed. "I've followed Sterlyn's lead by not asking you stuff on the way, but now that we're close, why don't you tell us what you know?"

"That's the problem," Griffin said sharply. "I don't know much. All Dick said is there's a problem and he needed to see me immediately."

"Wait. Then why am I here?" Killian sat back, not distracted by the sights any longer. "I thought they wanted me here, too."

"Like I said, there was a protection issue. That's all I know." Griffin licked his lips as he pulled over into a small section of the road that was open and out of potential traffic against the wall. "I figured the two of you should be here because you know security measures better than most everyone else."

Great. That wasn't going to sit well, especially not with the angels.

"Follow me." Griffin climbed out of the car just as Dick ran out of a small building across the street.

"He's here," Dick yelled toward the building he'd left and glared at Griffin. "And this whole thing is his fault."

CHAPTER FOURTEEN

GRIFFIN PAUSED mid-step at the venomous accusation Dick had thrown at him. Alarm and anger poured off him as he stared the man down. "What in the hell are you talking about?"

"Don't act like you don't know," Dick spat. "It's time to come in here and face the music." The soulless man glanced at me and then Killian as a cruel smirk spread.

We'd walked into a trap, and there was no getting out of it. Dick had something up his sleeve, and unfortunately, we were about to find out what it was.

The buildings reminded me of Shadow Ridge's downtown. Hell, most likely, Shadow Ridge was a replica to make Killian's discarded pack feel more at home. In this section, they were smaller, two-story buildings made of brick.

I looked around the street, surprised by the quietness. We hadn't seen or passed one car besides our own. Even in the main part of the city, people had milled around on foot, and for that matter, there was no traffic or even stoplights that I had noticed.

We need to leave. He linked. *Something isn't right.*

Oh, I agreed, but unfortunately, that wasn't in our cards. *He obvi-*

ously has an audience inside, which means if you leave, it'll work out even less in your favor. We were in a "damned if you do, and even more damned if you don't" situation. *We have to see what he's done and address it head-on.*

Killian stood next to me, his Adam's apple bobbing. A muscle in his shoulder twitched like he was preparing to fight or flee.

Why do you have to be so logical? Griffin teased dryly, still radiating discomfort.

Needing to be there for him, I held his hand and squeezed gently. *Everything will work out.* It had to.

I hope you're right, he replied, and the two of us walked side by side toward Dick. Killian jogged to catch up and flanked me on the left.

We approached Dick, who stood under the small metal awning, watching with apparent delight. He rubbed his hands together as his irises deepened to the color of coal. Even the pretty pinks, blues, and purples that danced around us from the top of the dome couldn't hide the darkness that oozed off him.

For him to be so gleeful, we had to be walking into something even worse than I'd expected.

Dick opened the door and said loudly, "I'm surprised you didn't run like the coward you truly are." He waved us in, and Griffin straightened his shoulders.

I stepped inside and felt like I'd traveled back in time. The walls and ceilings were dark cherry wood. Matching crown molding covered the corners where they connected with the intricate Shadow City emblem chiseled into the design over and over again. The floor was made of white marble, and in the center of the room, under a large, diamond chandelier, the Shadow City emblem had been incorporated into the design in golden stone.

"He did show." The dark, manly hiss echoed off the walls.

By the center of the far wall, seven people stood in front of a marble fireplace.

The man who had just spoken scowled, his sinister appearance matching his hissing voice. His light brown hair fell over his forehead, emphasizing his fair skin and teak-colored eyes. He stood regally, making him somehow seem taller than his perhaps six-foot frame. His scent, which reminded me of apples, made my mouth water. I remembered that vampires smelled sweet. Handy information I'd picked up from my mate.

"Matthew..." Alex, the vampire prince I'd met at Shadow Ridge Coffee only a few weeks ago, *tsked*. "Calm yourself." He pulled on the collar of his navy button-down shirt, which contrasted with his pale skin and soft blue eyes. He lifted his head, and the chandelier's light reflected off his sun-kissed brown hair as he moved to stand beside Matthew. They were the same height, but Alex had a more syrupy sweet scent mixed with apples.

The vampire prince had intervened, which meant there had to be a catch. We hadn't become friendly, and even though there was no vileness coursing off him, I didn't sense any warm fuzzies, either.

"I'm surprised, too," a man who had to be at least seven feet tall snapped. His spiked caramel hair put even more of an edge on his stoic face, and his all-black attire added to his commanding presence. His pure honeysuckle scent hit me, and I remembered Griffin informing me that angels smelled like flowers. Haunting winter-gray eyes focused on Griffin as the man's nose wrinkled in disgust, which told me everything. He had already determined Griffin was guilty of whatever crap Dick had set up.

Forced laughter pulled my gaze to one of the most beautiful women I'd ever seen. Even with the sneer, her full, blood-red lips were alluring, and her forest-green eyes surrounded by long black lashes flashed at the angel with malice. She was my height and wore a long black dress as if it were a second skin. Her sparkling amber hair shined with her goodness. "Azbogah, you aren't the official judge down here anymore."

That's Rosemary's mother, Griffin linked, keeping me informed.

"Ask the other angels, and see what they say. That is, if you're brave enough," Azbogah bit back. "Just because you don't like my decisions doesn't mean that I don't still get to make them."

Wow. I hadn't expected to meet Yelahiah so soon, but the formal introduction would have to come later. "What is this all about?" I asked.

"I'll tell you what this is about!" A short woman pushed through the two glaring angels, her scarlet-streaked black hair bouncing. She squinted her heavily lined, misty gray eyes in accusation at Griffin. Her body shook with rage as she pointed one long black fingernail at my mate. "You scheduled every single Shadow City guard to attend training, and the spell hiding the city from humans almost failed."

"*What?*" Griffin asked in shock. "Erin, there has to be a misunder—"

"Not only that," Dick interjected. "But you brought outsiders into the city without clearance. Your mistakes keep racking up."

Griffin lifted a hand. "I thought—"

"Oh...you *thought*." Matthew cackled, making my skin crawl. "Maybe that was part of the problem."

My throat prickled with rage, and my wolf slipped close to the surface. If I lost control now, Griffin would look even worse. I took in long, steady breaths, trying to calm the raging storm swirling inside me.

"That's enough," Yelahiah snapped. "Erin was able to restore the barrier, and the guards are on their way back. We can discuss it tomorrow at the emergency council meeting." Authority rolled off her.

Azbogah bristled but remained quiet.

And that put me even more on edge. The hate between the two of them was palpable, and for him not to argue with her made me wonder if he and Dick were planning something together.

That sounded like something they'd do, based on their inter-actions.

"Well, we can't let him leave—he might not come back." Erin

cracked her knuckles like she was preparing for a fight. "So what are we going to do with those two?" She gestured at Killian and me.

"I can escort them back to Shadow Ridge." Dick took a step toward me. "I'd be more than glad to since I need to check on the bar, anyway."

Dick didn't want me to be part of the meeting tomorrow. That had to be why he was so eager to take us back...which made me wonder why.

"If she goes, I go." Griffin's voice was low, bordering on threatening. "She's my fated mate, and I'm here declaring her to make it official and present her to the council. I refuse to be separated from her."

"That's what I thought." Yelahiah nodded at me and smiled. "Rosemary has spoken of you often."

Alex chuckled. "Isn't it kind of awful to have your fated mate working at the coffee shop? Or is that the kind of kink you two are into?" He waggled his eyebrows as he winked.

"Am I the only one who finds this hard to believe? Your *fated mate*?" Azbogah laughed loudly, hurting my ears. He shook his head and gestured at Griffin. "You expect us to believe that you're settling down after the number of women you've run through? I've heard enough stories about them over here; I can only imagine what you've done in Shadow Ridge."

A low growl escaped me before I could stop it. I wasn't stupid. I knew he'd been with other women, but for it to be flaunted in my face like that so maliciously—that was a hard pill to swallow.

Unless that was the point. They wanted me to come off as irrational to prove that not only was Griffin not a good leader, but his fated mate was unhinged. Dad had been right when he'd visited two years ago—corruption was still rampant here.

I had to take control over the situation. I smiled sweetly. "Was it necessary for you to say that?" I'd call his ass out, even though I had a feeling he would take exception. "You're a supernatural, so you know he didn't lie...unless your senses aren't as strong as they once were?"

Azbogah's smile fell from his face, and his hands fisted. "What did you just say?"

"Your senses might be going." I lifted a hand and looked wide-eyed at Killian and then Griffin. "Not only can he not smell, but he's lost his hearing, too." The best way to take control of a situation was to use the same tactic against them. I moved a couple of feet closer to him and cupped my hands around my mouth. I spoke loudly. "I said—"

"Oh, I heard you." He breathed raggedly, his nostrils flaring. His jaw clenched as he tried to rein in his anger.

"Good." I patted his shoulder, wanting to push him over the edge. "Dick had such a hard time understanding things the other day at Griffin's house, so I don't want to have to worry about another member on the council losing their edge." I smiled brightly, knowing that the stench of a lie wouldn't come. Dick thought he could threaten me and make me scared. And I'd tried telling him that it wouldn't work, but alas, here we were. He truly hadn't gotten it.

"Now listen here," Dick growled and marched toward me. His face turned red as his anger got the best of him. "I understood exactly what you said, and you don't know who you're up against."

"Up against?" Griffin asked coldly. *Wow, I've been an idiot for so long. He's been conspiring the entire time.* "Are you threatening her?"

"No, he's not." Azbogah jumped back into the conversation and stepped between us and Dick. The dark angel smiled charmingly, but the emotion was absent from his eyes. He was cold, heartless, and power-hungry. "This is all a misunderstanding. Isn't it?" He turned and arched an eyebrow at Dick.

Dick's face turned as red as a tomato.

"I think we're done here," Yelahiah said sternly, but the corners of her lips lifted. "The meeting is tomorrow at nine a.m., and if this woman is Griffin's fated mate, then of course she's welcome to stay here. Fate trumps all laws, as it is predetermined by the divine."

The divine? I'd have to ask Rosemary about that later.

"Well, Killian isn't your fated mate, too, now is he?" Alex beamed at Griffin and placed a hand on his chest. "Because it would kind of make sense if he were. You two are super close, and you even went so far as to buy the house next door to his."

Killian's mouth dropped, and Griffin went as pale as the two vampires in the room.

Laughter bubbled out. This was the first time I'd truly seen Killian speechless, and I kind of loved it.

"No!" Killian jerked his head side to side. "Definitely not. Not that there's anything wrong with that, but we don't swing for the same team."

"What is up with these Earthlings and their sayings?" Yelahiah sighed. "Ever since Rosemary started acclimating to the outside world, she's come back speaking another language."

"We don't agree on much anymore," Azbogah said, "but I feel the same way."

"Thanks, Dick," I interjected before anyone else could step in. "For offering to take Killian home. It means a lot that you care for his well-being." I batted my eyes.

"Actually, I don't need to go back to the bar." Dick cleared his throat as he rolled his shoulders. "I'll get someone to take him home, though. Don't worry."

In other words, he'd wanted me gone, and now that I wasn't leaving, he wanted to stay close by. He must be worried that Griffin had brought me here, but did he expect my mate to leave me behind? Dick didn't have a fated mate, so maybe he truly didn't understand. But the thought of being separated from Griffin after the shit we'd been through the last few days petrified me, especially knowing that an angel was working with Dick to discredit him.

My gut informed me that Dick was making his move. Not only did he want to discredit Griffin, but I was pretty damn sure he wanted to take the alpha title away from him. Instead of challenging him the way our wolves knew and respected, he was fighting dirty. Going behind Griffin's back, trying to gain the council's support.

The only reason I could come up with was that he knew he

couldn't win a challenge against Griffin, so he was taking power the one way he knew how.

I refused to let that happen to my mate.

Not now.

Not when he'd decided to step up and continue the plans he and his father had made together to improve things, not only for his own race but for the entire city.

Not when he and I planned to build a future in which all the supernatural races worked together to make things better as a whole.

They wouldn't take that away from us.

Killian glanced at me, seeming unsure how to proceed. At the end of the day, I couldn't force Dick to leave, though I'd love to be able to. Somehow, he'd set Griffin up, and we had to prove it. Griffin would never do something so reckless as to leave the city vulnerable.

I had to assume Killian and Griffin weren't linked because the knowledge of how to link between packs had been lost. One of the things on our first order of business would be to figure this pack bond thing out. Bart had been able to submit to me but still maintain dominance over his pack. I had felt it through our connection. Maybe bridging that gap would result in Killian's pack no longer feeling like second-rate citizens.

"Someone is already here to take him back to Shadow Ridge," Dick said authoritatively. "They just informed me that they pulled up."

They had bypassed Griffin and gone straight to Dick despite my mate being here. That irritated me. Another issue we'd address.

"We'll walk him out, and then I'll take Dove to the alpha home here in the city," Griffin retorted, making the insinuation that he was still the alpha clear.

You're extremely sexy right now. Seeing him take charge warmed my body. He'd been getting like this more and more frequently, and that proved just how much he was changing. *Maybe when we get there, you can show me your bedroom.*

Hell, yeah. He intertwined our fingers and turned so our backs were to the others. The power play was clear: he wasn't worried. However, his next words were equivalent to a cold shower. *Right after you meet Mom.*

Holy shit. I was heading to meet his mother. There was no telling how this was going to go.

CHAPTER FIFTEEN

I'D NEVER MET someone's parents before. In fact, Griffin had been all my firsts in every way that mattered. With the way my luck was going, his mom wouldn't like me, which would put even more of a strain on our relationship.

As if we didn't have enough to deal with.

Are you okay? Griffin asked, emanating confusion. *Your emotions were steady the entire time in the building, but now that we're leaving, you seem like a hot mess.*

Thanks. I could count on him to be honest. *That makes me feel so much better.*

We stepped outside, and the assortment of shifting colors made me almost dizzy. The air around me changed constantly, reminding me of the aurora borealis but surrounding me.

A Mercedes SUV waited for Killian at the curb, and the driver rolled down the window, waving him inside. "Let's go."

"Nope." Griffin shook his head. "I already took care of his transportation. Thanks, though."

The driver scoffed but took off, not even bothering to say goodbye.

It was time to get a hold on Griffin's reign before he couldn't take it back. Dick had been working hard against him for them to treat him so disrespectfully.

Killian turned toward us and lowered his voice so only Griffin and I could hear. "Are you sure I shouldn't stay?"

"Honestly, I'm not." Griffin pulled at his bottom lip.

I was. "You can't. That will give them even more ammunition to make Griffin look bad tomorrow." I was so damn tired of the broken link—something had to be done. "You two should try to connect like Bart and I did."

"What do you mean?" Killian asked, his forehead lined with confusion.

"Bart submitted to me back at the house, but he retained his position as alpha of his pack. I'm guessing that the two of you can do the same since Griffin is ultimately the alpha of both Shadow City and Shadow Ridge."

Griffin was stronger than Killian, but neither man had embraced their role in their pack until the past few weeks. "It'll give you both an edge since clearly, your two packs have been at odds. If you can coordinate with each other through the link, that will give us an advantage over Dick. He won't expect a full pack alliance." Most likely, over time, the Shadow Ridge alphas had resented the wolves who were tucked safely behind the tall city walls. As the respect was lost, the relationship between the two packs had deteriorated more and more. At least, that was what I'd gathered during my time here when I'd overheard the grumblings in the coffee shop and from the glimpses I'd caught of Dick's interaction with Griffin, Killian, Sierra, and his own daughter, Luna.

"But we're equals," Griffin said uncomfortably.

"Dude." Killian arched an eyebrow. "We both know that's not true."

Their friendship had been forged after their fathers' and strengthened by neither one wanting to step into their rightful place in their pack. "And because of your friendship, uniting the packs once more would make both packs stronger," I told Killian, then linked with Griffin. *You are stronger than him—you were just sheltered more, and he wasn't. In the past few weeks, you've grown and started to own your strength, but if you don't take your place among your people, Dick will steal it from you.*

Another Mercedes pulled up, but this time, Lars was in the driver's seat. "Here I am, sir, ready to take your friend home."

"One minute," Killian said, then averted his eyes to the ground. I watched his body shake—he obviously didn't want to submit. He was strong in his own right, so for him to willingly stand down, even for his best friend, went against every instinct.

A second later, Killian shifted his body toward me. His voice popped into my head. *You both are my alphas now. Don't make me regret it.* He straightened, and his eyes glowed as his wolf recognized Griffin and me.

My throat closed as yet another warm spot filled my chest. *I didn't mean for you to submit to me.* I hoped he didn't think I was trying to manipulate him into that bond.

He patted my arm and spun around, climbing into the car. *I know, but I never would've been willing to submit to Griffin until you came into the picture. It makes sense that I submit to both of you, as I consider you both my true alphas.*

As soon as the door shut, Lars hit the gas, and the car lurched forward. Griffin and I stood there, watching the vehicle disappear from our sight, heading back toward the gate.

We better go before the council members come out. Griffin walked across the street, not bothering to look both ways. Granted, we would've heard any vehicles coming, but it unnerved me. I'd grown up near a human town where we deliberately looked both ways before crossing the street as part of blending in. But in a strictly supernatural hub, I guessed no one had to pretend to be human. It would take some getting used to.

Following him, I hurried and crossed the street, unable to prevent myself from checking for cars. Some habits would take longer to break.

Wings flapped overhead, and I tilted my head as a familiar rose scent filled the air. Rosemary's mahogany hair flew behind her as she descended and landed next to me. Her twilight-colored irises darkened. "What the hell is going on?"

Honestly, I wasn't sure, so I needed Griffin to help explain things. "Why don't you get in the car? We're trying to get out of here before your mom, Azbogah, Dick, Matthew, Alex, and Erin leave."

"Oh, great," Rosemary groaned as she climbed into the back seat. She sat on the floorboard, hiding so no one would see her if they came out the door. "If those people are the only members involved and they're here, that can't be anything good."

"No." Griffin shut the door and started the car. The composure he'd been maintaining slipped away, revealing his worry. "The crystals almost lost power."

"Impossible." Rosemary crossed her arms and pursed her lips. "That can't happen. The guards would have contacted the witches when the power began to flicker."

"The guards weren't there." Griffin ran his hands through his perfectly gelled hair, causing it to stick up. "And Dick somehow has the council believing that it's my fault." He backed out of the parking spot and turned toward the heart of the city. As we pulled away, the group inside stepped from the building.

We'd left in the nick of time.

Their conversation baffled me. I didn't understand a word of what they were saying, other than the power flickering. "What are the crystals, and how are they important?" I asked. Magic circulating in the air could be powerful, but it was also short-lived, so I didn't understand how a witch could leave if their magic fueled the grid. I hadn't realized how large this city was.

"Crystals." Rosemary blew out her breath. "Varying types of gemstones in different sizes that stabilize the witches' spell to make it last longer and hold the protective shield in place."

"Well, if that's the case, how did the witches not know they were weakening?" Surely they couldn't blame Griffin for that. They should have the replenishments scheduled and not wait for someone to randomly call and ask the witches responsible to come recharge the crystals.

"It's not that simple." Griffin turned back onto the main road and glanced in the rearview mirror. "You can get up now if you want. None of them will be able to see you."

"All this is ridiculous," Rosemary grumbled as she lifted her body into one of the seats.

Griffin chuckled. "Who would've thought you'd become friends with my fated mate and we'd have to keep you hidden?"

"If you would've told me that three months ago, I would've thought you were insane." Rosemary rolled her eyes. "Not saying that I don't actually think that."

I almost felt like I was listening to Killian and Sierra talk to one another. Rosemary usually stayed on point. "Why didn't the witches know that the barrier was weakening?"

"Because the barrier keeps the city hidden from human eyes, there isn't an exact science to tell how long the spell will last. It depends on how many humans are in the outer towns at any given time." Griffin pulled onto the road that ran parallel to the buzzing metropolis. Even from where I sat in the passenger seat, I could easily see the divide among the races: the angels flew around the city sky in groups; the paler-skinned vampires with their overly sweet smell congregated on the side of the street; shifters were gathered, hanging out in front of a place called Shifters' Dive. Some hairy men who had to be bear shifters were laughing loudly while sipping foaming glasses of what appeared to be beer.

The herbal scent that Griffin had informed me signified witches hovered around a group perusing the wares at a stand that showcased crystals, herbs, and all things needed for spells.

I noticed that whenever two groups of supernaturals passed,

neither acknowledged the other's presence, as if the other people didn't exist.

It unsettled me. The lack of regard would mean horrible things in the future if it didn't get taken care of.

I tore my eyes from the beautiful buildings and focused on what had to be fixed first. "So...I'm still not following."

"The more humans who visit, the more magic must be used to keep up the illusion. If there aren't as many humans nearby, the spell will last longer." Rosemary broke the facts down for me. "So we have guards stationed at each gate that leaves Shadow City. The building containing the crystals is guarded by wolves because they had to step in for your ancestors. Someone is always on duty in case something happens or the city is infiltrated, but mainly to keep an eye on the levels. The spell has a signature they're trained to identify, and if it begins to fade, they are to alert Erin that someone needs to come refresh it."

"There are also other magical artifacts in a warehouse near the crystal building that have to be protected." Griffin cleared his throat. "We aren't privy to what, but the witches swear that if the items were to be stolen, there would be severe consequences."

"See, that's my whole point." I felt like a broken record. "The witches don't feel obligated to tell you what's at stake because they see themselves as a separate community. We need to bridge the gap and learn to work together."

"I see your point, but change won't happen overnight." Rosemary sighed. "This is how things have been for centuries."

Dick blamed Griffin, but why? "Why were the guards called off? And how?"

"I have no clue." Griffin tapped a finger on the steering wheel. "I didn't approve anything that would have directed them to leave their stations."

Obviously, the *how* was the leverage Dick had against Griffin, so we had to figure out what the hell it was. "Rosemary, your mom was there. Do you think you could find out from her what Dick told everyone?"

"Yeah, I should be able to do that." Rosemary sighed.

"And are all the guards wolves?" The question kept popping into my brain. "I mean, there are other races, too. Wouldn't they want to protect the city as well?"

"There are vampire guards who protect the vampire side of Shadow City and the bridge that connects the city to Shadow Terrace, which is on the opposite bank of the river from Shadow Ridge. The vampire gate is also how Shadow City vampires get their blood supply, since humans don't live here," Griffin answered, his voice tight. "And there are Shadow City police, but the force is small and made up mostly of shifters who aren't wolves so that the wolf shifter representatives don't have undue influence in case someone needs to be taken down. There aren't a lot of them, but they protect the artifact warehouse and have a few people on patrol."

That made sense and was great for checks and balances. If wolves protected everything, all Griffin would have to do would be to use his alpha will, and he'd gain access to anything he wanted.

We pulled up to a large golden building with a sign outside that declared it the Elite Wolves' Den with a wolf pawprint underneath. The building had to be forty stories high. Griffin pulled into an attached garage and scanned his badge to open a gate for the lower parking level.

"This is my stop." Rosemary opened the door and climbed out. "I'll get to the council meeting early. Meet me at the coffee stand inside the council building, and try not to act suspicious. I'll tell you everything I know then." The door shut, and she took off so fast that she blurred.

She obviously didn't want to be seen.

Do you think you should've told her that you two are related? Griffin's shoulders relaxed now that we were alone.

That had been the plan. *She left before I could.*

Well, you'll have plenty of time in the future. He pulled into a slot closest to the glass cubicle enclosing the elevator. *Mom is ecstatic to meet you, but she's out with one of her friends right now. Apparently, they're having a girls' night, but she said she'd come home early and ride with us to the council meeting.*

I wished I felt the same way about meeting her, but at least that had bought me a little time. Maybe a good night's sleep would put me in a more confident frame of mind.

He slid his badge against another buzzer, and the cubicle door clicked. He held it open and waved me inside. Once I stepped into the building, I sighed with relief. Inside the building we'd just left and here, the beautiful city lights vanished as if there was something blocking it out on the glass, and I felt more at peace. The lights were gorgeous but overwhelming, much like a nightlight that never turned off and grew so bright that you felt blinded.

Griffin hit the elevator call button, and the silver doors slid open. Once we were inside, he pressed his badge to a sensor and then hit the top floor. Within seconds, the doors slid open again, and my jaw dropped. I'd expected to walk out into a hallway. I wasn't prepared for the doors to open into Griffin's home.

Dark platinum tile floors greeted me with interior walls the color of stratus clouds and all-glass outer walls that overlooked a breathtaking view of the city. White leather couches were placed perpendicular to one another in the living room area with a white coffee table sitting in the center.

One section of the floor-to-ceiling windows had a sliding glass door that led outside to a covered balcony, where the same flooring continued. Two large gold chandeliers hung above several black lounge chairs, and a bar with a black-stone counter sat in one corner.

It was strange to see all the nice furniture outside, but inside the city, there was no horrible weather or wind because of the protection of the dome.

I hadn't realized how wealthy Griffin was. I felt stupid. No wonder Luna had been desperate to get her claws into him. A low growl threatened to escape me from just that simple thought.

Every direction I turned, everything looked almost identical. The same color scheme and style.

Griffin took my hand and tugged me toward the hallway in the middle of the room that led to another section of the apartment. *I know you deserve the tour, but right now, I need some alone time with you.*

That was something I wouldn't argue against. We walked past multiple closed doors until he stopped at the last one on the left. He opened the door, and once again, the gray color scheme stared back at me.

The room was about the same size as his bedroom in Shadow Ridge and featured a king bed against the center of the right wall. Instead of a headboard, pewter squares started at the top of the bed and climbed toward the ceiling. Crisp white sheets that had to have been ironed peeped over the top of a dark gray comforter. The wall overlooking the city was all glass.

Griffin grabbed the edge of the silver-dust-colored curtains and closed them so the view was hidden. "In case anyone flies by." His eyes glowed as he spun in my direction and raced toward me.

His lips crashed onto mine, and his tongue slipped into my mouth. His taste overloaded my senses, and my body heated immediately. Last time, he'd dominated me, teased me, but this time, I needed him hard and fast.

I shoved him onto the bed and straddled him, peeling off my shirt. I didn't know what had come over me, but with all the threats we'd just endured, I *needed* to connect with him in a way that only I ever could going forward. Maybe it was the insinuation of how many girls he'd slept with that fired my urgency, but I needed every single one of them erased from his mind.

My hands grabbed the edges of his shirt, and I yanked it over his head. His hands wrapped around me, unfastening my bra. As soon as he flung it to the floor, his tongue flicked against one nipple, making my skin ignite.

He rolled me onto my back and stood, unfastening my jeans and dragging them and my panties off me. *Damn it, your scent is driving me wild*, he told me, and growled.

I pushed up and yanked his pants and boxers down so hard that the button flew off. My eyes took in every inch of him as I slid up on the bed, spreading my legs wide for him. I was primed and ready, and I didn't want to wait anymore.

With eagerness, he climbed in between my legs and slammed inside me. He knew exactly how I wanted him. He thrust inside me over and over, but I wanted something more...something different. *I want to be on top.*

I'll never complain about that. He chuckled as he flopped on his back, ready for me to lead.

Turning so my back faced him, I slipped him inside me. We'd never done this position before, and he hit inside me at a different angle. I began riding him, and he groaned animalistically, which urged me to move faster. That sound was so damn sexy, and I needed to hear it more.

My legs began to burn from kneeling, but the pressure was building, and I ignored the ache.

He sat up behind me and slipped his hand around my front, rubbing the sensitive spot between my legs that was bringing me closer to the edge. My body moved faster, and he increased the pressure to where it hurt and felt incredible all at the same time.

Within minutes, we both fell over the edge and climaxed together, our cries of pleasure mingling. Fully sated, I turned and lay against his chest as my breathing slowed and my eyes grew heavy.

Right as my mind began growing foggy, the *ding* of the elevator sounded, followed by a female voice calling out, "Griffin, I decided to come home after all!" Heels tapped on the floor as they approached.

My blood ran cold as realization settled over me.

I was naked in Griffin's room, and his mom was home and heading this way.

CHAPTER SIXTEEN

ATTEMPTING to leap out of the bed, I got wrapped up in the sheets and tumbled to the floor. I landed on my shoulders, causing a deep ache to run up my arms as the covers shifted, exposing my bare ass. I'd never felt so clumsy before, and of course, it'd happen now. I didn't want Griffin's mom walking in and seeing me like this.

Sterlyn! Griffin said with concern as his head popped over the side of the bed and he took in the disheveled heap of me on the floor.

This was not a good look for me in so many ways.

He stood up, bare-ass naked, not even pretending to be bothered that his mom was here. *Are you okay?* He squatted next to me and lifted me into his arms.

Yeah, I'm peachy. My cheeks felt as if they were on fire as he sat with me on the bed. *Your mom is here.*

His hazel eyes sparkled with mirth. *Yes, I'm very aware.*

A knock on the door made my stomach do somersaults.

"Griffin, I decided I couldn't wait to meet her, so I wanted to surprise you two." She sounded so happy. "I mean, this is the woman who'll be giving me grandbabies!"

Wow. Even though that statement was true, I hadn't thought that far ahead in our future. With everything we were going through, the farthest I could picture was probably a year's time.

"You didn't think to tell me you were heading here?" he called through the door and chuckled, his face filled with adoration as he watched me.

She huffed. "I thought I'd surprise you two."

"You succeeded," he replied, then laughed outright, making me want to punch him.

The asshole knew why I was freaking out, and he was teasing me. *Not cool.* I bared my teeth at him. Maybe sometime in the near future, I'd find it funny, but not so much now.

"Oh." She sniffed. "I smell that."

Please, someone, kill me and put me out of my misery, I chanted to myself only. Even before I met his mother, she was smelling the scents of our desire from just a short while ago.

"Well, no time like the present to get started on those babies," she said, and giggled. "I'll wait for you in the den." The clatter of her heels grew fainter as she moved away from the door.

I punched him in the arm. *You enjoyed that way too much.* I'd rather hide in here the rest of the night, but she was waiting for us. If I didn't go out there, that would only make seeing her tomorrow even more difficult. I was stuck.

"Ouch." He smiled as he rubbed his arm. "Keep that up, and I'll have to punish you. Mom can wait, after all."

"No way." I stood and hurried across the room to grab my clothes. "That will not be happening. This is embarrassing enough."

"Stop it." He rolled his eyes and pouted. "But I'm serious. If you don't want to see her yet, I can keep your mind occupied."

He might be sexy as hell and able to make my body do things that brought such immense pleasure, but I wouldn't be able to focus on anything but the sound of his mom's shoes for the next little while. "Don't worry, I'll punish you later."

"Later, huh?" he asked and smirked as he watched me dress. "I could get behind that." He waggled his eyebrows, driving the innuendo home.

"Behave." I pulled my shirt over my head and ran my fingers through my hair to at least make it look somewhat tame. I didn't need to walk in there with sex hair since we'd already announced what we'd been doing clearly.

"Fine." He pouted but quickly dressed.

Once we were both somewhat put together, he opened his bedroom door. *Mom has been excited to meet you. I should've realized she might come home early, but the thought of having you in my bed was a little too tempting.*

I wasn't about to complain about the sex. Hell, I was all for it, but had I known there was a possibility of her coming home early, I would've gotten dressed before I started drifting off to sleep.

With each step closer to the den, my heart pounded harder. I hadn't liked nearly every person I'd met from Shadow City. They were pompous and only out for themselves. Rosemary seemed to be the one exception. I feared that Griffin's mom would be the same way, which could cause problems between the two of us. We had enough of those.

Hey, it's going to be okay. Griffin grasped my arm, pulling me to a stop. He cupped my face and looked into my eyes as he continued, *There's nothing to be nervous about.*

That was easy for him to say—she was his mother. *If you were meeting my father, how would you feel?*

His face slipped into a mask of indifference. *Okay, I'd have been nervous, too, but I swear there's no reason to be. There were only two things that my parents wanted for me. The first, and most important, was finding a mate who made me a better man.* He pressed his lips to mine. *And you're even better than that—you're my fated mate.*

I inhaled slowly, calming myself. If that was his parents' first wish, then maybe I was overreacting a tad, and freaking out would make me look bad. Dad had told me to pretend to be confident even if I was the furthest thing from it. Pretending would bleed into truly becoming secure. It was some sort of mind-over-matter trick that he was always teaching me. But he'd been right about almost everything else, so what did I have to lose? *And the second thing?*

Becoming the alpha that Shadow City needed. He shook his head as he dropped his hand. *I always assumed he meant the alpha of the wolves, but I'm beginning to think you and he were more similar than I realized. He wanted to unite the races the same way you do and not have us all be seen as separate beings.*

Be careful who you say that to. I took his hand. *If you aren't careful, Sierra will start accusing you, in some demented way, of sleeping with your father.*

Since she isn't here, you had to go there for her. He wrinkled his nose and booped mine. *But don't worry. That won't prevent me from ravishing your body again when we get back to my room. After all, I did promise you a punishment.*

My body betrayed me, and the spicy scent of arousal wafted from me.

I see you have no complaints. He smiled.

Refusing to give him any more satisfaction, I marched off in the direction of the living room. I entered the room to find an ash blonde woman standing in the center.

She ran her hands along the sides of her pewter sweater as her light champagne lips formed a warm smile. Her sapphire-blue eyes scanned me, but not in a critical way. Her gaze was more curious. She placed her hands in the back pockets of her dark jeans as she leaned on the high heels of her black shoes. "Sterlyn," she said. "It's so nice to finally put a face with a name."

That was when I realized I didn't know her name. Griffin always referred to her as Mom. "Hi."

"Ulva," Griffin interjected. "Mom's name is Ulva."

"But you can call me Mom, if you'd rather," she said a little too earnestly.

I wasn't sure how to respond. *No, thanks, I already had a mother* would sound too rude, but I didn't feel comfortable calling her that, either.

"Isn't that a little forward?" Griffin asked as he placed an arm around my waist. "You haven't known each other for a minute yet, and you're asking her to call you Mom."

"Ugh, you're right." She tilted her head back and sagged her shoulders. "I'm sorry. It's just...I haven't seen Griffin this happy before."

"Wait." He hadn't gone back to Shadow City since we'd gotten together. "Seen him?"

"Yeah, the night he had to bring Luna here when she was so drunk." Ulva sat on the couch. "I had to come to the gate to let her in since her parents weren't answering their phones. She was ranting that Griffin forced her to take a cab and refused to let her inside his house in Shadow Ridge. That her mother and father wanted them to be together, and why couldn't he just accept that? She deserved to be staying in his house with him. Didn't Griffin know who she was and what her father was capable of?"

That sounded about right. I'd met Luna only a handful of times, and each time, she'd left a worse impression than the previous one. Granted, she'd tried to kill me on the night Ulva was referencing. Griffin had said he'd gotten her a cab, and obviously, it was true. He'd just left out the part where he'd accompanied her to the gate, but he was right. She wouldn't have gotten in otherwise.

"He told me he was sorry to dump her on me, but he had someone to get back to before he messed things up even more." She looked at her son with a soft expression. "And that's when I realized someone had stolen his heart. When he informed me that you two were fated, that was just the icing on the cake. This was exactly what we'd hoped for him to find."

Kindness radiated off her, confirming her words. I sighed in relief, realizing that she was truly a good person. I needed that; I'd been worried that there weren't many great people in this city. "Well, Griffin thinks the world of you, too."

"Atticus and I were more friends than lovers, but we worked, even to Saga's horror." She chuckled and gestured to Griffin. "That's one reason why we only had one child. The sex was—"

"Mom!" Griffin exclaimed with wide eyes.

"Sorry, you're right." She swatted her hand. "I just meant that we wanted Griffin to find the kind of love that we hadn't been able to find ourselves. It's one part of why Atticus wanted so much to open the city. He wanted our son to find his fated mate. He'd be so happy to see that wish came true."

My heart grew for a man I'd never get to meet. He'd loved Griffin so much. I'd known that Griffin's mother and father were chosen mates, but I hadn't thought about what that meant.

"So, who's Saga?" I wanted to learn more. I wanted every single detail about Griffin and his family that I could soak up.

"Dick's chosen mate." Ulva smiled. "One of my close friends. The four of us grew up together, and, boy, Saga did everything she could to get Atticus for herself. But he and I were best friends, and he said he trusted only two people in his life—me, most of all, and Dick. I thought that it would cause a wedge between Saga and me, but when Atticus asked for me to be his mate, she surprisingly backed down, and she and Dick realized that they were compatible as well." She smiled sadly. "Atticus was so relieved. He was always wary of her back then, and he protected me, probably a little too much. He was a wonderful man and a good father."

"Mom, I hate to cut this short, but it's late." Griffin made his way over to her and kissed her forehead. "Tomorrow morning is going to be nasty, so we need to get our rest."

"You're right. I'm exhausted." She yawned.

He squeezed her hand and straightened. "You know you don't have to come to the meeting, right?"

"I refuse to let you protect me like your father did." Her face pinched as she shivered. "I wish I'd known that Dick was trying to use you as the scapegoat. You need every person who supports you there. The more people you have behind you, the stronger a leader you'll look, and I want to see who all the traitors are."

That was something my father would say. Despite Atticus and Ulva being chosen mates, she was strong, which must have been one reason he'd selected her.

"Okay." He nodded. "Fine. I just hate for you to watch someone else you love get hurt."

That was an odd thing to say. *What do you mean?*

She and Dad were at Dick's having dinner when he died. Griffin scowled. *She saw the entire thing.*

They'd been eating at Dick's? That was a little convenient.

"I understand, and I love you for it." Ulva headed toward the hallway, leaving the two of us behind. She spoke quietly, but I was able to hear her with my silver wolf ears. "Maybe if I'd been more involved and paying attention, he wouldn't have died in the first place."

I wanted to ask her what she meant, but I was pretty sure she didn't know I was a silver wolf with extra-sharp hearing. If she had, she probably wouldn't have said the words out loud at all, assuming Atticus had shared with her what he knew about my kind. I bit my tongue, but only because I wanted to protect her. The more she knew, the greater the chance she would be harmed.

"Night, Mom," Griffin called out as he winked at me. "I love you."

"Love you, too," she said with longing in her voice.

Once the door closed behind her, Griffin returned to me with a salacious smile. "Now, let's go have some fun." He bent down and threw me over his shoulder, and took off to his room.

However, I wasn't able to laugh or fully enjoy the moment. My mind kept replaying what Ulva had just said.

ULVA MET me in Griffin's bedroom the next morning with a black suit in her hands. "This should work." She placed the clothing on the bed, along with a lavender lace shirt.

The suit bottom was a skirt instead of pants, but I didn't want to complain. I didn't have my own clothes here, so I would graciously borrow whatever she was willing to loan me. "Thank you."

Griffin was on the balcony, waiting on me to finish getting dressed. He'd pouted when I made him leave the room, but after last night, I didn't want to be naked in the bedroom with him while his mom was here. I needed at least a day's buffer before that could happen again.

She turned to leave the room but paused. "I want you to know I meant everything I said last night." She looked over her shoulder, locking gazes with me. "I already see a difference in him. Before you, he never would've been brave enough to face the council like this."

"I'm doing nothing." She must have been able to see that. She didn't need to give me credit for something Griffin was doing on his own. "He didn't even ask if I thought we should run. He's making these choices, not me."

"Oh, I know." She pivoted and tilted her head. "But you helped ground him. He was struggling, messing around, just trying to get by. You stepped into his life and gave him purpose again."

"Maybe, but he's made me a better person, too." I was meant to be a warrior, and that would never change, but he'd made me softer. Not in a weak way, but the opposite. I was able to open up to Rosemary because of him...and see things in the ways that my father had because of him. "I guess that's why we're fated mates."

"They're meant to bring out the best in each other." She nodded. "And being locked in here, the wolves and the other races have lost that way because we were rarely able to find ours anymore. But things are changing, and people fear it. You and Griffin will be an excellent example of a positive change resulting from rejoining the world."

"I have a hunch that the people trying to blame Griffin for the crystals are the ones who want to close the borders again."

She nodded. "You're exactly right. Several council members think we have the strongest supernatural races within these walls, and we shouldn't have to deal with petty problems caused by shifters who weren't worthy to live here to begin with."

"Sterlyn. Mom," Griffin called out. "We've got to go, or we won't get there early enough."

"They'll crucify him if we can't figure a way out of this." Ulva frowned. "We can't let that happen."

I placed a hand on her arm and leaned forward, dropping my voice. "So...there's only one thing we can do." I arched an eyebrow. "We take them down. Are you in?"

CHAPTER SEVENTEEN

THE CAR RIDE to the council building was made in complete silence. Griffin tried to appear upbeat, but he wasn't fooling either Ulva or me. He drove his Navigator through town, attempting to keep me out of the view of others as much as possible. The fewer people who saw me, the less likely they were to guess my heritage. We passed only one other vehicle, which was heading out of the city.

Griffin's leg bounced the entire way, despite the forced smile he wore.

Fortunately, Ulva and I were in agreement. No matter what, we were going to make sure that Griffin didn't take the blame for the trouble with the crystals. Still, we were working with minimal information, and I prayed that Rosemary had been able to wrangle details out of her parents.

After a few minutes' drive through the heart of downtown Shadow City, the capitol building came into view. It covered an entire block, a white rectangle with a cathedral-like roof. The walls reflected the ever-shifting lights, making it seem as if the building changed colors constantly.

Griffin turned into an uncovered parking lot on the right side of the building. "Here we are," he said, his voice devoid of emotion.

It's going to be okay. No matter what, I'd make sure we came out of this intact. Even if I had to be the one to take the blame. *Rosemary will have something to tell us, and then we can build our case.*

I hope you're right. He opened his door and climbed out of the car.

His dismissal hurt, but I couldn't be overly sensitive. He was going through a lot, and I couldn't take it personally. I refused to add more worry on top of what he already carried.

I got out of the vehicle, slammed the door, and met him and Ulva in front.

"We need to go in as a united front." I was sure they both knew that, but sometimes stating the obvious helped others feel more in control of a situation. I walked to the other side of Griffin so that he stood between me and his mother.

A few people walked past us, not looking our way. Yesterday, everyone's indifference had bothered me, but today, I was grateful. If anyone tried to talk to us right now, I would likely come off as rude, which might hurt Griffin in their eyes.

We followed the walkway to the building's front entrance. Griffin opened the tall hunter-green door and waved us in. My eyes scanned him as I passed by, enjoying the sight of him in his navy suit. The slacks were tight enough to show off his ass, and I had to restrain myself from pinching it as I brushed by. Now wasn't the time for inappropriate thoughts.

His mom's heels clicked on the beige marble floor, and I cringed as I strolled behind her, making the same type of noise. I hated wearing dress shoes and skirts. They were terrible for fighting, and I was raised to always be prepared for battle. Worst case, I supposed I could try to use the slender heel to pierce the skulls of my enemies.

The entryway was huge and bare, ending with another hunter-green doorway midway through the building. The probably once-white walls were stained yellow from time and wear. On one side of the entryway, a man was sweeping the floor. He walked past us, and a whiff of decay hit me hard, making me gag.

What the hell is that? I'd never smelled anything like it before.

Griffin winced and blew out his nose. *A vampire who's being punished. For him to smell that bad, he's gone without blood for a long time.*

Wait. *They smell sweet, not like that.*

Unless they don't feed, he replied. *I've only ever come across one other person who smelled like that, and it was when Dad took me to see the prison when I was a little boy.* "Hey, Mom." Griffin snagged my hand and nodded to a coffee shop at the right. "Sterlyn and I are going to grab a coffee. Do you want anything?"

"No, I don't think that would be wise." She blew out a breath and adjusted the maroon jacket she was wearing over a matching dress. "I'm on edge enough without the added caffeine. I'll go on in and save Sterlyn a seat."

"I'll be right there." I tried to keep my attention on her, but my gaze flicked over to the small coffee shop. It was a stand built into a corner of the room with no tables. Obviously, people weren't meant to congregate there, which was kind of problematic, as Rosemary was nowhere to be seen. *Maybe we should wait a few minutes.*

We can't, Griffin said in defeat. He wasn't even trying to hide his despair now that we were alone. *The meeting will likely start a few minutes early in hopes that whoever they're targeting arrives on time. It gives the perception that the accused doesn't care about punctuality. A little tip that Dad shared with me before he died.*

These people were assholes. Someone needed to take them down a notch or two, and there was no time like the present. *Okay. Hey, wait.* I walked beside him as a thought unsettled me. *Does your mom know to call me Dove and not Sterlyn?*

Probably not. His body somehow grew even tenser. *I'll link and tell her now.*

Thank God I'd realized that before it was too late.

We walked up to the cash register and placed our order of two black coffees. I usually got something sweeter, but my stomach was already upset. I didn't want to put too much sugar in it and wind up getting sick.

As the man handed us our drinks, Rosemary's scent drifted in our direction. I turned to find her walking over to us. Her long hair was pulled into a Dutch braid, and she wore a white sundress that made her skin appear to glisten. Her black wings fanned out behind her, contrasting starkly with her outfit and giving her sweet look an edge. Like me, she wore white high heels, but hers barely made a sound. "Hello." She nodded formally as she ordered a coffee of her own.

The older fox shifter manning the coffee counter turned around to make her drink, and she took a step closer, speaking in a soft voice that only Griffin and I could hear. "So, we have a huge problem."

"That's kind of obvious," Griffin bit out, letting his anxiety bleed through.

Babe. I chastised him. *I know you're upset, but being rude to her won't get us anywhere. In fact, you could piss her off to where she doesn't tell us anything.*

Nah, she loves you too much. Griffin brushed off my concern, but I could feel a little bit of regret through our mate bond connection.

Needing to divert her attention from his rudeness, I tried to refocus the conversation. "Do you have anything specific to help us?"

"Yeah." She scowled at Griffin before ignoring him and focusing on me. "Apparently, Griffin signed an order for the guards to attend additional training in case someone ever tried to attack the buildings."

"That's true." Griffin shrugged his shoulders. "What's the big deal?"

"Because you ordered all of them to go at the same time, leaving the crystals unmonitored." Rosemary lifted a brow and stepped toward the counter, dismissing us as the fox shifter handed her the coffee.

I took a sip of my drink, and the bitter coffee burned my tongue. The pain was a temporary reprieve, giving me something to focus on for a moment. I could feel Griffin practically vibrating beside me.

Slowly, Griffin and I strolled toward the door that must lead into the council meeting room. We moved at a snail's pace as we tried to wait on Rosemary without being too obvious. A tall, commanding figure hovering near the doorway caught my attention.

Yelahiah.

I wasn't too shocked, since Rosemary was getting coffee, but the older woman's attention wasn't on her daughter. She was focused on me. Her eyes narrowed as if she were trying to piece a puzzle together, and even when my eyes met hers, she didn't look away. Instead, her interest seemed to be piqued even more.

Unease filtered through me, and I wanted to run away. I'd never experienced such intense scrutiny before. Normally, I was drawn toward a fight or confrontation, not repelled. That was how silver wolves were wired. But this was different. I didn't know how to explain it.

Remember those papers Dick stopped by to pick up at the house? Griffin sounded miserable, and his body seemed to shrink.

Yeah. I remembered that day clearly. Dick had tried to push me into leaving and had even tried threatening me when he saw that I had every intention of staying. The douchebag had wanted to make me run, and I'd thought it was solely because of his daughter. Luna had been desperate to make Griffin her own. *You didn't read the forms, did you?* I tried not to sound accusatory, but I couldn't help it. Dick had been desperate to have him sign those papers quickly, and now we knew why.

I did. He growled, making the vampire sweeping the floor pause. Griffin didn't even notice and continued with his tirade. *But I didn't know how it would impact the guards' watch schedule. I assumed they'd always keep at least one or two behind.*

Dick had banked on Griffin not scrutinizing the details. The conniving prick. *Did you ask any questions?*

No, it seemed so straightforward. He turned toward me. *I fucked up.*

You trusted the wrong person. That was what this all came down to. *But we'll figure a way out of this.* Dad had taught me not to fret even when there wasn't an obvious strategy. That was what the enemy banked on, and I needed to keep a level head in order to seize the next opportunity to turn things around. *That was you being naive and wanting to see the best in people. You did nothing wrong. Why would you ever think anyone on the council would do something to sabotage the safety of the city?*

I should've done something that day, but instead, I'd let the man go with the papers. I had known something wasn't right and should've followed up on my instincts. Because I hadn't, now my mate could lose his place within his pack and city. All those changes his father and he had dreamed of might remain just that.

A dream.

I was also to blame here. But beating myself up over it would be caving and doing exactly what the asshole wanted.

I was stronger than that.

Griffin and I were more powerful together.

We had to remember that.

Rosemary hung back, most likely due to her mother. We needed to pretend, at least for a little while longer, that we weren't allies. That bit of information needed to be dropped at the perfect time.

"Well, hello there." Yelahiah's musical voice sounded like a lullaby.

There was something pure and raw about her that made me feel safe. But I couldn't tell her who I was. She was angry about what had happened to her brother, but I was very far removed from him, my blood containing only a fraction of his after all these generations. "Hi."

"You seem awfully familiar to me." She arched an eyebrow, reminding me of her daughter. "Have we met before yesterday?"

"No, we haven't." We hadn't even been officially introduced. Instead, I had been an observer to the show.

Griffin took a step closer to me. "She's my mate," he said simply.

"I got that much yesterday." However, her focus stayed on me. "What's your name?"

"I have many." I forced a laugh and hoped that the sound wasn't as crazed as it seemed in my head. "But the one most people call me is Dove." That wasn't a lie. All the customers at Shadow Ridge Coffee Shop on the university campus called me by that name. Only my closest friends and family knew my birth name.

"Dove." She grinned, which made her look more human. The superior angel facade slipped away, if only for a moment. "I like that." She licked her blood-red lips and motioned for her daughter. "Word to the wise—you two better get in there. If I know Azbogah and Richard, they're about to begin the meeting five minutes early."

Griffin's lips parted, revealing his surprise at her support.

"Thank you," I said as I looped my arm through Griffin's, directing him inside. If I didn't know he was gawking at her because she'd helped him, I might have gotten jealous. She could easily pass for mid-thirties, despite being centuries old. Angels were immortal.

As we entered the room, I scanned the area, looking for Ulva. I spotted her sitting next to a dark-haired woman on the end of a row of chairs against the wall close to the door we'd walked through. More chairs were set around a rectangular table with a cut-out section that faced the door. Twelve people sat around the table, which I'd expected: three angels, three witches, three vampires, and the wolf shifters, representing the shifters as a whole.

Dick stood in the middle of the table facing the door, with Azbogah on his right and Alex on his left. Erin's deep brown eyes darkened even more as she glared at my mate from next to Azbogah, and the red in her hair seemed to emphasize her anger. Then each council member's seat rotated between the supernatural races. Based on what Griffin taught me, I was able to sniff out each one. The only two vacant seats were the ones closest to Ulva.

The wolves represent all shifters, Griffin explained as he ushered me to the seat beside his mom. *The original council refused to let every shifter have a representative because then that general race would have the most say. They wanted it balanced, and the one race every shifter trusted was the silver wolf, so a vote was cast that silver wolves would be the shifter representatives. After all, they'd been the ones to organize the civil war against the angels. The silver wolves left before the first council meeting, but the decision couldn't be undone, per the other council members, so the strongest alpha wolf took that spot instead.*

I wondered if Yelahiah had hoped that the silver wolves would come back for her brother.

Griffin led me to Ulva with a frown now marring his face as his mother and the woman next to her looked up at us.

"Is this the girl that you were telling me about?" The lady's hair was twisted into a bun, and her icy blue eyes scanned me. Her skin was a light olive that highlighted her beauty.

"Oh, yes." Ulva gestured to me. "This is...Dove. Dove, this is Dick Harding's wife, Saga."

I stilled. From the way people spoke about Dick's wife, I'd expected her to have a weak persona, but there was strength and determination in those eyes. And I could read nothing from her. "Hello."

"Luna's told me all about you." Her mauve lips pressed together in displeasure. "We all thought that Luna and Griffin would wind up chosen mates since we got pregnant near the same time and they grew up together. It's a shame what all you've put her through."

Her words were meant to rattle me, but I couldn't get past the fact that I couldn't get a read on her essence. It was like it was neither good nor bad...or it was hidden.

"She didn't do a damn thing to your daughter," Griffin growled, getting riled up enough for the both of us.

Dick heard his voice and spun around. "Griffin, you're here—" he started.

Azbogah cut him off. "Right on time. Almost late, in fact."

My body tensed, and I readied myself to defend Griffin, when he kissed my cheek and linked, *Calm down.* He held my gaze an extra beat and then made his way calmly to one of the last two spots at the table.

Shit. If he had to remind me, then I was closer to losing it than I realized. Taking a deep breath, I calmed myself and sat next to Ulva. Rosemary entered the room and took the vacant seat beside me, while her mom went to the last spot next to Griffin.

I wondered if Azbogah had done that on purpose, but it didn't matter. Yelahiah wasn't on trial. Griffin was.

"So we're here to agree that Griffin is guilty of circumventing an all-council approval and ordering our guards to take additional weapons training." Azbogah jumped right to the point. "All those in favor of removing him as the top wolf representative of Shadow City, say aye."

"Aye," Erin said, jumping to her feet with Dick following right after. Matthew agreed without batting an eye.

They weren't even going to give him a chance to defend himself. Dick's grin morphed into a smirk when Alex confirmed.

Five of the eleven voting members had now agreed to remove Griffin, making it clear that there was only one thing that could prevent Dick from taking control.

I jumped to my feet. "He can't be stripped of that title. I'm the rightful wolf representative of Shadow City, and I'm here to take back my position as upheld by the divine."

CHAPTER EIGHTEEN

AZBOGAH GLARED at me as he stood next to Dick and said, "We're in the middle of a vote. Sit *down*."

No. If I budged, they'd finish the vote, and then I'd have to try to reclaim the title from Dick. Staying firm and asserting myself before Griffin lost the role was my best strategy. "But he isn't the rightful representative," I repeated loudly. The more confident I acted, the more inclined at least a few of the other representatives would be in hearing from me.

"Sit *down*," Dick said through clenched teeth. "This doesn't involve you."

"But it does." I took a step forward.

Rosemary turned in my direction and shook her head marginally.

I didn't need a pack link with her to understand what she was telling me—sit down and shut up.

What are you doing? Griffin's fingers trembled on his pant legs under the table. *You can't tell them what you are.*

Luckily, no one but Saga, Rosemary, Ulva, and I could see him shaking. His face remained confident as he pretended to not be fazed —like any real leader would do.

Maybe. I had to admit that I hadn't thought this through, but something had to be done.

"I said"—Dick spat the words as his face twisted in disgust—"*sit. Down.* You aren't part of this."

"Actually, she's the current Shadow City alpha's fated mate. Weren't you planning on presenting her to seal your relationship in front of the council, and thus, the Divine?" Yelahiah lifted a hand in my direction.

Warmth flowed through our bond as Griffin stood and looked at me. "She is, and effective immediately, she's the alpha mate of Shadow City."

"You do realize you're about to lose that position?" Dick gloated.

"I wouldn't be so certain." Yelahiah motioned for me to come forward as she continued, "Technically, this is supposed to be an open environment where anyone can speak their piece. Is there a reason you don't want her to state her case?"

"Why would you ask such a question?" Dick placed a hand on his chest. "We were just in the middle of a vote. She can speak at a later time." The evil inside him swirled so thick that there was a faint mist around him.

I'd never been able to see it before. Usually, I could feel ill intent only within my soul like a coldness and ickiness that radiated off a person.

"I, for one, want to hear what she has to say before casting my vote." Yelahiah walked over to me and stopped at my side.

We faced the council down together, and the third wolf shifter representative's sea-green eyes sparkled with interest, contrasting against his olive skin. He was only a couple of years older than Griffin, with sable brown hair that fell naturally against his face. It wasn't gelled back like Dick's or Griffin's. He seemed more like a wolf shifter who lived outside of the snobbish city. But like several of the other council members, there wasn't anything notable about his essence—as if he were neither good nor bad. "I would like to hear what she has to say, too."

"Ezra," Dick hissed. "I said we don't need to hear her." His eyes glowed faintly like he was trying to force the younger shifter into submission.

So that was how Dick had managed to take the wolf vote by the balls. He bullied this representative into doing whatever he wanted, and Griffin had been so wrapped up in his grief from losing his father that he'd handed the control right to him. "Are you seriously trying to force him to take back what he said?" I would call Dick out on it if no one else would. "Everybody is here and can see you doing it!"

Dick's face turned pink as his nostrils flared. He was losing his composure yet again. He straightened his shoulders. "I'm merely looking out for his best interests. If you're able to sway these intelligent people with whatever insane story you're trying to weave, he would be the one kicked off the council, seeing as he is the weakest of the three current members."

"I wouldn't be so sure about that." I filled my lungs, making sure my voice remained steady. I wanted to give him pause and drive him crazy. "After all, you admitted that this council is intelligent, so why would you even try to prevent them from stating that they'd like to hear my very *interesting* story."

A smirk spread across Yelahiah's face as she rocked back on her heels like she was enjoying the show. "She has a point. Wouldn't you agree, Azbogah?"

Azbogah scowled at us, but he nodded. "Sure. Whatever she has to say, I'm sure it'll be a waste of time, but we can see if anyone else would like to hear her story." He gestured at Ezra. "So one person has agreed to hear her story. Would anyone else like to express interest?"

"I would." A thin man leaned forward in his chair, and his peony scent told me he was an angel. His white feathered wings spread behind him, almost blending in with the white suit he wore. The only color on him was his butterscotch-blonde hair and piercing sky-blue eyes. One of the purest essences I'd ever encountered warmed me inside.

"Of course you would, Pahaliah." Azbogah shuddered and

pressed a hand to his stomach. "You wouldn't want your precious wife to be mad at you."

So this was Rosemary's father. He looked nothing like I'd expected him to. With her darker complexion, Rosemary definitely took after her mom.

"What about you, Gwen?" Dick puffed his chest as his arrogance fell quickly back in place while his attention landed on a gorgeous woman who sat between Ezra and Pahaliah.

Gwen tapped her four-inch burgundy nails on the table as hate flashed through her chestnut-brown eyes. "I don't want to even hear from the wolves who are already part of this council, so that's an easy decision for me." She licked her cranberry lips, stopping to emphasize her sharp teeth, which screamed vampire, and ran a hand through her messy, shoulder-length ivory hair. "In other words, that's a no."

We had two yeses and one no. If they did a majority rule type of thing, we'd at least be at a draw, and then I'd share my story, even if they didn't want me to. I'd respect this little game they wanted to play since it was buying time from them all betraying Griffin.

The witch who sat between Pahaliah and Alex flipped her waist-length, deep forest-brown hair over her shoulder and leaned back in her chair. She ran a finger along her black-stained lip as her coffee-shaded eyes lit with mischievousness. "You know what? I'm in. I could use a good laugh."

"Breena," Erin scolded the younger witch. "We have a lot of stuff that needs to get done back at the coven. Why are you wasting our time?"

"What if she does have a story worth hearing?" The dark-headed witch shrugged. "I don't want to be too hasty."

"Don't worry, Priestess." A maroon-haired witch chimed from the end directly opposite Griffin. "I understand the importance of getting our work done, so I don't want to waste precious time on some desperate girl who's willing to throw herself under the bus for her mate." Her ebony eyes matched her soul. "It's kind of pathetic."

"See, you should be more like your sister." Erin chastised Breena once again and smiled sweetly at the redhead. "Diana, you always make me proud."

"Anyone else?" Azbogah asked, avoiding looking at Yelahiah. "I'm assuming Griffin is a yes, so all it would take is two more to hang the council."

"Then I'm all ears." Alex leaned forward, placing his elbows on the table. "I'm hoping Matthew will agree with me." His eyes sparkled with mischief.

"Fine," Matthew huffed. "I will humor you this one time, but it'll cost you."

"Do I even need to ask how you're going to vote?" Azbogah's head flinched back, and his gaze clouded as he glanced at the female angel.

Yelahiah batted her eyes, smiling victoriously. "You've never wanted to break protocol before, so why start now?" She touched my shoulder. "Yes, I'd like to hear the girl's story, especially since you and Dick seem almost desperate that we don't."

"Not desperate." Azbogah waved his hand at me, gesturing for me to take the floor. "Just trying to be efficient, but please, proceed. Delight us with your carefully crafted tale."

Oh, how kind of the prick. Anger tightened inside of me, but I couldn't let it take hold. All that would do would allow me to miscalculate and mess up this chance. "There is something that everyone here should know," I said the words slowly and deliberately, buying time so my pulse settled and my mind cleared once more. "You see, one of the wolf council members does need to step aside."

"Those are some bold words without backing them up, *girl*," Azbogah barked.

All my life, I'd been taught to hide my heritage. That being a silver wolf put a target on my back, and boy, had I learned it was true. Not only had my brother been kidnapped and my entire pack massacred, but someone was desperately trying to capture me. Yet, maybe staying hidden had given away part of our power. Instead of standing to fight and keep our place in this society, we ran and hid, allowing corruption to take an even stronger hold in those we'd left behind.

Sterlyn, what are you doing? Griffin sounded scared. *Don't sacrifice your safety because of me. We can figure something out without throwing ourselves on the mercy of the council.*

I'm doing what we should've done all those years ago. Maybe I was being stupid, but with Yelahiah standing behind me, I became even more certain. *I'm taking back our place in the world.* Proudly, I said, "I'm Sterlyn Knight, the alpha of the silver wolves, and the shifters voted centuries ago that my race should be the council's shifter representatives."

Yelahiah inhaled sharply, and her hand tightened on my arm.

I wanted to check on her, but I refused to avert my gaze from Dick's. He'd take it as cowardice, and probably many of the others here would, too. I lifted my chin, making it clear that I'd stand my ground.

"A silver wolf?" Alex gasped as he pounded the table. "That's not possible."

"But it is." I urged my wolf forward, feeling the tingle along my skin. I removed my suit jacket so they could see my bare arms as silver fur sprouted. Then I pulled back on my wolf, not letting her go any further. A partial shift was hard to hold, but the full moon was close.

"Oh, my God." Ezra's breath caught. "She is."

"This is impossible." Azbogah's hands fisted as he turned to Dick. "Did you know about this?"

"I..." Dick stuttered. "I didn't." The stench of rotten eggs poured off Dick, alerting everyone that he'd lied.

Murmurs filled the room as Azbogah closed his eyes and pinched the bridge of his nose.

"You *knew* about her?" Griffin rasped as his feeling of betrayal rushed into me. "For how long?"

"I don't answer to you." Dick scanned the room as if in search of an exit.

Dick had known about me all along. This couldn't be a coincidence. Even though I was relieved that my instincts had been right, I couldn't help but feel horrible for Griffin. He'd trusted this man for so long, and to find out that he'd not only been sabotaging him, but hunting me, made him feel responsible.

The way to right the wrong was to address it head-on. *Make him submit to you.* I could do it, but this was something Griffin had to do for himself. He needed to realize the strength he held inside him. Not just that, but he'd command respect from the others in the room. Griffin needed to do this for himself. If I took care of it for him, I'd insult him on so many levels.

I refused to be that kind of mate. He and I needed to support one another and make each other stronger, not try to outshine each other.

"Actually, you do." Griffin jumped to his feet and marched around the table toward the older man. "You aren't fit to lead the wolves or be any sort of representative for the shifters. You're selfish and conniving."

"I've sacrificed everything to earn this position," Dick said as he pointed in Griffin's face. "I made the hard calls while you screwed your latest conquest or got drunk with that pathetic alpha who was supposed to be in charge of guarding the city."

"I'm going to college to get the kind of education I can use to help this city grow," Griffin countered. "If my dad were still alive, he'd have been leading the city while I was away."

"Exactly," Dick snarled. "If he was still alive. He isn't, so you should've stepped up, but you were too weak."

"You *told* me to go to college." Griffin's eyes glowed faintly as his anger took control. "You practically pushed me out the gate, telling me I needed to set an example for others and attend the university so more supernaturals would come."

Once again, Dick had been manipulating him for who knows how long. There was no telling what kind of deceit he'd fed everyone, and though I hated to see Griffin spiral in front of the council, this confrontation had to happen. It was long overdue, and hopefully, the damage wouldn't be too terrible.

"Let's not forget how you dropped off the paperwork at my house for what you've put me on trial for, telling me you'd be back soon to get the signed documents. Paperwork *you* created." Griffin spread his arms out. "You risked letting the city be revealed to humans just to put me in this position so that you could take over as alpha of my own city. This stops now. You're no longer part of the pack, and you need to go."

"What? I did not." Dick stumbled back as the sulfuric smell assaulted our noses yet again. "You can't do that. We're about to vote you out. Besides, no one believes you."

"But he's not voted out yet." I put my jacket back on as I moved to stand next to my mate, showing my support for him. He and I would always be a package deal, and no one would ever take that away. "And everyone believes him. Or did you forget that supernaturals can tell when someone lies?"

Dick's face turned pale, and his attention shifted behind me, I assumed to his mate.

I wanted to turn around to see her reaction, but I had to remain focused, especially now. We already had a ton of stuff against us— Griffin with his flippant lifestyle before he'd met me, and the silver wolves running away, leaving the other races behind. They had to believe that we were different and would change the tides.

"She's right." Yelahiah took her spot back at the table. "We haven't voted, and it's clear that Griffin isn't the one who should be on trial. So the previous vote is now void, and a new one will begin. Isn't that right, Azbogah?" She beamed at the dark angel who had been in alliance with Dick just moments ago.

If he said no, he'd be discredited completely. His reputation was already partially ruined.

"Yes, a new vote shall be taken." Azbogah nodded.

"*What?*" Dick's shoulders slumped as if he'd been deflated. "But—"

"Who is in agreement that Dick should be removed from the council, effective immediately, and replaced by the silver wolf standing before us as decreed by the divine?"

One by one, each council member said "aye" until only Griffin remained.

My mate locked eyes with the man who had once been like a father to him, and magic pulled inside him as he called his alpha will. He bellowed, "You are no longer part of this council nor part of Sterlyn's and my pack. You have until tomorrow to get your affairs in order and leave."

Despite Dick being part of Griffin's pack, it was clear that he didn't respect my mate as alpha. He hadn't challenged him...yet. I was so proud of my mate for making the douchebag submit to him before he could cause any additional problems.

Dick bared his teeth as he averted his gaze and vowed, "You haven't seen the last of me," before stomping out the door.

"So what does that mean for us?" Saga asked from the back, not even bothering to follow her husband. "Does that go for me and Luna, too?"

"Yes." Griffin spoke low but clearly, and he didn't bother to turn around. "Your daughter tried to kill my mate. You all must leave, too."

"Fine," she whimpered, and the door slammed behind her, leaving the gawking council's attention on the two of us.

CHAPTER NINETEEN

THE SILENCE in the room almost overwhelmed me. I hated being the center of attention, but in this unfortunate situation, that was exactly what we had to be. It was important for the others to know we had the guts to lead, to prove that we were serious and would take down any adversary.

We needed to portray confidence and solidarity.

Griffin took my hand as we stared down the council together, practically daring them to challenge us.

I will die to protect you, he linked with me before adding Killian to our bond. *Kill, Sterlyn just informed the council who she is.*

Of course, she did, Killian deadpanned. *I thought we were keeping that shit secret.*

Secrets never stay buried, I told him. The truth could take centuries to come out, but eventually, it always caught back up to people. This was something I'd come to learn ever since Dad passed. *And by hiding, we were giving our enemies exactly what they wanted. Leverage. Control. The only two things that could make Dick hard.* Obviously, his mate didn't give a shit about him. She would've happily stayed here while Dick roamed the world outside.

I'd been so stupid. I should've shouted my heritage from the rooftops instead of keeping the secret guarded.

Killian burst into laughter through our bond. *Damn, I'm so glad I can link to you two. Sterlyn has a way of making me smile that no one else can.*

Everyone but Rosemary. I'd seen the way they looked at each other, but both of them were too damn stubborn to admit their feelings.

Watch it. Griffin growled, teasing, but it fell flat because of the severity of the situation.

Whatever, man. Killian sighed exasperatedly. *She's my sister. Let me know if you need me. You coming back today?*

No, it'll be tomorrow. We had to stay here and make sure that Dick actually left. If we left the city ourselves, it could make us look weak, even though that wasn't the case.

"That was unexpected." Alex chuckled, bringing me back to the present. He sat back in his seat as he steepled his fingers and looked at me. "And silver wolves are still alive. Who would've ever guessed that?"

A murkiness swirled inside the vampire prince. He considered me as if he were at a crossroads where he could go evil or good. Most of the council members had corruption rolling off them—all except for Rosemary's parents, Ezra, and Alex. Each member was out to get something for their race or perhaps even for their own personal gain.

"Definitely not me." Erin's nose wrinkled with disgust. "We've done just fine without them. There's no need for them to return now."

"I have to agree." Azbogah sneered. "But at least her coming here has helped accomplish something. I can finally finish what we started all those years ago. My judgment still stands that the silver wolves should die."

"Not so fast." Yelahiah moved partially in front of me with a wide stance. "When you came to Earth, you forfeited being the judge, which means that your opinions don't carry weight anymore."

There was so much tension and hatred brewing between the two of them. Even if I hadn't known the history, it was clear that something had happened in the past.

I couldn't help but wonder if everyone knew why Azbogah wanted us dead. He knew we contained the power to rally the races and ensure the angels never gained control again. But this was a piece of information that could hurt us if shared. We needed more alliances before the members got nervous, thinking whatever plans they had would be thwarted. These people didn't want to unite the land—they just wanted to gain power of their own.

"Opinions?" Azbogah's jaw twitched. "What I say is the law."

"No, it's not." Pahaliah shook his head as he pushed his seat back. "Your influence has been fracturing, and the whole point of this council is for everyone to have a voice. I agree with Yelahiah. No harm can come to Sterlyn."

Griffin's hand tightened on mine. *We need to get out of here before things get worse. You being here is going to make others act irrationally out of fear.*

That didn't make sense. Why would they fear me? I was here to make things better. *We can't.* That wasn't how an alpha handled problems. Everyone needed to take a step back and think things through. "Why is it so important to kill us all? We've been living for centuries, and now that you learned we survived, you're determined for us to die again?" I wanted Azbogah to admit to everyone that we were part angel. It seemed that our heritage had always remained a mystery, and there had to be a reason. But I was already rocking the boat enough. I'd leave it alone...for now.

"Wolves aren't meant to have powers beyond that of any shifter." Azbogah shook his fist at me. "The fact that you do means that something got perverted. Your kind should never have been created in the first place. The only way to purge the world of silver wolves is to kill each and every one of you." A scary grin flitted across his face as if he relished the thought.

My stomach revolted. Could he have partnered with Dick and

planned my pack's slaughter? But if that was the case, then he couldn't have known that they had meant to spare me and use me to breed more of my kind. He wouldn't have been okay with that if he believed everything he said. And I hadn't smelled a lie.

"Well, there's only one way to make that call, because the council was formed for situations like this." Yelahiah scanned every member of the council as she continued. "A vote on whether the silver wolves should be protected."

"Are you fucking serious?" Griffin spat as he spun toward her and glared. He growled as he took a menacing step in her direction. "My mate's life depends on a vote?"

Be careful, I warned. I didn't like it either, but this was how Shadow City operated. The last thing we needed to do was piss them off even more—they'd be out to kill Griffin as well. I had to trust that Yelahiah knew what she was doing. *Don't insult them, or we'll be on even more dangerous ground.*

This is your life, *Sterlyn*. Griffin's shoulders bunched. *Not some vote on what movie we're watching tonight.*

I almost smiled despite the seriousness of our situation. Sierra always made us vote on what to watch because there were three women to two men. Needless to say, she got to watch whatever she wanted each night because Rosemary and I didn't want to hear her whine about girl solidarity.

I get that, but if you act out now, they won't keep Dick out of the city. Even worse, they'll probably put him back on the council. He'll pretend to play by their rules. I hoped I wasn't making a mistake, but regardless, the suggestion was out there, and I could already tell that Azbogah approved by the corner of his lips tipping upward. *If they agree to kill me, we'll go from there.* We couldn't think about the worst-case scenario and be defensive until we knew we needed to be. Otherwise, we'd be creating a problem that might not exist.

"Fine." Azbogah pressed his lips into a line and nodded. "That is an excellent idea. All of those in favor of killing the silver wolves, say aye."

"Aye!" Erin shouted with such enthusiasm.

Wow, that was eager. I had no clue what we'd ever done to her, but she was going on my *keep an eye out for* list. Maybe Griffin had been right, but it was too late now.

Diana raised her hand. "Aye."

"Agreed." Gwen rolled her eyes and crossed her arms. "No way in hell am I talking like that."

Azbogah scowled but didn't say anything. Most likely because she'd voted in his favor.

Then silence descended, which didn't make sense. I figured the vampires would jump at the chance, too, but both men glanced at the floor as if they would rather be anywhere but here.

"What the..." Erin leaned over the table in Breena's direction. "Girl, if you don't—"

"Fine." She blew out a breath, making her bangs puff out of her eyes. "Aye."

"Wait." Rosemary jumped to her feet, not able to remain silent any longer. "Does that even count? She got bullied."

"Rosemary, shush," Yelahiah scolded. "We're in the middle of a count."

"Who else?" Azbogah asked through gritted teeth. "Including me, that's five in favor. Only two more votes needed for a majority."

No one made a noise beyond their breathing.

"Only two more votes are needed." Azbogah rubbed his fingers together and tapped a foot on the ground. "You have to say aye for it to count."

When everyone remained quiet again, I was ready for the dark angel to throw a tantrum. Maybe roll around on the floor like a toddler. Given how his face twisted, that might not have been a crazy possibility.

"I'm thinking the final tallies are in." Yelahiah beamed as she patted my arm. "Which means Sterlyn and her wolves are protected."

"For the time being," Azbogah retorted.

Thank God. Griffin wrapped an arm around my waist. "I think we've done enough for today, don't you agree?"

"For once, I agree with the pup." Alex twirled a finger. "I second that. The meeting is adjourned."

Everyone got out of their chairs and segregated into their own races except for Azbogah and Ezra.

I glanced at the other wolf shifter, who seemed to avoid my gaze.

Odd.

Let's get out of here. Griffin placed his hand on the small of my back, leading me toward the door. *The longer we hang around here, the greater the chance Azbogah will try to pull something.*

He didn't have to encourage me—I wanted to get out of there just as much as he did. *Should we talk to Ezra?*

No. Griffin didn't even bother looking back. *He likes to hang out after these things. I'll catch up with him later.*

Ulva opened the door, waving us through. Her irises had deepened to more of a cobalt, revealing her own worry.

I brushed past her, and the three of us rushed through the lobby with three sets of footsteps following behind us. Someone was hurrying to catch up, which meant that another argument or threats wouldn't be far behind.

My body was prepared for battle, but the scents of Rosemary and her family put my anxiety at ease.

"Sterlyn," Rosemary called as wings flapped, and soon, she landed right in front of us. Her black wings feathered out behind her, giving her an unearthly beauty. She continued, "We *all* need to talk, but not here."

Ulva glanced over her shoulder, back at the council room doors.

"Tomorrow, we'll be at Griffin's," I replied. "That probably would be the safest place to meet. Talk then?"

She nodded. "Sounds good."

Griffin marched past her, waving both Ulva and me on.

He wanted to get back to his apartment before someone tried

pulling something on me again. The farther away we got from the council, the safer I'd be.

Supposedly.

Not with Dick still out there, but one thing at a time. I made sure my back was straight and walked out of the building like I didn't have a care in the world.

My dad's words echoed in my mind. *Fake it if you have to.*

THE REST of the day remained tense. Saga called Ulva over and over again, begging her to do something about their family's banishment. As if she could, or would, even want to attempt to talk her son out of Dick's punishment. At first, Ulva had tried to be nice, but it didn't take long before she made the situation perfectly clear: Dick had tried to sabotage her son, and she had no interest in helping him or the rest of his family.

Something was off about the woman, but I couldn't imagine what it would be like to be married to a man like that, someone so heartless and power-hungry. He probably stepped all over Saga and Luna, trying to use them to climb his way to the top. Perhaps that was why Luna had been so desperate to claim Griffin as her own.

Griffin snored gently next to me in his bed. It was close to two in the morning, and he'd just dozed off. His mom had been pacing the apartment for hours, adding to our anxiety. When she finally went to her room, he'd calmed down enough to fall asleep.

However, my wolf stirred inside me. She was on edge and continued to surface, making my skin tingle faintly. I heard nothing out of the ordinary in here, but maybe if I checked the entire apartment, she'd finally calm enough to sleep.

Given Azbogah's push to murder me, I didn't blame her for being on edge. The angel more than hated me. Actually...hate was too mild an emotion.

He *loathed* me.

Or rather, the silver wolves.

I was pretty sure it wasn't personal, just my genetics.

That didn't sound much better.

Slowly and quietly, so as not to wake Griffin, I untangled myself from his arms. He grunted and tried to pull me close again, but I rolled far enough away that he flopped over on his side and resumed his gentle snoring once more.

Whew. I didn't want to wake him. The day had been traumatic, and even though he now hated Dick, tomorrow would still be hard on him. He'd grown up with Dick as a constant presence in his life, and I hated to consider all the possible ways that Dick had screwed Griffin's family over. In fact, it was safer if I didn't consider it.

I inched the door open just wide enough to slip through and padded down the hall. I tapped into my wolf, helping me to remain silent. It was strange being in Shadow City because the moon's pull seemed to be a little stronger inside. Maybe the glass dome somehow magnified the magic. That made sense to me.

As I entered the den, nothing seemed out of place. My eyes were slowly scanning the area when hands grabbed the balcony wall outside.

I ducked behind the couch and crept over to the edge so I could peek without being seen. I could have rushed out there, but I wanted to see how many intruders there were, and how the hell they'd gotten up here.

The person grunted as they lifted their body over the side. All it would take was a finger slipping for the person to hurtle to their death unless they had wings. But if they had wings, I doubted they'd be dangling like that.

Salt and pepper hair peeked over the top, informing me of who it was.

Dick.

A memory of Griffin mentioning that Dick's family lived next door and how he would sometimes hear him and Saga scream at each other filtered through my mind.

The asshole had somehow gotten from his balcony to Griffin's. He threw his legs over the side and tipped onto the balcony floor on his ass.

He grimaced and slowly climbed to his feet. He tiptoed to the glass door and pulled out a set of keys. Taking hold of one, he slipped it into the lock and turned. A faint *click* confirmed that he'd unlocked it.

Did Griffin know Dick had the keys to his home?

The door opened, and he removed his shoes. Once he stepped inside, he pulled a knife from its sheath.

He was here to hunt, but little did he know, he was now the hunted.

CHAPTER TWENTY

MY PULSE QUICKENED under my skin. No wonder my wolf had gotten antsy. Both my animal and human sides knew that Dick wouldn't just give up and walk away from all of this. He'd have to try something.

I'd expected him to try to frame Griffin again, or maybe cash in some favors with other council members.

Not murder.

Although, if he was, in fact, the man who wanted me for breeding, I shouldn't be surprised. Still, even if he didn't have a problem with ordering death, being the one to inflict it was a whole different story.

I knew it all too well. Every person I'd killed haunted my dreams, breaking my heart all over again. Yes, every single one of them had been trying to hurt me, and I'd killed in self-defense, but each life was precious. Taking someone's life wasn't something to relish or reminisce about. It festered inside you, and in some ways, I remembered those people better than even my own parents' faces.

That was telling in itself.

Dick scanned the den. However, his attention never went behind the couch or to the walls. He was too busy looking in the corners to check places someone would actually hide.

Dick had no clue what the hell he was doing.

A desperate gleam filled his eyes, and he began to shake. The moonlight reflected off the edge of the knife, casting diamond-like patterns across the room.

Rashness was both a blessing and a curse. Dick was willing to do whatever it took to stay in the city, but his foolishness had clouded his judgment.

His breathing was short and shallow, which informed me that his mind was unfocused. Taking him down should be easy, but I knew that underestimating your opponent made you cocky and arrogant. I had to prepare for the worst-case scenario in which he would be a formidable enemy.

"This will be over soon," he breathed. "Kill the girl, then Griffin, and it'll all go away."

If I were a normal wolf, I wouldn't have been able to hear the words, but he'd confirmed my suspicions about his intent.

He wouldn't be getting close to my mate.

"Are you sure about that?" I asked, staying crouched.

My voice faintly echoed around the room, making it so he couldn't nail down my location.

"Sterlyn?" He startled and sniffed. "Is that you?" He took a step deeper into the room, where he should have been able to pick up my scent now that he was indoors.

"Nope." I wanted to infuriate him. "It's the boogeyman."

He placed his knife back in its sheath as if he didn't think I saw it. "I just had something I needed to get off my chest and knew Griffin wouldn't answer my calls or open the door."

At least this time, he was being careful with what he said. There was no stench of a lie. "Is that so? What do you need to get off your chest?" I wanted to see how far he'd go. What all he would be willing to say. "I'm all ears."

"Funny." He chuckled lightly as he took a few steps closer to me.

He was sniffing me out but trying to pretend like he wasn't. "You aren't a man, so I find telling you hardly worthy of my time."

Did he think I was stupid because I was a female? Like he thought that I would just believe whatever he had to say. Wanting to throw him off-kilter, I stood, revealing my exact location. "You're right. I'm so glad you brought that to my attention. Now my boobs and vagina make *so* much more sense."

"Do you think your smart mouth makes you appear strong?" He faced me and frowned. "I don't understand why Griffin and Killian dote on you. You're just a woman trying to live in a man's world. Pathetic."

Pathetic.

That was what he had the gall to call me.

"Me? Pathetic?" Rage brushed against me, but I let it simmer. We weren't fighting yet, and there was so much I had to say. It was about damn time I got some things off *my* chest. "You're the one who tried to set up Griffin so you could steal his power instead of challenging him like a real alpha would do. You're the one who lives in this city, afraid to go outside the walls for too long because God knows why. You're the one who pushed his daughter to try to lock down a man who had no interest in being with her. And you're the one who will let others fight but isn't willing to risk your own neck in those battles. You're a coward, and now no one respects you."

He straightened his back as he marched closer to me, stopping in front of the couch I stood behind it. He sneered. "A true leader realizes that staying safe is the only thing that makes sense. Why should I be fighting the battles when I can pull the strings?"

"Because you should never ask someone to do something that you wouldn't do yourself." Dad had taught me that, too. He'd taught me so much that I'd taken for granted. My heart ached since I would never be able to thank him, but now wasn't the time for mourning. "A true alpha leads by example. If every one of the people who looked up to you followed your lead, nothing would get done. They'd be hiding out in their homes, waiting for someone else to do the very things they're too scared to do themselves."

"Don't act like you know me." His voice grew louder. "You don't know shit. You're just some alpha wannabe who landed Griffin for what he could get you. The only thing you're good for is breeding, but the angels won't let you live long enough for that to happen. You screwed yourself by coming out."

Maybe.

I had a feeling that a war was coming, but right now, the imminent threat was Dick. "You're just upset that they found out about me when you wanted to keep my existence hidden. Why exactly was that?" I wanted him to admit it. I needed to hear him say everything he'd done, not only to me, but to my former pack.

"Just like a woman, thinking I have to explain myself to you." His hand went back to where his knife hid under his polo shirt. "I don't owe you anything."

He was getting ready to attack. At least we were away from Griffin. There would be no risk of my mate becoming injured. I tensed and inhaled deeply, clearing my mind.

Just as I expected, he pulled his knife and jumped at me. His wide eyes locked on my heart, telling me exactly where he was aiming.

He had no training whatsoever. He'd been sheltered his entire life and had never practiced battling another wolf because of his position. His cockiness would be the death of him because I refused to let him live after this.

He'd had my brother kidnapped, slaughtered my family and pack, had me hunted, and now wanted to kill me and my mate. He put everyone I loved at risk with each breath.

I bent and rolled out of the way, making him land awkwardly. Standing to face him, I found the front half of his body slumped over the back of the couch. He'd expected the knife to lodge into my chest, keeping him upright.

Struggling, he tried to straighten, but before he could get off the couch, I punched him in the face. As I pulled back, he sliced my arm with the knife, and my blood spattered onto the couch. The metallic scent almost made me gag, but I breathed through my mouth, lessening the impact.

"You stupid bitch," he bellowed.

Sterlyn? Griffin's voice popped into my mind. *What the fuck is going on?*

Shit, I'd hoped we wouldn't wake him, but that had obviously been stupid. Dick wasn't leaving without killing us, so it wasn't like Griffin would sleep through it all. *Dick is here and attacking us.*

"I've been wanting to hurt you since the first day I laid eyes on you." Dick rubbed his jaw as he got back on his feet and stalked around the couch toward me. "I should've had you killed that day. It's one of the biggest regrets of my life."

One. Wow, the fact that he admitted he had regrets kind of shocked me. He seemed like the kind of guy who thought his shit didn't stink when everyone around him could smell it. "Well, you won't be living much longer to dwell on it."

"You think you're going to win?" He laughed maniacally. "You have no idea who you're up against."

"Oh, but I do." I knew exactly who he was. "A man desperate for power who's willing to sacrifice everything to get to the top. Maybe even kill his best friend so the man's son would spiral and he could swoop in and be the hero."

He laughed darkly. "You think I killed Atticus? I would never have done that."

I expected the stench of a lie, but it never came. I'd been so certain that he'd been involved, given that Ulva and Atticus had been at the Hardings' house for dinner. Atticus's death had led Dick into a stronger position, but maybe I did have that part wrong, which didn't sit well with me. "And yet, you set up his son? Doesn't that kind of counter the argument?"

"You stupid bitch." He held up the knife, making it clear what his next move would be. "I'm not telling you anything."

He lunged at me, the knife aiming for my shoulder, and I ducked the blow. I kneed him in the stomach, causing him to stumble back several steps.

Griffin's footsteps pounded down the hallway toward us, which made Dick's nostrils flare.

"You ruin everything." Hate filled each one of his words. "This was supposed to be easy, and yet, here we are again."

"You still have a chance to cut your losses and climb back over the railing to your own balcony." Ugh, I knew I needed to kill him, but I had to give him one last chance. People could be redeemed if they wanted it themselves. Maybe this was his rock bottom, but I doubted it. Darkness circled him like a plague.

"I can't." He sighed, and his face lined with regret or worry. "This is all I have left."

He attacked again, this time not using the weight of his body. Instead of aiming to kill, his intent was now to injure. He swung the knife around crazily, making it so I couldn't get near him.

I'm coming in from the other side, Griffin linked. *Just stay safe, I'll handle him.*

Well, that was easier said than done. Dick had completely lost his marbles. At this point, he wanted only to inflict pain, and he didn't give a damn about himself, which made me sad. Was power that important to him that he'd rather die and leave his family behind than be disgraced? What kind of mate and father did that make him? If anything, it put him in an even poorer light. I almost felt bad for Luna. There was no telling the kind of hell she'd been raised in. No wonder she was a psycho, too.

He picked up his pace as he rushed me, his face contorting as if fighting his alpha's call. With each step he advanced, I countered, looking for something to help me. My wolf surged forward, and fur sprouted along my body. Griffin was close, and I didn't want him to get hurt, which was quite possible with the way Dick was acting.

My bones cracked as my body shifted into wolf form. Before I was on all fours, Dick grazed my wolf in the shoulder, struggling to continue the fight as Griffin growled. At least it wasn't an injury that I couldn't bounce back from. I bit into his wrist, and the knife clattered to the floor. Then I lowered my head and steamrolled Dick into the wall.

"No!" he yelled as his fingers dug into my fur. His nails bit into my skin, but his hand loosened of its own accord.

The alpha will was finally taking hold.

Griffin flashed past me, running to the spot where Dick and I had been moments ago, but I had to stay focused on Dick.

I took a step back, snarling and baring my teeth at the older man. Now that Griffin was here, there was no way he could win.

"You need to stop right now," Griffin rasped from behind me. "Leave Sterlyn alone and get the fuck out of my house."

"Do you think it's that easy?" Dick snorted as he held his arms wide. "That you can cast me and my family out and we'll just go all obediently? You aren't meant to be the alpha here. I am."

I wished I could talk sense into him, but you couldn't rationalize with someone who'd lost their damn mind.

"Dick, please," Griffin begged. "Don't make it come to this. All you have to do is stand down. You can find another pack. It's not like this is the end of the world."

"But it *is* the end of the world." He breathed raggedly. "And I have to do whatever it takes to right the wrong." He reached for my neck, and I growled, ready to bite him.

"Damn it," Griffin bellowed as he appeared beside me with Dick's knife in hand. He plunged it into Dick's heart, and the older man gasped. His hands dropped to his sides as his back fell against the wall and he slowly slid to his ass.

My heart hurt that my mate had been put in this position. He'd loved this man at one time, and I'd never wanted him to have to live through this guilt and pain.

Ulva's footsteps came running down the hall, and they stopped when they came into the room.

I couldn't tear my eyes away from Dick until he was dead, so I couldn't check on her.

"You actually did it," Dick sputtered and glanced at the knife protruding from his chest. "I...I didn't think you had the balls."

"When it comes to protecting those I love, I've learned that I'm willing to do whatever it takes." Griffin ran his fingers through my fur as he kept his gaze on the man. "And you've made it clear that you have no problem hurting anyone as long as you get what you want."

"Ahhh, if only you knew everything." Dick chuckled as blood trickled from the corner of his mouth onto his shirt. "You think you have all the answers, but you have no fucking clue."

My blood ran cold at the implications.

"What do you mean?" Griffin tensed as he squatted to be on eye level with the man. "What don't I know?"

The question hung over us like a cloud as Dick coughed, splattering the blood now pouring from his mouth. His heartbeat was slowing, and he wouldn't be alive too much longer.

I urged Griffin to find out what he knew before it was too late. I growled, wishing I were still in human form now that his mother was here.

"Dick, please." Griffin sounded almost broken. "What do you mean? At least tell me that."

"I want you to know that I loved your father," Dick whispered as his black eyes lightened. The hate that was always present began to disappear. "When he died, I lost a part of myself, too."

Sincerity dripped from his words, and some of the darkness that swirled inside him began to dissipate, which didn't make sense to me.

"Okay, but what did you mean?" Griffin asked desperately. "Do you want to leave Luna and Saga behind with secrets hanging over their heads?"

Dick flinched and took a shallow breath as death settled over him. "You will never win." Then his heart stopped beating.

"Damn it!" Griffin yelled as he pounded his hand against Dick's chest. "Tell me what I need to know."

But there was no point. Dick couldn't answer him any longer.

I nuzzled Griffin's side, trying to comfort him, but my mate wasn't here with me. He continued beating on the dead man's chest, screaming for an answer.

Ulva gasped, and I turned to find her in the hallway in a pale blue nightgown. Her mouth dropped in horror as she watched her son in his frenzied state.

This whole situation was a clusterfuck, and I couldn't do a damn thing in wolf form. I hated leaving Griffin like this, but the thought of shifting back into human form in front of his mother didn't sit well with me. I could shift and return within a minute.

I rushed back to Griffin's room, passing his mother. She stood there, frozen, her hand on her throat, watching her son lose control. Her being unable to feel his devastation was a good thing. That was all on me, and it broke my heart. His feelings of hatred, love, and betrayal mixed together as he came to grips with the knowledge that even in death, Dick hadn't tried to help him.

When I entered the bedroom, I shifted back into human form, then quickly grabbed one of Griffin's long shirts and some boxers and threw them on.

Within seconds, I was back in the living room.

As I passed Ulva, she grabbed my arm and begged, "Please help him. You're the only one who can get through to him right now."

I nodded and patted her arm as I reassured her, "That's the plan."

"Of course it is." She waved a hand in front of her face like she was trying to dry tears before they fell. "You already knew that."

Giving her a sad smile, I walked past her and hurried to my mate. His face was the color of a tomato as his fingers, coated with Dick's blood, tugged at the edges of his hair. "No." Tears dripped down his face, causing sections of his gray shirt to darken. "He was supposed to leave in the morning. Not die."

My heart broke for him, and I took some of his pain into myself. "Hey." I placed a hand on his shoulder, hoping my touch and voice would at least pull him out of his current state. I continued, wanting him to know that I was here. "I'm sorry."

"You're sorry?" Griffin repeated as he shook his head. He looked at me and inhaled sharply. "You've done absolutely nothing wrong. He forced our hand."

"He did." I wanted him to know that I agreed with that. Sometimes it was easy to doubt our decisions. "I just wished I had killed him, not you."

"I won't lie." He reached out to cup my face but stopped when he saw his fingers coated with blood. He blew out a breath and dropped his hand back to his side. "He was determined to kill you. I would do it all over again because keeping you safe is my top priority." His love bled through our bond, so much stronger than the pain of losing Dick. "Your life will always come before anyone else's."

My life wasn't worth more than any other person's, but I knew that he'd disagree. So I said the only thing that made sense: "I love you."

"I love you, too." He kissed my lips. "And at least this is over."

"But is it?" Dick's last words haunted me. "He made it sound like he wasn't working alone."

"We know Azbogah is involved." He frowned. "So that's not shocking information. Dick was just trying to unnerve us."

That could be it, but I wasn't sure. Either way, we still had to deal with Dick's death.

"You two go get cleaned up," Ulva said as she appeared beside us. "I'll call some guards to take care of the body. Maybe we can get some decent rest now that this asshole is gone."

I wanted to argue, but my mate needed to get clean. The sooner he washed off the blood and got into fresh clothes, the better his mental state would become. For now, fortunately, the battle was over.

CHAPTER TWENTY-ONE

AFTER THE RESTLESS night at the apartment, which included the Shadow City police getting involved since Dick had died in the alpha wolf's home, I almost cried in relief when we pulled into Killian's pack neighborhood and I saw our house.

Just getting out of the city and away from all the politics put me more at ease...almost.

"Do you think when Julius and Bart get here that your brother might be willing to tell us information now?" Griffin growled. "I mean, he could've helped us before now."

Part of me wanted to take up for my resurrected brother, but Griffin was right. I understood that Julius didn't trust us, especially with how he was raised. However, I was done being patient. We had to make sure both he and I were safe.

I linked with Bart, *We're back at the house. How much longer until you two get here?*

We're walking into your backyard now, he answered. *Just know he's nervous.*

Oh, I knew that. I could feel it through our connection, but I worked to lock it down. I couldn't let Julius influence me. I'd been so concerned with his feelings and well-being that I'd put Griffin and myself at risk. That time was over. I just hoped that Dick had been the person in charge of hunting me and my pack. *Doesn't matter. Do you think he'll tell us anything?*

Yes, I think he's ready to come clean. Bart paused. *Hearing that you were attacked again bothered him.*

Well, there was that.

When we pulled into the garage, I opened the door, eager to get the conversation going. "I'm going to let them in. They're in the back-yard now."

"Okay, but Sterlyn..." Griffin grabbed my hand. *If he doesn't cooperate, we've got—*

I cut him off, not wanting to hear it. *I get it. The games are over. He puts everything on the table, or I'll have to figure out a way to punish him without him feeling like we're turning our backs on him.* He was family and a silver wolf, after all.

Appeased, he let me go, and I marched straight for the door. When I opened it, Bart and Julius were standing right there, their floral, musky scent invading my nose.

Julius averted his eyes to the ground, not even attempting to challenge me, and his usual animosity was absent.

My concern for him coiled inside me, and I had to make a conscious decision to push it down. "Thanks for coming so quickly. Please come in."

"I'm glad you're safe and well." Bart hugged me and kissed the side of my head. "But you are the alpha of our kind, so I'm also not surprised."

Being around him was nice. He reminded me of my father and had the same temperament. The association was bittersweet, but I clung to it.

I stepped out of the way, not wanting too many of the guards outside to take notice of them. Griffin had talked with the guards who were watching the back, but the fewer who knew about Bart and Julius, the better. They entered the house, heading directly to the living room, where Griffin waited, as tense as if he were preparing for a fight.

I hoped it didn't come to that, but I couldn't blame my mate for his demeanor. The best course of action was to get everything in the open and let things fall into place. That was something Mom taught me when having candid conversations with Dad. She'd say, "Men aren't mind readers, and they aren't very intuitive about certain things. Be assertive with them, and remember that it does not, in fact, make you a bitch or aggressive. Those are terms that men who aren't as confident as your father call women when women act the same as they do."

I pulled out a picture Ulva had given me of her, Atticus, Dick, and Saga, taken a few weeks before Atticus died. "Was this the man who gave the order to kidnap me?" I asked my brother.

His eyes flicked to the picture, and he grew pale. "Yes, that's Topper."

"I wish you'd known his real name." I tried keeping my voice even, but a little frustration leaked through as my throat tightened. "This is the man who was trying to steal Shadow City away from *my mate*."

"I didn't know that." Julius lifted his hand. "The way he talked and acted, I thought he didn't even live in the city."

"Wait." Griffin's hands clenched. "Dick wanted to *breed* with my mate?"

"No!" Julius shook his head, then paused. "At least, I don't think so. When he was talking about it on the phone, it sounded as if she was intended for someone else. Topper said that person was weak, but he needed an ally. That was almost two years ago. I haven't seen him since then."

My stomach dropped. He *did* have an accomplice. "Who was he working with?"

"I...I don't know." Julius sighed and walked over to the windows to look out. "I grew up with a woman who was disinterested in me, who made sure I had the bare necessities and trained hard each day with instructors they brought over with any sort of combat skills a non-shifting wolf could use. When he first met me at sixteen, Topper —Dick," he amended—"didn't seem comfortable with me and didn't want to be around me more than he had to. Almost as if he'd just found out about me. When he talked to some woman on the phone—I never met her, just heard her voice—she pointed out that Topper was meant to lead, and that some man named Atticus being dead was a blessing for everyone."

Heartbreak slammed into me as my mate heard how Dick had regarded his father. He'd already been through so much. I wished I could take this hurt away, but unfortunately, this was the world we lived in.

I wished, at least, that Julius knew more so we could take down every single asshole who'd caused our families pain. "Who sent all the people you trained?"

"Once again, they just showed up." Julius shrugged. "You have to understand, I was just trying to survive. All I knew was that Grace said that the people who saved me wanted me to train all those men because I had a natural talent for battle strategy, and if I didn't train them, they would kick me out. I had nowhere to go and no one to turn to."

I sighed, nearly over the conversation. The one thing we'd learned was that Dick was the contact, but there was someone else out there. "Where did you grow up?"

"In the house you were taken to." Julius pursed his lips. "I lived there my entire life, and two years ago, Grace left, right before Topp —Dick showed up. I've been on my own since then."

Most likely because they didn't want the lady to see Dick. Just another clue that there were so many more people involved than we'd originally thought. "How did you get your orders?"

"At first, Grace was the one who talked to whomever—until the day Dick appeared." Julius growled in frustration. "After that, he'd call me and tell me when people were coming, where to send people, and what training needed to be accomplished. They kept me out of the loop for the most part."

It was as if every time I felt like we were getting closer to the truth, we took several steps back.

I hated to keep pushing, but we needed answers. "I've seen at least two guys take their own life instead of being captured. You trained them—why did they do that?"

"Because if they're captured, their families will die." Julius grimaced. "It's for safety measures so no identities get released. I was willing to run because I didn't have anyone to risk."

His words hit hard. He was that alone.

"Look, he's telling the truth." Bart sighed. "We all know it. At least part of his hellacious past is gone."

Yeah, maybe. But I hadn't gotten much closer to the truth other than realizing that someone else was still out there. A woman—which didn't make sense, as Dick had such a problem with people of that gender being in charge.

"Look, I'm sorry, but...I need some time." Julius ran his hands through his hair, and his pain pulsed through me. "I...I just..." He turned and walked out the back door, rushing toward the woods.

I took a step to go after him, but Bart grabbed my arm. "It's best if you let him go for now. He's been on his own a long time, and has to process things his way."

"I hate that I caused him pain, but we've got to get some answers." The longer we stayed in the dark, the more death and chaos might result.

Bart patted my arm. "I know. But now he's connected with his wolf. He's mellowing out, though it's going to take a little time. Don't push too hard, or he might shut down again. Let me go run with him, and I'll connect with you later."

"Okay," I sighed as Bart hurried after him.

Still, I couldn't help but think that maybe this would've all been over if Julius had told us everything to begin with.

A few weeks later, Sierra entered Griffin's Shadow Ridge kitchen and yawned, placing several bags of food from Dick's Bar on the table. "So, what are we doing tonight?"

I'd hoped that they would change the establishment's name, but Saga had moved into the back of the restaurant in Dick's office and insisted on keeping it the same. Almost as if it would serve as a reminder of what we'd done to them.

I wanted Sierra to quit, but she was insistent that the tips made it all worthwhile. I finally relented when she promised she'd let us know if something went wrong or if anyone shady showed up.

"We?" Griffin arched an eyebrow and placed some canned drinks on the table. He sat in the seat closest to me and pointed at one of my best friends. "Why does she always assume that she's hanging out with us?"

"Because she's part of the group." I winked at Sierra and settled back, feeling the happiest I'd felt in forever.

Rosemary sat on the other side of me with Killian next to her. We had one open seat that Sierra had dubbed hers since the first night we'd all piled in here together.

"And I always feed you." Sierra pulled out a styrofoam box that had *Griffin* written on it. "But I mean, if I've overstayed my welcome, I can take this and the rest of the food back to my house."

"*Your* house?" Killian snorted. "Can you even still claim it? You're still staying here with the rest of us."

"Speaking of which, why are we all still staying together?" Griffin glared at everyone. "I mean, maybe Sterlyn and I could get acclimated to our *own* space."

"Sorry, but I want to spend more time with my distant cousin and be here, since this whole predicament isn't over." Rosemary snatched the container with her name. "We have a lot of catching up to do, and Mom thinks it would be wise for me to stay out of the city while things are so tense with the angels. She's afraid a civil war could break out at any second."

When I'd told Rosemary the truth about my heritage, her face had lit up with surprise and relief. She'd felt a strange connection with me that she hadn't understood, since I was all wolf. But the revelation of our real relationship explained our familial pull toward each other and mine to Yehaliah when I'd seen her in the council room. Apparently, it was my angel genes recognizing our family.

After Dick died and Luna and Saga were banished, the mood in Shadow City had darkened. The angels were beginning to divide, either siding with Rosemary's parents or Azbogah. Of course, the other races weren't thrilled about Dick being kicked out of the city and his subsequent death, but there was no denying that Dick had broken into Griffin's house. However, Griffin killing Dick had elevated his alpha status within the shifter community. The change was good, but I hated that it had taken that for the shifters to actually look at him as their leader.

A leader should inspire confidence, not instill fear, and I had a feeling that Griffin's acceptance was due to the latter at the moment.

Our best bet was to let things calm down and go back into the city in the next couple of weeks for the first council meeting after the entire debacle. We'd been gone for a few weeks now, and the tension was still at a boiling point. We weren't hiding, but we didn't want to stir up more drama by just being seen.

Yelahiah had visited us a few nights after we'd returned to Griffin's Shadow Ridge home and told me her side of the story. She'd shared with me her guilt and regret for not standing firm with her brother. She'd never thought it would go that far, but when she'd realized that his death was imminent, she'd taken a stand beside him.

By then, it had been too late.

She'd carried the guilt with her for so long, but she wanted to have a relationship with me and the rest of the silver wolves. She said that we were family and that our angel side was just as strong as it had been all those centuries ago. Angel magic didn't dilute even when they mated with other races—rather, the power manifested over generations and remained just as strong. That was why, when Griffin and I finally had a child, they'd be a full-blooded silver wolf, too, and the oldest would be the future true alpha heir of both packs with our second child being the spare.

"Speaking of tense, how're Julius and Bart?" Sierra asked as she plopped into her seat. "I figured we'd have seen more of them by now."

"We met with them yesterday." For now, they were staying out of sight. Until things were settled with Shadow City, I didn't want to make it easy for anyone to find the remainder of the silver wolves. I didn't want to risk them being slaughtered, too. "They're at the new location Dad was developing. Apparently, a few houses have been finished, so they're staying there."

"Is Julius still being ornery?" Killian asked, leaning toward Rosemary.

"Actually, he isn't." He didn't stare at me with outright contempt anymore. He'd finally shifted and was more settled with his wolf, which hopefully changed things. "He wasn't overly friendly, either, but he confirmed that Dick was who he'd been working with."

"I still don't trust him." Griffin took a bite of his hamburger and talked around the food. "He went against his own race and family once—he could be biding his time to do it again."

This was something he and I had agreed to disagree on. I couldn't blame him for feeling that way because if the shoe were on the other foot and someone had tried to kidnap Griffin, I wouldn't have been too forgiving, either.

"Okay, enough depressing talk." Sierra clapped her hands. "It's movie night. Now, show of hands, who wants to watch *Mean Girls*? Majority wins."

"Is there even a point to this?" Griffin sighed and shook his head.

Killian shook his head. "Nope, but we need to find another guy to hang out with us so it's a split vote. I swear, my pecs are softening from the amount of estrogen we're around nightly."

"Hey." Sierra jumped to her feet and grabbed her box of food. "Rules are rules, so deal with it."

GRIFFIN SHUT the door to our bedroom, then grabbed my waist and pulled me against his chest. He linked, *I swear, Sierra better be glad you enjoy those movies, or I'd throw a fit.*

I wrapped my arms around his shoulders and grinned. *Is there anything that you wouldn't do for me?*

Nothing, he replied, kissing me.

His tongue brushed my lips, and I opened my mouth, letting him inside. Every touch and time we were together was better than the last. Each day, I fell more madly in love with him, to the point that it was almost scary, but I wouldn't have it any other way.

The last week had been some of the best times we'd ever had. The fact that my secret was out was freeing. Our group had been able to run together without fear of someone finding out what I was. Despite the alpha duties we were attending to, we got a lot more alone time, and without a constant threat hovering over us.

You taste so good. He growled. *Better than any dessert.*

Really, now? I teased as my hand brushed down his chest and below.

He was hard and ready, and I was a very willing participant. I unfastened his jeans, ready to see him in all his naked glory. His body was perfect, and I couldn't wait for it to be all over me.

God, I love you so damn much. He pulled back and removed all of his clothes. His hazel eyes darkened to almost liquid gold as he advanced toward me. He stalked me like I was his prey, and I loved it.

He was the only person I'd ever been thrilled to feel that way with.

My body warmed just at the promise, and I was beyond ready for him. The back of my knees hit the side of the bed, and I fell onto the mattress, leaving my silver hair fanning out around me.

"You are so beautiful." He paused, studying me, his face filled with adoration. "I don't know what I've ever done to deserve you, but there are definitely no take-backs."

"Are you sure?" I teased. "I mean, maybe I could find—"

He covered my body with his and nipped my lips. *You finish that sentence, and you'll have to be punished.*

Promises, promises.

The scent of our arousal hung heavy around us, and his breath caught. He grabbed the collar of my shirt and ripped the material away from my body.

I gasped with surprise but also with need. He'd never done something like that before, and the possessiveness and desperation were the perfect aphrodisiacs. His hand unfastened my bra as his mouth captured my nipple.

My body arched against him, already wanting him inside me. *Griffin.*

He tensed as I slipped my hand between us, touching him. I stroked him, and his body coiled on top of me.

Oh, God. He moaned as he rolled to the side of me. He pulled back to yank down my yoga pants and growled. *No panties.*

I thought you might like that. I quickened my pace, enjoying the control I had over him.

Hell, yeah. His fingers slipped between my legs, and the two of us rubbed one another, bringing each other close to the edge.

The pressure built inside me, and I grabbed his hand, yanking it aside. I straddled him, guiding him inside me, and then rode him hard.

There was no gentle build to it, as close as I already was to the edge. He bucked against me while his fingers dug into my waist, turning me on even more. I spread my legs further apart, letting him slide in as deep as he could go.

Our bodies slicked with sweat as pleasure rocked through us. Our feelings merged together, making our orgasms even more intense as our bodies convulsed in pleasure.

"Holy shit," he rasped, raising himself to kiss me once more. *That was amazing.*

Yes, it was.

A loud knock sounded on the door, and Killian said, "We've got a huge problem. Two of the guards have disappeared, and their connection has gone cold."

The implication rang clear. "You think they're dead?" I asked.

"Yes," he said tensely. "And whoever is behind it all is here."

CHAPTER TWENTY-TWO

THE MOMENT of solitude and pleasure vanished. My body tensed as I hurriedly dressed again.

Both of us rushed, desperate to get outside and see what we were facing. Each moment we were blind to the threat meant the attackers had longer to get into prime position.

Dick said we had no clue who we were up against. That was what I'd been worried about when we returned home a week ago, but when nothing happened in those first few days. I should've known that our unknown enemies would wait long enough for us to let our guard drop.

He'd told the truth, and there was someone else after us.

Do you think it's Azbogah and his followers? Griffin asked as he buttoned his jeans.

I slipped my shirt over my head. *No, I don't. Azbogah is an in-your-face type of person. He wouldn't do a sneak attack. He wants a production to make himself feel more powerful. This is whoever was working with Dick...or whoever Dick was working for.*

Maybe Julius knew this was going to happen, Griffin growled, watching me put my jeans back on.

Thinking the worst of my brother was easy. We hadn't gotten off on the right foot with him trying to attack me and all, but he hadn't known that Dick had my pack slaughtered. *When he said Dick was the main person, he wasn't lying. You know that.* There had been no signs, neither smell or physical tells like a racing heart, of a lie.

More guards are being attacked. Killian connected with us again using the pack links we now shared. *The enemy is surrounding us.*

Any clue who it is? Griffin asked as he opened the bedroom door.

No, but they're all shifters, Killian said as worry pulsed through our pack bond. *I'm shifting and joining the fight now.*

We entered the living room just as Killian opened the back door, with Sierra and Rosemary right behind him.

"I'm going to fly around and see what I can see. I wish Mom and Dad could help, but they have their hands full in the city with all the problems Azbogah is creating." Rosemary looked at me. "From the sound of it, you need to get Bart and the silver wolves over here to fight."

I hated to do that, but the sounds of howls and screams wailed outside. Whoever was attacking us was pulling out all the stops, and the heartbreak pouring from Killian informed me that it was worse than I had initially understood. We needed backup, and it would take Bart and his pack at least ten minutes to get to us. Every second could mean another life, which was unacceptable.

Are you and the others able to get here quickly? I linked to Bart, not bothering to beat around the bush. I allowed my alarm to penetrate the bond. He needed to realize how bad of a situation we were in.

Of course. Bart answered immediately. *What's wrong?*

Whoever was working with Dick is here.

Shit. Bart sighed. *I'll get Cyrus and the pack, and we'll be there shortly.*

I hated to be that person, but I had to ask. *Are you sure bringing Julius is the right thing? If he knows the attacker...* I trailed off, trying not to say too much. However, my lack of words probably spoke volumes.

The one time I'd called my brother by his birth name, he'd flipped out on me. Yet, Bart had been calling him Cyrus since we'd first met him at my old house. I tried not to let it bother me, but I was slightly jealous that they'd gotten closer while my twin didn't seem to want much to do with me.

Look, I know things are strained between the two of you, but he's changing. Bart's voice softened. *I promise, if I see any hint of him going out of line, I'll deal with him. He still hasn't been able to control his emotions and thoughts very well when situations get intense, so I'll know.*

Even though I wanted to push the conversation further, we didn't have time to argue. The longer we took to spring into action, the more people would get hurt. *Fine, just...be careful getting here.*

We'll take the woods, Bart replied. *I'll let you know when we're near.* He ended the connection between us.

The new land Dad had purchased for us was even closer to Shadow Ridge than my hometown was. I couldn't help but wonder if Dad had thought the same thing I did when we were found—hiding wouldn't get us far. The closer proximity made me think that he had, that he was working on a strategic plan to announce our presence.

The best way to fight an enemy was to come out of hiding. That had taken me a moment to realize, given we were being attacked right now. But at least it was all coming to a head instead of the small attacks they'd been focusing solely on me.

I linked with Killian and Griffin, *They're on their way.* I ran outside after Killian with Griffin cursing behind me.

My steps slowed as I took in the horror. At least twenty enemies were trying to get to the house. Killian was fighting a sandy brown wolf who appeared to be almost as strong as he was.

I scanned the area, trying to determine who needed the most help. Two bear shifters were in animal form, fighting four guards in human form, while the rest of the fighters were wolves. A few of our guards had shifted, and the ones who had remained human were using their guns to fend off the bears.

My wolf surged forward, and my clothes ripped from my body as I landed on four legs.

Damn it, Sterlyn, Griffin said angrily. *This has to end.* His bones cracked as he followed suit, shifting into his animal form.

We should've taken Dick's warning more seriously. This was partially my fault, but remorse could be felt later. Right now, I had to focus on the matter at hand—kicking ass.

Sierra shrieked as a sable wolf attacked her mid-shift, the wolf taking advantage of her moment of weakness.

I'll help her. Griffin ran in her direction.

That was for the best because I wanted to help the human guards with the bears, who were large and not the easiest to injure. Only two other races were harder to fight, which were angels and dragons. However, Dad told me that the fae dragons kept to their realm, and the few that had moved to Earth had disappeared a long time ago, even before the birth of silver wolves.

Pushing off my paws, I reached our guards in record time. All of the enemy wolves were engaged in battle, and our people seemed to be holding their own.

A black bear threw his head back and roared as he stood on his back feet. The four guards paid attention to him, as he sounded like he was going to attack. But as they raised their guns to fire at him, the brown grizzly charged forward, using the other bear as a distraction.

The grizzly used its speed as its biggest asset.

The moon was near full again, and I tapped into my moon powers, tugging on them harder than ever before. My wolf raced across the small clearing, and I reached the grizzly just a few feet from his target. I bit into his shoulder as his head swung in my direction.

"Sterlyn!" the tallest guard yelled, aware of what was happening. He pivoted his gun toward the grizzly, but sharp teeth slashed into my side before he fired.

I whimpered, and my jaw slackened of its own accord. White-hot pain stole my breath, forcing my mind to race.

The bear released me, but his dark, soulless eyes stayed locked on me. Blood dripped from his mouth as he raised a paw to claw at my other side. He was purposely not going for kill shots, which petrified me.

Whoever was leading them still wanted me alive. I could only imagine why, and every possible thought churned my stomach.

A gun fired, and a bullet plunged right between the bear's eyes. The grizzly stumbled as the realization of what had happened settled over him. He crashed to the ground, causing the earth to shake. My side throbbed, but I didn't have time to focus on that. There were still so many shifters left to fight, and I could hear more battles farther away, which meant more enemies were coming.

The tall guard who had just protected me yelled to his friends, "The black bear is charging. Get a tranq and shoot him."

I climbed back to my feet and turned in time to watch the black bear sink its teeth into the thinnest guard's arm. The guard's blood-curdling scream churned my stomach.

"Not happening!" the shortest of the four yelled as he shot at the black bear, but the tranq whizzed past, missing its mark.

"Get back," the thickest guard yelled as he shot two consecutive rounds. The first bullet lodged into the black bear's front right leg, and the second nailed the chest. However, the chest wound wasn't fatal, and the bear didn't appear fazed. He jerked his head, thrashing the guard's arm. Crimson blood poured from the wound, soaking the grass.

The metallic stench turned my stomach, but I breathed through my mouth. I hurriedly limped toward the bear, desperate to injure him enough that he couldn't cause any additional damage. Each time I breathed or moved, my own throbbing side almost knocked me down, but I pushed through, focusing on the air moving in and out of my lungs.

"You asshole," the thick guard yelled, and he lifted his gun to fire more. His rage was getting the best of him; he wasn't paying attention to his surroundings.

A cream wolf ran through the trees, its focus entirely on that guard. Just as the guard fired, the wolf lunged, aiming for the guard's neck.

Crouching down, I pushed hard, leaping farther than ever before. I collided with the cream wolf in midair, and my acceleration offset his forward motion, causing him to fall backward. He hit the ground with a loud thud, and I landed on top. I ripped out his throat, reducing our enemy count by one.

Gunfire continued, and I rolled off the dead wolf and faced the guards once more. This time, the remaining three uninjured guards shot at the black bear one by one. Each hit caused blood to trickle from the wounds. The bear tried to retreat, but the guards countered each move.

Now that the guards had it handled and could help the injured one, I needed to move on and help someone else. It would've been nice if I had inherited angel healing powers so I could help the short guard and myself, but that wasn't part of the silver wolf package.

Another wolf ran from the woods, stopping me in my tracks. The golden-bronze fur and overly perfumed musk told me exactly who it was—Luna.

Her Caribbean-blue eyes sparked with loathing as she slowed and stopped.

What the hell was she doing here? I linked with both Griffin and Killian, *Luna's here.*

Fuck me, Griffin bellowed. *I should've killed the whole family. Banishment wasn't enough.*

The darkness I felt from her before was nothing compared to this moment; evil swirled around her like a tornado. She bared her teeth at me and growled, making her message clear.

She wanted me dead, and she knew I was injured.

But that wouldn't stop me from kicking her ass, so I howled in warning. I wanted her to know this place was mine and she needed to get out.

Luna gave me a wolfy smile that somehow made her look more sinister than dopey. She trotted a few steps toward me, refusing to step back and cower.

I expected nothing less.

A snapping branch to the right made me fully aware of what she was doing. She was distracting me, the same way the black bear had the guards. However, I wouldn't allow them to get the jump on me. I pretended not to hear a thing and bared my teeth. I needed them to think that my hatred had blinded my senses.

Bart's voice popped into my mind. *We're almost there. How are you all holding up?*

Not wonderfully, but telling him that would make his pack more frantic and desperate. In other words—vulnerable. I needed them on top of their game and fully engaged with their surroundings. *We're managing, but I won't lie. Knowing you're close thrills me.* Hopefully, the others wouldn't be prepared for a group of silver wolves to join us. Dick must have thought that Julius and I were the only ones left alive. This had to give us an edge, or at least I had to believe that it did.

While I kept feigning that Luna had my entire focus, in my peripheral vision, I could see a black wolf trying to sneak toward me. The animal hovered close to the tree line, his coat nearly the color of the night. However, my eyes could make out each strand of fur, and his yellow eyes seemed as bright as flashlights to me.

Luna pawed the ground, stirring up dirt and grass. She danced around as if she were considering attacking me. If I hadn't been alerted to the black wolf, which was now only about ten feet away, her peculiar actions would have alerted me to something. She had no intention of fighting me, or she would've charged by now.

The black wolf dove toward me, looking to take out one of my paws and not going for a kill shot. That was actually smart, seeing as I was injured on that side already.

I jumped, and my injured muscles burned like they were being ripped apart. However, I managed to make the black wolf miss me completely and crash to the ground.

Extending my claws, I slashed the black wolf's fur and skin as I landed on top of him. He whimpered and tried to roll away, allowing my claws to rip across his neck and twist his head. His neck cracked from the momentum, and he fell limply to the side.

A snarl from Luna forced my gaze away from yet another person I'd killed and back on her as she retreated into the woods. Now she was running scared.

Oh, *hell*, no. That bitch wasn't getting away. Not this time.

CHAPTER TWENTY-THREE

NOT WILLING TO LET HER disappear, I linked with Griffin and Killian, *I'm going after Luna. She just tried to distract me while another wolf attacked me.*

Are you okay? Griffin asked with concern. *Are you injured?*

I'll be fine. I couldn't lie because he could feel the pain through our bond. But if I told him the extent of my wounds, he would be even more upset about me going after Luna, and worse, he'd be distracted. *Nothing that won't heal.* In fact, my magic was already kicking in, and the pain was beginning to lessen as the moon rose higher in the sky.

Maybe one of us should go with you. Killian wasn't thrilled with my actions, either.

No, you're all engaged in battle as is. If one of them went with me, that would expose another of our guards to additional attack. Right now, looking around, it seemed that we were evenly matched, and I felt bad leaving them. But I had a feeling Luna was the key to figuring out who the hell was behind this mess. Saga must have contacted the person Dick had been working with. *Besides, I'm already in the woods.*

Damn it, Sterlyn. Griffin growled. *Couldn't you have waited for one of us since you're hurt? Wait for me, please.*

Annoyance flared through me, but I took a deep, calming breath and kept my eyes locked on Luna running ahead. Griffin wasn't being controlling or possessive; he just hated that I was doing this alone. It had nothing to do with my fighting capabilities. *I would, but remember that last time, they had a boat. I don't want to chance her getting away.* If Luna thought we were winning, I could see her zooming off and leaving her allies behind. She was that kind of a narcissistic asshole. *Look, Bart is close by. I'll get him to join me. Does that work?*

Fine. Griffin sighed. *But the first sign that you might be in trouble, please promise me that you'll retreat.*

Now *that* was an easy promise to make. *I promise. You can't get rid of me that easily.*

Do I need to still be part of this conversation? Killian groaned. *I mean, I'm glad that my brother and sister are together—it makes family events so much easier—but I'd rather not hear the mushiness. It's going to distract me from my fight because if it gets much worse, I'll have to vomit.*

Wow, you have been hanging out with Sierra. Griffin snorted. *You've grown so dramatic.*

You know what? You can kiss my ass, Killian retorted.

Nope, sorry, man. Griffin's voice grew proud. *There's only one ass I kiss, and yours is definitely not it.*

See! Killian's voice grew higher. *I don't want to hear that shit.*

The trees flew past me as I kept my pace, despite their banter. *Let me know if you two need me. I'm going to contact Bart like I promised.*

I love you. Griffin's tone grew serious. *Call if you get in trouble. I'll get there as soon as I can.*

Be safe, sis, Killian said.

Love you both, I said before shutting down the connection.

Luna cut left, heading in the direction of the water, as I'd feared. That must have been how they'd arrived. Boats putted down the river so regularly, it wouldn't have alerted the guards. We were going to have to include a river watch in the future. Our enemies must have surveyed us long enough to know the extent of the perimeter we kept an eye on.

One of the key strategies Dad had pounded into me and driven into the other pack members' heads was to be unpredictable. If you had a set schedule, your enemy could easily identify holes in your defenses, leading to attacks that could take out a chunk of your manpower. That was likely what had happened here, and even though Killian and the guards were amazing, it showed that they didn't have the training that the silver wolves did. It was time to break down the divide and for all wolves to work together, because at the end of the day, we were on the same team.

To ensure that I didn't close the distance between Luna and me, I had to constantly adjust my pace. I didn't want to gain on her but rather to play up my injury and make her overconfident. The water's trickling grew louder. Time to link with Bart. *Hey, where are you?*

About a half a mile away from Griffin's backyard, Bart answered immediately, including all the other silver wolf pack members into our connection. *What's the status? It sounds like the battle is still going strong.*

I hadn't been part of a group pack link like this in a month. My heart warmed as the connections flared inside me—which gave me an idea. Why were we still operating in silos? All three of our packs could talk and strategize at once. I linked Killian and Griffin into the conversation so we could all hear one another. *I was there a few minutes ago, and it seemed like we were on equal footing. I'm thinking it wouldn't hurt to have a few of the silver wolves help fight by the house and a few join me.*

But right now, the focus needs to be on backing up Sterlyn, Griffin jumped in, ready to lead alongside me. *She's running after Dick's daughter, and we should assume she's being led into a trap.*

Where are you? Bart asked, concern wafting through the bond.

Heading to the river. We were slowly approaching the area of our first large battle, only weeks ago. Blood from both sides had coated the ground already. We didn't need more blood spilled, and yet, here we were. *There's a small cutout where a boat can anchor and have easy access to the woods while keeping passengers relatively dry when they disembark. We're about a quarter-mile from it.*

The closer I got, the more scents I smelled. There had to be at least eleven other people there, one of whom was Saga. *Dick's mate is here, too. I smell her.*

I picked up your scent, Julius linked. *On my way.*

That's not comforting, Griffin growled, not thrilled with my brother being the one to come help me.

The truth was, I didn't like it, either. Dick was the person who'd worked with him, but being around people who might remind Julius of that didn't sit well with me. For all I knew, he could decide to switch sides again.

You come here and help the guards near the house, Killian said, siding with Griffin. *Griffin and I will go after Sterlyn. We just can't leave, or our people will be slaughtered.*

No, that will take more time. Let the silver wolves join me. I appreciated how loyal Killian and Griffin were to me, but we couldn't afford to toss strategy aside and let our emotions get in the way. *They're closer, so stand your ground. This is the best way to end it all.*

Shadow City reinforcements are en route, too, Griffin informed us. *They should be here in the next few minutes. I alerted them as soon as we knew of the attack.*

That was good. We needed all the guards we could get. There could be more enemy shifters coming, but if Saga and Luna were here, that probably meant every one of Dick's fighters were here, too, or they wouldn't have risked coming. They'd assumed that they would take us out, which solidified that they didn't know about Bart and the other silver wolves.

The river came into view between the trees, and Luna increased her pace. Three boats floated in the water with several people in each one of them, poised as if they were ready to take off at any time. *There are three large boats here.*

Darrell and I will go with Cyrus to help Sterlyn, Bart said. *That should be enough to get us by, and the rest of the pack will come help Griffin and Killian until more guards arrive.*

Fine, but if Julius betrays us, Griffin linked, allowing his feelings of distrust to be felt by all, *then I'll kill him.*

I'm on your side, Julius tried to reassure him, but it fell flat. Things always seemed to fall flat when it came to his interactions with any of us, which made Griffin not trust him even more.

He won't, Bart reassured. *We're near Sterlyn now.*

I slowed my pace a few feet from the tree line of the river, not stepping into clear view. The three motorboats were in front of me, and Saga walked to the side of the middle boat with a hate-filled smirk as Luna raced toward it.

She cooed, "Good job, Luna. You actually managed to do something right, for once, unlike your father."

Her hateful, mocking tone sent a chill down my spine. Her once hidden soul swarmed with an evil that I'd never seen before. It coated her so thickly that her skin took on a demonic reddish glow.

"And you got the silver wolf I wanted all alone." Saga lifted her arms outward as her eyes locked on me. "She's injured, which will make things easier for us. We still have big plans for her." She snapped her fingers, and three men walked up behind her while six more—three in each of the other boats—turned their attention to me.

Her words rang inside my ears.

She still had big plans for me. She'd been in on this with Dick.

My stomach revolted at what the original plan had been for me. A fucking breeder. But with whom?

Honestly, not knowing the answer was probably best.

Luna had purposely led me here, but I'd expected that. What I hadn't expected was for these people to seriously be listening to Saga, though the darkness clinging to her told me enough. She must have had someone help hide her true self inside Shadow City, which was why I hadn't felt either good or bad from her—a witch must have aided her, similarly to how my brother had been spelled to appear dead.

Maybe it was the same witch.

Saga laughed heartily and placed a hand on her chest. "Even in animal form, I can see your confusion. You thought you had this all figured out, but you know nothing."

The man on Saga's right, who had a long scar down one cheek, moved as if to get off the boat. Saga lifted a hand and commanded, "Don't use the real guns. Get the tranq ones. We can't chance killing her."

He obeyed immediately, rushing off to do as he was told, but five others stayed, leaving their rifles pointed at me.

Holy shit, there was no hesitation. He thought of her as his superior. But Dick had been so against women leading.

Realization washed over me, making dread weigh down my body. This whole time, she'd been in charge, not Dick.

Rosemary landed next to me, the purple of her eyes glowing in the moonlight as she stared down Saga. "What would good ol' Dick say about you taking charge?"

Hope sparked in my chest. Out of everyone due to arrive, Rosemary could not have been timelier. She and I thought similarly. Even though we didn't have the mind-linking ability, she'd asked the exact question I'd been thinking.

"Who do you think has been in charge since the beginning?" Saga retorted. "In fact, it was easy getting his attention, but I had to play the submissive role. After all, Shadow City wolves don't take female alphas seriously. You didn't even suspect me." She frowned and gracefully climbed out of the boat. She walked past Luna and toward me, not even acknowledging her daughter's presence.

That was why she'd wanted to mate with Atticus. She was an alpha forced to play down her own power, so she had to get the strongest wolf possible to pick her for a chosen mate. She'd been working this angle for longer than Griffin and I had been alive. This had been a cold and calculated plan—no wonder we'd felt like we were behind for so long.

Julius overhearing a woman on the phone say Atticus being dead was a good thing made sense. Saga had somehow gotten pregnant soon after Ulva, to try to come into power that way, and had used Dick to strong-arm Griffin, using his grief against him.

"You got pregnant on purpose, didn't you, right after Ulva did? Luna is only a few months younger than Griffin," Rosemary said with a sneer.

Her eyes glazed over like she was going back in time. "Yes, when Ulva got pregnant and we learned it was a boy, I got my backup plan in place." She gestured at her daughter.

How the hell was that possible? She couldn't have known she was going to have a girl...unless a witch helped her.

Rosemary shook her head, and her eyes widened. "You wouldn't use magic—"

"Yes, I would. I have witch friends—" She paused, pursed her lips for a second, and giggled. "Okay, 'friends' is a stretch. Nonetheless, I have witches who will do my bidding because I have leverage over them, but that's a whole different story."

I stayed still, afraid to move. Her ramblings were filling in some serious holes and giving Bart and the others time to get closer before I had to fight. Silver wolves were strong, but I couldn't take on nine men by myself, especially when they were armed.

"God, this feels so good." She strolled closer to me, placing a hand on her chest. "I mean...despite all the bullshit, here I stand, in charge like I should've been all along. Dick wanted to work with Azbogah, but I should be the real leader of Shadow City. I can do things no man could do."

Tilting my head, I tried to look fascinated to encourage her to keep going. It wasn't like I could ask her questions in animal form.

"You're crazier than your mate." Rosemary snorted. "Was it the same witch who found the silver wolves that stole Sterlyn's brother?"

"Yes, I stumbled upon her granddaughter and used her as leverage. To get her granddaughter back, she had to steal the alpha heir. He was meant to be Luna's breeding partner so we could take over the entire wolf race, but your dumbass brother couldn't shift," she said, turning her attention to me. She sighed and rolled her eyes as if it had been a mere nuisance. Like he'd put her out instead of her actions trapping him in his human body. "And I couldn't risk your pack desperately searching for their alive, kidnapped alpha heir. So I killed them, making sure I could start over with you."

The woman was insane. The way she talked about my pack's death as if it were nothing and why she'd pushed Luna so hard at Griffin. Since she couldn't breed with the silver wolf, she needed to get her child angled as alpha mate.

The guard with a scar appeared beside her with the tranq gun in hand.

Shit, the others should be there at any second.

Rosemary's eyes flicked toward me, and she nodded slightly. She was trying to buy time for the others to catch up to us. "But then why kill Atticus and Sterlyn's pack?"

"I pushed Luna toward Griffin and used Julius to train my warriors. When Griffin hit puberty, his attention strayed to every other girl but her." She pointed at Luna and sneered. "She obviously needed a helping hand, so I invited Atticus and Ulva over for dinner one night and poisoned Atticus's food. I was nervous that someone would figure out that his death was abnormal, but the herbs the witch gave me weren't detected, so his death was documented as natural causes. Just an abnormality." Her nose wrinkled, and she glared at her daughter, who whined and cringed back. "And yet, Luna *still* couldn't capture the attention of a man mourning his father."

Luna whimpered and pawed at the ground.

She'd killed Atticus so that Griffin would be stricken with grief, allowing her daughter to finally lock him down. All the hate I felt for the girl was now replaced with pity.

But after Atticus died, Dick was also spiraling, and Saga was able to get him involved in her plan. A growl escaped before I could clamp it down. I had never hated anyone as much as I did her.

"Oh, shush. You've caused a lot of problems." Saga shook her head. "If it weren't for you, Griffin would still be an unfocused mess, and Dick would still be alive, but I guess it's all worth it now. I found someone who still wants you and will make an excellent mating partner for you." She pursed her lips and tilted her head. "Well, time's up." She glanced over at the guards. "Catch her now, and kill the angel. It's time to go."

The man with a scar lifted his gun, aiming at my shoulder. It wasn't a kill shot—they wanted to injure me so I couldn't fight.

No, I had to figure a way out of this.

CHAPTER TWENTY-FOUR

MY HEART POUNDED SO LOUDLY that my ears rang. I didn't
see an escape. I tore my gaze from the guards and scanned the area
for anything that could help me out of this mess. Bart, Julius, and
Darrell were so close that I could smell their floral musky scents, but I
was on my own.

Every bad situation I'd experienced had been caused by this
bitch, and I let the pain and rage build inside me. Normally, I would
attempt to calm the beast, but I needed to channel her strength to get
myself out of this situation. Even if I had only a nebulous idea of
what that solution might look like—at the moment, nothing was
coming to me.

Rosemary took to the sky, spinning round and round like a
tornado as I glanced frantically from side to side, knowing that the
seconds were counting down. If I even wanted a slight chance of
coming out of this unscathed, I had to make a move.

A few trees covered me, but the men ran from the boats. I
couldn't turn my back on them or run off because they could stumble
upon the silver wolves that would be here at any moment. I needed to

buy time. I tried scooting backward, deeper into thicker trees, but a bullet could travel faster than I could move.

Still, I couldn't just stand there and do nothing.

I refused to give up. I wouldn't give Saga that pleasure. It would make her victory that much sweeter, knowing she'd broken me. I'd go down fighting, even if it was futile.

My side twinged with pain, but I'd take it. The sharp throbbing had diminished to an ache, which made it easier to move...for now. Unless I was injured again.

As I leaped for the protection of the tree, I heard the cock of the tranq gun Scarface prepared to fire. A sinister chuckle escaped him. Assholes like him enjoyed being the predator with its rush of power. Unfortunately, my life was in his hands.

"Do *not* kill her," Saga commanded, obviously picking up on the guy's intent. "You have the tranq gun for a reason."

It would have been nice if she'd said that because she cared, but she didn't. She wanted me for something worse than death, and I'd do everything I could to escape or die trying. Being her captive wasn't an option for me.

Dying would be the better alternative.

At least in death, I would find peace. But the thought of leaving Griffin behind gutted me. I *had* to make it out of this, for him. For *us*. We deserved to be with each other and make a life together. We couldn't let them take that away.

I slunk deeper into the green leaves, desperate to hide behind the trunk. Maybe I'd be able to use the tree as cover after all.

The asshole fired, and the crack of the gunshot mocked that thought.

There was no getting out of this alive. The dart would hit my left side just as I reached the tree. I braced for impact, but something black flashed across the sky and sacked me.

Rosemary's floral scent hit my nose as she wrapped her large wings around me. Then the sound of flapping wings reached us, disorienting me. She must have broken the sound barrier to reach me in time.

The *clink* of the dart bouncing off her wings amazed me once more. For her feathers to look so soft, they were stronger than anything I'd ever seen.

"Damn it, why do these angels keep getting involved?" Saga growled. "Get your asses out of the boat and kill the angel. Your guns won't work on her." She stomped her feet and glowered. "Ugh, this angel has caused enough trouble, especially since she and her parents decided to align with them instead of me."

Yeah, she was completely irrational. How had she managed to keep up the act for so long? Maybe Dick dying and her being cast out was the final straw.

We're here, Bart said as Rosemary lowered her wings, staring at the nine guards who were now climbing off the boat to get us.

Thank God. We needed more people, but we should be able to get by until the others could reach us. I linked with all three men. *There are four of us and eleven of them. Each one of you take three while I go for Luna and Saga.* I was being selfish, wanting to handle those two on my own, but they had caused so much suffering. I had the right to want justice.

As if Rosemary were part of the pack link, she turned toward the guards. "I'll take the big burly one and the other two with guns. You focus on the ones who aren't armed."

Aren't armed was a stretch. The other six had knives, but at least they had to be much closer to us to strike. *Follow her lead.* When I nodded my head, Rosemary took off flying directly at the others with Julius, Darrell, and Bart racing after her.

I focused on Saga. Luna stayed at the riverbank, avoiding eye contact like she would rather be anywhere but here. Granted, her submissive stance could be an act, so I kept an eye on her anyway.

Shots fired, and I sighed with relief as I watched Rosemary twirl around, fending off the bullets. The guards were desperate to injure her since she was the most durable one there. If they didn't focus on her, she'd kill them with her strength and wings, so their hands were kind of tied.

Good, let them sweat.

"Just because you have her on your side doesn't mean you'll win." Saga bared her teeth at me, reminding me of a vampire. Usually, wolves did that only in animal form.

She kept talking as if I cared what she said or she could somehow intimidate me. But that wasn't how this was going to work. Her running her mouth only made me more determined to kill her since she had absolutely no remorse. Instead, she sounded proud, as if I should be in awe of her.

She was the worst kind of coward. She hid behind everyone else to try to get what she wanted. She wasn't willing to fight her own war, even now. She watched as the guards fought on her behalf, and she tried to psych me out with her words.

I took long steady strides toward her. I wanted her to feel like prey...to feel weak and worthless. Killing her quickly would be too nice. She deserved to suffer for every life that she'd stolen, including Dick's.

"It's in your best interest to stop." She took a step back, revealing some of the nervousness she had attempted to hide. "The more you fight, the harder this will be on your friends and even yourself. If you come willingly, then all the hurt and injury can be spared. We won't even tranq you." The rancid stench of her lie almost made me choke. Even outside, it didn't appear to dissipate, which told me everything.

She wanted to hurt us all. No one was off the table.

Luna whimpered and rubbed a paw against her nose.

For once, I sympathized with her. She couldn't handle her mother's stench, either.

I growled and crouched, letting her know that I didn't believe a damn word that she said. For someone so strategic, she sure hadn't thought through the whole lie.

"Fine, you caught me." She lifted her head and smirked. "Every single one of your friends and family will die, including your bastard brother. I thought I killed them all, but I won't make that mistake again."

My self-control snapped, and I jumped at the lady, wanting to rip her throat out.

Her eyes widened, and she stumbled back. "Luna, attack now!"

I'd expected her to want someone else to fight her battles for her, so when Luna charged toward me, I fell to the ground and rolled, causing her to miss.

I jumped back up on all fours and snarled. I wanted this all over.

Luna's eyes deepened to navy as she turned to face me. Her breathing was quick and shallow, revealing the state she was in. She wasn't thinking clearly.

I took deep breaths, letting the adrenaline flow through my body. Most people thought being upset was the best way to get your body buzzing, but it wasn't. Adrenaline pumped through you when there was a threat in front of you. You didn't have to be a hot mess to get it to come, and channeling it appropriately could give you an edge over your opponent. Thankfully, the pain from my injury vanished as the hormone took control.

Luna lowered her head, telegraphing her next move. She wanted to bulldoze me on my injured side. I had to give her props for critical thinking, but she was clearly untrained, always broadcasting her next move. When she charged, I waited a few seconds before moving out of the way.

"Look up, you idiot," Saga yelled. "She's moved. You're going to run past her again."

If I were in human form, I would've retorted for her to come fight me herself if she could do so much better. No wonder Luna was so angry and full of hate—her mother had probably talked to her like that her entire childhood. That kind of emotional abuse could crumble even the strongest person.

A whimper left Luna as she stopped and lifted her head to find me. Her eyes locked on my shoulder, once again informing me of her next move.

There was no way this girl could ever win a fight. Obviously, neither Saga nor Dick had bothered to train their daughter in combat, yet here she was, expected to fight a silver wolf.

She attacked, and I waited until she was right on me to stand on my hind legs. Since I wasn't there to offset the impact, she propelled past me, and her face rammed into the ground. I jumped on her back, digging my claws into her skin.

However, I couldn't bring myself to kill her. It didn't seem right, seeing as Luna had suffered more than I could ever imagine. No wonder she'd been desperate to lock in Griffin with a mother like that constantly whispering in her ear.

Luna whimpered and jerked underneath me, making my claws go deeper. Damn it, she had no clue how to fight me off from this angle, and everything about this just felt wrong.

I took the opportunity to check on my packmates and friend and realized that they all had taken down at least one of their opponents. But every time I thought we were getting the edge, another surprise knocked us back on our asses. I feared that maybe Saga had another trick up her sleeve.

Warm blood trickled under my paws, and I detached myself from Luna and stepped to the side.

"How pathetic!" Saga yelled as her face twisted with disgust. "She doesn't even want to finish you off, that's how pathetic you are."

Luna tried to stand, but she couldn't. She stayed still, not even bothering to attempt to protect herself any longer.

Pain rocketed through me, and panic clamped my throat as someone from my pack got hurt. At first, I thought it was Griffin, but when I dug deeper, I realized it was Julius.

My brother.

I pivoted in his direction to find him crumpled in a heap with blood pooling underneath him. I couldn't tell where he was hurt, but the two guards standing over him smiled. The guard with the unibrow held a knife that dripped with blood and cooed, "Hell, yeah. I took down a fucking silver wolf."

Rosemary, Bart, and Darrell were still engaged in battle, but Bart and Darrell kept throwing glances at my brother. His link was still there, which was the only reason I wasn't losing my mind.

Focus on your fight, I linked with Bart and Darrell. I could come back to Saga later. She was too scared to do much of anything. *I'll take care of them.* I jumped, thrusting my legs against the ground, drawing power from the moon. My body buzzed as I snarled and charged the men.

Griffin's voice popped into my mind. *What's wrong? Are you injured?*

No. Julius is hurt, and I don't know how bad.

I'll be there soon. Griffin sounded funny for a second. *We got some reinforcements, and some are heading your way now. Just please be careful.*

I will. It was time to bring this to an end before anyone else got hurt.

Unibrow's eyes flicked to me before bulging. "Holy shit. Sean, get ready. She's coming."

"What?" Sean was smiling as he turned to glance at me, but his mouth dropped in pure terror. "That's what we get for trusting Luna to handle her."

Those assholes had expected an untrained wolf to take me down? I wasn't sure if I should be insulted or not. They were obviously idiots, which spoke volumes more about them than me.

The image of their smiles flicked through my mind, and I leaped at Unibrow. He was the one who'd hurt Julius, so he'd be the one I took care of first.

Unibrow lifted his knife, but his movement was too damn slow. The fact that Julius got hurt by this jackass blew my mind, but the proof was right before my eyes. Bart and I needed to work with him in wolf form.

I sank my teeth into Unibrow's wrist, causing him to drop the knife. He howled, which only made me chomp harder. I wanted him to feel the pain before I ended it for him.

"Don't worry, I got you," Sean cried, informing me that he was making a move. He was almost as bad as Luna.

I released Unibrow and spun just in time to see Sean swing downward. He was aiming for my back, and I moved away, leaving him to catch air. I sprang forward and slashed my teeth through his neck. Blood poured down his chest, and he tried to speak, but he only gargled words formed as he released the knife and clasped both hands around his neck.

"Sean!" Unibrow whispered as he watched his friend, and then his body coiled. He faced me, rage evident on his face.

This was the part I'd come to hate most. The inevitable deaths. But these people would never leave us alone. I prepared myself for the attack, which I welcomed, because I was *over* this entire thing. A certain cold-hearted bitch deserved some of my attention.

But instead of striking me, he kicked Julius. When he moved to kick him a second time, I swiped at his leg with my claws and lifted upward, causing him to fall on his back. Then I slashed through his neck, not wanting to taste any more blood and needing to end this.

"You stupid bitch! You keep ruining everything." Saga bent and removed a gun from around her ankle. "I don't need you." She stood and aimed at my heart.

CHAPTER TWENTY-FIVE

I'D GOTTEN out of one precarious situation just to land in another. What was it with people pointing guns at me? At some point, I'd like to not have the constant threat of someone trying to kill me. Being bored was underrated and exactly what I wanted.

Saga was maybe fifty feet away, and there were no trees close by. The best I could do was use Sean or Unibrow as a shield. They were already dead, so they wouldn't feel the pain, but something felt wrong about it.

I'm on my way, Bart linked with me as he fought off two men. He kept glancing at me, not paying attention to his own battle.

She fired, and I rolled out of the way, channeling the moon. I dodged the bullet by barely an inch.

Focus on your opponents, I told Bart. He wouldn't be able to reach me any faster, and instead of talking with him, I needed to determine a solution. If I didn't do something, I'd be lying dead right next to them.

As if Rosemary could hear my thoughts, she glanced in my direction. She paused, which allowed one of her opponents to stab her in the stomach with a knife. She clutched the knife, stumbling back as blood trickled down her stomach, coating her black shirt. She hissed, "You dumbass mutt."

A deep, threatening snarl escaped me. No. This couldn't happen. Rosemary was part of my family, and none of us were going down.

What's wrong? Griffin linked, including Killian in the bond. *Are you hurt?*

No, I said. *Rosemary's been stabbed.*

Killian's anger rang thick through the bond. *Son of a bitch. I'll kill the bastard.*

Not if I get him first, I vowed. I wanted to hurt every single person who had inflicted any sort of pain on my people.

"It ends now!" Saga yelled, and her finger tightened on the trigger.

Sterlyn! Julius shouted through the bond. The amount of pain he felt washed over me. I dove to the ground and shoved myself under Unibrow's body as best as I could.

His dead weight almost stole my breath as I crawled underneath him, and his body jerked from the impact of a bullet, making a few thick drops of his now congealing blood fall on my face.

Holy shit. That worked. I couldn't comprehend how I'd pulled that off. With me in animal form, I'd figured there was no way his body would shield me completely, just maybe prevent her from landing a kill shot.

"How do you keep doing that?" Saga screamed, and her footsteps grew louder. "You keep messing everything up!" Her anger propelled her toward me.

The closer she got, the better I'd be able to protect myself. When she was too far away, I was at the mercy of the firearm with limited ability to strike back.

I stayed still, wanting her to get as close to me as she dared. If I moved, she might stop and shoot again. I linked with my brother, feeling his pain exploding through our bond. *Julius, how badly are you hurt?* I couldn't lose him like this. There was too much we hadn't said, and we hadn't spent any time together. He was my twin, for

God's sake, and I had hoped that we had time to get some sort of relationship established. He and Bart were the only two people from my
parents' side left alive.

Please call me Cyrus, he rasped, even through our bond. *I
should've asked you to do that days ago.*

Stop. Fear coiled inside me, and I refused to acknowledge why.
You cannot die. I won't allow it. We have so much time to make up for.

But it was like he hadn't heard me as he continued. *I blamed you,
which is so fucked up, but you were the only one I could. Bart kept
telling me that I had to stop, but I didn't want to listen. I have so much
anger inside, and even though shifting has helped, it's still heavy in me.
What I'm trying to say is—*

Do not apologize to me now. He was saying goodbye, and I
wouldn't let him die on me. I didn't care what it took—Cyrus was
going to live. *We're making it out of this, and you're going to take me
somewhere nice and apologize to me there. Got it?*

I— He started.

Got it? I pushed as Saga's footsteps grew closer. She was beginning to slow but still moving forward. I held my breath to remain still,
hoping she thought I was injured. *This is not our end, I promise.*

He snorted then groaned in pain. *Ugh, don't make me laugh.*

Then tell me you understand. Even in this horrible situation, the
corners of my wolf's lips tipped upward. I hadn't realized the extent
of how badly I wanted a relationship with him, and now that it was
possible, I felt happy, despite the horrible current situation. *Or I will
be forced to make you laugh.*

I don't plan on going anywhere, he reassured me just as Saga
stopped.

She breathed in loud, short gasps, making it easy to determine
that she was standing at Unibrow's feet.

My head and chest were lodged under Unibrow's back, but if she
moved to my right, she could hit my back or my side. Either option
wouldn't kill me, most likely, but it would hurt like a son of a bitch.
However, if I moved, she could get an even better shot.

As if she read my mind, she fired, but I burrowed under him to the best of my ability. She must have been so angry that her hands shook, causing her aim to be off.

Keeping my head clear was hard with a dead man on top of me. The scent of his blood was overwhelming. His skin was already cooling, making his death harder to ignore. Damn it, I wanted her to come right up to me.

"Get up. You're coming with me," she spat. "Hiding under a body won't prevent what's going to happen."

I'm on my way, Bart linked as his paws hit the ground, moving closer to me.

No one else needed to get hurt on account of me. *Focus on your fight.*

Don't worry, he replied. *I took both of them down.*

Thank God. With his help, the fight would be over soon. From the sounds of it, they were getting things settled back at the house. I connected with all the silver wolves, as well as Killian and Griffin, and felt them begin to celebrate victory, but the fight wasn't finished. *Don't get overconfident. We might be winning at the moment, but that also means they'll grow desperate.* I repeated the words my father had beaten into my head. *Desperation makes people crazed. They'll do whatever they can to take down whoever they can.* In rare cases, their desperation could even give them leverage to come back on top, but I didn't want to worry the others more than I already was.

Got it, Killian said. *We'll be careful, but with the vampires here, hopefully we'll end this soon.*

Vampires? Really?

Yeah. Griffin sounded even less thrilled than me. *It was a shock. The vampire king, vampire prince, and a handful of their own guards showed up with the Shadow City wolves to help. They stayed back and watched until we were obviously winning before stepping in, but we weren't in a position to turn down help in case something went awry or we risked insulting them.*

That was true. *No, I get it.*

I'm on my way to you now, Griffin promised. *Things are under control, and Alex and Matthew are also heading your way. They have speed that could come in handy with guns.*

Those words would normally comfort me, but not now. I didn't want him to get here and be hurt, but if I tried to dissuade him, that would only get him to come faster.

"You do realize that you won't make it out of this alive," Saga continued, and her footsteps shuffled over, I assumed so she could shoot me in the back.

My body tensed of its own accord, bracing for impact.

Bart growled.

"What? No!" Saga screamed, and a gun fired.

Something crashed hard on the ground. I pushed the corpse off of me and scrambled to my feet. What I saw would forever scar me as Bart's pain washed over me.

Saga stood over my uncle and fired another shot between his eyes. Tears burned my eyes as hysteria licked throughout me. While she was distracted, I pounced on her back, forcing her to fall on top of my freshly dead uncle.

This bitch had taken so much from me. She'd not only kidnapped my brother but slaughtered my family members. If Cyrus didn't make it, I didn't know what the hell I would do.

"Get off me," she screamed as she tried to roll away from my uncle. I chomped down on her right arm, the very one she used for the gun. If I ripped her arm off, she'd never shoot anyone again.

For the first time, I didn't mind the taste of blood. In fact, I relished it. This woman deserved to bleed for every damn thing she'd done to us. My mind grew hazy with so much hate and anger that I felt like someone else.

Sterlyn, watch out! Cyrus yelled through the bond, snapping me out of whatever warped reality I'd been in.

I stumbled back and let go of the wretched woman, realizing I was acting just like she had—crazed with the desire to kill.

The other wolf! he screamed again.

Shit, I hadn't kept an eye on Luna like I'd planned. I pivoted to find her jumping toward me, her eyes locked on my neck.

I didn't have time to move.

Something flashed between us, sacking Luna mid-pounce. I blinked several times as Luna slammed against the tree and the vampire prince came into view.

Alex had saved me.

She snapped at him, trying to bite his arms, but he held her head firmly. Vampires had strength that normal wolf shifters lacked.

"Will you stop it?" he huffed. "You aren't going to get out of this. Hell, you're weaker than any wolf I've ever fought before."

"What are you doing here?" Saga bit out the words. "Haven't you interfered enough? Leave us the fuck alone!" She climbed to her feet as she held her wounded arm close to her body. Blood poured from it, and if she didn't slow the flow, she would definitely get dizzy.

"Do you want to die?" Alex asked with a chuckle as Rosemary landed next to him with a wince.

Matthew strolled into the clearing with Griffin on his trail. Griffin's hazel eyes found mine, and he raced toward me.

I inhaled sharply as Saga lifted her left arm.

No. Not again.

Her hand shook as she aimed the gun at Griffin. A cruel smirk filled her face.

Magic like I'd never felt before bolted through me, making the blood rush through my veins with incomparable power. My body propelled itself toward the woman with a speed almost as great as that of Rosemary and the vampires. I reached her within milliseconds, this time sinking my teeth into her neck.

"Imposs—" she started, but my teeth cut off her words as I severed her throat. Her body fell limply to the ground as I landed back on my feet, watching her. I tensed as I kept my gaze on her, waiting for her to move. Every time I thought we defeated our enemies, they surprised us again. At this point, if she'd popped up even missing half her neck, it wouldn't shock me.

Baby, Griffin said softly as he trotted up next to me. *It's okay.*

No, nothing is okay. My chest constricted, and air wheezed through my lungs. Once again, I might have lost my entire family. A family I had just found. I'd hoped to get to know Bart, but that had been taken away from me. *Cyrus.* My gaze flicked to him, and I found Rosemary standing over him, her hands glowing white as she healed him.

I should've felt better, but a huge part of me was just numb. I kept my body tense as I surveyed the area. Every enemy was now dead except for Luna.

Darrell's heartbroken howl pierced my soul as he leaned over his dead alpha. He lowered his head to Bart's body and cried once more.

Once again, the silver wolf pack had been torn apart, and this time, I'd be expected to put it back together. But I couldn't abandon Shadow City, either, since I'd demanded my spot on the council. I wasn't sure how I was going to handle both situations, but I didn't have a choice.

"Why don't you go home and shift back into human form, and we can figure things out from there," Alex suggested. "Matthew and I can handle this one." He nodded toward Luna, who had stopped fighting as her eyes latched onto her dead mother.

Regret flitted through me. Even though Saga was a horrible person, she *was* Luna's mother. In less than two weeks, Luna had lost both her parents at mine and Griffin's hands.

Griffin nuzzled my neck, trying to bring me comfort. *Let's go back and shift so we can take care of everything.*

He was right. I didn't have the luxury of staying here and breaking down, so I turned and slowly walked home.

WHEN GRIFFIN, Killian, Cyrus, Sierra, and I left our house again to deal with the consequences, my heart was still heavy. Dead bodies littered the ground, although this time, they were mostly Saga's allies.

But there was still at least a dozen of our own down with them. There was so much to do, and the first order of business we had to contend with was Luna.

Rosemary was pacing the back patio. "Mom has asked for you, Griffin, and me to head back to Shadow City to meet with the council. We have to deal with the fallout of Dick's and Saga's betrayal and decide how to handle Luna."

"I have to help my pack. They just lost my un—uncle." My voice broke on the last word.

"Let me be here for them," Cyrus said softly as he touched my arm. "Lean on me, and let me take care of them for you."

The sincerity flowing through our bond warmed my heart, making me feel a little bit more like myself. "Okay. But if you need me..."

"I'll let you know," he promised.

"One wrong move—" Griffin growled.

And Cyrus nodded. "I know. How about Killian stays with me and keeps an eye out?"

Griffin's shoulders slackened like the wind had been let out of his sails. "Uh...yeah. That sounds good."

I hated that it had taken *this* to get Cyrus and me heading in the right direction concerning our relationship, but at least we were finally getting there. "Is that okay with you, Killian?" I hated not to at least ask, since Killian had his own pack duties to contend with.

"It's fine." Killian hugged me. "Honestly, at this point, we all need to work together, right? Just one large pack."

"That's right." He understood what I'd always wanted. Just because we were technically three packs didn't mean we couldn't work closely together.

Snarling came from the woods, and Alex walked out carrying Luna. Her eyes locked on me, and she thrashed, trying to get free and foaming at the mouth with desperation.

She still wanted to kill me.

CHAPTER TWENTY-SIX

"DON'T WORRY." Alex beamed at me. "She'll ride with us. She won't harm you."

Luna twisted and writhed some more, but he didn't even seem bothered by her efforts. She could have been a baby doll for the amount of concern he gave her, which seemed to infuriate her more.

Of course, Alex and Matthew would be heading back to the city with us. They were two of the vampire representatives, after all. There couldn't be a council meeting without them, or at least not an official one, from what Erin had said before.

"Thank God." Rosemary sneered. "If I had to ride in the back seat with her, I'd wind up slicing her to make things even."

"You do realize she didn't injure you, right?" Sierra arched an eyebrow and wrinkled her nose. "Ignore that. I have no clue why I'm taking up for her. Slice the bitch."

"Because you enjoy arguing with me about everything." Rosemary sighed.

"To the point of siding with a psycho," Killian jumped in, taking up for Rosemary. He took a step closer to the angel while *tsk*ing at Sierra. "Maybe you'll reconsider in the future."

"Yeah, do you think that will actually work?" Sierra stood tall as if she were proud of having no filter. "I say what I think, and there are times when even I'm surprised by what falls out of my mouth, which is saying something."

You guys are weird. Cyrus chuckled through the link, though not using the mocking tone I'd grown accustomed to hearing from him. *It's like no matter what gets thrown at you, you all bounce back together...like family.* He sighed, and sadness trickled to me. *I'm jealous of that.*

Well, I have a feeling that you'll fit right in soon enough, I replied. The truth of the matter was that I wanted him to be part of our team. He was important to me and the only immediate blood family I had left. *If you're open to it.*

The image of Bart's body flashed into my mind, making my smile fall.

"We'd better go before Erin and Azbogah get tired of waiting." Griffin took my hand and turned, opening the door again to head back inside the house.

A council meeting seemed like a terrible way to end the night, but if we didn't show up, it would cause more drama. Things were already tense between Griffin and me and most of the others on the council. That was probably why they wanted to talk to us.

"You guys go. We'll take it from here," Killian said as he patted Cyrus's shoulder. "We'll get the packs handled and bury the dead while you're gone."

"We're leaving," Matthew said as he pulled the keys from his pocket. "And we'll meet you there." The corner of his mouth tipped upward like he was up to something.

Alex winked at me as he followed his brother, clamping his hand over Luna's mouth to keep her quiet.

Not even bothering to give the prince a reaction, I focused on my friends. "Let me know if you need anything." My voice sounded thick with emotion. I wanted to help pay my respects to everyone who'd given or risked their lives for us tonight, especially Bart.

"We will." Sierra hugged me tightly. "Just go take care of things. This will all still be here when you return."

My side had mostly healed, so her touch didn't hurt, and I was able to hug her back before stepping past Griffin. She was right. It would take time to heal and mourn the dead.

Rosemary's breath caught as she turned, once again reminding me of her injury.

"Why don't you heal yourself?" I asked and paused inside, waiting for her and Griffin to walk through. "Or can you not do that?"

"I can, but it takes even more magic." She gently touched her chest just above her stomach, and the clean shirt she'd changed into clung to her from fresh blood. "I need to recover from healing Cyrus, but I'll be able to do it closer to Shadow City."

At least there was that.

I glanced over my shoulder, watching as Cyrus, Killian, and Sierra headed over to several men who were already working on moving the dead. The men listened and looked at Killian and then Cyrus with respect as each man spoke, so I knew things would be okay. Cyrus was ready to learn to be a strong beta. The role he was always meant to play.

Forcing myself to move forward, I faced the front again and headed to the car.

ROSEMARY GROANED as we hit the bump where the land and the bridge that led to Shadow City connected. "Pull over."

"Now?" Griffin asked as he slowed the vehicle. "We just got on the bridge, and we need to get to the council."

"I know that," Rosemary snapped. "But stop. I need a minute."

She hadn't healed herself yet, and her attitude worried me. "I thought you said—" I began, but my words died off as a bright light started to glow from the back.

The light grew brighter, and as I turned to check on her, the whole back seat lit up brighter than the sun. All I could do was close my eyes, hoping that my retinas hadn't been burned to a crisp.

"Damn it!" Griffin bellowed as he slammed on the brakes, making the car lurch forward. "A little warning would've been nice."

I faced forward, stretching out my arms to brace myself on the dashboard. The seatbelt caught, causing my body to jerk. The light in the back seat ebbed.

"I did warn you." Rosemary's voice was clear now, without any evidence of pain. "I told you to stop the car."

"She's right." I blinked a few times, trying to stop seeing spots. "Are you going to light up again, or are we safe?"

She huffed. "I'm healed, and I couldn't do that again right away, even if I wanted to."

"Are you still hurt?" I looked at her and realized that her skin was a shade darker than normal. She still looked beautiful, but she looked tan. How the hell was that possible?

She shook her head. "No, I'm not, but it took a lot out of me to heal myself." She lifted her arms and examined her skin. "My magic is almost depleted. It's going to take some time for it to recharge."

Griffin glanced in the rearview mirror. "Is that why you look different?"

"Yeah, our power inside projects outwardly more than it does in other races." She rubbed her fingers together. "You can easily see our essence, though only angels can sense it."

Her words settled over me. "Wait, are angels able to see the intent of others, too?"

"Yeah, we are. That's one reason why I warmed up to you so quickly." Rosemary shifted around, stretching out her arms. "Your light was pure like Mom's, and of course, I felt the familial bond, though I didn't quite understand that since it was different with your wolf and all."

She'd warmed up to me *quickly*? The first time I'd met Rosemary, she was complaining about not being waited on fast enough, which I hadn't tolerated. When I'd pushed back, I'd somehow gained her respect, despite Carter bitching about how I shouldn't have told her off. But I wouldn't have called her reaction...*warm*.

"So I can see intent, too." I ran my fingers through my hair, pulling it away from my face. "That's why I don't trust certain people, especially the ones negativity clings to, like Luna, Azbogah, Saga, and Dick."

"Yeah, the wickedness around them is probably the worst I've ever seen, too. Granted, I haven't been around much in the world outside of the city." Rosemary blew out a breath. "God, it feels good to be able to move and breathe without hurting."

"I'm glad you're okay." I leaned over and touched her arm. "Seeing you get hurt..." I trailed off as my throat dried. I'd lost so many people I loved.

"Hey, I'm not going anywhere." She patted my hand awkwardly, clearly still uncomfortable with intense emotion. "So we're good."

A chuckle left my throat as I slumped in my seat. Rosemary being back to her awkward self comforted me.

Griffin pressed the gas, and the car accelerated toward the large gate. "Why didn't you do that back at the house before we got into the Navigator?"

"Because I wasn't strong enough yet, and I didn't want to do it in the Ridge in case any humans were close by. They didn't need to see the light." Rosemary cleared her throat and crossed her arms. "I waited until the witches' spell hid us."

The gate opened without Griffin even having to get out, just like the last time we came. "Should we be worried?"

"No, there isn't a threat inside, so someone was watching for us," Rosemary answered. "Mom probably put out the word to the guards on duty."

We pulled into the city, and within minutes, we were at the council building. The lights were on, making it clear that people were already inside.

"Alex and Matthew aren't here yet," Griffin growled as he parked. "Good, I wanted to beat them."

"They left before us." Rosemary opened her door and climbed out. "That's actually not a good sign."

Damn it, I hate to admit it, but she's right, Griffin complained as he got out of the car. *What if they don't show up? They'll say the wolves are siding with me because I'm their alpha.*

I tried to smile like I wasn't concerned, but the trepidation through my bond spoke volumes. It had been a shit night, and the vampires unnerved me. They weren't known for being helpful, and they hadn't asked for anything in return.

Rosemary marched to the front door, with Griffin and me following close behind. The city's ever-changing colors were more muted in the darkness. They didn't demand my attention quite like they did during the day and almost reminded me of lightning bugs in the fields in summer.

The front door opened, revealing Yelahiah. Her gaze landed on Rosemary and then me, and her body relaxed. "Ever since I learned you all were under attack, I've been so worried. But we couldn't chance leaving with Azbogah being the only angel in charge, so we mentioned the war to Alex and Matthew. Are any of you harmed?"

"No, we're good," Rosemary answered quickly. "I got hurt, but I'm fine now."

She glossed over her injury like it was nothing, which I found intriguing.

Now's my chance to get her back. Griffin smirked as he opened his mouth to rat Rosemary out, but I intervened.

If Rosemary didn't want to go into detail over her injury with her mom, then we didn't need to waste time. "Saga was the one coordinating the attacks. We had to kill her, and Alex and Matthew are bringing Luna here."

"They aren't here yet, and they have the one girl that can prove your innocence?" A muscle in Yelahiah's jaw twitched. "Azbogah is trying to paint you two as the culprits behind Dick's death and the attacks tonight, saying you're the common denominator. If you can prove that Luna and Saga were involved, that should satisfy the other council members who would side with you."

Great, we were back on trial. I shouldn't have been surprised. Azbogah would do anything in his power to get in a position to kill me and the others of my kind.

The door to the council room opened, and Pahaliah poked his head out. "Are you ready?" He gave his wife a sideways glance. "They're waiting for Griffin, Sterlyn, Alex, and Matthew."

Yelahiah replied sweetly, "We're on our way."

"Good." He gave Rosemary a solemn gaze before closing the door once more.

"Uh...what did I just miss?" I asked. Pahaliah's visuals had been a clue of some kind, but I wasn't sure what.

The older angel straightened her shoulders. "Azbogah has already begun working the room. That's one reason you all needed to get here as soon as possible. The longer he has to sway people, the harder it'll be to keep those in your favor."

I took a deep breath. I was so tired of having to prove ourselves, but there wasn't a better alternative. The only other option was letting Azbogah weave more control through the council. I wouldn't give the jackass the satisfaction.

"You two go first, since I'm not officially on the council." Rosemary motioned in front of her. "Let's get in there before the others get here." She nodded in the direction of the parking lot.

She's right. Griffin placed a hand at the small of my back and led me toward the council doors. *Who knows what those two vampire idiots will say? Let's at least say our piece first.*

I had a feeling that if the vampires sided with Azbogah, it wouldn't matter, but this was our best shot. We had to take it.

The four of us entered the council room. Everyone sat in the same seats as before, but each one glowered at us, clearly not happy to be there at this late hour. Ezra's hair was messy from either sleep or stress, but the witches and vampires were all made up, proving they enjoyed the nighttime.

Is Ezra okay? In all the commotion, I hadn't even considered the other council representative.

Griffin blew out a breath. *I don't know. When we were attacked, I couldn't get ahold of him. Maybe he was asleep. I had to coordinate the guards, which was one reason I needed to stay close to the house and be there when they came.*

I wasn't sure how I felt about the shifter.

"*There* are the troublemakers," Azbogah spat as he stood and pulled at his oddly crumpled button-down shirt. "It's odd that you all blamed Dick for your troubles, and yet, within weeks of his death, another deadly battle occurs with you two at the center. Maybe you were behind all of these supposed attacks and set the whole thing up for Dick and Saga to take the fall."

Hell, he jumped right to the point, making his assumptions sound like facts. No wonder Yelahiah wanted us to get here so quickly.

"We are innocent." Griffin tensed, his anger already bleeding through.

We needed to hold ourselves together, not come off as unhinged or easily upset. That would make us look guilty even if our words and actions rang true. We had to remain calm and purposeful. I looped my arm through his, showing our solidarity as we walked closer to the council.

Erin slammed her hands on the table, making her breasts bounce under a low-cut shirt that left little to the imagination. She leaned over the table, and I wasn't sure how they didn't spill out of the top. "That's what everyone says. Now let's vote that these two are the problem so I can get back to my date."

Yeah, *date* had to be a far stretch of the word, but I forced my lips to stay shut. The woman already hated me enough. "Well, at least two of the vampire representatives are missing, so shouldn't we wait for them?" This was a risky move, but there had to be something we could find to prove that we hadn't been the people involved.

"If the majority here votes to get rid of the two of you, then we don't need their votes." Azbogah smirked cockily. He appeared so confident that this would go the way that he wanted. "So everyone who agrees to remove both Griffin and the silver wolf from the council, say aye. We don't need people who cause this kind of drama representing the city. Gwen?"

The ivory-haired vampire flipped her hair over her shoulder, and her eyes sparkled with maliciousness. "Aye."

Diana fluffed her hair. "Aye."

"Aye!" Erin yelled gleefully and then glared at the dark-headed witch, who seemed to like to cause problems for her. "Now, Breena, tell them aye."

My heart sank when I realized that if Breena and Ezra voted in favor of Azbogah, we would be removed from the council, and then the dark angel would come after me. Strong wolves always wanted a higher rank, so if Ezra were the one who could make the final decision, I wasn't sure what he'd decide. No wonder the witch put Breena on the spot.

The young witch sighed dramatically and leaned back in her chair. She opened her mouth to cast her vote just as the chamber's double doors crashed open.

Alex cruised into the room with his hand clutching a now human Luna's arm. Matthew trailed in after them, wearing a smug look on his face.

"I can't believe you started without us," Alex chuckled, but there was a glint in his eye. "The whole council wasn't present, so I don't understand what's going on."

"We have your sister here," Azbogah explained, pointing to Gwen, "And if six people here want Griffin and Sterlyn removed, then your two votes wouldn't matter. It's not like you would vote for these wolves. You know better than that."

"Actually, we vote in favor of Griffin and Sterlyn staying," Alex said as he jerked the wolf toward him. "Luna and her mother attacked them in their very own home."

"Are you serious?" Diana hissed. "You're going to side with shifters?"

"No, I'm siding with the truth." Alex shrugged. "I mean, Azbogah seems a little too eager to get the wolves off the council. To me, it sounds like he has a vested interest in discrediting Sterlyn, maybe for his own selfish reasons."

"Hey, now!" Azbogah growled. "I'm for all races having representation. I have worked across races for centuries now."

"Yeah, you're a saint." Matthew shoved his hands into his pockets and stood on the other side of Luna. "But we can prove that Luna and her mother were the aggressors. Tell them, Luna."

She jerked her head, refusing to say a word.

"Well, then we will," Alex said, and winked at me. "We saw the fight, and actually, I'm the reason Sterlyn is standing here. I saved her from Saga, who was about to shoot her to death to avenge her husband. Dick and his family have been causing all the problems in the city and outside its gates, and Luna here can't say otherwise because we'd all know it was a lie."

"Tell them the truth," Rosemary hissed at Luna. "Tell them what happened. Remember what happens to those who need to be forced. We can torture it out of you. I wouldn't feel bad about it at all. One of your men stabbed me."

"No, you wouldn't." Luna's bottom lip quivered, and she shook her head back and forth.

Yelahiah played the part with her daughter. "We're angels. We're willing to do whatever it takes for the truth to be set free. If you're honest, you know the punishment won't be nearly as bad."

Luna swallowed hard.

"Now listen here, you don't get to threaten people," Azbogah shouted.

But Luna nodded her head. "It's true. Mom organized the attacks. All of them. Even the ones outside of Shadow City, with shifters fighting each other. She wanted to make Griffin look weak so Dad could take control. They had plans to take over the entire city."

"What?" Pahaliah said in shock. "Then that settles it. If she were lying, we'd all know it, and that means these two aren't guilty of anything."

Azbogah's face dropped in such disappointment it was almost comical. "Fine. Then what do we do with her?" He jerked a hand at Luna.

There was only one option that would work. It was the option that would hurt her the most. "Put her in jail and let her live out her days in solitude," I said.

"What?" Luna jerked her head toward me. "No. You don't get to make that call."

"I second the motion," Yelahiah stated, followed by Pahaliah, Griffin, Alex, Matthew, and then Ezra, even though the wolf shifter didn't seem too thrilled with that decision.

But that didn't matter right now because we managed to get the majority.

Before anyone else spoke, I stepped in, wanting to drive the knife deeper into Azbogah's chest. "That's seven votes right there, a majority rule."

The dark angel scowled at me as Luna screamed, "You bitch. I'm going to kill you. You wait and see!"

"Ugh. Take her to the prison." Erin waved her off. "Now I'm going back to my date."

"And we're going to head back to our packs to help bury our dead," Griffin said tightly. *Azbogah and Erin hadn't counted on a real council meeting. They wanted the vote done quickly, thinking there was no way we could come out of this ahead.*

I know. They had made that clear.

As we walked past Alex, he whispered just loudly enough for me to hear, "That's three favors now, silver wolf. Remember that."

My stomach dropped at the implication.

CHAPTER TWENTY-SEVEN

THOUGH I WANTED to ask what the vampire meant, I refused to give him the satisfaction of letting him know that his statement bothered me. He could try to turn this around on us, but at the end of the day, the damage was done. Even if he tried to take back his support, he'd obviously still claim that I owed him for the time they'd voted to hear me out when Griffin had been on trial by Dick, and then for helping us fight Saga. What was one more favor at this point?

Forcing my legs to continue to move without faltering, I pretended the prince hadn't said anything. If he saw that his words affected me, there was no telling what he'd do.

Vampires enjoyed manipulating and messing with their victims.

And the king and prince were just like all the other vampires I'd met or heard stories about, which had been my fear. I should've known that they weren't any different and would want something in return for their help.

Rosemary rushed after me and touched my arm, making me still. She said softly, "I'll fly back over there. You two go on without me."

"Okay, be safe." I nodded. She'd been spending most of her time with us, so I understood. "Let me know if you need us."

"I will." She patted my arm awkwardly, then headed back to her mother.

It might be better if she didn't try to be affectionate. Griffin chuckled as we stepped into the lobby. *I think she feels more uncomfortable trying than just being her standoffish self.*

Do not say anything to her. For her to want to connect with me in a more human way meant so much to me. It emphasized how important I was to her, and she probably didn't even realize it. I tried not to push her too hard, either, because even though I was more affectionate to her, I understood not wanting to be too touchy-feely. I was only comfortable hugging those who were close to me.

Griffin rolled his eyes but kissed my cheek. *Fine, but only because you enjoy it.*

When we stepped outside, the sky was still dark, but I wasn't tired at all. Adrenaline still pumped through me.

The sickly sweet scent of vampires hit my nose from where the king and prince had walked in moments ago. The unease I'd felt flooded back.

Griffin walked to my door and opened it. *Hey, are you okay?* His concern washed over me like a wave against the sand.

I'm just ready to go home and have you hold me. I'd tell him about the vampires, just not tonight. We'd already endured too much. All I knew was that with Griffin by my side and with our packs and friends, we could get through anything.

We had to.

I climbed into the car and tried to smile, but my mate studied me. He pressed. *You avoided the question, so that worries me. What happened?* He stood there, not budging.

He wasn't going to let it go, so I filled him in on what Alex had said on our way out.

Damn bloodsuckers, he growled as he slammed the door and marched over to the driver's side. *Let's get the hell out of this forsaken place.* He jumped in the car and had us heading back to Shadow Ridge within seconds.

Shadow City was supposed to be this glorious place that people coveted, but the harsh reality was that it was cruel and the opposite of what it should be. Something had to change, but it wasn't going to happen overnight. It would take time and, unfortunately, political strategy.

But until we could change things, I felt exactly like Griffin—I didn't want to stay here any longer than we had to. All we seemed to have inside were enemies within the different races. Hell, even the shifters were segregated. We were supposed to represent the bears, birds, cats, and everyone else, but the only interactions I'd had were with the ones who had attacked us.

As soon as we pulled back onto the bridge heading to Shadow Ridge, some of the tension left my body. I hadn't even realized how stressed I'd been until that moment.

The moon was high in the sky, and as we drove through the dark and bare downtown, it almost felt like Griffin and I were the only ones awake. I closed my eyes and enjoyed the warmth of his hand on my thigh.

There was no telling what we'd be walking into once we reached the house, so I took advantage of the peace of the moment.

This is how it should always be. Griffin's voice practically purred in my head. *I don't think I've ever felt you this relaxed before.*

Relaxed was pushing it—there was still so much churning inside me—but I actually felt like I could breathe for once. *I'm just trying to enjoy a moment of peace before walking back into that nightmare.* I hated that the woods surrounding our home were now full of bad memories. There should be good ones there of us all hanging out and running in the woods together. Maybe day by day, we'd make more good memories to help drown out the bad.

The rest of the car ride passed in silence, and when we took the sharp turn into our neighborhood, I sat upright. We passed by several Craftsman-style homes before turning into Griffin's driveway.

When we walked in through the garage, I was surprised to find Killian, Sierra, and Cyrus already there. Cyrus stood next to the living room window, looking outside, while Killian and Sierra sat on the couch.

"Is everything okay?" My body tensed, but I managed to remain calm because the three of them didn't seem to be alarmed.

"We just finished burying the dead." Killian yawned.

"Already?" Griffin asked with surprise. "There were so many."

"With the silver wolves, the Shadow City guards, and my pack working together, we managed to get everything accomplished in record time," Killian said, and pointed at Cyrus. "And that man is a natural leader."

That I already knew. He'd trained all those guards, and none of them would've listened to him if he hadn't earned their respect. He was born to be a leader even if he wasn't the alpha. A lot of wolves thought you had to be an alpha to lead, but that wasn't true. An alpha couldn't oversee everything at all times—that was setting a pack up for failure. An alpha was only as strong as the rest of the pack. "I'm not surprised." I walked to Cyrus and squeezed his arm. "He reminds me of our father in a lot of ways."

"Really?" His silver eyes lightened to almost white.

"You'd know if I were lying." I dropped my hand, not wanting him to feel uncomfortable. We were finally moving in the right direction, so I didn't want to push too hard and fast and ruin it. "Where are the other silver wolves?" I glanced outside to find a bare backyard.

"They went back to the houses that our father had purchased to move to." Cyrus chewed on his bottom lip. "They want to head home in the morning to get the rest of the pack. They're tired of being split up."

I wasn't sure I could afford to leave right now when things were so unstable. If we ran, Azbogah and his angel followers could come after us. "Like permanently back?"

"No." Cyrus ran a hand through his hair. "They're moving to the new land...Dad was working on. They...*we* want to stay close to you. They only went home to get their stuff for the move. We all want this pack to stay together, and we understand now that Shadow City needs us, too. We're stronger together than apart."

I had to agree with that. "I don't know if I can leave right now."

"Then let me do it," Cyrus said eagerly. "Let me help you. I've done so much to hurt you—I want to make it up to you and be there for our people. Losing Bart and almost dying, it puts a lot of things into perspective."

"Okay." I nodded and smiled. "If that's what you want, then I'm okay with you taking over Bart's role."

Babe, Griffin asked with concern, *are you sure that's a good idea? I mean, he does seem different, but—*

He is. I can feel it. Our twin bond hummed with a new kind of energy that didn't seem tarnished. The darkness that had surrounded him was gone, as if things were finally clear to him for the first time.

Then I can't argue with that. Griffin's worry lessened, though it didn't completely vanish. *I just want our packs in good hands.*

Our packs. I'd never heard him say that, and honestly, I hadn't said it, either, but I liked the sound of it. He was completely right. We were mated, and our packs needed both of us. *And I love you for it.*

"You want me to take over as their leader?" Cyrus beamed. "Are you sure?"

"I'm positive." It made sense for him to lead and report to me when I couldn't be in two places at once. "I think Bart would like that, too." My heart ached at the thought of my uncle, whom I hadn't gotten to know nearly well enough. "Where is he buried?"

"Close by, between here and the new pack neighborhood." Cyrus nodded toward the woods. "Under a large, strong tree. I talked to our cousin—Bart's daughter—and she wanted him buried where she could visit his grave when they get here."

That sounded perfect. Bart was tall and strong, so he should be buried in a place that mirrored him. "Will you take me in the morning?" I wanted to leave flowers and say goodbye.

"Right before the rest of the silver wolves and I head out to get the rest of the pack." Cyrus nodded.

"Guys, I'm not trying to whine here, but..." Sierra started.

"You're gonna?" Killian jabbed.

Sierra stuck her tongue out at him. "Oh, you think you're funny stuff, don't you?"

"Well..." Killian patted his chest. "When you're as good as me—"

"Oh, God." Sierra gagged and pretended to dry heave. "Please don't make me vomit."

"You better not throw up on our rug." Griffin's face twisted in disgust. "If you vomit, your ass is going to be buying Sterlyn and me a new one."

Cyrus chuckled beside me, making me grin.

"Anyway." Sierra sighed. "I'm too amped up to go to bed, so I say it's television time."

"Yes, and we're going to watch *Die Hard*," Killian said and pointed at Griffin. "Am I right?"

"Hell, yeah." Griffin sat on the loveseat and looked at me while he patted the open spot beside him. "It's our turn."

"We haven't voted." Sierra's mouth dropped. "Where's Rosemary?"

"Not here yet." Griffin chuckled. "So three guys to two girls. We win. Turn that shit on."

"Cyrus, don't you wanna watch *How To Lose A Guy In Ten Days*?" Sierra pouted like she thought that would make him agree.

"Uh, that's a huge no." Cyrus leaned against the wall and arched an eyebrow. "I'm with them. *Die Hard*."

"Maybe you're all right after all," Griffin said, and smiled at my brother.

At my mate's approving words, Cyrus's happiness flowed into me. I linked with Griffin, *Thank you. That made his day.*

I meant it. Griffin patted the spot next to him once more. *And I need you here now.*

Not wanting to waste another second away from him, I hurried across the room and sat as he slipped his arm around my shoulder.

"It's about damn time." Killian grabbed the remote and turned on the television and movie.

"This is not fair." Sierra crossed her arms and leaned back in the chair. "This was not how it was supposed to go."

"Oh, stop." I had to give Killian and Griffin credit. They'd been watching a ton of movies they didn't want to see. It was time they had their turn.

The sound of flapping wings rose outside the back door. Cyrus jumped up and ran to open it, and Rosemary came walking in.

She glanced at the television, and her brows furrowed. "What are we watching? That doesn't look like something Sierra chose."

"That's because you weren't here, and I got outvoted." Sierra's eyes lit up. "But you're here now, so that means we can revote."

Rosemary's head tilted as she watched the beginning of the movie.

"Tell them you want to watch something else." Sierra clapped, expecting to get her way.

"Actually, this kind of looks interesting." Rosemary walked over and took the spot between Killian and Sierra, her eyes glued to the screen.

"What?" Sierra gasped. "I couldn't have heard you right."

Killian leaned forward and winked at Sierra as he said, "You lose. Now shut up and enjoy the show."

My cheeks hurt from smiling so widely, and I snuggled into Griffin's arms.

Everything was going to be all right. Cyrus would lead the silver wolves, and Griffin and I would change things in Shadow City. With the people here in this room, I knew we could get through anything that came our way. As long as we were together.

ABOUT THE AUTHOR

Jen L. Grey is a *USA Today* Bestselling Author who writes Paranormal Romance, Urban Fantasy, and Fantasy genres.

Jen lives in Tennessee with her husband, two daughters, and two miniature Australian Shepherd. Before she began writing, she was an avid reader and enjoyed being involved in the indie community. Her love for books eventually led her to writing. For more information, please visit her website and sign up for her newsletter.

Check out my future projects and book signing events at my website. www.jenlgrey.com

ALSO BY JEN L. GREY

Shadow City: Silver Wolf Trilogy

Broken Mate

Rising Darkness

Silver Moon

Shadow City: Royal Vampire Trilogy

Cursed Mate

Shadow Bitten

Demon Blood

Shadow City: Demon Wolf Trilogy

Ruined Mate

Shattered Curse

Fated Souls

Shadow City: Dark Angel Trilogy

Fallen Mate

Demon Marked

Dark Prince

Fatal Secrets

The Wolf Born Trilogy

Hidden Mate

Blood Secrets

Awakened Magic

The Hidden King Trilogy

Dragon Mate

Dragon Heir

Dragon Queen

The Marked Wolf Trilogy

Moon Kissed

Chosen Wolf

Broken Curse

Wolf Moon Academy Trilogy

Shadow Mate

Blood Legacy

Rising Fate

The Royal Heir Trilogy

Wolves' Queen

Wolf Unleashed

Wolf's Claim

Bloodshed Academy Trilogy

Year One

Year Two

Year Three

The Half-Breed Prison Duology (Same World As Bloodshed Academy)

Hunted

Cursed

The Artifact Reaper Series

Reaper: The Beginning

Reaper of Earth

Reaper of Wings

Reaper of Flames

Reaper of Water

Stones of Amaria (Shared World)

Kingdom of Storms

Kingdom of Shadows

Kingdom of Ruins

Kingdom of Fire

The Pearson Prophecy

Dawning Ascent

Enlightened Ascent

Reigning Ascent

Stand Alones

Death's Angel

Rising Alpha

Ingram Content Group UK Ltd.
Milton Keynes UK
UKHW040642140623
422990UK00033B/280/J